TIGERS
OF WRATH

Jeanne Montague

CENTURY

LONDON   MELBOURNE   AUCKLAND   JOHANNESBURG

First published in Great Britain in 1987 by
Century Hutchinson Ltd,
Brookmount House, 62–65 Chandos Place,
London WC2N 4NW

Century Hutchinson South Africa (Pty) Ltd
PO Box 337, Bergvlei, 2012 South Africa

Century Hutchinson Australia Pty Ltd
PO Box 496, 16–22 Church Street, Hawthorn,
Victoria 3122, Australia

Century Hutchinson New Zealand Limited
PO Box 40–086, Glenfield, Auckland 10, New Zealand

ISBN 0 7126 1637 3

Typeset by Deltatype, Ellesmere Port
Printed in Great Britain by
Anchor Brendon, Tiptree, Essex

By the same author

THE CLOCK TOWER
MIDNIGHT MOON
THE CASTLE OF THE WINDS

For Alan

Thanks, my friend, for introducing me to
the wonders of the word-processor

With acknowledgements to and admiration for some of
the courageous explorers who penetrated the South
American wilderness. The accounts of their adven-
tures were inspiring and more than helpful: Lt.-Col.
P. H. Fawcett, Brian Fawcett, Robin Furneaux, Peter
Fleming and Alain Gheerbrant. Also to Alfred
Métraux for his book on voodoo.

The tygers of wrath are wiser than the horses of instruction

'The Proverbs of Hell' by William Blake.

BOOK ONE

The Stranger

I have been here before,
   But when or how I cannot tell:
I know the grass beyond the door,
   The sighing sound, the lights around the shore.

You have been mine before, –
   How long ago I may not know:
But just when at the swallow's soar
   Your neck turned so,
Some veil did fall, – I knew it all of yore.

Has this been thus before?
   And shall not thus time's eddying flight
Still with our lives our love restore
   In death's despite,
And day and night yield one delight once more?

'Sudden Light' by Dante Gabriel Rossetti.

Prelude

The drums had fallen silent at last. The air no longer floated with mysteries or pulsed with their insistent throb that had violently reacted on nerves and brain. The phantasms of the night were fast vanishing. Colour crept back into the mango trees and palms.

She stood on the verandah, staring out at the dawn. Her eyes were blank in a face haggard and ashen. The pale rays of first light played over it, fanning down from a sky, rainbow-hued in the east, still shrouded by night clouds westwards. It was that awesome moment of absolute stillness when the world seems poised on the brink. The cicadas had ceased chirring, the frogs from giving voice in the swamps, and the birds had not yet begun their hymn to the sun.

She drew in a deep shuddering breath and a shiver shook her from head to toe. Her skin was chilled by the damp mist hanging over the fields of sugar cane, creeping up from the sluggish river. The tops of the trees poked gaunt fingers through it. Each stem of cane was surmounted by a silver-grey ostrich feather that fluttered in the faintest breath of wind and turned the view into something unreal and dreamlike.

It seemed that she had been standing there for ever. Maybe she had. In moments of great shock the usual concept of time turns upside down – it could have been a second or hours. It was as if the whole of her life had been a pathway to this horror. What had gone before, though seemingly significant, meant nothing now.

Dazed, numb, she could not force movement into her limbs. Her thin hands were white-knuckled with tension as she clung to the wooden balustrade. It was her sheet

3

anchor. A vast gamut of emotions was at war within her. A duel in which her thoughts drove each other from the battlefield of the mind to that of the subconscious, and back again.

She became aware of a shiver in the air, nebulous, unreal, like a netherworld of whispered incantations. The sun filigreed the dark clouds with gold, thrusting them back into the arms of night. Animal life stirred and woke in the brooding jungle that surrounded the cultivated ground. It was scarcely held at bay, seeming to writhe and thrust forward greedy tentacles, eager to swarm over the house, the hutments, to claim this stolen land as its own again. Snakes slithered in its depths, or were they lianas shooting out suckers, resembling spotted snakes? Parakeets began their shrill chattering, the sound vibrating along her nerves all the way from her fingertips to her heart. Day had come – a day that she had prayed would never dawn.

The mist was melting away. In the distance she could see little trails of smoke rising from the huts of the plantation workers. Before long, one of the servants was bound to patter in on bare feet from the kitchen quarters. Run – screamed something inside her, panicking. Run! Run! She could not run, could not move. It was as if some monstrous spider had netted her in a sticky web, a prisoner till it thought fit to suck the vital juices from her body and eat her alive.

With a supreme effort, she prised her hands from the rail and half turned seeing, from the tail of her eye, a corner of the white-painted verandah. A riot of green, fleshy vines swarmed over its uprights, heavy with scarlet blossoms which emitted a sickly, cloying scent. A little lizard flashed up the wall, pausing with palpitating sides, alarmed into stillness, its glittering eyes fixed on her. When she moved again, it fled.

Slowly, every step an agony of apprehension, she turned towards the house. The sunlight, growing ever stronger, sent harsh beams slanting across it. She noted, quite dispassionately, the peeling paintwork and crumbling plaster, the air of decay and neglect which hung over all. A large colonial dwelling, pretentious in its heyday, but allowed to rot. Memories flooded up, none of them reassuring. Why had he allowed everything to rot? Including himself – and her?

Now she could see the glow of the paraffin lamp on the table, its light rendered feeble by the sun. Its frosted glass globe was gummy with the melted bodies of moths, flies and mosquitoes which had burned during the night, hurling themselves at it in compulsive fascination. There were glasses on the cane surface. One had tipped over, and a rapidly drying pool of rum lay there like blood. Bottles stood haphazardly, half-full or empty. Swamp-green, squat, secretive, like phials in an alchemist's laboratory, harbouring poison in their depths.

Her white skirt whispered as she walked across the bare planks. There was the scrawl of brown legs as a tarantula scurried from under the table and dropped to safety over the verandah steps. She ran a hand across her forehead. It was already unbearably humid, and she could feel the sweat trickling between her breasts and at her armpits. A bell clanged in the distance and she started. The peons would be heading for the fields. Not slaves. Slavery had been long abolished, but though free, their lot was almost as hard, nearly as degrading. Would they know, somehow sense what had happened? Like dogs that howl when the master dies?

Carefully, step by shrinking step, she advanced, averting her eyes from that which she knew she had to face. Across the verandah and into the sitting-room. It was flooded with a greenish hue cast by the shadow of a tree whose branches stretched nearly to the roof on the right-hand side. This spread of green sprouting from the gnarled, ancient trunk had been encouraged, even welcomed. Thus the room was nearly always pleasantly cool.

5

I used to pretend I was walking under the sea if I came in here when I was young, she thought – cool green sea of my childhood. Her thoughts came up against a barrier. She didn't want to think of those days, but they kept impinging themselves on her mind. Fragmented pictures passed across memory's darkened mirror, flashing there momentarily, then vanishing. The room, crowded with people – herself a little girl in a frilly white dress, Leila's big brown hand holding her small pale paw, bringing her down to meet the guests. She could hear the sounds of laughter, the clink of glasses, popular music blaring from the horn of the gramophone, and see her mother – beautiful then – watching him. People always watched him. He had been irresistible, the centre of attention wherever he went. And I, most of all, was bewitched by him, she thought.

No one accompanied her now. No one sheltered and protected her against fear. She was alone. No, not quite alone. It would have been better had she been. Her breath was rasping harshly in her throat, and the room was no longer cool. Fever seemed to rage in her blood, like malaria.

'I can't,' she whispered to the meshed windows, the familiar furnishings, the china ornaments, the cut-glass candelabrum, its crystal drops tinkling icily, bell-like. 'Please don't make me! Let me find it's been a dream. Let me wake in my room upstairs! Leila! Where are you? I didn't mean it! We shouldn't have done it!'

She was aware of another sound, a diabolical buzzing like bees swarming. The flies were beginning to gather, shiny, metallic blue-black, attracted to the feast. As compelled as the moths dazzled by lamplight, her eyes lifted and then she knew that it was no dream. All too real, horrible and stark, was the body in the wicker armchair.

'Look at him,' she moaned, punishing herself. 'Look well, and never forget.'

6

He was still partly sitting, head laid back against the padded frame. A big man in a crumpled white suit. His hands, broad and tanned, the backs furred with dark hair, were clenched on the arms of the chair. The watery light stole over him, pinpointing every detail: the wine and sweat stains, the dust on his boots, the flash of gold on the chain girding his slack, paunchy stomach. In the silence, she could hear the steady tick of his pocket-watch, remorselessly marking out the seconds between herself and retribution.

Till that moment she had still hoped, even prayed that something might have changed. Perhaps there had been a crazy mistake and he had only been asleep after all. She would enter to find him snoring drunkenly, as on countless dawns. With sickness sending the bile to her mouth, she looked into his face, and the sense of nightmare rushed back tenfold. It was useless to screw her eyes tight shut. She could still see that terrible face. It had grown even more horrible, setting into a death mask.

The flesh now bore the purplish patina of a bruised grape. The face of an old man, lined, sagging. The eyes were open, and the expression in them was one of terror. The whole face seemed carved with it – scribbled all over with pure dread, the mouth torn open as if in a silent scream.

She buried her face in her hands, but some power outside herself seemed to be forcing them down, so that she had to fill her eyes, her mind with that awful face. The room reeled, and wherever she looked, she saw it. No corner of her soul would ever escape it – no matter where she hid, it would haunt her. Falling to her knees, she tried to pray but the words stuck fast to her lips. She was doomed, damned, condemned. There was no escape.

Then a single ray pierced the green gloom. It struck sparks from the ring which, huge, ornate, circled the

7

little finger of the dead right hand. Like an eye, it seemed to stare at her – a yellow, malignant, all-seeing eye.

'Oh, God!' she whispered. 'What am I to do? I've killed him! Killed my own father!'

1

It was a raw November afternoon. The young Irishman, clad in an old pair of breeches and gaiters and a threadbare coat, found himself in Bell's Spinney, a big outlying covert a mile or so from Cleg Kennard's neat tithe cottage. Kennard managed the extensive estates of Armitstead House. It was because of him that Shawn was there at all.

His task was to take specimens from the leafless trees and undergrowth to the manager, who would then identify them, explaining things that he already knew like the back of his hand. Pompous old idiot! he thought. Bedad! It's like teaching your grandmother to suck eggs!

Taking out his knife, he began to cut at the new shoots without much enthusiasm, cursing when the wet ran down his arm as the branches, suddenly released by the severing of the selected twig, sprang back. Goddamn it! This was hardly the life for him. Surely he had not been wrong in his glowing expectations of something far better? Not him, not Shawn Brennan, who was usually blessed with the luck of the devil.

He meditated as he worked. Kennard had promised to take him along to meet Lord Ruthen. His visions were rosy-tinted. He saw himself making a most favourable impression on the great man. If he played his cards right, he would soon be installed as head agent. It was high time Kennard retired. He had held one of the plums of his profession for too many years. He should give a younger man a chance. If all went well and Ruthen took a fancy to him, it could be a golden opportunity. Yes, very soon he would step into Kennard's shoes, with a comfortable wage, a decent house rent-free, lots of shooting, a couple of hunters, and –

At this point he had reached a white gate at the edge of the covert. Away to the right stretched the wood, a collection of brown, naked boughs, except where the nodding crests of green spruce or Scotch fir broke through, dark against a grey sky where a sullen sun hung like a bloody ball. Ahead lay emerald pastures, wet with recent rain. A few last withered leaves spiralled lazily down, and an acorn dropped with a soft thud, but otherwise the scene was very still and peaceful. Shawn leaned over the gate, his nostrils filled with the pungent odour of decaying vegetation. It reminded him of other autumns, spent in the pursuit of game.

'What grand weather for hunting, to be sure!' he murmured aloud.

It had been a long time since he had done that though once, in the halcyon days of his boyhood, things had been different. Shawn came from an irresponsible, feather-brained family who had made a speciality of extracting the utmost enjoyment from life, and running through every farthing they possessed in the process. They had always been sportsmen. His father had hunted hounds, entertained on a lavish scale, and generally drained his cup to the dregs. Shawn remembered him with affection, that loud-voiced mountain of a man with the humorous green eyes under heavy brows. It had not mattered to him that his father had thought sordid financial considerations beneath the notice of a gentleman. In vain, his legal adviser had timidly ventured to bring them before him, on which occasions he would do one of two things. If he was in a good humour, he would lightly but firmly dismiss the subject in a manner that brooked no argument. In a less genial mood, perhaps after a heavy night's drinking and gambling, he would curse the poor man with every oath in his widely varied vocabulary, so that the well-meaning but unfortunate lawyer would make good his retreat with as much haste as possible.

Consequently, on his father's death, Shawn had found himself in possession of nothing but a few hundred acres of land mortgaged up to the hilt, a dilapidated manor house, muddled account books, and enough family influence to give him a chance. This took the form of learning estate management under a first-rate exponent, who only accepted pupils as a great favour. Kennard had been that man.

Shawn had arrived at Abbey Sutton the previous day, after being dispatched hence by anxious relatives, banished from the misty hills of Southern Ireland. He grinned wryly as he recalled how delighted they had been at having, without personal cost, done something for him, patting themselves on the back and going their ways.

Glad to see the last of me, I'll bet, he thought without bitterness. Although he romanticized about everything and had elevated creative lying to a fine art, he was never dishonest with regard to himself. It seemed as if every feckless, law-breaking characteristic in a long line of hard-living, hard-drinking squires, who had scraped by on their charm and their belief in a God-given right to rule, had reached its zenith in him. He had inherited dash and a handsome face, a tall, wide-shouldered body, curling chestnut hair and those light green eyes which, along with his peaked brows, gave him the quizzical look of a leprechaun. He was also the owner of a beguiling tongue that bewitched women, young and old, from Dublin Bay to the rolling Wessex downs.

He chewed on a length of grass and grinned remi-niscently. He'd been in England under a week but had already found the girls more than obliging. Servants, of course, or barmaids. Not really the sort of company a gentleman should be seeking, no matter how down-at-heel. But women were women, the world over. Warm, loving, welcoming to a man like him. They couldn't resist him. There had been trouble back home. Shawn knew everything there was to know about jumping out of bedroom windows, scaling roofs and skimming along tiles. He was a past master in all the feats of an accomplished philanderer.

These thoughts were wiped from his mind as a sound, faint yet distinct, reached his ears. He stiffened and his eyes narrowed. He listened intently. It came again, and there was no mistaking that noise so intimately bound up with his dearest memories. It swelled into a clamour. Then he spotted something white moving up the hedge-row – lost it for a second – saw it leap over a gate not two fields away. First one, then two. Thick and fast they came now, and as each cleared the gate, it took up that spine-tingling note of a hound hot on the scent. Shawn watched till the followers of the Sutton Hunt, having taken the fence or crowded through the nearest gate, had vanished into the woods.

'Mother of God!' Shawn muttered, his heart throbbing. It's no easy thing for a Brennan to endure being without a mount in the sight of hounds running. Damn my father! I should've been out there in the lead if he hadn't guzzled the money away! He stood, blood on fire, his eyes fixed on the fence that separated one field from another. It was a large expanse, and he measured it mentally. Not too high. It was the wide ditch beyond, with its crumbling, slippery bank, almost invisible from this side, that made it tricky.

He never expected to see a horseman so far behind the hounds, but he heard the thud of galloping hooves, and saw a big bay, obviously out of control, come tearing straight at the fence. He had a brief glimpse of its rider in a flowing velvet habit – flaxen hair spilling from beneath her top hat with the force of the charge. He shouted a warning. Too late. Crash! Over they went. The bank gave way. Horse and rider turned a complete somersault.

Shawn was there in an instant. He found an astonished and furious young woman sitting on the ground.

12

Her outraged expression at finding herself in this humiliating position was so comic that he shook with laughter.

'Are you all right, now?' he shouted.

Her eyes flashed sparks at him from beneath haughty lids. 'No, I'm not! Where's that bloody brute?' she snapped, stretching out an expensively booted muddy leg and rubbing it gingerly.

The horse, having scrambled up and shaken itself, was now out of sight. Shawn stood, legs spread, hands on his hips, and looked down into her beautiful face. 'There's a stile up there. Why don't you rest on it for a while? I'll try to catch him,' he suggested, his eyes going over her boldly. And she was well worth looking at – mud, temper and all.

He held out his hand. She hesitated for a moment, then gripped it with gloved fingers. He pulled her to her feet, retaining his hold a fraction longer than was necessary. He could see the quick rise and fall of her breasts under the figure-hugging jacket, the white lace of the stock wound around her slender throat, her flushed cheeks, and moist parted lips. She made no attempt to remove her hand, meeting his eyes questioningly.

Then, as if suddenly mindful of her station, she ground out: 'Thank you, pray do that, my good man,' and, turning her back on him, walked across to the stile.

Shawn watched her with amusement. Oh, she was trying to act the great lady with him, was she? But he had felt the warmth of her hand, heard her sharp intake of breath when her breasts had brushed against his chest. Great lady? Great whore, or he'd go to sea in a shipyard! Still chuckling and congratulating himself on recognizing an amorous little baggage when he saw one, he pursued the bay's tracks, finding him quietly grazing in the corner of the next field. He was a fine, upstanding animal, every inch a thoroughbred, from his long muscular neck to the swishing tail he carried so proudly.

13

Shawn talked to him in a soft, seductive voice, similar to that which he used with women. 'Come on, my beauty,' he whispered. 'To hell with her! It's me that should be after riding you.'

He was up in the saddle almost before he knew it. Instinctively, he lengthened one stirrup, then stopped and laughed. In for a penny, in for a pound, he thought. I might as well ride him back. And he adjusted the other.

The woman was perched on the top of the stile. When she saw him mount she started to wave and shout. He could guess the gist of her words. There was no way they could be flattering. How dare a lout like him take her place in the saddle? He waved back, smiling widely, thinking, she imagines that I'm a farmhand. I'll show you, lady. One day – one *night* – maybe sooner than I expect, if my luck holds.

It was then that the hounds gave tongue as they struck the scent of the fox. Shawn turned in the saddle. The notes swelled into a chorus. A lithe brown streak shot through a gap near the corner of the wood and fled across the field. A loud, involuntary view-holloo burst from Shawn's lips, such as had often awakened the echoes in his native land. He became oblivious of everything except the hounds streaming away on the line of the fox. He forgot time and place. He forgot the angry young lady.

The bay cleared the rails and they were off. Few riders gave chase, too busy chattering on the other side of the spinney. They were wary of the difficulties. The fence on one side and the ditch on the other made even the most experienced huntsman draw rein and contemplate the risks involved. Not so Shawn. The hounds were running in a compact phalanx, fast and almost silent. He gathered up the bay and drove him at the next hurdle as if the devil himself was after him. There was a sensation of rising high in the air, his heart swelling with the joy of it. A plunge. A jolt. He was over the top. What more

14

could a man ask for? He was blind to everything but the feel of the wind in his face, the bay's swinging gallop, the way the hounds were turning.

The fences leaped up at him. Shawn was aware of how neatly the horse took them, poising on his hocks, then giving a lift of his hind hoofs so that they just brushed the topmost twigs. Begorrah! but he's a flyer! he thought. Never had he known such a thrill as in this chase. It was one of those chances that come so rarely, but in the hope of which the huntsman continues even on the dullest day. Shawn was experienced and spared his mount, but the hounds were running like smoke. To be almost the only rider with them was an opportunity too precious to jeopardize by attempting short cuts. He rode straight in the wake of the flying pack, with a single rider on his right and not another soul in sight.

The going was clear. No wire, no treacherous banks, each brushwood barrier scalable. The horse was enjoying it too, going straight as an arrow, clearing fence after fence. Shawn's cap brushed against a low bough. His face smarted, scratched by briars, yet he was happy – the blood of his Irish ancestors beating strongly in his veins. He was invincible!

So caught up was he in this potent magic that he failed to see the water till too late. He sent the bay at it. The animal did not refuse, but jumped short. Shawn was catapulted into a shallow, ice-cold stream. Swearing violently, he scrambled out somehow and, with a heave and a pull, managed to guide the bay to a convenient spot a few yards down, where the bank was low. A fresh outburst from the hounds gave warning that the end was at hand, and Shawn had ridden no further than a couple of fields when they ran into the fox near a narrow lane. The lone huntsman, of whom he had been but dimly aware, was there at the kill.

Shawn, dripping, reined in near him. The man gazed at him curiously, but with a certain respect. 'You ride well,' he said, a big, strong, black-bearded man who looked as if he could carry on riding for hours yet. 'Your first time with us, is it? Can't say I've seen you about before. But, damned if your horse isn't a dead ringer for Lord Ruthen's Brandy. Might be his brother! Did you get him in this country?'

Shawn started, suddenly remembering the young lady he had left so far behind. 'That I did, and a pretty useful beast he is,' he lied. 'Whose horse did you say he's like?'

The huntsman was watching him with keen blue eyes that looked very bright against his muddy, tanned face. He was wearing a red jacket and buckskin breeches, now much the same colour by the sweat and muck of the chase. 'Lord Ruthen's,' he replied. 'It's bloody odd. He wasn't riding him today. He let his sister, Lady Josephine, have him. Unwise, I thought, for he's a powerful animal and inclined to be wilful, but she's wilful too, determined to ignore advice.'

'And who might you be, sir?' enquired Shawn, as they jogged back the way they had come.

'I'm Darcy Devereaux. I own Chalkdown Farm.' Shawn was again subjected to that shrewd, unsmiling stare. 'Are you going to hunt here regularly – Mr – eh?'

'Shawn Brennan,' he answered quickly, a dozen unpleasant possibilities presenting themselves as the excitement faded. He tried to laugh, adding evasively: 'It was a good sample of hunting, your Honour. I could wish for no better.'

Darcy Devereaux was wondering who he was, and how he came to be riding the horse that he had last seen Josephine mounted on so defiantly. He was certainly a scruffy individual, and had a thick accent. There was a confident air about him which was appealing. But then, the Irish tended to possess the grand manner even when they lay in the gutter.

Darcy scented something intriguing here and seized upon it to dispel the boredom which always beset him

16

when forced to attend a house party. Oh, the hunting was good, but the price was high. Because his farm was only a few miles away, he had managed to avoid staying at Selden's house last night, but even he could not be so churlish as to refuse to attend that evening's festivities. Had Brennan been invited too? Selden was noted for his unconventionality. His actions sometimes shocked the local gentry. The next few hours might be entertaining after all.

He adroitly turned his horse's head towards the direction of the manor. Shawn drew in, hesitating. 'I'll not come with you, sir,' he said. 'My path lies that way,' and he pointed towards the spinney in the distance.

'I see,' answered Darcy, who did not and was completely mystified. 'But that's nowhere near the house. It's a long way around.'

'I've got to go that way. I've left something there,' Shawn replied truthfully. 'I'll meet you later, perhaps.'

Darcy saluted with his whip and headed along the bridle path. Shawn glanced after him, then made way as fast as he could. It was a long, dull ride. The short day was drawing in, night clouds piling up on the horizon. It was cold and he was soaked to the skin. Depression settled over his usually exuberant spirits. So, he'd cooked his goose good and proper. Borrowed Lord Ruthen's horse, had he? And left his sister stranded. This was embarrassing, even for a son of Erin who could usually talk his way out of any situation. It might be possible to bluff matters for the moment, but he felt most uneasy when he thought about the possible consequences.

It was a considerable walk over rough ground to Armitstead House, so Lady Josephine, wife of Major Douglas Huxley, had been forced to wait. She glared through the gathering twilight with concentrated fury as Shawn loomed out of it. He was leading Brandy, and wore a martyred expression, relieved by a faint smile.

17

'Sure and your runaway's led me a terrible dance,' was his opening gambit.

Josephine slid from the stile, pacing towards him, her whip swishing against her damp skirt as if she wanted to hit him with it. 'You blackguard!' she stormed, stopping in front of him. 'What about me? I saw you joining the hunt. How dare you keep me waiting?'

'I'm sorry – I really am,' he exclaimed. Her rage was like a physical blow and he almost recoiled. 'You've had a long wait, but it's nothing to what I've gone through. Look at me! I'm soaked to the buff! Probably catch my death, and all in your service. I don't regret it. Oh, no – not one little bit. I've served you, and will always serve you, in any way you want.'

'All I want is never to set eyes on you again,' she shouted. 'I've missed the kill, because of you!'

'I had the devil's own job to catch him.' He managed to look deeply pained. 'He ended up in the stream, so he did, miles away. It took me ages to find my way back here to you.'

'Liar!' She glared at him, her breath hanging like mist between them, small and slim and infinitely desirable in the frosty gloom. Shawn wanted to drag her into his arms, and kiss her till she was dizzy. He did not move, merely staring deeply into her eyes, till she hesitated. Then he knew he was safe, using a ploy that had rescued him on more than one occasion, making his face appear honest and open, with bland, innocent eyes. He adopted a frank manner, and general air of one expecting and deserving gratitude. It totally disarmed her.

She was angered and perplexed having, during the wait, prepared the worst string of powerful insults that she could think of. Now she found herself wishing that she did not have to mount up and ride to the house to prepare for dinner. There was something secretive and exciting about being in the darkening woods with this handsome young stranger. He looked like a gypsy, wild and raffish, yet his voice was soft, cultured even, with that fascinating brogue.

'Am I forgiven?' he murmured, and she suspected that he was mocking her gently.

'Perhaps,' she conceded, and placed a foot in the stirrup.

Shawn was there, his hands at her waist, holding her lightly before helping her into the saddle. 'Good.' There was so much charm in his smile that Josephine's heart flipped over. 'I hope that we might be friends – perhaps ride together sometimes. I'm a stranger in these parts, and need someone to show me the ropes.'

'Ha! You've a damned sauce!' She tossed her head, and bobbed her heel against Brandy's side. As he moved wearily onward, Shawn walked alongside. 'I'm a married woman, I'll have you know.'

'Married, are you? Well, you would be, of course. A girl as lovely as yourself was bound to be snapped up by some lucky blighter,' he answered easily, and Josephine was very aware of his hand, resting on the rein, close to her knee.

'My husband is a military man, and terribly jealous,' she replied icily, but could not help sneaking a glance at him from behind the veil that kept her hat in place.

'D'you give him cause?'

'How dare you suggest such a thing? My God, I've a good mind to give you a taste of my whip!' she raged. Shawn twinkled at her, absolutely unrepentant, and highly delighted.

Josephine was not lacking in courage, indeed she had a reputation for being quite fearless, even reckless at times, but it was dark in the woods, the path narrow and winding and the house seemed miles ahead. She was alone with this man. She knew nothing about him, and was finding it impossible to pigeonhole him. He was too assured to be a labourer, yet his clothing was dirty and shabby. Who was he? Coupled with her growing alarm,

19

was a sense of raging annoyance because Darcy had made no attempt to find out why she had dropped behind. An imp of perversity was urging her to take this rapscallion back with her. Oh, Douglas would fret and fume, but she had never allowed her husband to dominate her. She knew exactly how to keep him sweet. All she had to do was pretend that she enjoyed sleeping with him. She despised men, despised this need they had which made them putty in her hands. It was so easy to please them. Just play the game their way, flatter their ego, pander to their masculinity. Easy? Yes, but not with Darcy. Perhaps this was why she was so much in love with him.

To her intense relief, she began to recognize landmarks. There was the lodge, and there the gates of Armitstead House. Acting on impulse, that trait which had landed her in trouble more than once, she drew the horse to a standstill. Shawn saw her face gleaming above him, unreal and wraithlike. Her eyes glittered like jewels.

'I'll bid you goodnight, my Lady,' he said, with an ironic bow.

'No. You must meet my brother. I don't know who you are or what you're doing here, but no matter. Come with me.'

The lodge keeper was already at the gates, massive wrought-iron creations shining in the light of the rising moon. Josephine and Shawn passed through.

Armitstead House had been designed to impress, and it succeeded. Positioned on a rise above Abbey Sutton, it commanded a fine view of the surrounding countryside. Away on its right lay the moors, bleak in winter, a purplish blue in summer when the heather was in bloom. It was there that the shepherds roamed with their dogs, hardy men and true, dedicated to the welfare of their flocks. To the left lay the sea, where trawlers harvested. Beyond the downs rose hills, misty in the distance, scarred with black holes in which miners toiled like dwarfs, grubbing a pittance from the depths of the earth.

Beyond that again, and far out of sight, huddled small old towns with higgledy-piggledy houses, some going back to Saxon days. Timbered in black and having overhanging corbels, they lined the narrow streets, peaceful mostly but crowded on market days when the farmers drove in their stock for sale. Then the air would be electric with excitement as gypsies harried villagers on these rare, much anticipated outings, with their offers of horses, paper flowers, and clothes pegs, persuading blushing maidens to have their fortunes told. Unemployed labourers, servants and dairymaids would be there too, putting themselves up for hire. Ale and cider was on sale, hot-pie stalls did a roaring trade and, sometimes, the showmen arrived with their rides and shooting ranges. There might even be a circus with a menagerie of wild beasts, or a play, staged in the town hall, were travelling actors performed their fantasies.

But all in all, the people of Wessex viewed strangers askance; they did not hurry to accept them. They had all the time in the world to become acquainted, once newcomers had proved themselves. Now their narrow concepts were broadening, despite their prejudices. The railways had long been established, destroying boundaries and aiding communication. The market towns were becoming congested with cyclists and horse-drawn vehicles and, more recently, the noisy, unpredictable motor car. The young people were leaving, seeking jobs in the cities, expanding their horizons in a manner undreamed of by their forebears.

Yet still the hierarchy existed, the class system rigidly maintained. Everyone knew his or her place in the general pattern of things. Of course, there were always the rebels, the agitators and tub-thumpers who envied the wealthy and sought to bring them low. These were in the minority. On the whole, the farmers were content to rent land and work for the master, the fishermen to give a percentage of the catch to the man who owned the port, the miners to hack coal from the feudal lord's seams. The old law survived, as it had done down the ages, and men like Selden Ruthen were thankful for it.

He was in an expansive mood as he lounged in his room and enjoyed a Havana cigar. His body glowed with health after the hard day's riding. On his return, he had gone to the master suite where his valet had prepared a hot bath. Stripping off his hunting pink, he had immersed himself and relaxed, while Jenkins laid out his evening clothes. The bachelor life suited Selden and he was disinclined to forfeit it by marrying again. He had taken on the yoke once, eight years ago, a not too satisfying plunge into matrimony. It had been short-lived. Twenty-five then, he had decided it was time he settled down and raised a family. It was only because I'd been ill, he thought, got that bout of pneumonia after a weekend in Paris with Tommy Lowndes. Too much champagne, late nights and visits to the brothels. Strange how a brush with death can weaken a man's resolve. Belinda netted me when my defences were down, or rather her formidable Mamma did.

A tight smile lifted his thin lips as he sat in the armchair by the fire roaring in the chimney breast, lit more for effect than to supplement the efficient heating system which was one of the talking points of his house. Belinda. He didn't think of her often. Blonde, pretty, emptyheaded child. For a few months he had been content to become a boy again, romping with his girl-wife. But, as time passed and she showed no signs of producing the desired heir, he had become bored, needing something more than everlasting frivolling. She was too timid and shy a lover to satisfy him for long. He had grown accustomed to the earthy charms of music-hall singers and opera-house dancers. Her prudish attitude to sex and her shrinking refusal to enjoy it had made him lose patience. But before the restiveness had had time to culminate in trouble, she had suffered a miscarriage. The cruel wind of reality had swept over the delicate plaything and, after a few days of agony and fear, her soul had fled. Standing by her deathbed, Selden had looked down at the still mask of her face. Though aware of little but intense relief, even he had found it a strange and disturbing experience.

Once the funeral was over, Selden had been perfectly prepared to resume his former life, and had already laid plans for a stay in London, looking up friends whom marriage had forced him to neglect, but he had reckoned without Alison. A frown settled over his brow, and he shifted impatiently. Were it not for her interference, he could have quite forgotten that he ever had a wife, but even here, in the bedroom, there was a painting of Belinda over the mantelpiece. Her face looked down from the bureau, a photograph in soft sepia tones, and a snapshot in a round silver frame stood on the bookcase. All over the house the same face stared from the walls, for Alison saw to it that no room was without a pictured reminder of the young mistress who had reigned for one short year. Stupid, sentimental bitch! growled Selden under his breath. It's got to stop. She's bloody well stifling me. How the hell am I going to get rid of her? Eight years! Jesus Christ, the colour was fading from the photographs. The pretty face with the large eyes and small, babyish mouth was growing cloudy and indistinct. If only Alison would remove herself, then he could forget Belinda completely.

Her name was never mentioned between them. A curtain of silence was drawn over that short, uneventful year during which Belinda had lived with him. He knew that Alison had convinced herself that he could not bear to refer to the past, thinking that he had been so much in love that his life had ended with his bride's death. She's too damned romantic! he thought scornfully. What she needs is a bloody good humping, but she'll never get it – not now.

He was realist enough to know that he had only himself to blame. Conscience-stricken by his lack of emotion as he had stood by Belinda's coffin, he had gone to his sister, white and haggard, and had spoken a few, ill-chosen words.

'You're in charge here now, Alison,' he had said, very manful and dry-eyed. 'We are alone together, and I shall never marry again! Do as you please with the running of the house. I shan't complain. I'll never care enough about anything to complain! My life's finished!'

To his horror, he had found that Alison had taken him literally. Though only eighteen at the time, she had made a solemn vow. Loyalty to poor Selden! Faithfulness, devotion, unending patience and tenderness to Selden of the broken heart, and the broken, blighted life. This had been all very well for a while. Alison proved an excellent housekeeper and perfect hostess, but Selden soon experienced a strangling sense of claustrophobia that increased as the years went by. Chance had made them brother and sister but they had not the smallest thing in common.

Thank God for my rooms in Jermyn Street, he thought. My retreat. Alison doesn't even know it exists. There was the large town house on Sloane Square, but this was her province when they went to London for the winter season. Twenty-eight Jermyn Street was his secret, and he gloated because he kept Alison in ignorance. The inestimable Jenkins was his ally, naturally; the soul of discretion and well paid for the privilege. It was he who saw to it that the apartment was opened up, aired and cleaned before a visit, that meals were sent in and the wine coolers filled. Selden had the feeling that Jenkins rather enjoyed scoring a point off Alison. Certainly, he acted his part to perfection,

24

keeping to his own quarters when the gamblers played deep into the night or flashy under-dressed and over-painted ladies called. Alison would have been scandalized had she known half of what took place in the Jermyn Street abode.

Why couldn't she be more like Josephine? he wondered, idly watching Jenkins' bland face as he moved about with quiet efficiency. The black evening suit lay across the wide bed, a crisp white shirt beside it. He took cuff links and collar studs from the silver box on the ornate mahogany dressing-table, placing them precisely side by side, and draped the long ends of the bow tie across his arm, waiting expectantly for Selden to cast aside his crimson silk robe and start to attire himself.

Selden was in no hurry to move. There was at least half an hour before the gong summoned everyone to dinner. Josephine would be there, of course, and her stuffy, unimaginative husband. He found it strange that sisters could be so very different from one another. Alison, in his eyes, plain and dull, and Josephine, beautiful and vastly amusing. It would never have occurred to her for a moment to sacrifice herself for anybody, let alone a brother. She's like me, he mused. Sufficient unto herself, selfish and egotistical. And again, like himself, was extremely attractive to the opposite sex.

Selden was handsome, titled and most eligible. He had no difficulty in obtaining female company, when he desired it. And he did desire it, often. This sometimes vexed him. In this respect he was not independent, possessed of a powerful sexual appetite, but even this could be assuaged by money. He had not yet discovered the woman virtuous enough to resist his good looks, his lordly bearing, or his generosity. This did not endear them to him. He used them for his pleasure and then left them, even if by that time they had been unwise enough to fall in love with him. No woman was going to put chains around Selden Ruthen again.

25

As he watched the blue smoke from his cigar curl up towards the plaster-encrusted ceiling, he congratulated himself on his latest stroke of good fortune. He had been half expecting it to happen one day, though no one could have foretold how long the old devil would live out there in Brazil or whatever god-forsaken hell-hole he had settled in. But some weeks ago Henshaw, his solicitor, had written to him, saying that Edgar Ruthen was dead. As the only surviving male relative, Selden expected to be heir to his uncle's title. His dearest wish was about to be granted. He rather fancied himself as the Marquis of Suttonbridge.

Not only had he inherited a thriving estate on the death of his father, Edgar Ruthen's only brother, but he had shrewdly developed other business interests too. He spent a great deal of time in London, meeting with financiers and brokers, realizing that there was money to be made in the fast-growing towns. There was a building boom. The middle classes were purchasing houses as never before. The factory owners were throwing up terraces of cottages to rent to their workers. Property was a sound investment, and he had the wherewithal.

Exeter and Dorchester were the pulse towns of Wessex, and Selden was seen feverishly buying up land there. Turning his avaricious eye towards his own area, in and around Abbey Sutton, he had seen its potential. Ten years earlier, he had pulled down the old manor house which had been his father's pride and joy and had erected a massive Gothic structure in its stead. He had employed the best architect of the day, Jonas Orde-Bunbury, the man who had designed many of the ostentatious buildings which had delighted the heart of the late Queen Victoria.

Armitstead House had been completed, but it was only a part of Selden's plans. For him it was more than a home. It was a show case by which he might impress prospective clients with money to burn and the need to

26

demonstrate to the world that they could join the ruling classes through their wealth. Unlike some other aristocrats, Selden entertained anyone at his table, provided they had money. Not for him the old idea that trade was a dirty word. It was trade that had made the British Empire a force to be reckoned with.

Trade! he rolled it around his tongue along with the rare old brandy sipped from the balloon goblet held between his long fingers. Trade! It had a fine ring to it. And the gentleman farmers and lordly nabobs would come around to the idea. What was the use of hanging on to old concepts in the midst of a changing world? The Boer War should have convinced the diehards that nothing was the same any more. Imperial power – the control of the Empire – these visions set him ablaze. Patriotic? Hardly. Practical was a better adjective when applied to Selden. Less charitable people hinted that he was greedy and self-seeking, ruthless too, quite unlike his revered father. Now there was a man who had lived like a gentleman and abided by a code of honour. Many doubted that Selden had even heard of the word.

In a mellow mood, he strolled through the high, vaulted corridors and down the sweeping staircase to the vast hall where his guests had gathered before going in to dinner. He never failed to be warmed by a glow of satisfaction when he viewed any aspect of Armitstead House, considered to be one of Orde-Bunbury's finest works. Externally it resembled a French chateau, but the flamboyant interior aped the most extravagant and theatrical achievements of baroque Italy. The effect of immense height in the hall had been obtained by raising the upper compartment in a tower, which was invisible from outside the house. Orde-Bunbury had excelled himself with his plaster work, combining illusion and reality; plaster curtains, tassels and trumpet-blowing cherubs; a painted sky, mirrors, real rope and real scythes, marble and bronze sculpture. At one end was a minstrels' gallery. Opposite it was a dais, lit by a splendid bay window with carved stone surrounds of cruciform shape and panes ornamented with stained-glass panels.

Electrically lit chandeliers shone down on the scene where the hunters, the men transformed in their black suits and snowy linen, the women drifting like colourful butterflies, were gathered in little groups, talking and laughing. Alison, an angular, earnest-looking woman, had undertaken to put everyone at their ease, but it was Josephine who saw Selden as he reached the foot of the stairs.

She swept forward, magnificently dressed in a robe of golden net covered with beaded embroidery of the same hue, the chiffon skirts poised one upon the other, softening the glare of the satin slip which clung to her, and fell into a train at the back. Encased in it, her body appeared of an incredible slimness, yet there was not a single angle or harsh, unlovely line. Her shining hair was dressed loosely, away from her face, twisted in a fashion which displayed the shape of her head. The gown was low cut, and diamonds clasped her throat, repeated on the bracelets which banded her wrists on top of the long white gloves.

'There you are, Selden. Where've you been hiding?' she cried, reaching up on tiptoe to kiss his cheek.

Selden met her blue-grey eyes that reflected the golden lights of her gown. They understood each other, neither caring if the other knew their little secrets and deceptions. There was a bond between them nothing could destroy. Both despised the patient, plodding endeavours of people like Alison.

'Having a rest and enjoying my own company,' he answered, then his eyes went down over her. 'But, my dear – such gorgeousness! Every bead a treasure. It must have taken months of work, and on a piece of perishable net. Hasn't Douglas read you a lesson on wanton extravagance?'

'*Decadence*,' she interrupted firmly. 'You must *always* call it decadence. And I perfectly agree. But the poor little *grisettes* had spent hours embroidering it, so someone had to pay, and Douglas might as well do it as anyone else. He was adamant that I have it. I just *happened* to take him to the dressmaker with me one morning, you see. He positively insisted. I wouldn't have dreamed of ordering it.'

'Humbug!' he laughed, taking her hand. Her heavily seductive French perfume wafted into his nostrils, and he felt a stirring of family pride in this fascinating woman. 'Is there any possible way of getting into the thing or do you wriggle in at the neck? The sleeves are a trifle brief, don't you think?'

'Perhaps, but it's the fault of my arms. They *are* so shapely! Look at that dimple. You wouldn't have the heart to hide it, would you?' returned Josephine, shutting one eye so as to peer with the other at the soft dents above the elbow. In praise or blame she was always markedly honest with regard to her own appearance.

'Josephine, really! You're impossibly conceited,' he chided affectionately, thinking, I wish Alison took herself a little less seriously. She'd get on much better and might find some man willing to take her off my hands.

Even when Shawn appeared at the door and came to a sudden stand as if dazzled by the glittering apparition near the staircase, Josephine seemed to see no reason for changing her pose, but continued to crane with undiminished interest. 'Hello, there,' she said. 'I'm showing Selden a dimple. This side, to the west! I can just see it like this, but I know it's beautiful viewed from the other side. I wear my sleeves short on purpose.' She straightened up, mischief shining in her eyes, adding: 'Selden, meet Shawn Brennan. He was kind enough to catch Brandy when he threw me this afternoon.'

Shawn returned Selden's nod, feeling himself being

29

scrutinized by a pair of cold grey eyes. His doubts returned, doubts which he had successfully pushed from his mind during the excitement of Josephine smuggling him into the house and ordering the butler to find him an evening suit to fit. The bedroom to which he had been conducted had surpassed his wildest dreams. Viewing himself in the pier-glass as the dinner gong boomed, he had known that he would pass muster, a dandified figure indeed.

'And where do you hail from, Mr Brennan?' Selden was saying coolly, as if it were the most natural thing in the world to have him arrive, uninvited, in their midst.

'I've a house and land in County Cork – Four Oaks, by name. You may have heard of my father, Errol Brennan – squire and magistrate. He was a great judge of horseflesh, sir. No one like him, at all.' Shawn had decided to brazen it out. Ireland was a long way off. It would take a curious person some weeks to find out that Four Oaks and all it contained was mortgaged almost beyond redemption. He refused to dwell on Kennard's reaction when he heard about this escapade.

'I don't recall the name, but you're welcome.' Selden was wondering if this young man was Josephine's latest beau. He knew that she and Darcy Devereaux were indulging in a torrid love affair but if, as he suspected, she was as lustful as himself, one lover would hardly be enough.

It was Shawn's first excursion into smart society, and its casual air delighted him. What struck him most was that none of them appeared to possess any surnames. They were all Algys and Billys and Lady Algys and Mrs Billys. Provincial that he was, he presumed that this was the customary method of address within the charmed circle into which he had been temporarily pitchforked. Josephine was being monopolized by her husband, a straight-backed gentleman with a waxed moustache and a military stance. Everyone seemed to be pairing up, and he obeyed Selden's request to conduct a Mrs Jack Something to the dinner table. He had considerable misgivings about his ability to entertain her. His apprehensions were unfounded. A short, searching examination satisfied the lady, before the fish was removed, that he had no aspirations towards smartness, and that therefore the barest need for civility was all he could expect from those who could lay claim to such qualification. Consequently, she met his well-meaning efforts at small talk with indifference, and devoted herself to a pink and white young gentleman in a high collar who sat on her other side.

This left Shawn with ample time to watch his fellow guests and to consume a most excellent dinner, a situation which he accepted with philosophical relief. There was plenty to occupy his attention. The splendour of the ladies' dresses; the magnificence of the hothouse flowers and the gold centrepieces which covered the table; the bewildering variety of dishes and the giants with powdered heads who proffered them; the high-pitched conversation and the shrill screams of laughter as some more than ordinarily facetious Algy set the table in a roar. What a contrast between the run-down manor of Four Oaks and the shabby wayside inns that had been his lot since leaving.

Alison Ruthen had noticed the arrival of the stranger. It had been most inconvenient and had upset her place settings. Trust Josephine to do something like that. Alison supposed he was one of her lame ducks. Really, both she and Selden had no sense of the appropriate. That Mr Claypole and his noisy, common wife! Selden had been most particular that they be entertained like royalty. He had some scheme in mind, she could tell. There had been quite an uproar among the squires when it became known that Claypole was to stay at Armit-stead House, for he was one of those millionaires who had descended, meteor-like, on English society within the last few years. The man was a haberdasher! He owned a chain of department stores, the biggest of which was in London's West End.

To the dire confusion of both Alison and her fellow-sufferers, it became abundantly clear that it was a matter of perfect indifference to Selden whether they accepted Claypole or not. He had been determined to invite him however much they grumbled. It had come to light since Claypole's arrival yesterday that he was the possessor of a house in Grosvenor Square where members of the Royal Family honoured him with their company, of one of the largest steam yachts afloat, and of a villa in Newmarket.

Oh, Selden, Alison sighed as she watched him where he sat at the head of the table, I don't understand you any more. Outwardly he was the same, with his long, lean face, deep-set eyes and sensual lips which always reminded her of ancestral portraits. For him a stock and fob would have seemed more appropriate than an evening suit. His colouring was like Josephine's except that his hair was several shades darker and his eyes slate grey. I don't resemble them, Alison thought gloomily, I'm the cuckoo in the nest. My hair's what's called rich mouse, and my eyes are a peculiar colour – like pewter, very dull.

This lack of rapport had not been present directly after Belinda's death. In his agony Selden had turned to her, and she had sworn never to fail him. Life had not been easy; he had not always been easy to get along with even in their childhood. But she had taken up the burden, expanding her energy and expecting little appreciation in return. She had not wanted thanks, all she wanted was to help. Little more than a schoolgirl then, she had been vaguely aware that it would prevent her marrying but, unawakened to sex, she had not fully understood what this privation entailed, and for years she had been content. She had her own house, her own place in the world; a life work worth doing, and which no one but herself could undertake.

But lately there was no denying that she and Selden were getting on each other's nerves. She searched her soul for reasons, deeply hurt. No one could have said she was not the most devoted of sisters, but a chill finger of doubt was penetrating her consciousness. Did Selden really want such devotion? She had done her utmost to be a clever housekeeper, careful and considerate of his comfort, but the bitter truth was that they were jarring on one another. Unspoken friction shadowed the air.

There was a growing restlessness within her. She found the daily routine stultifying. There was nothing to mitigate the increasing loneliness, the sense of isolation. Oh, they entertained frequently, when Selden was home. There was the bustle of preparing for trips to London, opening the house for the season, but Selden spent more and more time away. Seeking something to fill the empty hours, she joined several charities, meeting with other ladies, to sew or sort over clothing collected for the poor. There would be garden parties and fêtes at one or other of the big houses, perhaps a dance to celebrate some fortunate girl's engagement. Festivities to which she and her neighbours looked forward for weeks at a time. What volumes it spoke of the flatness of life in the country. How tired she was of it all. How she thirsted for a change. Even her talent for art gave her little pleasure these days. There was no one to share it with, no one remotely interested in discussing it. She spent less and less time in her studio, creativity at a halt.

Any claim I might have had to beauty is fading fast, she had thought as she dressed that evening. I'm twenty-six! What was it Selden had said the other day? 'You're getting on, Alison. Of course, you do understand, don't you, that if ever there was talk of marriage, you mustn't hesitate on my account.'

Did he suppose that no one had ever asked? What

33

would he say if he realized that she had already dismissed two worthy suitors who had offered not only themselves, but their not inconsiderable worldly goods? She had pointed out to them that her course was already set. But it had been pleasant to know that someone had cared. When I grow old and fat, she consoled herself, it will be nice to remember that I remained single from choice, not necessity. Perhaps she hadn't really been put to the test, not being remotely in love with either of them. But what was love? A pathway to the pain that Selden had suffered? The immoral liaisons with which Josephine amused herself?

It was nearly eleven o'clock when they finally left the dinner table and repaired to a palatial apartment known as the music-salon. An impromptu ball was organized on its polished parquet, with one of the effervescent young men operating the gramophone. The waltz and polka were danced first, but this did not prove exciting enough, so a set of Kitchen Lancers was improvised.

Leaning against a potted palm, lazily watching the proceedings, Darcy Devereaux was moved to observe sardonically to Selden: 'Lord, what a performance! Whoops! Look at them go! Kitchen is a good name for such a caper. It reminds me of the bars and gas lamps of a Parisian place of amusement that I've not visited since my misspent youth.'

'Claypole's enjoying himself,' Selden answered with satisfaction.

Darcy shot him a glance. 'And this is all that matters, I take it? You wish to please the oh so important store owner?'

'He and I are about to do business,' Selden replied, and his lips curled in a smile. 'I think I'll go and ask Mrs Daisy Claypole for the honour of the next dance.'

Josephine was signalling to Darcy with her fan behind Douglas's back and, knowing what she wanted, he strolled towards the conservatory which led from the music-room. It was filled with exotic plants and shrubs, the atmosphere moist and warm, almost tropical. Josephine was flitting from flower to flower like a big gold moth, bending her head to drink in the heavy perfume. The curve of her neck, the line of her cheek half hidden against the leaves, the slender body bent low from the waist, were graceful and alluring.

It was quiet there, the music beautified by distance, the gentle splash of the fountain giving an illusion of tranquillity. All at once she felt his shadowy presence, and the next moment his touch upon her bare shoulder sent her blood leaping. She drew in a sharp breath. He was such a handsome man, his face strong and craggy, skin tanned by constant exposure to winds and weather. No mere token farmer, she knew that he worked as hard as any of his hands, sparing himself no measure of the gruelling tasks on his lands. He was tall and powerfully built, with wide shoulders, slim waist and narrow hips. Whatever he chanced to wear looked good on him, be it tweeds, hunting gear or, as now, a perfectly tailored dinner jacket. He fitted into every situation, adapting himself, chameleon-like, to the farming community or the high life. Heads turned whenever he put in an appearance, and he could have had almost any girl in the county as his wife but, so far, had shown no inclination to marry.

His eyes looked particularly blue that night, his dark hair brushed back in deep waves, his closely clipped beard outlining his jaw. Her gown rustled as his arms came around her tightly. She glanced apprehensively towards the double glass doors which separated them from the others, but they were shielded by a thickly foliaged magnolia bush.

'I'll come to your room later,' she whispered, her voice unsteady. 'Of course, I may have to let Douglas make love to me first. He'll expect it, and be most frightfully put out if I refuse. That is, if he doesn't have too much to drink. He's quite useless then – can't raise a bean!'

'I hope you'll have a bath after,' Darcy growled, experiencing a feeling of distaste. 'I really don't like other men's leavings.'

She laughed, and the sound rang hollow. 'Make sure he drinks a lot, then I can leave him tucked up in bed, with his valet on the alert, armed with a bucket. He's sure to be sick all over the place.'

'And you call what you do with him making love?' Darcy said, a bitter slant to his mouth. But even as he spoke, her warm breath caressed his cheek as she turned her mouth up to his, begging for his kiss.

With her lips crushed under his, that melting, weakening sensation beginning to crawl insidiously through her limbs, a part of Josephine was thinking: Making love? Oh yes, she had loved Douglas once, with that youthful infatuation which could never be repeated. She had been wooed ardently by him, her hand sought in marriage, and had been in a seventh heaven of delight when she walked down the aisle on his uniformed arm. A virgin on their wedding night, she had found joy in his satisfaction. It was only later, as the months went by, that she began to wonder about her own right to fulfilment. She had attempted to talk to her husband about it, though shy and ignorant, suffering from lack of knowledge about the facts of life. Servant girls were better informed than she had been. In her sheltered stratum of society it was not considered nice for young ladies to be aware of such things.

So, even after the birth of her first child, she continued to take a passive role, becoming more and more frustrated as Douglas fanned the flames of her desire without ever quenching them. Her love turned to dislike. She was deeply disappointed and impatient with his lack of sensitivity. Before long, she began to experiment with other men, seeking completion, sometimes finding it, sometimes not, coming to the conclusion that men, no matter how much they boasted of their success with

36

women, rarely had the delicacy and understanding to play upon the female body like a finely tuned instrument, bringing it to ecstasy. Even Darcy, much though she adored him, had his off moments. Tonight when she crept into his bed, he might be on form, taking pains to give as well as receive pleasure, or he might be rough and ready, selfishly seeking his own release, leaving her throbbing with unsatisfied lust.

Much later, when the others were all set to spend time and money at the roulette table, playing Consule Planco, Selden gathered Mr Claypole and bore him off to the gunroom. Once there, he installed him in a leather armchair, placed a large brandy in his hand and lit up cigars. 'Well, sir, and how d'you like Armitstead House?' he began.

Claypole, short, stout, ruddy complexioned and heavily moustached, bared his teeth in appreciation. 'Grand, Lord Ruthen – it's grand!' he exclaimed, his eyes, set in a network of wrinkles, assessing the fine furnishings, his shopkeeper brain totting up figures relentlessly. 'My Daisy's most impressed, most impressed indeed. She'll not be happy with the one back home now. Won't rest till we've a country mansion just like yours. You know what women are – like something to swank about, don't they?' He winked affably, attempting to draw Selden into that confederacy of males who pampered and patronized the women in their lives.

'Good thing for chaps like me that they do,' commented Orde-Bunbury from the depths of his bushy brown beard. He was a thickset man, with powerful shoulders and massive hands, looking more like a stevedore than an architect of renown. He nodded as a footman approached with the brandy decanter.

'Would you build me one?' Claypole sat on the edge of his chair watching him through puffy lids, chubby legs crossed, white spats displayed over his shiny patent leather shoes.

'I'd take on the commission, sir, if you can find a suitable site.' The architect smiled in his beard, recognizing everything that was base, showy and ill-bred in Reginald Claypole, but prepared to fleece him. Selden had invited him that weekend with the express purpose of clinching some sort of a deal. He had dropped sufficient hints for Orde-Bunbury to cancel other engagements and catch the first train down.

Claypole cast his eye around the gunroom. It was panelled in oak. The heavy chimneypiece was based on a Norman example and surmounted by a huge mirror and clustered stone shafts. Everything was dark and heavy and ponderous, but undeniably extravagant. There were several glass domes of stuffed birds, the brilliant, scintillating plumes of rare breeds set against stones and shrubs and flowers. Another glass case contained wax fruit tumbling from a plaster cornucopia. Animal heads hung from the walls, alongside gun racks and sporting prints. Claypole had not yet learned to hunt but, by God he intended to, and fish and shoot, and he'd make damned certain that Daisy did likewise. He might not have been born an aristocrat but he'd bloody well see that he lived like one!

Selden was standing by the fireplace, one foot resting on the elaborately wrought brass fender. 'I think I might be able to help you there, Mr Claypole,' he remarked casually.

'You know of a parcel of land?' Claypole looked at him keenly, puffing at his cigar.

'I might, if the price was right.' Selden was an expert at prevarication. Let Claypole work up a sweat. He had danced with his wife, impressing her with his refined manners and good looks, listening with studied interest as she recounted her triumphs as a Gaiety Girl before accepting Claypole's proposal.

'Of marriage, I'll have you know!' she had chided playfully, rolling her eyes at him with heavy sauciness.

'Oh, no, there was no hanky-panky before the ring was on my finger! I'm not that daft!' Selden left her, assured that she'd give her husband hell if he didn't buy her a mansion on as grand a scale as Armitstead House, at the very least.

Claypole rose to the bait, eager to assert himself and show these people a thing or two. 'You're talking to a businessman, sir.' His chest swelled a little under the stiff white shirt-front, and the gold watch-chain that crossed his paunch stirred as if in agreement. 'I didn't make Claypole's Emporiums overnight, you know. A great deal of effort went into it, I can tell you – effort and planning and sweat, if you'll pardon the coarseness, but we're talking man to man – and talking money, what's more.'

'Let's not cross our bridges before we reach 'em,' advised Selden. 'You may not like my proposition, may not care for the land I'm about to offer.' He seated himself on the curl-backed horsehair sofa, and crossed one thin, elegantly clad leg over the other. He had an ace up his sleeve, but did not intend to play it, for the moment.

'That's true, I'll not deny it.' Claypole liked his style. Such matters must be approached with caution. 'Can you give me a hint, my Lord?'

Selden put down his glass, steepled his fingers together and smiled. 'What would you say to hundreds of fine acres containing parklands and arable grazing, woods filled with game and your own trout stream?' he asked slowly, then, giving Claypole no time to answer, he went on: 'There's an old building in a choice spot in the very centre of the plot I have for sale.'

'But Daisy don't want an old building!' Claypole exclaimed, showing more interest than he had intended. 'She wants a house like this one!'

'She shall have it, Mr Claypole,' Selden soothed, his taut smile deepening. He cast a fleeting, amused glance at Orde-Bunbury. 'Isn't this so, Jonas?'

39

The architect returned his smile and managed to conceal his impatience with the pompous little man who was about to part with money, a great deal of money. 'Quite so, my Lord. You may choose what style you wish, Mr Claypole. The existing house, little more than a ruin, might I add, can be demolished. I can show you plans of buildings like Armitstead House, copied from French chateaux, or you can have a Scottish castle, if you wish.'

'A castle, eh?' Claypole could no longer hide his interest, fired by grandiose schemes, and Selden's excellent brandy. 'Aye, Daisy would go mad about a castle, I'll bet my bottom dollar!'

'You'd like to hear more details of this property?' Selden beckoned to the dark figure who had been seated quietly in the background, watching and listening without a word. 'Meet Mr Jason Henshaw, of Henshaw, Horsefield and Bailey. My London solicitor, don't you know.'

'A pleasure, Mr Claypole.' Henshaw uncoiled his thin limbs and bowed. 'Your servant, sir.'

He seemed a tall man at first sight but, compared with Selden, he lost this semblance of height and retained only that of thinness. His hair was sparse, permitting only a few strands to be slicked back with macassar oil over his lofty bald cranium. His face was bony, and his mouth was a narrow slit between his prominent nose and chin, giving it an air of secrecy. On either side of his narrow head, his ears seemed unusually large, red and semi-transparent in the glow of the shaded lamp-bulbs.

'A month ago, Mr Henshaw brought me some extraordinary news,' Selden continued, idly swinging a polished shoe, his eyes fixed on it as if it was of far more importance than the present conversation. 'My uncle, the Marquis of Suttonbridge, has died –'

'I'm sorry,' Claypole blurted out, composing his flabby features into sorrowful lines.

40

'Thank you, but truth to tell, I can't remember ever meeting him. I was a schoolboy when he left England,' Selden went on, his eyes shifting from Claypole's rubicund features to that of Henshaw's lugubrious countenance, and then to Orde-Bunbury's keenly observant face. 'My father was his brother. We all use the old family name, very proud of it. I was next in line when he snuffed it some years ago. I knew that the Marquis had no children, and had departed for foreign climes in somewhat mysterious circumstances. As far as I was aware, no one had heard from him since.'

' 'Pon my soul, here's a rum go!' Claypole was agog, though not entirely surprised. He had hobnobbed with enough nobility by now to realize that they could be somewhat eccentric in their habits.

'A letter came to my office from Bahia, in Brazil.' The reedy voice of Henshaw was as thin as his frame. 'In it, I was informed that Edgar Ruthen, the Marquis of Suttonbridge, had died shortly before. This is all that it said – no details, no enlightenment. As Lord Ruthen's adviser, I wrote to him straight away. He expects to be the new Marquis. The Priory and its lands will belong to him, though it's not general knowledge just yet. There are formalities, you understand. These privileges can't be claimed by right. They are given by favour of the Crown, but we don't anticipate any difficulties.'

'I see,' breathed Claypole, with dawning comprehension. 'It's this house – this land, that you're offering to me!'

'It is indeed. How perceptive,' smiled Selden, through the fragrant haze of cigar smoke. 'Does it appeal, Mr Claypole?'

Claypole's store-owner instinct put an instant curb on his keenness. 'That depends,' he said cagily.

'There's no hurry.' Selden rose and stretched his limbs, an easy, graceful figure, very much the aristocrat. 'Take your time, I'll have no trouble selling it in other

41

directions. A most desirable property. Tell you what. Why don't we drive over there tomorrow and take a look at it?'

Claypole had just opened his lips to reply, when there came a sharp knock at the door. At Selden's call to enter, the butler appeared, standing stiffly to attention as he announced: 'There's someone to see you, your Lordship.'

Selden frowned, giving him a stern glance. 'At this time of night? Who is it?'

'He gave his name as Mr Rufus Godwin, and says his business is urgent.'

Selden waved an impatient hand and was about to order that the stranger be shown into the library where he could see him alone, when the door was flung back and a short, burly man in a fur-collared overcoat and large black hat strode in, bringing with him a blast of clean, cold air.

'Lord Ruthen!' Gimlet-sharp eyes peered at him, and he made no apology for this rude interruption. 'I must speak with you – at once – now. I'm the late Edgar Ruthen's executor.'

'What?' Henshaw was outraged, his professional pride under attack. 'You can't be! My firm have always handled the concerns of the Ruthen family.'

'Sorry, old chap, but you're wrong.' Godwin flung back the capes of his coat with a swashbuckling gesture. There was something vaguely theatrical about him, so squarely made, his nose of noble proportions, as high-bridged and sharp as a falcon's beak, his face lined, his eyes pouched but remarkably youthful despite his obvious years. 'I knew Edgar aeons ago. We were students at Oxford together. He made me his legal adviser after I'd taken silk. When he decided to pack it all in and go abroad, he asked me to keep an eye on things here. We've corresponded from time to time.'

'I don't understand.' Selden's face was pale, and his

eyes burned in their deep sockets. He stood by the fireplace, head high, staring down scornfully on the intruder. In his head a luminous haze widened and narrowed and danced – thickening, crimsoning into fury.

Godwin advanced towards the fire, holding out his strong, blunt-tipped hands to the flames. 'Damned cold night. When I got the telegram, I caught the last train from Paddington. Had a hell of a job finding a cabby willing to drive me out here. But the matter is urgent, sir. I've come to dash your hopes, I'm afraid.'

'What d'you mean?' Selden was aware of a sudden silence, as if the room, the whole house, perhaps even the universe, was listening.

'You can't inherit.' Godwin's crisp, deep voice broke it.

There was a gasp from Henshaw. 'It's not true! You lie, whoever you are!'

Godwin turned those bright, penetrating eyes on him. 'It is absolutely true, my friend. Edgar Ruthen left behind him a daughter. She's already on the high seas, and will be landing in England very soon to claim her inheritance.'

2

Alison escaped from the house, letting herself out of a side door. She took a deep breath of the clear, cold sparkling air and hoisted her bag on to her shoulder. She was warmly clad in a thick tweed skirt and cardigan, topped by a long coat, and had a muffler wound around her throat and a knitted tam-o'-shanter on her head. Under one arm she held a sketching pad, and her hold-all contained artists' materials.

She went around to the stable block to collect her bicycle and rode down the straight path, coming to a narrow avenue of bare beeches which led to a summer house thatched with heather. But instead of going to the grig-house, as it was called, she turned left, following a track which led between the paddocks, winding its way into a copse, where the naked branches soughed in the brisk northerly wind. Soon she emerged into the open, dismounting and pushing her cycle across the broad expanse of a field.

I must go there again, she thought. If what Selden says is true, the new owner will be arriving soon. Will she be friendly? Or will she shut herself off from us, her unfamiliar relations? Selden was angry, she could tell. Angry and disappointed and very bitter. She had been astounded when he had called her into the gunroom last night, and introduced her to the lawyer, Mr Godwin, abruptly laying the situation before her. There existed a cousin, a foreign woman, born to Edgar Ruthen late in life by a French lady from Haiti.

It was difficult to grasp this reality. Dazed and stupefied by the rage on her brother's face, trivial thoughts had flashed across her brain; of airing a room

44

for their unexpected visitor; of breaking the news to the vicar and his wife. When Godwin had retired, she had lingered on, hardly noticed as Selden pacified Claypole, assuring him that they would work something out. It all came to light then. He had been planning on selling the land to him, of pulling down The Priory. Even the faithful Alison found this an almost blasphemous notion. The Priory had stood on the site since the thirteenth century. True, it had not been lived in for years, cared for only by an elderly retainer, but to destroy it, and erect some monstrosity designed by Orde-Bunbury! Alison discovered that her patience with Selden and his schemes was wearing perilously thin. She could but hope that Camilla Ruthen proved to be a mettlesome opponent who would successfully foil any such plans.

After breakfast, Selden, relentlessly determined not to be thwarted, had placed himself at the wheel of his sporty Lanchester car and, with the Claypoles in the rear seat, had driven off to view The Priory. Alison had seen that set expression on his face before and knew it boded ill. She visualized a battle royal, or would their cousin be a meek girl and give in? She had no doubt that Selden would bring his considerable powers of persuasion into play. For her own part, she found the idea of a long-lost cousin rather thrilling, her lively imagination already at work. But whatever happened in the near future, it was bound to affect her own connection with The Priory.

For as far back as she could remember, she had loved the place. It lay only two miles from Armitstead House, and had become her refuge. Watkins and his aging wife lived in the lodge, and Alison was wont to roam through the echoing rooms alone, filled as they were with furniture shrouded, ghostlike, in dust sheets. Like most old, deserted houses it was reputed to be haunted. Certainly, Alison had not liked being there after twilight had turned the shadows into something deep and mysterious, hurrying away with the feeling of being watched by invisible eyes. But on summer days, when the sun was high, pouring light and warmth through the shutters, it had been her delight, and many were the sketches she had made, both inside and out.

I must do just one more, she thought as she hurried along. The days were brief at this time of the year and she must work while the light held. In the distance the weathercock glittered on one of The Priory's towers. She'd draw it from a different angle. This would be interesting. She already had a large collection of sketches of the house from every aspect, executed in all seasons, a dedicated artist even though her fingers might be stiff with cold, and her feet aching with chilblains.

She stopped suddenly, gripped by another thought. Would the new mistress keep the gypsy wagon or would it be destroyed as of no account? This must not happen! She forgot everything else, leaving her cycle leaning against a wall and running to the boundary of the manor's rear garden. Like the rest of the grounds, this had reverted to the wild. All lawns and beds lay drowned beneath a lake of weeds. In a far corner, beleaguered by briars, an ancient wagon stood under an ash tree, its tin chimney lost amongst the branches. There was no record of how this home of a wandering band of Romanies had found such an anchorage. Alison, Selden and Josephine had played there when children. Bossy Josephine, she remembered, had always insisted on being the Gypsy Queen, whilst she had been forced into the thankless role of Fly, the lurcher, tethered between the wheels. Selden, of course, had been King of the Gypsies. Things haven't changed all that much, thought Alison wrily.

It had been a pretty play-place then. Its former nomadic owners had carved their family name 'Lees' over the door. It was still decipherable. Its panels had lost the former glory of their paintwork, but it was possible to discern the outlines of leaves, dragons and prancing horses. There was something different about it today. For a moment her mind struggled with the problem, then she realized that smoke was drifting from the lopsided stove pipe which protruded through the bow-roof. Indignation welled in her. So the intrusion had already begun, had it? Without knowing why, she was blaming Selden, though it was illogical to think that he'd already been there. It was hardly a thing with which to impress that horrible Reginald Claypole and his stupid wife. No matter. Someone was usurping her stamping ground.

She brushed through the grasses and walked up the wooden steps. The top half of the stable door was open. She looked in. Old broken toys still lay on its floor. Torn children's books were heaped on its shelves, and bulging mattresses sagged on the bunks where once she and her siblings had bedded down for a night of joy and terror. I ran for home first, she recalled, frightened by the ghostly hooting of an owl. Selden and Josephine teased me about it for months, making my life a misery. Somehow, this memory added to her present annoyance.

They weren't there now, but someone else was, and she started with surprise. 'Good morning, Lady Alison,' said the man who was resting on his hunkers near the rusted iron cooking stove.

'Good heavens! Mr Turner!' she exclaimed, pausing on the threshold, her shadow darkening the interior. 'What a fright you gave me! I thought you were a tramp!'

He laughed and stood up, and she saw that he was wearing an open-necked shirt and corduroy jacket. He looked entirely different without his dog collar and clerical garb. 'No tramp, Lady Alison, though there are times when I'm tempted to take to the road.' He picked up a cloth and wrapped it around the handle of the battered kettle which had begun to sing over the flames. 'May I offer you a cup of tea? The mugs are clean. I've brought them over from my house. Mrs Barlow will have my scalp if she knows. An admirable woman and superb cook, but a mite impatient with my erratic comings and goings.'

Alison gave him an involuntary scutinizing glance, and had an impression of a long, lean jaw, light brown hair, and a line of eyebrow, unexpectedly dark. The whole effect was too thin and lined to look robust after the florid men she knew, but it was, nonetheless, instinct with force.

Reassured, she nodded and seated herself on the edge of the one wooden chair. The wagon was warm. The stove glowed and wood smoke scented the air. 'We were never allowed to light a fire in here,' she said, watching him arrange two pottery mugs neatly, add milk and sugar and then wait for the tea to brew in the squat brown earthenware pot.

She noticed his fingers, long and pointed, the nails filbert-shaped, and carefully manicured. His present clothing suggested a consideration of ease above fashion, but his hands were evidently tended with care. She approved of this distinction.

'When you were children?' He cocked an eyebrow at her, and she saw for the first time that he had rather fine brown eyes. They were humorous, crinkled with laughter lines at the corners.

'Yes, we played here sometimes, Selden and Josephine and me.' Alison, usually shy and awkward with men, was surprised to find that she could talk to him quite freely. I suppose it's because he's a curate, she thought. Churchmen aren't like the others, are they? I don't need to be on my guard with him.

'I see,' he answered, quietly smiling, and she knew that he did indeed see more than she perhaps intended. He turned to his task, adding: 'I do believe that capital pot is now ready. You do take milk and sugar? Or are you one of the lemon brigade? If you are, then I'm afraid you're out of luck.'

'Milk will be fine. I don't have sugar.'

'Sweet enough, eh?' His smile deepened. 'I've a sweet tooth, I fear. Can't resist buying toffees and chocolate when I take the children into Lacey's shop.'

'How are the children?' Alison knew that he had four.

'Wildly excited. Christmas is coming, and they're busily engaged in writing notes to Santa Claus and posting them up the chimney. Do you still believe in him, Lady Alison?' He sat on a stool near her feet, and gave her a boyish grin.

Alison sipped the strong, hot tea, and then smiled back. 'What a question! Me? Hardly. Christmas for me means extra work and organization. Selden will expect an enormous house party. The invitations have already gone out.'

'And you wrote them all, I suppose.'

'How did you know that?'

He placed his cup on the floor and clasped his arms around his drawn-up knees. 'I can't imagine Lord Selden sitting down and applying himself to such a boring task.'

Force of habit made her fly to Selden's defence. 'He's a very busy man, you know, and it's my job to help him.'

'So I gather.' His voice was level, expressionless. 'I know that I've not been in the village long, but they talk about you and what happens up at the house. I gather he's a widower and you've dedicated your life to him. Some people think it's a pity – a nice woman like you, wasting herself.'

'Well really! Those gossips! You'd think they had something better to do!' She could feel herself blushing and hated it. She knew that she looked awful when her face turned red, convinced that she wasn't one of those fortunate women who could blush charmingly. She was embarrassingly conscious that he had noticed it, and that his interest was heightened thereby.

'Don't be cross,' he said kindly. 'You're much prettier

49

when you smile. The gossip wasn't spiteful, not about you, at any rate. You're popular in the village.'

'Thanks very much!' There was such bitterness in her voice that he stared at her. Lord! she was thinking angrily. I'm not even interesting enough to give them anything to tattle about. Popular indeed! Did he think this pleased me? I'll bet Josephine isn't at all popular, but her carryings-on must give them a field day!

Frank Turner had arrived at Abbey Sutton in the summer, as assistant to the Reverend Mapley. He had seen Alison in church on several Sundays, when she was in residence at Armitstead House. His housekeeper, Mrs Barlow, was a limitless mine of information. Little happened in and around the village which did not reach her ears. So Frank was more acquainted with the happenings at Armitstead House than its owners would have credited. The Reverend Mapley was nearly as bad, whilst his wife had her ear constantly to the ground. Christian charity work was a wonderful excuse for minding other people's business.

Thus Frank was fully conversant with Lady Josephine's friendship with Darcy Devereaux, and also with Selden Ruthen's predilection for property expansion. He had also gathered that Lady Alison was at his beck and call. What he had not realized was that she was unhappy in her self-appointed task.

'I didn't mean to be rude.' He turned his face towards hers with a twinkling appeal. They were close together, and the smiling interchange of glances seemed a good and pleasant thing.

'Don't pay any attention to me,' she said, looking away. 'I'm feeling edgy today. There was a party at the house last night. Selden invited some rather objectionable people to stay.'

To her relief he asked no questions, but talked easily on mundane subjects, not waiting for replies, but content simply to fill in the time till her self-possession

50

returned. She was also waiting for it, but only so as to be able to confide and be comforted. That this stranger could find the right panacea for the wounds inside her she acknowledged with something approaching delight.

Perhaps I should go to church more often, she thought, wondering if religion was the answer. Contentment enfolded her, but she would not admit even for a moment that it had anything to do with the man at her side, the thin man with the kindly face, and clear, boyish eyes. Alison was not given to hasty friendships, but in this case there seemed no preliminary stages to live through. The moment of meeting had acclaimed a mental understanding which years of intimacy might have failed to bring about. Her inattention grew increasingly obvious, until at length he ceased speaking, and looked at her questioningly.

'You don't feel like talking? Shall I stay, and be quiet, or would you rather I went away, and left you alone.'

'Stay, please, and talk, but my mind is so full of problems that I can't think of anything else.'

'Poor little girl,' he said, so simply and kindly that there could be no offence in the familiarity. 'Very well then, let's talk of happy things.'

'Oh, yes! That will be nice. What shall we talk about?' She forgot that she had been unhappy, forgot Selden and Josephine and the Claypoles.

'Ourselves, of course,' he answered promptly. He laughed again, and tilted his head, meeting her eyes openly and gaily.

'Someone famous, I can't remember who, said that there was really no other subject to talk about but oneself, just as there was no other dish for breakfast but bacon,' she quipped, surprising herself. Normally she could never find a witty rejoinder until long after the opportunity had passed.

'I expect it was Oscar Wilde. Sounds like one of his comments.' He smiled into her eyes with a sense of

51

intimacy that sent her spirits racing upwards with a mysterious intoxication.

Wilde! What am I doing here, alone with the curate, discussing the man whom polite society would have forbidden me to mention? Somehow, she no longer cared. 'Are you fond of yourself, Mr Turner?' she asked suddenly.

He was refilling their mugs, bringing them across the tiny space. 'Devoted to me, of course! Why shouldn't I be? I'm not a bad fellow, by and large. My name's Frank. You can call me that, if you wish.'

She chose to ignore this for the time being, saying half-jokingly: 'It's the truth, I suppose. Most lonely people have no one to love save themselves, but the idea's rather shocking. Aren't we taught by the church to be selfless? Even if it's true. I don't think one should admit it –'

'I'm not saying that it's true of me now. That was ages ago, before I married.' His face had grown serious. Now she could see the lines about his eyes, the powdering of grey hair above his ears.

'Mrs Turner, of course. How is she?'

Alison had forgotten that he had a wife. She ferreted through her memory, trying to picture Mrs Turner. Yes, she'd met her at one of Mrs Mapley's sewing parties. Brown-haired, rather stout, with no dress sense at all. She had not had much to say, but Alison had put this down to natural diffidence, also it was nigh impossible to get a word in edgewise when Mrs Mapley was in full flood. A shy person herself, she could appreciate the woman's uneasiness, suddenly thrust into a strange community where everyone seemed to know each other.

'Elsie doesn't enjoy very good health, I'm sorry to say.' His shoulders sagged and his face had lost its buoyancy. 'She suffers a great deal.'

'Oh, I'm so sorry! I didn't know – didn't mean –' Impulsively she reached over and placed her hand on

52

his, then immediately recovered herself and withdrew it, blushing again.

'This is one reason why I left my calling in London,' he went on, looking not at her, but at the floor between his feet. 'I thought the country air – a change of scene –'

'And she's better?' She tried to sound hopeful, making her smile brightly encouraging.

'A little.' He made an effort to shake off his gloom. 'I mustn't burden you with my troubles. We're here to enjoy ourselves. Remember?'

'Why exactly are you here?' she asked. It was better when he smiled. She had not liked those grooves which had deepened each side of his pleasant mouth when they spoke of his wife.

'I was going to put the same question to you.' His voice was calm and level again, lifting the atmosphere. 'All right, I'll confess first, if you promise not to laugh.'

'I promise.' There was something exhilarating about sharing secrets. It was a pleasure that Alison had not known since her one childhood friend moved away from the area.

He shifted a little uneasily on his stool, then grinned up at her. 'I write.' He said it with a queer kind of pride.

'Oh.' Alison did not know what else to say. He had brought it out as casually as if he had said, 'I breathe. I eat. I sleep.' So nonchalant that it left her speechless.

'No one else knows. I've never mentioned it to a living soul – well, only to my publisher, naturally.'

'And what do you write?' Some comment was called for and Alison made the obvious one.

'Novels.' His face lit up and the lines were smoothed away. 'It's not the sort of thing a clergyman likes to own to.'

'Why? It's an accomplishment, surely? Good Lord, a writer who has actually been published! That's wonderful!' She was thinking of her sketches and how she had daydreamed sometimes of being exhibited in a public gallery. The Tate, perhaps? The Royal Academy! This man had done it. His creations had come alive in print. Her admiration rose by leaps and bounds.

It was his turn to flush. He seemed genuinely delighted by her praise. 'That's good of you. But you see, the sort of things I write aren't considered to be – well, you know – proper literature. I started doing it when I was at theological college, to make extra money, you see. My parents weren't rich and it was costing a lot for me to go into the church. I knew someone who wanted some hack work done. I've always found words come easily to me. Then, after I'd been ordained, I met Elsie and we were married. The four children arrived in less than six years. A curate doesn't receive a large stipend. I went back to writing to supplement our income, but on the quiet. In fact nobody knows anything about it. Even Elsie never asks where the occasional cheques come from. Small though they are, they help out.'

'So, where does this place fit in?' She glanced around at the caravan, so pleasant with the wintry sunlight pouring through the little latticed windows, and the fire crackling and popping beneath the kettle.

'Our house is small, nothing like as grand as the manse. The children are young and noisy. Elsie doesn't disturb me in the study – thinks I'm engaged on parish business, but I find it simpler to come here when I've some scribbling to do.'

A wild notion flashed through Alison's mind. There were so many rooms at Armitstead House. Why shouldn't she suggest that he use one of them for his work? Then she realized the ridiculousness of such a notion. What possible excuse could she give Selden? He'd only sneer and make fun of her, like he had when she'd dug in her heels and insisted on converting one of the garden rooms into a studio.

'What exactly is it you write?' Unconsciously she had drawn closer to him seeing, with a shock, how very bright his eyes were, hedged by curling sandy lashes.

54

'Penny-dreadfuls!' he replied promptly. 'Blood-and-thunder adventure stories for errand boys, and romances for maidservants. You see now why I hide my light under a bushel? It's not something to boast about. I'm sure the Reverend Mapley wouldn't approve. I use pen-names.'

'I think it's wonderful,' Alison breathed, and she meant it. 'But, oh dear, it makes my reason for coming seem pretty tame.' She took a deep breath and rushed on. 'I like to sketch and paint. That's why I'm here. I've done dozens of pictures of the old Priory. I've never shown them to anyone. Well, Selden's seen one or two. He calls them my daubings.'

He bowed, hand on heart. 'Your secret is safe with me, fair maiden.'

Alison rose, picking up her bag and pad. 'I'll leave you to your work, Mr Turner –'

'Please don't rush away,' he answered, watching her intently. 'It's refreshing to talk with a fellow artist. The next time I see you it will undoubtedly be in different circumstances – at some parochial meeting, a jumble sale, or choir practice. You'll be singing carols with the villagers?'

'If I can.' Alison had always refused other years.

'You'll come here again.' His voice had a new, deep tone.

'Tomorrow, if it's fine. But I don't want to disturb you –'

'I'll look forward to it.'

Alison left the wagon without a backward glance, but she knew it would be an impossibility to concentrate on drawing that day. She took a roundabout route home, unwilling to see its occupants so soon. She did not want to lose the glow which was warming her. She had found a friend. Someone with whom she could share her ambitions. It was no good calling them modest. She now knew that they were far from that. Once, many years before Belinda died, she had wondered if she might attend art school, but this had been frowned upon. Titled young ladies could not enter those rather worldly, Bohemian establishments, where models posed naked and the students were rumoured to be completely without morals. It was not the done thing.

It was so nice to talk to him, she thought, as she headed towards the village. She was already looking forward to the morrow. Dejection had given way to serenity. The day now appeared radiant, despite the bitter cold. Alison felt remarkably light-hearted, gazing around her as she walked through the woods. It was as if scales had been removed from her eyes, and she was inspired to make notes of what she saw, perhaps capture it later on canvas in her studio.

It was worth being out of doors, whatever the season, for then she was closer to nature, the only thing in the world that she had found unchanging in the drifting storms of personal relationships. The path beneath her cycle wheels was frostbound. Beauties hidden in the richness of summer stood revealed in the woods. The stately firs soared upwards from the silent earth, and carried her mind to the freedom of the pale sky above. The gnarled oak's twisted branches overshadowed the dead, brown leaves, and through them shivered a gentle rustle.

I think I like winter best of all, she thought, stopping to stare at a particularly entrancing view through an avenue of bare trees. *That* would make an impressive painting, if I can only remember it when I get home. Cycle parked against a bush, she unstrapped her pad from the pannier and did a lightning sketch, head to one side, pencil working swiftly as she stood there, absorbed.

She came to the perimeter of the estate between two ranks of beeches that gave entrance to the picturesque village, with its traditional duckpond and green. Thatched cottages showed tidy gardens, and the grey

56

Norman church dominated all. The vicarage stood beneath its shadow. Next to it was the small house called Dolby Wold, where the curate and his family lived. Alison had never paid it much heed before, but now as she pedalled slowly past, she noted the lace curtains in its windows, the smoke coiling from its chimneys. Two small children, muffled to the ears against the cold, were playing on a swing in the front garden.

The village street consisted of rows of grey stone gables, at the end of which stood a sundial-surmounted cross. A little further on was the Methodist chapel, red brick, ugly and out of place, unlike the mellow Norman church with its stained-glass windows and flying buttresses. Then came the sturdy Tudor almshouse. Over its porch and beneath the elaborately sculptured crest of the Ruthens, was an inscription saying that it was founded by Lady Margaret Ruthen in 1534. This never failed to please Alison. She liked to think that her ancestors had lived there and cared for the villagers for centuries. It made her feel worthwhile and secure.

There was a small milk float carrying a couple of metal churns, parked outside the imposing entrance of the ancient Red Lion inn, once a busy posting house. An old grey horse stood dozing between the shafts, waiting with patient resignation. Alison smiled. Stan Hoddinott was undoubtedly within, quaffing his lunch-time cider. Like the horse, housewives would also be waiting, but with less stoicism, for him to continue his round. He'd be unsteady, slopping the milk as he scooped it from the churns with a pint measure and transferred it to his customers' jugs.

Lacey's Store was situated opposite the inn, its stone walls hung with jewel-bright enamelled signs, advertising cigarettes, starch and metal polish. Leaving her cycle outside, Alison pushed opened the door. A bell tinkled, and her nostrils were immediately assailed by its familiar odour, a rich conglomerate of spices, corn, paraffin and cheese. Lacey's sold everything from boot-blacking to material by the yard. Its outer room, reached from the pavement by a single, brass-edged step, was so dim that on such a winter day as this, it was lit by handsome oil lamps. They were positioned so that their yellowish rays could fall on the set of wooden drawers beneath the counter where change was kept in dish-shaped containers. Though electricity had been run to Armitstead House and, at Selden's expense, the church too had been wired for this latest innovation, gas had never been piped to the village, and candles and lamps were still in general use.

The shop was stacked to the ceiling with commodities. The nearest big town was Ryehampton, twelve miles away, necessitating a journey by car or horse-drawn bus to Sutton Cross where a train ran once a day. There was no need to do this with a store like Lacey's within easy access. Only if one had exotic inclinations or fancied a day out.

Alison wove between open-ended barrels of sugar, rice, grain and flour, to the long, highly polished mahogany counter, behind which old Mrs Lacey reigned supreme. A wizened lady, whose knitting needles rarely ceased to flash, even when she was serving. Usually her imperious voice summoned her boy Jim, who was at least fifty years old. Jim would come running, grumbling and complaining, to weigh sugar on the brass scales and then, with the dexterity born of long practice, let it trickle in a snowy avalanche into a bag of thick, dark blue paper, neatly whipping the top closed. Or he might attack the huge round of cheese standing on the wooden board, slicing it through with a wire, using the skill of an axe-man severing a head. The scale would shudder as he tossed on the yellow, creamy wedge, applied the lead weights and stood back, squinting at the pointer.

More than two customers at once put both him and

his elderly mother in a panic. They might even have to bring in a recruit in the shape of Mrs Lacey's spinster daughter, Gladys. She would appear from behind the glass-panelled door at the rear which led to an inner sanctum. Gladys had worked in Ryehampton for a spell as a shopgirl and she was therefore respected. She specialized in fabrics for the home dressmaker. A heavy bolt of cloth would be hauled down from the shelf, spread out on a further counter kept especially for this purpose, and much consultation would ensue. Once the customer had made up her mind, out would come an enormous pair of scissors. Snip, snip, fold precisely, wrap the purchase in a sheet of crisp paper, the big ball of string revolving like a top as a length was drawn off.

Gladys also dealt with ready-made garments, some of which might be displayed in the tiny bow window; cardigans, knickers, liberty-bodices, socks, pinafores, a child's dress or two. She was an exceedingly thin lady, who considered herself to be genteel and spoke in a refined voice.

Alison heard her clipped tones as she advanced towards the counter where she could see large glass jars of colourful sweets. She was addressing the Misses Carpenter, two short, stout sisters, who were identical twins. They always wore matching outfits, and were so alike that Alison had long ago christened them Tweedle-dum and Tweedledee.

She came in on the tail end of a conversation concerning combinations. The elderly twins saw her, and bobbed a curtsy at one and the same moment. 'Good morning, Lady Alison,' they chorused in unison.

'Good morning, Miss Violet, and to you, Miss Priscilla.' Alison nodded and smiled. They were like rosy cherubs from an Italian painting, smiling at her with rather snobbish delight in having met her in the shop. She could not help teasing them a little. 'Are you anticipating a hard winter?' She indicated the thick white woollen undergarments displayed on the counter.

59

'Indeed, yes, your Ladyship.' Miss Priscilla ducked and bobbed.

'Very cold, to be sure,' her sister echoed.

Alison was aware that her toes were tingling with the sudden warmth from the cast-iron Tortoise stove that squatted behind its protective mesh guard. The three maiden ladies were looking curiously at the pad of paper under her arm, the canvas hold-all hanging from her shoulder.

'I've been sketching over at The Priory,' she vouchsafed, wondering why she was bothering to explain. Was she anxious to carry on being popular? It was true that she was invariably polite, hating to offend anyone.

'You're an artist, Lady Alison. My, so accomplished,' commented Gladys, not to be outdone, thin, big-knuckled hands resting lightly on the counter.

'Sketching! How clever,' the twins breathed admiringly.

'Not very, I think.' Alison shrugged it off, embarrassed. 'My poor efforts are not all that good.'

She was considering what they would say if they had known she'd been alone with the curate in a run-down gypsy wagon. But it was so innocent, she protested silently. I'm not like Josephine. He's a married man! Involuntarily, she could almost hear her sister's gay, lilting voice remarking: '*That* never stopped a good woman!'

'Can I help you, Lady Alison?' Mrs Lacey was poking an inquisitive nose in her direction, and peering through her gold-rimmed pince-nez.

Have they heard about Cousin Camilla's imminent arrival? Alison wondered. She knew that little happened above stairs which wasn't immediately a source of news in the kitchen and butler's pantry. The servants considered it their right to be in the know. Too soon yet, she decided. Give it a day, then it will be common knowledge. This will ruffle the serenity of the village.

She gathered her wits and rested her baggage on a bentwood chair near the grocery counter. Her eyes went to the sweet jars. 'Thank you, I'll take half a pound of peppermints and half a pound of mixed chocolates.'

While Mrs Lacey was weighing these out, the shop bell jangled, and Mrs Barlow clumped heavily across the floor. A middle-aged woman, her black skirts sweeping the brown linoleum, she had a basket over her arm and a shopping list in a black-gloved hand.

'Jim, take Mrs Barlow's order,' his mother said querulously. 'Get the bacon slicer going. You'll be wanting bacon, Mrs Barlow? And I've a tasty side of ham, fresh in.'

She nodded, another stranger in their midst. She had come with the Turners, keeping much to herself, a north-country woman with a broad accent. 'Happen I do, and other things besides.'

'Have you finally settled in, Mrs Barlow?' Alison asked courteously.

'Aye, thank you.' There was nothing servile about Mrs Barlow. She accorded Alison the respect she deserved, no more, no less, handing Jim her order meanwhile.

'It'll be your first Christmas here, won't it? We all look forward to it and celebrate in fine style.' Alison found herself eager to pursue the conversation. This woman was Frank Turner's housekeeper. She had probably been with them for some time and would have intimate knowledge of their lives.

'So I gather.' Mrs Barlow seemed disinclined to talk, soon busily engaged in ensuring that the goods served her were of the best, though not necessarily the most expensive. Listening to her, as Mrs Lacey weighed the sweets into cone-shaped paper bags, Alison came to the conclusion that the Turners were fortunate in their choice of servant. Unlike some, and staff were often problematic, there seemed no chance that she would

61

ever attempt to cheat them or cream off some of the housekeeping allowance to line her own purse.

She handed over twopence for her purchases, tucking the bags into her hold-all. These will do for tomorrow, she thought happily. I'll share them with my sweet-loving friend. As she turned to go, she heard Mrs Barlow say: 'I'll take a bottle of whisky, Jim – nay, not that one, it's far too dear. How much is the Glen Morran?'

'Mr Turner, he likes his little drop of grog, don't he?' Jim gave a gap-toothed grin. 'I never yet met a churchman what don't.'

'Happen he does.' Mrs Barlow gave him a severe stare. 'It warms him after working in that freezing vestry. It's high time the heating was reviewed. The choir've always got snotty noses.'

'I've heard the organist complaining about it too,' chimed in Miss Violet. 'Poor Mr Blake, he gets chilblains so badly. I've given him a jar of my herbal salve to rub on.'

'Wintergreen Ointment, that's the thing for chilblains,' answered Mrs Lacey, pointing to a sign hanging just behind her head. 'We stock it here.'

'Nay, best cure is an old northern one.' Mrs Barlow was packing necessities into her basket. Jim would carry the heavy cardboard box containing the rest of the groceries. 'Steep hands and feet int' chamberpot. But the water must be fresh, what you've produced on rising int' morning.'

This broad remark silenced the Misses Carpenter who retired, twittering and shocked to the material counter. They attended the Methodist chapel and were members of the Temperance Society. They were easily shocked. Mrs Barlow's face was perfectly straight but, as she met Alison's eyes, her lips twitched.

'And how is Mrs Turner?' Mrs Lacey took the money which Mrs Barlow drew from her purse, and counted out change.

62

'Not too well,' came the brisk reply.

'I've hardly seen her. She doesn't often venture out.' Mrs Lacey liked to see everyone who resided thereabouts. Her shop, which combined as a post office, was the hub of village life, even more important than church or chapel.

'That she don't.' Mrs Barlow checked the change and placed it in the depths of her black leather handbag. 'She's never been the same since little Effie were born.'

'The last child?'

'Aye, most definitely the last. She's been told not to have any more.'

'I should think not indeed,' sniffed Gladys who had been listening to this fascinating snippet of conversation. 'Why there's hardly a year between those children, is there?'

Mrs Barlow did not deign to reply. She reached across the counter and gathered up the bottle of spirits. 'I'll take that with me now,' she said firmly.

As Alison left, she was storing away all she had learned about Frank Turner. He had a sick wife who mustn't give birth again. He drank whisky, pretty often by the sound of things, and he was a writer. This was their secret. Those gossips in the shop would have given their eyeteeth to know of it! And he liked sweets. I'll indulge this fancy of his tomorrow, she thought as she cycled in the direction of the long, straight drive which led to Armitstead House. The sky was turning leaden overhead. Early dusk was settling, and the wind whistled through the waving tree tops, but she was unaware of its icy bite. Now she could face Selden and the rest of them. Her life had shape and purpose. There was someone with whom she could share her dreams. She had found a soul mate at last. Even the guilt she was experiencing because he was a married man had a thrilling edge. It added a touch of spice to the adventure. Perhaps I'm more like Selden and Josephine than I suspected, came the extraordinary thought, but in me the fires have been damped down and suppressed.

Twilight seeped through the room, purpling the shadows, bringing mystery. Josephine woke from sleep, stretching and yawning, her back curved against the naked chest of the man who lay beside her, his arms folded over her breasts, his long legs entangled with hers.

Her eyes opened and she saw the rapidly darkening room. The last rays of light flickered over the dusty panelled walls. Here was a portrait, a dead eye glaring from cracked canvas, a ruff, a jewel, and there a piece of gilded stucco edging the ceiling, a faded, faintly glinting coat of arms. Selden's right, she thought drowsily, it's time to have the old place destroyed before it falls down, though it's a damned useful love-nest for Darcy and me.

The bed smelt musty, and it was damp, she was sure of that, but neither must nor damp sheets could prevent Josephine's enjoyment when she was indulging her animal needs. At least it doesn't creak, she thought with a giggle. By God, it would take the efforts of half a dozen rollicking sailors who'd been at sea for six months to make this old thing shake. Solid! It was that, all right. A huge oak Elizabethan bed, with posts that looked as if they had been hewn out of tree trunks, intricately carved, a rearing headboard, inlaid with walnut and chiselled Tudor roses, and a tester from which were suspended embroidered curtains. We've put it to the test, good and proper, she thought, desire knotting her stomach as recent memories rushed in, but it's never as much as quivered!

She arched closer to Darcy, unable to get enough of his hairy, muscular body. He muttered in his sleep, his arms tightening. Josephine twisted around and ran a hand over his shoulders, his narrow waist, the sleek line of his thigh. She wriggled impatiently, wishing he would wake up. He was aware of her, she knew, even as he dreamed. His body was responding, hardening, pressing intimately against her rounded hip. Was he dreaming of her? she wondered idly. Or was there another seductress wooing him to passion, playing with him, goading him into sexual activity? Perhaps he thought he was in one of his haystacks, pushing up the skirts of some farm girl? Or in London, backstage at the Gaiety, his hands fondling the big, opulent breasts of an actress? Maybe Paris filled his slumber, with its gilded whorehouses offering manifold delights.

Whatever it was bringing about the desired reaction, Josephine knew that shortly she would be the recipient. She waited in tingling anticipation. They had almost been prevented from meeting that afternoon. Trust Selden to insist on driving the Claypoles to view the property, despite last night's dramatic turn of events. But they had returned in time for luncheon, though Alison had been absent. Josephine had eaten sparingly, having read somewhere that a heavy meal ruined one's sexual appetite, and gone out afterwards on the pretext of riding. It had been difficult to shake Shawn off. He'd been angling to accompany her. Selden seemed to have taken a fancy to the glib-tongued young Irishman, although there had been a scene with the estate manager who had come looking for him. Shawn had been shown up, not very happy about it, but ingenious in his explanation. Selden could admire these qualities and had responded by offering Shawn the post as second-in-command to Kennard, and also put him in charge of the stables, a position to which he was admirably suited.

While she continued to stimulate Darcy, Josephine was musing on whether or not she should encourage Shawn. A new admirer was always exciting, a challenge which she could rarely refuse. But oh, Douglas, she sighed, things could have been so very different if you'd been more sensitive to my needs. I loved you once. She

65

remembered how it had been when he was invalided out of the South African war, something of a hero for his exploits with the Imperial Light Cavalry. He was still handsome, still attractive, made even more so by the slight, rather romantic limp brought about by shrapnel in the leg. But he was becoming dull, too interested in the bottle and the companionship of old comrades. A man's man, who infinitely preferred to attend mess dinners where women were not included, to spend his time, as this afternoon, in the billiard-room at Armitstead House, drinking, smoking and talking with Selden, Claypole and Orde-Bunbury.

He could have been riding with me, she thought. Even now it could've been my husband here in bed, not Darcy – if only things had worked out differently.

Josephine was so easily bored. She found little interest in her children and certainly did not intend to have more. She had found pregnancy distasteful and had hated getting fat with none of her lovely gowns fitting. As for the actual process of birth! Though she'd had uncomplicated labours – 'I could've had it in a hedge-row, my dear, easy as shelling peas!' she had said to Selden after the first occasion – she was making sure that it did not happen again. Frequent trips to her doctor in Harley Street supplied her with pessaries and other chemicals guaranteed to prevent conception. She forbade her husband or her lovers to use condoms, disliking intensely this barrier between herself and her urges.

She had become a skilled lover, avidly reading any books she could obtain on the subject of amatory deviations. These were not generally sold over the counter in respectable bookshops, but Selden had contacts, as interested as herself, and therefore banned books littered his study and she had *carte blanche* to use them. He found it amusing that she did so, often discussing pornographic literature with her, an activity which both of them found stirring.

66

So to Shawn again – he was charming and handsome, and his green eyes twinkled so impudently every time he looked at her. But then there was Darcy with whom she was infatuated. Sorrowfully she accepted the truth that he probably wouldn't give a damn if she slept with Shawn. He was a hard man. Sometimes she teased him, saying: 'I don't believe you had a mother, Darcy. You were chiselled out of a block of granite!'

One day, she knew, she'd have to watch him leading another girl down the aisle. Not for years, maybe, but along would come some heiress and he'd see the advantage of such a match. Hers was a lost cause. Douglas would never divorce her; drunkard though he might be, he was strong on family honour, and he thought the world of the children. No, she'd be his wife for the rest of her life. Darcy did not care enough to fight for her, too selfish for heroics.

But he wanted her. There was no doubt about that. He was surfacing now, one hand finding her breasts, weaving its customary magic. She moaned and pressed against him, shuddering when his other hand roamed between her thighs. His mouth claimed her lips, pressing them open insistently, and pleasure started to course through her. Then she suddenly freed herself.

'Nature calls,' she said, disentangling her limbs from his and getting out of bed. She kicked against an empty wine bottle and it rolled away into a corner. 'I shan't be a minute.'

She found Darcy's shirt and put it on, then padded towards the door on bare feet. This chamber was the most habitable one in the house, and Josephine had first taken Darcy there after a ball, one hot summer night in June. She knew The Priory almost as well as Alison. It had been a prime spot for adventurous games during her childhood. The three youngsters had been left much in the care of the servants whilst their parents were abroad or in London. Their upbringing had been a curious

mixture of rigidity and astonishing ease. Perfect polite-
ness and obedience were insisted upon at all times, yet
they were allowed to run wild in the woods and fields, to
spend long unsupervised hours in the deserted Priory, to
sleep in the gypsy wagon on warm nights.

Josephine used the place for her own convenience, as
she did everywhere else. She did not love it as Alison did.
It would not devastate her if the Claypoles knocked it
down, apart from annoyance at the loss of a trysting
place. I wonder what this cousin, Camilla, will do with
it? she thought, as she opened the door and let herself out
into the shadowed passage beyond. And I wonder what
she'll be like? I hope she's not beautiful or I'll have
trouble with Darcy and his roving eye.

The floor was gritty under her bare feet. A few dead
leaves, blown in through a broken pane, drifted and
swirled as she passed. Exploration at an earlier date had
shown her that the rooms were very rich in oak carvings,
and the lofty stone chimneypieces proudly bore the
Ruthen crest. The walls were hung with original
tapestries that had been made for them, three hundred
years before. She remembered antique dressing-tables,
mirrors, and quaint embroidered coverlets. They were
still in place, but increasingly dusty, tattered and
dilapidated by the ravages of time and neglect. As a
child, she had been delighted to explore the chests and
armories containing queer old dresses and coats of
bygone periods, the identical garments which were
depicted in the many portraits throughout the building.

Josephine possessed nerves of steel, and was not in the
least worried about traversing the echoing passage on
her way to the small closet which contained an antiquated lavatory. The light steadily faded. The doors on
either side were like the black entrances to caves. There
was an arched window a little further on, giving a view of
the jungle of a garden. An owl swooped across on great
silent wings and the bats were stirring in one of the

towers, venturing out, their tiny, high shrieks filling the space with noise.

Josephine reached the closet, groped for the mahogany seat and found it. After a short while, she pulled down Darcy's white linen shirt, which flapped about her knees, and headed back for the bedroom, then she stopped, listening intently. She was sure that she heard the rustle of skirts, and what sounded like someone sighing. Damn! she thought. I hope Alison isn't lurking around with her bloody sketchbook. I don't want to run into her with Darcy tucked into bed in the Master Chamber. Of course Alison knows about us. Even she can't be so naive as to imagine our friendship is innocent, but knowing and seeing are two different things.

'Who's there?' she called loudly. Her voice bounced back at her. No one answered.

Josephine held her breath and stared into the gloom. There was a pair of brocade curtains hanging at the end of the passage where other corridors intersected. A window lay beyond them, its diamond panes glinting. Just for an instant, she could have sworn that someone, she had the impression it was female, drifted across between the drapes. She heard another sigh, then it developed into a sobbing which rang strangely in her ears. The fine down rose on Josephine's limbs, but she sensibly dismissed the sound as caused by the wind which was sweeping through the old building. A thousand thoughts came crowding in on her, but her only alarm was that of discovery with her lover.

My God, she laughed to herself, if Alison was with me she'd be prattling on about ghosts. What sport we used to have, Selden and I, jumping out and frightening her when we ran riot here in the old days.

A suspicion darted through her. 'Selden?' she shouted. 'Is that you? Stop fooling about!'

It would be like him to have followed her, just to be provoking. Then another thought made her smile again.

69

Perhaps it was more than an irritating prank on his part. Supposing he had been watching Darcy and her make love earlier, hiding and poking a spy hole in the curtains? This would be in character, and it neither shocked nor dismayed her. She found it amusing, even exciting but: The dirty-minded bastard! I'll make him confess to it, she vowed.

She chased down the corridor, hotfoot in pursuit of the intruder. Reaching the end, she stood looking left and right along the seemingly endless corridors which disappeared into complete darkness. They rang with a curious feeling of emptiness. There was no one to be seen.

3

Selden was in the breakfast-room. Beside his plate lay a copy of *The Times* and the *Morning Post*, also a pile of correspondence, much of which was certain to be greeting-cards, emblazoned with robins and holly. He glanced at the headlines in the interval between courses. The air was redolent of liver and bacon, coffee and hot buttered toast. Footmen stood to attention, performing their duties punctiliously at precisely the correct moment, whisking away dishes and presenting others.

He sat at one end of the long, oval walnut table, and Alison occupied a chair at the other. She was nibbling fastidiously at fresh fruit and wholemeal bread. Frank had taught her about vegetarianism, and now she shuddered in disgust at the thought of bacon, refusing to view it in its crisp and rashered form, obstinately harking back to the slaughterhouse. This sudden cringing from all meat dishes had exposed her to much barbed teasing from Selden, who had no time for what he considered to be crankish fads.

They were alone, though only temporarily. It was the day before Christmas Eve and soon Josephine and her family would be arriving to spend the festive season with them, besides Orde-Bunbury, the Claypoles and several other people. As Alison ate her frugal repast, her mind was buzzing. Though her housekeeper, Miss Tennant, was very well organized and Beckford, the butler, could have run Armitstead House with one arm tied behind his back, there was still much that was Alison's sole province.

She glanced around the room with satisfaction. It glittered with tinsel and paper chains. The whole house

71

had been similarly decked for the festivities, and an enormous fir tree took pride of place in the hall, garbed in shining balls and ornaments made of finest spun glass. Little wax candles waited ignition in their brass holders. Alison was looking forward to the wonder in the visiting children's eyes when they were permitted to view this splendour before being hustled off to bed in the nursery in the west wing, there to pin their stockings to the mantelshelf and tuck down under the quilts, listening for Father Christmas's sleigh bells.

This was the time for children, their moment of magic. Alison thought of the presents she had bought them. They lay beneath the lower branches of the tree, wrapped mysteriously in crackling coloured paper. There were gifts for everyone, piled high, an exciting mound to be opened on the afternoon of Christmas Day, when church had been attended and a leisurely luncheon enjoyed. Alison wished that she had children of her own. Maternal longings had only recently begun to torment her. Once she had accepted that she was fated to be a maiden aunt, but lately she found herself thinking more and more of holding a baby to her breast – her own baby, whom she had nourished within her body and blessed with the largesse of her milk.

It was not fair. There was Josephine who had grumbled all the way through her pregnancies, and was only too happy to hand her infants over to the care of a nanny. Josephine had always got her own way without even trying much. She had been a vivacious, lovely child and, though a born nuisance, had always beguiled people into doing what she wanted. Whereas Alison had been plain, grumpy, a trifle stout and over-sensitive, with straight brown hair and freckles, but clever in an academic way. Once she had mastered reading, she had become addicted to the printed word, needing it as a drunkard needs alcohol. Because Selden and Josephine closed ranks against her, she had wandered ever deeper

72

into the fascinating world of books, finding escape there. In this secret universe she could become anyone, perform anything – be a beautiful princess, a noble knight, or a powerful enchantress at will. It was then that she started to draw, committing her dream world to paper, but secretly, too thin-skinned to risk ridicule.

She was the middle child, an unfortunate position, neither the eldest nor the baby. Selden and Josephine had occupied these coveted places. He was the firstborn, filled with charm from the cradle. Nanny Hobson, who had brought them up, was fond of recalling his triumphant babyhood – the darling, the much desired heir, spoilt and handsome.

'My goodness,' she would say, eyes misting, when they visited her in her retirement cottage. 'I couldn't walk far without someone stopping the pram and remarking, "What a fine boy! Look at his eyes! And what a head of curls! He's an angel!" '

It was true – to outsiders. He had that indefinable something, that drew onlookers like a magnet. It put him in the centre of everything. People smiled when they saw him. It seemed that he made them happy simply by being there. And, as he grew, his beauty increased, the sort of looks that turned heads and encouraged a second glance. He had big eyes and long lashes, and bewitched strangers, but within the family he was capable of terrible bouts of bad temper, wilful, cunning and cruel. Also, he was not truthful. Neither was Josephine. But Alison, despite their greed, their violent tempers when crossed, their lack of self-control, loved and envied them. Their parents were vague, distant figures occasionally crossing the screen of their young lives. When their mother died, Alison had been distressed, not so much at her passing, but because she felt so little emotion. The same had happened on the death of their father, much later.

Her reverie was rudely interrupted by Selden, who

had started to open his letters. He slammed one down on the table, making the coffee cups rattle and causing the footmen to glance his way. His grey eyes were furious. His whole body seemed to spark with rage. 'She's arriving today!' he shouted. 'That bloody trickster, Godwin, has just written to tell me!'

There was no need to ask to whom he referred. The subject had been on everyone's lips for weeks, ever since that fatal night when Selden's ambitions had been toppled into the dust. Alison glanced at Beckford who, with an almost imperceptible gesture, dismissed the footmen and then retired himself, closing the door carefully.

'That will be nice,' Alison said calmly, though her hands were clenched in her lap, hidden by the damask tablecloth. 'A new cousin, who'll be spending Christmas with us.'

'You're a fool, Alison!' he snarled, flinging his napkin down and getting to his feet. 'A sentimental fool! I don't want her here.'

'There's nothing you can do about it,' she sparked with sudden spirit. 'Even you can't get your own way in this!'

'Can't I? We'll bloody well see about that,' he muttered, standing before the fire, legs wide spread, thumbs jammed in his waistcoat pockets. He flashed her a glance beneath his frowning brows. 'Don't you go siding with her, Alison. You know damned well that the Claypoles'll be here. He still wants The Priory estate. Damned keen!'

Alison rose slowly to her feet. She was simply dressed in a long grey flannel skirt, neatly belted around her slim waist, and flaring out to a gentle fullness at the hem. Her white blouse was high-necked and had full sleeves, tightly cuffed. Her swept-up hair was kept in place with tortoiseshell combs. Selden had not failed to notice that she was taking care with her appearance lately, and a part of his mind was toying with the reason for this sudden change, but not seriously. He had matters of far greater importance to brood about.

'She may be a very nice person.' Alison held her fine-boned hands to the blazing coals, standing close to her brother. 'How can you judge till you've met her? You don't know the first thing about her.'

'I know she's a blasted nuisance. Why the hell wasn't the family informed of her existence long ago, eh?'

Alison glanced at his sulky expression and smiled. Selden was still the same, a spoilt brat at heart. She knew that he wanted her to agree with him, but a latent obstinacy, for which she had difficulty in accounting, prevented her from granting his desire. She persistently looked the other way in silence until he was forced to speak again.

'You must agree that it's put me in a devilish awkward predicament.' He was succeeding in causing her to feel guilty, as if she was somehow to blame for his frustration.

'One of your own making, Selden.' A moment before she had been decidedly pale, now there was a suspicion of temper in the flush of her cheeks. Her lips were pressed together as she struggled to keep in check impetuous words – words that should have been spoken years back. She had never had the courage to be so bold before, but Frank had given her confidence in herself.

'You obviously don't understand,' he said loftily, moving towards the window, drawing a cigarette case from the pocket of his Norfolk jacket as he went. Every morning of his life he took up this position after breakfast, smoked a cigarette, digested the morning's news, and plotted his course for the day. 'Thank God, Josephine is coming.'

He did not have to add more. Alison flinched, pain lancing her. Oh, yes, Josephine would commiserate with him, and they'd put their handsome heads together and concoct a mischief. But the hurt was not so sharp as it

75

might have been a short while ago. She was cocooned against their injuries, able to remove herself from the ache, to observe it from a distance.

When Selden had finished his cigarette and gone off to consort with Kennard on estate matters, she went to find Miss Tennant and, after instructing her to prepare a further guest-room, collected her outdoor clothing, picked up a book of carols from the music-salon and opened the front door.

The old church had that expectant air of excitement and anticipation which always pervaded it on festive occasions, be it Easter, Harvest Home or the Nativity. It was arched with elaborate fan vaulting, and its pulpit was particularly fine. A beautiful filigree screen was a notable feature, also the beautiful glass windows behind the gilded altar. It contained some monuments of her ancestors and plaques very suitable for brass-rubbing. A cross-legged crusader was stretched on a stone bier; a noseless knight and his lady rested beneath a carved canopy, all erstwhile members of the Ruthen clan. Legend had it that during the Civil War five of the bells had been removed from the tower and broken up for shot to defend The Priory against the Parliamentarians. The octagonal Tudor font was in a good state of preservation, and there were a few old rusty helmets which Alison thought would have looked better hung on the walls than placed upon the capital of a column.

The organist was performing a few practice runs, filling the nave with thunderous waves of sound. An odd wheezing came from the bowels of the organ, as if the antiquated instrument had asthma, but it was only the heaving of the bellows, operated by Ben Martin who had performed this office for forty years, without fail. The usual members of the choir were absent, their practice would come later, but the choirmaster was about to rehearse those who had offered to go around the village singing carols in aid of the poor and needy, a charity

76

organized by Mrs Mapley. They had been meeting once a week for a month. Frank Turner was much involved – so was Alison.

He was there. She saw him as she walked down the aisle. He looked up and smiled. He was different, a neatly attired curate in a black suit, a white round collar beneath his chin. She saw with a shock that he had had his hair cut. Remembered that he had told her when she saw him last a few days ago that he was going to Ryehampton to be made smart for Christmas. So short, cropped about the ears. It made him look older, more gaunt. It saddened her, for she liked his hair when it grew long, falling over his brow.

She stood by Gladys Lacey and found the first carol in her book. Frank was with the men, who shuffled and cleared their throats. The organ struck up 'Holy night, stilly night'. The voices rose, wavering at first, then growing stronger. Gladys was tone deaf and she droned away in Alison's ear, enthusiastic but off key. Her eyes rested on the crib, set before the altar, the shepherds, the angels, Joseph and Mary and the Holy Babe.

'On yon virgin, mother and child,' she mouthed the words, but her thoughts were whirling in pain.

I'm a virgin, but I want to be a mother! She looked across at Frank. The light was shining through the window forming a halo above his bowed head – red, yellow, green. Elsie's a mother. She's borne his babies! I mustn't see him again! It's wrong. He's a married man with four innocent children.

They had not met often lately, both so busy about their separate preparations for Christmas. But when they did – ah, then, Alison came alive. The carol performed to the choirmaster's satisfaction, they sang several more. She wasn't aware of what they were. We don't do anything wrong, she thought, arguing with herself. Only talk. The hours flash by when we're together, there's so much to talk about.

77

I must not see him again. She accepted it with dull grief. I'll write to him, leave a note in the wagon. He'll find it when he has time to go there after all this is over. She hated Christmas, she who had always loved it – hated it because it condemned them to be so occupied with trivial, unimportant things. It came between them. What shall I put? How can I write and say – I'll not see you again because – because you're married – because I'm frightened! Terrified of –

'So it's arranged then, we'll meet at the village cross and proceed to the almshouse.' The choirmaster's nasal voice sounded faintly in her ears, a thousand miles away. Then she was jerked back to earth as he repeated her name. 'Lady Alison? I asked you if this suits you. We can visit the old people, it will give them such pleasure, then the Red Lion, and finish up at Armitstead House. Will this be convenient for Lord Ruthen?'

It's the tradition, isn't it? she wanted to scream, impatient with his stupid face with its perpetually red nose. Like Mr Blake, the organist, he always seemed to have a cold. How can he possibly teach singing? What does he know of the problems of human nature or the passionate yearnings that inspire art and music?

'Perfectly convenient. I'll make sure that there are mince pies and mulled wine for all,' she answered jovially.

People were leaving, filled with seasonal goodwill, petty enmities glossed over. Alison hung back. Frank was in conversation with Mr Blake. Alison pretended to be admiring the holly wreaths with which Mrs Mapley's band of loyal helpers had decorated the church. She heard a door bang on genial farewells, then a single pair of footsteps coming towards her. She did not dare look around. She felt his presence behind her, could almost smell him.

'Alison,' his deep voice was hushed. 'I've not been able to come to the wagon. So much work to do –'

'I know.' She still did not turn to him. 'I too have been busy.'

'I've finished the book,' he said, standing so close but not touching her.

'I'm glad.' Then she could look at him. This was better, general not intimate things to speak of. 'You're happy about that?'

He grimaced. 'It's a job well done. We need the money.'

'You'll start another after Christmas? Can't you begin the one you've been telling me about – your master-piece?'

'It's impossible to talk here.' He glanced over his shoulder, nervous not for his reputation, but for hers. 'I'll meet you in the usual place, in an hour.'

I can't go, she thought. Aloud she said: 'All right. In an hour then.'

I can't write to him, she decided as she left the church. That would be cowardice. And ingratitude too. He's helped me, made me conscious of my own worth. I must see him once more, to tell him – I know what I can tell him! Camilla is coming. We'll not be able to use the gypsy wagon any more.

Josephine threw herself down on the couch in the gunroom, crossed her slim legs at the ankles and accepted the large glass of brandy that her brother offered. 'Lord – Christmas!' she exclaimed. 'I'm abso-lutely exhausted! Thank God the preparations are behind us and we can now look forward to letting our hair down!'

'All that shopping in London. That's what's done it,' Douglas grinned, winking at Selden. 'The poor old girl had the awful burden of spending an afternoon at Harrod's.'

'You may well mock.' She looked at him severely.

'Men know nothing about these trials and tribulations. Absolutely nothing! Those children of yours have been demanding the moon! And they'll get it, if you've a hand in the matter. You spoil them, Douglas.'

'They're grand kids,' he rejoined, a little shamefaced. 'Someone has to love 'em, as their mother ain't all that keen!'

'Stuff!' Josephine rolled her eyes at her brother, exasperated. 'They lead a charmed life. The little devils! I don't think they notice my lack of maternal interest one bit!'

'What about another drink?' suggested Selden, and picked up Douglas's glass. 'I've got news for you. Cousin Camilla is arriving at any time.'

'Good grief! Here's a go!' commented Douglas, watching his wife as he twirled his waxed moustache into even sharper points.

'For Christmas? She's staying here?' Josephine remained unmoved, though her mind was working feverishly. Bang would go the Master Chamber at The Priory. She lived with Douglas in Erwarton Hall, his family seat some three miles on the other side of the empty house. It had been easy enough to meet Darcy from there. But now? Sometimes they contrived a night of passion in London. She had even slipped over to his farm, when Douglas was away, but Camilla's possession of The Priory was going to seriously curtail their activities.

Selden's handsome features were composed into an expression which she knew meant trouble. A thrill tingled along her nerves, and she hoped that he would never look at her in that positively sinister way. He took no more kindly than she did to being baulked of his will.

'I suppose she'll have to stay. Unless she books in at the Red Lion,' he muttered ungraciously.

'That wouldn't look very good, would it?' she remarked, having a fair idea what was passing through his

80

mind. 'You've got to box clever on this one, brother dear. Have you a cigarette?'

Selden held out his case and she placed one in her long jade holder, drawing the smoke back into her lungs when his lighter flicked. Her eyes met his in a glance filled with understanding. Whatever transpired she was, and always had been, his ally.

Douglas wrinkled his brow, puffing at a cigar. 'I don't see what all the fuss is about. It'll be interesting to meet a girl from Brazil, won't it? Liven Christmas up a bit.' He was regretting the fact that he could not spend the holiday in London. There were bound to be jolly gatherings in his club. 'Fascinating country, what? Knew a retired officer who went out there, joined an expedition into the interior or some such. Answered an advertisement in *The Times*, don't-cher-know? Damned brave. Wonder what happened to him? Never heard of again. Disappeared up the Amazon River.'

'Eaten by head-hunters, no doubt,' Selden answered sarcastically. 'Lot of damned savages there.'

'Lot of damned savages in Africa too. Why, I remember when I was trekking across the veldt –'

Seeing that he was about to launch into wartime reminiscences, Josephine cut him short. 'Who else will be among the welcoming committee, Selden?' she asked, eyes slitted as she stared up at him through the cloud of bluish smoke.

He smiled down into her lovely, wayward face, thinking how beautiful she was, this sister of his, too good for someone like Douglas. 'The Claypoles and Orde-Bunbury. The Pinnegars, you know them, the Colonel's the Master of the Hunt – their two handsome daughters – and Devereaux.'

Good old Selden! Josephine relaxed against the damask cushions of the deep couch. Trust him to ensure that she was not lacking a partner. And who would be warming his bed at night? she mused. He was a dark

81

horse. Rarely could she wheedle the names of his mistresses from him. 'Those girls are growing up. Been away at finishing school, in Switzerland. I hope they haven't become too handsome,' she pouted, raising an arched brow at him meaningfully. 'Or d'you have your eye on one, or maybe both of them?'

'Really, Josephine, that's going a bit far, ain't it?' Douglas found her puzzling. Gone was the sweet, gay girl he had married. She had grown hard, brittle, too fond of strong language and outrageous opinions. Now she was fluffing the sides of her hair with her finger-tips, her enormous hat cast aside. Most striking in her fitted coat of fine burgundy wool, with a black feather boa, yards long, drifting around her shoulders. She had filled out since he first knew her, and her figure was seductive, the much sought after hourglass shape. He knew by the bills presented to him that she was obsessed with clothes, never having enough even though her wardrobes were bulging. He liked to indulge her, was proud of her, desired her, but he sometimes sighed, wishing that she could find it in her heart to show affection to both him and their children.

'Oh, Douglas! Grow up!' she retorted irritably, wondering if she dare ask Selden when he was expecting Darcy to arrive. 'Why shouldn't I express an interest in Selden's love life? Damn it, I'm not a bloody nun!'

'Please don't use that sort of language,' Douglas floundered, experiencing his usual discomfort in their company.

'Why not? Gentlemen swear.'

'Not in front of ladies,' her husband objected.

'Damn it, Douglas, your notions are as dead as the dodo.' Her cheeks were flushed under the rouge and her eyes flashed. 'We're living in the twentieth century now. Why d'you suppose that women should obey their so-called lords and masters? You don't own us, you know, just because we're your wives or sisters. Don't you agree, Selden?'

Selden was staring out of the window. He knew perfectly well that she was seeking to pick a quarrel with Douglas to salve her own conscience. She was not a social reformer and did not give a damn about votes for women or the Suffragette Movement. Josephine, as always, was only concerned with getting what she wanted, and would use any argument to do so. Sometimes, he felt a twinge of pity for Douglas, but the man was a dolt. He had no idea how to handle someone as headstrong and high-spirited as Josephine. Darcy, on the other hand, knew his business with women. If she was my wife, I'd give her a good hiding now and again, he thought, then take her to bed for a week. That would stop her.

Seeing that he was not about to enter the lists on her behalf, Josephine yawned and played with the mink muff that adorned her left arm. 'Isn't it nearly lunchtime? Where's Alison? And when will the others be here? Can we play whist tonight?'

'Alison's gone to practise carols in the church.' Selden regarded her with amused eyes, reading her like a book. Let her stew a little, let her appetite be whetted. He'd acted as her pander, inviting Darcy to stay. Of course, he had a perfect alibi. The man was a bachelor. There was no harm at all in asking him to spend the holiday with them. Who knows, he might even find one of the Pinnegar girls to his taste? This would be amusing. The fur would fly! Josephine wouldn't like it at all.

'How frightfully noble of her!' Josephine remarked, reaching for another cigarette. 'There's a girl who knows her place. Perhaps you should have married Alison instead of me, Douglas.'

'The idea has occurred to me,' he answered drily.

'I think I can hear a car coming up the drive,' Selden broke in suddenly. 'Perhaps it's the Claypoles.'

'Or Darcy.' Josephine sat up, slipping her arms out of her coat, smoothing down her skirt, straightening her lace blouse. 'Shall you go and see?'

'I'm going to have another drink. What say you, Douglas? I suggest we're topped up before our peace is shattered.'

Josephine was fumbling with her bag, drawing out a hand-mirror and prinking, her eyes stormy as she stared over it at her annoying brother. He was aware that she had to keep an outward display of decorum and he traded on it for his own twisted entertainment. At such moments, she almost hated him.

A tap on the door and the stately Beckford appeared, announcing in stentorian tones that Lady Camilla Ruthen wished to see Lord Selden. There was a second's silence. Time seemed to be in suspension. Then Selden collected his wits and nodded for admittance. Josephine held her breath, eyes fixed on the door, conscious of the tension emanating from him, almost rejoicing in it. Serve him right! she thought savagely, reverting to childhood spite. Tormenting, selfish pig!

Beckford returned, to fling wide the door and declaim loudly: 'Lady Camilla Ruthen!'

She stood on the threshold for a moment, and there was that split-second hush which pays silent tribute to a successful entry. Selden stared, Douglas goggled, and Josephine gasped. So *this* was Cousin Camilla!

They saw a woman of above average height, wearing a bizarre outfit the like of which made Josephine green with envy. She did not move for an instant, permitting them to experience the full force of her power and regality. She wore a full-length sable coat, a matching fur hat on her piled-up hair which was the colour of ripe wheat, a tumbling, tawny mass of curls loosely secured by exotic jewel-headed pins. Her skin was honey hued, kissed by a tropical sun, and her eyes were most unusual, slanting up at the outer corners, amber flecked with green, staring haughtily from between long black lashes, her brows arched and finely marked. Her face, broad at the brow, narrow at the chin, had pronounced cheekbones, and her mouth was too wide for classic beauty, the lips red and full.

When she moved towards the astonished group near the marble fireplace, her coat swirled back, revealing a black velvet costume beneath – not a skirt, but pantaloons tucked into the tops of tight, high-heeled boots of scarlet leather, and a vividly patterned jacket of eastern design. She had a graceful walk, sensuously languid yet vital, her body swaying from the hips, a woman aware of its power and using it to the full.

Selden recovered first, stepping to meet her. 'Camilla! How delightful! Welcome home to England. I'm Selden Ruthen,' he said and, taking her extended gloved hand, he raised it to his lips.

Just look at him! thought Josephine, getting to her feet, drawing herself up and girding her loins for battle. What a turncoat! My God, I can just see his crafty brain working. A lovely woman, quotha! A *single* woman, to boot. I'll bet he can hear wedding bells pealing already. Not marry again? He'd do anything to get his hands on The Priory and its lands. He'd even sell his soul to the devil, if it wasn't already in hock to that gentleman!

Not to be outdone, she glided over to them. 'I'm Josephine Huxley, Selden's sister. How marvellous to see you, Camilla! And what a lovely costume. Where *did* you get it? My word, I've read in the fashion magazines that this is the latest vogue, but it's the very first time I've actually seen anyone with the nerve to wear it.'

Camilla looked at her, eyes very clear and level, subjecting her to a cool glance. 'I visited Paris and London before driving down here. Paul Poiret and Jacques Doucet designed some clothes for me. Poiret used to work for Doucet, but he's recently opened his own shop near the Place de l'Opera.' Her voice was low, attractively husky, with a curious accent, part French, part Portuguese, wholly intriguing.

'And he's advocating trousers for women? How very

innovative! You'd best look to your laurels, gentlemen!' Josephine laughed lightly and gave a sidelong look at her husband and brother.

'They're most convenient for driving,' Camilla answered, taking the seat by the fire which Selden drew up for her. She removed her hands from the sable muff to which she had returned them, took off her gloves and held her wrists to the blaze. She wore a large antique ring on the forefinger of her right hand. It shone in the light of the dancing flames, diamonds flashing around the central yellow stone. 'Your country is so cold. I've not been warm since the *Empress* berthed here. Paris was no better.'

'May I offer you a cigarette?' He pulled out his silver case.

She shook her head. 'I prefer a cheroot,' but she permitted him to light the thin brown cigar which she took from a pack in her bag. The fragrance of Havana's finest tobacco coiled like incense through the room.

'You drive a car?' Selden was exuding charm, turning the full blaze of his smile upon Camilla.

'Certainly. We started out yesterday, resting in a hotel in Ryehampton last night. I've a sports model, a Mercedes, but it's only a two-seater. Leila rode beside me, but poor Sam had to travel in the dickey-seat. My chauffeur is following in the Rolls-Royce, with the rest of the luggage.' Whilst devastatingly lovely, Camilla spoke in a straightforward, unaffected manner, almost mannish in appeal. A strong, independent girl, if appearances were to be believed.

Selden was fascinated. He had never met anyone quite like her. Accustomed to women responding immediately to his looks and masculinity, he found her an irresistible challenge. She did not blush or simper, answering his questions frankly, her regard slightly wary, as befitted a stranger meeting relatives for the first time, feeling her way, sounding them out.

'I say, I'd better introduce myself.' Douglas was on his feet, smiling down at her. 'I'm Douglas Huxley, Josephine's husband.' Camilla nodded and he rushed on: 'I'd like to talk to you about South America. Most interesting place, so I've heard. Had a friend who went there once –'

'You've servants waiting in the car?' Selden could not have been a more considerate host. 'I'll ring for Beckford to take them to their quarters, and then Josephine can show you to your room. You girls can have a nice cosy chat, about clothes and what-have-you. Lunch will be served soon. I expect you're hungry after your journey. I'd like to see your car – have a Lanchester myself – noisy beast but it works up a speed. Does a good sixty miles an hour on a straight stretch. I'll take you out in it this afternoon, if you've nothing else planned.'

Don't overdo it, Selden, Josephine thought. Slow down, old bean. She doesn't look the kind of woman to be taken in easily. But she was hoping that he would succeed in seducing this intriguing, too attractive cousin, dreading her meeting the highly susceptible Darcy.

'Thank you, but no.' Camilla rose gracefully, working her fingers into her gloves.

'Perhaps you're right. You'd like to rest before meeting the others? I've several other guests coming to celebrate Christmas here with us.' Selden brushed aside objections, certain that she could not fail to respond to his charm. Others always had. Why should a colonial behave any differently? She should be grateful that he was showing her so much attention.

'I shan't be staying.' There was a hard ring to Camilla's voice that made him decidedly uncomfortable.

'Not staying? But I thought – I assumed –'

'I'm eager to see my house.' Her eyes were feline, and like a cat with claws retracted, she stood her ground, watching him.

Selden stared at her in astonishment. 'But you can't live there, it's impossible. You don't understand. Didn't Godwin tell you? It's derelict. It hasn't been occupied for years.'

'Then it's high time it was.' Camilla walked to the door, turning as she opened it. 'Goodbye, Selden – Josephine – Douglas.'

'You'll at least come to dinner on Christmas Night?' Selden was almost eager, as if unable to bear losing sight of her, the property of small consideration now.

Camilla smiled, a deep, considering smile. 'I may,' she said, then let herself out. The door closed softly behind her.

Alison sat in the wagon and shivered. Nerves were making her shaky, but not only this, the temperature was well below zero. As one of the carol singers had remarked: 'It's too cold for snow but won't be any warmer till it's down!'

A white Christmas? It was more than possible. Anything was possible in the capricious English climate. She had known it to be mild in winter and then snow in April, the golden heads of daffodils poking hopefully through the drifts. The clouds were growing heavier and greyer, the wan sunlight breaking through sometimes over the drear, bleak hills. She had walked from the church with the east wind biting a way through her thick coat.

She knew that she should be going back to Armitstead House for lunch. Selden would be expecting her to be there to greet their guests. She was aware that, despite his denial of her, he would want her support should Camilla arrive, particularly if Josephine had been held up. None of this mattered.

Where was Frank? Was Elsie ill? Had Mrs Barlow run to the vestry with a message demanding his urgent return home? She knelt by the black, sullen stove, opening its front and poking at the dead embers. Her knees were shaking. There was no paper, no kindling of any kind. Frustrated, she sat back on her heels, glaring at it. It became the inanimate object of her fury and despair. Without its warm glow, the wagon seemed squalid. And why not? she thought bitterly. It *is* squalid, a dingy little love-nest without the love. He's never touched me, never kissed me. How many times have I sat here with him, unable to stop looking at his mouth – wanting – aching –

He was behind her before she knew it, taking the poker from her hand, leaning against the miniature over-mantel. 'You shouldn't do that. It's man's work. Shall I light the fire?'

She shook her head, standing now. 'I mustn't stay. It's nearly lunch-time.'

'You've been crying.' He took both her hands in his. 'I don't like to see you sad.'

She hadn't been aware of tears, but now she felt them, salty on her cheeks, stiffening, drying there. He drew her down on the bench that ran under the side window, useful seat, with lockers beneath.

'I'm sorry,' she said, but the root of her sorrow could not be put into words.

She knew that he was going to take her hands again, and she did not draw away. The silence, the cold, that odd grey dimness of light, her tears, were conspiring to alter manmade laws. I can't go on being brave, she thought, and she let the tears flow. Leave me! her mind cried, leave me alone. Can't you see –?

'Alison, dear girl.' He was looking at her seriously. 'Is it Selden? Has he been unkind again?'

'No, not Selden,' she sobbed, groping for and being unable to locate her handkerchief.

He took his own from an inner pocket and gently wiped her face. 'I know,' he said quietly. 'I know what it is.'

89

'What are you saying?' Terror filled her. The words must not be spoken. If they were, then she was lost, condemned to the black pit of hell for ever. She made to rise but he pulled her back.

'Simply this.' And he held her close, his mouth against hers, one hand behind her head. It was so strange, so much a part of her imaginings that she could not protect herself, could only stay there, his mouth warm and alive on hers, drawing out her strength till she had none left.

Then his lips were on her eyelids, tasting her tears, and his hand took the pins from her hair, letting it fall, its weight over his arm, his fingers touching her neck, stroking softly. Tranquillity lapped her. So it was done. Much might follow, the ultimate union of their flesh, but his action was the seal upon their future, nothing could prevent it now.

His arm came around her shoulders, his hand resting on her breast, feeling her rapid heartbeat. Alison would have been quite ready to die in that moment, to sacrifice anything if she might remain there for a little while with her head pressed against his chest. Everything else paled before this need. She forgot Selden, forgot Elsie – wanted Frank with an urgency beyond all reason. His hand was exploring further. She felt the chill air on her skin as he unbuttoned her blouse, exposing her breasts.

One part of her mind was still shocked, still inhibited. It struggled for supremacy. 'No, Frank,' she whispered. 'No. You're married.'

He stopped and, like a sleeper awakening, stared into her eyes. 'Married? Yes, but what a mockery.'

'What d'you mean?' Her body was disappointed. It had begun to stretch luxuriantly under his caresses, purring with pleasure, a wanton thing without control. But her mind made her sit up, leaning away from that tormenting hand. 'You love Elsie, don't you? She's your wife –'

He sat hunched into himself, his face as bleak as the hills outside. 'Love her? I hate her!'

'Frank! How can you say such a thing?' She was bewildered, yet even as her mind battled with the terror of his words, so her body wanted to be back in his arms.

'God help me! I've tried to be patient, tried to tell myself that she's ill – but oh, Alison, if you only knew!' There was anguish in his voice. She longed to kiss him, to cradle his head against her breast, to console him.

She clenched her hands into tight fists to prevent their wayward drift towards him. Anger – stir up your anger. There, that's better. 'But her health was broken by giving birth to your children – the children you wanted. How can you be so unjust as to blame her?'

His faced was planed by shadows, gaunt, hollow-cheeked in the dimness. 'I know that. D'you think I haven't blamed myself? That I didn't try to keep away from her after the first two were born? She wouldn't have it. She was so possessive then, jealous, afraid of physical passion yet needing it. Her last confinement was complicated, but it wasn't that which turned her. No, it had begun to happen long before. I've thought so much about it. There's a weakness in the strain. Her father was the same.'

'Insanity!' Alison felt as if the freezing wind had penetrated her bones. She wrung her hands together, missing his touch, refusing to permit them to creep into his for warmth and comfort.

A faint echo of the smile he usually reserved for her curved his lips. 'Of a sort,' he said grimly. 'She drinks, as her father did – whisky, gin, anything she can lay hands on. When I first found out, I refused to believe it, making excuses – she'd had too many babies too quickly – the fact that we couldn't sleep together any more because of this – perhaps she didn't like London.' He reached out and gripped Alison's hands. She could not stop him, did not wish to.

'Oh, Frank, how terrible,' she murmured, sympathy welling up. 'But doctors? This can be cured?'

91

'I've tried everything.' She had never seen such despair on a man's face before and it broke her heart. 'There's no cure because she doesn't want one. She enjoys her affliction. What right have I to take it away from her? Sometimes she's better of her own accord, but not for long. One drink and she's off again. Mrs Barlow looks after the children and my wife. She's a saint, that woman.'

'And who looks after you, Frank?' she asked slowly, freeing one hand and gently trailing her fingers over his face, his hair.

He shrugged. 'She does that too. I've said, she's a good woman. Sorry for me, I expect. She must be for she never speaks of it outside the house, and rarely within it, shielding the children from Elsie's moods and tempers, her ravings and abuse, usually directed against myself. But you see, Alison, when she's sober, she's a sweet soul, wouldn't harm a fly. Quiet, too quiet, very reserved. I love her once, adored her, and for years I've thought she would get over this craving. But now I find her repulsive, disgusting when she's been drinking. I can't trust her with money. Mrs Barlow handles all that. We try to restrict her drinking to a single bottle of spirits a day.'

'The villagers think it's you who likes to tipple.' It was strange how humour could be found in the most dire circumstances.

He smiled in response. 'I know. The Reverend Mapley has taken me to task about it.' Then his face grew serious again. 'I love you, Alison.'

'I know,' she whispered, happy but grieving. 'And I love you, Frank.'

'Oh, my darling.' He turned her towards him with a slight movement so that she might see his face, might look into his eyes, deep brown eyes in which she could feel herself melting. 'What are we going to do?'

'Nothing.' She gathered her sanity, gathered her principles, pushed him away from her. 'You're married.

There are the children to consider. We're neither of us free. We have responsibilities. The church –'

'Damn the church!' She had never seen him so angry before. It frightened and excited her. 'I should never have become a parson. It's not my vocation. My parents wanted it, not me. I've no calling, I've not seen visions or heard the voice of God demanding that I serve Him! How can an intelligent man believe all that claptrap? Now the church is going to try and prevent me having the woman I love. But I shan't let it! Love me, Alison – love me now –'

He took her hair in his hold and drew it around them, tightened it till she could not escape. His hands were at her breast, on the warmth of her body. 'Frank! Don't!' she cried.

'Let me touch you, please,' he breathed against her face. She did not realize what he was doing at first, lifting her skirt under the coat, caressing her thighs, finding the waistband of her cotton knickers, tugging at them. She wanted to tell him to stop, but his mouth would not let her speak. He's going to hurt me, she thought, and she was shivering with expectation and longing, thinking of that act, the bare facts of which she knew about, though never realizing – never knowing –

Ah, the joy of being held, fondled and loved. Why must he demand more? If they stayed like this, pleasuring each other with caresses, then there would be no sin – no adultery. But Frank's hands were trembling as he sought the innermost softness of her body. She knew this would not content him, though for her it was enough, that quivering, aching feeling that made her cry out, unable to endure such pleasure.

'You mustn't!' she whispered, pleaded. She tried to fend him off, but her arms were powerless, refusing to obey her.

'Darling, please – I'll not hurt you! But just a little – please!' He was a stranger suddenly, his eyes intense

93

above her, his body urgent. Not Frank – not her dear companion, but a monster in the grip of a powerful force that demanded release.

She twisted from side to side, crying out: 'No! No!' trying to protect herself – from him – from her! Then a sound held them both still. Wheels were crunching across the weeded, frosty gravel of the drive leading to The Priory. Frank released her. She crept to the window, her thoughts numb. The hedge was too thick. She could see nothing through it, but the car was close now – passing, its engine noises fading into the distance.

'It must be Camilla!' she gasped. 'She's expected. She's here!'

'Your cousin? That'll put the cat amongst the pigeons!' Frank was at her back, his arms clasping her to him, his hands crossed over her breasts.

'I was going to tell you.' She turned in his arms, looking into his face. His hair was ruffled, short and spiky, the firm line of his mouth softened by so much kissing. 'We shan't be able to use this place again, unless she's kind and permits me to come here sometimes. But I can't let her know about us.'

She found herself thinking back to the first simplicity of their meetings, almost with regret. It would never be the same again. They were friends, yes, they'd always be friends, but they would be lovers very soon. Had Camilla not arrived, by now the act would have been committed, irrevocable, binding. He was gentle again, less alarming, but his eyes were still full of things she dared not interpret.

His hands tightened on her, slipping inside her blouse. They burned there, his thumbs stroking her nipples. His warm breath was against her hair. 'We'll find some-where private. It doesn't have to be here. The vestry, perhaps, late at night – in the dark, beloved.'

This shocked her. Not the church where her ancestors lay, where the services were held. 'My studio,' she gasped, arching her throat, eyes half-closed as desire washed over her. 'No one goes there but me. I'll point out the window when you come tomorrow evening, with the singers.'

Then she was buttoning her blouse, brushing down her skirt. They could not find her hairpins. Found them at last, scattered over the dusty floor. He was helping her pin up her hair, his hands trembling as much as hers. She was ready, as ready to leave as she ever would be. He held both her hands and kissed her mouth, then her eyes and she closed them against seeing his, and letting him read all that was in hers. He put his arms around her and held her pressed to his heart for a long moment, then let go. She stood still, eyes still closed. Heard his footsteps cross the floor, felt the vibration of the wagon, heard the door shut behind him. And she felt in that second as if she would run after him, go with him then, face the scandal, brave the world's cruelty, never leave him.

She did not do so. Common sense prevailed. She waited for a while before venturing out. A flake of snow blew into the wagon as she opened the door. It struck her gently on the nose, and then the air was full of them, thick, white, swirling feathers drifting down from a rapidly darkening sky.

'What is it, missy?' Leila was staring through the windscreen at the dancing whiteness which blotted out the serpentine meanderings of the overgrown drive. 'Looks like the work of devils to me.' She sounded ill at ease, huddled in the fur-lined cloak which Camilla had insisted on purchasing for her.

'It's snow, Leila – frozen rain. You've seen pictures of it, haven't you? There's plenty of it up in the Andes. It can't hurt you, except for the cold which you're not used to.'

She was peering through the windscreen, driving

slowly and carefully. She too had never before seen snow, but she had learned about it at school. It had not occurred to her that Leila and Sam would be surprised by it. There were so many things strange about England. She was not sure how her two servants were going to like it, the harsh climate, the grey cities. It would have been better to have waited till the spring, she thought, I've heard that spring is lovely here. But I couldn't. It would have driven me mad to have remained in Bahia after –

The car lurched on the frozen ruts of the neglected drive. Camilla's hands were sure and experienced on the wheel. Her father had owned one of the first cars in Bahia, always keen to keep abreast of inventions. She had learned to drive in 1897, when she was twelve, coping with the beautiful, belching monster, built on the lines of a horse-drawn carriage. That Daimler was the forerunner of many, and the one she had sold before leaving had been a sturdy Wolseley in which she had jolted over many an uneven track, assisting him in his obsessive, never-ending search.

Really, it was quite impossible to see where she was going, the snow settling on the windscreen like icing sugar. Camilla leaned forward, straining her eyes, contemplating the advisability of stopping, getting out and rubbing it away. Then a huge black shape loomed out of the dazzling mass. She drew in a sharp breath as the car rocked to a halt before a flight of crumbling, snowy steps. As the engine died, the silence was so intense that it almost hurt the ears, every sound muffled by those crystallized flakes falling from the sky as if they would never stop.

I should be feeling some emotion, she thought. This is my ancestral home. *Mine*, every stick and stone, every blade of grass, each acre of land. Visions of how it would be had haunted her for years, though her father had rarely spoken of it. The subject had been taboo. The merest reference to The Priory had invariably thrown him into a black mood. But the bits of information she had painstakingly garnered now passed through her mind like tattered banners fluttering in the wind. It was very old; it had belonged to the Ruthens for centuries; her father had been a nobleman; she would own it one day. It had seemed too fanciful to be believed, but here she was, face to face with the reality.

'Come along, Leila,' she said with forced cheerfulness. 'Let's take a look.'

The snow crunched under her boots as she mounted the steps, staring up at the massive façade. As she did so, the silence shattered, a sudden wind howling around the house, driving the snow against her face with a wild shriek, whipping at her coat, smarting in her eyes, stinging her cheeks. It held a triumphant note, more boisterous than threatening, as if recognizing her and claiming its own, a huge elemental force at play, wanting her to join in the sport, to rush through the empty house with it, waking the shadows into life.

In that odd, yellowish light, the power of The Priory struck her forcibly, though the widespread destruction was glaringly apparent. The graceful pilasters that intersected the lofty mullioned windows were falling to pieces, and the fantastic stone pinnacles above and on the carved gable ends were fast disappearing. A solitary place of broken, creeper-covered walls and breast-high weeds, vast, maze-like, confusing.

Leila and Sam were close behind her. Their dark-skinned faces seemed darker still in contrast to the snow. Leila was a haughty *mambo*, in cahoots with the spirit world, well able to protect her charges with strong magic, but she was apprehensive as she followed her mistress. Her son, Sam, brought up the rear, dragging his crippled right leg. A lad of eighteen, Camilla's junior by three years, his body was misshapen but his wits were sharp. At the top of the steps there was a frowning stone archway. The massive oak front door was open, hanging crookedly on rusty iron hinges.

Camilla paused under the portico, smiling at Leila. 'I didn't need the key that Mr Godwin gave me. It's so heavy, weighs a ton.'

'That door must be mended, right away,' Leila declared. 'Sam will fix it. You don't want just anybody walking into your house, missy.'

She was a mulatto, half-black and half-white, a superbly handsome woman in her middle forties, with broad shoulders and a narrow waist, long-legged and having a haughty carriage that a duchess might envy. Her every gesture expressed an inborn elegance. There had been no question about her coming to England. The idea of deserting Camilla never entered her head, but she viewed the old, eerie house with a feeling close to aversion. Muttering incantations, fingers creeping to the talismanic necklace she wore, she stepped inside.

They were in the Great Hall, shrouded in an even deeper silence, a vacuum almost, with the storm buffeting outside. Dark – a dusty darkness lit only by snowlight; suits of armour standing in corners, sightless eyeholes in helmets, rusted weapons hanging askew against panelling, ragged pennants; the cold examination of long-dead eyes staring down on the intruders from portraits. Above the staircase, they saw the sky through a jagged hole where part of the roof had caved in. They crossed to a lofty reception room. Most of its ceiling lay in chunks on the filthy carpet. A section of floor had collapsed so that there was a crater in its midst.

Leila stood in the doorway, head up, listening. 'Ah, missy, but this room was once fine, filled with people – handsome men and lovely women. Voices and laughter and music beat against the walls and drifted out into the night. I hear it still. I see them, the dead ones – they welcome you, for their blood runs strongly in your veins.'

Camilla was more intent on a tour of inspection than conversing with her ancestors. But there was no denying that she felt at ease here, despite the awful chill, the wind gusting through broken panes and exposed rafters. She supposed that Leila was right, she invariably was, and she could not help but respond to the atmosphere. The building was too large to explore at that moment. She must wait till tomorrow and do it in daylight. So they went no further than finding the kitchen, the privies and the main bedchamber. Everywhere there was that air of ruin and decay, but Camilla refused to be downhearted. She had told Selden that she was going to occupy it, and stay there she would! The kitchen was a ramshackle room, stone-flagged and freezing, with a huge open fireplace where sooted pots still hung on cranes suspended from the chimney. Sam had already taken himself off to examine the outbuildings, returning, his black hair white with snow, his arms piled high with dry kindling.

Soon a fire roared in the hearth. Leila had attacked the pump which stood beside the stone sink. Creaking and protesting it had at last yielded up spring water, which was soon boiling in a big black kettle. Leila liked cooking over an open fire, beginning to hum under her breath as she worked. Sam had a broom thrust into his hands and her sharp instructions to sweep the floor. Meanwhile Camilla trudged backwards and forwards from the car, unloading. She had taken the precaution of buying groceries in Ryehampton, sufficient supplies to last until they could visit the village store. Also they were carrying enough clothing to manage until the chauffeur arrived next day in the Rolls. She had purchased three feather-filled quilts in London, of the kind used on the Continent. Contrary to what Selden thought, Godwin had told her what to expect, and she had left nothing to chance. They would be well-fed and warm during their first night at The Priory, luxuries could come later.

It was dark outside by the time Leila had prepared a meal and laid it on the table which she had made Sam scrub. Camilla had discovered some candlesticks in a

cupboard, and these held the white wax candles she had
had the forethought to bring. The house was well
furnished with every commodity, albeit old-fashioned
and grimed with age. Thus fine china adorned the table,
cutlery too, and crystal glasses which, thoroughly
doused in hot water, now held ruby wine within their
depths.

Camilla sat back in her wooden chair, warmed by
Leila's cuisine, slightly tipsy from the good Burgundy
she had purchased in London. Sam leaned forward and
lit her cheroot. She mused as she smoked, watching the
fire as it spat and hissed, devouring the logs greedily with
a leap of sparks and a flaring roar. Leila moved quietly
about the kitchen, her shadow flung, huge and high,
across the beamed ceiling, singing to herself, sometimes
murmuring as if holding a conversation with unseen
things. As far back as Camilla could remember, this
woman had been there, a solid, comforting presence in
her life.

A Creole, she spoke English in a singsong negroid
patois, but her French was perfect. Born and reared in
Haiti, as a young girl she had been taken into the service
of the Gontard family in Port-au-Prince. Camilla's
mother, Hélène, had been the only child. She had met
Edgar Ruthen shortly after he arrived in the West
Indies. Before he had moved to Rubera, a village a few
miles north of the busy port of Bahia, her father had
given his permission for them to marry. Leila had
accompanied her beloved Hélène, passionately devoted,
fiercely protective. This strong love had also been
lavished on their daughter. Before Hélène died, she had
placed Camilla in Leila's care, a duty that she had
faithfully carried out.

After the upheaval of Edgar Ruthen's sudden death,
Leila had been the one who stood by her. It was she who
laid out his body and performed the ceremony to free his
spirit long before a Christian priest was informed. She

too who had taken the ring from his hand and purified it before giving it to Camilla, saying that she was now protected from its influence. It would never harm her but she must respect its power.

Drowsing by the fire in The Priory kitchen, Camilla looked down to where it adorned her right hand. It was magnificent. The stone in the middle was a tiger's-eye, surrounded by diamonds and set in a heavy gold band damascened with strange symbols. She had never seen her father without it. He had let her play with it sometimes, when he was feeling paternal. This had not happened often. And now it was hers, along with everything else he had owned. The Estancia Esperança on the outskirts of Rubera; the cocoa and sugar planrations; shares in the rubber boom of Bolivia and in the meat-canning factories of Argentina; The Priory and its acres. Rufus Godwin had explained it all to her, saying that she was a woman of substance now.

Rich? He said she was really rich, as it was understood in Europe. In Rubera one was rich if one owned a couple of goats and a dried-up patch of soil. There had been a deal of wealth in Bahia, where Camilla had attended a convent school. She had mixed with the haughty Brazilians, been their guest and experienced sumptuous living, wondering sometimes why her father chose to reside at the *estancia* instead of buying one of the palatial houses in Bahia. She never asked him. One did not question Edgar Ruthen. She had accepted that they must live on the fringe of the jungle so that he might fit out canoes and embark on those dangerous trips into the interior, from which he invariably returned disillusioned and malaria-stricken, a crazed look in his eyes.

After his death, letters had arrived from his London lawyer. It was necessary that Camilla travel to England. She had been glad to go, feeling that she would become insane if she remained in Brazil a moment longer. A steamer was booked to Rio de Janeiro and from there she

101

had boarded the *Empress*, a luxury liner bound for Liverpool. Shipboard life had prepared her in some way for the existence she must now lead – that of a young heiress. Amongst the people she had met, had been a youngish couple named John and Amy Marchant. They had given up the struggle to make a life for themselves in South America. He had gone there as a chemist at the Liebig Company's Extract of Meat factory on the River Uruguay. It had been a good job, but they had left on account of the health of their daughter, Harriet.

'That poor baby.' Leila's voice disturbed Camilla, bringing her back to the present. The *mambo* had a knack of picking up on other people's thoughts. She liked the Marchants – John so suntanned and broad, his wife wearing that wasted, aging look which so often settled upon emigrant European females, and would have helped them if she could, but the child had a mysterious malady for which there was no cure.

Camilla had been shocked the first time she saw her, down in the Marchants' cabin. It was almost impossible to believe that she was five years of age. She was like a beautiful doll, no bigger than a six month old baby. Her face was as if fashioned in wax. It wore the blank expression of a doll. No answering warmth, no smile animated it. Her blue eyes held not the slightest flicker of movement or recognition. But it was her hair that was so uncanny. She had not grown but *it* had, seeming to possess a life of its own – long, so very long, falling over her small, shrunken form like a shining mantle of gold silk.

The Marchants owned a house in London and Camilla had stayed there before driving down to Wessex. They had called in the most skilled paediatricians, but nothing could be done for Harriet. Leila was wise in the ways of medicine, but she sighed over the problem and said again: 'Poor baby.'

'Leila, is it *wanga?*' Camilla asked, holding out her cup

102

for more coffee. She had tried to draw the Creole out on the subject before, but she had remained obstinately silent.

Now she shook her head, playing with the talisman, almost as if she was 'telling' the beads of a rosary. 'No, Missy Camilla. No *bocor* priest roused the *loups-garous* to fly in at night and suck the blood of that child.'

'Then if it wasn't the work of a sorcerer, what *is* the matter with her?' Camilla persisted. Leila threw her a sharp look.

'You mighty pushy. Supposing I don't want to tell?' Dark eyes resting on Camilla, deep, all-knowing eyes.

'Don't be silly, Leila. I'm your pupil, aren't I? You've taught me everything I know about Voodoo. You can trust me, surely?'

'This ain't nothing to do with Voodoo. It's a secret known only to slaves.' The *mambo* held her head a shade higher.

'There are no slaves any more, and even if there were, you know where my sympathies lie. If there's anything you can do, anything at all, then it's your duty to aid Mrs Amy.'

'There's nothing any doctor can do, nor medicine-man either,' Leila answered slowly, staring into the fire. 'I've seen such cases before. She's never going to grow up to be a woman. Mrs Amy'll have a helpless baby on her hands till the day Missy Harriet dies.'

'But she wasn't an imbecile when she was born. Amy says she was perfect and very bright.'

Leila's face grew still, the firelight touching its darkness with crimson. 'Someone must've held a grudge against the Marchants, or maybe just against all whites.'

'But you've just said it wasn't *wanga*.'

'No need for magic to do what was done. D'you remember that soft spot on a baby's skull? It pulses with the heartbeat and the bones have to knit and protect the brain.' Leila paused, still hesitant to betray an age-old

103

weapon used vengefully by the oppressed, then she went on: 'Someone took a long, sharp needle and thrust it into that tender part of little Missy Harriet's head.'

'How horrible!' Camilla cried, but she knew something of the appalling history of slavery. The Negroes and Indians had often been treated with savage barbarity. They still remembered and did not forgive.

'The wound can't be seen, but the child's damaged beyond mending. Nothing can be done.'

There's no emotion more powerful than hatred, Camilla thought. Hatred of cruel white masters, hatred of the bully, the brute – hatred of a domineering father. Stronger than love, stronger than faith, a force that drives one on remorselessly.

Whilst listening to Leila and thinking about this, Camilla was also ruminating on the people she had just met. There was not much to be made of them yet. Time would tell, but there had been something about Selden which put her hackles up, and Josephine's patronizing attitude had been infuriating. As for Douglas, he had had a tail-wagging friendliness, like a large mastiff, probably harmless enough. Godwin had warned her that Selden was none too pleased to hear of her existence.

'Watch him,' he had said, as they discussed business in his chambers in London. 'Selden Ruthen's a slippery customer. Not to be trusted an inch.' Camilla, listening, had found her liking for his cold, clean-cutting frankness growing in her. Rufus Godwin was a man to be relied on, and she fully intended to do so, when necessary.

It was growing late and they had had a tiring day. After making sure that the fire was banked down, Leila lit candles and led the way to the upper floor. Camilla had already taken over the Master Chamber. It was cleaner than the others and she agreed with Leila that it looked as if someone had been occupying it recently. They had decided that it must have been a vagrant, using the house unbeknown.

104

'I'll keep Sam with me, in the dressing-room.' Leila was spreading the feather quilt on the rumpled coverings of the four-poster. 'Off you go, Sam. I shan't be long. I'll see Missy Camilla ready for bed and brush her hair before I come. Don't forget your prayers, now. To serve the *loa*, you have to be a good Catholic.'

Sam lingered by the fire which he had lit earlier in the wide stone fireplace. Its glow threw his dark face into relief. 'Tell it again – tell the story of God and the saints and the *loa*.'

Leila smiled at him, white teeth gleaming. 'You just want to stay up late, eh?' But she did not hurry him, thinking that he would be nervous until he acclimatized himself to these new surroundings. She took a lawn nightgown from Camilla's valise and spread it over a chair near the fire to warm. Then, sitting Camilla down before the dressing-table, she unpinned her hair and began the nightly ritual of brushing the thick curling mane.

Camilla relaxed under that familiar touch, watching Leila's reflection in the cheval-glass, seeing the room at her back, part shadowed, part lit by firelight. Leila's voice ran on, like the soothing babble of a stream. 'When God created the earth and the animals, He sent down twelve apostles to keep order. But they done grow proud and saucy. They ended up rebelling against God, so He sent them to Africa to make them mind. It's them and their children who, as *loa*, help their servants and comfort them in trouble. But one of them refused to obey God, and gave himself up to sorcery and changed his name to Lucifer.'

After this, Leila shooed Sam out of the room, and helped Camilla undress. 'How strange it is to be here,' Camilla said, when at last she was propped up in bed, her dressing-robe over her nightgown to keep out the cold. 'No mosquitoes. No netting. I can hardly believe it, Leila.'

105

'Your fate, missy, your destiny.' Leila folded away her clothes, then stood for a moment at the foot of the bed, looking at her. 'Are you sure you don't want me to sleep in here, on the couch?'

'Quite sure. This is the master's room, isn't it? I'm master here now.' Camilla refused to admit, even to herself, that she was not perfectly at home. She could not deceive Leila.

'I'm not certain it's wise. Things have been done here, unclean things – recently and in the distant past.' The *mambo* seemed to be snuffing whatever it was out of the air. 'I've placed a few little objects in the doorway. They should protect you. Tomorrow I must set up my *houmfor*. Then the *loa* will truly be able to guard us.'

When she had gone, Camilla eased herself down against the pillows and pulled the duvet up around her chest. She had her pen at hand, and intended to take the opportunity of bringing her diary right up to the moment. She had kept it for years and it contained her most private thoughts. There had been so much to add lately and further scribbling kept her occupied for some time, but gradually tiredness overtook her, warmth pervading her down to her very toes. She could hear the storm threshing against the windows in the embrasure behind the thick, faded velvet curtains. The firelight cast peculiar shadows on the ceiling and in every corner. A damp stain on a far wall looked like a grotesque face.

I'm not afraid, she told herself sternly. Why should I be? This is my home. Somewhere, she could not recall how or when, she had been told that the Ruthens were renowned in the past for their tumultuous passions and impetuosity. Now she knew this to be true, in the heart of their stronghold, prey to atavistic stirrings deep within her that proclaimed that she too came from a stock as wild and uncontrollable as the blizzard raging outside.

She turned her head to one side on the pillow, sleep weighting her eyelids. The fire crackled, then collapsed

106

in a shower of sparks, its glowing embers resembling wicked little eyes. The wind rumbled and moaned in the chimney like a slumbering volcano. I'm going to be happy here, she thought sleepily. I'll explore it thoroughly in the morning. I must find workmen to begin the repairs. It's going to cost a fortune. How lucky that father was so rich – disgustingly, shockingly rich – so rich – so sad – my father. The tiger's-eye glowed on her finger. It felt heavy as lead.

She had entered that weird state where voices, images at variance with anything she had ever known smothered her brain. Suddenly, she jerked awake, sitting up with a start, staring into the room which was darkening quickly as the fire sank lower. Somewhere, around, above and below her, she heard a woman crying. So close, so strange – it seemed to come from inside her own head.

4

The cold gleaming of dawn crept across the heavens. The silver crescent of a waning moon hung between enfolding clouds. There was no promise of a bright day, for the sky grew heavier, pregnant with more snow to come.

Why didn't I stay in my warm bed back at Armitstead House? wondered Shawn. I must be bloody mad! But there was a restlessness stirring in his blood, a compulsion to be out in the open. Not that he was dissatisfied with life. Far from it. His plans were working out better than even he, the eternal optimist, could have hoped. He had secured a good post, been given practically free rein in the stables and, because of his titled Irish connections, was treated not as an employee but more as a trusted friend helping out. He often ate at Lord Ruthen's table, was encouraged to take part in entertainments, and was expecting to share in their splendid feasts over the next few days. Then there was the delectable Josephine, flirting with him behind the backs of both husband and lover. No, life wasn't at all bad.

But, nomadic by nature, he needed the thrill of the road beneath his horse, the tracks rendered iron-hard by frost, the crispness of the newly fallen snow untrodden save by the creatures of moors and woodlands. A flock of sheep wandered down the hilly slopes, gazing at the man riding out so early in the wintery light. A hare skittered from the hedgerow, paused inquisitively, then lolloped off, leaving his queer little footprints. I could track him, if I felt inclined, Shawn thought. If I'd brought my old lurcher with me from Bantry, he'd enjoy the sport, and I could ride home with the kill dangling from my saddle, taking it to the kitchen for Miss Tennant to jug. There were the clear markings of a pheasant's feet halfway across the road. They stopped short suddenly as their owner panicked at the sound of Shawn's approach, rising in a flurry of golden-brown plumage, screeching as it hurtled for cover.

'Don't worry, little feller,' shouted Shawn. 'I've left my gun behind.'

The air was like wine, and Shawn filled his lungs with it as his horse plodded through the snow. Though a gregarious person, there were times when he liked his own company. He was invited to lunch at Armitstead House, knew that Josephine would be there, had already met her when, bored with bridge, she had found her way to his room last evening. Nothing had happened. They had prowled around one another like courting cats, and indulged in verbal fencing. He had been amused by her teasing, seductive manner. She was attracted by him, he could tell, and was content to bide his time.

Of course his reasons for this chilly excursion were not entirely concerned with communing with nature. His mind functioned like most people's, a complicated interweaving of motives, some clear cut, others buried deep in the subconscious. Shawn habitually had his eye on the main chance. It was as natural to him as breathing. If he could acquaint himself with facts which would be to his benefit, then he never hesitated, keeping both ears and eyes open and his mouth shut, until it was advantageous to speak.

He knew exactly where he was heading and what he intended to do when he got there. But this did not detract from his appreciation of the scene around him, with the rolling hills glistening, snow wreaths twining around clefts and crevices, the dawn advancing slowly between the ragged edges of driving clouds. Above his head were the intricate traceries of branches sparkling with a myriad diamond points at the tips of the outermost

109

twigs. Pearly mist rose between the trees, softening their gaunt shapes.

He drew rein when he reached the boundary of The Priory. Smoke drifted from several of the many chimney-pots. He smiled thoughtfully, his horse tossing its head, its breath echoing the smoke rising into the frosty dawning. She'd been as good as her word, then, that mysterious Ruthen cousin. He'd heard what had happened when she first stepped into Armitstead House. The kitchen had been buzzing with it. A foreign woman, bold as brass, so the servants had said, driving a car and wearing trousers! Defying the master, telling him exactly where he got off! No flies on her, by the look of things. And she'd vowed to take over The Priory at once, never mind that it was a wreck, and supposed to be haunted. Darkies with her too, servants or somesuch – heathens, no doubt. What was the world coming too? they had asked, scandalized and delightedly shocked.

It was worth investigating. Shawn clicked his tongue softly and gave a gentle tug at the bit. The Priory already seemed different, and this was not solely due to the softening effect of the snow. It now wore a slightly smug, lived-in look. Shawn had been there before, prowling the perimeter of the old building, entering it sometimes, to stroll through its once magnificent rooms, trying the handles of locked cupboards to see what might come his way, frustrated in his attempts to open them. But he had discovered two useful pieces of information on his visits; Josephine and Darcy used it for love-making, and he had seen Frank Turner slipping into the gypsy wagon, Alison too, on more than one occasion, and noticed their cycles nestled side by side under the hedge. He liked Alison and had no intention of telling tales on her. In his opinion she got a raw deal. If she could find some joy with the curate, then good luck to her! He speculated on how the four guilty parties would react now that Cousin Camilla had taken up residence. It was hardly likely to endear her.

Boldly he traversed the carriageway, and that too was altered. He had become used to seeing it as a curving sweep of moss and thistles, nettles and docks. Its avenue of sycamores had seeded among the stones closer to the manor, so that their saplings sprang from the brushwood of weeds. Ground ivy had crept up the steps and over their balustrades. Fungi had sprouted from the brick-work, and swelled like cysts from the trunks of the trees. Privets, once a trim hedge before the lower windows, had grown tall, curtaining the glass and brushing the sills. All this had been obliterated by snow. It had taken on the guise of a story-book castle, its iced pinnacles reminding Shawn of a wedding cake. As he drew nearer, the wind sighed through the naked branches, like the travail of a troubled spirit.

There was no sign of life, apart from the chimney smoke. Still in the saddle, he guided his animal around to the back. This was where he had made his first entry some weeks ago, finding a broken window and swinging his long legs over the sill. As he entered the courtyard, he saw a lad coming from an outhouse, his arms full of logs. Each was as startled as the other. Shawn recovered quickly. He stared down at the boy, registering a bent frame, a twisted right leg. Black curls tangled on his forehead, his melting dark eyes had that tender, melan-choly expression typical of children of mixed blood, strangely appealing. His nose was thin, almost hooked, a refinement in his brown face that was striking.

Shawn's eyes sharpened. There was something about the lad which was disconcerting. He rummaged in his memory to discover what it was, couldn't find the answer, tried to dismiss the odd conviction that he had seen those features somewhere before.

'*Bom dia, senhor,*' the lad said. In spite of his disability, there was a touch of pride in his posture. This was no plantation slave. He had been born a free man.

'Come again! Can't you speak English? I don't understand your lingo.'

111

There was mischief in the lad's eyes. 'Good morning, sir,' he pronounced carefully.

'Top of the morning to you, sonny,' Shawn answered, while all about them the light grew steadily stronger.

'I'm Samuel – Sam to my friends.' He heaved the logs into a more comfortable position, keeping those lustrous eyes on Shawn the while, slightly questioning.

'Well then – Sam,' Shawn smiled down on him. 'Can you be after telling me where Lady Camilla might be at this ungodly hour? Is she still abed?'

'Oh, no, *senhor*.' The logs were obviously giving trouble and Shawn swung down from his horse, at his side in a couple of long strides.

'Here, let me help you.' Without waiting for an answer, he took some of the load in his own strong arms. It was perfect excuse for getting into the house uninvited. From what he had already heard about Camilla Ruthen, she was just as likely to send him away with a flea in his ear, unless he could justify his intrusion.

The kitchen was as he had seen it before; uneven stone floor, wide low sink; rusted pump. But it was clean now, and warm. A lively fire glowed beneath the pots. His nose twitched as he breathed in the good smell of strong coffee, and bread cooking in the bake-oven alongside the vast chimney alcove. This was more like it! Why, the old place was looking almost welcoming. Damned if it didn't remind him of his own tumbledown manor, Four Oaks!

He met the unblinking stare of the statuesque black woman bending over the fire with a ladle in her hand. 'Sorry to intrude so early, ma'am.' Shawn doffed his hat and conjured up his most dazzling smile. 'I was riding this way, and it occurred to me that you might need a bit of assistance. My name's Shawn Brennan, and I'm estate manager over at Armitstead House.' He wasn't exactly that yet, but it had a fine sound to it.

Leila did not answer for a moment, opening her mind to the stranger's vibrations which conveyed more to her

112

than physical appearances. Vigour and vitality breathed out of him. He gave the outward impression of confidence. Was more sensitive than he cared to admit. No prejudice or air of condescension. No pretence of accepting her and her son, but despising their colour inwardly. He was genuinely friendly, yet could be cunning too, and was adept at looking after himself. A survivor. This she read within seconds of meeting him.

'You're welcome, sir,' she said simply. 'Please to be seated. You'll be cold. Would you like some coffee?'

'Indeed I would.' Shawn straddled a chair, crossing his arms over the back, still smiling, still observing and storing impressions away at the back of his mind. So these were the heathen servants. He'd met surlier treatment in the cottages hereabouts where he was looked upon askance, because of his assertive manner, Irish accent and devastating effect on females.

Leila brought him over a cup, placing it on the table. Shawn noted that it was made of fine china, noticed too that the shelves of the pine dresser which ran the length of one wall, were now gay with colourful plates and dishes. Sam was seated by the fire, polishing brass utensils. They'd already begun to raid the cupboards, had they? Those tantalizing locked doors which contained Lord only knew what treasures. And why not? It all belonged to Camilla Ruthen. She had a perfect right to do what she willed with it. Eat your heart out, Selden, you arrogant bastard! Shawn thought good-humouredly.

He chatted brightly to Sam and Leila, charming away their reservations, making them laugh with his anecdotes about English village life, gently warning them to expect coldness from the inhabitants of Abbey Sutton, particularly the chapel-goers. 'A stuffy lot. Don't seem to like people having fun. I'm a Catholic myself, but there's no church here. Have to drive to Ryehampton if I want to make my confession.' He threw this in for Leila's benefit, having read somewhere that most Brazilians were of that faith.

113

'We'll get used to it.' Leila impressed him with her calm dignity. 'Missy Camilla has some kind friends in London. We stayed with them. She met them on the boat. Mr John Marchant and his wife.'

'You must give me a shout if you want any help.' Shawn nodded for a second cup of coffee. 'The house needs repairing, and I can organize men to do it. I'll come over in my spare time and lend a hand.'

'Don't trouble yourself. I'm quite capable of arranging my own workforce.' A melodious voice addressed him from the doorway to the hall. 'I don't think we've met. Who are you? What are you doing here?'

Shawn swung around and leaped to his feet, surprise giving way to amazement as he looked at Camilla. She was wearing a woven skirt, a heavy knitted cardigan, topped by a shawl. Her hair was loose and, like Leila, she wore gold hooped earrings. She looks like a gypsy, by God! was his first thought. Christ! What a beauty!

'I'm Shawn Brennan.' He recovered himself at once, bowing and smiling. 'Don't wish to appear rude. Just a natural neighbourly interest.'

'Did Lord Ruthen send you?' Camilla brushed past him, going over to the fire, standing there before the hearth, her eyes regarding Shawn without any emotion.

'That he didn't. He doesn't know I've come.' Shawn couldn't get over his sense of wonder. This was perhaps the most beautiful woman he had ever seen, and his experience was wide, his interest in the female face and form deep and abiding.

'Do you work for him or are you one of the family?' Camilla accepted the coffee Leila presented, seating herself in the wooden armchair at the head of the table with as much grace as if she was attending a banquet.

He slanted her a glance. 'Well now, how can I explain? I've only been in this country a short while. I come from Ireland, you see. Lord Ruthen's taken me on as assistant manager, and I run the stables for him. As

114

for being a part of the family? I'll say this for him, he's made me feel at home – Lady Josephine too.'

Camilla could well believe that the woman she had met briefly yesterday *would* welcome such a goodlooking young man. I wish I could rid myself of suspicion, she thought. Selden and his sister were kind, yet I felt their animosity. This man. What are his motives for coming to The Priory? He seemed harmless enough, but Camilla had learned through bitter experience that people were devious and underhand, usually demanding something of her, rarely giving freely.

Her golden, gleaming eyes were watchful above the high cheekbones as she considered Shawn, hardly listening as he rattled on about his important post on the estate, his friendship with the family. Untidy chestnut hair, worn rather long, curling lashes lowered as he gesticulated, his hands square and powerful. Horseman's hands. A nice smile, but one which he switched on and off at will. He was used to a warm response from women, men too probably, if he didn't offend them with his air of brash assurance. A tall, spare body and long limbs. Oh yes, he would have much appeal for someone as bored and spoilt as Josephine had seemed to be.

'I take it that you're familiar with this house.' Camilla interrupted his flow.

Green eyes were suddenly full on hers. A tenseness in his face, as if he was struggling to hide his thoughts. His skin was tanned, but fine and clear. He obviously spent much time out of doors. 'I'll confess that I've been here once or twice.' He smiled disarmingly. 'I was curious. It seemed odd that such a huge old place should've been deserted. I've heard that it's haunted. This was enough to make me trespass. I hope you don't mind.'

'Haunted?' Camilla glanced at Leila, who was listening without comment. She nodded slightly, lips pursed as if to say, 'I told you so, missy.' Camilla remembered the night, that disembodied, doleful crying which had faded by the time she called Leila. 'And who haunts it, Mr Brennan? Have you seen a ghost here?'

Shawn was pleased. He had captured her attention. His nimble brain skipped through Irish folklore. County Cork abounded in apparitions, though a great number of these unearthly manifestations were reported by gentlemen staggering home from the taverns after having consumed vast quanitites of porter. As for The Priory? Shawn was a member of a superstitious race. Though intent on purloining goods from the building if able, he had not liked to linger there, aware of something strange, cold spots in certain areas that made the hair rise at the nape of his neck. Sounds too, sometimes, though they could have been nothing more than the gusts and crying of the wind.

'Oh, well, Lady Camilla,' he answered, his eyes caressing her, 'there's the obligatory hooded monk or two, so I've heard tell. The usual stories that circulate about any ancient, deserted house. But the only spirits I ever encounter are those found in a bottle!'

'There *is* a dead one here!' Leila spoke with such suddenness that Shawn jumped. The Creole was standing very stiffly, her head tilted at a listening angle, eyes glazed as if seeing things invisible to ordinary mortals. 'The rituals weren't observed. The *gros-bon-ange* is angry and frightened, unable to leave the place where she died.'

'You think it's a woman?' Shawn was prepared to go along with anything provided he could linger in Camilla's company. Despite his cynicism, he was impressed by Leila. She reminded him of his maternal grandmother who had been said to have the 'sight'.

Leila's large dark eyes rested on him, her consciousness returning to the kitchen and its occupants. 'I *know* it is a woman. A sad woman, tormenting the living because she died violently and wasn't given a worthy burial place.'

116

'You must help her, Leila,' Camilla said earnestly. 'I want no tortured souls walking my house.'

Leila nodded, busy stirring a mixture boiling in a small black pot standing on a trivet over the flames. The pungent smell of herbs rose with the steam, and the contents bubbled gently. Shawn was a trifle apprehensive, thinking that Camilla might be frightened, but she was taking her black servant's words calmly, as if used to such procedures.

She left her chair, coming across to stand close to him. He saw the fiery glints in her tumbled mass of hair, saw the honey-gold of her satin-smooth skin, caught the challenge in her eyes, but ventured the thought that vulnerability dwelt there too. Her perfume drifted up to him, exotic, exciting, whispering of adventure, of star-filled tropical nights and deep, sinister jungles. Shawn tingled, not so much with desire, but in sheer enjoyment of anything as perfect as Camilla Ruthen. Jesus! he thought, Josephine had better beware. When Darcy Devereaux claps eyes on this pretty darling there'll be trouble.

'If you know your way around, you'd best come with me on a tour of inspection.' Camilla was moving towards the door. With a wide grin, Shawn followed her.

'Can I come too, *patrão*?' asked Sam, throwing down his polishing rag and clambering to his feet.

'If you wish,' Camilla smiled at him warmly. She was fond of Sam. He had always been a part of her life, nearly as much as Leila. His skin was lighter than his mother's. Camilla had never been told who had sired him. Leila did not mention his father, ever. It had not seemed important, and Camilla rarely thought about it, assuming Sam to be the result of some youthful indiscretion.

Contrary to her expectations, Sam already seemed to know his way around The Priory, pointing out rooms, hidden nooks, passages and secret stairs as if he had lived there before. Shawn found it disconcerting. He

117

would have much preferred to have been alone with Camilla, impressing her with his knowledge. Sam was stealing his thunder, hobbling ahead of them enthusiastically.

There was so much to see, an atmosphere of dirt, muddle and decay hanging over everything. Camilla, a bunch of keys in one hand, stopped in the great hall, paying particular attention to a grandfather clock with a brass face. Shawn helped her to adjust the weights and set the pendulum swinging. It needed the services of a competent clockmaker, wheezing like a grampus, but Camilla's face lit up, and her hands smoothed the dingy rosewood case lovingly. It was as if she was trying to establish possession, showing The Priory that both it and its contents belonged to her. The tick of the clock punctuated the fitful rushing sound of the wind through the empty corridors.

Shawn's eyes widened as Camilla unlocked door after door, cupboard after cupboard. The long stagnant years had brought dust, damp and mildew, the timbers had been under attack from woodworm and deathwatch beetle, but the grandeur of the architecture remained, beautiful and untouched by time. Outside it had battlemented towers and turrets and buttressed walls, a noble-looking structure, with numerous shields and heraldic designs carved upon the masonry. Within, some of the rooms had the crests of the families who had intermarried with the Ruthens emblazoned in painted glass in the tops of the mullioned windows.

'It's a fair old heritage, Lady Camilla,' Shawn observed, standing with her and looking out on the snow-covered landscape. Sam had hobbled off up a winding staircase, and they were alone for a moment.

'I intend to keep it that way, Mr Brennan.' Her voice echoed across the room, strong and clear.

Shawn was aware that whenever she spoke of the property it was in decisive terms. No doubt she thought

118

he would go running back repeating her every utterance to his master, Selden Ruthen. Her lack of faith in him was troubling. He found that he wanted to win a smile from her lips, a favourable glance from her fascinating eyes. Don't be such an idiot! he chided himself. What the devil's got into you? Shawn Brennan getting mushy over a woman!

'I wish you'd call me Shawn,' he murmured, gazing down into her face. 'You're as jumpy as a high-strung filly. No need, you know. You can trust me.'

'Can I – Shawn?' Her lips smiled but her eyes were wary. 'Aren't you Lord Selden's creature? Or possibly Lady Josephine's?'

'That's a cruel thrust, and damned unfair.' He grimaced wrily. 'Sure, I work for him, but that doesn't make me his property. Spying isn't my style, I'll have you know. As for her Ladyship? I'll admit she's a mighty fine woman, but fickle as the wind. Kind of predatory, if you know what I mean. There's nothing gentle and feminine about her. I like to make the running, not for the woman to be after doing it.'

Camilla stepped back from the window, drawing her shawl closer. It was bitterly cold in this room they had chanced upon at the base of one of the turrets. The faded arras, telling in stiff figures an allegorical tale, shook as the winds crept between it and the wall. 'A woman's lot isn't an easy one,' she said, walking away from him, reaching the cobwebbed mantelshelf and running a finger over the dust. 'Not in South America and, I suspect, not in England either.'

The front of an oaken dower-chest, the fading surfaces of ancient mirrors, all gave back faint reflections of the dazzling snow-light outside. Shawn caught up with her, itching to fondle her, to stroke that mass of hair, bury his face in it, sink into the perfume of her skin. She swung around, defensive, as if she could feel his hands touching her neck, the edge of her blouse, her throat. Hardly

119

breathing, she held his eyes, unable to move for the vividness of her imaginings, the terror it engendered, and could not stop thinking of it. Then one hand flew to her face. Shawn saw the ring glinting there. It was like an eye warding off attack.

'Hey, don't look so scared,' he said gently. 'What's the matter? Who has hurt you? Tell me, and I'll break every bone in his body!'

Camilla pulled herself together with a tremendous effort. It was foolish to be so frightened just because a personable man made no secret of the fact that he found her desirable. *It's the past. I can't forget. God help me, I had thought – hoped – that here, in Wessex, the phantoms would have been laid for ever. Not so. One can't run or hide from irrevocable things and deeds too awful to contemplate. Leila. I want Leila. She's the only one I can trust.*

'What makes you think I'm scared?' Outward calm cloaked her once more. She was aloof, detached. She even managed a throaty laugh. 'If I were of a nervous disposition, I'd hardly decide to move in here, surely? You're allowing your imagination to run away with you, Shawn.'

The vulnerable moment had passed, so quickly that Shawn was not sure it had happened at all. Taking his cue, he accompanied her back to the kitchen, chatting of inconsequential matters. Leila welcomed Camilla, as if relieved that she had come to no harm when out of her sight. There was no sign of Sam.

'That rascal! Always wandering off. This house and grounds'll be a paradise for him,' she complained, shaking her bandana-covered head.

'He's happy here, Leila. He really likes it.' Camilla was steady now that she saw her.

Leila was wielding a long knife, deftly chopping herbs on a wooden board. 'It's as well that someone is, missy. The house needs happiness – happiness and love and the sounds of children's voices. It's been alone too long.'

120

Shawn realized that they were waiting for him to leave. He didn't want to outstay his welcome, so he picked up his hat and fastened his overcoat. 'I'll be off then. D'you want me to drop in to the shop and place an order for you? Have you everything you need? Don't forget, it's Christmas. You'll want to stock up. Won't be anything open for three days at least.'

Camilla could not help responding to his apparent zeal and good will. Perhaps she had been hasty in her judgement. To make up for her coldness, she walked with him to the back door. 'Thank you, but don't worry about us. I'm expecting Simmonds and his wife to arrive this morning. He's my chauffeur and handyman, whilst Mrs Simmonds is my housekeeper. My friends in London selected them for me, and they seem an efficient couple. No doubt they'll have stuffed the car with food. They'll know what is necessary for Christmas in England. We celebrated it in a different way in Bahia.'

'You'll be visiting Armitstead House?' He hesitated in the cobbled yard, reluctant to leave her and he could not explain why, even to himself.

She shivered, clutching at her shawl, the icy wind tossing her hair. 'I've been asked to dinner tomorrow night.'

He grinned. 'Wonderful! I'll look forward to that. You've met the members of the family?'

'Not Lady Alison.' Camilla wished he would go. There was so much to do inside and she had not yet finished exploring.

Shawn was twisting his hat around in his broad hands, looking into the lining as if seeking the answer to some problem there. Then his green eyes twinkled as he looked at her again. 'You'll like her. She's not like the others. A good woman, if ever I saw one. Now, what about the repairs?' He cast an eye at the crumbling gutterings.

'After Christmas, Shawn. I can't think about it yet.

121

I'll be seeking women who aren't afraid of hard work. Even the rooms that are habitable need a thorough cleaning from top to bottom. As for the rest, it'll take months before The Priory's former glory is restored.'

'I'll help,' he said eagerly.

'We'll see.'

'Goodbye then, for the moment.' Unable to wheedle further promises from her, Shawn clapped his hat on his head, saluted with his whip, and went to find his horse.

Camilla thought about him several times during the morning, but her attention was soon occupied by the appearance of the Rolls which braked at the front steps and disgorged both Mr and Mrs Simmonds and a mountainous heap of parcels and boxes. They were a well matched pair, forever arguing in a friendly way and seeming completely devoted to one another. Wilf Simmonds was approaching fifty, spruce in his smart uniform, always unruffled and polite. He possessed a sense of humour, good health and stamina, coupled with courage and loyalty. His wife, Beryl, had been carefully trained in one of the big houses, serving her apprenticeship from the age of fourteen, starting in the humble position of tweeny and working her way up through the strict servant hierarchy. Both had excellent references.

Camilla had interviewed them in the Marchants' London house and, impressed by their cheerful manner, had engaged them without seeking further. Beryl, a neat woman with a broad, homely face, cast a businesslike eye around the kitchen and set about making friends with Leila, a not too easy task for the Creole jealously guarded both her mistress and her mistress's possessions. Camilla prayed that they might soon reach a compromise.

Later Beryl stood in the Great Hall and looked about her. So much dirt was a challenge which she met with alacrity. First of all, she sent her husband and Sam searching for more wood. 'What we need, Lady Camilla, are fires lit everywhere, to dry it out. That one there for example,' she pointed to the fireplace which was big enough for a man to stand in, its stone canopy stretching towards the dimness of the rafters.

'Probably find they're clogged up with fallen masonry and birds' nests, my dear,' predicted Wilf, winking at Sam. 'Maybe even a bat or two.'

His wife was not to be discouraged. 'There's only one way to find out. Get to it, Wilf!'

Camilla, content to let her take charge, retired to the library, but Beryl was hot on her heels, insisting that a fire be lit on the hearth, declaring that her Ladyship would take a chill if she tried to work there without one, what with her but recently come from a hot country and all. Whilst Wilf and Sam hefted in kindling and large branches, busy as beavers beneath the great carved overmantel, Beryl attacked the room with broom and dusters. Camilla tried to ignore her, examining the bookcases which lined the walls from floor to ceiling. Thick, leather-bound volumes stood, exuding cobwebs and learning, behind dingy glass.

'Don't bother to clean those yet.' She fended off Beryl's attempts to do so. 'I want to work, and must have some peace. You've made it livable. That will do for now.'

'Very well, ma'am,' Beryl replied reluctantly. 'If you're quite sure. I'll go and see what else can be done. Come along, Wilf, and you, young Sam. Is there anything you require, my Lady?'

'A cup of coffee at eleven.' Camilla seated herself in the imposing carved chair before the desk, a pile of papers which Rufus Godwin had given her, stacked on the Morocco leather surface. 'I don't wish to be disturbed till then.'

The room fell into studious stillness, and she worked steadily, becoming absorbed in the documents, most of them crackly with age, the copperplate writing fading.

Amongst them were the deeds of The Priory, and there was an interesting map showing the extent of the estate, boundaries clearly marked. She perused this for a long while, wanting to become fully informed about every aspect of her property. The brass ashtray became filled with cheroot stubs, the air sweetened with fragrant smoke. Pausing in her labours, resting her head against the padded back of the chair, Camilla saw that the ceiling was painted with cupids and clouds, albeit very dirty ones. The darkly panelled room was furnished in the eighteenth-century Chinese manner. A pair of flowered vases stood on identical buhl tables. There were two lacquered chests across which golden dragons sprawled. Beryl will have the time of her life putting all this to rights, Camilla smiled to herself. And this is but a fraction of the furnishings, if the inventory I have here is correct.

With the arrival of a tray with silver coffee pot, cream jug and sugar basin, served punctually at eleven, Camilla thrust her task aside, determined to take the map and view her land. The weather looked decidedly inclement, but this did not deter her, neither did Leila's gloomy predictions about pneumonia, and broken limbs caused by stumbling into snowdrifts.

However, once she had left the shelter of the house, Camilla's resolution almost failed. The snow had fallen heavily in the night, silent, unhurried, covering everything with a thick soft mantle. The entire world seemed snow-bound, transformed into something alien to which she was totally unaccustomed. The sky was iron dark, the earth white, muffled in a blanket through which a stream snaked, black and lipped with ice. The trees and hedges, already strange to her Brazilian eyes, were loaded with their icy burden, branches protesting under the weight. She glanced back at The Priory. It was like a squat beast crouching beneath its hood of snow.

Her cheeks burned with the cold. Her breath hung in

124

the air. She huddled into her fur coat, boots moving in a floundering tread as she struck out towards the fields. The map was in her pocket, and she stopped near the road, taking it out, refreshing her memory. It was not easy to determine the boundaries, for long drifts lay under the hedges and across gateways, curved and sculptured by eddies of wind into strange shapes and solid, arrested waves. Everything was noiseless and still.

Camilla had come some distance from The Priory. It was as if she had journeyed to the ends of the earth, so solitary and remote did she feel. She struggled across one field, and then another, sweating with effort by this time, regretting her impetuosity but stubbornly refusing to turn back. As she pushed through a small gap in a frosted iron gate, she saw sudden movement – white fleece which looked grubby against the virgin snow. The sheep heard her from afar, assuming that she was bringing hay. They came towards her in a seething, bleating mass.

Camilla tried to scramble to safety. Her boots could not grip on the icy surface. She skidded, lost her footing, sprawled in a deep drift. She lay there for a second, winded and furious, cursing the silly creatures and, above all, the person who had put them there. Godwin hadn't mentioned sheep. Oh yes, there were many belonging to the estate, but they were scattered on several different farms, cared for by the manorial tenants. Someone was usurping her land! It was tantamount to stealing. What right had they to trespass, just because the master had been long gone?

It was then that she saw him – a horseman silhouetted against the skyline. Skilfully, he guided the animal down the treacherous hillside towards her. Camilla hauled herself up by an overhanging branch, showered with freezing droplets, clinging to it till she regained her balance. He was coming closer, making in her direction. He wore a weather-proof greatcoat with triple capes

125

which served to emphasize the width of his shoulders. Black hat, black hair, black beard, swarthy skin and, as he pulled in beside her, she saw that his eyes were of an intense blue in a powerfully handsome face.

'Are you all right?' he asked, his deep voice ringing across the complaints of the hungry sheep.

'Yes, thank you.' Camilla had lost her dignity and was not pleased. 'Those stupid animals!'

He gave a low chuckle, his eyes lighting with amusement. 'They thought you were the shepherd, bringing them their supper.'

Aware that her cheeks were flushed with anger and embarrassment, Camilla brushed the snow from her skirt. 'Who owns them? They don't belong to The Priory. Has he permission to use the land?'

Darcy Devereaux gave her a slightly mocking, quizzical glance. 'The fields have been empty for years. Such a waste of good grazing.'

'But was some arrangement made about this? Has there been a financial agreement? If not, then whoever owns those beasts will have to remove them, at the double!' Camilla shouted, aware of one thing only – some bandit was using *her* land, and this was not to be tolerated.

He raised a cynical eyebrow, at ease in the saddle, completely at home out there amongst the snow, his horse lowering its head and nibbling at the whiteness. 'What concern is it of yours?' he enquired evenly, though by her accent he had already guessed who she was.

'I'm Lady Camilla Ruthen. The Priory is mine. The land is mine. No one shall use the grazing unless I give them leave.'

'Ah, so you're the late Marquis's daughter. I might have guessed.'

Darcy was more than just pleased. Well, what a gorgeous young female, if a fiery one with a fiendish temper, by the look of things! Unabashed by her fall,

126

unafraid of *him*, she was glaring up, an infuriated ice queen who'd like to have the power to shout: 'Off with his head!'

He feasted his eyes on her warm complexion, the colour heightened by rage, on her amber eyes sparkling with indignation, the loosened tumble of curls that flowed from beneath her wide-brimmed felt hat. Edgar Ruthen's daughter, eh? Heir to The Priory. This know-ledge seemed to give her an air of power and authority, despite her youth and her foreignness. It showed in the way she carried herself – the faintly regal tilt to her head, the wilful set of her chin. Beautiful, aye, she was that all right. She reminded Darcy of a Pre-Raphaelite painting – *Monna Vanna* by Rossetti, perhaps. In comparison, Josephine's charms seemed suddenly overblown. In a flash he realized that he was heartily sick of her.

'I've taken over The Priory and intend to stay,' she announced loftily. 'I want to talk to the man who's had the gall to steal my fields. D'you know him?'

Darcy threw back his head and gave a bark of laughter. 'Oh, yes, Lady Camilla, I know him very well indeed!' Then he sobered, and the look in his eyes made her conscious that she was alone with him in a remote spot. 'I confess that I'm the villain you're seeking. I live on the other side of the hill, at Chalkdown Farm.'

'Then I suggest that you remove yourself and your sheep back there at once.' Camilla had not been so angry with anyone since her father died. This man, with his arrogance, his mocking manner, roused the same un-controllable passion in her that Edgar Ruthen had done. How dare he sit there laughing at her?

'Can't be done, your Ladyship.' His expression was imperturbable.

'It *will* be done! Or I'll take you to court!' Comforting visions of Rufus Godwin's burly figure and trenchant tongue flashed through her mind. He'd know how to deal with such a high-handed brigand!

127

'You wouldn't win.' Darcy was maddeningly confident. 'Anyone who knows anything about farming will tell you that it's good for the ground to be grazed. The manure enriches it, the animals keep it cropped. I brought the sheep down from my top fields two days ago when I saw that snow was coming. Just as well that I did, or I'd have been digging them out of drifts this morning.'

'I don't care if you and your damned flock are buried twelve feet under – you'll move them!' Why am I so angry with him? she wondered, her emotions in a turmoil. Am I substituting him for Selden? Is it really Selden who should be bearing the brunt of my fury? It was imperative that she take a stand. She was sensitive to the fact that if she showed herself weak in any way, then her enemies would attempt to wrest her rights from her, bit by bit.

'Tut! Tut! That's not a very nice thing to say,' he reproved, his blue eyes mocking and admiring her.

'You'll learn soon enough that I'm *not* very nice when I feel injustice is being done,' she answered grittily.

'You'd not see my poor little baa-lambs perish in the snow, would you?' His smile was teasing but his eyes were keen. 'We're in for a bad winter. They'll struggle for survival up on the hills.'

If he cherished the hope of appealing to her pity, she demolished this with a brief, chilling reply. 'That's your concern. Not mine.'

'By gad, but you're a hard woman, Lady Camilla,' he said in a slow, sardonic way, his eyes feeding on her in a manner which shattered her confidence in her own strength. The horse fidgeted restlessly and he reached down a gloved hand to pat his long, strong neck. 'You know nothing of the English winter. We farmers face it philosophically, but never without misgivings. We always hope it'll last no more than a week, perhaps less, but we can't be sure that it won't be with us for three months or more. I've know snow fall in December and

128

not melt till April. I remember one year when the moor was buried so deep in frozen snow that one could walk over the hedges on top of it, and be lost for lack of landmarks. Several people died of exposure that way. The sheep died in hundreds, and in some parts cattle and ponies too. Snow, when it comes, is always ominous.'

She was about to make a stinging retort when she saw three figures plodding down the hill, lugging large bundles of hay. They were muffled to the eyebrows, and wore sacks over their shoulders for extra protection. The sheep could hear and smell them from afar. Their frantic bleating rose loudly as they clustered round the gate.

Camilla clung to her stand obstinately. 'They shouldn't be here. When will you move them?' She repeated with determined energy.

'I'll come and discuss it with you at The Priory,' he asserted rather than asked.

Camilla scrambled back to where the path should be, watching the approaching shepherds resentfully. They were mobbed by the sheep as they struggled through the gate. The hungry beasts almost swept them off their feet, tearing at the corners of the bales as they threw them down. A quick slash of a knife and the trusses tumbled apart. The sheep fell upon them, fighting over the hay like famished wolves.

Camilla brushed the hair back from her face, her eyes burning as she looked up at him. 'You'll have to call after Christmas. My lawyer will be here then.'

Darcy bowed low over his horse's mane and raised his hat. 'I'll be honoured, Lady Camilla. I'm sure we can reach a not too painful compromise. May I accompany you to the gates of The Priory?'

'No, thank you.' Camilla turned her back on him, trudging doggedly across the field, following her own tracks which were deeply pressed into the snow. Darcy watched her disappearing into the distance, sharp black against the white, as the short afternoon started to die.

The wind was rising, the snow swirling around her, and deep and muffling underfoot. Camilla was glad when The Priory reared up out of the gathering darkness, a solid habitat for humans looming amidst the cold and dark that froze her blood and sinews. She was so glad to return. Thankful to enter her home where the simple blessings of shelter awaited her. Food and fire, warmth and comfort, and the love of Leila and Sam.

But even as she stood in the kitchen while Leila fussed and Beryl produced a bowl of hot soup, so her mind was wrestling with a single question. The stranger with the searching blue eyes. Who was he?

Alison was in her studio, waiting for Frank to come. Her heart seethed with love. The surge dried her throat and beat in her body. It had been like that ever since he had kissed her in the wagon, held her in his arms. Never had she been so intimate with any man before. And there was more to come. By morning she would have been initiated into the mysteries of sex. She wanted to experience it but was, at the same time, terrified.

She had come into the studio about eleven-thirty, with the excuse that she was tired and wanted an early night to prepare herself for the rigours of Christmas Day. Selden, Josephine and the remainder of the guests declared that they were not ready for bed yet, though by the glances her sister kept shooting Darcy, Alison guessed that she was more than ready. But she no longer despised her, suddenly understanding the mad passion which could sweep over the most sensible of women, driving them to take steps which defied the laws of man. Was she herself not about to embark on the hazardous course of adultery?

She shivered, though the studio was warm. Adultery. It was an ugly word with unpleasant connotations. Six months ago – no, less than that – she would never have

130

dreamed she could become involved with it. Adultery. She said it again under her breath and it did not become more palatable with repetition. It smacked of dingy hotels, of stolen weekends darkened by guilt, of private investigators and scandal. It has nothing to do with Frank and me, she whispered. Our love isn't like that! It's not dirty and furtive! But wasn't it?

Undefinable feelings, latent in her, had stirred into life when Frank kissed her. Every one of her principles, the cornerstones of her existence, had vanished. She saw this clearly and bitterly. I'll become like Josephine, she thought. What women do not live their lives behind a veil of dissemblance? Are we not all harlots at heart? I'm a fraud, she decided. I had very greatly wanted to be good. Wanted to be self-sacrificing – up to a point. Wanted to be the devoted, patient sister. But now I see that it was a sham – easy to do when I wasn't in love. It only needed the right man to come along to upset the applecart. This sad moment of clear-sightedness left her depressed.

She glanced at the ormolu clock on the mantelpiece. Its gilt hands pointed to a quarter to twelve. She could hear sounds of revelry in other parts of the house. The children were long gone to the nursery. It was grown-up games that were now being played – probably Murder-in-the-dark or Hide-and-seek, capital excuses for snatched kisses in corners, for quick embraces and whispered assignations planned for later.

The studio was softly lit by the single ornate standard lamp with its fringed shade, that Alison had left burning. It was her sanctum which, when Armitstead House was under construction, she had prevailed upon Selden to assign to her. Situated on the north side of the building, it was splendid for painting, a central glass cupola flooding down light whatever the weather. Double French windows led out to a paved terrace which connected with the garden by a flight of shallow steps. It

131

had its own small bathroom adjacent. Alison had furnished it with a divan, covered by an oriental bedspread and heaped with Eastern cushions. Thus, if she worked late, she could spend the rest of the night there in comfort, away from her room upstairs where she could not escape the intrusion of her personal maid, Edna. A piano occupied pride of place near the large windows, a green shawl draped over it, silk fringes shivering in every movement of air. Alison could play, though not to a high standard, but sufficent to entertain herself. She could never be persuaded to perform in the music-room when there were others present. Unlike Josephine who could not wait to be invited, pouncing upon the Steinway with an enthusiasm which compensated for her lack of talent.

A couple of large easy chairs, shelves of books, cabinets of curios, potted plants and colourful rugs completed the studio's decor. Reproductions of her favourite paintings hung on the white walls, along with a few original landscapes which had come from the old family home. Here she could keep personal paraphernalia, relics of childhood; her china-headed doll, with its jointed limbs and opening and closing blue eyes, its wig of real, curling hair, its wardrobe of miniature clothing; that scaled-down baby-carriage in which it still sat, safe now from the vandalism of Selden and Josephine. Precious items which she valued.

Apart from these, the place contained the tools of an artist; stacked canvases, an easel supporting a half-finished work, a long bench littered with tubes of oil paints, a smeared palette, bottles of linseed oil and turpentine, a pile of drawing paper. Small-sized replicas in marble of the *Venus di Milo* and Michelangelo's *David* stood on plinths each side of the fireplace.

Alison wandered amongst her treasures whilst she awaited her lover. It was almost as if she was bidding them farewell. When next she visited them, she would be changed, the innocence gone. She would know the secrets of the Venus's beautiful, armless torso, would appreciate with a new eye the sensuality of the boy David's muscular perfection. She was tempted to ignore Frank's tap at the window, to pretend that she wasn't there, longing to remain as she was, part of her a child still, undeveloped, unaware – happy in her cloud-cuckoo-land.

This could not be. The path was set, the die cast. She had known this all through the evening, meeting at the church for a service before carol singing. The village had turned out in full force, and she had noticed two strange faces in the congregation. The whisper went around that these were the chauffeur and housekeeper from The Priory. Lady Camilla had not come! Why not? the round eyes and round mouths questioned. No one had seen her yet, though the Misses Carpenter vowed they'd spotted her car as she drove away from Armitstead House yesterday. The lofty church had rung with the joyous songs of the Nativity. Candles had glowed on the crib. The Reverend Mapley had given his address whilst his wife beamed with pride. Alison had listened to his plethora of words without taking any of it in. With splendid complacency he had stood at the main door after the service, wishing everyone who passed the compliments of the season.

'Merry Christmas, Lady Alison.' She had not been able to avoid this. He had smiled benignly, more than middle-aged, his face florid and rounded with good living, his eyes bright and bulging. The breath on which this greeting had travelled had been tainted by brandy.

'And to you, Mr Mapley,' she had replied in the proper voice of the gentry.

Seeing Frank standing with the carol singers, she had burned with a gem-like flame. Kindled into pulsating, vigorous life, she had walked by his side through the snowy night. Once, when they paused outside the almshouse, his shoulder had brushed against hers as they shared a carol book, bending beneath the lantern to read the words. It had been hard to sing when they entered Armitstead House, harder still to remain there when, carols over, he had departed with the others, the air filled with merry voices, a little slurred after libations from the Red Lion and Selden's generous cellars.

A few muttered words in the shelter of the porch. 'You'll come?' She had hardly dared breathe it.

'Around midnight.' His eyes blazing into hers, holding them, spearing them, and then he had gone.

A dragging hour during which she had pretended to enjoy the Christmas Eve celebrations, so many people to entertain, a grave responsibility to see that each and every one was comfortably settled. Then a hurried trip to the nursery wing, there to help Miss Gearing, the harassed governess of Josephine's children, Andrew and Flora. He was a naughty six-year-old, and his sister a weepy, over-excited four. Stockings had been pinned to the mantelshelf and warnings solemnly issued that if they weren't asleep within five minutes Father Christmas would deliver their toys to better behaved boys and girls. They wouldn't even find an orange or a sugar mouse there at dawning. Two pairs of wide eyes had regarded Alison over the tops of the sheets in the identical small beds as they promised to be good. Smiling, she had dropped a kiss on each little head and gone to her own room to change.

This was, in effect, her wedding night, but Edna, ever watchful, was there, so Alison had performed the customary ritual, shrouding herself in a cowl-necked, balloon-sleeved gown of warm flannel, and topping it with a matching peignoir. Neither garment was in the least romantic, bought to be serviceable rather than alluring. It had been difficult to remain calm, but if her cheeks were pinker than usual, she trusted that Edna would put this down to the excitement of Christmas. She

134

had dismissed her maid at last, and when she had gone, had finished brushing her hair so that it fell about her shoulders, and then crept down to the studio.

The waiting was agonizing. Supposing he could not come? There were his children, especially the youngest, Effie, of whom he was particularly fond. What if Elsie was having one of her bad days, and refused to let him out of her sight? No! Oh no! Fate could not be so cruel! He'll come – I *know* he'll come –

There was a sound. A sharp knock on the window. She switched off the light. The room was plunged in darkness smeared with crimson from the fire. She felt her way across to the curtains, pulled them back, peered out through the glass. He stood there on the terrace. She turned the key. A blast of cold air numbed her. He stepped in and closed the door quietly behind him. She went into his arms and it was as if he had not let go of her since the last time, as if they had stood there like that always, shadows in the dark.

'Frank – oh, Frank –' she breathed against his cold lips. He tasted of snow, of the dark wintry night.

'Hush.' He put his fingers over her mouth. She kissed them, worshipped them. 'We'll not talk – not yet.'

He found his way to the fire, his arm still around her. Drew her down. The embers glowed, so that after a moment she could see his face, his smiling lips, his eyes. Her fears died as he looked at her. Then his hands were on her breasts. He was unfastening her nightgown. He bent his head, kissing her throat, her bare breasts, her naked shoulders. He was undressing her and she had waited for this as she had waited for him. The firelight gave the room a feeling of secrecy and warmth. He was breathing hard as if he had been running through the snow, running from his home and all its demands, running to her arms. He held her tightly. It was a hard, hungry, unbreakable hold, his kisses almost brutal, and he sank with her to the hearth rug and there, hidden

135

away from the world, they lay together in a close embrace, their appetites heightened, fed on kisses and caresses.

Alison was trembling, the sweetness of desire making her arch her back and grit her teeth against it. 'Frank!' she cried in her terror and ecstasy.

'Ssh – be still. I won't hurt you, my darling,' he whispered, so tender, so gentle. 'Don't be afraid.'

Her body lost its identity. She was as nothing compared to the passion swelling in him, sweeping towards her, engulfing her. Then there was pain, so intense that she cried out again – pain which went on and on – unendurable – but she clenched her teeth and found the strength to bear it. This was what he wanted. She *must* give him what he wanted so desperately. It was over. Frank lay still beside her. She could feel the pounding of his heart, hear his laboured breathing, feel his sweat against her naked skin.

This was better. At last she could lie quietly in his arms, safe again. This is love, she thought. 'Frank, are you asleep?' she whispered. She touched his face, his shoulders, the hollows of his back, unsatisfied but not sure of what she needed.

He turned his head and kissed her again, lazily, the urgency quenched. She wanted to be fondled, for the caressing to continue, for pleasure to return, that secret pleasure she encountered on her own sometimes. She longed for it, and the sweet release it brought, could hardly believe it was true as he began to touch her again. Frank was doing it for her, giving it to her. Pleasure so exquisite that she writhed, her body opening, yearning – the feeling going on and on, climbing higher, peaking – drowning her in sensation.

She lay quietly, face turned to one side, buried in the cushion beneath it. His hand stroked the softness of her thigh, and she moulded her nakedness against his. He's my man, she thought sleepily. I want nothing but to lie naked with him in the firelight and whisper of love, dreams, plans for the future. He disengaged himself from her embrace, sitting up, reaching for his discarded shirt.

Her eyes snapped open. 'Where are you going?'

'Home.' He saw her whole body shiver and her shoulders hunch with pain, but he did not spare her. 'I must go back before I'm missed. Elsie's dead drunk and Mrs Barlow's in bed, but Effie has a cold and is quite likely to wake and call for me.'

'I see.' Her voice was a wan, lost sound in the darkness. This is how it would always be, she supposed, no matter how much he loved her there were others who had a prior claim. Anger smarted within her, but she, unsuccessfully, tried to temper it with logic.

'I'm sorry, beloved.' Frank had his trousers on, his shirt thrown on loosely, the front unbuttoned. He leaned over her, smoothed her hair, kissed her mouth. 'There's nothing I can do about it – yet.'

Alison sat up, the flames turning her skin to gold, deep shadows beneath her breasts, on the insides of her arms. 'Yet? You've a plan, Frank? Tell me.'

He ran a troubled hand through his hair, staring down at her. 'I don't know what to do.' There was a pain in his voice. 'All I'm sure of is that I love you, Alison. I've never felt like this about a woman before.'

'Not even Elsie.' She had not intended her voice to be accusative, but it was.

Frank groaned. 'We were young then. I didn't understand what I was doing. Now I do, and I know this is the real thing.'

'But you're going to leave me, tonight of all nights.' She knew she was being unreasonable and did not care. She wanted him, wanted to lie beside him through the dark hours, to see his face on the pillow beside her as dawn streaked the sky. Why should he be allowed to go, scot free? To return to his wife and children, leaving her with nothing but memories.

137

With a seduction which she was learning fast, almost with a sense of remembering something once familiar, she rose to her knees, clasping his legs, pressing her face against his thighs. She felt his hands in her hair, was aware that they trembled. Neither spoke as he bent, lifted her up and sat down in the armchair, settling her on to his lap. She wrapped her arms around his neck and buried her face in his neck.

'Must go,' he said hoarsely. 'If I don't, I'll be here for ever.'

'Stay then – stay –' It was madness. If they were discovered it would be disastrous. They'd have the wrath of the whole county descending on their heads. She could almost see the headlines in the newspapers – Curate seduces titled lady. Adultery committed after carol-singing! Sick wife refuses to comment! 'I belong to you,' she murmured. 'I want to sleep in the same bed with you, even if it's only for an hour. Please, Frank –'

He tumbled her from his knee and, taking her hand, led her to the divan. With one hand he threw back the covers and she slipped between them, the sheets icy against her hot flesh. Her heart beat fast in the cage of her chest. I'm not going to think of anything, only of this. His body and mine in the firelight. Then he took her as she had wanted him to take her from their first meeting in the wagon. She had been stirred then, as she was now by this sweet madness in her blood, rejoicing in it, shutting her mind to everything except loving and being loved in return.

5

'Wilf, I want you to drive me over to Armitstead House at seven o'clock. You may return here, if you wish, then collect me at midnight.' Camilla gave the chauffeur his orders in the library, before going to the Master Chamber to change.

It was dusk, though not yet five. The sun had been shining for most of Christmas Day, a picture postcard scene, with red-berried holly bushes, a robin in evidence, cheekily demanding scraps at the back door, and the distant pealing of church bells. It was as if England was putting on a display for its exiled daughter, showing her that it could match any exotic view displayed in South America. Camilla was impressed but coldly so, both inside and out. A child of the sun, she missed its heat, this pale, red-glowing apology was not the Ra she worshipped. The chill foreign scene did not move her. Her soul was shrivelling. She could almost see it becoming a crisp brown thing with ragged curling edges, like a dead leaf.

In her diary, dated December 24th, she had written:

Leila has carried out some of the ceremonies performed for this winter solstice. She's rather upset because there's no Catholic church around here, as she always goes to mass on Christmas Day after being up all night taking part in Voodoo rites. On one hand she likes to celebrate the birth of Christ, and on the other prepares magic to afford immunity from sorcerers and evil spirits.

This is a strange Christmas Eve for us. At other times I've gone with Leila to the house of the Guede, where drums are beaten all night, and a spicy, herby smell fills the air. There

139

was always a lot of dancing, and people busy pounding mixtures with pestle and mortar. The drug that results is so strong that whilst using it for his magic, I've seen the *hungan* reeling as if drunk.

My father didn't approve. He dismissed such things as mumbo-jumbo, foolish man, but my mother had been brought up to respect the power of Voodoo. Leila never failed to include me in all but the most secret rites, and I was about to be initiated into those, when we left Brazil. So I've seen the congregation dance for hours on end, seen Leila possessed by the *loa* Brise, changing into a harsh, furious god, whip in hand, throwing herself on the worshippers, lashing them to make them dance with more fervour. I truly believe they *are* taken over by spirit entities. I believe too that the Voodoo rituals mingle the best of African and Christian ideals into a powerful, very personal religion. Leila has always said that I have the gift, being able to scry in my crystal. I used to enjoy it, but not any more. I've put it away, not gazed in it for a long time.

Anyhow, to get back to the Voodoo Christmas celebrations. They use it as an opportunity for healing, which can be no bad thing. I wonder how many Christian revellers aid their fellow creatures in such a way? Not many, I'll bet. I've seen what could be called miracle cures. I'd stake my life that no such good will be done tomorrow night at the gathering at Armitstead House. It will be interesting to meet my cousins again, and to be introduced to Alison. I wonder about Shawn Brennan. Leila swears he's a harmless person under that rather cocksure exterior. We shall see.

Note: the ghost of The Priory. Shall I hear her again? I can only presume that she was crying for my benefit last night. I wonder what it is she wants of me? When I've settled in, and sounded out the rest of the Ruthen brood, I'll concentrate on her.

Leila came to help Camilla get ready for the party, clicking her tongue in reproof of her mistress's choice. 'That gown's not ladylike. Your Mamma would never've worn such a thing. How you going to impress those lords and ladies if you insist on dressing like a Scarlet Woman, eh?'

140

'Scarlet fiddlesticks!' Camilla looked at her reflection in the pier glass and found nothing wanting.

It was true that her mode of dress did not resemble that worn by other women whom she had met on the liner or in London. It was, as Josephine had correctly stated, in a completely new style. There was a freedom about it which suited Camilla's outlook on life. Not for her tight stays which gave the female body the appearance of a pouter-pigeon, or the high choker collars popularized by Edward VII's queen, Alexandra. Camilla was used to liberty. She had often run barefoot in the grounds of the plantation house. Swimming naked in the nearby pool had been a joy, lying in the sun too, absorbing the rays which coloured every inch of her skin to a golden brown.

She had found an echo of this striving for lack of restriction in the dress designers of Paris and, spending lavishly, had amassed a completely new wardrobe, becoming a devotee of Art Nouveau in the process. Intoxicated by the representation of plant forms that grew and burgeoned, budded and blossomed over every yard of fabric, and coiled sinuously around wood and metal, she had ordered curtains, furniture, lamps and ornaments. Her heart sang in response to the sensuous lines, the flowing curves which made one think of waves, of women's hair, of twisting smoke. Above all, she was captivated by the jewellery and had purchased several fine pieces by René Lalique.

The gown she had selected for her very important emergence into Wessex society was extravagant and luxurious, simple in line yet feminine and exotic. Made of rich purple velvet, the bodice and right sleeve were overlaid by chiffon patterned in leaf greens and lilac. This was softly draped at the back and billowed into a train.

Standing watching her, hands on hips, lips in a disapproving slant, Leila remarked: 'A girl of your age should be wearing white!'

141

'Like a virgin?' Camilla gave a low chuckle, but her eyes held a fierce light. 'You know this would be untrue, Leila. Would you have me a liar, besides being unladylike?' An unwelcome picture of André de Jaham presented itself in her mind's eyes. 'You should be glad, my dear *mambo*. If I died, it would save you the trouble of deflowering my body when you came to wash it before burial, to protect my soul from being raped by that unsavoury *loa*, Baron-Samedi.'

'Missy Camilla, what a thing to say!' Leila lifted eyes and hands to the ceiling as if beseeching assistance from the gods. 'Why must you be so bad?'

'You should know the answer to that. *You* raised me!' Camilla said briskly as she added pendant earrings to her attire and pinned a strangely beautiful brooch to her corsage.

It was her favourite piece, a decadent, *fin de siècle*, example of Lalique's art. A huge, misshapen pearl hung beneath the brooding, mysterious face of a woman, carved out of crystal, wearing a headdress of purple-black flowers upon her flowing black hair. Leila did not much like this either.

Camilla swept up her coat, a flamboyant garment made of leopard pelts, paused before the dressing-table for a final spray of perfume, then, seeing that Leila was still cross with her, flung her arms about her impulsively. Such a staunch, comforting woman, so good to cling to, and love welled in Camilla's heart.

'Missy – oh, my dear little miss, do be careful,' Leila warned, looking into the almost barbaric beauty of her face. 'I've a bad feeling about those folk of yours. They'll do you a mischief.'

'You'll guard me, Leila. You always have, always will.'

Leila sighed, her wise eyes concerned. 'I can't protect you from yourself, *ma petite*. You're like your Papa.'

Camilla stiffened and disengaged herself from Leila's embrace. 'Don't say that. I've no wish to be like him.'

'It's in your blood. You can't escape it.' Leila picked up a beaded bag, feather fan and gloves, handing them to her. 'Haven't you noticed the likeness in the portraits of your ancestors? The faces are the same. Wild eyes, wolf's eyes, and the mouths pleasure-loving yet cruel too.'

Camilla had noticed and did not want to be reminded. She changed the subject, giving Leila a parcel which she had prepared earlier. 'It's for you. A Christmas gift – one of the nice things people do in Europe. I've left one for Sam in the kitchen, and there's a package each for Wilf and Beryl.'

Leila adored receiving presents, and she chuckled as she untied the ribbon and opened it, giving a delighted gasp when she saw the scarlet silk shawl, boldly embroidered with gold roses and swinging fringes at its edges. 'Oh, missy! How fine!' She draped it around her shoulders and skipped a few steps, gazing at herself in the looking glass. She preened, tossing her dark head, eyes and teeth gleaming in the candlelight.

'When the house is finished, I'll give a grand ball, inviting half the county. You shall wear it then.' Camilla was feeling light-hearted, tingling with anticipation of the evening to come. It was a challenge which she accepted joyfully. There were fresh fields to conquer, and vitality flooded her. 'We'll show 'em that we're not a pack of uneducated savages, won't we?'

'We will indeed, missy!' Leila grinned, and Camilla knew that she was forgiven.

As the Rolls purred along, the wind blew up the icy surface of the road where the crust of new snow was flattened into long glissades like a band of metal. Camilla sank back against the plush upholstery of the rear seat, her satin slippers tucked into a fur-lined foot-warmer, a rug across her knees. The back of Wilf's peaked cap was turned to her, his eyes fixed on the treacherous road. He did not speak much, no more than

143

a passing comment concerning the weather and, in a short time, they were turning into the drive which led to Armitstead House.

Tall trees on each side, glimpsed briefly in the glare of headlamps, black above, white below. Then light ahead, shining from every window of the house, and at either stately pillar at the top of the steps leading to the front door. Wilf manoeuvred the car to a halt, leaped out and opened the door for Camilla, as upright and dignified as a general. There was ice in the wind which chilled her. The moon hung white for frost. It was bright already, shining on the purity of the snow, turning it to silver-blue.

In a few moments she was out of the cold night and into the glowing warmth of the hall. Selden was there, immaculate in evening dress, his hair slicked back, his grey eyes admiring her, his compliments effusive, as seductive as the serpent. A maid, smart in black and white, offered to take her coat but Camilla shook her head, leaving it swinging from her shoulders as Selden led her into a vast drawing-room. Faces. People. Strangers. All staring, all smiling but with eyes that questioned, criticized, envied – veiled of course, but there nevertheless.

'You've met Josephine, haven't you?' Selden's hand was cupping her elbow, squeezing it slightly beneath the cover of the leopard skin, unpleasantly intimate, as if they already shared secrets. 'But not Alison, I believe.'

Camilla saw a tall, thin young woman, registered that her dress was plainer than the other women's and that such severity suited her. Brown hair, dark grey eyes, pleasing features – nervous, for some reason which was connected with her forceful brother. She wanted to be friendly. Camilla could feel it when Alison took her hand and they exchanged a greeting kiss. Soft skin, fine too, and delicately perfumed. Yes, she liked Alison. How on earth could such a sensitive creature be related to wily

144

characters like Selden and Josephine? They've bullied her! Camilla was certain of it and, like a cat sensing danger, she felt a tingling run up her spine.

'I'm so glad you're here,' Alison said, and she meant it, seeing before her a woman whose beauty put Josephine in the shade. It was gratifying in the extreme.

'And I'm very glad to meet you.' Camilla replied, thinking, I've found someone who I can very nearly trust. 'You must come over and see me at The Priory.'

'I'd love to.' Alison flushed with pleasure and guilt, remembering the wagon, wondering how soon she dare broach the subject, and if Camilla would be annoyed and refuse her access to it. 'I know it well. I think it's my favourite place in the whole world. I've even done some paintings of it.'

'Can I see them?' Camilla was not just paying lip-service to her newly acquired relation, she was genuinely interested. Casting her eye round the group of people who were waiting to be introduced to her, she decided that this was probably the most worthwhile person present.

Alison's blush deepened, rising to her temples. 'Oh, they're not very good, I'm afraid. I've never had much training, you see, just a drawing master at school, and what I've picked up from books,' she stammered in self-deprecation. 'But if you'd really like to – well, perhaps we can go to my studio later.'

'Don't monopolize our guest, Alison,' Selden interrupted brusquely, but when he spoke to Camilla his tone was almost tender. 'The others are all dying to meet you. You're quite a celebrity, you know.'

'Like the prodigal son, you mean?' Camilla gave him a cool stare, angry on Alison's behalf, refusing the arm which he offered. 'Or am I rather in the position of the fatted calf?'

His mouth hardened, though he kept on smiling. 'In the name of heaven and all its pink angels, what have I done to deserve such a rebuke?' he asked mildly.

145

'Nothing – yet.' She gave him a swift disdainful look, then controlled herself. There was nothing she could put her finger on, but every instinct warned her that he was treacherous. Dissemble, she decided, be nice to him. Lull him into a state of false security, then perhaps he'll unwittingly show his hand. It could be that you're too much influenced by Leila's predictions, but she's rarely been proved wrong.

'I can understand your reticence and it does you credit,' Selden purred, ignoring her last thrust. 'I assure you that you'll find my friends entertaining.'

'Excuse us, Alison.' Camilla smiled at her and placed a hand on her arm. 'I promise to come to your studio presently, when I've performed my tiresome duties.'

A hubbub of voices rang through the room. Alison felt herself to be in a little centre of silence among the shrill women, the loud-laughing men. Dismissed from Camilla's presence by Selden, she wandered among them accompanied by her silence, longing for Frank. He had left her in the small hours, and it was as if he had taken her soul with him. Woefully she accepted that it was unlikely they could repeat their brief, sweet meeting often, and she dreaded facing her bed alone. Having tasted the joy of sleeping in his arms, of waking to find him there, her solitary couch would be a barren place indeed. Nothing would satisfy her now but spending every second of every day in his presence. I want to be his wife, she thought, his lifelong companion and helpmate.

'Are you all right, m'dear?' A kindly voice made her start. She who had prided herself on her integrity, was suffering the unease brought about by guilt and fear of betrayal. 'Christmas is a strain, ain't it? You look all in.' It was only her brother-in-law who had paused in his limping perambulations, killing time till dinner was announced.

'I have a headache,' she lied, and knew that she had already entered the world of deceit and duplicity which she had once despised so much.

146

'Ah, nasty things, headaches.' He stood with his hands joined behind his back, staring at the crowd, and Alison wanted to ask him what had gone wrong between him and Josephine. Why had she decided to enter upon a series of love affairs when she had him and the children? Once, these personal questions had scarcely skimmed the outer edges of her consciousness but, having experienced the powerful force of physical passion that drew men and women together, they were now uppermost in her mind.

Convention forbade such intimate probings, and they both remained standing, each locked in their own private hells, Alison fidgeting with her fan to occupy her hands, and Douglas touching a finger to his moustache. Together, two solitaries, they surveyed the convivial assembly.

The gilded reception room, decorated with wooden pillars painted to look like marble, and more than life-sized statues, seemed, like the rest of the residence, primarily designed to make the inhabitants appear insignificant. 'I think not, Lady Camilla,' protested Orde-Bunbury when she mentioned something to this effect as she stood talking to him later. 'My aim was to display Lord Selden's power and influence to advantage, not to denigrate him. Folk admire impressive buildings. Why, I've an order for a castle from Mr Claypole. Isn't that so, sir?'

She had been presented to the shop owner and his wife, also the Pinnegars, a well-meaning couple from a neighbouring estate whose sole topic of conversation appeared to be hunting. Their daughters, as solidly built as they were and equally horse-mad, were talking animatedly to several other young people on the far side of the room. By the glances they kept throwing in her direction, Camilla guessed that she was the subject under discussion. Josephine, rent with envy, had been gushingly enthusiastic about Camilla's gown. She had

now retired to one of the leather-upholstered chester-
fields, and her golden head was bent close to Shawn's,
but Camilla noticed that her eyes kept darting to the
door, as if she was expecting someone more interesting to
arrive.

Claypole was eyeing Camilla closely, wondering if
such outlandish garments would take on, and if he
should have a few samples in his London shop. He had
even gone so far as to ask her where she purchased her
gown, looking impressed when she told him Paris. Now
he paid attention to the architect's remark, adding: 'Aye,
that's right, Mr Orde-Bunbury. I'm very pleased with
your first draft, very pleased indeed. You like it too,
don't you, my love?' This to his simpering wife. 'That's a
grand bit of land. I can just picture a castle there.'

'Where's that, Mr Claypole?' Camilla was finding it
less difficult than she had expected to make small-talk.
She had memorized everything Rufus Godwin had told
her about Selden and his plans to sell the estate to
Claypole. She was biding her time, letting him make the
running, even finding amusement in imagining their
consternation when she dropped the bombshell of
absolute refusal to even consider the proposition.

'Why, it's that old place you own, Lady Camilla.'
Claypole came straight out with it. He'd never been one
to beat about the bush. Selden had told him to speak to
her, seeming confident that she could be persuaded to
part with it. What would a beautiful young foreigner
want with a lonely, ramshackle building like The Priory?
Having met her, Claypole had managed to convince
himself that she'd be far happier in London or Paris. She
was a dasher, without a doubt! Soon find some duke or
other to marry her and give her palaces galore.

Camilla stared at him. Her arched brows lifted in
mock surprise. 'The Priory, Mr Claypole? You can't be
serious?'

Misunderstanding her, Claypole permitted himself a

smirk, believing that she knew nothing about the male world of high finance. 'Oh, I am, dear lady. People'll call me mad, I know, but I'm willing to make you a handsome offer, a more than generous offer, for the house and lands.'

'Reggie's set his heart on it, Lady Camilla,' Daisy Claypole piped up, wearing a Claypole's Emporium creation, well-corseted, with a sweeping skirt, and corsage brief to the point of immodesty. Her swelling bosom, which had been the pride of the Gaiety Theatre, bore an ornate diamond necklace with cascading, shimmering drops, and her white, pudgy arms were loaded with expensive bracelets. 'And he always gets his own way.'

Not this time! vowed Camilla inwardly. I'd rather be seen dead than allow that coarse little man and his tarty wife even to set foot in The Priory, let alone demolish it!

She turned to Selden who was watching her quietly. 'Is this true? Did you tell him that he could purchase the estate?' she asked calmly, but if Leila had been there she would have known that when Camilla was so sweetly reasonable she was at her most deadly.

'Actually, I discussed this with him before I even knew of your existence, cousin,' he answered smoothly. 'But when the glad news reached me, I continued with these plans, feeling confident that you'd fall in with them.'

'A trifle premature, surely?' Camilla had by now signalled to the maid to take her coat away, dominating the group in her purple gown, idly waving her large peacock-feather fan with perfect confidence and grace. 'How could you assume so blithely that I'd not wish to live in The Priory?'

Selden shrugged, as if dismissing such a wild notion. 'But my dear, it needs a fortune spent on it! Foolish to contemplate wasting money on that ruin. If you want a country house, then I'm certain Orde-Bunbury would

149

be delighted to build one for you, on this side of the village, perhaps.'

This was too much for her hard-won self-control. She flashed Claypole a single glance from her kohl-lined feline eyes. 'My cousin has been labouring under a misapprehension, sir. I've no intention of selling. I shall restore The Priory and live there for just as long as it suits me. You'll have to look elsewhere for a site for your castle.'

She had expected anger from Selden, but instead she found him charmingly solicitous. With a few, well-chosen words, he smoothed Claypole's ruffled feathers, making suggestions about other beauty spots he had at his disposal. Taking his cue from Selden, the architect added a word and Claypole, still grumbling but slightly mollified, agreed to visit them whilst he was in the area. Further discussion was halted as the butler, a magnificent personage in deepest black and pristine white, announced that dinner was served.

As the guests moved towards the dining-room, each lady accompanied by a gentleman, Camilla rested the tips of her fingers on the arm Selden extended. He seemed concerned about nothing but putting her at her ease, throwing her off guard so that she began to question her own judgement. Certainly he was proving to be an entertaining companion, and seemed to bear her no resentment for foiling his plans for Claypole's establishing himself on The Priory grounds.

As they sauntered across the hall, he pointed out various striking features of his house and she could not deny that the structure was on a grand scale, but it totally lacked the subtlety which The Priory, even in its present sad state, possessed. Orde-Bunbury's building displayed a passion for the baroque, but it lacked restraint and a sense of fitness. Others might not be sensitive to this failing, but in Camilla's eyes it fell short of the rich beauty he had striven to achieve, showing instead vulgarity and clumsy ostentation.

150

'You'll enjoy the gardens. I've altered them very little from the original ones that surrounded the manor that stood here for centuries. When the snow clears, there's a multitude of delights hereabouts which I hope you'll permit me the honour of showing you,' Selden was saying as they almost reached the open, double doors which gave access to the dining-room.

He was interrupted as a man entered from the vestibule, flinging overcoat, top hat and gloves into the arms of a footman and striding across the polished parquet towards them. 'Sorry I'm late, Selden. Hope you've not held up dinner on my account. My skewbald mare decided to drop her foal as I was about to leave. We've been waiting for her to produce it for days and she has to choose this particular moment. Contrary creatures, mares – just like women.'

'That's all right, Darcy. We're only just going in.' Selden stopped, turning with Camilla on his arm. 'You simply must meet the star of the evening – my cousin from Brazil, Lady Camilla Ruthen. Camilla, my dear, this is Mr Darcy Devereaux from Chalkdown Farm.'

She found herself looking up into a pair of vivid blue eyes set in an intensely masculine face. An involuntary gasp escaped her lips. 'You?' she cried.

Selden frowned, surprised, but Darcy's laughter rang beneath the chandeliers. 'I've already had the pleasure,' he said, and the look on his face made her heart thump with fury, and something else too – a feeling that she recognized and dreaded.

'You've met?' Selden did not seem pleased, and she felt the muscles beneath her gloved hand tense.

'We have,' she answered frostily.

Those mocking eyes of an unholy blue regarded her with delight. 'You're none the worse for your tumble in the snow?' he asked, a bantering note in his deep voice.

'None at all.' Camilla's thoughts were whirling, the hot surge of indignant rage making her almost incoherent.

151

'What the devil –?' Selden began, glancing swiftly from Darcy's taunting, handsome features to Camilla's beautiful, furious ones.

'Don't worry, old chap. We happened upon one another near Bell's Spinney yesterday afternoon. She was being attacked by my starving sheep – practically eaten alive. Isn't that so, Lady Camilla?' His ironic smile encompassed her so impudently that she longed to smack his face.

She had thought the evening going so well, triumphing over Selden, Claypole and the rest, showing them that she was made of stern stuff. But this man's emergence on the scene had thrown her completely. She could not deny that the thought of him had tormented her since their first meeting. She had fired her rage almost frenziedly, to smother her curiosity to know more about him. Oh yes, he'd made a deep impression on her, and she was too honest not to recognize that it had not been an entirely unpleasant one. She was frightened as she stood between him and Selden in the hall, more terrified than she cared to admit. There was something dark and dangerous about Darcy Devereaux that stirred a response deep inside her. One other man had had that power. André de Jaham, the father of her dead baby.

'What a lovely place!' Camilla exclaimed when Alison conducted her into the studio much later that evening.

'It's my glory-hole. Everyone should have a nook they can call their own. Don't you think?' Alison answered shyly, switching on the shaded wall lights and the standard lamp.

'You're so right.' Camilla threw her bag and gloves on the divan and strolled around the long room, examining everything. If Selden showed a lack of taste in his decor, it was certainly not repeated here. 'I see that you're an admirer of Art Nouveau,' she added, warming to Alison by the minute.

There was something self-conscious and assertive about the studio's plainness, a striking contrast to the rest of the house, which was cluttered with pictures, ornaments, bric-à-brac and draperies. Here the furniture was tenuous and tall and appeared to be made of unstained oak or elm. The Rönisch boudoir grand piano was of some bleached wood and almost white. The only patches of colour were from the canvases on the walls, and the cushions strewn on the divan.

'Oh yes, I positively adore it.' Alison expanded in her own domain, less hesitant, more confident. 'I think your gown is wonderful, and that jewellery! It's breathtaking. Is it made by Lalique?'

Camilla stopped prowling, settling on the divan, crossing her slim legs and accepting a cigarette from a pewter box. She put it in an amber holder as long as a pencil, and lit it with a match from a tasselled case. Alison did not usually smoke but, wishing to share everything with this intriguing woman, she lit up too, choking a little as the unfamiliar fumes caught the back of her throat.

'The brooch is Lalique's work, but this is an example of the craftsmanship of Feuillâtre.' Her hair, swept into a loosely gathered cascade of curls at the crown of her head, was ornamented by a comb of gold filigree with the delicate, remote profile of a girl wearing a headdress of enamelled butterflies wings, set with tiger's-eyes.

'It's gorgeous,' Alison murmured happily. Just for a few moments she could forget that persistent ache in the region of her heart, as she discussed her other love – art. 'Those stones match your ring.'

Camilla contemplated the jewel glimmering on her right hand. 'It belonged to my father. He always wore it, set great store by it, and now I own it. Leila says it's cursed, but that it won't harm me, because of her magic.'

There was a peculiar note in her voice. Alison's happiness wavered. Camilla was quite unlike anyone

153

she had ever known before, fascinating but a little frightening too. 'Who is Leila?' she asked.

'Madame Leila la Floret, *mambo* of the Voodoo cult, my guide, mentor and friend.' The rich, lilting voice with its odd accent was almost hypnotic.

'What does *mambo* mean?' Alison sat beside her, unable to keep her eyes off such powerful beauty. Burne-Jones would have loved to paint her, she thought. Perhaps she'd sit for me.

'It's the Creole word for high priestess,' Camilla explained, and Alison's grey eyes were filled with wonder. She's a baby in so many ways, Camilla thought. Though she must be older than me, I feel her senior. Her life has been sheltered here, though unfulfilled. 'Tell me about yourself,' she urged, entrancing Alison with her smile.

'There's not much to tell.' Alison smiled in response. 'I'm the old maid of the family. I look after Selden. He's a widower, you see. So tragic – his young wife died eight years ago. She had a miscarriage and it killed her. Poor Selden. He was heartbroken. I had to to stay with him.'

'Did you, my dear?' Leila had trained Camilla astutely so that she found it easy to pick up on people's happiness or sorrow, a mixed blessing for it left her vulnerable, though she had learned to detach herself. Thus she knew that Alison was troubled, and that this was connected with Selden. 'Life's made chains for you that you find hard to break. But they're slackening. Someone, or something has been supplying the oil. Another creak or two and you'll be breaking loose, and going off at a tangent that will astonish everybody. Haven't you ever been in love?'

Alison shook her head. She could feel her cheeks burning and was terribly aware of the divan on which they reclined. Only a few hours before she had been making love with Frank between its sheets. She had the frightening feeling that Camilla was conscious of this too. But it was impossible! she tried to console herself. Camilla's a stranger. She's never met Frank. How could she possibly guess, unless she possesses supernatural powers?

She glanced uneasily towards the bathroom, hoping that her cousin would not wander in that direction. Then she chided herself for her foolishness. What if she did? She'd be too polite to comment on the sheets soaking in the bath. Alison had removed them from the bed before anyone was up, alarmed by the tell-tale blood stains which seemed to shriek aloud that she had just lost her virginity. She knew that if she did not do something about them quickly one of the maids was sure to come in to collect the laundry. It was quite possible that she would think nothing of it, assuming that her Ladyship was menstruating, but her guilt forced her to take no chances. The servants were shrewd and ever watchful. In her presence they always preserved an expression of concentrated vacuity which she was certain denoted acute curiosity. So she had run a tubful of cold water and plunged the sheets into it. She would wring them out later and dry them over one of the radiators, then put them on the bed again before the housekeeper noticed. For tonight, blankets would suffice.

Dragging her mind back to what Camilla had just said, she clasped her hands nervously in the lap of her dark blue silk gown. 'I don't quite understand you, Camilla. I'm perfectly content with my lot.'

'Are you?' Camilla's amber eyes stared into hers and Alison could not look away, mesmerized by them. 'You strike me as being pot-bound, like stale old ferns. You nccd uprooting and shaking and planting in fresh, strong earth. My God, you've got talent! Just look at that painting of The Priory on the easel. It's powerful, Alison. It has captured the brooding atmosphere to perfection. Don't waste yourself. Selden doesn't need you.'

Camilla had touched a raw nerve and Alison reacted

violently. 'What do you know about it?' she demanded sharply, jumping up as if about to flee the room. 'You've not been here more than two days. How dare you presume to pass judgement?'

Camilla tapped the stub of her cigarette into an ashtray calmly. 'I dare because it's true. I dare because I'm concerned for you. I can speak freely because there are no ties between us, and I'm not yet trammelled by the petty conventions of society. You and Selden don't touch within miles. It's not your fault and it isn't his. No doubt you've both done your laborious best to live together, two utter strangers who happen to have been born brother and sister, for eight long years without once resorting to violence. That in itself is incredible! But I can read the signs. Undoubtedly, inevitably, a change is at hand.'

'There *has* been a change, of course.' Alison tried to be flippant and failed miserably. 'You've come.'

Camilla compassionately spared her, feeling that she had taken it far enough, for the moment. She adroitly turned the conversation to less personal matters, encouraging Alison to show her her work. There was no question but that she was gifted, though her earlier drawings were childlike. But the more recent paintings, like that of The Priory which glowed, forbidding and sinister on the easel, displayed a depth and passion which betrayed that her emotions had been profoundly stirred by someone.

Alison blossomed under her attention, losing her reserve, but one thing was troubling her. She had the almost uncontrollable urge to confide in Camilla. If anyone would understand about her love for Frank, it would be her wise cousin. The words trembled on her tongue but – I can't! I daren't! and the moment of temptation passed.

'I suppose we must return to the party.' Camilla stood tapping a satin-shod toe against the kerb. The firelight

156

shimmered on her jewels, her hair. 'How terribly tedious. When will you visit me? Tomorrow? I'm eager to begin planning reconstruction. You can advise me on the best carpenters, builders, and cleaning women in the area.'

'It's Boxing Day tomorrow. It's my lot to go around the cottages of the poor with gifts of food, clothing and money. Selden and Josephine should come with me, but they never do. They'll be hunting – another Yuletide ritual. Such charity work will be your duty too, now that you're mistress of The Priory. Not this year perhaps, it will hardly be expected as you've only just arrived.'

Camilla had sauntered to the heavily curtained window which overlooked the garden, pushing aside the drapes and staring out at the moonlit snow. 'The view must be charming in the summer,' she remarked, then stiffened and peered more closely. 'There's some-one there. I can see him clearly. He's standing under the monkey-puzzle tree and looking this way.'

Alison's throat constricted as she too stared out. Yes, it *was* him! He must have been waiting for the house to fall into silence and darkness. Poor darling, he'll be frozen! I'll warm you, Frank, in my arms, in my bed. Your chilled flesh will turn to fire!

'I expect it's one of the gamekeepers,' she answered casually. How easy it was to fall into the habit of lying. 'The foxes are hungry this time of the year. Even the keeper's gallows doesn't deter them.'

Camilla thought this unlikely but she did not say so. Alison's colour was hectic, her eyes bright, a little mad even. 'I must go back to the party,' Camilla said, letting the curtains fall into place. 'You'll come?'

'No. My headache's worse. I'll have an early night.' Her mind was already streaking ahead – locking the door behind her cousin, running to the window, flinging it wide – his arms – his lips cold with the night – burning against hers. Frank. Frank.

157

Camilla seemed to be moving agonizingly slowly, her chiffon drapes floating as she picked up her bag, her gloves. 'By the by,' her tone was level, carrying the faintest flicker of interest. 'Who or what is Mr Darcy Devereaux?'

Concentrate on her question, don't think of Frank out there in the snow. In a few minutes, we'll be alone. 'Darcy? Oh, he's a friend of Selden's. Took over Chalkdown Farm about ten years ago. Came from Norfolk, I believe – inherited the farm from an uncle.'

'I see.' Camilla thoughtfully brushed her lips with the tips of the blue-green feathers of her fan. Her eyes were remote, and it was as if she had forgotten Alison's presence. Then she roused herself. 'Goodbye, my dear. If you can't come tomorrow, then make it the day after. I want you to meet Leila. A remarkable woman. If you like, I'll ask her to carry out a divination for you. Wouldn't you like to know your future?'

And Alison smiling and agreeing. Yes, yes, that would be fun. The day after tomorrow then. Good night – sweet dreams. Camilla was at the door, smiling, kissing her. The latch clicked as it closed. Alison heard her light footsteps fading along the corridor. She shot the bolt, her heart thudding so much that she leaned against the wood for a second. Desire seemed to melt her bones, drain her of strength, fill her veins with fire, make her breasts ache to be touched. Frank out there in the darkness. His hands would be cold on her flesh. Her nipples hardened at the thought.

He came in as she opened the French windows. 'What are you doing here?' Alison whispered.

He closed the door, remained quiet inside with her. 'I can't stay away. I think of you all the time. Even today, in church, even as my children played with their new toys. Effie had a doll, but I couldn't give her my attention. It's you who fill my mind, my dreams.'

His hands were on her shoulders, smoothing the silk,

158

feeling the warm skin beneath. She sank against him as if she were drunk, his hand cupping her breast, her head tipped back against his arm, mouth parted to receive the benediction of his kiss.

Camilla was much in demand when the dancing began. The men wrangled playfully for the privilege, and took it in turns to operate the gramophone or thump out tunes on the piano. Selden stayed on the sidelines and though he talked with various members of the party, his possessive gaze never lost sight of the slim figure in purple velvet as she was whirled around the music-salon.

He could not fathom her. She baffled, bewildered and fascinated him. Her lure lay in something infinitely more subtle than mere beauty. In her eyes he had read an eternal challenge, an eternal question. So, she wasn't going to co-operate in the matter of the Claypole deal? Selden did not brood about this, he simply shelved it for the time being. Changing tactics, he was setting out to woo her.

Watching her closely throughout the evening, he had asked himself if she really was aware of her power. There was nothing consciously provocative in her glance; her manner with men was indifferent to the point of boredom, yet there it was – a turn of the head, a droop of the lips, a tone in the rich low voice that proclaimed her to be an enchantress, the type of woman who from childhood to old age was destined to be served and worshipped, desired and loved. He thought with grim irony, that were she to be shipwrecked on a desert island, she'd find a knight-errant behind the first palm-tree! Yet the strong feelings she induced could also be perilous, inspiring envy and hatred.

At dinner her behaviour had been unconventional, to put it mildly. She had entered into lively discussions with the men on matters political, voiced loud opinions on behalf of the Women's Rights Movement, talked knowledgeably about cars, casually recounted hair-raising adventures in the jungle, and spilt wine on the table-cloth. There was something primitive, almost savage, in her naturalness of mien. He had been amused by the raised eyebrows of the ladies, and the way in which Josephine had sat there glowering.

Darcy made no secret of his admiration for this gorgeous, outrageous addition to the social scene. He had captured her at last, his arm placed lightly around her waist as they waltzed. 'I thought I'd never get near you,' he murmured. There was a disturbing expression in his eyes as they rested on her flushed countenance and, as she encountered that look, her heart beat so painfully fast that she was certain he must see her pulse racing.

'I love dancing,' she answered, very aware of his handsome face and fine physique, though muffled bells were clanging in her brain like those warning sailors of shoals shrouded by fog. 'We danced a great deal in Bahia.'

'Formal ballroom dancing?'

'Not always.' Clarity vanished. Gone was the gilded salon, the gramophone playing the lilting waltz *Songe D'Automne*. She heard drums beating with a passionate violence, saw black fingers on the taut skins of the *radas*, felt the savage rhythms in her blood.

'England must seem very strange to you.' His voice recalled her, his arm tightening. Her cheek was close to his white shirt-front. His body breathed out scented soap, clean linen, a musky male odour all his own. Like André's, yet unlike too. He had had a liking for heavy perfumes, using them liberally. Whenever he had left her after a night of love, that perfume had clung to the sheets, the pillows, her skin.

'It's certainly different,' she conceded, matching her

160

steps to his. He was a good dancer, moving with lithe grace.

'You'll come hunting tomorrow? Everybody who is anybody always hunts on Boxing Day.' His voice was an intimate murmur against her ear, and it was as if he spoke endearments.

'I've no proper dress for it.' She met his eyes and smiled coolly. 'I don't suppose it would go down very well if I appeared wearing South American chaparejos, a poncho and a sombrero.'

'I'd be delighted, and the stir would be uproarious!' His lean face broke into an engaging smile, even white teeth contrasting with his tanned skin and clipped beard.

At that moment, they danced past Josephine who was partnered by Shawn. The glance of undiluted venom she shot Camilla left her in no doubt as to her proprietorial interest in Darcy. 'Josephine doesn't look very happy,' she remarked lightly, testing him.

Darcy stiffened. A muscle twitched beside his jaw, but otherwise his face was closed and unrevealing. 'I expect her husband's getting drunk.' Then steering her away from his annoying mistress, he returned to the subject of the hunt. 'Well, if you won't come chasing foxes, will you attend the Hunt Ball? It's always held at Colonel Pinnegar's place. He's a bit of a boring old ass, but a first-class horseman. He always puts on a splendid party. Most of the gentry will be there. You'll come?'

'I'll think about it.' She was all too aware of him, aware too of Josephine's jealous eyes boring into her back.

'I shall be at The Priory at seven thirty to collect you.'

'You're very persistent, Mr Devereaux.'

He gave her a charming smile, but his eyes were like blue steel. 'You've no idea just how persistent I can be when I see something I want. Why don't you call me Darcy? You know as well as I that this pretence of

161

formality is quite useless. By the way, can you give me one cast-iron reason why you don't want my sheep on your land?'

'Money, Mr Devereaux!' She said, chin up, eyes sparking defiance.

The music had ended and one of the younger men was cranking up the machine, whilst the Pinnegar girls squabbled over the records. Darcy had not released Camilla, his arm still about her waist. Their eyes held for a second longer, then she wrenched herself free.

It was late, well after midnight, when she left Armitstead House. Wilf had been waiting for over half an hour, ensconced in Miss Tennant's parlour, drinking port and catching up on the local news. The night was bitterly cold, the icy blast slashing her cheeks like knives as she got into the car. There would be no snow for it was far too cold. Leila had waited up for her, as she always did when she was out late. As Camilla walked into her warm bedroom she remembered other nights – nights of the owl, nights of passion under the stars, the wind heavy with the drugging scent of bougainvillaea.

While she prepared for bed, she indulged in the customary ritual of discussing the evening's events with Leila. The *mambo* liked to keep abreast of happenings, considering it her due. Camilla was open about Alison, but neglected to dwell for long on Darcy Devereaux, though she knew perfectly well that little escaped Leila's shrewd observation.

'I've invited Lady Alison over. She seems nervy and unhappy. I think Selden's at the bottom of the trouble,' Camilla said as Leila stood behind her, brushing her hair. The room was already beginning to take on her personality, more welcoming now. Leila nodded sagely, and Camilla fell silent, suddenly tired. Quietness held sway, broken occasionally by the crumbling and settling of the logs in the grate.

When she was alone, Camilla went to the davenport,

pulled note-paper from its drawers, sat down and wrote to a Savile Row tailor, ordering a most expensive riding habit. Her lips curved in a small, cynical smile as she sealed the envelope and then addressed it. Why was she bothering to do this? It was not for the sake of the sport, that was for sure. She sighed deeply, knowing that she must sleep to obtain the energy and tenacity required to grapple with the difficult situations presenting themselves. Selden. Alison. The villagers. Above all, Darcy.

As she sat in bed with her journal, her pen hesitated for a moment, then she wrote: 'December 25th. I don't want to become involved with Darcy Devereaux. He's too handsome, too attractive. His type of men are poison to me, but I find them hard to resist.'

Leila had made her peace with Beryl though, at first, they had stalked around one another warily. They had one thing in common, however, a devotion to their young mistress. Beryl, the newcomer on the scene, had taken to Camilla during that first interview in London and Wilf, whilst appearing to be the strong one of the two, always bowed to the judgement of what he liked to term his 'better half'. Not only this; though loyal to a fault once they had given their allegiance to a master, they were a practical couple and could see that this was an opportunity for a settled home in the country with possibilities of advancement. They would be serving a young lady, not some dictatorial man. This too was an advantage, or so they thought. In this they were mistaken. Camilla would be as hard a taskmaster as any feudal lord.

Beryl was a lively, friendly Londoner and, whilst a stickler for the pecking order among servants, had no colour prejudice. She was rather intrigued with both Leila and her son, setting out to win them over. Once she established that Leila's real concern was acting as lady's maid to Camilla, rather lazy and slapdash about household management, she had no difficulty in taking over in the role of housekeeper. She had the impression that the black woman was relieved and, with her co-operation, had gone to work with a will. Little could be achieved until the holiday period was over, but she had done what she could, and the habitable rooms at The Priory had yielded to broom, carbolic soap, beeswax and elbow grease.

'Just you wait till the fine weather comes,' she announced, flourishing the big earthenware pot in the kitchen, sending a stream of reddish-brown tea into four sturdy mugs. 'Good gracious, you'll see the dust fly then, Leila. What we need is a couple of hefty washerwomen. All that linen needs a thorough laundering. Lovely stuff, most of it. And the blankets'll have a good airing, and all those drapes and curtains. It'll give the moths a shock. We've enough work here to keep us going for months on end.' She beamed at Sam whose mouth was smeared with mincemeat from the tarts she had just drawn from the oven. 'That's the ticket, lad, tuck in! You're a mite too scrawny, could do with a bit more flesh on your bones to keep out the cold.'

Undismayed by the crude cooking arrangements, she had treated Leila and Sam to traditional Christmas fare, with turkey, plum pudding, trifle and cream, cold pork, cranberry sauce, brandy butter, and other delights which had made their eyes goggle and their mouths water. Camilla had given her and Wilf free rein to order whatever they considered necessary, and they had sallied into Fortnum and Mason's before setting out from London. Beryl was looking forward to taking the village shop by storm just as soon as it opened again. She'd show these country bumpkins a thing or two! They'd be ordering items they'd never even heard of before she'd done with them!

Leila sipped the hot tea, her shining dark eyes resting

164

thoughtfully on the small, energetic woman. 'You're a fine cook, Madame Simmonds,' she said in her soft drawl. 'We celebrate the Holy Birth in Haiti and Bahia, but in a different way. There's food too, lots of it, and another *fête*, The Feast of Yams, after the first harvest, around the middle of October.'

'Mercy on us, what's a yam?' Beryl seated herself, elbows on the table, a mug between her hands, prepared to listen to yet another from Leila's fund of stories.

'It's a sweet potato,' put in Sam before his mother could reply. 'On the night of the *fête* it's boiled up with fish and everyone feasts.'

'Lor' love a duck!' Beryl exclaimed. 'Whatever next, I wonder? You from Haiti then? Must say I don't know much about such faraway places. You ain't a slave, are you? Don't hold with slavery. Nasty business.'

Leila's face was serious, a queenly tilt to her head, with its glossy, blue-black hair smoothed back from a centre parting and coiled into a tight bun at the nape of her slender neck.

'I was born in Haiti. It's part of the island of Hispaniola. No, I'm not a slave, madame. Slavery was abolished there more than a hundred years ago. My ancestors were slaves, when they came from Africa, but the great leader, Boukman, a Jamaican negro and *hungan* of Voodoo, gathered a large band of slaves in the forests and slaughtered the white masters.' The Creole's eyes were alight with a fierce pride in the triumphs of her forebears. 'My great-grandfather fought by his side, and tales about him have been handed down through my family.'

'Ooh, well don't that beat all!' Beryl was so excited that she had to have another mug of tea. She passed the brandy bottle to Leila. 'Take a slurp, deary.'

Leila added it to her cup, and continued: 'I'm a mulatto, and the white part of me is French. My Pa was respected in Port-au-Prince, and I served the Gontard

165

family, maid to their daugher, Hélène. She was Missy Camilla's mother.'

For a further hour she expounded on the parts of her life story that she considered would impress them. The less reputable side, she kept to herself. They lingered over their meal, and the contents of the brandy bottle sank. Leila instructed Sam to fetch a jar of rum from her own private store. This too was mixed with the tea, and it was a hilarious, friendly group who washed the dishes before retiring to their beds, glowing with good-fellowship and drinking a final toast to their mistress.

Because the servants' quarters in the attics were uninhabitable as yet, Beryl and Wilf had been given one of the guest rooms in a wing not far from the Master Chamber. Beryl had insisted that Wilf kept a fire burning there night and day, and had spent much time airing the mattress and blankets. He found several oil lamps, cleaned them and fitted new wicks, so the light they now provided was a vast improvement on candles. Even so, she had dubbed the house creepy, especially after dark, thankful to have Wilf's strong arms to protect her through the night hours, snuggling up to him in the canopied bed.

Leila had no such solace, only Sam in the truckle alongside her couch in Camilla's dressing-room. She had already transformed a corner of it into a shrine, with the black cross of Baron-Samedi, Lord of the Cemeteries and Chief of the Legion of the Dead. Because she was priestess of Mâitresse Erzulie Fréda Dahomin, the Venus of Dahomey, a print of the deity hung in the place of honour over the altar. In reality it was a crude oleograph of the Blessed Virgin, from a painting in the style of Sassoferrato. The head of the Virgin leaned to one side, and her eyes were rolled upwards in ecstasy or pain, while one forefinger pointed to her scarlet heart, which was transfixed with seven rapiers.

The Catholic priests frowned on these images, but

166

their saints had become inexorably mixed with African deities. There were thousands in use – in Haiti, in Bahia, in New Orleans, and male worshippers who had become the secret husbands of Erzulie, dedicated every Tuesday and Thursday to their goddess, driving their human wives from their houses on those days, for Erzulie was famous for her jealousy. Then, quite alone, and with the use of certain drugs, they spent the night in a state of orgy, summoning her. Perhaps she did appear as a succubus, draining them of their sexual energy, certainly the belief was very strong. When controlled by her during rites, the entranced acolyte acted like a coquettish woman, flirting with the men and paying them indecent attentions. It was small wonder that Christian priests were appalled, unable to equate this wanton creature with Our Lady of the Seven Sorrows.

Leila did not find it a paradox. On the altar, a prayer book stood cheek by jowl with the playing cards and rattle of a seer. She knew that whatever the religion or creed, it was simply a means of tapping the powerful force of creation. She made obeisance to the Baron and Erzulie, taking a wax taper to the fire in the grate and sprinkling incense over the charcoal in a brass censer. The perfumed smoke coiled like a snake, wavering, swirling, strengthening and filling the room with blue mist.

Taking up her *asson*, the sacred rattle, she passed it over her sleeping son. Standing there for a while, she prayed, then placed certain consecrated objects at his head and feet to protect him from the dreaded *loups-garous*, female demons who sucked the blood of slumbering youngsters. Sam slept on peacefully, his long lashes lying like fans on his cheekbones, the skin of which was no darker than an Italian's or a Spaniard's. In those quiet features, she detected those of the man who had planted this single seed in her womb – he who had seduced her into loving him more passionately than her revered gods – more than life itself.

167

Chanting to herself, Leila began to feel out the Master Chamber, circling it, crouching like a wary dog, her nose twitching. Her mistress was at the Hunt Ball. There was no likelihood of interruption for when Darcy Devereaux had called for her, he had said that such parties usually continued till dawn. Leila had observed him as he stood in the Great Hall waiting for Camilla, a mighty fine gentleman to be sure but, the doorway of her senses unlatched, she had felt his presence like an oppressive stone upon her heart.

Camilla's eyes had been bright, her colour heightened when she had swept down the magnificent oak staircase to meet him, radiant in a green and gold gown, an emerald mantle swirling around her, but there had been a taut awareness in her too. She was excited by him, Leila could tell, but he had not yet scaled her defences. Leila had sighed as she closed the front door behind them and heard them drive off in his car. She did not want to see Camilla suffer again because of a man. Poor child, she had been tossed on a cruel sea of emotions, beginning with her father, continuing through André de Jaham, and culminating in Edgar Ruthen's death.

Whilst appearing to be engrossed with the Simmonds in the kitchen, her mind had been battling with an undertow of terror that thundered warnings like surf gnawing at a beach. Not for herself, not for Samuel, but for her mistress. In the glowing embers of the fire, faces had formed, remaining briefly, then melting in the flames, one replacing the next. The sorrowful eyes of Hélène, a girl like herself when she had entered her service; the handsome, ruthless, features of Edgar Ruthen; Camilla, whom she had brought into the world, taking her into her arms at the moment of her birth; André de Jaham; the numerous men who had appeared at the *estancia*, worming themselves into Ruthen's trust, drinking with him, gambling the nights away, setting out with him on his fruitless expeditions.

168

The Priory had been Ruthen's home. Here he had first seen the light of day. His ancestors had owned it, lived, loved and died in it. It was steeped in their atmosphere, in the memory of their deeds both fair and foul. The very walls seemed to breathe it out. Passion and hate, the lust for power and wealth, cruelty, remorse, lionlike courage, honour and shame. It was all there, locked in time, its force waiting to be used again, like a corked genie pleading to be released from a bottle.

Leila had already prowled most of the house, rattle held before her like a shield. It was made from a gourd, dried and emptied of its flesh and pips, covered with a network of china beads mingled with snake vertebrae. When she had been ordained as a *mambo*, this had been consecrated by baptism before she had been put to bed with it. But though she had gone through cellars, reception rooms, salons, galleries and passages, she was always drawn back to this chamber, as if the psychic powers at work were centred there.

The house held no fears for her. She respected it and its dead ones, blessed them and asked their pardon for her intrusion, neither did she sense any threat to Camilla. It was external foes who would damage her if they could – evil human beings, not those of the spirit world. Living men and women, but chiefly men. The positive masculine element had always brought trouble to Camilla. She was too susceptible to it, too responsive, despite her pride and fearsome independence.

Alone now, the building soaked in sleep and silence, Leila whispered to the *loa*, begging their aid. There was no sound but the regular and monotonous clicking of her rattle. The air was charged with a waiting quality. Then, suddenly, she heard a wind blowing outside the door, sounding like a river plunging through a gorge. There were other dallyings too, noisy eddies – voices raised in anger, a woman's sharp cry. Leila tried to follow the sounds which resonated somewhere in the distance. The corridor outside, perhaps? She opened the door and, using her senses like antennae, walked its length. The noises continued but not there. Ears pricked, Leila paused, puzzled. Now they were from inside the Master Chamber which she had just left. The quality of those unearthly sounds changed. A solitary voice now – a woman crying, but not mere human weeping – more like the howling of a tortured animal.

Leila returned whence she had come, following the trail like a hunter. She shuddered as she entered the candle-shadowed room, sending up a prayer to St Michael, the bane of demons. The evil in the air was almost tangible, but the trouble was not there, not quite. Where was it? Linked with the room, filling it with abhorrent things, but as if spreading like a muddy flood from elsewhere.

'Where are you, spirit?' Leila shouted, then she repeated a few Catholic prayers only to switch abruptly to a potent Voodoo incantation.

With a shivering sigh, an arras at the far end of the room slithered to the floor. There was a door behind it, small, arched, of heavy oak, studded with iron nails. Leila's breath rushed from between her lips, and she thanked Erzuli for her help. Her eyes glistened in the dim light, blank, glazed, in that half-world state of near trance. The howling and shrieking intensified. Leila's hand came to rest on the handle of the door. It burned her palm like fire. She shook it, but it did not yield. Where is the key? She sought it in her mind. The davenport! She hunted through the drawers, unearthing old papers, letters tied up with rotten ribbon, relics of the past. No key. Her long, slim dark fingers probed and searched, her mind concentrated on it. These pieces often contained secret compartments. She had come across them in the West Indies, articles which had once belonged to wealthy French settlers. Pulling out one of the drawers, she noticed that it was shorter than its

170

fellows. Out came the one next to it, her fingers slid into the gap – a small push and a little narrow, boxlike container was revealed. She turned it upside down and a key dropped into her palm.

The door was stiff, even after the lock had clicked. It hadn't been opened for years. Hidden by the arras, no one would have noticed its existence. Leila was strong. She leaned her shoulder against the wood. It gave with the protesting squeal of corroded hinges. Beyond lay darkness, deep and impenetrable. Leila fetched the candle, holding it high in one hand, the *asson* in the other. Complete silence fanned down. The crying had stopped as abruptly as it had begun.

The candle lit up the small room, white, uncertain, the flame wavering. Small puffs of dust drifted across the floor, disturbed by her entrance. Cobwebs brushed her face. The air was stale, overlaid with an odour reminiscent of rotting leaves, morbidly enticing. No light penetrated the thick drapes drawn across the windows. The room was exactly as it had been left, years ago, the fireplace heaped with dead ashes, the table littered with playing cards, wineglasses in which the dregs had dried, a bottle with its contents soured, a saucer with the brittle stubs of cigars lying amidst lavalike dust. The surrounding chairs were uneven, as if they had been pushed back in haste. The whole scene gave the vivid impression of people leaving in a hurry, fleeing perhaps from heaven only knew what horror.

Leila thought she caught a humming sound. Yet not, more like a drumbeat, muffled, far away. Strain as she would she could not identify the noise. The sound was gone. The room was extraordinarily cold. She could not move, rooted to the spot, knowing that she was not welcome there. The room rejected her. It was pushing her away. The silence was heavy with the unspeakable. The candle flame burned up suddenly and there, above the carved overmantel, hung the portrait.

171

It was as if he looked straight at her, younger than when she had first met him, Hélène Gontard's suitor. How magnificent he was, with dark hair, and tawny eyes like Camilla's. Tall, with good shoulders and strong hands. It was a full-sized portrait, and he was wearing a hunting outfit, red jacket, white stock, buckskin breeches, shiny black boots. Two hounds were at his side, gazing up at him as if hypnotized. The arrogant owner of The Priory, which was depicted in the background, glimpsed through dark trees.

The painting dominated the room, and it seemed that he was there in the flesh, but beneath this suave portrayal of a wealthy landowner, Leila knew him for what he had really been – a harsh, cruel man, embittered, cynical and uncontrolled, given to dissipation, driven by mad devils of ambition and greed. So this had been his lair, had it? She shuddered away from thoughts of the scenes which must have been enacted there. Remembering him in his later years, his good looks coarsened by drink, drugs and his numerous intrigues with women, both aristocratic and from the lowest dregs of the port. This was the man whom Camilla had hero-worshipped until her love had changed to hate.

Strength flowed through Leila's limbs. She walked across the floor and stood directly below the portrait, staring up into those eyes which seemed filled with mockery, that face alive with malevolent sexuality. Even now she felt it, after all those years.

'Edgar Ruthen, you wicked man,' she said softly, her deep voice ringing across the stillness. 'You're dead. Stay dead. Leave us alone.'

6

'You're seeing far too much of her! Damn it, Darcy, what about me?' Josephine demanded, staring down at him angrily from the saddle of her chestnut gelding.

He stood by one of the barns at the back of Chalkdown Farm, the spring sunshine slanting over his dark head. His blue working shirt was open at the neck. He looked larger than usual, suddenly quite rough, almost as if he were a labourer, and this impression combined with his striking physique was sufficient to make her journey well worthwhile.

'Good morning, Josephine,' he said, cocking an eyebrow at her. 'I suppose you're referring to Camilla. Trouble is I'm not seeing *enough* of her. She's too bloody virginal! What brings you out so early?'

'You know that I want to talk to you. You've been avoiding me for weeks.' She reined in her horse and dismounted, tying him to the fence. Josephine was a superlative actress, and she lingered there momentarily, aware that she made a most elegant picture against the backdrop of the mellow old farm. As indifferent to the animal as she was to her children, she now talked softly to him, and he answered, whinnying gently, nudging against her, snuffing for an apple. She patted his neck and kissed him beneath his long forelock.

'I've been busy, what with lambing and the bad weather.' Darcy watched this performance cynically, while his flesh, as always, responded to her lush body.

She was dressed in a tailored riding habit, her blonde hair confined in a demure net beneath a small, low-crowned topper. The black velvet jacket, cut like a man's, was uncommonly modest compared to her usual décolletage, but it clung to the outline of her breasts. Such attire, with a high neck and long sleeves, should not have been seductive, but Josephine transformed even this into something tempting.

'Tosh!' she snorted indignantly. 'Don't use that as an excuse. You've been deliberately avoiding me. Don't you want me any more?'

It was a mild morning, quiet, still, without any wind. Only the rooks moved on the grass, like sable imps, strutting and cawing to one another. Across the field behind the barn came the sound of chopping, and the dull rhythmic thud of an axe on timber. On the far side, two men were laying a long beech hedge. The faint, sweet scent of fresh-cut wood hung on the air mingled with the smell of trampled earth, grass and cow dung.

Deny it though he might, Darcy did still want her. Perhaps it was a form of love, he didn't know, but there was no denying the strong physical attraction between them. That should have been enough. Why was he torturing himself by chasing after rainbows? Camilla was aloof and impregnable, still harping on about him trespassing, even though they had come to a financial arrangement under the guidance of her lawyer. Anger simmered as he recalled the maddeningly condescending way in which she had given him permission to use her land on their last meeting, formally conducted in the library of The Priory. Yet he knew there was passion beneath the ice. Melt her and she'd be insatiable. Her mouth, that was what told him, and her eyes. But he was hardly going to give Josephine the satisfaction of learning about his frustration.

'What nonsense you talk.' He smiled down on her charmingly and placed his hand on her arm. She felt the weight and warmth of it through the cloth. 'You must know that my motive for spending time with her is avarice, pure and simple. I've no intention of altering my habits, or giving in to her damnably high-handed demands.'

174

Josephine had galloped the distance between Erwarton Hall and the farm, feeding her fury, working herself up into a fine rage. But now another emotion was making itself felt, a delicious sense of triumph as she recognized the desire in him. There was no one about, the farmyard deserted, save for a couple of cats sunning themselves on the wall and, through green, sly eyes, observing the pigeons preening and courting on the grey slate roofs. Douglas was in London; the children having breakfast with Miss Gearing; the servants, knowing that she was gone, would be idling in the kitchen, drinking tea and wasting time. Let them. She did not care. A shiver of expectation ran through her.

'How's the new foal coming along?' She looked away from him towards the stable, drawing off her gloves as she spoke. Even this simple action was suggestive. Her movements were languid, the riding skirt clinging to her rounded hips, and he was intensely aware of her ripe body that he could see clearly in his mind's eye though she was fully clothed.

'Sheba's a good mother,' he answered huskily. 'I'll be putting them both out to pasture very soon.'

'Are they in the stable? Can I see them?' Her eyes slanted at him beneath the long lashes, dark at the base, spun-gold at the tips. Her pink tongue flicked out to pass over her red lips. He remembered it, that soft, clever tongue and her soft, clever fingers working their magic on his flesh, the thought rousing him to the pleasures that he knew all too well.

He had been in an irritated mood, his manhood offended by Camilla's constant refusal to let him as much as kiss her. That anger had to find an expression. Josephine would provide the vehicle by which he might relieve it in another, equally violent way. Without answering, he took her by the hand and led her into the dim, hay-sweet stable. The mare and her foal were in one of the stalls, nuzzling at the manger. Duty-bound to

175

show a modicum of interest, Josephine paused, commenting on the little one's glossy coat, though her tongue stumbled over the words, and her head was dizzy. It was warm inside, shafts of dust-grained sunlight streaming in from a narrow, unglazed window up near the timbered roof.

She glanced at the silent Darcy, admiring him afresh. God, but he was handsome! Such thick black hair, and those devilishly blue eyes, such a well-trimmed luxurious beard. How soft it had felt brushing over her as his lips had sought the secret places of her body. No foreign bitch was going to have him, if she had anything to do with it! He was *hers*.

She shivered as she felt his fingers running lightly up her back. They traced the nape of her neck, the line of her jaw to the lobe of her ear. In an instant, she had spun around, her arms clasping him fiercely as she ground her body into his. Just for a moment, he hesitated, his eyes staring into hers with almost a look of hatred. Then, with that wildness and need which she remembered so vividly, he pulled her down on to the hay behind the stall.

'We can't, not here. Someone will come – anybody can come in – anybody,' she protested faintly, knowing that she'd die if he stopped. With a grunt of amusement, he covered her mouth with his.

His big, tanned hands pushed up her skirt, and he smiled tightly as he did so because she usually wore breeches under the riding habit. Not today though. She'd come to him prepared for this. There was not even the bastion of delicate knickers to hinder his exploration. Her thighs were bare above the tops of her black silk stockings, no stays to encumber his searching fingers. The stockings were supported by crimson satin garters. Her hips arched against his hand. He knew what she wanted but, taking a perverse satisfaction in thwarting all women through her and Camilla in particular, he did not do it.

He guessed that she was starving, and had been looking forward to a sensual feast and then ecstatic release. Vengefully, he denied her. Ignoring the breasts that she had bared in yearning for the touch of his hands, he unfastening his breeches and rolled over on her. With the sensations of revenge, anger and lust mixed together, he thrust into her flesh.

Disappointed, Josephine wrapped her legs around his hips, striving to gain a measure of enjoyment, and failing. He was crushing her into the straw, pounding away, seeking his own release. As she braced herself to the assault, her only satisfaction lay in the thought that while he was spending himself in her, he was not doing it with anyone else. Hotfoot on this came the anxiety that perhaps she wasn't normal. Even as his animal cry denoted his final spasm, even as she moaned and faked orgasm, she was wondering if there was something wrong with her. Did other women have this difficulty in climaxing with their partners? Was her desire for a slow, creeping softness, a yearning to be fondled, nibbled, consumed, an unnatural perversion? The gates of memory sprang open and she unwillingly recalled herself and a girl at school, nights filled with waking warmth, sensitive hands stroking her, stirring in her thighs such undulating waves of pleasure, the like of which she had rarely experienced with men.

Darcy withdrew from her, lying on his back, one arm flung over his eyes. She curled against him in her crumpled clothing, a tremor of repugnance in her stomach, her skin reeking of his sweat, wetness spreading between her legs. If only he would speak kindly to her now, tell her that he loved her. He didn't have to mean it, but the words would soothe her bruised ego. He said nothing, his ragged breathing becoming deep and even. You selfish bastard! she thought. I'll not let you go to sleep!

'That was wonderful,' she sighed, almost convincing

herself that the lie was truth. 'Oh, Darcy, you're a superb lover!'

While her hands fondled his beard and trailed over his lips, nose and cheekbones, a hot coil knotted in her loins as she planned what she would do when she reached the privacy of her bedroom at Erwarton Hall. She'd finish what he had begun but left uncompleted. The warmth increased as she pictured how she would go to the wardrobe and, from a carefully locked drawer, take out the pretty oblong box which contained the strange present that Selden had given her some time ago.

'Good God, where on earth did you get such a thing?' she had laughed when she had unwrapped it and lifted out the contents, finding it gross but fascinating, so thick, hard and long, an erect phallus substitute.

Selden's eyes had been very bright, his lips curved into a pensive smile. 'I'm a customer at a certain discreet shop in Soho where many devices can be purchased, coyly labelled "Marital Aids". It's more effective than a candle, so I'm told by ladies of my acquaintance, even better than the real thing! I thought it was time you discovered that there're more ways than one of skinning a cat.'

Excitement had thickened in Josephine as she was struck by the rather shocking and novel idea that her brother would enjoy watching her experiment with the thing. 'Perhaps you should buy one for Alison,' she had giggled, filled with malicious glee. 'She must be frightfully frustrated.'

'My dear girl, I doubt she'd know what to do with it,' had been his drawling response.

So, when lying in the arms of an inept lover while he humped and groaned and expended a deal of energy, she had often amused herself by thinking: You bloody, clumsy fool! D'you *really* imagine that I'm anywhere near approaching the peak? What earthly use are men, except to provide women with money and, horrible thought, children? They're a nuisance, that's what! And she would dwell fondly on the contents of her pretty box, thanking Selden for his understanding.

Yet her vanity needed men, her body too, for she still dreamed of finding the perfect lover, one who would satisfy her completely. She thrived on compliments, loved to tease and torment, never happier than when she had roused a man so that he could no longer hide his desire, greedy to witness that hardening of his flesh which indicated yet another conquest. She was jealous and possessive, feeling slighted if someone whom she considered to be her property cast his eye elsewhere. Consequently, she had developed a violent hatred for Camilla. She had spent much time planning her wardrobe for the Hunt Ball, only to be eclipsed by the Brazilian. Even Douglas had fawned on her, forgetting to drink for at least an hour whilst he waited for his name to come up on her dance-card. It was most vexing.

Darcy stirred, sitting up, giving her a crooked smile as he adjusted his clothing. 'Well, Josephine –?'

'Well, Darcy –?' she smirked back, eyes heavy-lidded and dreamy. 'Shall I come for a repeat performance tomorrow morning?'

'I shan't be here.' He was standing now, looking down at her where she sprawled wantonly in the hay, those beautiful legs fully exposed to his gaze, skirt hitched above the fair, curling triangle at the apex of her thighs.

She scowled and scrambled to her feet, knocking away bits of straw that clung stubbornly to the velvet. 'Oh? And why not?'

'It's market day. I'll be off to Sutton Cross at dawn.'

'Alone?' She tried not to show interest, but it was impossible. Her cheeks burned with anger, her heart was a heavy, discontented lump in her chest. He was treating her like a whore whom he'd just used and now contemptuously dismissed. Uncaring. Callous.

'No, I'm taking Camilla with me.' His eyes warned

179

her not to start an argument and, biting back the flood of hot words which sprang to her lips, she walked with him into the yard, fuming and vowing to get even with that tantalizing bitch who was obviously weaving a strong web around him.

Camilla was uneasy and could not sleep. She rose from her bed and padded to the window on bare feet, her white silk nightgown whispering as it skimmed the floor. There was no need to pull back the heavy tapestry curtains. The embrasure was so deep that there was room for a dozen people inside. She knelt on the padded seat which ran the length of the stone bay.

It was deep night, but the darkness was broken as the horizon flared suddenly all along its rim, a bloody glow which grew into lurid flame. It spread out, engulfing the blackness like a massive monster with yawning, slavering jaws, widening and deepening till the clouds were tinted with orange hues and the very sky seemed to smoulder. There was something ominous in that fire by night. It was like a red portent, though of what Camilla could not guess.

Darcy had warned her to expect this, the sacrificial March fires that blazed the way for spring. Yet, even while understanding it, she was disturbed. He had said that in this month they fired the moor, letting the flames leap like snakes amongst the gorse, heather and bracken, charring and blackening everything in their path. When she wanted to know why, he'd replied that it was to clear off the old, spent growth, to make way for the new and discourage the heavy accumulation of scrub.

This was only one of the many lessons he had taught her about the land and how to preserve it. Still staring at the fire, bewitched by it, she visualized other fires, other rituals, also concerned with fertility. Was the civilized English farmer so very different from the peons she had

180

lived among in Rubera? Certainly the moors and uplands here were deserving of superstitious respect.

During her lonely rides over her acres, she had observed the ancient barrows, dark against the skyline, crowning the hilltops with mystery. There was something fascinating about these strange round tumuli. Wilf had explained that they were burial mounds and under them lay the remains of great warriors. She had discussed it with Leila in depth. The Creole was already aware, but could not tell her who it was that had lain for centuries under the red earth and white stone, up there on the moors. Perhaps it would be revealed to her in dreams.

Many aspects of this particular corner of Wessex had been presented to Camilla as she careered across the countryside. She had found isolated farmhouses with grey stone walls, slate roofs, chickens clucking in the yards, and dogs that barked at her approach; locals leaning over their gates, who gave her fixed unsmiling stares as she passed; narrow lanes, small gurgling streams spanned by arched stone bridges; wide expanses of high, open ground, rugged and windswept, dotted with sturdy sheep and occasional herds of wild horses drifting across the slopes.

The swaling fires had an unsettling effect on Camilla. She knew that sleep was now out of the question. Somewhere, in the depths of the house, she heard the longcase clock chime three times. She was in a dull, lethargic mood, her movements slow and languid as she crossed the room and stirred the embers in the grate with the brass poker. The smouldering logs burst into flame, their dancing, ruddy glow echoing those outside. The silence was like a coffin lid, banged shut. She crouched by the fire, holding her hands before it. The crimson light made them almost transparent. She withdrew into her thoughts, immobilized, hardly breathing. The minutes blurred together like raindrops on a windowpane.

181

Gradually, she found something impinging on her awareness, urgent, undeniable. The room. That small, secretive room which led from this one. Coming home late from the Hunt Ball, she had found Leila there, on her knees before the portrait, stiff with cold, in a trance. Gently, knowing the rules and the correct procedure, Camilla had roused her. Together they had explored the hidden chamber and she had been strangely drawn to it. Next day, she had gone there as soon as she woke, pulling back the heavy curtains, letting the snowy light pour into ever corner. She knew then her search was over. Before, she had wandered the house like a lost soul, knowing that somewhere lay a spot which she could call her very own, private, concealed from prying eyes – a place for study, for developing the arts which Leila was still teaching her.

Without external guidance, she had found the dusty tomes behind cobwebbed glass. They consisted of maps, ships' logs, accounts of the adventures of long-dead travellers. So, the tropics had called to him even then. The Priory and its lands had not been enough. The room, overshadowed by his portrait, was filled with evidence of his obsession. This had not come upon him on arrival in Haiti. It was that which had driven him there. She had stood for long minutes on end, staring up at that decadently handsome face which never stirred in response. So different from how she remembered him. In the painting, he was at the peak of his powers, radiant, godlike, but there was something missing. The hand clenched round the riding crop was bare. He did not wear the ring that now adorned her finger. This had startled her, for he had prized it so greatly that she had assumed it to be an heirloom.

I must go there again, Camilla thought, rising from the hearth. Perhaps tonight I'll understand him. She was finding it impossible to shake him off, though to keep pawing over the memories of their life together and his appalling death, was bordering on necrophilia. The lamp on the table had an expectant air. Holding it high, she opened the oak door which slid back easily. Wilf had taken his oil can to the hinges. Her reflection confronted her, murky and dim, in the glass of the bookcase. She was smiling.

The lamp light fell in pools of brightness that penetrated the Stygian gloom. The windows looked stark. There was no moon. Outside a hoarse-voiced owl called again and again in flight. Camilla was conscious of belonging, as she was when she rode on any part of her land. It was as if, with just a little more effort, she would be able to vibrate that chord of racial memory locked away in her genes, on the verge of plumbing the depths of some amazing knowledge that would transform her existence.

'What is it, Papa?' She held the lamp even higher, flashing it across the painted features. 'What do I have to know?' Then, defiantly, she added: 'D'you still want dealings with me, the daughter who killed you?'

Her ears began to ring with a disembodied humming, reminiscent of bees around a hive, or flies hovering over a corpse. It grew so loud that the room shook with it, and the light in Camilla's hand trembled and wavered, dimming to a pinpoint. From the darkness, the uncertainty, came fear. For the first time, she began to sense a threat. Not from him, not from the portrait, but from somewhere in the blackness of space, coming closer – closer. It was in the room. She could smell it, a fetid odour that crawled insidiously into her nostrils, and a sound, a slithering step as of someone walking with mud clinging to their feet. Cold, cloying, damp. The air was rancid with it.

Camilla peered into the dimness, seeing nothing, hearing much. The open doorway behind her constituted a threat. As when in the rain-forest by night, she felt the urge to have something solid at her back, lest she fall prey to an attacker. The noise had transmuted itself to a low keening which rose to a howl like that of a witch's cat, a black obscene demon. The doorway was blank. The thing had taken possession of the room.

She felt a touch at her back. Her heart jumped, its pounding a pain in her chest. In a paroxysm of terror she swung around. The lamp in her shaking hand regained its brilliance. It struck the carved stone of the fireplace surround. Just for a moment she could not believe what she saw. There was movement over its surface. Yes, there it was again, crawling over the stone like some horrible tarantula, the blood-stained imprints of a small hand! Each one faded as she stared, to be instantly replaced by another, up and up, over the carvings of fruit and acanthus leaves, reaching the central coat of arms, hovering on the Ruthen crest. Here the fingers lingered, then like water sinking into arid sand, they vanished.

She was perched precariously at the top of a stepladder when Selden was shown into her presence. The Priory was a hive of activity. A troop of workmen in overalls, commanded by Obadiah Makepiece, local carpenter, wheelwright and undertaker, were encamped there. The sounds of hammering, sawing and the West Country drawl of the labourers rang through the once-deserted rooms.

Camilla was hanging curtains in the library. The old ones had fallen to pieces when Beryl and her band of village charwomen had lugged them into the garden for a beating. New ones had been ordered and had only lately arrived from London. Whilst perfectly in tune with the panelling and painted ceiling, these were of thick linen printed with a William Morris design, tendrils of leaf-green interlinked with orange tiger-lilies. The drapes were long and wide, and the library made a superb foil for such breadth of pattern.

184

'Camilla!' Selden stood at the bottom of the steps, looking up at her. 'What *are* you doing? Why don't you leave it to servants?'

Frowning in concentration as she struggled with the weight of the fabric whilst slipping the brass hooks into the thick wooden rings of the mahogany curtain poles, Camilla did not spare him a single glance. 'The servants are busy in other directions. The whole house is in an uproar. Once the workforce moved in, all hell broke loose. Not that I'm complaining. I want it completed as quickly as possible, but the neglect of years cannot be put right in five minutes.'

'I did warn you.' He rested a booted foot on the bottom rung, head flung back as he stared up at her. From that perspective, her legs, in calf-length culottes, seemed longer than ever, spine stretched, head poised on that slender neck as she fought a winning battle with the obstinate rings. 'You should've accepted my invitation to stay with me whilst all this was happening.'

Camilla swished the secured drapes backwards and forwards, then settled them in elegant folds each side of the tall window. 'I wouldn't have missed it for anything. It's so exciting, like a voyage of discovery. Wonderful old house! I love it!' she observed as she began to climb down.

Selden gave her his hand and she jumped the last few steps. He caught her in his arms to steady her. She gave him a frigid stare and freed herself. 'You're so fearfully independent, my dear,' he sighed, with a meaningful look. 'I wish you'd let me help you.'

'I've plenty of help. Sit down, Selden, if you can find a chair. There's one under that dustsheet over there. I'll ring for someone to bring in drinks. Whisky suit you?'

Selden did as she bade him, unearthing a solid, leather-covered armchair, whipping off its shroud and brushing his hand across the seat before risking his clean riding breeches. Camilla was like a restless flame,

185

striding across to the worsted bell-pull and tugging it vigorously. She then settled on a corner of the desk, crossing her legs, resting her elbow on her knee, chin in her cupped hand as she stared at him.

'What d'you want, Selden?' she asked with that blunt frankness which in turn delighted and piqued him.

'My dear girl, what a question!' He feigned surprise whilst searching his mind for an answer which would not send her flying off in a tantrum. 'I'm naturally concerned for your welfare. So much work!' He glanced around at the chaos of the room.

'Don't worry about me. I've recruited a grand team. I've the Simmonds from London, and several local girls applied for jobs as skivvies, parlour and chambermaids. Not much for them to do yet, but I told them that if they wanted me to employ them, they'd have to start now, roll up their sleeves and whale in. Every one of 'em agreed. I think they're all dying of curiosity about me. Couldn't wait to get into the house. And then there's Shawn – he's been great. Got stuck in like a good 'un.' Camilla's deep drawling tone was an odd contrast to the unconventional, even slangy mode of speech she used.

Selden was struck anew by its exaggerated, boylike bravura, and found himself thinking that she really ought to reform. But on the other hand how much less amusing it would be if she did! She was right in her assumption that people were talking. Nothing quite like her had hit Abbey Sutton before. Jenkins had kept him informed, a frequent visitor to Lacey's shop. Camilla had breezed in there once or twice and ordered, amongst other things, boxes of cheroots which she let it be known were for herself. This alone was enough to give Mrs Lacey a seizure! As for the vicar – he had called on her one day, all solicitous nosiness but, after a blistering argument with her concerning religion, had left in high dudgeon. Apparently those engaged in the tremendous task of restoring the manor, could not praise her enough.

She was a just but tyrannical taskmaster, expecting the highest quality workmanship for which she paid an equally high wage. The repairs must be costing a fortune! Selden dourly reflected that she could well afford it. The income from the estate and investments, held in trust for her all these years, was hers to do with as she pleased.

Leila came in with a decanter and glasses on a silver tray. Selden had heard about the Creole but had not met her before. His first impression was that she was a splendid creature. Through all his various amatory escapades he had never had a black woman, and the thought of doing so was titillating. This died abruptly. Her eyes, as expressionless as a snake's, were bent on him. A curious spasm convulsed her face, every line, every hollow showing its chiselling.

'Thank you, Leila.' Camilla saw that she had already formed an unfavourable opinion of Selden, and resolved to question her later.

Leila was her rock. Without her guidance, she felt that she would not be able to carry on. On the night when she had first seen the ghostly hand prints, even her considerable courage had cracked. She had shouted for Leila, who had come running, expressing no surprise at such a grisly phenomenon. Together, they were not only engaged in putting the house to rights, but also seeking to pacify the unquiet spirit that haunted it. With such pressing matters on her mind, she could hardly bother to attend to Selden.

'So that's your nigger.' He nodded towards the door as Leila closed it after her.

'My friend.' She corrected him with such a severe look that he almost flinched.

'Friend – servant – whatever! She's still a darkie, ain't she? Been with you long?' He smiled affably, sipping his drink, attempting to break through the barriers which she seemed intent on throwing up between them.

187

'All of my life.' Camilla wished he would come to the point of his visit. She had so much to do and, after her morning's work, planned to blow away the cobwebs with a canter on the moors.

It seemed that her wish was to be granted. Selden set down his glass and leaned towards her. 'I say, Camilla, can't we be friends?'

'I'm too busy for friendships –' she began, but he reached out and put his hand on her thigh, a pleasant tingle going right up his arm at the feel of such soft, yet resilient warmth.

'You can find the time for Darcy,' he grated, and his grey eyes were smouldering.

'Not at all.' She wanted to move, but remained there as if made of stone, showing no emotion. 'He's a business associate.'

'Like hell he is!' Selden sneered, fingers digging into her leg. 'You let him take you to the Hunt Ball, and he's called here frequently, so I've been told. Didn't you go to Sutton Cross market with him the other day?'

Camilla shook off his hand, withdrawing to the further side of the table. 'So? He's a farmer. I need to learn about farming.'

'Farmer be damned!' Selden exploded, voicing a long-standing resentment. 'He didn't know one end of a pitchfork from the other ten years back. Comes from an old Norfolk family who've grand titles but are poor as church mice. He inherited Chalkdown Farm from his uncle. Deuced lucky for him. It enabled him to pay off some of his debts, skip out of London just in time to avoid a couple of nasty law suits, and hide away down here in the country.'

His jealousy of Darcy was so obvious that she would have laughed aloud, if something in his manner had not restrained her. Instead, she reminded: 'I thought he was one of your cronies.'

'He's a good huntsman and, as it happens, has proved

188

to be a competent farmer.' Selden had risen to his feet
and was now standing over her. Tall, lean, his fair hair
ruffled from his brisk gallop, he was perfectly attired in
Harris tweed jacket and beige breeches, a silk scarf
knotted casually beneath his chin, the epitome of a
country squire, till one looked into those cold, almost
reptilian eyes and saw the ruthless thrust of his jaw. He
shrugged, an unpleasant smile twisting his mouth. 'I get
along with him reasonably well. It's always useful to
have a bachelor on hand if one has an over-abundance of
females at parties. But with regard to friendship,
Josephine would know more about that.'

Camilla had already heard the rumours, had formed
her own suppositions when she had met Darcy and
Josephine at the same gatherings, watching them, seeing
how her eyes devoured him, whilst he did his best to
avoid her. Beryl, hobnobbing with her coterie of stalwart
cleaners, had picked up most of the village gossip,
relaying it to her mistress. It was common knowledge
that Darcy Devereaux and Lady Josephine were lovers,
but in her heart Camilla had hoped that the affair was
over. Certainly Darcy had dropped several hints in that
direction, whilst never coming out into the open.

She decided to play Selden at his own game, presenting a blank face to him. 'I don't quite follow you –'

His lip curled in a faint smile, one eyebrow shooting
up as he continued to stare at her. 'She's his mistress.'

'She *was* his mistress.' Camilla could not help herself.
The words left her lips before she was able to prevent
them.

His expression was sceptical, though his voice was
smooth as he replied: 'They still meet, my dear. Such a
passionate liaison. Of course, poor old Dougie's in the
dark. The husband's usually the last to know, so they
say.'

Camilla was studying her hands. The tiger's-eye
flashed as she turned it around on her finger. 'I thought
it was over.'

'He told you that?' Selden's mocking laugh jarred in her ears, bringing to mind other mockery, other cruel laughter. He was a blond replica of her father, endowed with those pronounced Ruthen features which were recognizable in the family portraits, and in the faces of several lowly members of the community thereabouts, proof that they had never been snobbish when it came to the pursuit of their vices.

'No.' Her voice was very low. 'We've not discussed it.'

'At least he hasn't lied about that. One point to his credit.' He wanted to touch her bowed head, to grip that tumbling mass of corn-gold hair and force her to look at him. He thought he had found her Achilles' heel, congratulating himself that this meeting was proceeding according to plan.

Then he was transfixed by her tilting catlike eyes, and the expression in them silenced him. Selden no longer felt like laughing. 'How do I know *you* aren't the liar?' she hissed.

Giving himself a mental shake, Selden regained his composure. The poison was working. He knew precisely how to feed a woman's jealousy and breed distrust. 'Josephine and I are pretty close. We keep no secrets from one another, well, hardly any. She's told me that she's been going to his stables, at an early hour before anyone's up. They used to rendezvous here, you know. In the Master Chamber, of all the cheek! Haunted or not, this wouldn't deter my sister from rogering.'

The Master Chamber. Her own room. She remembered remarking to Leila when they first arrived that the bed looked as if it had been slept in. Nausea choked her throat. She swallowed hard, grappling with the ache deep inside her. Until that moment, she had not realized how cleverly Darcy had wormed his way into her trust, though not completely. No man would ever have the power to do that again, but at least she had begun to enjoy his company, to look forward to their meetings.

190

I've not been honest with myself, she sighed. It wasn't to learn about farming that I encouraged him, it was because I find him attractive and was hoping – hoping. For what? Not for love, you fool. Love is hurtful, destructive. You want no part in it.

If Selden had been expecting a violent outburst, he was disappointed. She fastened her attention on something else he had just said. 'Haunted? You think this house is haunted?'

Was she more interested in visitations than Darcy? Had he been mistaken? For an instant, Selden doubted himself and this was unnerving. 'So I've been told. We played here when we were children, and I must say I had a spooky feeling sometimes. Alison was in a blue funk more often than not. Josephine and I used to scare the living daylights out of her.'

What an unpleasant pair, Camilla thought angrily. She had seen much of Alison during the weeks since her homecoming. Most days found her at The Priory, lending a hand. She seemed pathetically grateful for any show of friendliness. 'I'll speak to Alison about it. Maybe there's some old legend that will account for the ghost. D'you know what form the manifestations take?'

Impatient to return to more personal issues, Selden said offhandedly: 'Josephine declares that she's heard a woman crying, but she exaggerates wildly about everything. Always sees herself in such a dramatic light. Wouldn't be surprised if she'd had a bit too much to drink, or was trying to pull a fast one on Darcy.'

'This happened recently?' She was trying not to think of Darcy and Josephine together in the bed in which she now slept, but obscene visions obscured the reality of the muddled, half-finished room, the spring morning, her cousin's eyes.

'A few days before Christmas.'

This was better. She had not yet looked on his splendid body and handsome, bearded face. She could very nearly forgive what he had done before they met. But if he had been making love to Josephine since, then that was a very different matter. It was absolutely illogical, and she knew it, repeating over and over that he meant nothing to her, except as a troublesome neighbour who considered it his right to ride rough-shod over any corner of her land that he fancied.

'To get back to Darcy and your sister.' She rose to her feet, perfectly cool, perfectly controlled. 'I can't think why you're bothering to wash their dirty linen in public. I don't give a damn what he does. It's immaterial to me.'

Selden was taken aback. Was she lying? There was no telling with women. Deceivers from the cradle. 'I'm most happy to hear it. I was rather hoping that you'd consider a day out with me soon. I've to go to Ryehampton next Saturday. Will you come?'

Why not? she asked herself unhappily. She did not like Selden, he was as slippery as an eel, but for her own sake she must not grow to rely on Darcy for male companionship. That way was the sure road to the delirious insanity which she had known once, and vowed never to repeat.

She was walking towards the door, and said, over her shoulder: 'There are several things I need. A trip to Ryehampton would be useful.'

He caught up with her, placed a hand on her arm and swung her around to face him. 'Capital! We'll have lunch in the Ruthen Arms, and I'll show you the sights.'

She almost changed her mind, reading his thoughts. He'd like to get me drunk. It was as clear as if he had spoken. He wants me. More than that, he seeks to compromise and discredit me. 'I haven't yet said that I'll come.'

'Don't disappoint me,' he pleaded with that almost shy, boyish grin which he had used since nursery days to quell opposition. 'You won't need Leila as a chaperone. I'll look after you, Camilla.'

192

'Will you, Selden?' Her clear eyes probed into his. In them he saw no shadow of the doubts which beset her.

His hand tightened, his other arm clipped her around the waist, pulling her against the hard wall of his chest. 'What about a kiss to seal the bargain?' he coaxed. 'Just a friendly kiss between cousins, eh? Why d'you shut yourself up here, living like a nun? You were made for love, Camilla. It breathes out of your pores. The villagers are somewhat dismayed by such impeccable behaviour. They're not used to it in the aristocracy. You should give them a little food for gossip.'

'They expect me to be a hussy, because I'm foreign?' Camilla was testing her own reaction to his nearness. All she felt was the overwhelming desire to escape.

'Something like that,' Selden whispered, then he swooped like a hawk, capturing her mouth with his before she realized it. His violating tongue slipped between her lips, betraying him.

Camilla tore her face away, holding herself like an icicle in his grasp. 'Let me go, Selden!' she snarled, eyes blazing. 'I've dealt with tougher customers than you. Don't force me to knee you in the crotch!'

He released her with a light laugh. 'My dear girl, spare me that! I hope to father legitimate offspring before I'm done.'

Camilla did not move. Let him do the retreating. 'What a loss to mankind if you weren't able to add further vipers to the Ruthen nest!' Her sarcasm coiled around the room, and his lips thinned.

'A great pity.' He adjusted his cravat calmly, resisting the urge to strike her. 'Particularly as I was hoping that you would be their mother.'

Surprise knocked Camilla off balance for a second, then: 'Is this a bad joke or a rather crude proposal of marriage?' she snapped.

'I'm not joking.' Selden picked up his hat and crop from a side-table. 'What could be more agreeable than a match between us? I'm most damnably in love with you, Camilla.'

'In love with me or my money?' Her voice was hard, her eyes like golden spears.

He sauntered over to the entrance, then glanced back at her. 'Does it matter? Both, I suppose. I desire you and that, for me, is tantamount to love.'

'I don't need a husband.' Yet even as she spoke she was considering the idea dispassionately. Marriage without love's torture might not be a bad scheme. What had it been called in days gone by? A marriage of convenience. So sensible. So safe. With property and the breeding of strong heirs the prime objective. No risk of being flung into the maelstrom of tormenting passion.

'You need children. A woman like you should have a nursery filled with babies.'

The words knifed through her, piercing her armour, though he could not know what he was saying. Babies! The thought was bitter-sweet. Babies to erase for ever the memory of that tiny coffin laid to rest in the graveyard at Rubera. It would please Leila to rock an infant in her arms and croon Creole lullabies, but Camilla felt in her bones that the *mambo* would not approve of Selden for its sire, even though she had a sensible head on her shoulders and would not be blind to the advantages of such a match.

'Aren't you rather jumping the gun?' she asked, resenting his manner, but giving him grudging credit for his outspokenness.

Selden was studying her with an excitement which his jaded appetite had not known for a long while. Unstable, promiscuous and incapable of fidelity, he was constantly seeking fresh challenges. There was something about Camilla that marked her as untamed. He liked her style, liked the flamboyance of her clothing, her furs, her jewellery, visualized walking into the London theatres or smart clubs with her on his arm, drawing every eye.

Despite her youth, she gave the impression of being wise in the ways of the world and he rather doubted that she was still a virgin. This did not matter to him. Virgins were over-rated in his book. He'd rather have a woman who knew how to use her body for love.

Thoughtfully, he thwacked his whip gently against the side of his breeches, still observing her the while. 'I don't think I'm being precipitent. We're adults, aren't we? Do we have to beat about the bush? You strike me as a girl of perception. We'd make a fine couple, Camilla. Dammee, it would be the wedding of the year.'

In her imagination she caught the fleeting, satisfying picture of Darcy's face if she gave her consent and an engagement was announced. He wouldn't like it, of that she was convinced. It would almost be worth the inconvenience, just to witness that. If only she could find it in her heart to like Selden or at least tolerate him. Her instinctive distrust was not based on anything solid, apart from his schemes regarding Claypole. He was handsome, well-connected, appeared to be popular, and mixed in the right circles, yet there was something wrong. She could not put her finger on it, but it existed, secretive, malignant, like an obnoxious fungus beneath the soil.

'We're first cousins.' Here was a concrete reason for refusing him. 'I don't think this would be acceptable.'

'It shouldn't stand in our way. Lots of cousins marry.' Selden was not to be put off. 'Do I take it that you're not turning me down out of hand? You'll think about it?'

It was the least she could do. Their estates were too close to make an open quarrel tolerable at this juncture. 'Yes,' she replied as they walked out into the Great Hall.

'Good. And I'll pick you up about ten in the morning on Saturday. Will this suit you?' He could not have been more charming, more courteous, nodding to the stately Obadiah who tugged his forelock respectfully as he passed, bowler-hatted, dark-suited, wearing a stiff white

195

collar, followed by an underling weighed down by two enormous cans of paint.

'Very well, Selden, if you're sure? You may find it extremely boring. I really do have some serious shopping in mind. I can't possibly be hurried when it's something important concerning the house. Trivial to you, perhaps, but there's some yardage of curtain material that has to be matched. We need it at once. Can't wait for it to be posted.'

'A highly commendable attitude, my dear,' he said indulgently. 'You're very practical, and this is an admirable attribute, rare in one so beautiful.'

They stood at the head of the steps for a few moments longer, and Camilla could see two of the gardeners digging up weeds. Already the grounds were being tamed, the undergrowth attacked, paths, sundials, sunken gardens, yew hedges beginning to reappear from the rampant tangle. Would it be finished by mid-summer? It was then that she was planning to hold her first party, opening the old house to light and laughter and music. And love? There's ample time for decisions, she thought. Selden and Darcy must prove themselves. I'm not at all sure that I want to share The Priory with either of them.

It was later than she intended when Camilla was at last able to mount her horse and escape into the open, yet there was still a wealth of light and colour left in the day. She breasted a rise, pausing to drink in the view spread out before her like a huge patchwork quilt. It glittered under the noonday sun, filled with warmth and interest and all the delights of spring. Green fields bordered the vast, rolling reaches of the moor, deep combes slid into clumps of woodland, white farmhouses stood on the hillsides, and small shining streams tumbled between boulders.

196

Setting spur to her horse, she rode down to the river, trotting between high hedges of feathery blackthorn. Water poured from clefts in the rocks to fall in sparkling rivulets across the path. Primroses and violets starred the deep banks, butter-yellow cowslips nodded to clumps of bluebells. Joyous life ran strong in Camilla's veins. It was good to shake off the worries besetting her. Scents, movements, the touch of leather under her bare hands, the feel of the horse beneath her, these renewed her courage, her faith, and sent dismal, dark things scurrying back to Hades whence they came.

The busy river rushed full and clear over its bed of glossy pebbles, winding away under a small bridge. Now, amidst the chuckling of water, the shrilling of birdsong, she heard another sound. Hooves rang on a hard road and bridle bits jingled. They were heading for the inn at the crossroads. Usually isolated, it now bustled, riders coming from all directions, clattering and talking, mounted on horses of every sort – thorough-breds and sturdy cobs, ponies and small solid beasts whose beige noses hinted at moorland blood. There were family groups and single riders. Carriages and a few cars disgorged servants with hampers, hip flasks, rugs, and changes of clothing for their masters.

Camilla saw Darcy almost at once, arrogantly at home in the saddle of his high-mettled black steed. She tried to look at him objectively, but he was heart-stoppingly handsome, so lean and angular, the bone structure of his face clear in that bright light – strong bearded jaw, slender nose slightly flared over the straight lips. He was hard and muscular, his body designed to wear clothes well, be it evening suit, country gear or, as now, huntsman's attire – the blazing red coat, white tight-fitting breeches, black hat and top boots.

She was about to hail him, when she saw Josephine canter up, leaning across to place an intimate, lazy hand on his arm as she smiled into his face, her gelding so close that her knee bumped against his. Camilla remained where she was, half hidden by trees. There was an extra stir. The crowd who followed the hunt on foot made for the open gate opposite the inn. The hounds gave tongue, controlled by their handlers. Colonel Pinnegar, Darcy and one of the gamekeepers were grouped together, discussing the fate of the animal they had selected for culling. A stirrup cup was passed around. At last all was ready. A horn blared, and the riders moved off towards the moor.

Camilla watched them go, the air rent with the excited noises of the leading hounds, the thrilling note of the horn. She felt suddenly lonely, wishing that she, not Josephine, jogged along at Darcy's side, remembering, too late, that he had told her they were hunting that day. She was about to turn her animal's head in the direction of the higher slopes from where she would be able to observe the hunt's progress, when a voice spoke behind her.

'Why aren't you with them, Lady Camilla? There's a big old stag to be pulled down today.'

She swung around to see Shawn's smiling face. He too was in hunting pink and riding one of Selden's best horses. 'I'm hardly dressed for it.' She indicated her gaucho trousers and fringed jacket, her shallow-crowned, wide-brimmed hat. 'You're late. You've missed the start.'

He pushed his black cap to the back of his head and his green eyes went over her admiringly. 'No. I was here, but I've been watching you. Far more rewarding than joining that crowd of show-offs. I like your outfit. You look as if you've been herding cattle on the prairie. How's the house coming along?'

'Fine, thank you.' She was listening to him with only half her attention. The cries of the hounds could be heard in the distance, calling intermittently, punctuated by the horn and faint voices encouraging their efforts.

198

'The harbourer told me they're after a wily buck who's getting too old to be boss of the herd. He'll know the ropes, all right, and lead 'em a dance, to be sure,' Shawn commented, leaning his forearms on the saddle-bow and squinting into the sun. 'I'll bet he's well away by now, heading into that maze of woods over there at the foot of the hill. That's what I'd be after doing if I was in his shoes.'

'Deer don't wear shoes.' Camilla found his presence vaguely irritating, though normally enjoying his company. He often dropped in at The Priory, a cheerful, willing helper, only too keen to assist her, lending his considerable muscles to move heavy pieces of furniture, his banter chivvying up tardy workmen.

He chuckled, those penetrating eyes returning to her. 'A figure of speech, no more. Bejabers, but you're solemn today. What's up?'

'Nothing.' Camilla bobbed her heels into her mount's flanks and moved away.

'Where're you going?' He was behind her, and she broke into a canter to escape him.

'Up higher, where I can get a good view of the hunt.' Her voice trailed on the wind, her face turned towards the moors.

'Be careful. I don't like the look of the weather,' he warned, dropping back.

What nonsense, she thought crossly, urging her horse into a gallop. It's a beautiful day. She glanced over her shoulder once, and saw him wheeling, to follow in the wake of the huntsmen. Good. She didn't need company, wanting nothing but the feel of the wind tearing through her hair. It tugged at her hat, only the leather chinstrap preventing it from blowing away. Now the inn dwindled to toy-size below her, the woods too as she gained height. She caught sight of the riders, a long line of tiny, galloping figures strung out to keep pace with the running hounds. The deer could not be far ahead. Then

199

she saw him, a flash of rust-brown, poised for a second at the top of a bank before leaping it and streaking up the slope on the other side. The pack streamed out in pursuit, till her eye could no longer hold them. Their sounds faded. Silence closed in on her.

Lost in thought, she had not realized how far she had travelled till she rested her horse some time later. Without boundaries or hedges, the moor was like a green-gold, undulating ocean. She had reached its heart. The desolation and emptiness was daunting. Utter and complete solitude. A curlew called suddenly, breaking the spell, making her feel less lonely. It stopped abruptly, as if strangled by some giant, invisible hand.

The sun had gone, swallowed up by thick clouds which now advanced over the clear ground like a white wall, moving swiftly down to engulf her. She felt the wet breath of the mist on her face. A hostile world of absolute blankness coming upon her without warning. Nothing stirred. The fog was opaque, without form or dimension, a muffling blanket through which she heard the faint bleating of sheep. That feeling of being surrounded by a strange inhumanity intensified. It was as if the spirits of the moorland were jealous of their stronghold, resenting strangers. She was alone, yet had the uneasy feeling there was something observing her – something alien and unfriendly.

Which way to go? She had completely lost her sense of direction. There was nothing to see save drifting whiteness. Landmarks had vanished. Slowly, she moved forward, talking to her horse whose ears were twitching nervously. It would be pointless trying to find her way back to The Priory until conditions improved. She cursed herself for not bringing a compass, but it had never occurred to her that she might need it. Wessex moors were a far cry from uncharted jungle regions. Or were they? The instinct for danger sent the fine down rising along her limbs. Though the day had been

200

pleasantly warm, when darkness fell the cold would be intense. She had not come prepared for this and, if she was not to risk exposure, needed to find shelter fast.

She became aware that the quality of her horse's motion had changed. The turf under his hoofs felt spongy. Every step he took was accompanied by a squelching sound, black ooze plastering his fetlocks. Till then, they had been thudding over grass. Camilla dismounted to investigate. The heels of her boots sank into yielding, treacherous ground. In the hollows under the tussocks, cushions of wet, matted moss were interwoven with slimy grasses and water plants. As she put a hand down to test it, she was startled to feel humid warmth breathing up into her face, heavy with a feral, swamplike smell which she recognized.

'Wonderful!' she exclaimed ironically to the horse, the reins looped over her arm. 'We, old friend of man, are lost in a dense fog in the peat bogs! Now what do we do?'

She spoke loudly, defying whatever it was that ruled such a fearsome place. Not even an echo answered. The horse merely nudged her with his nose, his mane glistening with drops of the same moisture that dampened her hair. In her mind, she raked over everything she could remember Darcy telling her about these dangerous areas. It wasn't much. *I couldn't have been attending, too busy looking at his incredibly blue eyes, no doubt! You're an ass, Camilla Ruthen. Won't you ever learn?*

The wisest move would be to stay exactly where she was until the mist lifted, but she was getting cold. The billowing mass seemed to be seeping into her bones. Recalling tactics used when crossing swampy, trackless wastes in the Brazilian forests, she began to pick her way with the utmost caution, guiding the horse as she did so. The silence was broken by weird gurglings and poppings, a sighing, settling sound. Little broken rills came from nowhere, running between the tussocks. Flies

201

were humming over the rich pickings of decaying matter.

Despite the treachery of the terrain, she was certain that there must be a safe way across if one knew how to walk and where. In the jungle she had been taught that rushes liked their roots firmly anchored. It was safe to step among them. She gingerly tried out a patch of green moss and the liquid peat swelled out. These then, were to be avoided at all costs. If only she could find some means of accurately judging her direction. For all she knew, she might be travelling away from The Priory, becoming even more deeply enmeshed in this threatening place. It was too cold to stop, too perilous to go on, but there was no alternative.

Speaking reassuringly to the jittery horse, she led him along a reasonably stable path covered by a sturdy mat of heather. It led past a deep, still pool. Camilla shuddered with more than the chilly damp. It was a forlorn spot, the mist hanging thickly over the oily surface, blocking the view of its farther bank. It might have stretched on to the ends of eternity. Perhaps she had died without being aware and this was the River Styx. Soon Charon would appear out of the blackness in his boat, ready to ferry her shade to Hades.

The idea sickened her. What a hellish spot. How horrible to sink beneath the black water where rotting branches reared up like prehistoric monsters, dripping foul slime. Tired, chilled to the marrow and hungry, her strength was at a low ebb. Camilla was not easily alarmed, but now as she stumbled and splashed, up to her knees in peaty mire, she was filled with an intense fear that threatened to rob her of both caution and reason. This wouldn't do at all. One thing her father had taught her was to keep a cool head. It had been the only way to survive in the jungle. God, but you've been in tighter corners than this, she chided herself. At least there aren't bushmasters here and you're free from tormenting mosquitoes. As for hostile tribes? Well, the natives in these parts aren't too friendly!

She grinned into the fog and control returned, but suddenly the horse went down, chest-high in the clogging mud. Panic heaved him out, whinnying, eyes rolling, with arched spine and legs that kicked free from the greedy bog. Camilla could feel the sweat breaking out at her armpits and under her breasts. She patted the trembling beast, clinging to him, careless of the filth that matted his coat.

'There, boy, it's all right. You're safe. Good boy, brave Jeddah – come along, we'll soon have you back in your cosy stable.'

She was certain that it was growing darker, night clouds joining those of spectral fog. The going was slower for every step had to be carefully tested lest they stumble into a black, bottomless morass. The quaking ground inclined gradually. The mist deepened and the quagmire squelched and sucked ominously. Something loomed straight ahead, and Camilla gasped. It seemed to be advancing, a huge, sinister figure – seeking her – meeting her!

It was as if she had been turned to granite. Then she gave a shaky laugh as she recognized what it was. A slab of grey rock, ten feet tall, thrusting upwards like a warning finger. A standing stone. She had seen many similar ones scattered across the countryside, sometimes in circles, sometimes positioned like this solitary sentinel. No one could tell her for what purpose they had been upended, giant monoliths of ages past. Leila avoided them, muttering about sacred groves and sacrificial rites.

Recovering from her fright, Camilla inched towards it, though she wanted to run in the opposite direction. She had the eerie felling that it was watching her. It's only a stone! she bullied herself. What can a big fat ugly rock do? The ground looks firmer all around it. Christ, it would have to be or such a massive lump would have sunk long ago! Doubtless, it can be seen for miles in clear weather. If I stay in its shelter, someone is bound to find me. Aren't they?

The idea was formidable. She was getting the same vibrations from it that she had experienced when exploring creeper-covered mounds left by the Incas. A brooding presence, unseen, dominant and compelling. Something dark, primeval, like a sleeping dragon coiled beneath the sod. Walking in a waking dream, she at last laid a trembling hand on the cold, yet vital stone. She sank down on her haunches at its base, back pressed against it. Jeddah stood patiently beside her, his head lowered, occasional shivers trembling through him.

The mist shifted and whirled, thinning slightly. She could see the pool. Mesmeric, it drew her eyes. She was not sure if she slept, dreamed or was still awake. Something moved in the murky depths. Surely that was an arm, a thin white hand gripping a tortured, blackened branch? Gripping, then slipping back – back. Was that the sound of weeping or was it the wind beginning to keen? Nightmare visions floated somewhere in her subconscious, baffling her brain, leaving only the sick, raw taste of fear.

'Camilla!'

She started, fully awake, hearing her name called from out of the mist. A horseman sat there motionless. For a second she did not recognize him, her eyes blinded by phantoms, then: 'Darcy?' she croaked, her legs wobbling as she tried to stand. 'Darcy, is that really you?'

He was out of the saddle and at her side, his arms catching her as she crumpled. 'Of course it's me. What did you think it was? The spectre of the Brocken?'

'I don't know.' She clung to his warmth, his strength, his reality. 'Oh, Darcy, I was lost, you see – I couldn't find my way.' He was a living, breathing human being. It was miraculous. She had never been more thankful to see anyone in the whole of her life.

204

He held her against his chest, his hands in her wet, tangled hair, then running down to stroke her back, gently, soothingly. And he was moved by the sudden transformation. She was no longer arrogant and self-sufficient, just a frightened girl whose weakness awoke a chivalrous response.

'My God, Camilla, you gave me a scare! That was a silly thing to do, riding out here by yourself. The bogs are extremely dangerous, and we treat them with great respect. It's not wise to go near them on horseback, and much easier and safer to ride around, even if it does mean a lengthy detour.' He lectured her, his sternness softened by a disarming smile, white teeth shining in the gloom, against the greater density of his beard. 'When Shawn caught up with us, he told me that he'd seen you heading for the moors. We guessed that the weather was about to change. It was raining by the time we made the kill, so I took a short cut which I knew was safe, and came looking for you. Why didn't you let me know you were at the inn?'

'Josephine.' She leaned her head against his red-coated chest, too weak with relief to play games.

She could feel his silent chuckle vibrating through her body and, looking up into his face, saw an expression there which rocked her senses. 'Damn Josephine!' he growled. 'Who's been gossiping about me? My affair with her is over – has been for some time.'

'Selden said otherwise.'

'Selden?' His brows swooped down in an alarming scowl. 'Ah, I see – he's a deep 'un, and cunning as a fox.'

'He thought that I should know the truth.'

He muttered something under his breath and she was glad that she had not caught it all. The few key words she heard were graphic enough, then he added loudly: 'The truth? What truth? The truth according to Lord God Selden?'

'But – but –' she stammered weakly.

205

'No buts. Listen to me, Camilla. Selden lied because he wants you and, through you, your lands. He's a man without a soul.' As she opened her lips to protest, he prevented her. 'Let me finish. Yes, I was Josephine's lover but, believe me, all that's in the past. Since I first saw you – ah, Camilla –'

His mouth, from the instant it closed on hers, was hungry and demanding. He gave her no time to protest or prepare herself. His lips were on hers, possessive, provocative, persuasive. Fear had made her rationality retreat into itself, leaving her defenceless and responsive. His kisses were good. She sank into them gratefully.

BOOK TWO

The Outcast

The glory of the sun upon the violet sea,
The glory of the castles in the setting sun
Saddened us, made us restless, made us long to be
Under some magic sky, some unfamiliar one.

Oh, Death, old captain, hoist the anchor! Come, cast
    off!
We've seen this country, Death! We're sick of it! Let's
    go!
The sky is black; black is the curling crest, the trough
Of the deep wave; yet crowd the sail on, even so!

Pour us your poison wine that makes us feel like gods!
Our brains are burning up! – there's nothing left to do
But plunge into the void! – hell? heaven? – What's the
    odds?
We're bound for the Unknown, in search of something
    new!

'Travel', Flowers of Evil by Charles Baudelaire, translated by Edna
St. Vincent Millay.

1

There's nothing more evocative than one's sense of smell, so potent and powerful, thought Alison as she wheeled her bicycle through the woods. It's as emotionally charged as music, with that same feeling of excitement, opening the floodgates of memory. I shall never breathe in the scents of the countryside without recalling this magical time of my life.

It was a beautiful morning filled with space and light and the promise of new life. A cuckoo called indolently, while more responsible birds chirruped as they flitted busily in the leafy greenery, engaged on urgent nest-building. From the fields came the plaintive cries of newborn lambs, and the anxious bleats of ewes. The shepherds would be heaving a sigh of relief now that the fraught work of lambing was over. The gamekeeper's job was not yet finished. To him fell the task of protecting the young. There was the constant threat of predators: the vixens with their own broods of hungry cubs, the scavenging crows and ravens. His gallows would be freshly adorned with bloody carcasses.

Darcy had been in the thick of it, Alison knew, attending his valuable flocks, up all night with difficult deliveries, coping with the disappointment of still-births, lambs rejected by their mothers, ewes who had lost their own babies and were given orphans to foster. Josephine's bad temper was a clear indication that she was being neglected. Alison had refrained from adding fuel to the fire by telling her that she had met Darcy coming away from The Priory several times recently. Camilla was close as a clam, mentioning him casually in passing, but Alison, senses honed by her own love affair,

209

observed that her cheeks were pinker than usual and her eyes like stars. She denies it vehemently, even to herself, she had concluded, but I know that she's in love.

As yet, she had not dared ask her cousin about the wagon, though she had craftily drawn her attention to it by presenting her with a canvas painted last summer. It depicted the gypsies' bygone home, set against a backdrop of thick undergrowth, seeming to be a part of it, wanderings done, taking root beneath the trees. Camilla had shown interest, and promised to make sure that it was not destroyed by over-enthusiastic gardeners. Alison longed to take her into her confidence but did not quite dare. There was something chillingly remote about Camilla at times, as if she had built a fortress around herself, lowered the portcullis and raised the drawbridge.

Alison turned down the path leading from the top of the woods to where the noisy stream ran through the narrow valley to the ford. Crossing by the footbridge, she continued towards her rendezvous with Frank. It was not easy to meet and discretion was the key-word, but lovers have a knack of providing themselves with secret, sheltered spots. Frank and Alison were no exception. Now that the harsh winter was over and summer just around the corner, they would be given ample opportunity to make love in lonely woodland dells, on beds of fern at the edge of the moors, under the hot sun or on warm, starry nights. Alison's skin tingled with anticipation, and she hurried as she pushed the heavy-framed cycle, that trusty steed which gave her the freedom to roam far afield. Her increasingly frequent jaunts into the outdoors caused little comment at Armitstead House. Fortunately, it had been her habit to wander off for hours on end. They knew and were placidly indulgent of her desire to be alone with the impressive scenery and her sketch book.

'Such a harmless hobby,' Selden had declared patronizingly. 'Keeps you out of mischief, my dear.'

210

If only he knew! Alison had never been more happy or more racked with guilt. Not remorse. This did not come into it. They were committing adultery, but she had succeeded in persuading herself that Elsie had asked for it. She obviously loved drinking more than Frank, therefore it was no sin for him to find fulfilment elsewhere. Sometimes Alison worried about the children. She had met Effie, the last-born, a dainty, feminine creature. Going into Lacey's one day, her heart had jumped in her breast when she had seen Frank standing there, the child's hand in his. Solemnly, he had introduced her, and Alison had admired his control. Never, by the blink of an eyelash, had he betrayed anything more than a curate's polite interest in one of the members of his parish.

'Hello, Effie,' Alison had said, bending down to the child, seeing Frank in that small, elfin face, the long fair ringlets caught back with a pert bow of pink ribbon. 'My! What a big girl! And when will you be five?'

Effie, who had been staring at her with large blue eyes fringed by straight blonde lashes, removed her thumb from her mouth long enough to answer: 'When I've finished being four,' then tucked it back between her lips again.

Frank often spoke of the child, repeating some of her precocious remarks. She was much brighter than her three brothers. Alison experienced a pang of jealousy, though scolding herself unmercifully for being so petty as to resent his affection for his daughter. If only *she* could have been Effie's mother, instead of a drink-sodden wreck like Elsie! It's just not fair! she would storm silently in moments of depression. Why couldn't I have met him years ago, before he became mixed up with her? Why aren't they my children? Oh, God, I love him so much!

She was so engrossed with her thoughts that she paid no heed to the glory of the spring-laden hedges that

211

bordered the winding lane leading to a copse some distance from the ford. Then the persistent cooing of amorous wood-pigeons penetrated her consciousness. She stopped looking inwards, realizing that she was almost there. Under the trees, down a slope, to where the bluebells made a carpet that reflected the cloudless sky. Her feet rustled the stiff leaves, and the sultry scent wafted up to be stored in memory's treasure house.

Frank was stretched on his back, arms clasped under his head, staring up into the vast green spread of an oak tree. He roused when he saw her, jumping up and running to take the bicycle, prop it against a bush and enfold her in his arms. He kissed her deep and long. She heard wanton sounds issuing from her throat, while her body responded in that warm, fluid way that inevitably led to making love.

'Oh, my darling.' His voice was husky with emotion as he raised his head, consuming her with the intensity of his gaze. 'How long can we keep up the charade? When I saw you in church on Sunday, I wanted to take you on the pew, then and there. I couldn't concentrate on the sermon. What are we going to do?'

'I don't know,' she said on a note of desperation.

'We'll think of something.' He hated to see her sad, cupping her face between his hands, stroking her lips with his thumbs. His gentleness always roused her nearly as much as his passion. She had known precious little gentleness in her life.

'Will we?' Freeing herself from him, she sat on the grass which was imprinted with the long length of his body. Resting her arms on her humped knees, she stared up at him, unaware of the accusation in her eyes. 'When, Frank? When are we going to be together all the time? I want to share your dreams, your daily life, your bed.'

Suddenly seized with a burning impatience at the subterfuge, the lies, Alison's desire grew cold. In the beginning, she had been stunned by the revelation of bodily passion, grasping greedily at what little time was alotted to them, snatched from busy routines, duties, responsibility to others, even grateful for such small mercies, but lately she had begun to dwell on what *could* be, if they had the courage to escape. More to the point, if *he* had the courage!

Frank knew what was passing through her mind. She did not need to put it into words. She wanted him to leave Elsie, to abandon his career in the church. He longed to do this too but, older than Alison, less wealthy, less protected from harsh realities, he was aware of the pitfalls hazarding such a course of action. They loved each other now with a passion that he had doubted would ever come his way, but how would that love survive possible poverty, the shame of living as illegal man and wife, shunned by friends and acquaintances, treated as outcasts, almost as lepers? Elsie would be vindictive, particularly if he was unable to support her in even so humble a state as he now did. She would deny him access to the children, dramatically enjoying the role of the wronged wife. It would give her the perfect excuse to drink excessively. She actively disliked Effie, illogically blaming the child for the traumatic birth that had robbed her of her health. He shuddered away from visions of Effie being left unprotected in her hands. But, if labelled an adulterer, there was not the faintest chance that any court of law would place her in his care.

There was no point in going over it again. Often before, they had wasted precious moments together in this unsatisfactory fashion, finding no solution. Slowly he walked across the green-carpeted glade, and crouched in front of her. Alison's heart felt physically sore as she looked into his face. It ached painfully – with love, with fear, with forebodings about their future. She noticed new lines etched there, and this hurt her too. He had been worrying. She had added to his troubles when all she wanted was to lessen them.

213

'So, what's to do?' he asked softly, bending forward and brushing her lips with a kiss as soft as spring rain.

She shook her head sadly. 'There's no answer, is there, Frank?' When he was close, she could never resist touching him. Her fingers brushed through the brown, silver-streaked hair above his ear. 'I only know that I come alive when I'm with you. When we part, there's no joy any more. You take all the colour with you. Everything is grey. Is it right that we should live like this?'

'Right? Wrong? I don't know one from the other any more.' He lay on the grass beside her, pulling her down into his arms. 'I want you, Alison. Call me selfish, call me wicked to make you suffer so, but I can't do without you.'

The dell was hot with the sun held between the high trees like a bowl of warmth. In the golden glow, the mystic pervading green, Alison's senses swam. The problems of how and why slipped away. She was no longer plain Lady Alison, charity supporter, dutiful sister. He was no longer a curate on the wrong side of thirty, tied to a drunken wife and four children. They became pagans, Eve and Adam, nymph and shepherd, god and goddess, forgetting everything except their need for each other.

Following an instinct as old as time, she turned on her back, urging him to follow, to cover her. In normal life she was stiff and self-conscious through force of habit, but with Frank she relaxed, eager for his flesh to be pressed against her own. Nothing mattered but getting closer, having more, giving all. Her soul opened up, and all that she was belonged to him. Joyfully she gave him every part of herself, and did not feel drained by the giving but filled to overflowing, receiving him in return.

Frank levered himself above her with straight, rigid arms, his eyes glazed with passion-induced blindness. 'I love you, Alison,' he gasped. 'I love you.'

'I know,' she whispered, and cupped the back of his head, burying her fingers in his thick hair till they touched the scalp.

Gradually he relaxed the muscles of his arms, and lowered himself on to her gently. He kissed her mouth, then pressed his face into the warm, naked hollow between her shoulder and neck. She could feel his heart pounding and the quickness of his breathing.

The perfume of crushed wild flowers was as intoxicating as wine as they celebrated the holy rite of man and woman. Alison drew it into her lungs, into her memory, as if to bottle it against the lonely times when he would not be lying in her arms.

The sunshine streamed into the breakfast-room of Selden's magnificent bachelor quarters in Jermyn Street. It lent additional brilliance to the dazzling yellow of the daffodils, the vivid red of the tulips which lined the window-boxes outside under the gaily striped awnings, and flashed on the plate and crystal which covered the well spread table.

The room was furnished with mahogany in the main, with a set of antique dining chairs and an oval lyre-legged table which had been sent up from the country. A few sporting prints and signed photographs of stars of the variety stage hung on the walls; a Ruff's guide and a racy French novel, a pile of daily finance papers and weekly sporting press were tossed carelessly on the chiffonier.

Selden sat at the head of the table, wearing a resplendent smoking jacket of blue and black brocade, struggling with the problem of the English breakfast. He had told Jenkins repeatedly that all he required after a hectic night was a pot of hot coffee, but the valet, no doubt driven by some unconfessed paternal urge which compelled him to try and fatten Selden up, insisted on

215

producing bacon and eggs. He pushed the plate of congealing rashers away, and waved an impatient hand at Jenkins indicating that he should refill his cup.

The valet obliged but with a sour cast of face. Though he never said as much, he carried about him a faint air of disapproval. 'Wouldn't you prefer a cup of tea, your Lordship?' he suggested gravely. 'Why not try to eat something? What does your Lordship say to half an anchovy on toast?'

Selden let loose a string of scathing profanities, telling Jenkins, in no uncertain terms, exactly what he could do with his tea and toast. Jenkins retired, offended, leaving Selden to the black coffee and his own black thoughts.

He had arrived in London yesterday and had been up very late the previous evening having gone out on the town. A quiet little dinner at the Corinthian Club with some particular cronies, had been followed by a box at the Eldorado, where more friends were discovered, both male and female. There was a Covent Garden ball to which he had certainly never intended to go, but to which he nevertheless went. That meant supper with a ravishing little brunette, a rather genteel girl of the upper echelon who was, in fact, no more than a high-class prostitute. He had drunk a great deal of champagne and wound up in her rooms and in her bed. Dismally he considered the possibility of winding up with a great deal more, a dose of the clap to be precise, if he was unlucky.

He had only a vague recollection of the evening's events, being uncertain as to whether he did or did not invite the whole company to go down to Armitstead House for the weekend, where he had assured them that his sister, would make them welcome. The whore too? He thought that her name might have been Violet, and in the cold light of day swore softly under his breath as his imagination called up visions of the remarkable possibilities of such a visit.

Selden was not happy. His emotions were a conglomeration of anger, bruised vanity, frustrated greed
and desire. In a raging fury, he had slammed out of the
house and driven to London at breakneck speed, hardly
giving Jenkins time to pack a bag. That bloody Brazilian
bitch! Who the hell did she think she was? Temper no
way improved by a colossal hangover, Selden dragged a
crumpled letter from the pocket of his jacket. Reading it
over again was like sucking on a nagging tooth.

'Dear Selden,' Camilla had penned in a large, scrawl-
ing hand.

> Sorry to disappoint you, but I'll not be taking you up on
> your offer of driving me to Ryehampton on Saturday next.
> As for the other matter we spoke of, well, I'm sure you'll
> agree that it was meant in jest. You couldn't possibly have
> been serious, could you? At any rate, I've made up my mind
> that such a thing is out of the question. I don't think we're in
> the least compatible. Yours sincerely, Camilla Ruthen.

'Bitch! Bitch!' he muttered. The paper was scented with
a heavy perfume that stirred his senses, reminded him of
her. He crushed it in his fist. It was only the second time
in his life that he had ever offered a woman marriage,
and she had had the temerity to refuse him! More fool
her! No woman turned him down without living to regret
it. Now I'll never get my hands on The Priory estate, he
thought, scowling and brooding, not while she lives, that
is. He was second in line, due to inherit if she died
without legitimate issue. Oh, he might be made
Marquis, if the Home Secretary thought fit, but what
about the land?
He knew why she had changed her mind. Abbey
Sutton was too small for anyone to as much as sneeze
without it being noised abroad within the hour. Darcy
Devereaux was at the bottom of it. He'd saved her from

217

the boggy moors or somesuch quixotic act of gallantry which, without a shadow of a doubt, had been motivated by desires not so very far removed from Selden's own. Josephine was furious, white-faced, thin-lipped, the archetypal woman scorned, out for Camilla's blood.

But, as he was driving along the London road, with Jenkins in the dickey-seat, hanging on for dear life, a plan had begun to formulate in the dark, convoluted recesses of Selden's mind. Subconsciously, this had been one of the factors which had set him winging there, besides the natural desire to escape, fling himself into congenial company, get drunk, and find a willing whore to hump. He had never been satisfied with Godwin's story and his cousin's abrupt appearance in their midst. Oh, there was no way he could disprove her claim. She was Edgar Ruthen's brat all right, but he had been worrying at the problem like a terrier with a bone.

He would have been quite content to let the matter rest, had she agreed to marry him. Now, all his energies were at white-heat, concentrated on finding out more about her past. She had hardly mentioned Brazil, never referred much to her life there, apart from dazzling party-pieces concerning jungle treks. The black woman knew. He was sure of that, but she was unlikely to be coerced into talking. He had already considered this possibility and rejected it. No, if he wanted to discover what had really happened in Bahia, then he must either visit the place himself or send someone else. Should he be able to unearth damning facts which would discredit her and if he contested the will, the English law courts might come down heavily in his favour. He was acquainted with several judges who were never averse to a generous bribe, and other law-men on whom he would not have the slightest compunction about using blackmail.

A cunning smile twisted Selden's thin, deceptively aesthetic features and his fist tightened on the letter with a force which he would have liked to vent on Camilla. If

218

what Josephine and rumour said was true, he needed to work fast before Darcy managed to slip a ring on her finger. He would be a formidable foe, and Selden was well aware of it. Darcy worshipped property, power and money as much as he did. Almost as possessive, very nearly as ruthless, he would fight to the last ditch and fight dirty, to preserve what he considered to be his by right.

Jenkins returned, standing to attention at the door. 'There's a *gentleman* outside, my Lord,' he announced starchily, laying doubting emphasis on the title. 'He says you asked him to call this morning.'

The coffee was clearing Selden's head. His memory returned, and with it an excitement comparable to that of the hunter closing in on his quarry. 'Show him in, Jenkins,' he said calmly, giving no indication of the thrill gripping his gut.

It was all coming back to him with a rush, and he rose to extend his hand to the man whom Jenkins ushered in. He was slight and dark, of some thirty-five years, and his quiet attire, a charcoal grey suit, with plain silk tie and pearl pin, contrasted strongly with the casual apparel of his host.

'Ah, Captain Martingale,' Selden greeted him affably, though repulsed by the man's flabby handshake.

'Lord Ruthen.' Martingale bowed slightly. 'I've come, as you requested.' His smile was oily, his accent difficult to place. It had a common twang though he called himself Captain. He had risen through the ranks in the Boer War, perhaps? Selden thought it unlikely.

'Sit down,' he waved a languid hand towards a chair. 'Have you breakfasted? Help yourself. My man will be only too delighted to have someone appreciate his cooking.'

'Thank you, sir.' Martingale eyed the loaded table with a look which indicated that he had not eaten, and probably did not know precisely where his next meal was coming from.

219

Selden resumed his seat and regarded the man closely, sipping his coffee the while. 'You've thought over what I mentioned briefly last night?' he said at last.

Martingale diverted his attention temporarily from the excellent cold pigeon pie. He dabbed his lips with a napkin, eyes wary but eager. 'I have, sir. Right up my street, if I may say so.'

'What is it you call yourself? A private investigator? Is that correct?' Selden drew a cigarette from a silver box, lit it and permitted a coil of blue smoke to drift from his nostrils.

'That's right, sir. I'm a great admirer of the writer, Conan Doyle, sir.' He had already invested his presence there with the vague importance of a secret mission.

'Ah, you model yourself on his fictional hero, the famous detective, Sherlock Holmes, do you?' The ironical twist of Selden's lips was lost on Martingale who was engaged in helping himself to another cup of coffee and some devilled kidneys from one of the silver entree dishes.

He nodded, mouth full, then swallowed hastily. 'Reading those novels inspired me to take up this sort of work, I'll confess.'

Selden was not interested in past history, only present and future results. He sat up, steepled his lean fingers together and stared at Martingale in a disconcerting way. 'You're free to work for me? Or have you too many other pressing assignments?'

As he had correctly surmised, Martingale was down on his luck. He was wearing the same suit as the night before. His collar was grubby, his cuffs frayed, his boots scuffed. Though he bore himself with a jaunty air, his eyes carried the haunted expression of a man who stayed away from his lodgings for fear of running into his creditors. Various subordinates and hangers-on had turned up in force at the Eldorado. He had been one of them, wangling an introduction. Selden had decided then that he would suit his purpose admirably.

'I am deuced busy,' Martingale lied, accepting a cigarette. 'But I might be able to squeeze you in. As it happens, the divorce case I was working on has just come to a satisfactory conclusion.' He leaned forward confidentially. 'A peer of the realm, no less. Hired me to watch his wife. Followed her to a hotel in Brighton where she met a man. Oh, I could tell his sort first off. One of those gigolos, if you take my meaning, years younger than her. A regular lounge-lizard. It wasn't easy, but I know the ropes. Managed to take some pictures of 'em with my camera. Caught 'em red-handed, strolling along the prom, arm in arm. Top-hole invention, cameras. Bet naughty wives hate 'em! They don't lie, you see, not like the ladies in question. I was paid a handsome fee for that – most handsome.' He did not add that this was six months ago and he had not worked since.

'You'd not find me ungenerous, should you decide to avail me of your valuable services,' Selden drawled, disliking this shabby man intensely, but convinced that he would be malleable.

Selden had perfected the highly effective trick of casually slipping questions into a conversation, and his friends had unwittingly told him all he needed to know about Martingale. He had the reputation for being a card-sharp; he was obsessed with betting – the horses, the dogs, prize-fights, anything at all which offered the precarious element of chance. On the surface it might appear that the odds on trusting him were abysmally long, but Selden enjoyed manipulating people. There was a fascination second to none in rooting out their little foibles and transforming them into destructive weapons. This shoddy 'Captain' would do what he wanted, with no questions asked, if the carrot dangled before his nose was attractive enough. And, when Selden had finally finished using him, no one would be the wiser if his body was found floating in the Thames one dark night. He would die unmourned and unsung.

Now Martinglae was hunched forward, looking imploringly at him. There was a patina of sweat dewing on his face, a crawling eagerness in his eyes. 'I'd be most honoured to do you a service, sir. You dropped a hint or two last night. Can you be more explicit?'

Selden lounged back in his chair and cocked his expensive shoes up on the table, well tailored legs crossed, seemingly preoccupied with examining his nails. The breeze wafted through the half-opened windows, stirring the drapes, bringing with it the rumble of the busy London streets, the cries of vendors, the noisy putt-putt of car engines, the clatter of hansom cabs as they bowled down Piccadilly. Dragging out the interview, amused by keeping the man in suspense, Selden yawned lazily as if he hadn't a care in the world.

Then, with an abruptness that made the detective jump, he suddenly swung his legs to the floor and sat bolt upright. Grey eyes as hard as quartz, voice equally hard, he hurled the words down the table at Martingale: 'I want you to go to South America.'

The clouds were gathering, the sun had gone, and the open window framed the illimitable space of the western sky, pale luminous flame, with night marching along the horizon. Like giants the sepia clouds towered up from the edge of the moor, fluid, ever-changing, solemn shapes passing across the vault of the heavens. In the garden, a solitary blackbird defied the encroaching darkness with a last sweet song.

Camilla paused, captivated by the beauty of the twilight seen from her bedroom window. The fullness of the year was fast approaching, and a soft southerly breeze ruffled the warm air. In a few weeks it would be Midsummer Eve, when she would hold her first party. The house was almost ready. Obadiah and his men had worked well and she was more than pleased with them.

Bonuses will be paid, she decided. They had certainly earned them, and a grand feast too, on the night of the solstice, with marquees set up on the lawn, trestle tables groaning with food, cider and ale flowing like water. Anyone who wanted to come from the village would be more than welcome. While they feasted out of doors in celebration of the house's debut and summer's pagan festival, she would be entertaining the nobility. Fireworks! Good old Sam, he had reminded her that she must order plenty. The groundsmen would organize bonfires. Oh, yes, much later when the more sober of her guests had departed, she'd dance with Leila round a bonfire. Sam would play his sacred drums. He was a qualified *tambourie*, deserving of fame and honour, but driving Beryl almost demented with his constant practice. It was nigh impossible to escape the *manman's* sonorous, throbbing rhythm, wherever one went in the house or gardens.

'Ah, there you are, Missy Camilla.' Leila came in at the door, for it was time for her to attire her mistress for dinner. 'I thought you were still outside.'

Camilla smiled, whirling around and plunging into the task of getting ready, while Leila helped her, shaking her head dubiously as she did so, although her dear charge bloomed with health and happiness. But when Leila remembered the cause, she was troubled. It had started on the night that Camilla had been trapped in the mists. A terrible night when Leila had thought never to see her again. Then, after dragging hours of anxiety, the horses had been ridden in. Darcy Devereaux had supported Camilla as they entered the house. His arms had been about her, such a big man, so tall and black-bearded, with an expression in his eyes from which the Creole had instinctively shrunk. If the devil himself had darkened the threshold of The Priory, she would not have been more scared.

Every time they met afterwards, and this was often for

he now came and went at will, he seemed to be searching
her face for something that he was disappointed not to
find. Was it her approval he sought? If that was so, then
he was doomed to disappointment for ever. Leila did not
like him, and that was that.

It had not taken Camilla long to recover from her
ordeal. She was young, strong and resilient and had been
through much worse trials than that, but whilst outwardly the same, those who knew her intimately were
aware of a change. She was every whit as interested in
the progress of the work. No aspect of the refurbishing
escaped her eagle eye, yet beneath her boisterous high
spirits there was an alarming preoccupation. Leila
would catch her gazing into space, eyes veiled and
dreamy, full lips slightly parted, curved into a musing
smile. She had seen that look on her face once before, and
had fervently prayed never to witness it again. Hélène
Gontard too had worn it once, long ago in Haiti.

Now, whilst Camilla held up first one gown and then
the other, uncharacteristically indecisive about which to
wear, Leila stared at the coloured glass at the top of the
window as if it were a magic mirror wherein her vision
might overpass the last twenty-three years. She was
transported back through time and space to the
luxurious colonial house in Port-au-Prince, finding
herself in Miss Hélène's exquisite bedroom where
everything, walls, rugs and drapes, was of pure, snowy
white. It was a hot, starry night, and those stars were
reflected in Hélène's eyes as she talked of Edgar Ruthen.

'I love him, Leila. He's asked Papa for my hand in
marriage.'

Detached, as if watching two other people act out this
scene, Leila saw herself as a handsome young woman
with dark features of extraordinary delicacy and
regularity, a sable Venus wearing a skirt of stiff scarlet
taffeta, a white blouse, a brilliant shawl, necklaces of
coloured beads, gold earrings. Her hair, an unbroken

224

sweep of shiny black, fell almost to her waist. Her finery denoted that she was about to chaperone her young mistress for an evening out – a ball, perhaps, a party. Whatever it was, Ruthen would be there too, as reckless a swashbuckler as any of the pirates who once haunted the waters around the island.

'Missy Hélène, you've fallen in love too fast,' the young Leila warned, apprehensive about him, that handsome aristocrat but lately arrived from England, bursting like a tornado into their lives, shaking the sleepy port out of its complacency. Not only was he devastatingly goodlooking, but also intelligent, cultured and witty. More than this, he glowed with a dark, destructive energy, hurtful to himself and fatal to those who fell beneath his spell.

'I don't care what you say, I'm going to marry him!' Hélène stared at her defiantly, so beautiful in her frilled white gown.

She was like a fragile magnolia blossom, her complexion very pale, the cheeks touched with the faintest cameo tint. Although born in Haiti, her background was French in every way. The lime and chestnut trees of the Paris she had never seen would have been a much more appropriate setting for her than bread-fruit and palms. The Gontards' only child, their baby, their jewel – indulged, adored, and pampered.

So, to please her, they had let her have Ruthen. It had been a splendid wedding, a costly affair with no expense spared. Hélène had never looked more radiant than when she walked down the aisle on Ruthen's arm and out into the baking heat of the crowded square. Poor girl, so ignorant, so totally unprepared. Leila's blood had run cold when she heard her screaming on the wedding night. Next morning she had crept from the bridal chamber subdued and frightened, a sensitive flower broken by a savage storm. She never smiled again from that day forward. Very soon, Ruthen had bundled his

225

household on to a boat and sailed for Bahia. Leila had no choice but to obey and go too, her thoughts locked in combat within her. By that time Camilla already lay in Hélène's womb.

The good time was over, for Hélène, for all of them. Ruthen made money fast with his cocoa and sugar plantations, his shares in the meat-canning factories, his interests in rubber, but he was a man blinded by a mirage in the pursuit of which he stumbled, year after year. Many others before him had also become what was known as *quaqueros*, those who wander in the *llano* and forests seeking lost treasure.

The history of South America was a bloody one; the persecution of the Indians by the Spanish and Portuguese; the arrival of the first slaves from Africa; the haphazard settling of European emigrants, the use of its rivers and coasts as hideouts for filibusters of all nations. Its gold, silver and diamond mines drew men like magnets, despite the hardships. The legends about buried treasure were legion, but it was not an ill-gotten pirate hoard that Ruthen sought. There was more to it than that.

Even before they reached Rubera, his true nature had been revealed. He was selfish, utterly heartless, and became violent if thwarted in any way. He could not resist women, and made no attempt to conceal his adultery from his wife, indeed he delighted in flaunting it in her face. He drank heavily, and grabbed greedily at every sensation that came his way, but through all and above all, he hunted for an elusive prize, the secret of which he guarded jealously.

Helplessly, Leila watched Hélène age prematurely. Her beauty faded and finally vanished under his tyranny. There was only one person who did not tremble in his presence, and that was his child, born nine months after they were married. Camilla adored her father, regarding him as an omnipotent god. For the early years of her life, he reciprocated this adoration, proud of her prettiness, her wit, disrupting routine by insisting on scooping her up from her cot, setting her high on his shoulder while she squealed with merriment, showing her off to his disreputable companions. He ignored Hélène's objections to the child being exposed to a gang of drunkards, wasters and cut-throats. He cursed Leila with a fluid stream of filthy epithets if she as much as hinted that what he was doing was unwise.

This idyll of mutual admiration between father and daughter ended with brutal abruptness. One night, the child rose from bed on hearing him come in. She inadvertently burst into the midst of a vicious quarrel. Ruthen was mad with drink, her mother half insane with jealousy and grief. Camilla saw him knock her to the floor, saw him battering her, heard her screams for mercy which he did not heed. From that moment on, her love turned to hate. The feeling intensified when Hélène died shortly after. It grew like a demon foetus within her as she matured, blossoming to terrible fruition when –

'Leila! Don't stand there dreaming! Which d'you think suits me best? The gold satin or the crimson silk?' Camilla's voice, so like her mother's, catapulted the Creole back to the present.

She was wearing a black slip, the bodice brief, the skirt flowing down to her satin slippers where it foamed into lace flounces, like the dress of a flamenco dancer. Her skin was a darker hue, for the days had been sunny and she had, more than once, indulged in her immodest habit of swimming nude. There was suppressed excitement in her every movement, and it was not hard to guess the cause. Darcy Devereaux was coming to dinner.

Leila stood, knuckles digging into her hips, struggling to push back the memories that still clouded her mind. There was a puzzled frown between Camilla's brows. She expected Leila's approbation, was lost and uncertain if it was lacking. The Creole glued a smile on her

227

face and gave her attention to the pressing problem of Camilla's evening wear.

'Why you so choosy all of a sudden? You know you'd look gorgeous in an old sack-bag!' she grumbled as she picked up a heap of discarded gowns, flung carelessly across the back of a chair. 'Don't know why you're bothering to ask me. You don't listen to a word I say no more.'

Camilla was instantly contrite. She hated to be at cross-purposes with Leila but, coax as she might, she could not extract a single word of praise from her lips concerning Darcy. When she thought about it in rare moments of good sense, her heart plummeted, for Leila's intuition had always been proved right. She had been successful in silencing the warning voice inside her own head that had advised caution, but it was difficult to deny Leila.

Because she was afraid, she lifted her determined chin obstinately. 'I can't see why you're in such a horrid mood because I've invited Mr Devereaux to dine,' she said haughtily, seizing the silk gown and pulling it on over her head.

'It's not right and proper, Missy Camilla, and you know it!' Leila's mouth shut like a rat trap as, grimly, she fastened the small row of gilt buttons that closed the scarlet material across Camilla's tanned shoulder blades. 'You've no business entertaining a man alone. Only bad girls do that. Bad, bad girls with bad reputations.'

'Poppycock!' Camilla glared at her in the cheval mirror with was suspended on turned pillars in the centre of the dressing-table. 'We're in England now, not stuck in some backwater.'

'Same rules apply,' Leila replied stubbornly. 'Bad girls are bad girls all the world over, and men're out for themselves. All they want is to do rude things to 'em.'

Camilla laid her hairbrush down with slow deliber-

228

ation, turning on the stool to confront her. It was high time they had this out, once and for all. 'Listen to me, Leila. I may have made a shocking mistake once, but I don't intend to repeat it. I shall never give myself to a man again until I've a wedding ring on my finger. D'you understand?'

'I understand that you believe what you're telling me at the moment.' Leila lost none of her severity. 'You're one hell of a good liar to yourself, Camilla Ruthen, and take that uppish look off your face when you're talking to me! You've not grown so mighty grand or so big that I can't wallop you!'

'Don't scold, Leila.' Camilla's arrogant front collapsed. She sank her head in her hands with such a despairing gesture that Leila touched her bowed shoulder. Sensing her softening, childishly in need of sympathy though she could not quite fathom why, she leaned against her solid body, breathing in the smell of Leila which had been a source of comfort for as far back as she could remember. 'You know that you can sit in the dining-room and chaperone us the whole time, if you want. I'm not about to leap into bed with him or anything like that. I'm lonely. Oh, yes I am! Don't start saying that this is ridiculous because of the constant stream of workmen, and Sam, Wilf, Beryl and you. I'm still lonely. I need a man to lean on. A man of my own to share this great place with.'

She could feel a chuckle shaking through the *mambo*. Her deep voice was filled with laughter as she said: '*You*, missy? The most self-willed little puss ever born, who likes nothing better than to queen it wherever she goes? *You* in need of a lord and master?'

It was ridiculous, and Camilla knew it, but it was the truth. No, not precisely. She was too honest to cheat. It was not just any man she needed – it was Darcy. It was all past hope or remedy and she could hardly tell how it had come about. After the personal tragedy in Rubera

229

that had left her like a sick, wounded animal, she had
vowed to isolate herself from male company, to go out no
more, to avoid all change in the convent-like way of life
she had adopted. She had been desperately ill, sick in her
mind even though her body had healed, so sick that she
had allowed hatred to corrode her soul, a black, vitriolic
hatred against the man whom she blamed for her
unhappiness, knowing no rest until she had engineered
his death. Even then there had been no peace – not on
the liner or in London or Paris, not even at The Priory,
until the night when Darcy had taken her into his arms.
It was as if she came to herself then, having passed
through some ghastly nightmare, waking to light and
joy.

Then she spoke the words that Leila had been
dreading. 'I think I'm falling in love with him.'

The Creole sank to her knees beside her, velvety eyes
staring up into her face. 'Don't do it!' she pleaded, hands
clasping hers with a fierceness that hurt. 'Stay as you
are. One day you'll find a man worthy of you, but not
this one. Have I ever been wrong? Didn't I warn you
about André? You took no notice, and look what
happened.'

'But why, Leila? Why don't you like Darcy? He's a
fine man. He's not tried to seduce me. All that he's given
me is laughter, affection, knowledge of the land. He'd
make a good husband, I know it.' Camilla's eyes shone
with that bedazzled light which stabbed through Leila's
heart like a sword.

'Not for you,' she answered firmly, rising and folding
her shawl about her, struck by a sudden chill wind
blowing from an icy future.

'Why?' Camilla insisted, standing too, back straight,
head high, willing her to find one good reason for
doubting his integrity.

'He's too much like your father.'

Camilla flinched. The lamp-lit room seemed to

230

darken. Leila's voice woke the echoes, calling up those slimy things that lurked in the depths of memory. Anger whipped through her, roaring into flame.

'You lie!' she shouted, snatching up the lamp and running towards the secret room. 'He's not like him. Come and look, you stupid woman!'

The small room was cold. It always was, even when a blazing fire roared up the chimney. It did not frighten Camilla. She had taken up the gauntlet, challenging it with her own strong personality. The most rare and beautiful objects in the house had been gathered there, as if such perfection dared anything twisted and ugly to survive. She had eased herself into its atmosphere gradually, making her peace with the portrait of her father as a young man and, after taking the proper precautions, opening herself to that other – the sad, sobbing entity who haunted it. She had not seen the hand prints again, wondering if it had been a figment of an overwrought imagination, but sometimes she felt a presence, heard a sigh, smelled that stagnant odour. Just sometimes, when the moon had dwindled to a faint, thin crescent and the night was dark. It was a shy ghost and, in common with most psychic phenomena, refused to come out when called. Leila and she had sat there for hours on end, performing rituals, encouraging it to show itself. Nothing had happened, the room was placid and innocent as a summer lake. But, when she least expected it and had almost forgotten about it, there would come that feeling of being watched by something invisible.

There was nothing in the room on that evening, only the portrait with its mocking half smile and the eyes which seemed to follow wherever she went – nothing but Camilla's anger which buffeted the walls and disturbed the figures on the Gobelin tapestries. She faced the painting, making herself examine those hated features minutely to see if Leila spoke the truth.

The Creole was at her shoulder, and she crossed

231

herself as she too stared at the canvas image of Ruthen. 'I was right,' she whispered hoarsely. 'It's what I've felt about Mr Devereaux from the first moment. They're too alike.'

Camilla had always loved and respected Leila, looking upon her as a second mother, but now she was possessed of the violent urge to hit her. Leila started and backed off, hands outstretched as if to push away something evil. This was not the girl she had reared! She hardly recognized her, so demoniacal and dangerous in her rage. This creature with the venom pouring from her blazing eyes could not deny her parentage. In that fraught moment, she was Ruthen's daughter, through and through.

'You're crazy!' Camilla stormed. 'Darcy is Darcy, and no one else! He bears not the slightest resemblance to that devil up there! You insult him if you think that!'

Before Leila could form a reply, they heard Beryl's cheerful voice at the bedroom door. 'Lady Camilla! Mr Devereaux is here.'

'Very well, Beryl. Show him into the drawing-room. I shan't be many minutes.' Camilla gave Leila a final, searing glare and hurried over the completion of her toilet, before running down to meet him.

Well, Leila need have had no fears for my virtue during dinner, she thought some time later, glancing at her newly appointed butler and several footmen who, impeccably dressed and solemn as judges, waited at table. It gave her a deal of quiet satisfaction to be seated there in her own establishment, entertaining a man such as Darcy. The Priory was something of which to be justly proud, hardly recognizable from the wreck into which she had stepped at Christmas.

The dining-room was magnificent, every Tudor feature lovingly cherished and painstakingly restored. The paintings, dispatched to Sothebys for cleaning, had come home to roost, as fresh and glowing as the day the artists put brush to canvas. She had discovered a set of rare Breughel miniatures tucked away in an obscure corner. These had been given pride of place. Throughout the main rooms, the ceilings, when washed, had revealed a great diversity of friezes and decorated pilasters. She was particularly pleased with this one which had a painted *rainceau* of fanciful figures. The furniture charmed her, some elaborately carved Elizabethan pieces, others designed in the eighteenth century. Silver had been unearthed from the backs of musty cupboards, and a huge selection of fine china. If Beryl reported some essential item lacking, then Camilla ordered it from London.

'You've managed to secure the services of an excellent cook,' remarked Darcy when the footmen took away the final course. 'I've never tasted such delicious food except in France. Congratulations, Camilla.'

She was smoking a cigarette as they lingered over coffee and liqueurs. 'I'm glad you approve. Mrs Williams has just joined us. She's one of the housekeeper's friends.' She gave a nod of dismissal to Harvey, the butler, who bowed himself out. Damn Leila, she was thinking. I'm not a child to be ordered about in my own house!

There had already been ructions when Camilla had moved the Creole and her son from the tiny nook next to the Master Chamber, returning it to its original use as a walk-in dressing-room, complete with racks for clothing, chests of drawers, and long mirrors. Now that the rest of the bedrooms were habitable she had given Leila an apartment of her own, some distance down the corridor. Annoyed and alarmed, Leila had protested that it was too far away. Supposing Camilla needed her in the night? What of the *duende*? Camilla had replied confidently that she would deal with the ghost, but she did concede to Leila's pleas to have a bell in operation between their rooms.

Warmed with wine and good food, Camilla relaxed and crossed her silk-clad legs beneath the rustling crimson gown. Darcy was a most pleasant guest. He had a fund of amusing stories, many of which concerned country life and his boyhood in Norfolk. Camilla was testing him every inch of the way. Despite Leila's worries, she was acting with the utmost caution, sounding him out, watching his reactions, trying not to be blinded by his stunning good looks. He exuded male arrogance and a kind of animal magnetism, mixed with a powerful charisma all his own. In the normal way such characteristics would have made her run in the opposite direction. She had good cause to avoid sexually attractive men, but his other qualities were disarming. He was well educated, a man equally conversant with politics, art and literature, certainly no bumpkin. Yet when he spoke of his herds, his farm and lands, his eyes glittered with a genuine enthusiasm which was infectious.

'You like it here, in Wessex?' he asked, leaning towards one of the candles to light his cigar. The shining table, the panelled walls, swallowed up the soft gleam and left only his face, with a halo around it, and the darkness beyond.

'Oh, yes, very much.' Camilla spoke calmly, but her nerves were vibrating at his closeness.

They had never been alone in this way before. It was almost a domesticated scene. What would it be like, she wondered, if we could sit like this every night, talking, drinking, smoking and exchanging views? And later, in the bedroom? So far, he had only kissed her once, in that hour of mist and fear. She had waited. Oh, she admitted it. But he had not attempted such intimacy again. Was it out of respect? Or didn't he find her desirable? Was he, perish the thought, still finding satisfaction with Josephine?

She stole a quick glance at his face. The planes and hollows were lit from below by the candle's flame.

Deep-set eyes, hawk nose, finely shaped head with the hair curling about his ears. In the golden glow his skin looked dark as an Arab's. The sun was strong and he spent much time out of doors. Was the rest of his body sun-kissed too? The thought sent an ache stabbing through her loins, shaming her. There was the flicker of a smile beside his mouth that showed he was sensitive to her bewildered feelings.

'I believe that we're behaving in a somewhat irregular manner,' he remarked, resuming his seat, long legs in snug-fitting black trousers stretched towards hers under the table. He laid his head against the back of the chair, exhaling smoke through his nostrils up towards the scrolls ornamenting the ceiling. 'All very well in the racy, artistic set of Chelsea, but not in Abbey Sutton.'

'Oh? I wasn't aware of anything improper. I'll call in Leila if you like. I'm sure she'd love to sit in a corner with her tatting and make certain that I don't endanger your reputation.' There was a sarcastic edge to her voice as she struggled to play down the growing sensuality that was reaching out towards her from his recumbent body.

His eyes crinkled with laughter at her attempt to be pompous. She relaxed and laughed too. He noticed that she had a delightful, ringing laugh and realized that he had not often heard it. 'I only meant that it's a little unusual for a couple who aren't even engaged, to spend an evening alone like this. Selden would be furious if he knew.'

This sobered her and her eyes sparked. 'Selden? What's it to do with him?'

He shrugged in answer and reached for his cigar. 'Well, he does have a rather, shall we say, *possessive*, attitude towards you. Almost as if you two had some sort of understanding.'

'The damned nerve of the man!' Her capable fists were clenched on the inlaid wood, the tiger's-eye giving off sparks. 'I've given him no cause. In fact, he had a letter from me not long ago advising him quite bluntly not to entertain hopes in my direction.'

As he looked at her angry face, he stubbed out his cigar and moved his chair closer. Her subtle perfume fascinated him. The fire of her rage excited him. He felt the muscles in his groin tighten. When he had first set eyes on this exotic woman, he had determined that she should belong to him. He was too cynical and world-weary to call his emotion by the fanciful name of love. Frankly, he had never experienced that self-sacrificial fire which drove the most sensible men mad, knocking them off balance so that they behaved in a most abnormal way. Desire was a much more comfortable bedfellow, and he had felt desire many times over. That was something he *could* relate to.

The sober golds and russets of the walls repeated their highest note in her burnished hair. He liked the fine texture of her skin. The proud line of her lips appealed to him, as did her direct gaze, and he was aware of the thickness and length of her lashes. Her anger was electrifying. He was glad it was directed towards Selden, not himself.

'I'm relieved to hear it. Does that mean that I'm in with a chance?' Before she could move, he lifted her right hand to his lips and her skin burned as she felt the brush of his beard on the back of it. She did not pull away, allowing it to remain linked with his. Then one of his long, sun-browned fingers touched her ring. 'I noticed this the day I met you. What an interesting piece.'

'It belonged to my father.' Her heart was thundering so hard that she was surprised he could not see her breasts shaking. Still she did not deny her hand the comfort of being held in his. He was no longer subjecting her to his disturbing gaze, his attention focused on the tiger's-eye. Taking a deep breath to steady herself, she added: 'I discovered a portrait of him in a room upstairs and the ring was missing from it. This is puzzling, as I don't recall ever seeing him without it on.'

236

'May I see the painting?' His blue eyes fastened on her face, rendering her tongue-tied for a second.

Then: 'I suppose so – but it's in my study – leading from my bedroom –' she faltered, praying that he did not think she was being coquettish and giving him an open invitation for a further, much more private, meeting.

'So? We'll just have to take Leila with us, won't we?' His smile was sardonic but, as he spoke, his arm came to rest on her shoulders, hand turning her towards him. His smiling lips hovered over hers, so close that she could see the individual silky hairs of his beard, and the point where the long sideburns joined it each side of his lean jaw, and the quality of the tanned skin between.

He was going to kiss her. She knew it, her mind arching away from the encounter, her body yearning towards it. There was but an instant between his intention and its completion, a moment when a hundred thoughts chased through her brain, denial, longing, possibilities. Then Harvey sailed in like a flagship, a stately, liveried being with much gold braid about him. He stood at the door and looked into the distance, over their heads.

'There's a personage in the hall, your Ladyship, asking to see Mr Devereaux. He gave his name as Josh the Cowman.'

Darcy swore under his breath, throwing down his napkin and getting to his feet. 'Excuse me, Camilla.' He gave her a bow, whilst she thanked heaven for the interruption. It gave her a breathing space during which she might marshal her flagging forces. But even as he strode towards the door her wayward instincts were admiring him. What a charming, handsome fellow to be sure. What impressive shoulders, elegant waist and sleek hips.

He was only gone for a few moments, frowning when he returned. 'Damn it! That was my herdsman. I'm afraid I'm going to have to leave you.'

237

She was on her feet, wide eyes searching his grim face. 'What's happened?' Her own disappointment was swallowed up in concern for him.

'My prize Devon cow is having trouble delivering her calf. Josh can't find the vet. He must have been called out elsewhere. I'll have to see what I can do. She's too valuable a beast to lose.' He spoke crisply over his shoulder, already halfway to the door.

'May I come too?' Now why did I say that, she was thinking as he nodded and she followed him into the Great Hall. Of course, I'll convince myself that it's to learn another farming lesson. In reality, I know that I can't bear to let him go.

Josh waited there, a smallish man, clad in cord breeches and gaiters, his face weather-beaten and wrinkled, his moustache and beard sparse and grizzled. Camilla found a wrap, while Darcy stood in muttered conversation with his cowherd as he shrugged his shoulders into his overcoat and clapped on his hat.

'Ready?' He looked up sharply as Camilla ran down the stairs.

'Ready,' she answered, velvet cape clutched about her, aware of informality coupled with a sense of fitness, as if she was his long-standing partner, accustomed to going out into the night with him.

A great, full orange moon hung in the sky. The air was warm. Somewhere in the woods a nightingale staged an operatic performance. Darcy led the way on his horse. Camilla climbed into the gig in which Josh had covered the distance from Chalkdown Farm. She was not sure of the way, though once, in daylight, she had circled its perimeter on Jeddah, reconnoitring enemy territory. It was odd to think that she had looked on Darcy as a foe. Was it only six months ago? It seemed that she had lived a lifetime since then.

The shaggy little cob trotted briskly, the gig's wheels bumping over the uneven track. Its oil lamps gave off a pallid light. The bushes were full of rustling sounds; shadows lay like still pools beneath the dark spread of the trees; once, twice, eyes glowed red in the hedgerow, flashed and vanished. The sound of the hoof-beats of Darcy's mount changed, no longer thudding over the dry dirt road, now a hollow clatter crossing the stone bridge. Unseen water rushed below them, darkly swirling, rippled by moonlight. On between fields where horses, disturbed by their passing, kicked and neighed and galloped behind the fences, like elfin steeds, ghostly grey, flecked with dull white.

A yellow glimmer shone ahead. 'We're 'ere,' grunted Josh, addressing her for the one and only time.

Shapes gained form and substance, turning into a long, low house, with a beetling thatch above dormer windows. A dog began to bark. Josh steered the gig towards the barn. The door was open, sending forth a beam of misty light. Darcy swung down from his saddle, threw the reins over a rail and, without stopping for Camilla, ducked his head under the lintel and disappeared from view. Josh scratched about beneath his battered hat and climbed out of the gig stiffly.

' 'Tis m' bad back, milady – damp's got in m' bones,' he grumbled, wiping a hand down the side of his breeches before offering it to her. Camilla grasped it firmly and alighted. The yard had been swept clean, but even so she picked her way carefully. Her attire was most unsuitable for a visit to a cowshed.

I must be out of my mind, she thought. I could be tucked up in a comfortable bed by now, not acting the midwife to a stupid cow. Oh, lord, I'll be in for a lecture from Lcila in the morning. She'll not believe me, of course, having convinced herself that I was off spooning with Darcy in the moonlight. It was difficult to discern details, but she did catch sight of another shed, its roof supported by pillars, cart-shafts gleaming within, steep-sided wagons, the dark solid bulk of a steam tractor. Attracted by unusual noises so late, cattle were drifting across from the fields beyond, great white horns lifted expectantly, ponderous, short-legged, their red coats turned to rusty black by the moon, white tail-tags swishing. Their deep lowing was echoed from within the barn.

Holding her skirts high, Camilla trailed after the men. Josh was leaning with his forearms on the stall wherein stood the labouring animal. Hat pushed to the back of his tousled head, face deadly serious, he offered advice and the benefit of years herding cattle. Extra lamps had been hung on hooks from the beams. Darcy had thrown aside his coat, fastened a leather apron about his waist and rolled his sleeves up beyond the elbow. Josh glanced curiously at Camilla, then back to the drama of birth, finding it of much greater significance.

'The poor old gal's been strugglin' fer hours,' he observed, the length of straw stuck between his teeth moving from side to side. 'She's gittin' tired, sir.'

'Pity you couldn't get hold of that bloody vet!' snapped Darcy, forehead rucked. 'He's off boozing somewhere, like as not. Did you try the pub?'

Josh shook his head. 'Tried 'em all, sir – not a sign of 'im. 'Course, I did 'ear as 'ow ole Jarge Pugh's got the belly-ache. 'Ee don't 'old wi' doctors, allus' calls the vet out – swears by 'orse pills 'stead of med'cine, 'ee do.'

'That's a fat lot of help!' Darcy was in a black mood. This was the cow's first calf. She was a fine beast, a perfect example of the Devon Red, and had won several rosettes at the last agricultural show. He had entertained high hopes of breeding from her, and could have strangled the vet with his bare hands for not being on call. It wasn't as if he hadn't alerted the man that his help might be required. He turned to his second-in-command. 'Come on, Josh, it's all down to us, I guess.'

'What can I do to help?' Camilla asked, feeling inadequate, uncertain as to why she had come.

240

'Go and make a billycan of tea.' Darcy did not even bother to look up, intent on examining the cow. 'Kitchen's on the right. Mrs Loftes is away. I expect you'll find where everything's kept. Oh, and bring the brandy bottle too.'

It was a strange night, with events blurring into one another. First the large kitchen, warm, homely, with cats snoozing before the range. She knew that Darcy had a housekeeper, but had never been inside the farmhouse before. It was shining and clean. Obviously Mrs Loftes was a good manager, and it did not take Camilla long to locate the things needed. She set the can on the trivet to bring the tea to the boil, remembering that men usually liked it strong. It was a little reminiscent of the times she had cooked over campfires, living rough as she trekked through the wilderness with her father. Milk stood on marble slabs in the dairy-room, set between two thick inner stone walls for the sake of coolness. She added it to the reddish brew, ladled in sugar, gave it a hearty stir, found the brandy and a tin filled with fruit buns, and placed the lot on an outsize metal tray.

'Mind 'ow you goes, milady,' Josh cautioned, broad face wreathed in smiles as she reappeared in the barn, staggering under the burden. 'My word – fancy you comin' along. Still, if you'm goin' ter be a farmer's missus, you got ter git used ter the birthin'. No good bein' squeamish like.'

Farmer's wife? Camilla mulled this over during the next few hours. Squeamish? She was that, all right, particularly when she saw Darcy's arm disappearing inside the cow as he tried to manipulate the calf. The sweat ran down his face in rivulets. Great wet arcs spread out at his armpits and up from his waist. He swore continually, while the patient beast permitted his interference trustingly, head lowered, mournful sounds issuing from her.

Camilla pitied her anguish, mind swinging back to a

241

hot, steamy night in the previous year when she too had writhed and strained to bring life into the world. Alone with Leila, in a hut on the edge of the forest, riven with pain, with shame and, in the end, with black despair when her child had been born dead.

'I can't shift the little bugger.' Darcy's voice recalled her to the barn. 'One of its damned legs is stuck in the way.'

At long last, with the aid of a rope and his considerable strength, the calf made its reluctant appearance, wet and shiny, to be lowered tenderly to the straw by Josh. There was a tense silence, then it jerked its folded limbs and gave itself a shake while the cow nuzzled it. Her big soft tongue caressed, fondled, licked the little creature clean. Camilla walked out into the dawn with the pale stars twinkling and the moon still visible, pondering on the mystery of birth, and that even greater riddle – death.

Darcy stood in the yard, stripped to the waist while Josh worked the pump. The cold water cascaded over his muscular torso and darkened the hair on his chest while he gasped at the shock, laughing too, pleased with the night's work which had given them a fine bull calf.

'He'll be a good 'un, Josh. His sire's a champion. We'll have him servicing the heifers when he gets older,' he shouted, running his hands through his dripping black hair and shaking droplets from his beard. Then he caught sight of Camilla and his grin broadened. He seemed not in the least perturbed because she had come upon him when he was half-naked.

She stood there motionless, unable to drag her eyes away, her breath lodged somewhere in her throat, an odd curling feeling in the pit of her stomach. It was as if those clothes which he normally wore were an artificial camouflage he was forced to adopt to fit in with his everyday surroundings. Without them, he seemed larger, even more powerful. His wet hair glistened darkly. There was a sheen of moisture on his bare chest,

242

his wide shoulders. The dark trousers emphasized the slimness of his hips. There was a dangerous quality about him. It frightened Camilla, even while she responded to it. In stunned fascination, she watched as Josh handed him a towel and he rubbed it over his body, in no hurry to dress, taking his time, aware of her eyes. She was relieved yet disappointed when at last that glorious, sun-browned flesh was hidden by his white shirt.

'I'll take you home,' he said as he walked across to her, leading her to his horse, swooping her up and placing her at the front of the saddle. 'But first, there's something I want you to see.'

Both of them had gone beyond normal weariness, coming out on the other side of it with that light-headed feeling which follows being up all night. Out of the grey void a bird piped aloud, then another, to be answered by trills of ecstasy. Before ever the sun edged up over the horizon, when only the faintest perceptible glow indicated approaching day, the birds awoke and sang. They roused the barnyard roosters who added their raucous challenge to the ever-increasing chorus. Camilla heard the notes and rejoiced.

She was content yet disturbed as she leaned back against Darcy's chest, his arms around her as they rode, the damp smell of his hair intoxicating her nostrils, mingled with that musky, masculine body odour with which she was all too familiar. Her flesh responded to it, making her ache with desire. It was so long now since she had been loved by a man. Up and up they climbed, two solitary people braving the daybreak wildness of the moors. Vaporous wisps hung over the woods, presaging a hot day. A pearly haze was spreading out over the east turning to molten gold. The dark clouds were fading to delicate duck-egg blue. Everything sparkled, fresh-washed with dew, the clear air like chilled champagne.

Camilla and Darcy stood in the middle of a circle of

stones. Shards of light caught them, flickered over them. Large, eerie, the ancient mystic ring dwarfed the human man and woman. Placed there by long-forgotten tribes whose history had never been recorded, they dominated the plateau, and all around was the emptiness of the moor.

'It's wonderful.' Camilla was filled with awe. What hands had hewn these monuments? How long had they stood like sentinels on this spot? They were as mysterious as the barrows, keeping their secrets, hugging their magic to themselves. They did not speak to her for she was a *mambo's* pupil, giving her allegiance to far older gods than the Celtic ones.

Darcy's arm was around her waist, his face upturned to the sky. 'It's believed that if you dare to stand inside the circle, bad luck will dog you if you don't follow the sun from east to west.'

'Do you believe it? Are you superstitious, Darcy?' As he looked at the broad vault above them, so she filled her sight with his face.

His eyes pinned hers, expressing indomitable energy and fire though dark ringed from the sleepless night. 'One can't fail to be, living out here so near to the earth.' His arms tightened, pressing her close to the heat of his body. 'One thing's for sure. I'll follow the sun, Camilla. I don't want my luck to turn, not now I've found you.'

'You think it's luck that has brought us together?' she whispered, though all coherent thought had fled. 'You may live to regret it, Darcy. I've never considered myself lucky. Be careful that the misfortune that's haunted me doesn't brush off on you.'

He laughed confidently, head up, beard jutting towards the sky, hair tousled by the breeze. 'I defy fate! If you love me, if you'll consent to be my wife – let it do its worst! Nothing will succeed in parting us.' Then those blue eyes returned, devouring her. 'Do you love me,

Camilla? Will you dare heaven's wrath? Will you give me your solemn vow, here in this magic circle?'

Ferment stirred in her. Was she prepared to give up her hard-won independence? For love, for that fragile thing composed of desire, need and loneliness? It offered a pale hope of sharing, of touching souls. How elusive, how impossible a dream.

'Camilla. My Camilla, you'll not refuse me, will you?' His breath was against her mouth, his beard soft as velvet brushing her cheek. It was impossible to resist, and part of her did not want to, that wild reckless part which Leila knew so well and dreaded so much.

She was laughing, almost crying, answering breathlessly: 'All right. I'll marry you, Darcy – if that's what you want.'

His hands were on her shoulders, gripping her, shaking her, the first rays of the sun reflected in his eyes. 'Do *you* want it? Answer me!'

He seemed almost heroic as he stood towering above her, masterful, audacious, beautiful, at one with the strength and power of the stones. 'Yes! Of course I want it!'

His magnetism was so compelling that she cast aside her fears and yielded herself freely to his hard embrace. As his mouth closed over hers and the hot blood surged through her, beating in fierce turbulence like a stormy sea, her ears caught a faint sound. Mingled with the breeze whistling around the stone circle and the high, sad lament of a curlew, she heard the throbbing of drums.

She started, quieting, straining to catch their message. A fierce note, calling, insistent. The fine down rose on her limbs, for these were not joy-drums. They held a dark, rolling, warning note.

2

The gypsy wagon creaked as Alison started up when Frank mounted the wooden steps. Then she was in his arms, hugging him to her with a more than normal urgency.

'There's something I must tell you!' She buried her face against his white shirt front, inhaling summer, the scent of hay and flowers, the strong masculine sweat engendered by his cycle ride from the village.

He held her slightly away from him, looking down into her face, his eyes humorous, questioning. 'What is it, darling?'

'I'm pregnant,' she burst out, forgetting all the carefully prepared speeches she had been rehearsing ever since she came back from Ryehampton.

His eyes widened. Joy flashed across his suntanned features. 'Alison! Is it true?'

How grateful she was to him for that moment. Had he been annoyed, afraid, hesitant, then her own worries would have risen in a muddy flood to swamp her happiness. But his reaction had been an instinctive one of unalloyed delight because the one he loved was carrying his child. All the difficulties of the situation would surface later, but just for a few, precious seconds, they could stand there in the dusky warmth of the wagon, holding each other, rejoicing and welcoming the new life growing secretly inside her.

She gave a shaky laugh. 'Oh, I'm sure, all right. I've missed two periods, so took myself off to the town, pretended I was married and made an appointment with a doctor I don't know. I wore Mamma's wedding ring, good job I kept it in my jewel case, and found it amazingly easy to lie. I didn't even blush. Aren't you proud of me, Frank?'

'Very proud.' His hands were smoothing her back and her skin tingled, even though it was covered by her thin lawn blouse. 'So what did the medical man have to say about my woman and my child?'

'He was pleased with me, said that I was perfectly normal and there was nothing to worry about.' She did not add that it had been terribly embarrassing, having to undress behind a small screen and lie on the high, hard examination couch. The leatherette covering had been cold and slippery, the smooth sheet tied across it too impersonal, hygienic and clinical.

A prim, gaunt, crisply starched nurse had been present, and Alison had imagined a suspicious gleam in her frosty eye. Had she guessed the truth? Dr Greenway could not have been more encouraging however, telling her not to be tense, assuring her that it would not hurt. Gentle pressure on her stomach, gentle rubber-gloved fingers slipping into her vagina. Yes, she was two, almost three, months pregnant.

As she told Frank about it, her eyes sparkled, and the warm tones of the midsummer heatwave flushed her face. She was happy, fiercely, radiantly happy. Even her walk was different. She had noticed it herself as she left the doctor's surgery and passed along the busy Ryehampton streets towards the station. There was a bounce in her step and, catching a glimpse of herself in a shop window, she had slowed down, thinking: That person reflected there is going to be a mother. In January, Dr Greenway had said, beaming, kindly, pleased to be the bringer of such good news. It didn't show, so far. Her stomach was flat, her waist slim, but her breasts were heavier, a tracery of faint blue veins marking the creamy flesh, the nipples darker, more prominent.

Frank was aware of them, unbuttoning her blouse and

247

slipping a hand inside. 'Our baby won't go hungry,' he murmured, then he patted her hips with his other hand. 'The doctor was right. No trouble there. You're built for childbearing. My dearest love, I can't believe it!'

This jarred, and the world began to intrude. She found his statement slightly ridiculous. After all, Elsie had borne four children. Hadn't it occurred to him that conception would more than likely take place? But I knew, she thought, and it didn't stop me from sleeping with him. She had been terrified when her period was late and then did not happen at all. So terrified that she felt sick every time she thought about it. At first, she had tried to tell herself that it had been late before, then remembered that, in those days, she'd been a virgin, not feverishly coupling with her lover at every possible opportunity.

She had decided to say nothing to him until she was sure. Days of anxiety had followed. Each morning when she woke she would say to herself, it's bound to start. I can't be pregnant! The slightest twinge of an abdominal pain, the smallest niggling backache and her hopes would rise. This is it. I'm coming on. Yet even as she examined her knickers for the longed-for staining, so something within her was satisfied to find nothing. Lying in bed alone, she would touch her stomach, her breasts. They were sore, the nipples tender. Oh, God! I *am* going to have a baby! Panic, then gladness, a seesaw jumble of emotions.

'There it is, Frank! Can't be denied. Does it surprise you?' She was alarmed to find that she wanted to burst into tears.

He looked bewildered, and the worry had started. There were creases around his eyes, between his brows. 'Well, no. It was on the cards, I suppose. I tried to be careful, but it wasn't always possible.'

He released her and sat down on one of the lockers. The sunlight streamed in through the tiny window,

248

running fingers of gold through his unruly hair. Alison sensed his withdrawal and a chill touched her heart. 'What are we going to do?' she whispered and sank to the floor near his feet, resting her head back against his knee.

'What we should've done months ago.' She felt his touch on her head, stroking, soothing. 'We'll go away together.'

She twisted around, her grey eyes huge, staring up at him with hope and alarm. 'How can you? Elsie. The children. Your work!'

'What work?' he said bitterly.

'The church – your calling –'

'To hell with it!' This was a new aspect of Frank. Before her was a man filled with impatience, with unfulfilled ambitions, with rebellious longings. 'I told you – I have no calling. God doesn't speak to me. I don't know that I believe in Him.'

'But your wife.' She hated to see that almost cruel look in his eyes, yet something dark in her responded, satisfied, vengeful.

'I loathe her. I've lost all respect for her. I can't live with her any more.'

Alison made one last attempt to cling to everything in which she had been so carefully indoctrinated. Decency, honour, caring about other people's feelings. 'Then the children. You don't hate them.'

'I'm indifferent to the boys. Elsie has made certain that they are her creatures. It's only Effie –' He suddenly sank his head in his hands and a groan escaped him. 'I can't leave her with that drunken harridan!'

This was better. Alison could cope with it now. Frank had softened. He needed comforting and she rose to her knees, her arms about him, drawing him close to her. 'We'll take her with us. Oh, listen, Frank. I've thought about it so much since I suspected about the baby. I've money. There's no need to worry about that. We'll go to London and buy a house somewhere. I thought perhaps

249

in Chelsea, the artists' quarter. Apparently those sort of people aren't likely to worry whether we're married or living in sin. It was always out of bounds for me. Not Selden, of course, he goes wherever he wants – Josephine too, I shouldn't wonder. As for Elsie, we'll send regular amounts of cash for her and the boys.'

He still looked very worried. 'But Alison, I can't live on your money. It wouldn't be right.'

'Nonsense.' Her fingers dug into his shoulders. She shook him in her eagerness. 'What does that matter? You'll be able to work – really work on your books. Not hack stuff, something important. And I'll paint –'

'With two children to look after?' He gave a rueful grin, wondering how she would manage in more strait-ened circumstances. She was a romantic whereas he, the realist, could visualize the troubles ahead, not the least of which was Elsie. She would have to leave the curate's cottage. Where would she go? What would she do?

Alison airily brushed aside the domestic problems of their new life. 'We'll be able to afford help – a nanny, cook and housekeeper. Don't look on the black side, think how wonderful it will be. Imagine it, Frank, a home of our own with a garden, I quite like gardening, and friends calling in. Oh, yes, we'll make friends amongst the writers and painters. Freedom! Freedom of thought, of expression. I've always wanted it. Never had it! No more Selden and Josephine ordering me about. No more pretending to be something I'm not. No more clandestine meetings – we'll be able to sleep together every night.'

Holding his face between her hands, she kissed him passionately, pushing him down on the locker. He turned on his back, drawing her on top of him. She moaned in pleasure, rubbing her body against his, every nerve, every drop of blood reaching out to enfold and engulf him, longing to be fused with him. She sat up momentarily to tear open her blouse and push aside her

250

skirts, on fire with desire and that heady, glorious feeling of liberation.

'We must be careful. Camilla's gardeners!' Frank protested faintly. 'Wouldn't do to be caught until we've laid our plans.'

'I know, I know –' she muttered, but now her busy fingers were unfastening his clothing. 'They won't come near here. She's ordered them to give this place a wide berth – I'm not to be disturbed when I'm painting –'

Her hair had come unpinned, flowing down over him like a silky brown curtain. There was a wildness in her eyes that was almost frightening, yet exciting in its intensity. This was an alien Alison, a ruthless, pleasure-seeking woman. She had thrown off her bondage to family, conventions and duty, knowing what she wanted and pursuing it remorselessly.

She straddled him, lowering herself on to his hard penis, head thrown back, throat arched, eyes slitted in ecstasy. Swept up by her passion, Frank groaned and bucked beneath her, hands gripping her hips as she rode him to completion. The wagon juddered on its rotting wheels. It was filled with heat. The sun beat down on its roof and Alison slumped on Frank, bathed in sweat.

'When we've our own home, we'll bath together,' she murmured into his neck. 'I've never shared a bath with a man before. Water, cool water, Frank. I'll soap you all over – just think of it. We're going to be so happy.'

When she had withdrawn and stood, straightening her clothes and putting up her hair, Frank lay propped on one elbow, watching her. 'How and when are we going to leave?' he asked, then smiled. 'You seem to have everything planned, you temptress.'

'We'll do it on Midsummer Night,' she mumbled through the hair-pins gripped between her lips. 'It's lucky that Camilla's throwing a big party. They'll be so busy over the next few days, no one will notice if I'm acting strangely. I'm practically invisible to Selden and

251

Josephine anyway, unless they want me to do something for them.'

'That gives us less than a week to make arrangements,' Frank was buttoning his trousers and smoothing a hand over his tousled hair.

'We'll go after dark, when the party's in full swing. Can you drive?' Alison was calm now, on the surface.

'I can,' he replied, amused because she had so quickly reverted to her role of organizing spinster.

'Then we'll take one of the cars and go to Ryehampton. There we can get a train to London, book in at an hotel and start house-hunting. I've enough money here, and can draw more from the bank in town.' Her steady tone belied the excitement churning within her. 'Will it be possible for you to snatch Effie?'

'No problem. Elsie and the children have already been invited to the shindig at The Priory. Everyone in the village will be there.' He paused, coming to stand beside her, looking down with love and concern. 'Are you quite sure, Alison? There'll be one hell of a rumpus. You'll be a social leper, shunned by decent folk.'

'Decent folk? My God, Frank, they're a bunch of hypocrites, the upper crust! D'you know what goes on beneath that veneer of respectability? The infidelities? The mental and physical cruelty? The dirty, despicable things which must never, never be brought out into the open?' He had never seen her more serious or more fired. 'I don't give a damn for their opinions. I've a chance of happiness and nothing or nobody, is going to stop me.'

'Now, tell me about him. Don't deny it, Camilla. I just know there's a 'him' somewhere. Nothing but love gives a woman that certain sparkle,' Amy Marchant said, as the guest-room door closed behind her.

Camilla had met her and John at Sutton Cross station. These were by far the most important of her guests and she had insisted on driving the car herself, instead of trusting the job to Wilf. He had his work cut out anyway, helping Beryl and Leila prepare for the party. It had been a busy, exciting time as The Priory was decked for the gala occasion. Camilla felt a mixture of pleasure and apprehension as she anticipated the evening to come. At the height of the festivities, she would announce her engagement to Darcy. It had been a closely guarded secret. As far as she was aware, not even Leila knew, though she did keep throwing her odd looks, and there was a certain discomforting stiffness between them.

She smiled at Amy, delighted to see her. They had not met since before Christmas, though corresponding regularly. Amy looked in much better health. She had filled out, her complexion was no longer sallow, and her fair hair was brighter, fashionably styled beneath a small, feathered toque. John too seemed fitter and happier, though the news concerning their child had not been promising. Despite thorough examinations by the most eminent physicians, nothing could be done to cure her illness. Camilla had not the heart to tell her friend that nothing *would* be done. Let her continue to hope for a miracle. Let her seek the advice of other doctors, of faith healers and spiritualists. It would give a shape and purpose to her life and possibly comfort too. They had not brought Harriet to The Priory, and Camilla was of the opinion that a few days away from the worry and care of the tiny invalid would be good for them.

Leaving John to tour the stables in the company of Rufus Godwin, who had arrived the day before, the two women had slipped upstairs where luggage now stood waiting to be unpacked by Amy's maid and her husband's valet. Not yet though, first it was essential that they talk. Camilla needed to confide in someone. Despite her self-contained hardness, her apparent confidence, she was as nervous as any young woman approaching matrimony. She would seek Amy's help in

253

the enormous task of organizing the wedding. Usually this was accomplished by the bride's mother, aunt and sisters, but Camilla had no such comforting bevy of experienced relatives, and did not know where to begin.

She patted the padded seat beneath the windows which were flung wide to the newly acquired glory of the garden. 'Come and sit down, Amy. You're right, of course. Oh, dear, is it as obvious as that? I thought I'd been controlling myself.'

Amy looked into that lovely, vital face and gave a droll smile to hide the affection in her eyes. 'I'm sure no one else guesses, only me and I'm a wily old bird wise in the ways of women. What other reason can you give me for this elaborate beanfeast?'

'To show off my wonderful house! To impress my neighbours and convince 'em that an eccentric foreigner, like me, can settle down and run an English country estate with the best of 'em.' Then she stopped pretending, tucked her feet up under her, clasped her hands around her knees and began to tell her friend everything about Darcy, ending lamely with: 'That's about it, I'm head over heels in love. He reduces me to curds and whey! For better or worse, I'm going to marry him as soon as I can!'

Amy gave her a keen look, wondering at the rather tense determination in her voice. It was almost a touch defiant. Though not knowing Camilla for long, she had quickly learned to love her, not only for her fascinating beauty but for her strength of character, her impulsive kindness and open-handed generosity. There wasn't a mean, petty bone in the whole of her shapely body. Though so tough on the surface, Amy had sensed, right from the start, that she was vulnerable. She could only hope that Darcy Devereaux was worthy of her.

Camilla, confession over, uncoiled her limbs, stretched widely and jumped up. Life was good. Her friends had come. There was to be a party. Relief flooded her now that she had actually voiced the words, I'm going to marry Darcy! I really am! she thought. No more doubts, no dark shadows of foreboding. Like the prince and princess in a fairy tale, we'll live happily ever after. We shall share everything, the lands, the house. Together we'll build our future here, making it a home in the true sense, a place to return to at the end of each day. And children! She drew in a sharp breath. Yes, she wanted a child at once. Maybe next year her baby would lie in the old oaken cradle she had found in the attics. Her son. Darcy's son. He would like that. Resolutely she pushed away the tiny ghost from Rubera. He must never know about it. She had already learned that he had a temper to match her own, and shrank from the thought of having it directed towards her.

He was under the impression that she was a virgin, and had been respecting her as such. Though desire was like a searing flame between them, glowing white-hot whenever they were alone, he had not attempted to seduce her, always stopping himself from taking the ultimate step of complete possession. She would have been unable to prevent him, had he tried. Her own passionate nature demanded satisfaction and she made love to him as best she could, given this one restriction. She loved him for being prepared to wait, was terrified that her boldness would give her away, but could never refrain from intimate caresses or conceal her own hot-blooded response when he pleasured her.

'We must be married very soon, Amy.' Restlessness animated her and she took her friend's hands, pulling her to her feet. 'When d'you think? How long will it take for the preparations?'

'Autumn is a lovely time.' Amy linked an arm with hers as they walked to the door. 'I was an October bride.'

'But that's ages away,' Camilla wailed, stopping and swinging to her, golden eyes wide. 'I can't wait so long. Let's make it no later than the end of August.'

Though Amy was tired after the journey, she good-naturedly allowed herself to be guided through the house, while Camilla explained precisely what state it had been in when she took it over and went into details of the restoration. She talked fast, as if it were safer to be talking fast, walking fast, to escape her own thoughts. Amy nodded and smiled, praised and commented, yet underneath she was thinking: Camilla's not one hundred per cent sure about this man. If she was she would be calm, not prancing about like a nervous colt.

A leisurely luncheon followed, eaten in the open air on the shady terrace beyond the dining-room, an intimate meeting of friends and supporters. Camilla looked upon Godwin more as an adopted uncle than a lawyer. She contemplated his reaction when he heard of her impending marriage, having the uneasy feeling that he would be none too pleased. When all was said and done, she was an heiress and, as such, a prey to fortune-hunters. Memory registered that he had been less than cordial when he met Darcy earlier in the year.

'My dear young lady, what a transformation,' he now commented, glancing round at the mellowed, ivy-clad walls that surrounded them on three sides, illuminated by the strong, overhead light of summer. The lawns lay lazing in the sunshine, and the trees were heavy with the fullness of leaf sweeping down to meet them. The sweet scents of blossom suffused everything. 'I'd never have believed that The Priory could look like this. The place has come to life after all these years. It's like it was in the old days, when I used to stay here with your father, both young men then, if you can believe a doddering ancient like me was ever young.'

He twinkled at Camilla while she served him with a further helping of strawberries and cream, and she smiled in response. He was a square-cut man of medium height, his shrewd face dominated by a jutting chin, a large nose and bright eyes. He looked more like a buccaneering sea captain than a lawyer. 'That's made my day. I'm glad you approve. You may not be so happy about it when you see what it's cost.'

'Worth every penny, I should imagine.' He was assessing the view. 'Can't lose, if you put your cash in property. Must say I had my doubts when I first clapped eyes on you. Lot of responsibility for a woman, a great place like this, but it looks as if you're managing admirably. I'll take a glance over the accounts later, but not today. This is a time for feasting and merriment, eh?'

'I agree. We'll put business behind us,' John said, smiling fondly at his wife and reaching over to take her hand in his. 'This is a holiday, and we've Camilla to thank for it. What are you ladies going to do this afternoon? I've noticed that you have croquet hoops set up over there, Camilla. I'll challenge anyone to a game who feels like it.'

Godwin declined, announcing his intention of finding a quiet spot and snoozing the hours away, but Camilla and Amy agreed and soon the tock of wooden mallets striking wooden balls pervaded the somnolent atmosphere. It was a scene of perfect peace, the fluttering white dresses of the women and John's flannel trousers and striped blazer epitomizing gracious English country life. Yet Camilla was seized with a frightening sense of unreality. Was she truly there, the lady of the manor? From some mysterious storehouse of the brain, other scenes arose to obscure the present – heat and steamy tropical vegetation, the languid inertia, the relentless, enervating sunlight. Drums – drums always throbbing somewhere in the background, a monotonous sound to which the ear became accustomed so that it was at one with the pulsing of blood through the veins. She'd heard them again, up there on the moors when Darcy proposed, and she shivered at the recollection.

The lazy afternoon stretched out. The shadows grew longer on the velvety grass. As the hotness of the sun's

257

breath was slowly withdrawn, the air was filled with the smell of cooling leaves. Walking as in a dazed dream, Camilla went to her room to bathe. The night was very nearly upon her – the party for which she had worked so hard and planned so assiduously. Soon Darcy would be there.

The converging roads were filled with an unending stream of vehicles, and the dust rose in clouds above the hedgerows. The women wrapped themselves closely in motor-cloaks and veils, the pace slackening to a crawl as the congested lines merged together at The Priory gates. Once that point had been passed, the dirt of the highroads was replaced by refreshing shade from the great avenue of trees and mock oranges overflowing with blossom. Members of more conservative households came by carriage, attended by postilions. The villagers walked, dressed in their best, leading their children by the hand, making a beeline for the huge marquees that had sprung up like toadstools on the lawns. Under the stern eyes of Beryl, Wilf and Harvey, the servants had not only prepared a feast for the gentry within the house. In the tents, wooden trestle tables groaned under a mountain of food, and the landlord of the Red Lion was in charge of the barrels.

Rather self-conscious in their blue uniforms, the members of the local brass band were taking their places on a raised platform outside the biggest marquee. The sunset gleamed on their gold braid and the highly burnished surfaces of trumpets, trombones and bassoons. Obadiah Makepeace had abandoned the tools of his trade for the day. He was now the bandmaster, assuming a rare importance. Attired in red, his moustache twirled into aggressive points, he commanded his platoon of musicians. Rising to the toes of his black boots, he lifted stiff arms aloft. There was a flash of sparkling white gloves. His baton sliced through the air, and the strident sound of a brisk, military march resounded across the lawns, startling a noisy gaggle of starlings who were wheeling and calling above the oaks.

Camilla smiled as she heard the strains floating from the discreetly arranged distance. She was ready, wearing a new gown especially designed for the event, well aware that she was about to be scrutinized by dozens of curious eyes. Just before she went down to greet her guests, she slipped into the secret room. The light was scarlet and gold as the last rays of the sun struck through the arched windows. It flamed on the portrait, and she was sure that Edgar Ruthen's expression was more sardonic than usual.

'Well, you old devil, and what would you say about all this?' she addressed the canvas aloud, standing before it, hands planted on her hips. 'You tried to ruin my life, but I've beaten you. There's nothing you can do to hurt me now.'

She could almost hear his mocking laughter, and his voice, deep and cynical, drawling: 'Think you're clever, eh, my girl? Imagine you can get away with it now that I'm dead? Don't be so sure. I stopped you having André de Jaham. Had him snuffed out, removed, murdered. And as for your bastard baby? Did you really think I'd permit such a blot on my name? It had to die, daughter.'

Camilla clenched her jaw, eyes slitted as she stared upwards. 'Stop it – stop it!' she grated. 'Leave me alone, dead thing. I'm here, in your own family home. It's mine. I'll do as I like in it, and I'm going to marry Darcy. I defy you and your master, Satan, to try and prevent me!'

She closed her ears to the hint of jeering laughter that polluted the atmosphere, spun on her heel and left the room, turning the key in the door. Fan and evening bag in hand, she squared her shoulders and went out to meet the foe, as resolute as a gladiator about to enter the arena. Will it be thumbs down for me? she wondered.

Later, Shawn moved easily through the reception

259

rooms, mingling as if he had spent his life at such gatherings, superbly confident. The Priory rang with polite laughter and refined voices. A string quartet played selections from popular musical comedies from their perch in the minstrels' gallery overlooking the Great Hall. Ever alert for anything that might prove advantageous to Erin's representative, Shawn adopted a nonchalant gait, ears open and eyes peeled. He was proud of Camilla's achievements, annoyed when he caught snatches of unflattering conversation from amongst some of the visiting gentry who had come motivated by spite or curiosity, more than willing to criticize her.

She's done well, the beautiful colleen, he thought, as he wandered towards the ballroom. A fine woman, too good for Darcy Devereaux and his ilk. Now, by all the saints, why is she not after looking at yours truly? You'll have to do something about that, Shawn, my lad! Meanwhile, if that ain't Lady Josephine over there, giving you the glad eye! She'll fill the gap, for the time being.

He passed through the crowded, elegant, high-ceilinged rooms, their contents and occupants endlessly reflected in great gilded mirrors. A million diamonds twinkled from the cut-glass chandeliers; delicate Sevres vases shone on the mantelpieces and carved court cupboards; family portraits and pastoral scenes glimmered dimly in gilt frames. Magnificent drapes hung at the windows, their colours blending with the shimmering satins, heavy silks and delicate muslins adorning the female guests. Underfoot were thick Aubusson carpets or highly polished parquet. Against the dark oak walls glowed the muted hues of tapestries. There was the repeated sparkle of silver and crystal as the brigade of quiet-footed servants offered trays of refreshments and wine. It all aroused in Shawn a satisfaction, and a longing amounting almost to avarice. It was a world he coveted, a world he fully intended to possess, though he was not prepared to barter his soul to do so. Unlike many of those present, he did have some scruples.

He had reached the long room just outside the dancing area, where the chaperones rested on couches, fanning themselves languidly. Their young charges, dressed in white with ribbons in their ringlets, chattered and giggled, peeping at the black-suited men from beneath demure, lowered lashes. The air about them quivered with overt interest and curiosity about those strange, forbidden male creatures. It was alive with a repressed sexual quality that made Shawn smile. Given half the chance, they'd be out there in the darkening woods with 'em, skirts up, legs spread, he thought. As eager as the village belles to lose their virginity and find out what all the fuss was about. There was the scent of banked flowers and mingled perfumes. Soft music drifted from the other room, and over all came the faint clink of glasses and the discreet pop of champagne corks.

Josephine bore down on him after freeing herself from a group of admirers. 'Are you going to sign my dance card?' she demanded, coming to rest at his side like an exotic bird of paradise.

'Oh, so you do believe that I can write?' he countered, his green eyes staring down into hers. He noticed that the lashes had been darkened and blue cosmetic shadowed the lids. 'I was under the impression that you thought this impossible for a fellow fresh from the Irish bogs.'

'You're a difficult beggar sometimes, Shawn,' she answered pithily, and her eyes kept darting beyond his shoulder, seeking – watching. 'I'm not in the mood for your sarcasm tonight.'

'What's the matter, your Ladyship, Devereaux not paying you much attention?' He cocked a questioning brow at her, though aware of her bare arm brushing his dinner jacket, the perfume of her scented flesh drifting up to tantalize his nostrils.

261

'Devereaux hasn't paid me any attention for weeks,'
she answered, nodding at passing acquaintances, smile
brittle as glass, a taut line to her lips.

'No?' Shawn followed her to the ballroom, thinking
how seductive she was, her hips swaying provocatively
beneath the gown of transparent turquoise silk over an
opaque azure ground.

'No.' She shot him an annoyed glance. 'Don't pretend
that you don't know all about it. He spends every
moment of his spare time with Camilla. I'd like to
throttle her!'

'Tut! Tut! Such harsh words from so fair a lady!'
Shawn said, a smile hovering about his mouth as he
slipped an arm around her waist when the orchestra
struck up a waltz. Her body was pliant yet possessed an
intriguing feeling of strength. He could well imagine that
she would be tireless in bed, a demanding, hungry
mistress.

'You haven't heard anything yet,' she warned, yet
even as she spoke, so she leaned against his chest, arm
about his shoulder, hand clasped in his. Her thigh
pressed against his as they danced. Desire thickened in
him.

'Steady there,' he growled, arm tightening. 'Not long
ago Irishmen were barbarians. Pillage and rape, my
dear Lady Josephine.'

'Don't worry,' she breathed against his cheek. 'I'll
whisper "Help!" Though I must admit I'm surprised to
find you here, and not outside with the peasants. Much
more your style.'

'Bitch,' he muttered, deliberately holding her against
the hardness of his loins, knowing by her quickened
breathing that she was aware and desirous. 'When am I
going to sleep with you?'

'I've not made up my mind that you are.' Her voice
was unsteady, a drugged look in her eyes.

'Oh, but I am. Make no mistake about that, your

Ladyship. The only question is – when? Tonight? Why not? We've been pretending too long. You know that our mating's inevitable.' His accent was thicker, an intense look on his handsome face that thrilled her. His arms were strong, his body needful. Josephine had never before had a working man as a lover. Though Shawn laid claim to Irish nobility, she suspected that he was exaggerating. The notion of a rough wooing was titillating.

'You assume too much, Shawn.' She feigned anger, trying to pull away. He refused to relinquish his hold. 'I've high standards, you know. I expect a man to be a skilled lover. I doubt you'd know how to please me.'

'Then you'd be wrong, achusla.' Shawn reversed easily, whirling her round to the sugary strains of the 'Blue Danube'. 'On the contrary, I know exactly what a woman wants. I've made a study of it. I like women, you see. I adore their bodies and admire their minds. I promise that you won't be disappointed.'

At that moment the waltz finished and Harvey's voice boomed over the sprinkling of applause, requesting that everyone gather in the Great Hall where Lady Camilla was about to address them. A ripple passed through the ballroom. They were intrigued, mystified, wondering what further surprises the foreign woman had in store. Selden came across to take his sister's arm, his eyes warning Shawn off as he led her away. Shawn shrugged and took his time in following them.

Alison trailed into the Hall with the rest, taking up a position near the stairs. She had hardly been aware of the crowd, far too occupied by her own feverish expectations. Frank was in the garden with Elsie and the children. She had not been able to speak with him that night but, over the days, had been putting their plans into operation. Now her outdoor clothes were ready in her room and she'd packed a case secretly, not an easy matter with her maid poking her nose into everything.

263

There was money in her purse, and a car selected. She hoped that Frank would remember all that she had told him to do.

After she had changed into a Romney style gown of grey tulle, she had gone down to her studio before the guests started to arrive, breathing its familiar atmosphere for the last time. She was sad to leave it, but had given Camilla her paintings to look after, though not betraying her intentions, and storing her artist's equipment in a tea chest, trusting that Selden would have it sent to London later, though not too hopeful about this. He was bound to be furious with her, and spiteful in consequence. Her other possessions could follow at leisure. She was not over-concerned. All she wanted was to leave Armitstead House with the least possible disturbance. Nothing mattered but being with Frank.

Seated at her writing desk, she had drawn paper towards her and penned two letters; one to her brother explaining that she was going to London to study, and another to Camilla. In that she told the truth, confessing her love for Frank and the fact that she was pregnant by him. She promised to forward her address as soon as they were settled. Camilla would be the only one who would understand. Alison had no illusions. Selden would hear that Frank too had left home. He would ferret out the facts soon enough.

Now, from her place by the towering staircase, she saw Frank at the back of the Great Hall. He was standing there with Elsie, that plain, dowdy woman who had the right to call him husband. Her face was flushed and her eyes glittered. There was a vacant smile curving her slack lips. Her gown was of an unfortunate shade of red that did nothing for her complexion. No doubt she had been indulging in the freely flowing alcohol. Frank would be making sure that she became inebriated as quickly as possible to facilitate their escape. For once, her craving would be of benefit, and he would use it in a calculated fashion.

264

The heat, the tension were making Alison feel sick. Sweat bedewed her upper lip, and she thought that she was going to faint. The scene whirled and she put out a hand to steady herself, gripping the wooden satyr that ornamented the newel post. He seemed to leer at her knowingly. Alison trembled. In the midst of a crowd one could be so horribly alone. Among the hundreds of guests crowding the house and the lawns outside, not one had cared to pause at her side. Other girls less attractive than herself had flitted about with attendant cavaliers, or formed the centres of jolly groups. Not even Selden and Josephine gave a damn. It was a hateful thought. Alison fought against it, telling herself that this didn't matter now. But her heart ached as she acknowledged the truth that they would be happier without her. Her mind leaped at the sight of the one man who did care, who would have come swiftly forward, unsatisfied, unseeing, until he had gained her side. Soon it will be like that always, came the warm, glad thought. This is the last time, the last night that I shall be ignored. For ever after I'll belong to Frank.

Camilla appeared at the head of the stairs and descended slowly, pausing halfway down. Darcy stood at the bottom, looking up at her. The noisy crowd hushed, every eye turned to their hostess. She wore a trailing gown of a soft green, and over it a diaphanous cloak, elaborately embroidered in silks. Her tawny hair was banded by turban-like-folds of gold tissue, fastened by a diamond brooch holding an ostrich plume in place. Her expression was vivid, one of transfixing beauty and radiant audacity. She was striking, commanding instant attention, like an autocratic empress about to issue an edict to her subjects.

'A chip off the old block,' muttered one aging squire to another, both members of the Sutton Hunt. 'Dammit, if she ain't the spittin' image of Edgar Ruthen. I remember him, you know. Strange fellow – damned strange.

Always thought he had a bit of a screw loose somewhere – didn't seem like one of us at all. Confounded good horseman, though –'

'My friends,' Camilla began, holding up a hand for silence. The tiger's-eye ring blazed like fire. 'Welcome to The Priory. This is a very special night for me. The midsummer solstice. The celebration of The Priory's emergence from retirement. And there's something else much more important. I'm very happy to tell you of my betrothal to Mr Darcy Devereaux!'

A gasp arose from the spectators. In that sudden astonished moment, Leila caught her breath in horror. Half concealed as she was near the green baize door of the servants' quarters, she stared out and upwards. Camilla was like a lurid comet on the stairs, but everything else had vanished, leaving only her, suspended there in a dark void. Silence, blackness. The Hall had gone, the house too. Camilla floated, insubstantial as mist and Leila prayed, gripped by terror. Then she saw him – saw Edgar Ruthen reaching down to seize his daughter. Behind him appeared another wraithlike being. Wan-faced, awful.

With a roar that almost deafened her, the present shattered that other dimension. The denizens of the nether regions vanished. Leila clapped her hands to her eyes, blinded by brightness as the Hall righted itself and exploded into sound. Darcy had bounded up to stand by Camilla, one arm about her as they both smiled down at the milling crowd. Men were on the stairs, shaking him by the hand, pummelling him on the shoulder. Women were gathered into little knots below, smiling, talking, staring at her, some with envy, some with malice, a few with genuine goodwill. She had drawn the glove from her left hand to display the engagement ring Darcy had given her. Everyone loudly admired the sapphire in its diamond setting.

'Here's a turn up for the book,' commented Shawn,

masking his surprise and that queer sensation of betrayal.

'So he's done it, the crafty swine.' There was a fixed smile on Selden's lips as he watched the couple. The steely quietness of him made Shawn's scalp crawl. Selden had made no secret of his own ambitions regarding Camilla, and such calm was unnerving. Shawn had the distinct impression that he was plotting something.

'Damn him! The dirty, conniving bastard!' Josephine hissed, face like chalk, eyes flashing with temper. 'And damn her too!'

'Now, now, keep cool, sister dear. People are watching you. Don't want the whole county saying that you couldn't control your feelings because your lover's given you the go-by,' Selden said smoothly, and his fingers tightened painfully on her arm. 'Come along. We must congratulate the happy pair.'

Shawn went to get a drink, staring broodingly down into his glass before raising it and silently toasting Camilla. He had lost her, and even this brought a rueful smile to his lips, lost her and she'd never guessed how he felt about her. He hadn't realized it either. The raw hurt within him was a revelation. He'd thought himself immune to the pangs of unrequited love. He took up another bumper of champagne, knowing that he'd have one hell of a hangover in the morning. What was it they said about champagne? A headache in every bubble. Ah well, *c'est la vie!* Josephine would need consoling and he swore that before the night was out he would forget his disappointment between her lovely thighs. He set off in pursuit of his prey.

Alison was less amazed than the rest. She had guessed, long before, how things lay with Camilla and Darcy. All she could think of was: Thank God! Thank God! Now there'll be even more excitement and roistering. Frank and I will slip away totally unobserved. With

267

something of a shock she realized that love was making her self-centred. She no longer cared much what happened to others, just as long as she had what she wanted. I *am* like Selden and Josephine, she thought, then edged towards Frank, glad to see that Elsie had already returned to the beer tent, and that he had Effie by the hand. Mrs Barlow was taking care of the boys outside somewhere. Doubtless they were seeking a vantage point from which to view the firework display that was about to commence.

Camilla walked down the stairs on Darcy's arm. Well, it's done, she told herself and was aware of a tremendous sense of relief. Come what may, I've made a public declaration and thrown in my lot with this man. A moment later, her thoughts had flown back on the wing of feminine impulse to another – her dark first love, André. How often she had once dreamed of a similar announcement, a betrothal for which she had longed with all her heart. She had reckoned without her father. André, like many another high-born Creole, had black ancestors. If there was one thing Edgar Ruthen could not abide, it was Negroes. He was perfectly willing to use and exploit them, but in his eyes they were less than human. He despised them, reviled them. When he had learned that his daughter was in love with one of them his scorn had been blistering in the extreme. His rage after hearing that she was pregnant by André had been the unbalanced fury of a madman.

'Darling, you were superb.' Darcy's voice pulled her back from the nightmarish past. 'By Jove, this has given the locals food for gossip. I'll bet I'm the envy of every manjack amongst 'em.' His eyes were faintly amused.

'I think congratulations are in order, old man.' Selden emerged from among the sea of faces, the press of evening suits and expensive gowns. 'You've stolen a march on us, to be sure, snatching our beautiful cousin.' His voice was smooth, the grey eyes switching to Camilla's face betraying no emotion.

268

'Thank you, Selden.' Darcy was equally controlled, equally insincere. 'I trust that you'll attend the wedding.'

'My dear chap, I wouldn't miss it for anything.' Selden bowed over Camilla's hand, raising it to his lips. Though the touch was light, his mouth seemed to scorch her skin.

People were dispersing, returning to the dancing, the drinking, the feasting, and Shawn overheard a snatch of conversation typical of the comments being bandied about. ''Struth! Darcy must've taken leave of his senses,' one debonair beau was saying to another as they stood by the buffet tables helping themselves to caviare.

'How so, Johnnie, old bean?' replied his companion, heaping ham sandwiches and lobster vol-au-vents on to a plate and passing them to a tastelessly dressed plump girl with protuberant eyes. Her expression was like that of a dreamy sheep. 'Ain't she just about the most gorgeous filly you've ever clapped eyes on?'

'Oh, she's a stunner, I'll grant you, Charlie,' the other replied airily, eating black grapes from a gold plate. 'But she comes from Brazil, don't-cher-know, and everyone says that people out there all have a touch of the tar-brush somewhere along the line.'

'You mean she's a darkie?' squeaked the girl, giving a high, shrill laugh. 'Crikey, how droll!'

'As much a nigger as that servant of hers,' declared Johnnie. 'Did you see her hanging about the Hall? Looks like a deuced witch-doctor, don't she? D'you want some ice cream, Pru? There you are. Tuck in, old thing.'

'But Lady Camilla's fair-skinned,' protested Charlie. 'Bloody marvellous hair, what?'

'No she ain't, she's tanned,' Johnnie went on doggedly, determined to prove his point. 'Anyhow, that don't signify. Could have been a long time ago, colour running out, weakened by too much breeding.'

'I think you're mistaken, Johnnie. She don't strike me

269

as being a darkie. Any road, she's the late Marquis's brat, so what's the odds? Better be careful or her black mammy'll put a ju-ju spell on you. Your willie may drop off or something.'

'Ooh, Charlie, you are awful!' shrieked Pru, convulsed with laughter.

The noise had attracted several others of the younger set. They were agog, ready to pick faults in their hostess. Shawn was holding his tongue with great difficulty, alarmed to find that these silly, ill-informed comments hurt him. It was as if they were directed against himself. The final straw came when a thin, weak-chinned youth, hair slicked back and shiny with brilliantine, snorted down his nose like a thoroughbred horse and said:

'She must have a bun in the oven. Poor old Darcy's had to do the decent thing and marry her.'

'I suggest you take back that remark,' Shawn broke in belligerently. Half a dozen pairs of eyes swivelled towards him.

'I say, that's going it a bit strong. Who the devil are you?' sneered the trouble-making Johnnie.

'I'm not talking to you, boy-o, though I'd as soon take the lot of you on single-handed!' Shawn's blood was up, a red haze dancing before his eyes.

'Good grief, it's that Irish lout Selden employs, ain't it?' drawled the one with the receding chin. 'Take me on, would you? I'd beat you to a pulp in a couple of seconds, no sweat.'

Shawn's hand shot out and gripped him by the collar, dragging him close till he could stare down into his eyes. 'Come outside and prove it! I'll not be after staining our hostess's carpet with your rotten blood!'

It was now an affair of honour. The young man could do no more than accept the challenge. The ringleader, Johnnie, took over with tipsy solemnity and, leaving Pru with her twittering girlfriends, they made for the courtyard, strolling off casually so that no one would guess there was going to be a fight and try to stop them. A circle was formed, the coats of the antagonists neatly folded and laid on a garden bench, then shirtsleeves were pushed up and fists bunched. Shawn fought ferociously, blacking his opponent's eye, before landing him a right hook to the nose. He heard the satisfying crunch as it broke, saw him crumple, blood streaming down his face. Camilla had been vindicated. He felt on top of the world, so dusted his hands, put on his jacket, and continued his search for Josephine.

She had finally succeeded in cornering Darcy. He had done his best to avoid her, but Josephine would have none of this. She had put him in the position where he could not refuse to dance with her without being downright rude. Trembling with rage, she frowned up into his bearded face as they circled in a waltz. Hate him she might, because he had wounded her so deeply, but her blood ran hot at the sight of his craggy features. He was just too handsome, dark as a Bedouin chieftain, except for those deep blue eyes.

'You cad!' she grated, all too aware of his powerful body beneath the immaculate evening suit. 'What about *me*? Or don't I figure in your future plans?'

Darcy did not reply for a moment, and the controlled quietness of him terrified her, then: 'You, my dear, will find another lover soon enough, I don't doubt. Spare me your insults. You knew from the start that one day our affair would end,' he answered, keeping his voice down.

The room swirled, couples swept past Josephine, expressions vacuous or smiling, and it seemed to her that everyone knew of her humiliation. 'How could you? After all we've meant to one another?' She could think of nothing new to say, the trite phrases of the betrayed woman springing to her lips.

There was a taut smile hovering around his lips as he glanced down into her flushed, furious face. 'Oh come, Josephine! Don't play the tragedy queen. What *did* we

271

mean to one another? We satisfied our lusts, nothing more, and it was fun while it lasted. But there was always Douglas lurking about in the background, and you couldn't keep your roving eye to yourself.'

'Beast!' she snarled, but pain throbbed within her, and it was as if a yawning abyss was opening before her. A blankness, an emptiness of body and soul. No more Darcy to tease, torment and take her to the heights. 'Does *she* know about us?'

'Camilla?' Darcy guided her through the dancers, manoeuvring adroitly. 'Yes, she knows. She also knows it's been over for some time. Why can't you accept defeat with at least a pretence of dignity?'

Somehow, Josephine had been clinging to the hope that he might be using Camilla for his own ends, marrying her for her money. This she might have found just tolerable, if he had remained her lover. But the look in his eyes told her plainly that he had no intention of continuing to meet her behind Camilla's back. It really was over, as far as he was concerned.

'Is that your final word?' she asked, vowing to get even with him if it took her the rest of her life.

'What did you expect?' he countered, as they glided to a graceful halt when the music died. 'Secret assignations? That I should be as unfaithful to my wife as you are to your husband?'

'That would have been in character.' The venomous words shot from her lips but she had never been more frightened or felt more alone. As they turned away to join Camilla and Selden who had completed a final twirl close by, she added: 'I don't believe you, Darcy. Leopards don't change their spots. I can't see you as the devoted husband, and I very much doubt that you've fallen in love at last – not with a woman. With her lands maybe, her money, but that's all.'

Shortly after, she was seated by herself in the conservatory, struggling not to cry, when Shawn came upon her. 'Where's the Major?' he asked abruptly.

272

Josephine looked up at his broad-shouldered, athletic form and the serious, watchful expression in his slightly slanting eyes. 'Flat on his back somewhere, sleeping it off, I expect. He's been drinking since lunch, always starts parties too damn early so that by the time they begin, he's no idea what's going on,' she answered irritably.

'Good.' Shawn reached out a hand and touched her shiny golden hair, letting his fingers trail down the soft curve of her cheekbone. 'You've never visited my little cottage, have you? Why not let me show it you now?'

Josephine had been trying to drown her sorrows in champagne, but her mind had remained painfully alert. 'Why not?' she said suddenly, and stood up shakily, her filmsy shawl trailing around her. 'Anything's better than having to see Darcy fawning on Camilla, so pleased with himself, the bastard. Ha! she must be a fool to be taken in by his lies! Stupid bitch!'

The sky was shot with colourful stars as the fireworks flared, wheeled and screamed. Loud 'oohs' and 'ahs' arose from the spectators. Frank made sure that Elsie was at the bar in the marquee, then he found Mrs Barlow and said that Effie felt sick. Lady Camilla had offered one of the cars and he was going to take her home and put her to bed. Alison, hovering in the vicinity, exchanged a few words with him, very low, then went to the studio to fetch her case.

She was shivering, although the night was warm. The garden twinkled with fairy lights. They glowed orange and pink as she slipped into the courtyard where Frank waited for her in Camilla's runabout. Effie sat in the passenger seat, thumb in her mouth, hynotized by the rainbow stars flashing briefly before dying in a shower of sparks. A rocket went up with a rush, trailing fire. Night had hung its own lantern in the sky – the great, shining full moon.

'We'll go to my house first,' said Frank after he had swung the starting handle, waking the engine into throbbing life. 'My case is there, ready packed, and I've included some things for Effie. Are you all right, darling?'

'Yes, oh, yes. Come on, Frank. What are we waiting for?' She lifted Effie and took over the seat with her nestled on her lap.

He found the gears and, with a slight jerk, the car moved forward, gathering speed. Soon they had passed the lodge gates, and the road widened before them. Alison slipped her free arm through Frank's and leaned her head against his shoulder. It was really happening. They were leaving. Ryehampton lay ahead, then London. Her new life had begun. She hugged Effie, but the child made no response, staring fixedly at the pyrotechnics flaring over the rooftops of The Priory.

Shawn was the only one who saw them go. He turned back at the small gate that led to the path in the woods, catching the glare of headlights. He stopped, though Josephine was already forging ahead, and his eyes narrowed thoughtfully. Now where were those two going? And wasn't that a child on her knee? he wondered, and knew a quiet amusement. The curate and Lady Alison, slipping off in Camilla's sports car? Well, good luck to 'em. It was no business of his. He had other fish to fry, and most delightful fish at that.

Selden had assigned Shawn a small cottage not far from Bell's Spinney. There he lived alone, catering for himself when he did not eat at Armitstead House. He liked his surroundings to be neat, and Josephine was surprised to find that the moonlit garden was well tended. Pruned trees shaded the gravelled path with its edging of cockleshells. There were flourishing herbaceous borders, and potted plants on the cobbles outside the front door, where honeysuckle and climbing roses made a perfumed arch.

274

Tiny doormer windows stared down, like black eyes peering from beneath a fringe of thatching. Excitement gave Josephine goose pimples. It was such an enchanting night, filled with an expectant hush broken only by the occasional whoop of a distant rocket and a gay cascade of rainbow sparks. She felt Shawn's brief touch on her shoulder, then he unlocked the door and entered first, explaining that he must light a lamp, and would she be careful not to bump her head? The beams were dangerously low in places.

Heart thumping, Josephine waited in what appeared to be a living-room, approached directly from outside. She could see Shawn's dim shape as he moved about and, in a few seconds, his disembodied face appeared above the strengthening yellow glow of an oil lamp. He was smiling in her direction.

'D'you want a drink?' he asked, placing the lamp on a sideboard and reaching for the decanter standing on the oak surface. It was like a dark mirror. She saw the wavering light, saw his features. Her own close by.

'Why not?' She attempted nonchalance, accepting the glass.

'May I take your wrap?' He was beside her, courteous, unhurried, lifting the soft folds of her shawl away from her shoulders and spreading it over a chair. His every movement held the quality of an intimate caress.

Within the portals of his own domain, Shawn seemed even more independent, slipping his arms out of his coat sleeves, lighting another lamp, refilling their glasses, master of all he surveyed. He acquired another, more interesting dimension and Josephine glanced around the room curiously. It was plainly furnished, but showed good taste. The cottage was obviously very old, with six-foot-thick stone walls and low latticed windows. There was a wide fireplace which occupied most of one wall. It contained stone seats within the curve of the chimney breast and, as it was too warm to merit a fire, the alcove had been filled with a brass wine cooler containing flowers.

'It'll be mighty cosy in the winter,' he said, seeing her interest. 'You'll come here then, and we'll make love on the hearth rug. There's nothing quite like doing it by the warmth of a roaring fire.'

Josephine raised her eyes to his, feeling the colour rushing up into her face at the look in them. 'You're very sure of yourself,' she replied with difficulty.

He grinned at her engagingly, and rested against the edge of the refectory table that stood, rock-solid, in the centre of the faded carpet. His legs in their tailored black trousers, were long and well formed. His white shirt fitted comfortably across the breadth of his shoulders, and contrasted sharply with the bronzed column of his throat exposed as he took off his bow tie. Chestnut hair curled at the opened collar.

'You've furnished the place yourself?' She took a chair, pretending that she was not aware of his almost flagrant virility, concentrating on her surroundings.

'Your brother let me have things from the house. I raided the attics. Nothing of much value, but it does for a bachelor living by himself.' Though Shawn spoke matter-of-factly, he could feel the tension stretching between them. It seemed to be gathering force in his loins. 'There's a scullery at the back,' he went on. 'And a bedroom upstairs.'

Josephine nodded and allowed him to conduct her up the winding narrow flight that led from a doorway in the wall next to the fireplace. Moonlight shafted through a narrow aperture halfway up. He was ahead of her. He reached down to take her hand. There was no upper landing. A few steps more, and she stood beneath the low ceiling of the bedroom. The windows were on a level with the floor, under the eaves. They were open, the smell of the night creeping in.

It was a strictly masculine room, dominated by a wide

oak bed. There was a shaving stand with a mirror supported on a twirled walnut frame, a wardrobe with a matching chest of drawers, a small bedside table on which Shawn placed the wine decanter and glasses. He had already lit the candlestick that provided the only light. Like the downstairs rooms, it was astonishingly neat, and smelled of pomade, leather and shaving soap. Up to that moment, Josephine had always felt in control of any situation in which they had been alone, but the balance of power had been changed. She experienced a slight twinge of misgiving.

This vanished in the next instant as Shawn came to her and took her in his arms. He held her gently, and his fingers carefully roamed over her face, following the line of her neck to the lobe of her ear. Josephine tingled, the caress awakening a pleasurable echo between her thighs. She drew in a sharp breath of surprise because of the effect of his touch on her body.

'What a lovely little ear,' he whispered. 'Sure and it's begging to be kissed.'

Then it was his lips that nestled against her lobe. She could feel the warmth of his breath, hear the quickness of it. For a moment this alone betrayed that he was becoming as excited as she – but then, not only this. Now his sex was hardening, pressed against her. His mouth remained soft, working its way across her cheek to the corner of her mouth, resting on her lips. He went slowly, making no attempt to use his tongue. Gentle, seductive warmth, a creeping movement, until it was she who opened her mouth to him.

Having savoured its sweetness, he lifted his head and said, huskily. 'You're beautiful, Josephine. D'you know how long I've waited for this moment? I'll tell you. Ever since I saw you take a tumble from Brandy during the hunting. I made up my mind then and there that one day we'd wind up like this.'

Josephine, smiling, flustered, was almost forgetting

277

Darcy's cruelty. It was flattering to know that this personable man had wanted her all along. 'I thought you were devoted to Camilla,' she demurred.

'Och now, and what would be after giving you such a notion as that, at all?' he whispered beguilingly.

Josephine shivered in delight at the sound of his pleasant, vibrant voice, softened and muted by the Irish accent which he had never lost. It was a voice that could woo seductively and caressingly, as Shawn knew only too well, using it quite blatantly to advance his chances with a woman. At other times it could hold a metallic ring that commanded obedience. The key to his whole personality seemed to lie in that voice of his.

'Everyone seems attracted to Camilla,' she said. 'Even you.'

'Faith, achusla, don't be silly,' he gently reproved, and began lightly to fondle her shoulder blades. 'You're the only attractive woman hereabouts.'

'D'you mean that, Shawn?' she almost purred under his tempting touch, letting her head loll back against his arm.

'By all the saints, I swear it,' he protested, but he was careful to keep his fingers crossed.

Yet in a way he was sincere. Shawn invariably adored the woman he happened to be making love to, whilst he was with her. He might forget her five minutes after, but during the time that his desires were concentrated on her, then he knew a form of love. Women were to him entirely delightful creatures, and he infinitely preferred their company to that of men. Their opinions were so much more interesting. He was tolerant of their faults, fascinated by their conceits, fancies and machinations. He had no faith in them, but this did not make him bitter. On the contrary, he treated them indulgently, as if they were charming, wayward children, but was never patronizing, bowing to their superior intelligence. It amused him to hear men talking loftily about the ladies

278

in their lives, for he knew that the mere male was no match for their cleverness.

With perfect timing, he now patted the side of the bed. 'I really should go,' Josephine protested weakly, but she joined him on the white marcella quilt.

He unfastened the chiffon overdress she wore, while she sat mute as a statue. She felt naked without it. The satin slip worn below revealed her full breasts with the faint, dark circles at the tips. Involuntarily she arched her ribs, breasts jutting towards Shawn's hard, capable hands. She drew in a breath as he touched the delicate points. Pleasure shot through her, right down to her womb, and she trembled.

'By God, how I've longed to have you here like this.' His voice was lilting, sounding like music. 'I've lain on this bed at night, tormented by visions of you. The pain was so bad sometimes that I've had to relieve it myself, if you take my meaning.'

Consummate liar that he was, Shawn omitted to mention that, far from lonely and frustrated, he had spent many evenings with obliging servants or the barmaid of the Red Lion. Knowing nothing of this, believing him, Josephine went weak with the images his words evoked. There was something exciting about the idea of him using her as his sexual fantasy.

'Now I'm going to take your clothes off,' he said softly, having discovered long ago that women liked being talked to when love-making.

Yes, this time Josephine should be naked, but maybe not always in future encounters. He sometimes relished the urgency of a half-clad woman lying beneath him, the sensation of satin underwear, of fine lace and silk stockings. With an ease that spoke of considerable practice, he began to undress her. This did not take long for Josephine wore nothing under her gown, and Shawn smiled into the dimness. He had guessed as much.

When she was naked he went on his knees on the rug

279

and drew her to him, pressing his face against her stomach, kissing the soft flesh. His slips slowly descended, caressing her all the way, and when they reached the fair hair on her pubis, his tongue found and licked silkily over her clitoris. Josephine shuddered and closed her eyes, fingers fastened about his head. Shawn took his time, enjoying it as much as she did. He did not bring her to orgasm just then, but led her almost to the peak, then turned his attention to her nipples that swelled under his insistent lips, rising to meet them.

When she was limp and almost screaming for release, he deposited her lightly on the bed and began to strip off his garments. His body gleamed in the light of the candles, a white band about the hips, gold everywhere else. There was thick hair around his genitals and a lighter covering on his chest. Then he was beside her, reaching anew for her breasts, and, with a sense of plunging disappointment, she felt the erect phallus prodding her stomach. Damn! She thought. Now he'll want to put it inside me. I'll never achieve a climax. She knew that once that swollen organ took possession, her chances of fulfilment were over. He would hump and grunt for a few seconds, then slump on her, replete, leaving her aching and unsatisfied. This is how it had been with other men. Even Darcy had rarely taken the trouble to stimulate her into completion, assuming that what she wanted was the sensation of him taking her.

She stiffened, waited, anticipating that he would throw a leg over hers, rear up, supported on his elbows if she was lucky, prise her thighs apart and then thrust into her body. But to her amazement, Shawn did none of these things. Instead, he reached down and began to caress her feet, her ankles, calves and knees. Slowly, sensuously, his fingertips explored each curve and hollow, sliding to her inner thigh and beyond, parting the soft flesh, the silken hair between.

Josephine gasped and writhed against his hand. 'Easy now,' he soothed. 'Be patient. We can prolong this –'

'But how can you? Why don't you –?' she protested, hardly able to believe that he was real.

He smiled, having the uncanny knack of reading a woman's mind, knowing exactly what she wanted. 'I can wait. I want to see you reach the heights first. You like this, yes? You want me to continue? I will – I will – just a little more, then I'm going to stop, allow the wave to recede, then gently work it upwards to a peak again –'

My God! thought Josephine. He *is* real! He's bloody wonderful! For once Shawn misjudged his timing. Before he could remove his hand, she suddenly pressed hard against it. Waves of acute pleasure, so sharp that they resembled pain, rolled over her. The sensation focused, blossomed, became uncontrollable. A cry was torn from Josephine's lips as she climaxed in an overwhelming, breathtaking rush.

3

The noise of people departing, laughter, voices, rising into that calm darkness which precedes dawn. The slamming of car or carriage doors, sounds of horses or engines, crunch of gravel under wheels. It awakened Rufus Godwin. He stirred, leather chair creaking, in the billiard-room whence he had retired at around two in the morning. With a grunt, he pulled away the handkerchief spread over his face and squinted into the dimness. Lamps still glowed behind opalescent shades, but beyond the windows there was a faint, grey smudging.

'Christ above! What's the time?' he growled and, after fumbling in his waistcoat pocket, drew out a solid gold hunter and consulted its face. It was almost half past three. 'Confounded parties. Haven't they any homes to go to?'

He was stiff. His arm had gone numb through leaning on it for too long, and he had a crick in his neck. This in no way improved his temper. Groaning, he sat up, carefully swinging his legs from the footstool on which they had been resting. His bushy brows drew down into a thunderlike scowl as a manservant, face grey with fatigue, came in with a tray, collecting glasses. There were dirty ashtrays everywhere; plates smeared with scrapings of gritty, green-black, bilious-looking caviare; flakes of pastry nestled against crusts of bread, curling and dry as toast; a few half-eaten dishes of strawberries, juice dyeing the cream an unappetizing pink. A glass of wine lay tip-tilted on the carpet. Its spilled contents made a purple stain, as if there had been a murder on the billiard-room floor during the night.

Parties! Rufus grumbled to himself. I'm getting too

old for such shemozzles. What a mess! People are like animals. No, they're not. Animals know how to behave themselves. Even pigs don't leave litter like this. Poor Lady Camilla. I hope she won't find too much damage or, perish the thought, a few of her valuables missing. Rufus had no illusions about the feckless members of the upper class. They got themselves into debt just like the lower orders and were usually far less scrupulous about finding the means to extricate themselves.

'Get on with it, my good man,' he said aloud to the servant who was hovering nervously, wondering if he intended to finish the glass of whisky at his elbow. 'Take the damned thing away. I can't drink whisky at this time of the morning, goddamn it!'

'I can,' came a voice from floor level.

Rufus stared, could see no one, then spotted a trouser leg ending in a black silk sock and patent leather shoe protruding from beneath the billiard table. 'What the deuce –?'

'It's only me,' said Douglas, inching out a little further, propped on his elbow and regarding him from between the bulbous legs. 'Don't you really want that whisky? Pass it down, there's a good chap. God, I'm dry! Got a mouth like the bottom of a parrot's cage.'

Rufus obliged. 'What are you doing under there, Major Huxley?'

'Quiet retreat. Needed a kip.' Douglas drained the glass and cast his eye around for any other that might have been abandoned. 'Where's my wife? Bloody woman's always disappearing. No wonder I drink.'

'I haven't seen her. Been asleep myself. I think the mob's on its way out. They've scoffed the hostess's food, guzzled her drink and torn her reputation apart, so they'll leave happy.' Rufus lumbered to his feet. Catnaps always refreshed him, and he now intended to find his way to his room, have a bath, a shave and change into more comfortable clothes.

283

Douglas crawled out of his refuge, staggering to his feet. His evening suit was crumpled, tie half undone. His face was waxen, his eyes red-rimmed. Tousled, haggard, with a stubbly jaw, he was not an inspiring sight. There were bottles and fresh glasses on the sideboard. He made for it with the urgency of a man lost in the desert for weeks.

'Oh, my head!' he moaned, tossing the liquor down with a shudder.

'That's the last thing you need.' Rufus eyed the bottle and regarded him in that strange light, half artificial, half dawning. 'You look terrible.'

'I feel bloody terrible! Where's Selden? Where's everybody gone? Where's my goddamn chauffeur? I want to go home.'

He slumped on the edge of a chair, whisky glass held in one large bony hand dangling between his knees. Rufus's eyes were thoughtful under those formidable greying brows. He did not know Douglas well, had only met him a couple of times before, but he had already formed his own opinion about his wife. A slut, if ever he saw one! And the Major seemed so dejected and alone. He felt quite sorry for him.

'Why don't you stay and have some breakfast? I'm sure Lady Camilla's arranged it. There's nothing more pleasant than sitting on the terrace of a gracious old house, drinking coffee, eating fresh hot rolls and watching the sun rise.'

Douglas pulled a face at the mention of food. 'Ought to be getting back –' he mumbled, then stopped.

There was nothing to go home for. Josephine was hardly likely to be there, though she could not be with Darcy Devereaux. The thought caused a spasm of amusement, as sour as the taste in his mouth. He really didn't care any more what she did or how many men she slept with. Once, ah, once, it had been a different matter. Pain so severe that he had found comfort and ease only in

284

drink, but not now. To hell with her! His attitude to his own loss of feeling was ambivalent. He both welcomed and deplored it. There was a void in his life that nothing could fill. Oblivion was the only answer.

'You look in a bad way, old son,' commented Rufus. For one horrified moment he thought Douglas was going to break down and cry. 'Come, come. It's only a monumental hangover, I expect. You'll feel better in an hour or two.' To jolly him up, he added briskly: 'What about the bombshell Lady Camilla dropped, eh? This engagement. What d'you think about it? I must say, I didn't much care for Mr Devereaux when I met him in January. What sort of a fellow is he?'

Douglas lifted dark-circled eyes. They were like burning holes boring a way into his skull. 'You'd do better to ask my wife.'

'Friend of hers, is he?' Rufus was accustomed to piecing facts together from hints, tips, ambience of tone, trifles which might have escaped a less astute observer. It was his job.

'Was,' Douglas corrected him, stared moodily into his half empty glass, swirling the honey-brown contents slowly. 'I doubt he'll find her any friend of his after this evening's announcement.'

What the devil's going on here? Rufus mused, getting up and peering out into the garden. The trees and bushes looked ghostly. Birds had begun their endless twittering and, in the distance, he could hear a cockerel giving voice. Just for an instant, his mind slipped notches and it was as if it was more than a quarter of a century ago, and himself a young man – presentable then, slim too, a keen athlete, the world opening before him. And his pal, Edgar Ruthen. They had often wound up playing billiards in this very room after a party, in their shirt sleeves, cues to hand, smoking cigars, drinking, chewing the fat, discussing the local talent, planning seductions. Edgar – that dazzling, fascinating man! And now he was dead and his daughter ruled in his stead.

But there was something in the atmosphere that sent a warning prickle along his scalp. He had been aware of it when he first set foot in the place yesterday. What was it? Apprehension? Danger? Was it directed towards the girl who owned it or did it emanate from her?

As if conjured by his thoughts, Camilla suddenly appeared in the doorway. The long night had left no traces on her features. She looked radiant. Darcy was with her, holding her hand.

'Ah, there you are, Mr Godwin!' she cried gaily, running over to him. 'Just the very person I've been looking for. This is the best time of all, don't you think? When the last of the tiresome guests have gone and one can settle down with a few cronies, duty done. I want to show you something. A room we've unearthed. No one knew it was there. The windows were hidden by ivy. Couldn't see them at all from below. Will you come with me?'

'I'm going home,' muttered Douglas. 'Is my chauffeur in the servants' hall?'

'Harvey will find him. Don't worry, Douglas. Yes, I think you should go. You look all in.'

Douglas limped past her but stopped dead in front of Darcy, glowering. 'Where's Josephine?' he demanded, truculent and still drunk.

'I've no idea.' Darcy's tone was light, his eyes wary.

'Ha! That's a joke. No idea, eh? For the first bloody time in ages you don't know where she's hiding or who she's been whoring with!'

'That's enough, Major.' Rufus was at his side, taking his arm between spatulate fingers. 'Watch your language. There's a lady present.'

Douglas shook him off, swaying, head down like a bull about to charge, but a fighting bull at a *corrida* worn down by the matador's cape. 'Sorry, Camilla, didn't meant to upset you – last person I want to upset. You're a nice girl. I like you. You're too good for that crowd. I'll

286

take my leave. Lovely party – good night or good morning or whatever.'

'Let me help you.' Rufus encouraged him out of the room and into the passage. Here he tried to go down a stair that did not exist and nearly fell forward on to the carpet. He turned and looked rebukingly at the place where he imagined the step ought to have been.

'Dammit, where am I?' he muttered. 'Why doesn't the bloody floor keep still?' He turned to leave the house by the back door, but Rufus steered him to the front, guided him down the flight of stone steps to where his car was already waiting, a bored, uniformed driver leaning against the bonnet and smoking a cigarette.

As soon as they were alone, Darcy took Camilla into his arms. 'My darling,' he whispered, his lips against her ear, hidden by curling fronds. 'I can't believe it's really true. We shall be married soon. I'll be here with you always and, when friends depart, we'll be able to go up to our bedroom together and shut out the world.'

'Did it go well? Were they impressed?' It was so good to have a companion at last, someone with whom she could share her experiences. She realized how lonely she had really been. Oh, there had been Leila and the others, but this was different.

'I should say they were! Did you see Claypole's face when he walked in? His eyes nearly popped out of his head.' Darcy laughed, and set one of her pendant earrings swinging, watching the diamonds sparkle.

'He offered to buy The Priory, if I was interested in selling,' she answered with a smile. 'Said it was superb. Promised not to alter a single thing. Selden looked as if he could murder him.'

'You won't sell?' He sobered suddenly, and there was a shadow in his eyes.

'Not on your life, but it was satisfying to know that he'd had no idea the old place could look like it does. Selden and Orde-Bunbury were stringing him along –

hoping to make a packet. The poor man had simply no idea. They could have sold him anything, no matter how preposterous. I expect they'll still try. I hope it's not too close. Don't fancy him and Daisy as neighbours.'

'Selden's an unscrupulous hound.' Darcy hung an arm lightly across her shoulders. 'I'm glad we've spiked his guns.'

This was good. She felt safe, defended, she who was perfectly capable of fighting her own battles. What a joy to be able to hand some of the responsibility over to him. I'm tired of being so practical and strong, she thought. They all look to me – even Leila. Their welfare, maybe their lives depend on my planning. I'm sick of being the *patrão*, the boss-man. It's time I had a husband. The cards are stacked against a woman trying to go it alone.

'And now you're going to take me to that mysterious room you've been telling me about.' Darcy kept his arm about her as they strolled out through a side door into the garden. 'Can't think why you've not granted me the privilege before, Camilla. Is it so very special?'

A moment's strangeness, feelings that she could not explain, even to herself, a reluctance to involve him in that odd room. She had successfully avoided it for weeks, though he seemed curious, eager, with a keenness that in itself was daunting. She drew in a deep breath, to steady herself, to mark time, then:

'We'll go when Godwin comes back.' She attempted a laugh which rang with insincerity in her ears. 'After all, no corner of your new kingdom should be denied you, should it?'

'Quite right, there must be no secrets between man and wife.' His lordly tone jarred. Uneasy thoughts swirled like dark mist through her mind. What am I doing, handing my destiny into a man's keeping? My father – and now my husband!

She suddenly needed Leila, but the Creole had been deliberately ignoring her for hours. Camilla had passed

288

her on the way to the billiard-room, stopped, put out a hand, but Leila's dark eyes had been blank, as if her mistress was invisible. She had seemed preoccupied with the disordered rooms, demonstrating her disapproval by bustling about, picking up oddments, sweeping up crumbs, straightening chairs, or moving them aside to reach untidy litter dropped behind them. This was Beryl's job really, and there was an army of servants, but Leila was intent on doing it. Camilla noticed that she had cast aside the crimson shawl which, at Christmas, they had planned she should flaunt at the first big party in the house. How proud she had been of it earlier on, she remembered, magnificent with its red silk draped over her erect shoulders, the fringes reaching almost to the floor. In that moment no one could have doubted that her African forefathers had been tribal chiefs. There had been something awesome about her that had impressed the guests despite themselves, and Camilla had experienced a warm glow of pride. But now –?

She's angry with me. The thought had been like a barb thrust into her heart. She's never liked Darcy. Defiantly, she had stuck her nose in the air, striding past Leila, her arm deliberately linked with his. Well, she can like it or lump it! Who is she to try and rule my life? But she was unhappy and disappointed, chilled with fear too, for Leila could see into the future. What did she forecast for the years ahead that made her so opposed to the match?

Standing by one of the deserted marquees with him, the rising sun changing everything with its divine flame, she still felt that isolation, as if only she was there to hear the birds singing of the passage of time and the dawning of a new day. This is how it will be, something told her, he won't be here in the future. You'll be by yourself, day after weary day, looking – seeking – for what?

Then the sensation vanished. Darcy was speaking to her. He *was* there, warm, alive, physical hands on her

289

physical flesh. Laughing, the sunlight glinting on his
black beard. The impact of his reality was like a blow.

'Darling, come back! You're asleep on your feet. My
poor girl, you must be exhausted. Let's have a quick look
at your study, then have breakfast and go to bed for a few
hours. Separate rooms, alas, but not for much longer.'

Rufus was found, collected and carted upstairs. He
talked all the way. This new sighting of the ancient house
seemed to stimulate him. Reminiscences poured out like
a torrent in full spate. Camilla glanced at him in
astonishment, for he had not been like this on his visit in
January nor even yesterday. But then on that first
occasion the place was still a ruin, and we were too busy
to think about it before, she reminded herself as, skirts
lifted above her ankles to keep up with his hurried stride,
she sped along the corridors towards the Master
Chamber.

It must be the early hour, the comparatively sleepless
night, he was thinking. His mind seemed to be function-
ing on several levels at once. The present was there all
right, flashing by second by second – Lady Camilla, so
beautiful in her evening gown. On her such finery did
not appear garish in the fresh morning light. What a
beautiful woman. And Devereaux certainly looks
splendid, ideal man to be her mate. What a fine couple
they are, to be sure. So outstandingly handsome, so
confident. But beneath these prosaic observations,
other, confusing images were passing across his inner
vision. The Priory, not quite the same. Tilting, shifting,
back it went – back to Edgar's day – like an old
photograph superimposed over a recent one. That other
scene was in sepia tones, a faded print.

'Here we are.' Camilla had opened a door, was
standing back, welcoming them in.

Rufus stopped, shivered, stepped over the threshold
into the past. My God, I'm getting old! He felt it
suddenly, looked down at his hands, seeing the gnarled

knuckles, the corded veins, the flesh freckled, an elderly man's hands. How much longer have I got? Ten years? Less? Time! What a cheat! What a thief! It doesn't seem five minutes ago that I was here with Edgar. An acquaintance dies and you merely shuffle one place up the line, till it's your turn to drop off the edge.

The room was so overpowering that it succeeded in stabilizing him. Camilla went across to the deeply recessed windows, drawing back the heavy, sumptuously patterned Genoese velvet curtains. These were the same as Rufus had once known. She had merely had them cleaned and rehung. The drapes around the monumental four-poster bed were familiar too, ornamented with seventeenth century crewelwork, a sprawling flurry of stylized fruit and flowers. But even in the glory of that English summer morning, the whole effect was one of gloom. All the furniture was black with age, upholstered in very dark green velvet. The enormous carved chimneypiece reached from floor to ceiling. On the other side of the bed was an Italian inlaid chest which supported a large Venetian mirror in a gilt and oak frame.

It's damned theatrical, he thought, but then Edgar was always dramatic. Should have been an actor. Had that kind of personality, liked to be the centre of the stage, the star of the show.

Every item there seemed to shout of its former master. Edgar had been fascinated by the weird, the exotic. Relics of his almost obsessional craze for collecting stood everywhere, forcing themselves on Rufus with renewed clarity. The room was fitted up with numerous shelves and cupboard-like recesses, all filled with a medley of Eastern brass ornaments, idols, dishes, incense burners, strange vases filled with peacock feathers, oddly fashioned candlesticks, Chinese monstrosities in bronze. Even the paintings adorning the walls were not cheerful. Well executed, at least two hundred years old, no doubt worth thousands of pounds, their subjects were of fantasy, dream-world landscapes, where winged dragons and demons ruled the skies, and sea serpents sported amongst storm-thrashed waves.

'It hasn't altered one bit,' he said. 'But, my dear Lady Camilla, don't you find it rather oppressive?'

'I love it,' she returned simply.

'I would have thought you'd have cleared out all this stuff and shipped in new furniture from London,' the lawyer went on.

She turned to stare at him, her eyes fierce, slanting and golden. Edgar Ruthen's eyes. 'Oh, no, that wouldn't be right. It's perfect.'

'Rather like something out of Poe's *Tales of Mystery and Imagination*, my dear,' Darcy demurred, eyebrow raised quizzically, strolling around and examining everything. There was no point in letting Camilla know that the room was all too familiar. He glanced at the bed, thinking of the hours he and Josephine had spent there on its coverlet. Of course, it looked very different now, but he could still almost see her rounded, shapely limbs, her golden hair spread out on the pillow, eager lips hungry for his kiss.

'I'm very much at home,' Camilla replied levelly. 'The feudal lords of The Priory have always occupied it. Most of them were born in that bed and died there too. It was always out of bounds to strangers. Any unauthorized person found trespassing here was turned out of the parish.'

She was watching his reaction. He was not aware that she already knew of his clandestine meetings with Josephine in the Master Chamber. Bravely, she told herself that it did not matter any more, then knew that it wasn't true.

'First time I've entered these sacred portals, Mr Godwin. Camilla's most possessive about it. Had to buy her an engagement ring before she'd consent to show me,' Darcy lied as he lifted Camilla's left hand. The sapphire shot blue sparks, but Rufus's eyes focused on her right forefinger which was dominated by that large yellow stone. He was again puzzled by the ring, as he had been when he was first introduced to her. Where had he seen it before? The memory continued to elude him, half grasped, then fading tantalizingly.

'Your other ring, Lady Camilla. A most unusual piece. Where did you get it?'

'It was my father's. It became mine when he died. I didn't have to have it made smaller. He always wore it on his little finger, and it fitted me perfectly. My hands are rather too big to be ladylike.' She was looking down at it, caressing its polished surface with her thumb. 'I took it to a London jeweller to have it valued for insurance purposes. He was most interested, said he'd never seen another like it. Found it quite impossible to date, and thought it must be very, very old.'

Camilla spoke calmly, but it was impossible to block the pictures flashing across her brain; the Estancia Esperança; her father's dead body; the ring glowing against his bloated skin.

'Strange. I never saw him wearing it. Must have acquired it during his travels, after he left here,' Rufus declared, seeing her stillness, her control, yet troubled by nuances that made his mind scramble faster. 'Typical sort of thing for him to collect. Did he ever say where he obtained it?'

She shook her head vaguely, stepping towards an arras hanging on the wall opposite the windows. 'No. I only know that he prized it greatly.'

'And now she's promised it to me, haven't you, darling? You said I could have it on our engagement.' Darcy's powerful figure seemed to fill the room, over-shadowing Camilla, tall though she was. His face was bent a little forward so that his hooded eyes missed nothing, the harsh, handsome lines of it accentuated by

293

an enigmatic smile. 'Well, there's no time like the present.' He held out his hand, palm-upwards.

She hesitated for an instant, regretting the impulse which, in a mad, enchanted moment not long before, had made her willing to give him anything – promise anything. They had been swimming in the lake near the house, lying on its banks afterwards, naked, entwined, in the dark. The moon must have blinded me, she thought. The moon and the scents of night. My ring! I don't want to part with it.

'It's rather tight.' She pretended to tug at it. 'Oh, dear, I don't believe it will come off.'

'You're not trying.' Darcy still smiled, but with his lips only. That tight smile did not reach his eyes. 'D'you mean to tell me you've never removed it?'

'Never,' she repeated, wishing that Rufus was not watching them. There was an expression on his face which she did not much care for. Wry amusement? Cynicism? The doubt that they were suitably matched? 'Leila took it from my father when she prepared his body for the funeral. I put it on then and I've not taken it off, not even to bathe.'

'Why not wait a bit? Try soapy water,' Rufus suggested. There was something distasteful, very nearly obscene in the way they were struggling with the ring. Then Darcy twisted her wrist and, despite her yelp of pain, yanked it from her finger.

'There you are! I said it would come off.' There was a note of triumph in his voice. It echoed around the room. With an odd laugh, he pushed it on the outer finger of his right hand. Holding it up, he watched the sparkle and flash of the diamonds, the almost transparent lemon glow of the central stone. 'It looks much more at home on a man. Don't you agree?'

Camilla stared at him. A sudden unconquerable repugnance began to creep over her. A dark, woeful nub of sadness weighed her heart, so heavy and hurtful that it seemed to be spreading out, swallowing up the whole room. Slowly she clenched and unclenched her fist. How light it felt without the ring, how empty. Had it been necessary for Darcy to be so brutal in its rape?

Then common sense insisted on a return to a vestige of normality. 'It looks fine. Suits you well. But do you have to wear it on that hand?' Her smile felt stiff, as if her face had been coated with plaster and allowed to set in that position.

Darcy's features swam above her, blue eyes blazing. 'Why not? It fits like a glove.'

Why not? A dead hand, a thick swollen hand, furred with dark hair. A hand once tanned, sinewy and strong, then aging, grotesque – lax in death – rigid within an hour, the body putrefying with unusual rapidity even for that humid climate. Stinking by nightfall – the interment hastened. Why not indeed?

'Try the other hand. Please, Darcy!' The cry seemed forced from her.

He shrugged, looked at Rufus as if in league with him on the folly of women, then indulged her by trying it. 'It's no good, Camilla. It's too slack. I may lose it. No, here it belongs and here it'll stay.' He smiled slightly, the nicely graduated smile of an indulgent parent who had been forced to reprove precocity.

Camilla grew angry with herself as the fear inside her continued to churn and grow. How irrational, how silly. What could be more natural than the exchanging of betrothal rings? A custom as old as time. I won't think about you, she vowed as her father loomed larger in that space inside her head, in the centre of her forehead, almost between her eyes.

Shaking off the spell, she pushed aside the arras, turned the key in the lock and thrust the arched door wide. She stood for a second outlined against the light radiating from within, flooding like golden smoke through the unshuttered windows, filling each recess, banishing every shadow. Darcy gave an exclamation of surprise and followed her in. Rufus frowned. He had visited that extraordinary bedchamber on many an occasion, but Edgar had never told him about this further apartment.

The sunlight was dazzling. He put up a hand to shield his eyes, expecting warmth as he advanced to join them, meeting a cold so intense that it was as if he was approaching an iceberg. Shivering, he made himself go in, goaded by the curiosity inching through him.

'My God, Camilla! What a room! Is that your father? It's got to be him!' Darcy's voice, breaking through the shimmering mist, the freezing air.

Rufus's sight cleared. He shook himself. Must have had more to drink last night than I realized, or else I'm going potty! he thought as he looked around that horrible place. He could not understand it, feeling physically sick. As in some delirious dream the furniture, the drapes, the bookcases, things and forms in themselves so commonplace and harmless, inflicted a terror of anguish within him.

'You like it?' Camilla's voice seemed to screech as she addressed her lover.

'Like it? I'm mad about it!' he cried, and they stood together, hand in hand, staring at Edgar Ruthen's portrait. 'Your old man was quite something.'

Mesmerized, Rufus stared too. 'That's him to the life,' he rasped, the words seeming to cleave to his tongue. 'But why did he never tell me about this place or the portrait – or anything –?' he ended lamely.

Camilla gave a deep-throated laugh, musical, vibrant. 'He enjoyed his secret, perhaps. Were you that close to him, Mr Godwin?'

'I thought I was.' But how could one be sure of friendship, how trust another human being or know what really went on beneath the surface? 'We were at university together – had rooms in the same college. He

296

asked me to look after his affairs when he went abroad. No one knew. Messrs Henshaw, Horsefield and Bailey were most put out when I turned up and informed them that he had a daughter.'

'By God, but it's going to be a scorcher today,' Darcy said abruptly, and hooked his fingers in his tie, unknotting the black bow, then loosening his collar. 'This room is a suntrap. It's like an oven in here already.'

Rufus was nonplussed, hardly able to stop his teeth from chattering. I must be running a fever, he thought. Camilla and Darcy seemed perfectly at ease. She was rushing from bookcase to bookcase, flinging open the glass doors, showing him the contents. Their excited voices seemed to echo as if from a mountain top. The Alps, the Himalayas, the Arctic Circle, somewhere devastatingly cold. All Rufus could see were wastes of frozen snow as far as the eye could reach. Then sun on the snow, crimson sun – spreading, deepening into pools of blood against the whiteness.

'What larks we had, old chum! D'you remember London? Paris? Champagne Charlie's?' There was a low, mocking voice in his ear, in his brain. Its timbre was instantly recognizable, even after so long. Funny, how one never forgot a voice. 'And the girls? Those pretty little horse-breakers. Remember the Burlington Arcade? How they stood there every night, beautiful blossoms waiting to be plucked. All one needed was the readies, and we always had that, didn't we? Plenty of tin. A couple of young swells. And at the theatres, Stagedoor Johnnies, armed with flowers and chocolates. Never could resist that, could they?'

Rufus found that he was staring at his reflection in one of the gilt-framed mirrors hanging against the panelling. His image, but not the burly, beak-nosed fellow of later years. It was a young face, not exactly handsome perhaps, he'd never been that – but distinguished, even dashing. Flashily dressed. Yes, he'd always been a sharp dresser. The sort of man who, with his air of breeding, his obvious wealth, had never found a shortage of willing thighs ready to fall apart for him.

'D'you remember Maisie and Pearl?' that insidious voice whispered. 'A couple of crackers!' and a wave of perfume coiled about Rufus, an unusual, powerful scent. There had only been one woman he had known who had used it – Maisie Hughes, Edgar's devoted mistress.

'What?' He said out loud. The image in the mirror fractured across. He saw an elderly man there, face scored by a life lived to the full. Only the eyes were the same, though lined, pouched.

'I was asking you if you ever heard tales of The Priory being haunted,' Camilla replied, her features swimming into focus as he turned. She was smiling at him questioningly, but in her eyes he read her awareness. She *knows*. She feels it too. I'm not alone in this, he thought with an overwhelming sense of relief.

'Haunted?' he repeated the word, wanting to retain the moment, to grasp it like a lifeline. 'No, Lady Camilla. In all the time I spent here with your father, there was never any talk of ghosts.'

'I don't believe that,' Darcy looked over his shoulder to remark, then turned his attention to rifling through the bookshelves. 'Old houses like this always have weird reputations. No Grey Lady or Headless Horseman? How disappointing.'

Rufus was feeling better. Life returned to his chilled limbs. The room lay before him, deceptively calm. And it was a beautiful room. There was no doubt about it. I must have been having a funny five minutes, he assured himself. A touch of the sun, I expect. I did spend a lot of time in the garden yesterday without my hat.

'I'm sure Edgar would have made the absolute most of it, if there had been.' He could even smile, though his lips felt stiff. 'Frightening guests would have appealed to his, shall we say, unusual sense of humour. Sorry, and all that. Why d'you ask, Lady Camilla?'

She was about to reply when Wilf tapped on the outer door. 'Come in,' she said instead, putting aside the many questions she longed to ask the lawyer concerning her father.

'Milady, a man's just brought your car back, the one you loaned Mr Turner last night.' Wilf stood there in his bottle-green uniform, stiff as a poker, his eyes fixed on some point just above her head.

'Oh, yes. Good. Have you put it in the outbuilding?' she returned, wondering why he was still waiting, and what exactly he was waiting for. This was a trivial matter and could have been dealt with later yet he had the appearance of a man bearing weighty tidings.

'Yes, milady. He's gone now. A stranger, milady. Said he brought the car from Ryehampton station.'

'The station? I don't understand. What was it doing there?' Camilla felt a slight impatience, an unease.

'I asked him that, madam. Didn't like the idea of just anyone driving your car. Thought for a moment that he'd pinched it. He seemed honest though, said he'd been approached by a lady and gentleman just before they caught the last train for London. They asked him to drive it back here, paid him handsomely to do it, and gave him two letters, with instructions to make certain one was delivered to you, and the other to Lord Ruthen. Apparently, they had a child with them, a little girl.'

Selden rolled on his side under the covers when Jenkins tiptoed into the darkened bedroom to which he had retired an hour before. Groggily, he squinted up at the lean, black-suited figure of his valet.

'What the bloody hell d'you want?' he snarled. 'Christ, I've only just gone to sleep. Come back at noon.' He thrust his head under the pillow.

'I'm sorry, your Lordship,' Jenkins murmured deferentially, knowing his master's erratic temper,

299

unpredictable at the best of times and evil when he had had too much to drink. 'But there's a Mrs Turner to see you. Says it's very urgent.'

'Mrs Turner? Who the blazes is she?' Selden's voice was muffled.

'The curate's wife, my Lord.' Jenkins poised by the side of the ostentatious brass bedstead, balancing himself on his small, neat feet, like a spindle-legged stork.

He was a dark-visaged man of sombre mien, with immaculately brushed hair. His features were haughty, slightly supercilious, as befitted a gentleman's gentleman, but this was softened by a pair of mild hazel eyes. He had been with Selden for years and, if anyone understood him, it was Jenkins. He usually acted as a buffer between his master and unwarrantable interferences, but even his considerable skill in such matters had been ineffectual with Elsie Turner who had positively refused to take 'no' for an answer when she appeared at the servants' entrance ten minutes previously.

He attempted to explain this to Selden, but every word he uttered exacerbated his irritability. 'Damn and blast her!' Selden flung the pillow at him, sat up and ungraciously accepted the coffee Jenkins had discreetly placed at the bedside. 'Women! God's curse on the male species. Ain't that the truth, Jenkins?'

'If you say so, your Lordship.'

'I do say so! Diabolical creatures, put on earth to torment us. What does she want?'

'She didn't say, my Lord, but she seems very distressed.'

'I'll give her distressed, rousing me at this ungodly hour!'

He had sought his couch in a bad mood. Camilla engaged to that upstart, Devereaux! Of course, Selden had seen it coming. Gossip had been rife about them for weeks, but he had continued hoping. Hoping for what? Marriage to that free-speaking, independent bitch? Yes, he admitted it, that was what he had wanted. And now that he couldn't have it? We'll see, he had muttered darkly to himself, alone in his silk-sheeted bed. A couple of reports had come through from Captain Martingale who had gone to Brazil as instructed. Nothing of value, so far, but the fellow was working on it.

As he got out of bed, thrust his feet into his slippers and shrugged his thin shoulders into his silk robe, Selden's impatience with the fair sex was reaching boiling point. Useless, the whole lot of 'em! There was Josephine sulking last evening because of Devereaux, face as long as a fiddle. And then, to cap it all, a messenger had turned up at Armitstead House at dawn, with a letter from that fool, Alison. Even now it lay on the dressing-table where he had tossed it. Damned woman! Some bloody nonsense about going to London and attending art school. By God, I'll make sure she doesn't get accepted in any of 'em! he vowed, reaching for his cigarettes. I'll telephone the Slade at once, and Heatherley's in Newman Street. That damned place prides itself on having been the first school in London to admit women students on equal terms with men. I'll soon put a stop to that. Jesus, I'll be hanged if I don't see the place closed should they consider teaching my stupid sister. Art classes, indeed!

'Where have you put Mrs Turner?' he snapped, as Jenkins leaned forward to flick the silver table-lighter.

'In the morning-room, my Lord.'

This was the pleasant, sunny place where, had there been a mistress of Armitstead House, she would have consulted with the housekeeper, decided on the day's menus with the cook, written letters, answered or issued invitations. Alison had fulfilled this role, and Selden's anger redoubled. Why had she run off? It was her job to deal with troublesome petitioners from the village.

In high dudgeon he at length traversed the long, winding carpeted corridors which yielded continually

shifting vistas through round-headed arches and between smooth, cushion-capitalled pillars. Reaching the
wide staircase, he descended rapidly and strode across
the echoing hall and into the morning-room. A figure
stood there, dwarfed by the marble fireplace. It was a
woman in no way pleasing, either in dress, face or form.

Selden cast a jaundiced eye upon her. 'Good morning,
Mrs Turner, and what can I do for you?'

'Good morning, my Lord. Thank you for seeing me.
I'm sorry to trouble you – but – but –'

To Selden's embarrassment, her puffy pale blue eyes
swam with tears, and she clapped a handkerchief to her
mouth, stifling a sob. He was unaccustomed to dealing
with the in-between ranks. Servants, yes, grooms,
coachmen, chauffeurs, but the grey areas which were
neither fish nor foul baffled him. Unless they were scum
like Martingale who he could use, or prostitutes, again
things to be used. But as for churchmen and their
families? They were beyond his ken. A fresh upsurge of
anger against Alison swept through him. This was her
province.

'Be seated, Mrs Turner. Don't distress yourself. Pray
explain the problem if you can. Take your time.' Selden
lit another cigarette, wondering what on earth to do with
her. She did seem genuinely upset.

Elsie Turner was quite simply out of her depth. She
had awakened that morning feeling ill and would have
remained in bed, as was her custom after drinking
heavily, had not Mrs Barlow brought up the letter.
When Elsie first read it, she thought herself the victim of
a practical joke. It was Frank's writing, and she assumed
for a moment that he was pulling her leg. Bleary-eyed,
foggy-headed, the full import of that carefully composed
missive was slow to penetrate. She read it several times
before grasping that this was no joke, no prank on the
part of her husband.

She had sat on the edge of the bed for a long while, the

302

letter in her hands, trying to marshal her jumbled wits. Slowly, the shock had given way to panic, then indignation followed by rage. The boys had already gone to school and Mrs Barlow had stood there in the small cluttered cottage bedroom, wondering what was wrong. The storm of Elsie's outraged feelings broke over her head, and it took Mrs Barlow some time to calm her and make any sense of her ravings.

'Read it! Read it!' Elsie had thrust the letter under her nose. 'The villain has left me! Gone to London! Taken Effie with him!'

After Mrs Barlow had perused the contents, she had advised Elsie to dress herself and pay Lord Ruthen a visit without delay. Stunned, almost mad with grief and bruised pride, Elsie had followed her advice, but not before fortifying herself with half a tumbler of gin.

As she walked the distance between the village and Armitstead House, she kept repeating to herself: 'How could he? Why has he done this to me?'

She no longer loved him, but she was dependent on him, and firmly believed that this was a normal development between married couples. The passion died, the romantic feelings, but surely, a deeper affection should grow? Suddenly, as she passed beneath trees heavy with summer, her skirts brushing the grass, she remembered how it had once been with them and, for the first time in years, felt desire flood through her. Frank! He was hers. Her husband! And now some aristocratic Jezebel had taken him away from her.

She sobbed into her handkerchief there in the morning-room of Lord Ruthen's house, trembling at her boldness in coming, overawed by the splendour surrounding her. She had never been there before, never seen such a place. Hesitantly, she had gone around to the back to beg admittance, not daring to ascend the urn-flanked flights of steps to the front. And here she was, confronting his Lordship, in that beautiful room where every inch of walls, floor or ceiling was adorned with a riot of colour and patterns, electrifying in its grand scale that met her eye on every side.

Lord Ruthen frightened her too, so handsome in his casual brocaded robe and white trousers, his face grave, his grey eyes concerned. Such perfect manners! What a gentleman! She took comfort and a modicum of courage from his concern. Sniffing, she tucked the handkerchief back in her handbag, very aware of her shabby dress, catching a glimpse of her reflection in the great mirror above the fireplace. She was possessed of the queer regret that she was not still wearing the gown which the local seamstress had run up for the party at The Priory. Such a lovely colour. Carnation red. She had been almost pleased with her appearance last night. True, she had put on weight, once a slim slip of a thing, but this had given her a fine bustline. Mrs Barlow had taken the curling tongs to her lifeless brown hair and added a satin bandeau of the same shade as the gown. Nervous, shy, she had felt more confident after a few nips of gin, strolling in the manor grounds on Frank's arm, proud because he was accorded respect by everyone they met. What a fool I've been, she thought. He was planning to leave me all along. Even as we walked together, his mind was filled with *her*.

'Your Lordship, I want you to read this letter,' she said, and handed a folded paper to him.

He did not fail to notice that her gloves were dirty and that there was a hole in the left one. His dislike of this wretched, plain-faced creature grew. He stared down at her. The morning was hot and she had obviously been hurrying. Little beads of sweat lay on her brow beneath the lank fringe, and dampened the down on her upper lip. The stale odour of her body reached him, overlaid but not disguised by Yardley's Old English Lavender soap.

'But surely this is a private letter? You can't want me to –?' he protested.

'Please, my Lord. It concerns you.' Her watery eyes

looked up into his, and Selden experienced repugnance mixed with an odd sensation of curiosity. What would she be like in bed? he wondered. A pity that she wasn't a pretty supplicant so that he could go into his lord of the manor act, impressing and possibly seducing her.

'Very well, if you insist.' He opened the letter, then became still and silent as he read its contents.

'My dear Elsie,' Frank had written.

No doubt this will come as a great shock to you and there is no way in which I can break the news gently. I'm leaving you. By the time you get this, I'll be in London. I'm taking Effie with me. You never really loved the child, and she's all the world to me. I may as well tell you now, as soon it will be common knowledge, I'm not going alone. Lady Alison Ruthen is coming too. We have been lovers for months.

Try not to think too badly of us. We are very much in love and wish to make a life together. Effie will be well cared for. Don't worry about money. I enclose fifty pounds and will send you a regular sum. Even if you have to leave the cottage, and I suppose this is inevitable when a new curate is appointed, you should be able to move away and rent a little house somewhere for yourself and the boys. Why not go and stay near your married sister at Weston-super-Mare? The boys would enjoy living at the seaside.

I expect you will start divorce proceedings and I'll co-operate to the best of my ability. I shall be leaving the church and intend to write full-time. I hope that we can be divorced as I wish to marry Lady Alison as soon as possible. In this way, we may be able to prevent our expected baby from being illegitimate. I hope you will remember the love you once bore me and help me in this. I'll write again soon, but please don't try to find out my address. Alison and I wish to be left alone in peace.

Believe me when I say that I'm truly sorry to cause you grief, but you know that there has been nothing between us for years. Although you are my wife, and I should have supported you to the end, I'm not a saint, Elsie, and your drinking habits have proved to be untenable.

Yours, Frank.

Selden stood there rigid, lips pressed in a hard, straight line. His feelings were those of contemptuous anger. That fool of a sister of his. All right, so even her juices had not completely dried up through enforced spinsterhood, but did she have to get pregnant by the curate? That was about her mark, the silly, sentimental, brainless idiot! The curate! God, how absurd! Mrs Turner was looking at him, waiting for pearls of wisdom to fall from his lips. Another fool. He wanted her out of the house. Her ugliness offended him. No wonder Frank Turner had left her, though Alison wasn't much better. Damn them, those tiresome little people who were now going to make his life complicated. There would be an almighty scandal and he'd be caught in the crossfire. He was already searching for the means to ensure that the blame could not be laid at his doorstep.

'My sister! I can't believe it!' he exclaimed, with just the right amount of pathos. 'Oh, Mrs Turner, say it isn't true!'

'I'm afraid it is, sir, every word of it,' she cried, springing up, daring to lay a hand on his silk-covered arm. 'I'm sorry, so dreadfully sorry to be the one to tell you.'

'Alison! What madness possessed her? A woman in her position –' Selden succeeded in looking broken. Josephine would have applauded such a performance. 'And your husband? It's like a bad dream.'

'What are we going to do?' His tragic aspect caught at Elsie's heart. She had been so afraid that he might blame her, turn her away, refuse to discuss it. But instead he was so kind, so sincere. Her eyes grew wider, her face more flushed beneath her shapeless hat.

When she was not drinking herself into that sodden state of oblivion when nothing mattered, Elsie was an avid reader of romantic novels of the type Frank wrote unbeknown to her. In fact, she had read several of his without realizing that the author of this pulp literature was her own quiet husband. Now Selden seemed to be the personification of the handsome heroes of these impossible tales of noble love, betrayal and self-sacrifice.

'I don't know how to advise you, Mrs Turner, but rest assured that you shan't suffer for my sister's misdemeanours,' he answered, his voice husky with emotion. 'To snatch a child from its mother's arms. How heartless! How cruel!'

Such histrionics were infectious and Elsie gave full rein to her feelings in the drama of the moment. 'Oh, yes! My little Effie! My baby!' she cried piteously.

This was pretence and, deep in her heart, Elsie knew it. What Frank had written was perfectly true. She did not like Effie, and had resented her from the time of her conception. Another baby, when they already had three small sons. It was just too awful. Dirty, human lust was the cause. That uncouth act which her mother had taught her it was a woman's lot to endure, for the sake of the marriage vows, and to obey God's command to reproduce. An act which husbands enjoyed and their wives suffered to please them. Her mother had been deeply religious. The bible was her rock, her reference book. She instructed her children that the Almighty was a wrathful being, and the sinful went straight to hell, there to suffer eternal torments. Spiritual love was pure, physical love a sin.

Elsie, so carefully brainwashed, had been thrown into confusion when she met Frank during one of her mother's prayer meetings and he began to court her. She found to her horror that her response to this attractive man was one of bodily passion. After they were married, she would lie in his arms, thinking: I'm wicked. I shouldn't be enjoying this. It's my duty, nothing more. I've no right to be experiencing this excitement culminating in glorious release. She struggled with her urges, drove them underground, repressed them as best she could.

The birth of her first child seemed God's punishment, the agony, the humiliation of it beyond all expectation. Two more pregnancies in rapid succession, two more agonizing deliveries convinced her that she was being made to suffer for the sin of fleshly delight. Then Effie, and this time the confinement was so gruelling that God decided to forgive her. He spoke through the mouth of the doctor, who had attended her, saying that there must be no more children.

Frank suggested that they use methods of birth control but Elsie would have none of this. Only prostitutes and evil women prevented conception by artificial means. She withdrew from her husband's arms, from his bed, and sought solace in strong drink, unconsciously following in her father's footsteps. It was only now, as she stood near Selden Ruthen, that her dammed emotions broke the barriers she had so painstakingly erected. She denied that her response to him was anything but mental. He was a good man, she could tell. He would help her in her hour of need.

'Don't worry, dear Mrs Turner, your daughter shall be restored to you.' Selden's face shone in the sunlight striking through a high oriel window of stained glass. It formed a halo around his head.

'Oh, thank you, my Lord. I knew you'd help me,' she breathed.

His mind was working furiously as he considered the dowdy woman who was staring up at him with such a rapt expression. The last thing he wanted was for the whole village to be talking until he had decided what course to take. His eyes misted thoughtfully as he raked back over the past months. There had certainly been something odd about Alison's behaviour – this sudden fervour for church-going, the hours she had spent away from the house. Painting, she said.

He turned away, moving towards the chiffonier and pouring brandy into two goblets. 'Would you like a drink, Mrs Turner?'

'Oh, no, your Lordship. I never touch it,' Elsie answered, though her eyes were fixed on the decanter longingly.

Selden raised an eyebrow. He could have sworn that he had caught the taint of gin on her breath. 'No? Then your husband was lying, was he, when he spoke of your liking for alcohol?' He carried the glasses over and placed one in her hand.

'Sometimes I'm forced to take a little, for my health, you see – I have these funny giddy turns – that's all.' The way Elsie's fingers closed about the brandy gave the lie to her statement.

Selden's lips curled into the semblance of a smile. 'I'm sure that you need it now. Brandy is excellent for shock, and this is a particularly fine vintage.'

In the next instant, her glass was empty. Selden refilled it, putting her in a further flurry of embarrassment coupled with something else – a dark skein of dangerous feeling to which she would not admit. The brandy trickled over her tongue and settled like fire in her stomach. It suffused her with a warm, confident glow. Somehow, it no longer seemed strange that she should be sitting here in this sumptuous room drinking with his Lordship.

'You really shouldn't be waiting on me, my Lord,' she said, rolling her eyes towards him. 'It's not right, you being who you are, and me one of your humble parishioners.'

Good God, she's being positively coquettish! thought Selden with an inward shudder. Aloud, he said: 'Nonsense, my dear lady. We're fellow sufferers, are we not? Both compromised by the selfishness of others.' He took the vacant chair next to hers and leaned towards her, his grey eyes boring into hers. 'Let us put our heads together, shall we? Now, can you tell me anything which may throw light on this distressing matter?'

'I know nothing. What can I tell you?' she fluttered,

309

confused by his closeness, the scent of toilet water that
wafted from his skin, combined with that disturbing
male odour that she loved, hated, feared above all
things.

'Ah, I apologize for distressing you.' His hand rested
briefly on hers. 'But these are the kind of questions you'll
be forced to answer if the matter comes before the
divorce courts. Tell me, have you noticed anything
peculiar about your husband's behaviour over the past
months? Has he changed his daily habits, done anything
which you thought odd?'

Elsie found it almost impossible to think coherently. A
further brandy did not help, simply firing her desire to be
of service to this magnificent man. 'Well, let me see – he's
always shut himself up in his study, working, but around
Christmas, I did notice that he began to go out and not
come back for hours.'

'Have you any idea where he went?' Selden's voice
was soft, and he wore that cherubic smile which Nanny
Hobson always used to suspect so deeply. 'Master
Selden's up to no good,' she would say.

'In the direction of The Priory, I believe. Mrs Barlow
saw him once or twice.' A rabbit before a serpent could
not have been more mesmerized than Elsie Turner at
that precise moment.

'The Priory?' Selden permitted himself to look
puzzled. 'You think he went to see Lady Camilla? Is she
somehow involved in this?'

'I don't know, your Lordship,' Elsie answered, then,
to please him, she rambled on: 'Maybe she is. There's
talk of her in the village, and those darky servants of
hers. She's not like one of us, is she? A stranger, a
foreigner, with outlandish foreign ways. I wouldn't put
anything past her.'

Selden was only listening with a section of his mind.
He was thinking of Alison, trying to remember. Where
did she go, pedalling like mad down the drive, with her

310

innocent-looking sketch pads, her pencils, her brushes? He knew for a fact that she had spent much time with Camilla whilst The Priory was being restored.

'So you can tell me nothing further?' He made to rise, about to dismiss her, but Elsie again laid a hand on his arm.

'Wait, there is something. It's coming back to me now. He took Effie with him not long ago and, when she came home, she said that she'd been playing in an old gypsy wagon.'

This stopped him in his tracks. The gypsy wagon in The Priory grounds. Memories of childhood, of Josephine and himself tucked up for the night on one of the bunks. Her hot, wriggling body had made him feel odd, excited. How she had giggled! How she had squirmed yet liked it when he lifted her nightgown, curious, exploring, experimental. It was then that he'd discovered what he had long suspected. Girls were made differently from boys. Then, just when the panting excitement was at its height, Alison had screamed in terror from the other bunk, frightened by an owl. They had had to take her home. She always had been a damned nuisance.

In a flash, Selden knew that she had been meeting Frank Turner there. So, his skinny, plain sister had been coupling with the lean, middle-aged curate in the wagon. The picture presented was ludicrous. Had Camilla known about it? Selden relaxed. This could be used to advantage. The villagers were already suspicious of her. It would not be difficult for this ill-feeling to be carefully fostered. All grist to Selden's mill. His clever brain threw up something else.

'When was the letter from your husband delivered?' he asked, almost casually.

'Mrs Barlow found it propped on the mantelshelf early this morning,' she answered earnestly, never taking her eyes from his face.

311

'So he must have left it there last night. What happened at the party, Mrs Turner?'

Then she told him how, during the firework display, Frank had said that Effie felt sick. Lady Camilla had offered her car, so that he might drive the child home. Selden listened without comment, then rang a small silver bell on the table.

Jenkins appeared in answer to the summons. 'Yes, my Lord?'

'Jenkins, can you tell me who brought that letter this morning?'

'It was no one I knew, your Lordship. A roughish sort of man. So rough, in fact, that I was surprised to see him driving a very smart motorcar.' Jenkins showed no curiosity or emotion to find his master drinking with the curate's wife.

'A car, you say? What car?'

'It was a sporting model, my Lord. A Mercedes, I believe.'

'Like the one owned by Lady Camilla?'

'Very like, my Lord.'

'Thank you, Jenkins. That will be all.'

'What can this mean?' Elsie, never quick-witted, was baffled.

'It means, Mrs Turner, that I very much suspect Lady Camilla knows more about your husband's affair with my sister than we imagine.' Selden was looking up at the Saracenic ceiling, as if seeking inspiration from its eight-pointed central star. Then his gaze returned to her, wistful, a little dreamy, totally captivating. 'May I ask a great favour of you?'

A favour? This noble being was actually asking *her* for a favour? Elsie was bowled over. 'Of course! Anything!'

'Will you say nothing of this to anyone for a while? Leave it to me. If I have any news, I'll inform you right away. I know this will be hard. Your neighbours are bound to ask questions. Can you do it?'

'Oh, yes. I'll tell Mrs Barlow to keep a still tongue in her head. In fact we don't mix much with the villagers, being strangers ourselves. I can let it be known that Frank has been called away on church business.'

'I knew I could rely on you,' he beamed, but there was a dismissive air about him. He led her to the door. 'You say that Lady Camilla's not well liked? A pity –'

'Will you ask her about Frank?' Elsie paused in the doorway, glancing back regretfully at the morning-room, the like of which she might never enter again. She wanted to prolong the interview, to remain in Selden's presence. Within her formed the determination to come again. All she had to do was to send a message claiming to have further information.

'I'll ask her. Have no worries on that score.' Just for a moment, the look in his eyes was frightening, then it was gone, leaving only a bland grey stare. 'There are a number of questions I intend to put to Lady Camilla Ruthen.'

4

'Daddy! Daddy!' The child's voice penetrated Alison's dreams.

She opened her eyes and instantly remembered where she was and why she was there, last night's events clear in every detail. With a choke in her throat and joy in her heart, she saw Frank beside her in the wide bed, sleeping on his back, one arm flung over his face. She reached out to touch him, but the door opened and a small figure in a white nightgown stood there.

'What is it, Effie?' she asked, withdrawing as far as possible from Frank.

'Where's my Daddy?'

'He's here,' Alison held out a hand towards her, encouraging, smiling. Effie advanced crabwise, thumb between her lips, regarding her with large, distrustful eyes.

She paused by the bed, staring first at her slumbering father, then at the strange woman with the long brown hair hanging down over her bare shoulders. Suddenly conscious of her nakedness, Alison tucked the sheet up under her armpits. This solemn-faced tot was making her more uncomfortable than she had felt when signing the register as Mrs Turner, watched by the inscrutable concierge of the Faulkner Hotel.

'A double room for myself and my wife,' Frank had said, haggard in the pearly dawning light. 'And an adjoining one for our daughter.'

'You wish for breakfast and room service, sir?' The manager had been formally polite. 'That will be ten shillings and sixpence per night, sir, plus two and sixpence for the child.'

This was an entirely new departure for Alison. It was not often that she used hotels, but when she did, money had never been openly discussed. She had simply been presented with a bill at the end of her stay or it had been added to the Ruthen account. Should she have made a flying visit to the capital when it had not been worth opening up the town house, she had always chosen the Westminster Palace Hotel in Victoria Street where the family were respected patrons of long-standing. But to go there now had been out of the question. So, after leaving Paddington, they had taken a taxi to Villiers Street near the Strand and booked in at this one. She was no longer Lady Alison Ruthen, but a fugitive seeking anonymity as Mrs Frank Turner.

The manager had been courtesy itself, calmly accepting their arrival at so early an hour. 'Will you be staying long, sir?' he had enquired urbanely.

'Possibly for a few days,' Frank's aplomb had been admirable. 'We're house-hunting.'

'Ah, I see, sir. May I ask if you have an estate agent?' that polite voice had rolled on. 'If not, I suggest that you visit W. Rowntree and Sons, 33 to 39 Westborough and York Place. They have an excellent reputation and I'm sure you'll find their service most satisfactory.'

'But isn't that a shop?' Alison had put in, hand tucked into Frank's arm. He was holding the sleeping Effie, whose small head nestled into his shoulder. 'I'm sure I've visited a large showroom there. Yes, I'm certain of it. I bought some yardage of Liberty fabric.'

'Madam is quite correct,' the manager had smiled, stroking his waxed moustache. 'But they are also house-agents.'

He seemed perfectly satisfied that she and Frank were a respectable, well-to-do married couple, no doubt assuming that their personal servants would be arriving later. Soon they had been conducted through the spacious, gilt and plush foyer that bore the hushed

315

solemnity of a cathedral nave, and into a lift which whisked them to an upper floor. A neatly uniformed page-boy, pillbox hat at a jaunty angle, had carried their luggage. There had been no one else about, and Effie had slept throughout.

Tiredness had swept over Alison in waves. She still seemed to be on the swaying, rattling train. Even first-class tickets had not saved them from two tiresome changes necessitating lengthy waits on bleak platforms before the journey was completed. Then the smoky, noisy station, the press of early morning travellers, the bustle of a big city depot. She had stood forlornly, a grizzling Effie's hand in hers, as Frank went off in search of a hackney carriage or a taxi. Whilst attempting to soothe the fractious child, her eyes had been drawn to the gaudily clad women leaning over a barrier. Red hair, gold, black – vast hats loaded with artificial flowers and nodding plumage, feather boas, tightly laced waists and low corsages, the smell of cheap perfume. Their strident voices had reached her, larded with oaths delivered in Cockney intonations as they solicited passing men. One of them was obviously pregnant, and Alison had shuddered and closed her eyes momentarily. Poor creatures. What circumstances had brought them so low? The dregs of the streets, leaping like scavengers on men arriving from far corners of Britain. Brazen, raucous, displaying their wares, hoping for customers. There, but for the grace of God, go I, she had thought, with a feeling close to terror.

She remembered them now as she looked at Effie, and guilt racked her. I too am a fallen woman, she mused, though mocking herself for the melodramatic phrase. But this is different, surely? Ours is a union of true minds. Our baby is a love-child. I can't think of it as a bastard. But in Effie's eyes she imagined there was a gleam of condemnation, and some of the warmth and excitement abated, leaving a bad taste in her mouth.

316

Frank had been too tired to make love to her when they went to bed. He put one arm about her and held her close against him, his hand warm and hard between her shoulder blades. She had kissed him gently, thinking, we are one. Nothing shall ever come between us. But, listening to his even breathing, she had known disappointment, feeling foolish in her seductive nightdress. It was black chiffon, semi-transparent, bought in anticipation of something approaching a wedding night. What a waste, but there'll be tomorrow morning. No, morning is already here. Well later, anyway.

Though exhausted, she had lain awake for some time, listening to the sounds of the hotel springing into life, watching the light stealing in at the edges of the macramé-trimmed green blinds. The room was large and comfortably furnished. The ceiling had a lofty frieze, richly moulded. The walls were covered with pale lemon paper that resembled watered-silk, and the lower half was hung with thick, embossed imitation panelling. Besides the pseudo-Gothic double bed with its high, half tester, it contained large fitted wardrobes, a vast walnut dressing-table on which a lace-edged duchess-set glistened like frost, a writing desk supplied with hotel stationery, two deep armchairs and a couch, protected by antimacassars. It was rather old-fashioned, though boasting electricity in every room and telephones too. The marble mantelshelf over the cast-iron grate was crowded with china ornaments, a chambermaid's nightmare. There were a profusion of pot-plants poised on mahogany whatnots, dominated by a jungly monster of an aspidistra. A bathroom was reached through a door on the right, wherein, on lion's paw feet, crouched a massive tub, its white glaze festooned with sprawling pink cabbage roses. There was an equally gargantuan washbasin and a lavatory to match, the whole tiled from floor to ceiling in eastern arabesques, turquoise blue on a cream ground, edged with gold swirls.

317

The decor was overblown and pompous, and the establishment geared to provide everything that money could buy. This was no sordid lodging-house or squalid backstreet *pension* where no questions were asked. But its very air of smug gentility made Alison aware that had the manager an inkling of their unmarried status, he would be thundering on the door, demanding that they leave at once, turning them out on to the street, bag and baggage.

What was it Frank had said? 'You'll be a social outcast. A pariah.' She had denied it vehemently, but was already experiencing qualms. They would go house-hunting, but she would have to be careful not to shop in areas where she might bump into acquaintances. I hope we find a house soon, she prayed. A place where I can hide myself away and live only for Frank and the baby. And Effie? asked a small, sneering voice in her head. Of course, Effie too, she answered defensively.

The child now leaned across her father and lifted one of his eyelids with a small, insistent finger. 'Daddy, I want to go home,' she declared, her voice petulant. 'Where's Mummy? Where are the boys? Where's Mrs Barlow? I'm hungry. I want my breakfast.'

Frank woke then, smiled and pulled her to him. 'What's all this, pet? We're on holiday. I'm going to take you to Regent's Park Zoo. You'll like that, won't you? I'll ring for breakfast in a minute. Give me a chance to wake up.'

Effie wriggled into bed, worming her way between them, giving Alison a triumphant and hostile blue stare. She lay there in the curve of Frank's elbow, thumb wedged into her mouth. This was not what Alison had been expecting. She had dreamed of waking with Frank, to lie where Effie now was, planning their day, discussing the house, then gradually succumbing to passion before they rose, had a bath together in that decadent tub and dressed in a leisurely, teasing, amorous manner.

I should have known, she chided herself. What did I imagine was going to happen to Effie whilst this pleasant interlude took place? The poor little darling must be dreadfully confused. Telling herself firmly that she loved her because she was Frank's, and that she wanted to get to know her, to be her friend, she tried to make the best of it. She snuggled against the child, and Frank's hand came to rest on her shoulder, Effie in the middle. Suddenly, Alison stiffened, aware of a warm, unpleasant dampness.

'Frank, we'll have to get up,' she exclaimed, horrified, and reached for her negligee, trying not to remember the high hopes with which she had purchased it. 'Good heavens, she's soaking.'

He grinned, but there was a wry slant to his mouth. 'Oh, yes, I forgot to tell you that she wets the bed, didn't I, darling?'

Without answering him, Alison went to the window, looking down at the traffic passing below. The morning was well advanced, the sun like a white-hot disc above. The smell of melting asphalt, of dust, dung and motor oil rose up to meet her. The noise was deafening, reaching the fretted balcony on which she stood. The rattle of iron-bound wheels, honking taxis and horse-drawn buses, the steel-studded tyres of private limousines. Over the macadam road they made a hissing sound like a cross between a high wind in the leaves and a heavy shower of rain. Londoners went about their business, weaving their way dexterously between vehicles. Traders cried their wares, beggars hung about on street corners with their whining hard-luck stories, ragged women loitered with baskets, selling matches, flowers. Office staff released for lunch, typists, clerks and department store workers, were heading for the nearest tea-shops.

Alison seemed to be looking down on a sea of hats. The women's were huge, firmly skewered on their high-piled

319

hair, decorated with a variety of fake blossoms, ospreys, gauze and tulle, their escorts top-hatted, bowler-hatted or sporting dashing straw panamas. They strolled past the big stores, window-gazing. Wealthy ladies, very bedizened, alighted from their electrically driven broughams in which their chauffeurs sat upon a box in front which offered no protection. These free-spending customers were greeted by liveried major-domos under the striped canopies of the emporiums, before disappearing through revolving doors. Everyone seemed totally engrossed in their own concerns, self-absorbed, indifferent. Alison was bleakly certain that they would ignore, probably not even see, someone dying on the pavement at their feet.

Terrible isolation possessed her, homesickness as acute as a physical pain. She remembered how much she really disliked London, always happy to leave it. A longing for the countryside swept up, the green fields, the fresh air, the lack of rush and urgency. It's no use, she thought. I mustn't feel like this. I can't go home.

Behind her, she heard Frank laughing as he helped Effie put on her clothes. She was giggling as he tickled her. Alison glanced at them, clutching the now absurdly revealing garment about her, certain that Effie had noticed her nudity. But father and daughter were absorbed in one another. It was as if they had forgotten her existence. Jealousy gripped her like a serpent. It sickened her and she tried to be rational. I can't be jealous of Frank's child, she's a part of him. And of Elsie?

She took a deep breath and fixed a wide smile on her lips. 'Ready to eat, Effie? There's a good girl. When we've eaten, we'll go to Harrod's and buy you a doll, shall we?'

Effie fell silent, then climbed on to her father's knee. She stared at Alison, and there was nothing in her eyes but a faintly disdainful curiosity.

*

Camilla was not surprised to read the contents of Alison's letter. Her first reaction was: good for her. It was high time she did something for herself, instead of being Selden's slave. Then, as she read it through for the second time, the ramifications began to make themselves clear. She had been in England long enough to know that there would be a frightful scandal. The guilty lovers would be thrown to the lions, and she was already implicated by Alison's request to make sure that Selden sent on her belongings. She would forward an address, she had said, once she and Frank were settled, but on no account was Camilla to let her brother know it. Camilla shook her head, gazing down at that hurried, almost breathless writing. She had the gravest doubts about obtaining Selden's co-operation. He was much more likely to make things as difficult as possible for his rebellious sister.

After breakfast, Darcy went back to Chalkdown Farm and Rufus retired to his room. He had eaten nothing, was unusually quiet and preoccupied, so Camilla had not questioned him about her father. There was no sign of John and Amy, and Camilla gave orders that they were not to be disturbed. For her own part, she was too strung up to sleep. It had certainly been an eventful night and now there were further problems looming on the horizon so, summoning Leila, she went down to the lakeside. The Creole was still silent and withdrawn, but Camilla decided to ignore this, trusting that she would come around to the idea of the engagement in her own time.

Wearing a martyred air, Leila humped the basket containing her lace-making equipment, whilst Camilla carried a bottle of lemonade, some fruit, cheese and bread for their lunch. In a silence no way amicable, they marched resolutely along, the brilliant light of summer striking between the trees as they left The Priory behind. The lawns wore a deserted look. Already the marquees, the bunting and every trace of the party had vanished as if by magic. Confused by lack of sleep, Camilla wondered if she had dreamed it all. Perhaps it had not happened. There was no Darcy, no wedding plans. She gave Leila a suspicious stare, knowing her hypnotic powers. Were these disorienting thoughts springing from her?

Grabbing reality like a drowning man clutching at a straw, Camilla gave herself a mental shake. This is nonsense, she lectured inwardly. I know precisely what's happening and where I'm heading, and so does Leila. My desire to swim naked in the lake only lends force to her all round disapproval of my behaviour.

When the brambles, nettles and undergrowth had been beaten into submission by Camilla's team of gardeners earlier in the year, an interesting feature had come to light. They discovered that the narrow, meandering river had once been dammed into a miniature lake at the edge of the extensive grounds. The general opinion was that it may well have served as a carp pond for the monks, or could have been constructed during that fever for rearranging views that had fired eighteenth century property owners, giving them no peace until they had converted their manor houses into replicas of baroque palaces visited on The Grand Tour of Europe. To fit in with these ideas, the grounds were then landscaped by skilled artisans like Capability Brown, who had seen that money was to be made from this fashionable craze for the picturesque. Lakes had sprung into being, sham ruins, follies, temples and grottoes, cascades and irregular sheets of water.

Although no one had tampered with the architecture of The Priory, its gardens had come under attack. The result was now pleasing, mellowed by one hundred and fifty years of seasonal change and growth. Camilla thanked whichever ancestor it was who had designed it, for the pool provided a secluded place in which to swim or lie on the bank soaking up the sun. And that was not all. That earlier, innovative Ruthen had ordered a summerhouse to be built on its shores. Camilla did not doubt that there would be detailed plans and bills for this quaint bit of nonsense somewhere in the archives.

It was a rather eccentric piece of work, resembling the witch's gingerbread house in 'Hansel and Gretel'. When she first examined it, Camilla had silently congratulated its builder. Now refurbished, it was an ideal spot for picnics and intimate evening supper parties. It amused her to think that her forebear probably had it designed with liaisons in mind, so private, so perfect for illicit assignations. Certainly his descendant had taken full advantage of this, meeting Darcy there by moonlight.

Why didn't Alison tell me about her affair with Frank? she wondered as its fantastic little chimney pot came into sight. I could have let them borrow it, but of course the gypsy wagon had proved equally convenient. No wonder Alison had been so insistent that she was not disturbed. Oh, dear, she *should* have confided in me, her mind ran on. Perhaps I could have advised her on a method of preventing conception. Then she laughed at herself. I'm a fine one to advise anybody on such a subject. Look what happened to me!

'You going to swim mother-naked again?' Leila dumped her burden down in the porch. She always said that, every time they came.

'I am.'

'Then you mind the spirits. That Baron-Samedi, he done like girls with no clothes on. You going to get raped, Missy Camilla – raped by an ugly demon,' Leila predicted gloomily.

Camilla opened the door of the cottage-like structure and went in. The roof was low and thatched, the walls made of the trunks and branches of pine trees used in their rough state, though cut in ordered lengths, to give it an exotic texture and pattern redolent of the forest.

323

Inside it consisted of a single room, and she had had some furniture brought down from The Priory; a table, two benches, a chair, a divan, some colourful rugs. Cups and plates stood on wooden shelves and there was a kettle on a trivet near the tiny fireplace. She never entered there without thinking of Darcy, glancing at the couch, the hot blood of recollection singing in her veins. Perhaps we won't go away on a honeymoon, she thought. We could spend our wedding night here.

Leila had already hauled the rocking-chair outside, seated herself and taken up her work. She was exceptionally skilled in lace-making, colourful bobbins sticking up like porcupine quills from the stuffed pillow she carried in a special, high-sided basket, weighted at the bottom to keep it firm and steady. Venetian lace was her speciality, delicate and complicated, and much of Camilla's underwear was edged and inserted with it. Mouth closed tightly, she began sticking pins in the pillow to enlarge the pattern. Camilla had the uncomfortable feeling that she was wishing it was a mommet she pierced, a death-doll shaped as Darcy Devereaux.

With a shrug, she undressed, wrapped herself in a white cotton robe, took up some cushions and a blanket and padded, barefoot, past Leila and down to the water's edge. It was the Creole's job to watch out for unwelcome visitors. The only path to the pool wound in front of the summerhouse. No one could get by without confronting the dark-skinned sentinel. No one dared try. Camilla spent most fine days lazing there, drowsily listening to the cool trickle of the stream, the incessant trilling of the birds, the click of Leila's bobbins, pins and prickers.

The hot sun burned her shoulders as she discarded her robe. She poised on the edge for an instant, then dived in. The cold shock was exhilarating. There was a moment of enveloping darkness, then she rose into sunlight, pushing her hair from her eyes. The water was glassy under

324

the bank, tranquil, of a dark bottle-green with a slightly oily surface on which pond-skaters skimmed, mysterious, uncanny-looking creatures – insect phantoms walking on the water, but with very greedy appetites. She watched one seizing a floating fly. He skated away into the shade to devour it. The sun did not penetrate far below the surface and weeds drifted there, long fronds coiling and uncoiling like tenacious, slimy fingers.

Leila's disturbing remark about haunted pools could not be forgotten and, as Camilla swam, her thoughts turned to the Voodoo belief that the souls of the dead spent at least a year and a half in rivers, pools or wells. She remembered ceremonies associated with this, for the spirits became tired of drifting in eternal wetness. They warned their relatives that they were getting cold, and longed for the warmth of the sun. This nostalgia for the earth was so strong that if the one to whom they appealed turned a deaf ear, he was quickly struck down with illness from which he could be saved only if the correct ritual were performed.

As a powerful *mambo*, Leila had often been called upon to lead the rite, usually carried out on behalf of a whole list of dead, for it was a long, costly business and several families usually clubbed together to pay for it. It was no use putting it off. Leila had told her that she had done this once herself, ignoring the messages sent from beyond the grave by her brother. She had lost her strength, growing weaker daily, wasting away before everyone's eyes. She was too clever not to know the reason. The dead, growing impatient, had seized her. It had been necessary to carry out the required ceremony without delay, or she would have died too, joining her impatient brother beneath the water.

In an English lake, beneath an English summer sun, Camilla mused on this. That crying thing in the Master Chamber and the little room beyond? She recalled its slithering footfalls. Someone walking through slime, through mud, through murky liquid? Was this a spirit who needed freeing from lengthy immersion? Perhaps if I could persuade Leila to perform the extraction of the dead from water, the ghost will be laid to rest? She would be a job to catch, of course, they always were, those floating wraiths, and then she must be taken to a sanctuary where she would be transformed into a guardian *loa*.

I'll do it when Darcy and I are married, she resolved. There's too much to think about before then. You won't mind waiting a while, will you, ghost? she addressed it respectfully. I've not been aware of you recently. Perhaps my preoccupation with Darcy has blocked my perception. I'll have to tell him about you, in due course. Don't be disappointed if he denies your existence.

There was no answering echo, no chill which indicated psychic breezes blowing from the barren wastes of the infernal regions. It was almost too quiet, too peaceful, like the lull before the storm. Camilla left the water, wading through the shallows, her skin shining and golden, bedecked with a million sparkling diamond drops.

Grass beneath her feet, then the softness of rugs. Camilla threw herself down on the heap of cushions and stretched on her back, one leg flexed, the other straight, her arms flung out on either side, eyes closed in the blissful warmth. If I was a cat, I'd purr right now. She allowed her mind to wander down avenues too misty to be called thoughts. Strange incidents, strange conversations with people she had never met in real life, things which she forgot immediately when she came back to herself, only to drift off again, stupefied by the heat.

Blessed sun! It poured into every corner of her being, banishing the cobwebs, revitalizing her with the energy coming from its blazing core, radiating around her as she lay there, its worshipper, pressed against the slumbering earth. To her this was prayer, more so than in any church. Churches were cold, austere. The sun, the giver of life, should be praised in the open. Naked, body relaxed, every part exposed, the acolyte, drugged by heat, surrendered to the fiery god.

Suddenly, Camilla became aware of a chill. She gazed upwards through slitted eyes. A dark shape stood between herself and the sun. Like night, like winter. 'Go away,' she said clearly. 'Remove yourself, black object.'

She knew it was Selden, yet at the same time, half asleep, thought it was an apparition. There was no fear, no embarrassment because she was naked, only annoyance at being disturbed at her meditations. Leila, hearing her speak, was there in a flash.

'You shouldn't be here, Lord Ruthen. This is Missy Camilla's place,' she said in her careful, though accented English, and Selden, looking into her black eyes, found himself staring at a void so dense and unfathomable that he shrank back.

Camilla sat up and pulled her robe about her. 'It's all right, Leila. I'll deal with this.' Her tawny eyes considered him, from the top of his shiny black hat to the toes of his shiny black boots. 'You wish to swim, Selden? Go ahead. I'll not stop you.'

Still subjecting him to that look which seemed to freeze the marrow in his bones, Leila returned to her rocking-chair, her bobbins and that sharply pointed implement which she wielded with additional vigour.

Selden was nonplussed. He had ridden over from Armitstead House, taking a long route, cutting across fields and arriving lower down the river, quietly clopping towards the summerhouse. He had reined in behind screening willows, watching Camilla leave the water. Tall, wide-shouldered and straight-backed, with that slender waist and high, beautifully shaped breasts, she had seemed even more formidable without her clothes. Like a goddess, he had thought. A pagan from the dawn of time, maybe one of those legendary warrior women, called Amazons, of whom she had spoken during a dinner party, quite upsetting a number of ladies present, and not a few of the gentlemen. They were supposed to inhabit the remote regions of her country. Selden hadn't much liked the sound of them, for they were reputed to be ferocious fighters who lived without men, merely capturing a few when needing to breed, and slaughtering them after they'd served their purpose. The subsequent babies were killed if they were male and kept if female.

He removed his hat and tucked it under his arm. 'I didn't come to swim. I've an urgent matter to discuss with you.' He stood there motionless, save for the whip lightly tapping at the top of his riding boot.

'Then please move aside. You're blocking the sun. You've a damned big shadow, Selden.' Camilla did not suggest that he joined her on the rug, so he perched himself on a nearby tree stump.

'I expect you know why I'm here,' he began. His eyes were cold, heavy-lidded, with faint shadows under them.

'Do I? Is it to offer me further congratulations on my impending marriage? Perhaps ask what I'd like for a wedding present?' Camilla glanced away, busying herself with rubbing her hair with a towel.

Against its fluffy whiteness, her skin was almost shockingly brown. Selden wondered briefly if there was any truth in the rumour that she had coloured blood. It in no way detracted from her allure. In fact, he was uncomfortably aware of tightening in his loins, and envy twisted in his gut when he thought of Darcy enjoying such perfection of face and figure.

'That isn't why I came but, if you're fishing for compliments, I'll add that Devereaux's one hell of a lucky fellow.' Selden stroked his chin thoughtfully with the whip handle. 'Haven't you heard what's happened?'

Slanting amber eyes stared up at him from between a curtain of tangled hair. She pushed it back with one hand. 'I've heard many things.'

Provocative bitch! Selden gritted his teeth against the bodily urge that was spoiling the cut of his breeches. 'I had a letter from my sister this morning.'

'Josephine?' Camilla showed the faintest trace of interest, arms linked around her hunched up knees.

'Alison.' Selden's brows were drawn down into a scowl. 'She's run off to London. Wrote that she wants to attend art school or somesuch damn fool nonsense, but that's a red herring.'

So he didn't know the rest of the story? Or did he? Selden was cunning. One had to box clever. 'That will be nice for her,' she answered coolly. 'I've always thought her immensely talented.'

His hand shot out and he gripped her upper arm, pulling her nearer to him so that his eyes might bore into hers and gouge out secrets. 'Talent, my foot! All right, Camilla, time to stop playing games. I've had a visit from the curate's wife.'

'Well, aren't you the lucky one? What am I supposed to do? Jump up and down with excitement?' Selden's patronizing, yet vicious attitude always set her teeth on edge. She could never refrain from exercising sarcasm on him.

His smile thinned, his fingers bit into her flesh. Camilla sent a mental call to Leila. Her arm became a red-hot branding iron, searing him. With a start, Selden dropped his hand.

The next moment he had forgotten why, but he did not try to touch her again. 'Frank Turner's missus. She too had a letter, and in it her husband confessed that he and Alison had gone to London together. He wants a divorce. What d'you know about all this?'

'Only that Alison wants her belongings sent on, when she's ready to receive them.'

'Ha! What a bloody nerve! She'll get nothing from me – nothing, and you can tell her so, if you know where she is.'

329

'I don't know, and if I did, I'd not be informing you.' She was on her feet now, a fiery-haired virago. 'Why can't you help her? Look at the sacrifices she's made for you over the years! She's not asking you for money. All she wants are those things personal to her, but no doubt she'll get by without them. She's found something far more important. Something you'll never know, Selden Ruthen. She's found love!'

'What are you raving about? Love!' He mouthed the word like an obscenity. His handsome features had become ugly. 'Romantic drivel! What can a shrivelled old maid like her know of passion?'

'I'm not speaking of lust, which is the only thing you can understand.' Anger choked her. She was battling for Alison, for herself, for all women reduced by the tyranny of men.

He too was on his feet, his head topping hers by only a few inches. It was good to be a tall woman, good to be strong, well-muscled, able to defend oneself against the beast that dominated, not through intellect but by brute force. If he struck her, then she would return the blow. Her fists were already knotted, the knuckles white against the tan, a pale circle on her forefinger where once the ring had rested. She saw the emptiness. Felt it. Regretted it. Wished that it was there, not adorning Darcy.

'You're at the bottom of this.' Selden's fury matched hers, the brooding resentment of months, the bruised ego, the desire. 'Don't bother to lie. You loaned them your car.'

'So? Effie was ill.'

'They've taken Effie. Kidnapped her. Removed her from her mother's care. The authorities will be informed.' He snapped out the words with a kind of vindictive triumph, never doubting that might, if not right, would be on his side.

'If they find them.' She was defiant, daring him to

make as much trouble as he willed. She would oppose him every step of the way.

He smiled his slow, serpent smile. 'Oh, they'll be found. I've already been in touch with the police.'

'Why, Selden? Why are you doing this? Why can't you leave them alone? It's not through moral principles, surely?'

He turned from her, gazing across the still pool where a kingfisher darted in flashing array. 'How could I refuse Mrs Turner's appeal? She wants her husband back. She's desperately worried about her daughter.'

'Unusual for you to be philanthropic. Is she sober enough to know what's going on?' Beryl had kept Camilla informed about the habits and peculiarities of the villagers.

Selden ignored this. 'She'll do as I advise.'

'And that, I take it, will be to hound your sister and Frank Turner.'

'I'll see justice done.'

'Justice? Don't make me laugh! What would you know about that?' The contempt in Camilla's tone stung like a whiplash.

What was happening to Alison seemed to be the culmination of her own persecution. André – her father's brutality – her dead baby. I'll not see harm come to her, she vowed. Alison *shall* be happy. Her child will live and thrive and be a blessing to her.

She did not know Frank or his wife, could only begin to guess the causes for the disintegration of their relationship. The laws of men meant little to her. In this she followed her father's example. In retrospect, she saw that there had been a subtle change in Alison over the months, a change which she had been too engrossed with Darcy to ponder upon. When she had first met her, she had looked into her face and realized that she was capable of deep, passionate emotions. Despite Selden's sneers, she knew that his sister had none of the easy

331

sentiment of the average woman and now, having met her mate, the richness, the sensuality of her nature, once dormant, had sprung into being. Camilla rejoiced for her, could feel little pity for Elsie Turner, took up the banner for the runaway lovers, and made up her mind to thwart Selden at every turn.

A little breeze rippled the willows, the silver coils of the stream where if ran over an artificial waterfall into the pool. It touched Camilla's warm skin and she felt it, like wintry breath on her spirit. Selden turned slowly, and there was that in his barbed gaze more bleak than the coldest winter.

'You'll learn that I know a great deal about justice,' he said with slow deliberation. 'I've friends in the profession, clever men who'll give me the benefit of their experience in this case and any other in which I show an interest. You'll be unwise to meddle, Camilla. If you know of my sister's whereabouts, then you'd do well to help me. I can make life deuced difficult for you, if I set my mind to it.'

'Is this a threat?'

He shrugged, and walked to where his horse was cropping the short turf under the trees. 'I'm warning you, that's all.'

Camilla watched him mount and, turning in the saddle, salute her with his whip before he rode off. She stood for a moment as he dwindled in the distance. The sun seemed to have lost some of its heat, though it was at its zenith. She became conscious that she was not alone. Leila stood on one side of her and Sam on the other. They too were staring after Selden, alert, hackles up, like watchdogs protecting their mistress.

'Him a wicked man, *patrão*,' said Sam, his eyes switching to Camilla's face. Involuntarily her arm came out to rest on his narrow shoulders.

'Missy Camilla draws wicked men to her. She challenges them. They done want to wear her down, but she stay firm, like a rock, and they smash themselves against her.' Leila's eyes were clouded, head up, gold earrings gleaming. 'That one's heart is black as coal and twice as hard, but he'll be broken. You'll see.'

'He'll destroy himself without much effort on my part.' Camilla returned to the rugs, wanting to recapture tranquillity, but the enchantment had vanished.

'So will the other.' Leila did not move, held rigid by visions. 'You've set the wheel in motion. You gave him the tiger's-eye. Yet it's not you who'll destroy them both, but something bigger, more powerful than any of us.'

'Top o' the morning to you, Mrs Lacey, and to you, Miss Lacey.' The shop bell jangled shrilly as Shawn pushed open the door. 'Faith, and isn't it the grand morning, to be sure.'

Prompted by a spirit of devilry, he could never refrain from emphasizing the fact that he was Irish when he encountered any of the villagers. They were so very insular. Even someone from the next hamlet was regarded as an alien. One had to live in Abbey Sutton for a lifetime before being accepted. If I'm still here when I'm ninety, and Lord save me from such a fate, when I snuff it they'll come to my funeral, he thought as he doffed his hat and made an elaborate bow to Gladys Lacey.

'Good morning, Mr Brennan,' she replied, making an unconvincing show of being more interested in checking the rolls of cloth on the shelves behind her than she was in the young man who was looking at her with sparkling green eyes. 'And how are you today?'

'In spanking form, Miss Lacey, thank you kindly.' Shawn cocked a booted leg over the stool by the counter and leaned an elbow on its polished surface. Chin in hand he regarded her mother, who did not glance up from her knitting. 'And you, Mrs Lacey? Are you still being troubled with the rheumatics?'

333

'I'm a martyr to it, a positive martyr,' she answered with a deep sigh. 'But I don't complain. There are folks far worse off than myself.'

'Bejabers, how true.' Shawn composed his features into an expression of pious agreement.

He had come here to sound out the general atmosphere. There were rumours flying. He had heard much talk in the Red Lion over the past week. Not for years had there been such food for conjecture as was provided by the disappearance of the curate and Lady Alison. More disturbing for him were the dark hints about the foreign woman up at The Priory. He knew that Camilla and her staff, the London-bred Simmonds as well as the Creoles, had always been treated with reserve. Their arrival at the manor had been quite sufficient to put the locals on guard without this additional upheaval. Shawn had offered no comment, but he had not liked the tenor of the conversation. Musing over his pint of ale, it had not taken him long to deduce that Selden Ruthen was the malicious *agent provocateur* who had been dripping poison into their ears. Not openly, of course. He seldom visited the Red Lion. He must be using others for his unscrupulous ends. Shawn intended to find out what plots were being hatched in his warped mind.

Lacey's shop was the place where information was exchanged. There one learned more about one's neighbours than even at the public house, the Methodist chapel or the church hall. Shawn had deliberately made a habit of popping in, chatting idly for a few moments whilst he purchased cigarettes or a few groceries. This enabled him to keep a finger on the pulse of Abbey Sutton. Familiarity had bred, if not contempt, a certain guarded acceptance. The Laceys and their customers had tacitly agreed to put their opinion of Shawn Brennan on hold. They would wait and see about this one.

As was usual at about that time in the morning, Miss

Violet and Miss Priscilla Carpenter made their entrance. Shawn leaped up and opened the door for them. The spinster sisters were like two fluffy, overweight birds, bright-eyed and inquisitive. They glanced shyly, even apprehensively, at Shawn, then rustled towards Mrs Lacey. Greetings were exchanged, in almost the exact words that they had used yesterday and on every other day for years.

'Good day, Mrs Lacey,' they began. 'And how are you feeling?'

'I mustn't complain, as I was just telling Mr Brennan.' Knitting tucked under her arm, she took their shopping list and began to gather items from the shelves and bins. 'The Lord has been good to me. I may be crippled with the rheumatics but at least I had a devoted husband, God rest his soul. Never a harsh word in fifty years.'

Miss Priscilla, the more dominant twin, acted as spokeswoman for them both. 'That must have been such a blessing, Mrs Lacey. You'll have happy memories of the dear gentleman. Of course, Violet and I have never been married and, from what we hear, not all wives are as lucky as you were.'

'You never spoke a truer word,' Gladys broke in, her voice stilted, rather refined. 'Papa was a good man, a real Christian. There wasn't a Sunday when he didn't attend church. He was a sidesman, you know. I'm very glad that I remained unmarried. Things aren't what they were. Some folk treat the matter so lightly these days. Marriage vows mean nothing – less than nothing to them! It's a disgrace. Why, at one time, a decent person would never have considered divorce! It's not what women want, I'm sure. It's the men.' She fixed Shawn with a cold eye, as if he was the embodiment of male perfidy.

'Oh, how harsh!' he exclaimed, but mitigated the criticism with a dazzling smile. 'How can you be so cruel, dear Miss Lacey? Not all men are cast in the same mould. If I were to marry now, I'd never consider divorce. I'd be a devoted husband, so I would.'

Just for an instant Gladys had a stunning vision of what it would be like to be married to him. She read a great deal, mostly books with a moralistic bent, but she had happened upon the works of Ouida in the Rye-hampton lending library, and had immediately responded to the high-flown prose of this writer. As she looked at Shawn, so she thought of her favourite character whose name gave the title to the book *Pascarel*. She had read it so often that she could clearly recall the description of him: 'The moon shines upon his delicate dark face; his straight, poet-like brows; his dreaming eyes, that have at once the scholar's sadness and the soldier's passions.'

Shawn was chestnut-haired and green-eyed, bearing no resemblance to this hero of the Florentine Renaissance, but handsome men were thin on the ground in Abbey Sutton – and there was something about him. With an odd dark thrill, she loved to whisper the words 'the scholar's sadness and the soldier's passions.' She had been brought up in a narrow-minded household where the late Mr Lacey, a weak man but a bully, had ruled through his capacity for rousing negative, guilty feelings. She knew nothing of passion, but the words inflamed her. Particularly 'the soldier's passions', with its colourful connotations. Passions for killing, for domination – for blood? Blood like that which flowed from her every four weeks? Shameful, disgusting blood.

Unprepared, when it had first come upon her at twelve, she had thought she was going to die. It was the Almighty's punishment because she had disobeyed her mother, who had said: 'You must never touch yourself down there,' pointing below Gladys's waist. She had hidden the blood for a year of confusion and fear, trying to prepare herself for death, until her mother had found out, crossly remarking: 'You'll get this every month from now on,' and giving her a pile of linen cloths to wear. This had been her only sexual instruction.

Sometimes she thought passion meant love, devotion, and tenderness, though vivid images of a more basic kind would spring to mind. The farmyard. The massive bull serving the cows; dogs mounting bitches; the cock treading his hens. At night she would hear the alarming, intriguing shouts of the drunken men leaving the Red Lion at closing time. Lying tense in her narrow bed, arms folded across her breasts, legs pressed close together beneath the shrouding white flannel robe, she would stare at the lithograph of the dead poet, Lord Byron, which hung on the wall opposite. The sound of male voices outside in the darkness, the sight of his romantic, melancholy features caused an ache in forbidden areas of her body.

Now she felt it again in Shawn's presence, that disturbing sensation. Pascarel! Her breathing quickened. A flush spread up from her neck to her cheeks. She retreated into hauteur, saying: 'How can you be so sure you'd be a good husband, Mr Brennan? I understand that men are apt to make rash promises, in order to capture their victims.'

She hadn't meant to say that exactly. Wasn't certain what she wanted to say. Only knew that the idea of being *his* victim was exciting. Shawn's smile deepened, aware that he was the cause of her agitation. It happened every time he set foot in the shop. Poor thing, he thought. If she wasn't quite so plain, I'd be almost tempted to put her out of her misery. Her age did not worry him. Quite a few of his mistresses had been older women. Indeed, he had cause to be grateful to one of them. It was she who had initiated him into the art of love. Still a virgin at sixteen, though by circumstance rather than choice, Shawn had been her more than willing pupil. He remembered her with affection, that woman of the world who had retired

337

to a house near Four Oaks. An attractive, well-preserved widow of fifty who loved taking boys into her bed. It was she who had trained him, making him curb his eagerness, turning him into an expert when it came to delighting women.

'Ah, Miss Lacey, you've a low opinion of us men,' he said, adroitly managing to place his hand close to hers on the counter.

Gladys was now completely flustered, her face crimson, but her mother had kept an ear on this talk of men and marriage even whilst she was busy with her customers. 'You're right, Gladys.' She measured rice into a bag. 'I don't know what the world is coming to, I'm sure. When churchmen start misbehaving – well!'

'Churchmen? You mean Mr Turner?' Shawn had found the opening for which he had been angling. 'What have you heard, Mrs Lacey? What's going on at Dolby Wold Cottage?'

'Well might you ask, sir,' Mrs Lacey replied darkly, packing the goods into a basket for the twins.

'Mrs Barlow shops here, doesn't she? Has she told you about it?' Shawn lit up a cigarette and blew smoke rings towards the side of bacon hanging in its cheesecloth web up near the beamed ceiling.

'Mrs Barlow says nothing.' She did not add 'that northerner', but the inference was plain. 'I've seen poor Mrs Turner herself.'

'And how has she taken her sudden plunge into single life?' Shawn drew in the smoke, held it, sent it out through his nostrils. Gladys watched, fascinated.

'She's calm, dignified, never complaining,' she rushed in, wanting to capture his attention, almost elbowing her mother aside in her eagerness. 'I admire her spirit.'

Spirit or spirits? He wondered, subjecting her to the full force of his charm as he replied: 'Plucky, is she?'

'Oh, very. He's left her flat, you see, and she was so afraid she'd be homeless. The Reverend Mapley will be forced to engage a new curate and Dolby Wold goes with the post, but Lord Ruthen has most kindly offered to rehouse her. She said he'd been so sympathetic. Only right and proper, I suppose, seeing as how his sister is involved.'

'It's true, then, this talk of her running away with Frank Turner?' Shawn asked as casually as he could. 'I must say, I find it hard to believe. She always seemed such a quiet lady.'

'Still waters run deep,' said Miss Priscilla sagely.

'A dark horse, as you might say,' added her sister. 'She's an artist, you know.'

'That would explain it.' Shawn kept a perfectly straight face. 'We've all heard about artists, haven't we? An immoral lot, painting ladies without any clothes on.'

Miss Violet gasped and her eyes widened with most enjoyable shock. 'Oh, Mr Brennan!'

'So you think she led him astray.' Shawn dropped an eyelid in the suspicion of a wink as he looked across at Gladys, drawing her into a kind of intimacy. She withdrew her hand and moved to the far side of the counter.

'It looks very like, though from what Mrs Turner said, it seems that Lady Camilla may have been at the bottom of it. Encouraging her, stuffing her head full of foreign nonsense. She loaned them her car, you know,' she replied, unable to stop herself, the words leaving her lips in a torrent. 'She doesn't behave as a lady should – racketing around like a wild thing, coming in here, buying cigars, dressed like I don't know what. And that black woman and her crippled son. Gives me the creeps! Goodness knows what horrible rites they perform up there at The Priory! Witchcraft and black magic, I shouldn't wonder. It's a pity they ever came here. We may all be in terrible danger. I think Lord Ruthen's right. She's corrupted his sister, and Mrs Turner is suffering for it. She doesn't know what she'd do without

339

Lord Ruthen. Says he's acting like her guardian angel, making sure that her boys want for nothing, promising that he'll do all he can to find little Effie.'

I hand it to you, Selden, you crafty swine, Shawn thought. So this is how you're doing it, absolving yourself from blame and discrediting Camilla into the bargain through the dependent and obviously besotted Elsie Turner. D'you keep her supplied with booze too? Are you perchance humping her? No, this might put her off. If she's anything like Gladys, the fleshly reality would spoil the image. She'd prefer to worship you from afar. Noble Selden! Saviour of deserted wives and fatherless children!

'That's putting it strong, ain't it, Miss Lacey?' he suggested, but cautiously. 'Didn't you enjoy the midsummer party, the fireworks? I thought Lady Camilla gave an extremely generous show.'

'It was all right, but now she's got her hooks into Mr Devereaux too. Someone should warn him.' Gladys was not aware of the viciousness of her tone.

Phew! But Camilla's certainly succeeded in putting up the backs of the local harpies, he thought. Strange how they tolerate Josephine, yet Camilla seems to inspire them with nothing but jealous envy. He experienced a prickle down his spine, a warning chill which he never failed to heed. He needed to find Camilla, to awaken her to the danger. A sex-starved spinster like Gladys would be the first to lead a witch hunt, and the Witch-Finder General would be Selden Ruthen, halo, wings and all!

He was the first to hear hooves and the jingle of harness outside the shop. Instinct told him who it was but before he could stop her, Camilla stalked in, pausing on the step, the crown of her sombrero almost brushing the lintel. There was a sudden, intense silence. Every eye turned to her.

He broke it. Tried to alert her. *'Ill-met by moonlight, fair Titania!'*

'You idiot, Shawn,' she laughed. 'It's in the middle of the morning, not a trace of moonlight. What are you doing here?'

'I need to eat.' He spread his hands wide, indicating the loaded shelves. 'I'm a bachelor, as you know. I've no sweet little wife willing to run errands for me.'

'Don't expect any sympathy from me. I'm sure there are a dozen lovelorn girls hereabouts only waiting for the chance.' She spoke with a light, jesting easiness. Gladys was consumed with envy. Their eyes met over the counter and Camilla said: 'A packet of Romanoff Cigars, please, Miss Lacey.'

She was wearing *campo* riding gear, leather trousers, a man's white shirt, fringed jacket slung over her shoulders, Cuban-heeled boots. Shawn thought she looked good enough to eat, but he did not fail to notice the glances of the other women as they went down over her. He had the urge to put a protective arm about her. Camilla was accustomed to being stared at and took no notice. Gladys, having served her, took the offered coins with her fingertips and dropped them into the dish under the counter.

'Thank you, my Lady,' she said icily.

'Thank you, Miss Lacey, and did you enjoy my little party the other night?'

'Yes, thank you, my Lady.'

Camilla frowned slightly, as she turned towards the door. She knew that the villagers were suspicious of her but had been hoping that the work she had provided and the midsummer gathering might have allayed some of their doubts. Such coldness as was now being meted out both wounded and angered her.

'Are you riding back towards The Priory?' Shawn asked, following her.

'I'm meeting Darcy,' she answered thoughtfully, still troubled as she placed a foot in the stirrup and swung herself into the saddle.

341

'And I'm meeting Josephine,' he grinned at her as he too mounted.

'Oh, Shawn! Not Josephine.' She shook her head, wheatgold hair falling across her shoulders from beneath her hat.

'Someone has to console her for the loss of Darcy, and it might as well be me,' he answered amiably. They began to move off together, watched through the shop window by Gladys's envious eyes. Then he gave Camilla a sideways glance. 'Come to that, I need a bit of consoling myself.'

'You Shawn! Why?' She sounded disbelieving, not looking at him, keeping her eyes on the dusty road that led away from the village.

'Because I've lost you to that great black-bearded ruffian. By George, but I should call him out. Pistols at dawn!' He declaimed dramatically.

Camilla laughed. He could always make her laugh. They shared a mutual sense of humour, bordering on the ridiculous. As if not quite daring to be serious they mocked everything, using their own code of nonsense as a defence against hostile circumstances.

'You don't look as if you've been crossed in love.'

'I have to keep up appearances for the sake of my public. The clown who dons his grease paint to amuse the crowd even though his heart is breaking. On with the motley, and all that.'

'How heroic! And I don't believe a word of it!'

They turned into a deep, narrow lane, its sides touched by ferny banks. It was cooler there, a shadowy tunnel with branches meeting overhead. He was wondering how to convey the uneasy feelings that had gathered momentum in Lacey's Store. He suddenly reined in, and she paused too, looking at him questioningly.

'Camilla, be careful.' All laughter was banished from his face, replaced by unusual seriousness.

'Why?' Her eyes were no longer gold, turned to sherry brown by the purple shadow of her hat brim.

'Just a gut feeling. This business of Lady Alison and Turner. The villagers don't want to blame her for it. She's one of their own, you see, born and bred. They want to find a scapegoat.'

'And you think it will be me.'

'You're the likeliest candidate.' He wanted to lean over and touch her, in friendship, in support, but kept his hands firmly on the reins. Parody saved him. 'I'm sure that they believe that you and Leila and Sam indulge in blood sacrifices up at The Priory, by dead of night.'

'We do!' She entered into it with gusto. 'When there's a full moon, Leila flies on her broomstick, Sam turns into a werewolf, howling like fury and rushing about seeking victims for his horrible appetites, and my teeth become fangs. I haunt the graveyards, waylaying maidens and drinking their blood! Young men too, if I can find 'em. Of course, I rob them of their honour before feasting!'

'I knew it!' He grimaced in burlesque terror. 'Holy Mary! Gladys was right! The pure, unsullied Virgin Gladys! Back, fiend! Back to your coffin! You corrupt the glorious face of morning!'

Bursting into peals of laughter, they rode on. The lane rose gradually. They came out into the open where everything was warmth and light. The hedgerows were thick with blossom. Bees toiled from one abundance to the next, almost too heavy to fly. On either side the fields lay drowsing, deep with tall mowing grass, sheened with bronze. Sheep, naked from shearing, sought shade from the hot noonday sun.

Simultaneously they stopped again, for here their paths diverged. One road led towards The Priory, the other to Bell's Spinney. Shawn knew that Josephine would be at his cottage, hot from her gallop from Erwarton Hall. Hot with passion too, eager for him to

343

arrive. Yet even though she was a tempting morsel and he was enjoying making love to her, he would have given anything to have remained with Camilla.

I love her, he thought. I want her. Every part of her – her smiles and her sorrows, her beauty and her wildness, her past and her future. I don't care what she's done or how many lovers she's had. This has nothing to do with us. I shall leave her now, tumble into bed with Josephine and maybe she'll do the same with Darcy, but it doesn't matter. An interlude, nothing more. We're marking time until the real thing happens. Shawn seldom struggled against the tide. He went with the flow. It was no use cursing fate and trying to change events. All would fall into place eventually. He knew, deep in his soul, that more – much more, lay ahead for him and Camilla.

She was watching him, her eyes bright, her lips glistening where her tongue had moistened them. 'Goodbye, Shawn. Thanks for the warning. I'll be on my guard, but I'm going to help Alison.'

'D'you know where she's living?' Shawn returned her steady gaze, prolonging the moment.

'Not yet, but she'll write to me. I'll visit her in London. I need to go there soon, shopping for my trousseau.'

'Ah, yes, the wedding. When is it to be?'

'At the end of August.'

His lips formed into a wry smile as he asked: 'Am I invited?'

'Naturally. I'll need my court jester.'

Light bantering words, both of them aware of much left unsaid. He shifted in his saddle, his eyes on the sweeping downland that stretched away for miles, rippling and shining in the breeze, green and purple, melting into the distance to meet the vast blue vault of the horizon. Her land, soon to be Darcy Devereaux's.

'Watch Selden Ruthen,' he said sharply.

'I always watch him.' Her voice sliced firmly through the air. 'Don't worry about me.'

'I never worry, but I'll be there, if you need me.'

Then she gave a slight jerk on her reins and bobbed her heels against her horse's sides. He did not move for a moment, watching her go. She cantered away without looking back, merely lifting an arm in a final wave.

'Damn it! Damn and blast it!' He flung at the uncaring trees, the impervious sky. Then he kicked his mount into a gallop and rode with his head well down, an expression on his face that few people would have associated with the carefree Irishman. Using his spurs, his whip, he made straight for the cottage and Josephine.

5

Clouds gathered in the hot stillness. The atmosphere was like lead. Beyond the curving bay window, Camilla could see that the sky had turned lead-coloured too, curdled through with an unnatural livid orange-brown. No birds called in the garden. No sounds of bleating sheep or lowing cattle drifted from the uplands.

She brushed back the hair from her brow. The skin was damp yet burned as if she had malaria. Her fountain pen had run dry. Listlessly, she refilled it from the ink bottle reposing in a small recess of the escritoire. The Master Chamber drew darker, but she continued writing, her journal opened on the leather-covered desk top.

By this time tomorrow, I'll be Mrs Darcy Devereaux. Will it make me feel any different, I wonder? Everything is ready – the house, the reception, my gown. Am *I* ready? Yes, I am, but I do feel tired. My head aches and there's that something in the air which presages a storm. Darcy will be furious if a deluge ruins his crops. They've been working like galley slaves to get in the harvest, and before that there was the tremendous task of sheep-dipping. I've hardly seen him lately. He's so busy, and I've been frantically getting ready for the Big Day.

There had been so much to do. Amy had been a staunch ally and Camilla had spent some time in London with her, visiting dressmakers, milliners, shoe shops and the big stores. Although she already had plenty of clothes, it

346

seemed that even more had to be purchased for her role as a bride. Beryl had come too, armed with an enormous list which she had placed in the hands of a caterer, who, in turn, had sent it to their branch in Dorchester. As the day approached, so presents had been delivered to The Priory daily. The number was astonishing, and they were on display in the Great Hall. Camilla had not thought there would be so many people wanting to wish her well. Even Selden had brought along a splendid gift in the shape of a bronze figure.

It was of a woman seated on a magnificent steed, very much in the Art Nouveau vein that Camilla liked so much; a powerful armoured beauty, her flowing hair mingling with the mane of the arched-necked, nostril-flaring animal.

'It's of Brunnhilde astride Grane,' Selden had told her as they both stood admiring it. 'She was a warrior maiden of German mythology, daughter of Wotan and leader of her eight sisters, the warlike Valkyries. I understand it's the work of the sculptor Clare Coline. I just *had* to buy it. She reminds me of you, Camilla. I can visualize you swooping down out of the sky and collecting the bodies of dead heroes from the battlefield, flinging them over your saddle and bearing them to Valhalla.'

'Really,' she had answered, not certain whether to take this as a compliment or an insult.

'You know Wagner's *Ring Cycle*, I take it?' he had continued suavely. 'When you and Darcy visit London during the winter, you simply must let me take you to Covent Garden to see those wonderful operas. I've a box there, you know. I'll try to arrange it so that we can hear a really first-class tenor singing Siegfried.'

'At home, we had some recordings of Jean de Reszke in the role,' she had said, a shade defensively. There was no way she was going to let Selden assume her to be an ignorant savage. In fact, she knew and loved the music of

347

the German composer, but doubted somehow that Darcy would consent to spend a night at the opera, particularly in Selden's company.

'Did you? Splendid.' Selden had patted the bronze lovingly. 'I can never get Josephine interested. She's an absolute Philistine when it comes to music.'

'The educated South Americans are very musical, the natives too, in their own fashion.' Camilla had been possessed of the urge to impress him with her knowledge. 'Many Italians have emigrated to Argentina, and there's a fine opera house in Buenos Aires, the Teatre Colon.'

'You don't say?' Selden had watched her in a disturbing way.

Why is he being so amiable? Camilla had wondered, but had merely said: 'I can't promise that I'll persuade Darcy to come. We're not planning on a winter season anyway. Those months are generally rather busy on the land here, especially if the weather's bad. Thanks again for the present.'

'Don't mention it, my dear,' he had said, as she walked to the door with him. 'Goodbye for now. I'll see you at the wedding, eh?'

Now she glanced towards the window again, hearing ominous rumbles and mutters of thunder, distant, but coming closer. Rising, she walked across the dusky room towards that weird light. As she stood by the casement, a few splattering drops of rain fell on to the parched earth below. Suddenly the heavy clouds dissolved into a curtain of torrential rain coming straight down from the heavens. It reminded her poignantly of the wet season in Brazil. Homesickness took her unawares. My God! I miss it! The thought was astonishing.

Tropical and unrelenting, the rain poured on to the roof, gushing in arching jets from every gargoyled spout, flooding the garden within seconds. All the while the thunder came nearer and nearer, its giant voice bellowing above the downpour. The storm was right overhead.

348

Lightning flickered, draining colour and substance from the scene, turning the trees into elaborate silhouettes, eerie and ephemeral.

There was a strange beauty about it, very reminiscent of the awesome storms that swept the jungle. A fury had fallen upon the world – the sounds, the vivid flashes, expressing demonic anger. Leila will be at her prayers, kneeling before her altar, lighting placating candles for the deities, Camilla thought. I suppose she'll blame me for this, like she does everything since I became engaged to Darcy. She's not forgiven me. She could almost hear her voice: 'The storm demons are cursing your marriage. No good will come of it.'

Was she right? It was easy to believe, seeing those ponderous, inky clouds, the vicious forks of lightning, the murky sulphurous light. These combined to create an atmosphere of crisis. Monstrous elementals were battling it out in the ether. In a moment the earth would be rent asunder, the sky would explode, the last trump would blare, and mortals would be tipped over into unutterable darkness.

Camilla forced back these dire visions and made herself return to her journal. Time was of the essence. This would be the final entry whilst she was still a free agent. Tomorrow she was hardly likely to find the opportunity to add more. It would have to wait till later, much later – maybe during the honeymoon, maybe after.

'We're in the middle of a great storm,' she scribbled hurriedly.

I can barely see, but here goes. I had a letter from Alison this morning. The first one since she left. She's bought a house in Cheyne Walk, Chelsea. She's over the moon because it's not far from number 16, where once dwelt Dante Gabriel Rossetti. Apparently she wanders past the house, hoping to catch a glimpse of his ghost. I expect she genuflects. He's

349

practically canonized in her eyes. The greatest artist that ever lived! I must ask Selden about her things. Strangely enough, he's being really friendly these days. Walking around as if butter wouldn't melt in his mouth. Not so the local yokels. Oh, the servants are all right, I pay them generously, but when I go to the village, my reception is frosty, to say the least, and I had to rescue Sam the other day when I found him cornered by a gang of louts who were throwing stones at him.

I wanted to see Alison when I was in town, but she'd not been in touch and I didn't know where to find her. She's invited Darcy and me to visit. Of course, I'm sworn to secrecy with regard to her whereabouts. I don't know if he'll agree – in fact, I hardly know what goes on in his mind at the present time. It's the farm work. There's so much for him to do. Things will improve when we reach Paris. The ferry is booked, the hotel too. I'm looking forward to it so much. To have him to myself for as long as I like. No farm, no Priory, no responsibilities.

The door crashed open behind her. The sudden blast of wind whipped the pages, and Camilla whirled around. Darcy was framed there. 'Bloody weather!' he snarled. 'Could have finished, only one more field to go. Now the corn will be flattened!'

Why had he come instead of going to Chalkdown Farm? This had been the arrangement. They were not to see one another again until they stood before the altar, exchanging vows. A short parting, then unity for life. She had been anticipating spending these last hours alone, of meditating and composing her mind, of going to bed early and sleeping late, to rise refreshed in the morning. She was confused by her reaction. But I love him, don't I? I want him with me. I don't care about tradition. I don't believe that it's bad luck for the bride and groom to meet before the wedding.

The room was almost completely dark. Full of night

and storm and unnamable things. She was suddenly aware of their presence. It was as if the lid had been lifted off Pandora's box. It's Leila, she thought angrily. She's not praying to the Christian saints. She's rousing the devil-*loa*, Ti-Jean or Ezili-jé-rouge. She wants to prevent our marriage. It is they who have created this storm!

'Go away you wicked *baka*!' she hissed. '*Têtetête*! I'll set the snake-god, Damballah, on you. He'll bite you! Oh, yes, he will! Bite and sting and drive you back to hell!'

Darcy stopped dead, staring at her in puzzlement. His face was wet with rain. In the flashes of lightning, his hair seemed shot with silver, his beard too, the blue-white light glistening on its blackness. 'Are you talking to me?'

'No, not you.' She shook her head, straining her ears against the discord of the heavens. 'Hush! Listen! Can't you hear them?'

His eyes were glinting, wary. He was none too pleased with his reception. 'Who? What's going on? I can't hear a damned thing except the bloody thunder.'

It was true. She knew it. He did not see or hear those otherworld creatures. Many a time she had been with him here, or in the secret room and known that the sorrowful ghost was with them, seeing the faint crimson hand prints on the fireplace reaching up towards her father's portrait. But Darcy's inner eye was closed, his senses too. She did not know whether to pity or envy him.

'It doesn't matter. It's all right.' She took up the matches and went around the room. A flame leaped high behind the translucent globe of every lamp. The incense burners were the next to receive attention, and Camilla added a pinch of aromatic herbs calculated to banish harmful spirits. Leila had cause to be proud of her pupil, but tonight she might regret instructing her so well. Mentally, Camilla was holding a blazing sword outstretched, forming a golden circle around herself, around Darcy, around the room. She could see it clearly. Now they were protected from external forces, but were they protected from themselves?

'I had to come.' Darcy took off his coat, shook the water from it. His boots left muddy smears on the rugs.

'Why?' She was watching him steadily. Her face, illumined from below, was planed by strong shadows, eyes slanting like a predatory puma's, lashes spiked.

'Do I have to give a reason?' He was smiling but irritated. 'I need you. You'll be my wife tomorrow. I want to sleep with you tonight.'

'No.' She was conscious of breathlessness, the muscles of her stomach tightening. Frightened of the emotions he evoked, she took a stumbling step backwards.

Darcy moved like the lightning flaring through the casement. He dragged her into his arms. 'Don't be silly, Camilla. A few hours – what does it matter? Christ, I've been patient, haven't I? D'you know what torment you've put me through?'

He's different! she thought, grieving. But it was a difference that had been developing steadily over the weeks since their engagement. She could no longer pretend. He had changed, subtly but surely. More domineering, more rough, less considerate of her feelings and opinions. She tried to laugh it off. 'Oh, come on, Darcy! If it's only a matter of hours, then you can wait, surely? What are you? Some rutting animal?'

He raised his fist, and for one astounded moment she thought he was going to strike her. 'How dare you! Don't you ever say that to me again. D'you hear? I'm no animal, but I'll soon be your husband and you'll obey me.'

'Are you threatening me?' Cold rage stiffened her, and she glared up at him.

In the next instant he was passing a hand wearily across his eyes, his shoulders bowed. He grinned at her shamefacedly. 'I'm sorry, darling. I'm so damned tired, been slogging in the fields for days. Not sleeping too well either. Been having strange dreams. Forgive me.'

She hated to see that expression in his eyes, hang-dog, exhausted, and quickly filled a brandy glass, placing it in his hand. 'Come and rest, my love. There, don't worry. I understand. I want you too, you know. I'm not made of stone.'

He slumped dejectedly in a chair by the bed, staring down into his glass. 'Sometimes you seem too independent, Camilla. Makes me feel inadequate. I get to thinking that you don't really need me, and can manage perfectly well on your own.'

She dropped to her knees beside him, gripping his free hand in hers. 'That's not true. Oh, Darcy, I'm longing for tomorrow. I want to be married to you but, yes, I do like my own way about everything. I'm used to being master around here. If I see something that needs doing, then I order it to be done. Not any more.' She leaned her head against his knees, rubbed her cheek on the damp, harsh fabric of his breeches. 'I promise. I'll be as meek and biddable as a geisha-girl. I'm already dressed for the part.'

She was wearing a Japanese kimono, an exotic affair of white silk, lavishly embroidered. It was girdled around the waist and she wore nothing underneath. She had donned it after her bath, imagining that she would have no further visitors that evening. Darcy glanced down at it, always entertained by her unusual mode of dress.

'You?' A doubting smile lifted his lips. 'That'll be the day! You'll do exactly as I tell you?'

'Why not? I'm sure you'll not abuse the privilege.'

'You can start now, if you like.' His hand was stroking over her burnished hair. His ring reflected the lightning. 'There's something I want to know.'

'Ask away, O Lord of my life,' she murmured, and her resistance was weakening under that seductive touch. Why not? Why wait until tomorrow night? I love him. I trust him. Nothing can go wrong.

'When are we going to Bahia?'

His voice seemed unnaturally loud, louder even than the storm. Camilla tensed. 'I'm not planning to return – ever,' she answered firmly, yet found that it hurt her to say it. Like a betrayal. Bahia! The very word had a magical ring to it.

'But you've a house there – plantations. Don't you want to know what's been happening during your absence?'

'I don't care.' The very thought of the *estancia* clogged her mind like a dreary fog. 'There's a caretaker, and Ranger Hogan manages the fields. It's paying for itself. There are profitable returns in my bank. I leave everything to Lloyds.'

'Well, I'd like to see it. Why don't we go when we come back from Paris?' he persisted.

'Because I don't want to!' She was up now, more disturbed than she cared to admit.

'There you go again – the spoilt child who only does what *she* wants.' His smile was tigerish, his tone that of the logical male dealing with an unreasonable female.

It was maddening, but holding her temper in check with more patience than she knew she possessed, she said evenly: 'I have my reasons, Darcy.'

'Oh, and what are these? Memories of your old man? It's plain there wasn't much love lost between the two of you.' He eyed her suspiciously, twirling the glass between his hands. 'You never speak of him in kindly terms. Why is this, Camilla? Was he the only one who ever said 'no' to you?'

'You're asking a great many questions tonight. Did you come here to interrogate me?' She went into the attack, though inside she was thoroughly alarmed. Darcy must never find out about her past. She knew him well enough by now to realize that he would be unlikely to be either tolerant or sympathetic. He would side with her father. Use it as a weapon against her.

354

'I came here to make love to you. You're the one who started arguing,' he answered with steely patience. 'Just tell me the real reason for pretending that you never lived in Brazil. I would've thought you'd long for the sun, want to see your old home. You were born there, after all's said and done.'

Then something cracked in Camilla. She hated his stubbornness, mourned his lack of sensitivity. Why couldn't he leave her alone? 'Very well, Darcy. If you insist. I'll do more than tell you. I'll *show* you. Come with me.'

Taking up a table lamp, she went into the study-room and, with a quizzical lift of one dark, curved brow, he followed. The thunder had drawn slowly off. The rain still fell, but no longer with intolerable force. She noticed that one of the windows had been left open. The curtains were soggy. The lamplight wavered, then was supplemented by another as she touched a taper to the wick. Her movements were deliberate. By doing so she could control the thumping of her heart.

Darcy leaned against the doorpost and watched her. She never failed to fascinate him, particularly when angry. Her mouth was exquisite, a little parted, expressing her indignation at his demands, and her hair, loosened about her shoulders, framed that face of unusual beauty which held such arrogance, stressed by the slightly oblique lids of her eyes. Desire, heavy and urgent, weighted his loins. That, and a need to subjugate her. Not only her body, her mind too.

Camilla ignored him. Walking straight to one of the bookcases, she felt around at the back of it, and pulled open a hidden compartment. From this she drew out a single slim volume, and carried it to the table. Frowning, curious, Darcy strolled to her side, leaning over, one arm laid across her shoulders.

'What's this?' He stared down at a tattered book, obviously old, much stained and dog-eared.

355

'This is the reason why my father lived as he did, died as he did, was cruel to my mother, and had no time for me.' Her voice was low, chilling. 'This is why I never want to see South America again.'

She hated touching it, that document that she would have left behind, had not Leila insisted it be packed amongst her belongings. A small book, hand-written, with parts of it barely legible. It possessed a power greater than love, than hearth and home, than all the things mankind normally desired. Leila had known where Ruthen had hidden it – under the floorboards, wrapped in oilskin. It should be blood-soaked, Camilla had thought when the Creole gave it to her. My God, enough blood has been shed in the possessing of it. Knowing it too dangerous to leave unguarded, she had reluctantly consented to bring it to England.

Darcy picked it up, intrigued yet amused by her vehemence. 'Is it valuable?'

'That depends on one's viewpoint. Some have valued it above their immortal souls,' she replied, and drew her robe closer about her, as chilled as if an unseen miasma breathed out of the manuscript, infecting her, a legacy from the sombre, fever-breeding forests.

The rain had stopped. Beyond the windows the rags of breaking clouds showed wisps of sky. The treetops scolloped the teeming stars, casting shadows as dense as their own substance. The moon was rising and the air was cool and fresh, but in the room there was too much darkness and silence.

'You're being most mysterious.' He laughed and squeezed her waist. 'Devilish intriguing, in fact. Come, witch-woman. Reveal its secrets. We shall soon be one, remember, and you must keep nothing from me.'

There's no escape, she thought. I had hoped it would never come to this, but it seems that I'm committed unequivocally to this course of action. Perhaps when I tell him, he'll realize why I've shaken the dust of Brazil off my feet for ever. If he loves me, he'll know it is the only way I can break the evil spirit.

'I've no idea how it came into my father's hands. All I do know is that it was his bible. He never moved far without it, spent hours poring over it, squandered a fortune on the mad dreams it evoked. Was mastered by it, he who mastered everyone else.'

Darcy was turning the yellowish pages. 'There's a map,' he said suddenly, with a finger marking the spot.

'Yes. It's an area deep in the Brazilian hinterland, heading towards the Matto Grosso. It consists of huge tracts of unexplored jungle, swamps and rivers.'

'Go on,' he said intently.

'This is a log kept by an English explorer in the middle of the last century.' Camilla's tongue felt thick, and she had difficulty in forming the words. It's my own reluctance to speak of it, she thought. I hate and fear it so much.

'What does it say?' His expression was alert, almost frighteningly so.

'He set out with a few companions and half a dozen negro slaves, accompanied by some Indians. He was seeking a legendary gold mine. He didn't find it, but, according to these notes, he penetrated far into the forests and stumbled upon a ruined city. Perhaps it was built by an ancient civilization. Who knows? There are a host of similar legends in South America. He described it as being deserted, and the massive buildings had been devastated, as if by some long-ago earthquake.'

'Amazing!' Darcy broke in and, to her despair, she caught a look in his eyes horribly familiar to that which she had seen so often in her father's. 'And then – ?'

'He found temples, palaces built of huge blocks of stone. Look, here are drawings of the hieroglyphic inscriptions he claimed to have copied from some of them.' She flipped over the pages.

'Good God! So it had to be true? No one could make up such a yarn, could they?'

357

'He was convinced that there was a fortune hidden there, treasures beyond the dreams of avarice, and intended to return to civilization and organize a large expedition. This account was completed after he'd managed to escape when they were attacked by hostile Indians. He got back to Bahia, bringing some gold coins and small pieces of statuary. The last half of the book is strange, incoherent, almost the ravings of a madman. He seemed terrified of something. I don't know what happened to him in the end.'

'And your father? How did he become involved?'

'I've no idea, but somehow the log fell into his hands and he was obsessed with finding the lost city.' Camilla closed the book, intending to return it to the drawer, but Darcy's hand came down on hers with shocking force and determination.

'May I read it?'

'Why should you want to do that?'

'What harm, if it helps me to understand you?'

They stood with it between them, old leather, old paper pressed against the surface of the table. It grew, reared up like a wall, transformed itself into dense matted undergrowth, green and impenetrable. Camilla could no longer see Darcy. The room vibrated with the sound of drums.

'You think I'm being foolish?' Her voice was stilted with too much to say. It was as if she was conversing with a stranger from a great distance.

'I still don't understand the connection between your father's laudable interest in seeking out an ancient city, and your fear of going back.'

That wall! She struggled, but waving lianas wound themselves around her limbs. She saw it all, a misty picture-show jerking before her eyes. The Estancia Esperança; the white colonial house; the men who tramped in there at all hours, deep in conversation with her father far into the night – drinking, cigar smoke drifting. Hard-bitten explorers, ex-army men, rogues who fed Ruthen's ambitions with their extravagant tales of having glimpsed such a city, of having seen that fabled tribe of white-skinned men with red hair rumoured to inhabit uncharted areas. And the expeditions he had organized, costly, wearing. Near, oh yes, he claimed to have been near, yet each attempt had ended in disaster. Aggressive Indians, the shortage of game, the inability to find food to support more than a handful of men, the difficulties of using pack-animals because of lack of fodder and the ravages of vampire bats.

She tried to tell Darcy, but he remained unconvinced. 'What an adventure!' he interrupted. 'And you went on some of these trips? My dear girl, you've got guts!'

'I had no choice,' she answered tersely. 'He expected everyone to share his enthusiasm. I was useful to him because I knew something of the native dialects. Not much, but better than nothing, later I became more fluent, and the tribesmen liked me. I seemed to have a rapport with even the most primitive.'

'It must have been wonderful. To go where no white man had ever been before. Tell me more!' He was like an excited child, his eyes clouded by dreams.

'I suppose it was amazing, but I wasn't aware of it at the time – more concerned with thirst, with hunger, with humping loads, coping with scared bearers, covering endless miles in canoes down those endless rivers, with my father so impatient. Obsessed! Possessed! Mad!'

'I wish I'd known him.' Camilla could not believe what she was hearing. It was as if she was living through a bad dream.

'No one knew him,' she whispered, and glanced at the portrait. 'His cronies imagined they did, but they were wrong. "Good old Ruthen. What a stout fellow! Such stamina! Tackle anything, he will," they would say at first, but after travelling with him for a few days they'd change their tune. He expected obedience, you see. Was

359

brutal and quite ruthless. Whatever he said went, no arguments, no quibbles. He didn't care much what happened to his companions, only in so far as it affected the enterprise. I've seen him leave men behind with no hope of survival, if they fell lame or were injured. He was callous, disregarding life, dismissing it as of no account. He enjoyed killing animals too. Not simply for the pot, but for the sheer love of wanton destruction.'

'Plenty of hunting there, I'd imagine,' Darcy put in, smoothing her fingers in his attempts to make her relinquish her hold on the log. 'Paradise for a sportsman.'

'You're wrong, Darcy.' In her mind she was back, trudging through *banados* of mud and water. 'Where we went there's a singular lack of wild life. The swamps are too poisonous, the mushy undergrowth inhospitable. Everything rots in the damp, enclosed heat. It's dark in there – green, dripping darkness. The branches meet overhead, heavy with moss. It's infested with mosquitoes, fire-ants, the motúca fly that opens up such gashes in the flesh that the blood runs in streams, and the pium fly that comes out at night in dense swarms. Their stings turn into spreading, festering sores. Then there are the snakes. The bushmaster, the *fer de lance*, the cascabel, all killers with venomous fangs. A person has to be crazy to go there.'

'Has it nothing to commend it? You say your father returned again and again.' Darcy was leaning forward, drinking in her words. She had been trying hard to scare him off, but now saw that nothing would deter him.

'It's fascinating. Probably the most fascinating place in the world,' she replied slowly, finding it difficult to describe the spell it wove. 'Magnificent in its way, with mighty rivers and swirling rapids that crash over towering waterfalls. Everything is on a huge scale. Insects grow to a staggering size – beetles, spiders, butterflies. There are hundreds of miles of grasslands, mountain ranges – everything! The earth must have been like that millions of years ago, savage and untamed. It's said that once you've seen it, much as you hate it and struggle against its fatal lure, you can't stay away for long.'

'But there must have been some game,' he insisted, not really listening to her, remembering only the city. 'You couldn't have survived otherwise.'

'On the rivers, yes, if we were lucky. There are tapirs and capivara, peccary too. My father particularly enjoyed shooting alligators. They make good eating, but he often killed more than we needed, just for the hell of it.'

Against the screen of her brain Camilla could see boiling brownish water. A huge beast, six bullets in its head, refusing to die, whipping up the bloody foam with its enormous tail, blindly lunging with its jaws, carving circles around the canoe, straining through the water with its mangled head high. No fool, no coward, cunning and malignant. Her father fired again and again, standing in the prow, hurling abuse at his enemy. At last it dragged itself out on the bank, thrashing from side to side in agonized death throes, livid belly uplifted to the sun. And the vultures wheeled lazily in the molten blue sky. There were always vultures drifting on the thermals over Brazil.

'Give me the book, Camilla. Let me read it.' Darcy's voice in her ear, recalling her.

'No!'

She struggled. Her arms were locked at her sides, her body crushed against his hard strength. He made a grab for the log. The table rocked. She feared for the lamp, for its spreading oil, for the fire that might start. She was conscious of many things as she strained in his arms. Of anger, fear and desire. Nor fear of him, but fear *for* him, fear of the things seeping from the pages of that evil document. I should never have shown him, but I

361

thought, I imagined, I hoped that he would understand –

Far from that, it had served to inflame him. Darcy had no intention of denying himself the two things he wanted. Camilla and the map. He seized her by the shoulders. Shook her. 'Don't fight me! Don't make me hurt you!'

She stopped struggling. Weakness paralysed her. Now he cradled her head and held her to his mouth. She was shivering, long tremors running through her. She was captured. Could not move. She returned his kiss without thinking what she was doing, needing reassurance and forgetfulness. Knew that he had put the book in his pocket, was angry that he had successfully diverted her attention, then no longer cared. She melted against him, her body fitting his as if designed to do so. He swept her up in his arms and carried her through to the other room. He laid her on the bed.

His hands were on her skin, under her robe. They were trembling, then gripping hurtfully. The air on her naked body, and his flesh hot against hers. His lips on her breasts, hands, mouth travelling over her, feasting, needful and urgent. The tester above was like a roof, like a tent, like twisted vines. Fashioned of wood, it had once been part of a forest, of a jungle. The soft hiss of rain on the windowpanes, against the top of the tent, the bed-curtains becoming dirty-white, transparent – mosquito netting.

Then darkness, kissing and tasting, his body like crushed velvet beneath her hands. His knee between her legs, pushing them apart. But he'll know. He'll find out that I'm not a virgin. She tried to close them. He was insistent. 'I won't hurt you. God, I want you! Let me – don't stop me, Camilla!'

And he was there, on her, in her, lying on top of her, his face against her neck. He had given her no time to soften, to moisten. She was too alarmed, too filled with the darkness, the foreboding. His possession was a knife thrust, painful, but not difficult enough. She felt him hesitate, could read his mind in that instant before his driving urge blanked out thought, the rhythm quickening compulsively till his body jerked and he spilled himself inside her.

He did not speak, lying heavily upon her, his breathing slowing down, the rapid beat of his heart too. She waited breathlessly for the question, the condemnation she dreaded. The moments dragged out. He still said nothing. In the dimness of the bed she saw the alligator. It stared at her with its one remaining eye from its proud pulped face. Shreds of skin, bits of muscle. Blood oozed over its scales.

The hot sun poured across the harvest fields, flooded the village and beat upon the roofs. It was noon and, in contrast to the furnace blast outside, the interior of the church was dim and cool. Stepping inside had been a relief and Josephine relished it, for her hobble skirt, no more than a yard across at the hem, was a most fashionable but uncomfortable thing to wear in August. She had been determined not to be outshone by anything her cousin might choose as a bridal gown. Its design had been a closely guarded secret, but Josephine would have staked her life on it being outrageous and stunning.

Resentful though she was at Camilla capturing Darcy, wild horses would not have kept her away from the wedding. She sat in a front pew, fidgeting slightly, but satisfied at the stir her own outfit had caused amongst the assembly. The church was packed. Everyone had turned out to see Lady Camilla marry Darcy Devereaux. They were watching Josephine. She could feel their eyes on her back, curious eyes wondering how she would react when she saw the foreign woman exchange vows with her ex-lover. Where was Shawn? she wondered, vexed. He's late. It was Shawn, more than anyone, to whom she wished to display herself. He'll just die when he sees my skirt, she thought. It's slit almost up to the thigh so that I can walk! And it's made of satin. He loves to run his hands over satin. As for my hat! Well, I'm glad I'm not sitting behind me. It's as big as a cartwheel and loaded with feathers.

'Here's your hymn book, old girl,' murmured Douglas, handing it to her. 'Don't sing too loudly. You always manage to be out of tune.'

Lord, what a bore he is! she sighed. How I wish Shawn was sitting by me instead. I'd cross my legs, ever so casually, so that he'd see my black silk stockings. God, I've never had a lover like him. The answer to any maiden's prayer! I confessed to him about the dildo last night and he laughed, told me to bring it along at our next meeting. Not in the least bit shocked. He knows exactly what I like. Darcy wasn't a patch on him, but even so, I don't like the idea of Camilla having him.

Her attention was drawn to her children, seated further down the pew. Flora was wriggling. I'll bet she wants to go to the lavatory. Annoying child! Yes, I was right. There goes Miss Gearing, leading her away. But it would have been civil of Camilla to have suggested her as a flower girl. I wonder why she didn't? Though I'd not like the little beast as my bridesmaid. She made a mental note to add another mark to the score against her rival.

Selden arrived, sliding into the seat at the right of Douglas. He had never looked more distinguished, immaculate in morning suit, grey top hat and striped trousers. She was pleased to see the respect everyone accorded him. No smirch on the family escutcheon because of Alison, then? The scandal had died down, no more than a nine days' wonder, even though it was now common knowledge that she was pregnant by that horribly insignificant little man, Frank Turner. She must be mad! Josephine reflected. Might at least have

364

waited until she had netted an elderly peer as a husband. Then she could have let her hair down with whoever she chose. Never did have any sense, Alison, nor any taste either.

A stirring near the main entrance. Darcy walked down the aisle, accompanied by a stranger, some friend from his youth who had been invited to be best man. Josephine did not turn her head as they passed, but every nerve tingled as she caught the shadow of Darcy's upright form. Music drifted pleasantly under the Norman arches. The organ wheezed a trifle, but Mr Blake had obviously been practising. His playing was really quite acceptable today.

The atmosphere was electric. Everyone kept peering towards the door. Then, at a signal given by one of the ushers, the organ suddenly burst into a rousing anthem as Camilla appeared on Rufus Godwin's arm. There was a rippling sigh from the women. Here at long last, was the bride. Josephine fastened her eyes on the back of Darcy's head. She'd be damned if she'd give Camilla the satisfaction of turning to look. He was staring resolutely at the altar where waited the Reverend Mapley, white-gowned, bedecked, like a principal actor in a play.

The frou-frou of silk, the slither of satin, a waft of orange blossom, the very faint hint of mothballs from Godwin's black suit. Then Josephine glanced up. Jesus! She's done it again! A sheath-gown, tubular, straight, close-fitting, showing off her height, her slimness. Draped white lace, a satin overskirt hitched up at one side, fastened with a bunch of roses. It trailed into a train at the back. Her hair, flowing over her shoulders, was banded by a diamanté head-dress from which a delicate veil cascaded for miles, seemingly. Josephine gritted her teeth as the service commenced.

With a clearing of throats, a rustle of garments, the scraping back of chairs, the congregation rose to sing the first hymn. And Camilla stared up at the stained glass window, seeing the Christ displayed in jewel-bright colours, thinking of Oxalá, the African god of procreation and harvest. Forced to accept the Catholic religion, the black slaves had used their wits, still worshipping Oxalá but renaming him Jesus. Lord of fertility! Lord of rebirth! Let this be a new beginning for me, she prayed, aware of Darcy on her right, of the mass of people, of Leila somewhere at the back. Leila who had helped her dress as sorrowfully as if she was attiring her for her funeral. Amy had lightened the atmosphere, excitedly providing something borrowed, in the shape of a lace-edged handkerchief.

'Now for something old,' she had exclaimed.

'My bangle?' Leila had suggested, slipping the wide gold band from her wrist.

Camilla had hesitated, wondering if she had put a hex on the thing but, hoping this meant that she was giving her blessing, she had accepted Leila's offering. The need for something blue was fulfilled by a pair of frilly garters.

So here I am, she thought as the choir led the final verse of the hymn. The complete bride. Wearing traditional white, superstitions obeyed. My relatives are on one side of the aisle, Darcy's on the other. Not many of them had arrived; a distant cousin or so; a couple of sisters and their families. He did not keep in touch with them much. So far, they were but dim faces to Camilla. He had invited several friends, again unknown quantities, including the studious, bespectacled best man, a relic from university days. Some of the servants had come from The Priory, and Beryl was there. The good-natured Wilf had offered to oversee the preparations for the reception to give her and Leila the chance to attend the ceremony.

And what is going on in Darcy's head as he stands there so quietly? Camilla wondered, sneaking a glance at his hawklike profile. Is he regretting it? He had said nothing to her last night, merely kissing her briefly, rising from her bed and leaving for Chalkdown Farm. She tried to convince herself that he had not noticed her lack of virginity or, if he had, was not bothered. He was, after all, a very experienced lover. Maybe he was broad-minded too, considering that what was sauce for the gander was also sauce for the goose. I shall know tonight, when we're alone. If only I didn't feel so afraid!

It was a comfort to have the support of Rufus Godwin, who had been overjoyed when she asked him to give her away, accepting with alacrity. His calmness had steadied her nerves as they drove to the church in an open horse-drawn carriage. There had even been a few cheers from the villagers lining the central street. It's going to be all right, she now tried to assure herself. Concentrate on the service. Be happy. You're about to be married to the man you love.

The congregation sat again, and the Reverend Mapley began the address. 'In so far as we are gathered together –'

Camilla found her attention wandering. She wished it was over. Mapley was a long-winded, boring orator and the service meant little to her. This English church was so grey, so grim, so unlike the beautiful cathedrals in Bahia. As a convent schoolgirl, excursions to these had been a part of her education. She had learned to know and appreciate the genius of such artists as the crippled mullato, Aleijadinho, who had lived in the eighteenth century. Physically a monster, his features so deformed by disease that he wore a sack over his head, yet the beauty inside him was expressed in the work he left behind. But no church ceremony, however solemn, had the significance that Camilla felt at the Voodoo rituals. I wish we were being married by a *hungan*, she thought.

After what seemed a dragging eternity, Mapley reached the passage where the congregation were advised to speak if they knew of any reason why the couple should not be joined in matrimony. A hush had

367

fallen. The service was nearly over. People were hardly listening, looking forward to stretching their legs, walking out into the sunshine, going to The Priory to enjoy the wedding reception. In the pause that followed Mapley's words, it seemed as if the world held its breath. A few more moments and Camilla would become Darcy's wife. No one expected an interruption. No one could really believe it when the unbelievable happened.

'I know of a reason!' a man shouted from the rear of the church.

A gasp arose from a hundred throats. Heads turned. He came down the aisle, a stranger, wearing a dark suit and a bowler hat. The Reverend Mapley stared, aghast. In all his thirty years of officiating at weddings this was the first time such a thing had taken place.

'Who are you?' he stammered, totally unprepared for such an eventuality.

'My name's Captain Martingale. I've just returned from Brazil.' The stranger came on, not pausing until he reached the altar.

'How dare you interrupt this wedding, sir? What have you to say for yourself, eh?' Rufus swung around from Camilla's side to face him, instantly disliking the furtive eyes, the cheap suit, the swaggering air of the fellow.

'He's a private detective. I instructed him to go there.' Selden rose, and as he pushed his way past Josephine, he murmured: 'I told you to leave it to me, didn't I?'

'But why, Lord Ruthen? I don't understand.' Rufus had to shout to make himself heard above the uproar. Some of the congregation were shouting, others arguing, some demanding silence so that they could hear what was being said by the chief protagonists.

'I wasn't satisfied about my uncle's death.' Selden stalked towards Camilla who stood as if turned to stone. 'I suspected that there was much more behind it.'

'Why couldn't you keep your confounded nose out of it?' Darcy roared, his face like thunder. 'It was spite, damned spite because Camilla preferred myself to you!'

368

'I've done you a favour, my dear Devereaux,' Selden answered calmly, but his eyes were bright with a kind of feverish, suppressed excitement. 'You'll thank me when you hear the truth.'

'Gentlemen, gentlemen – please. Keep your voices down. This is God's house,' protested Mapley, mopping his sweating face with the sleeve of his surplice. 'Am I to understand that Lady Camilla is already married? If this is so, then I can't possibly continue with the service.'

'Oh, no, she's not married, though she should have been,' Selden went on triumphantly. 'She bore an illegitimate child in Bahia.'

'What!' Darcy grated, then he gripped Camilla's arm, forcing her to look at him. 'Is this true?'

She nodded, feeling as if the very floor was disappearing beneath her feet. 'Yes, I had a child but it died.'

'And you weren't married?'

'No.'

'You bitch! You've deceived me!' His face was working furiously, the lines so bleak, the eyes so hard that she flinched as if he had struck her.

'She's deceived us all,' Selden drawled, and his smile was poisonous. 'There was a rumour in Bahia that she was not only a black man's whore, a Voodoo priestess practising foulest rites, but something far worse. A murderess! She killed her father!'

369

6

'Are you quite sure you'll be all right? Won't you change your mind and come to London with us? Let things cool down here?' Amy said, as she hovered uncertainly by the car.

Camilla shook her head, still wrapped in that ice-cold mantle of reserve that had enfolded her during the revelations at the church. 'I'll stay here, Amy. Thanks for asking me, but I want to lick my wounds in private.'

Early September, and hotter than August. Already at nine in the morning the sun burned her neck. There was a haze of heat over the land, turning the hills to blue and silver. The Priory appeared to doze; solid gables, the hues of lichen-shaded slates, pleasing shapes of chimney stacks, square bell tower, luxuriant growth of ivy, all combined together to give a false impression of peace. The windows reflected the sun like diamonds. Camilla longed to retreat within its walls. She was glad that John and Amy were leaving, grateful to them for staying longer than they had intended, Amy positively refusing to abandon her in her hour of need, but it would be a relief to be alone.

'Well, if you're quite sure —' Amy still hesitated, until John, already seated in the rear of the Rolls, called to her.

'Hurry up, dear. We'll miss the train.'

'Will you visit Alison and tell her what's happened?' Camilla stood by the shiny maroon door as her friend climbed in. Amy was a staunch ally, trusting and trustworthy. She had had no qualms about giving her the address in Cheyne Walk.

'I will. I hope she won't mind. I don't know her all that well.'

'Give her my love and say that I'll see her soon.' Camilla shut the car door after her and stood back.

She watched the limousine glide smoothly down the drive, Wilf at the wheel, and Amy's anxious face staring from the back window, gloved hand lifted to wave. Camilla returned the salute, then walked up the steps, passed beneath the massive stone arch and carefully closed the front door on the world. She wanted nothing to do with it now, and for a long time to come. Like a hounded she-wolf, she had retired to her den, there to let her injuries heal.

The house was as hushed as if there had been a recent bereavement. Over the past days, the servants had crept about on tiptoe. No one wanted to meet Camilla's eyes. Masses of flowers had decorated it for the wedding. These had been hastily removed but their perfume lingered on, reminiscent of funeral wreaths. As she crossed the stone-flagged Great Hall, she saw the familiar, comforting things, the oak beams carved in rich tracery, the heavy elaborate furniture, the portraits of her ancestors. There was one of Cornelius Ruthen, dated 1613. He had added to the original monastic building. The family likeness was noticeable. Pausing by one of the fireplaces, she looked up at the coat of arms centrally placed above the canopy. It held meaning for her. Every quartering on that ancient shield emblazoned in red, black and gold, had a legend attached.

The sight of it brought comfort to her bruised soul. She was a part of that heritage, part of its history, its nobility or baseness. Ruthen blood was in her. Good blood? Bad blood? It was immaterial. She needed to feel at one with something, no matter what. Needed roots, a justification for her existence. Hundreds of years ago, in the dim dark ages, each of those quarterings had been a device worn by a knight on his heavy shield. It was his cognizance in the field of battle or at tournaments. Perhaps a Ruthen had borne it at Agincourt, at Crécy or

371

Poitiers, or in the lists in some fair lady's honour. The escutcheon was an emblem of the days that had been, and would never be again.

The sun had been shining down from one of the high, narrow windows, but now a cloud passed across it and the hall became shadowed. Like my reputation, Camilla thought. Family pride has been tarnished. And I care. Oh, yes, despite the stubbornness that won't let me show it, I care most desperately!

'I said that I'd break you,' Selden had hissed under cover of the pandemonium when Camilla had stood in the church, waiting for Darcy to declare that this news made no difference, that he would stick by her no matter what, and that Mapley should continue with the service.

But he had turned away, consulting with his best man, with Rufus, with one of his sisters alarmed at the fuss, while mayhem reigned around them. She had seen Josephine's sneering smile, caught the satisfied expression on Gladys Lacey's thin face – on Elsie Turner's. Everyone was staring at her, mouths gaping, taking an almost prurient pleasure in witnessing an interrupted wedding ceremony. This in itself would have been exciting enough, but when it had happened to a foreigner about whom wild rumours were circulating, this was an added bonus. She had felt herself surrounded by enemies – only Beryl there, taking her arm, and Leila too. Between them they had led her away, Rufus indignant and furious, demanding that Selden come to The Priory, bringing his nasty little spy with him, and give an account of himself.

They had come, Selden and Captain Martingale and Darcy. The servants had been lined up in the Hall, ready to offer their congratulations. The tables were laid out in the centre; long, oaken and solid, their surfaces spread with damask cloths, laden with delicacies, dominated by the white, frosted, three-tiered cake, adorned with miniature silver bells, slippers and horseshoes. Beryl had immediately taken command, drawing Harvey aside, explaining, while Camilla had been helped into the library by Rufus.

The ensuing scene was etched forever on her memory, though at the time she had been so stunned that she had remained silent, white-faced before Darcy, as if already on trial. She had wanted to run into his arms, to be comforted and petted, to lay her head against his shirt front and feel the brush of his beard against her temples. She still believed that he would kick Selden out of the house, affirming that he believed in her and fully intended to marry her. He said many things during the heated discussion, but this was not one of them.

'What proof have you to support these allegations?' Rufus had shouted, his stocky form planted firmly in front of Selden.

'Enough to stir up a hornets' nest,' her cousin had replied coldly, lighting up a cigarette. 'I intend to take the matter to court.'

'But Ruthen died of a heart attack. I was in communication with his Portuguese doctor.' Rufus had never been more angry in his life. Selden did not know it, but he had found a formidable opponent. The lawyer may have been old in years, but he possessed the unquenchable fire and energy of a much younger man.

Selden's lips had lifted unpleasantly, smoke coiling from his flared nostrils. 'No doubt he was bribed to say that, or possibly blackmailed.'

'Your methods, my Lord? Don't judge everyone by your own standards.' Rufus had not minced his words. 'If you take this to law, I'll fight you every inch of the way. You'll lose the case, and when you do, I'll advise my client to sue you for defamation of character.'

'Sue away.' Selden's eyes had been fixed on Camilla. Snake's eyes, coldly malicious. 'It won't help her. She'll be in prison by that time, awaiting the offices of the hangman, I shouldn't wonder. I knew from the first that there was something fishy about all this. Inherit The Priory, would she? Over my dead body!'

'That can be arranged!' Darcy had growled, his blue eyes mere slits in that dark face. 'What's your game, Selden? You don't need The Priory.'

'There's been a crime committed, a monstrous injustice done. I want to see it put right.'

'You bloody liar!'

'Be quiet, Mr Devereaux,' Rufus had cautioned. 'Now then, my Lord, let's hear this so-called evidence that your ferret has managed to unearth.'

They had talked for what seemed hours. Camilla was not spared. Martingale came forward and went into a detailed recital of her past. It was all there; her affair with André de Jaham; Ruthen's refusal to allow them to marry; her pregnancy and the young man's sudden death; her violent quarrels with her father and her vow to see him dead. Black despair had engulfed her. The list of her indiscretions was damning.

She had wondered just who Martingale had talked to in Brazil. Servants, perhaps? Some of her father's cronies? Most of them were heavy drinkers. It would not have been difficult to persuade them to admit to almost anything if Martingale had plied them with money and alcohol. Bribery and corruption, nepotism and favour ruled in that country where politics were complicated and some revolution or other always in the offing, led by hotheaded, quarrelsome agitators. No one was to be trusted. All were venal.

'But how can you prove that she was instrumental in her father's death?' Rufus had asked at last, as the shadows grew longer, painting the panelled walls with crimson. 'All this is so much hearsay.'

'Exhumation. The body needs to be examined by an English doctor under controlled conditions.' Selden had sounded so sure of himself.

At that Camilla had laughed, drawing their eyes to

374

her – a wild laugh, mirthless, horrible. 'D'you know how quickly a corpse decomposes out there?'

'Ah, no doubt you relied on that fact, murderess!' Selden had retorted. 'No matter. We'll leave it to the judge to decide who's speaking the truth.'

'You think you've won, don't you?' she had snarled, goaded beyond endurance. 'But I haven't started fighting back yet. When I do, watch out!'

'You're in England now, cousin, not some lawless foreign port. You'd find it hard to kill me here and get away with it.'

'I shouldn't count on it.'

'Did you make a note of that, Martingale?' Selden had swung around to the shabby detective. 'She's threatening me.'

'Please, Camilla, don't say any more.' Rufus had come across to take her cold hands in his. 'Leave the talking to me.'

'There's nothing more to say.' Selden had picked up his hat, and strolled towards the door. 'You'll be hearing from Messrs Henshaw, Horsefield and Baily in due course. Probably have a visit from the police ere long. Don't make any attempt to skip the country, will you, Camilla?'

Now she came back to the present, standing alone in the Great Hall. Was it only a day or so ago that her life had fallen to pieces around her, just when she was sure that she'd left the past behind? Rufus had sat her down and made her go over every detail of her father's death. It had been agonizing to remember things that she had pushed into a dark corner of her mind, but she had been as truthful as she dared.

No, she had not touched him. She had discovered his body at dawn one morning. He had died during the night. She had spoken convincingly while inside she was riddled with doubt and guilt, remembering so much else. Conversations with Leila – 'I hate him! We've got to get

375

rid of him. He's a monster. He killed André. Because of this I lost my baby. A ceremony to bring about his death! Do it, Leila – please –'

She admitted to Rufus that the rest of it was true. She *had* quarrelled with him about André, even threatened to kill him, but of course she'd not done so. The lawyer had heard her out, then assured her that there was really nothing Selden could do except stir up a lot of dirt. He had added grimly that this was enough to ruin her credibility in the area. The newshounds would soon get wind of a sensational story, and the repercussions were bound to be unpleasant.

'You'll be cleared, without a doubt,' he had said, then added gloomily: 'But mud sticks!'

'He's successfully broken up my relationship with Darcy.'

Rufus had crinkled up his shrewd eyes, and looked at her thoughtfully. 'Maybe that is not such a bad thing.'

'He'll never take The Priory away from me! I don't care what happens. I'll not leave it!' She had declared with such wrathful fire that Rufus had wondered if she had been entirely truthful about Ruthen's death. 'It's mine! No one else shall have it! I'd rather burn it to the ground!'

He left shortly after, heading for London and the Temple, there to consult with learned colleagues on the matter. And Darcy? Camilla leaned her head against the surround and gave herself over to despair. Darcy had refused to speak to her, slamming out of the house. Time had no meaning any more, and she rested against the Hercules who formed part of the support until the stone became warm under her cheek. How quiet it was. The quietness of the tomb. I could kill myself and no one would be aware, she thought. Perhaps I should do that. Who would miss me? Who mourn? I could join my little dead baby and André in the waters of oblivion. André loved me. I can see him now, with his olive skin, black hair, eyes of soft peat-brown. That aristocratic Creole, mostly Portuguese and French, but with a portion that was Negro. How would life have been with him? He was flirtatious, a ladies' man. By now I might have been a wronged wife. My father recognized this flaw. They were two of a kind. But he shouldn't have had him killed. Dragged into a dark alley in Rubera and battered to death like an animal!

A footfall on the flags jerked her from her reverie. She jumped violently, thinking to see God knew what – André! Her father!

'I've come to say goodbye,' said Darcy.

Her hands were at her throat, her mouth. She stared at him, her lips parted. 'Where are you going?' she managed to croak.

'To Bahia.'

'To clear my name!' Hope waved its tattered banner. He's forgiven me! He'll be my champion!

'To find the lost city.'

The plunge down into the pit again. I can't bear it, she thought. Aloud, she said: 'Don't be a fool.'

His face was empty and cold, the blue eyes bleak and remote. 'I've read the log, Camilla. I must go.'

'But what about us?' Her eyes shimmered with unshed tears, the first that had filled them since that calamitous wedding morning. He couldn't really be leaving, could he? With so much unsaid between them? Why didn't he stay and fight Selden?

'There's no future for us any more.' His voice was lifeless as if he had fought a terrible battle and lost. 'You should have told me about your past.'

'And what would your reaction have been?' She did not dare look at his face.

'I never much cared for second-hand goods.'

She braced herself and glanced up at him and what she saw filled her with anger. 'And what of you and your numerous affairs? What about Josephine? She was more than slightly shop-soiled, wasn't she?'

377

'I didn't ask her to be my wife.'

His words did nothing to soothe the confusion and fury rioting through her. She needed something more than excuses that sounded insincere. She wanted to punish him, so pushed it further. 'You believe that I killed my father?'

'I don't think you're a murderess.' For a long moment Darcy looked at her, his lips twisted in a tight smile.

'Then you're going because I once loved a man and bore him a child. You've no compassion for this youthful lunacy that brought me so much trouble.' Forgetting pride, she placed a pleading hand on his arm and said breathlessly: 'Oh, Darcy, give it time. I know that I should have told you, but I love you. I was afraid to lose you.'

Unemotionally, he removed her fingers, 'I think it best if we forget that we were to be married. Nothing you can say will make me alter my decision.'

'You never loved me!' Her voice rang out under the rafters. She stared at his face, but beyond the coldness in his eyes, the features revealed nothing.

'I was closer to loving you than any other woman I've known, but it won't work, Camilla. I've found something more important.'

Her heart sank like a stone. 'The fabled city. You had already made up your mind to look for it on our wedding eve – when I told you about it – even after we'd made love.'

'I realized then that you weren't a virgin.' He shut his eyes against the memory. When he opened them a split second later, pain was very apparent. 'I was hurt by your deceit, but I sat up all night at the farm, reading the log over and over, and suddenly nothing mattered but following in the tracks of the explorer who wrote it. I've been feeling restless since our engagement, almost trapped. I was about to settle down, and I'd never really seen much of the world. All this came to me with renewed force when I read that book.'

378

Camilla's emotions were so raw that she had no thought for his, never realizing that he was as ashamed and angry for what had transpired as she was. 'But you would have gone through with it?'

'Oh, yes, though I'd have wanted to know about your former lovers, and given you no peace until you consented to travel to Brazil, but now I can go alone.'

Strength drained out of her. Argument was hopeless. She could have conquered anything else, another woman, an addiction for drink, drugs or gambling, but this was too strong a pull. She had seen it before, had experienced its devastating power. 'When are you going?'

'Now. I'll drive to Ryehampton, then catch a train to London to arrange a few things.'

'Be careful, Darcy.'

His mouth curved in a crooked smile. 'You're concerned for me?'

'God help me, I've not stopped loving you. I wish I had!' Holding her back ramrod stiff, she stared in the other direction, no longer able to bear the sight of the man who had led her to believe that it was safe to indulge desire again.

'Look here, Camilla, perhaps I'll feel differently when I come back. If I get this out of my system, maybe we can pick up the pieces,' she heard him say. He's trying to salve his conscience. He's hoping I'll meet someone else while he's gone. She did not reply and he went on: 'I've engaged a manager for the farm. Should anything happen to me, I've willed the place to you.'

'Buying me off, are you, Darcy?' Her voice was flat, jeering. 'Is that what you've always done when you tired of a woman and wanted to go on to something more entertaining? You're like a child – a little boy seeking adventure. Gold! Lost cities! My God, I've heard it all before! You'll not come back. You'll die out there, and the world will be a sweeter place without you.'

He made no retaliation, but his jaw tightened and his eyes were like blue ice. They stared at one another in anger, in sorrow, and at last she could bear it no more, burying her head in her hands. He said nothing further. She heard his footsteps retreating down the hall, and then the soft click as the door closed behind him. Slowly, her hands came down from her face. She gazed at the emptiness, lost, alone, and took a hesitant step forward.

'Missy Camilla! My poor baby!' Leila appeared out of the dimness and Camilla threw herself into her arms as the storm of weeping broke over her.

The black woman held her, rocked her, murmuring in French, in the Creole patois – dark skin contrasting with her mistress's, ebony hair rendered darker by the tawny head pressed into her shoulder, eyes inky and deep, all-wise. She patted the shaking shoulders, and made no attempt to stem the tide of grief. Like a septic wound that must be lanced, so Camilla's sorrow must run forth, lest it turn inwards and poison her.

After a while, she encouraged her to mount the stairs to the Master Chamber. They needed to have a serious talk. Leila knew that there was work to be done. This house would never prosper until they had laid the apparition to rest. Ever since they arrived there, she had been aware of that doleful shade knocking on the portals of her senses, demanding admittance. She could not do it alone. Camilla was a part of the design, but she had been so occupied, first with the restoration of the building, then with her passion for Darcy. She had squeezed out everything else. But now she must be made to see that this was important. Nothing would go right for her until it was resolved.

'What am I to do?' Camilla sobbed, collapsing on the walnut daybed by the window in her room. 'He's gone, Leila.'

'He would have gone anyway, honey.'

Leila stood in the centre of the floor, dressed in scarlet

with touches of black. Though her waist had thickened slightly with the years, she was still a handsome woman. Many men had wanted to marry her in Bahia and she liked handsome men whatever their colour, still tormented by a restless, unquenchable urge. But here, in this cold, unfriendly country, Leila had had no suitors. She had concentrated her energies on her religion.

Camilla looked up at her, the tears drying on her cheeks. 'How d'you know he would have left me?' she demanded, and Leila was relieved to see anger breaking through the sorrow.

'I *know*,' the Creole nodded sagely. 'Even before you gave him the tiger's-eye, I could see what sort of a man he was. That ring affected him, like it did your Pa. And then you showed him that old, bad book. On the same night that you let him have you.'

'You were spying on us.' Camilla retreated into dignity.

'I was watching you for your own good. I saw him come like a devil out of the storm. I listened at your door. I hid in the shadows when he left. When you were asleep, I done crept in and looked for that cursed thing. It was gone.'

'How dare you! Peeping and prowling! Really, Leila, sometimes you go too far!' Camilla leaped up and began pacing the room, hugging herself, rubbing her hands up and down her arms to warm them.

'I promised your Mamma that I'd care for you always. I knew Darcy Devereaux weren't no good. But you wouldn't listen to me. Oh, no, too uppity-proud!' Leila looked at her with grim amusement. 'So now, high and mighty Missy Camilla Ruthen, you got to heed me. It's this here *duende*. She's a-crying and a-wailing, and you just got to listen to her. Do that, and then we'll deal with Lord Ruthen and all the rest of 'em, easy as pie.'

'But Darcy – ?' Camilla began, then stopped in her tracks. She was conscious of a lightening of the burden within her. She suddenly knew that there was something terribly important she had to do. Head up, she walked around and around the room, scenting the air like an animal, seeking the right spot to commence her work.

'Get out your crystal, missy,' Leila commanded. 'The scrying-ball. You've not been practising with it lately. The sight is a gift, and you ignore it at your peril. You're lucky. The magic sphere remains blank for me. I divine the future in the cards, in the bones, but I can't scry.'

'I don't want to use it.' Camilla's voice held a ring of defiance. 'I've not looked in it since we left Brazil. I'm too busy. There are too many material matters demanding attention. I haven't the time to be a prophetess. I've been threatened! I've been abandoned by my lover! Selden will try to take the house away from me, and you want me to crystal-gaze!'

'You're afraid of what it might show you,' Leila hissed softly, and her eyes had a hypnotic stare.

'I'm not!' Camilla stood there defiantly, her chin tilted. 'It's never shown me anything connected with myself. You know it doesn't work like that, any more than you can predict your own future with the cards. Good God! If seers could do that, they'd all back the winner of the Derby and end up millionaires!'

'The blessed *loa* are merciful. They stop the sighted from using it for their own gain. You'll not do this for yourself, but to aid a tormented spirit. Go on, missy. Fetch the crystal.'

Camilla could not tear her eyes from Leila's. They were like liquid jet. A great power surrounded them, very wise, very ancient and, like a sleep walker, she went to a drawer and took out the crystal. Unwrapping its black silk shroud, she walked into the secret room. When the Creole followed, she found her seated cross-legged on the carpet, her hands clasped lightly around the shining ball. Leila sank down opposite her, and began to beat out a rhythm with her *asson*. Unable to resist, Camilla

382

opened her mind and looked into the crystal. At first she could see nothing but reflections of the room. She had trouble switching off her thoughts. Darcy dominated them.

As far back as she could remember she had been familiar with that small globe in which strange images would form and fade. Leila had given it to her, and from the time she was a toddler it had seemed a natural part of her life. Whenever she looked into it visions would appear, only to vanish in quick succession. Better than books, this toy had never failed to amuse her with pictures which were as gaily coloured as printed ones, but had the advantage of being alive. As she grew older, Leila warned her that it must never be treated lightly. It was not a game, but an instrument with which to tap the unknown.

I've neglected it since being in England, she thought guiltily. The truth is that I was afraid of seeing my father, then frightened that I'd find out something unpleasant about Darcy. Perhaps I've lost the gift. Perhaps this is why misfortune has overtaken me. I must give myself over to a higher power. But it was some time before her mind became a tranquil pool. Silence filled the room, broken only by the gentle swish of Leila's rattle.

Then the crystal appeared to sway and move and lose all shape. In its place came a thick dark mist that spread until it enveloped all the space before Camilla. Slowly, in the blackness, she saw a long winding drive. A house. The Priory. Yet different. It was askew, like a negative carelessly placed over a familiar photograph. Its doorway advanced rapidly towards her. She felt herself being sucked inside. Up the stairs she drifted, up and up until she reached the attics. Into them, through them, doors and walls parting like water. Dust and cobwebs, a jumble of broken furniture, boxes, damaged portraits, abandoned toys, lumber which is too good to be discarded yet never used again. She came to a sloping area where roof joined wall. Wooden beams, a cupboard hidden behind an old coffer. The vision shifted, changed. Now she was in another room. It was occupied but she could not see by whom. She heard voices raised in anger – a woman's – a man's, sounds and sights and searing things that burned with a cold fire. The vision began to swirl, faded, was obliterated by a crimson flood. Camilla closed her eyes, sick and trembling.

'What is it, *ma petite*?' She lifted her lids to see Leila's watchful face close to her own. 'What did you see?'

Camilla's eyes were misted as if awakening from a deep sleep. 'The attics. Something's hidden there.' Her mind was like a stone and she wanted to run. She dropped the ball. It rolled across the carpet, then lay there, radiating prism rainbows. 'I can't! Leila, don't make me!'

A look of disapproval crossed Leila's face. 'That's wicked talk! You must obey the *loa*.' Her voice lowered, filled with passionate entreaty. 'Promise me you'll never throw the crystal away. Always look, Missy Camilla, in mirrors and waters and the ball. God has given you the vision. See always, my beloved pupil.'

Then Camilla lost all fear, somehow accepting that this was her destiny. She had no choice but to obey. 'Come upstairs with me,' she said.

She was burning with impatience now, possessed of an urge that banished everything else. She seized Leila's hand, dragging her along with her. There was no one about. It was Beryl's day off and Wilf had driven her into Ryehampton. Harvey was in charge below stairs, and Sam had gone fishing, though warned not to stray beyond the garden boundaries, for his own safety. The villagers had turned against the whole household. Stones had been hurled through the downstairs windows and, even more dusturbing, there had been a series of obscene, anonymous letters which mysteriously appeared out of nowhere.

384

Camilla sprinted up the winding stairs that led to the garrets. Like every other portion of the house, they had been thoroughly cleaned and renovated. The lumber had been either thrown out or burned, unless particularly old and interesting, when it had been restored and put into use. It was a positive labyrinth, and several of the rooms had reverted to their original use as servants' quarters; quaint, with white plastered walls, rough-hewn beams and bare wood floors, comfortable and cosy. She pushed open the door of the storeroom. This large oblong space had been kept as a depository for suitcases and the hundred and one things highly necessary when needed, but a nuisance when not. Sunlight penetrated the small, clean windows, making patterns on the floor, though shadows lingered around the massive chimney stack rising from the floors below, and darkened corners receding under the eaves.

Camilla put out her hands, groping almost, shutting her eyes and seeing it as it had been within the crystal, but when she opened them again although the dimensions were the same, it didn't seem the same at all. Too neat and tidy by far. Not a speck of dust, not a spider's web in sight. A rocking-horse stood under one window. Tattered saddle, cracked, dappled paintwork, a few strands of mane and tail remaining, vandalized by generations of romping children. She caught the faint echo of their voices. Then there was the ancient oaken cradle, with the Ruthen crest carved on its hood. A chest containing old-fashioned clothing, ruffs, farthingales, cloaks and hats. She had kept them for future fancy dress balls. And the cradle? She shuttered her mind against the dream of laying Darcy's child within it. Further boxes contained books and letters, things which she had put off looking at, promising herself that she'd tackle them on a rainy day when there was nothing else to do.

The sunshine dimmed, then returned. A ray glinted on a coffer standing against one wall. Camilla started.

Tension was like a hot wire binding her nerves. 'Help me!' she cried to Leila.

A heave. The chest was heavy, but once they had got it moving it slid across the boards. Clean floor behind. Clean corners. A cupboard built into the wall and obviously as old as The Priory itself. No mystery there. The small door opened easily. One of the workmen had given it new hinges, they gleamed back at her innocently, unrusted, well oiled. She could not remember what she had expected to find within it. Mouldering bones? A corpse?

'Bring over that candle, Leila.' Her fingers fumbled with the matches. The wick caught. Yellow uncertainty wavered inside the cupboard. It was empty. But it was waiting.

She felt around the wooden walls, tapping, probing. Could hear Leila's quickened breathing behind her. The recess was lined with a piece of old worn carpet, curling at the edges. She seized it and tugged – felt an entire floorboard come up in her hands. Beneath it, covered by a film of dust, was a bundle of letters tied with discoloured ribbon, and a thin book with a faded red cover. An exercise book, such as a child might use at school.

'Wasn't it an absolute hoot?' said Josephine, lying across Shawn, her big, beautiful breasts pressed against his naked, hairy chest. 'I don't think I've ever enjoyed anything so much in my whole life. Trust Selden to come up with the goods.'

'I suppose you mean the wedding.' He looked up into her treacherous, wayward face, poised above him in the twilight gloom. 'I'd hardly say that. It was a fiasco.'

'I know! That's the joy of it!' She laid her head down, nibbling teasingly at his nipples. When she looked up again, her expression was the embodiment of malicious devilry. 'And I hear down the grapevine that Camilla's now receiving poison-pen letters.'

'It wouldn't be you that's after sending them, would it?' His hand gripped her head, forcing her to meet his eyes, her own oddly tilted by the pull of those relentless fingers on her scalp.

'I may not like her very much but that's not my style. I'd rather have an out-and-out slanging match!' She laughed and wriggled against him, rubbing a foot down the length of his leg.

It was the first time they had met since the wedding. Remembering Camilla's stricken face, Shawn had been avoiding her spiteful Ladyship. But there was no denying that she was a pleasing mistress, game for anything. There was nothing she refused him, nothing they had not done, except discover that they loved one another and that each mating was any more than a fierce coming together of two healthy animals.

'Then who's sending them? Your brother?' Shawn released her and heaved himself up against the pillows, wedging one behind his back.

Josephine rolled over, kicking the bedclothes aside, hands behind her head, stretching her body with a contented sigh. 'No. He's in London, in collusion with his lawyer friends. No doubt digging up further dirt about Camilla. He's really got his knife into her.'

'I can't see why, devil take me if I can.' Shawn lit a cigarette, took a drag at it and, when she pouted, placed it between her lips.

'He wanted to marry her himself. He'd actually proposed and she turned him down. No one does that to Selden and lives to tell the tale.' Josephine flexed one shapely leg, holding it high and admiring her ankle.

'He's not in love with her.' Shawn did not believe Selden capable of loving anything.

'Heavens, no! I wouldn't think so for a moment. He doesn't like having his carefully laid schemes disrupted.

387

And she certainly did that all right when she took over The Priory and sent old Claypole packing. So many exciting things happening. What with Alison kicking over the traces and running off with that blighter, Turner, and then Selden's sleuth arriving at the eleventh hour. But most exciting of all, of course, is you, my wild Irish rogue!' Josephine turned to him, mouth parted, yearning towards him, yearning to feel once again the pleasure he had recently lavished on her.

She shaped her body to his, hands wandering familiarly, down over his chest, his hard flat belly, fingers brushing the hair which ran in a dark line from his navel to his groin. She expected an immediate response, but instead Shawn pushed her aside and got up. He stared at her for a second with a rather grim, mocking smile, though in reality he had the urge to smack her. He knew that if he had to stay there much longer listening to her vicious remarks, he *would* smack her!

He turned away and began to pull on his clothes. 'Isn't it time you went, Josephine?' he asked coldly. 'You'll be late for dinner.'

'It's not till eight, and Douglas is captaining the village cricket team. He won't be home for ages, drinking with them in the Red Lion. Come back to bed, Shawn,' she cooed, but her eyes had a hard glitter.

'Not now, Josephine,' he sat on a chair and pulled on his boots. Dusk of evening spread through the room as the sun sank and the moon rose in the east. He could see it just above the trees outside the window, a great full moon, casting long shadows, the harvest moon by whose light men would still be lifting the sheaves.

Rising, he ducked his head through the open casement, breathing in the scent of thyme and honeysuckle, hearing the last cries of sleepy birds. The afterglow of sunset reached out to meet the moonshine. All the land was bathed in a double radiance, filled with magic under

388

the indigo velvet sky. Shawn turned to pick up his thick tweed jacket and a heavy Inverness cape. The nights were getting colder, and the vigil might be a long one.

'Where are you going?' Josephine bounced up angrily, tossing her tangled fair curls back from her face.

'That's my business.' His tone was light but firm. 'I've done my duty by you, now I'm off.'

At that she came raging to her feet. 'Blast you, Shawn Brennan! Duty, indeed! I give as good as I get, don't I? You're a rude Irish pig, that's what you are! Why don't you go back to your bogs and your potato patch?' She began tugging on her garments, swearing as she laddered a silk stocking in her haste.

'I might just do that one day soon.' He watched this show of temper with vexation mingled with amusement. She was so predictable. This was not the first time there had been arguments, recriminations, quarrels. She was fiendishly jealous and possessive.

'Good riddance to bad rubbish!' she retorted, then suddenly she paused, staring at him through narrowed lids. 'Oh, but you won't go anywhere, will you, Shawn? Much too devoted to Camilla.'

He shrugged. 'No woman has ever stopped me from doing what I wanted.'

'This one will. Now Darcy's slung his hook, you'll be there like a devoted puppy dog,' she continued nastily. 'D'you know what I think?'

'I can't imagine.' He was bored, eager to be off, swinging his hat by the brim.

'I think you're in love with her.'

He gave her a long, cool stare, suddenly tired of her shrill voice and aggressive manner, her physical appetites that bordered on the gross, her viperous tongue and callous disregard for human feelings. 'You're right,' he said quietly. 'I *am* in love with her.'

Josephine let rip with a string of profanities that made him wince. Like a woman bereft of reason, she flung on the remainder of her clothes and flounced out of the room. He heard her running down the stairs and the crash of the front door. Shawn experienced a lift of the heart and a sense of relief. She was gone, and he knew the affair was over. He pushed the window wide to permit the night air to banish the odour of her cloying perfume.

A little later he let himself out of the cottage, saddled his horse, and rode through the still evening towards The Priory. A beech coppice closed around him. He guided his mount along a bridle path. It was the one that Josephine had always used when she came to see him. On the far side of the wood, another track branched off, leading eventually to Erwarton Hall. Shawn smiled as he stared into the dimness, imagining her furious ride home. The arch of whispering trees thinned. Now he could see the moon again and the meadow that marked the boundary of Camilla's estate.

Spurring his horse into a gallop, he covered the distance swiftly, took a short cut which meant crossing the stream, and was soon cantering up the drive. The scene was bathed in moonlight. He paused, entranced. The Priory was hunched there like an aged dragon amidst its lair of sentinel trees. A hulking monument to the Ruthens. Fantastic chimneypots poked black fingers into the star-frosted sky. There was the pale shimmer of windows, not lighted from within but reflecting the night. An owl stirred and gave her hunting cry. Another answered, dismal, haunting, almost frightening. Shawn's scalp crawled. Someone's just walked over my grave, he thought.

It was different when he stood in the kitchen. Warmth, good fellowship, the smell of the supper recently enjoyed by the staff in the dining-hall off right; Wilf snapping the tops off two short dark bottles of stout; Beryl seated by the range, a glass of sherry in her hand. Some of the servants were present, enjoying an hour's relaxation before bedtime. There had been a moment's

390

silence when Shawn appeared at the back door. The men, in braces and shirt sleeves, had given him hard stares, while the women waited to see what they would do. After all, he worked for Lord Ruthen, their mistress's enemy. There was a spy in the camp.

But then Wilf had removed the pipe from between his lips and asked him in, adding: 'What can I do for you, Mr Brennan?'

Taking their cue from him, the others resumed talking amongst themselves, joined by a few more who wandered in. Shawn accepted the mug Wilf offered. 'Is there anywhere more private?'

'The housekeeper's room. You coming, Beryl?' Wilf picked up the bottles and led Shawn along a passage and up a few stairs. The lamps were already lit there, and Beryl invited him in.

When they had settled themselves at the round table, Shawn took out his cigarette case. 'D'you mind if I smoke in here, Mrs Simmonds?'

'Smoke away. Wilf always does.' She smiled at him encouragingly, a robust, pink-cheeked woman, with a refreshing honesty and openness about her. A breath of fresh air after spending time with Josephine.

Shawn lit up, then leaned his elbows on the crimson cloth. 'Look here, I'm worried about these anonymous letters that are rumoured to be arriving. Have you any idea who's sending them?'

Wilf's face creased into a frown. 'Damned if I have. I'd like to catch whoever it is. They wouldn't do it again.'

'Is Lady Camilla very upset about them?' Shawn's eyes were pure green in the lamplight.

'What do you think? She don't let on, but of course she's upset.' Wilf topped up their glasses.

'They're filthy!' Beryl flashed indignantly. 'She showed me one. I've never read anything so disgusting. Whoever's writing such things must be barmy!'

Wilf was staring intently at Shawn. A kind-hearted,

big-souled man, he was devoted to Camilla and, through this crisis, had done his best to protect her from the mundane things that had to be taken care of. It was he who had promptly boxed up the food prepared for the reception and ordered that it be whisked out of sight. Mrs Mapley had received the bulk of it for the poor families to whom she dispensed charity. Aided by Harvey, Wilf had carried the wedding cake out to the Rolls and driven to the village. It had provided a treat for the old folk in the almshouses for days to come.

'Why are you so concerned?' he asked Shawn, stuffing tobacco into the rosewood bowl of his pipe. 'I thought you might be on the other side, Lord Selden's man – or Lady Josephine's,' he added, a twinkle in his eyes.

Shawn reddened under his tan, not exactly proud that this pleasant couple should know he had been humping Selden's sister. The damned village is a hotbed of gossip! he thought angrily.

'I admire Lady Camilla,' he answered, deciding to ignore the last part of Wilf's remark. 'She's done a splendid job on the old place, and settled in remarkably well, under the circumstances. She doesn't deserve to be treated so shabbily. Devereaux merits a kick up the backside for leaving her in the lurch.'

Wilf nodded in agreement and stopped being suspicious. He had come to know Shawn quite well, for the young man had spent much time at The Priory, before the work on it was completed. Despite the talk concerning him and Lady Josephine, it was impossible not to like the Irishman. There was a salt and freshness about him that was endearing. He was an entertaining, thrusting talker, humane and humorous, and was not afraid of hard work.

The minutes ticked by and the air became blue with tobacco smoke as the three of them discussed how best they could aid Camilla. 'I've watched out carefully,' concluded Wilf, 'but those damned letters just appear out of thin air, sometimes left at the back door, sometimes at the front. I've even found one inside, on her Ladyship's desk.'

'Is one of the servants in Ruthen's pay?' Shawn suggested.

'It's this house!' Beryl declared with a shudder. 'I swear it's haunted! I can never get warm here, and I have the most horrible dreams in which a dark figure, I can never see the face, keeps trying to give me a rotting rat skin!'

Wilf looked at her with husbandly indulgence. 'You'll have to stop eating cheese for supper, my dear. There's no such thing as ghosts.'

Shawn made no comment. He wouldn't say there was, but then again he wouldn't say there wasn't. He'd never seen an apparition, but had felt chills sometimes in old buildings, even out in the open, odd pockets in the ether which were not quite normal.

'I don't think spooks leave letters lying about.' He smiled across at Beryl. Then he turned to Wilf. 'Would you have any objection to my patrolling the grounds tonight?'

His request was met with such relief that he realized just how worried the Simmonds were. Wilf had many duties and needed his sleep. He could not spend nights on guard, and did not quite like to trust the job to any of the footmen. Besides which Beryl was obviously frightened and wanted him with her during the hours of darkness. So, before long, Shawn was stationed in a corner of the garden where an angle of the wall met a large, sheltering tree. It was a fine vantage point as it overlooked both the front of the house and a pathway leading around to the back. He had a hip flask of brandy in the pocket of his cape, a new pack of cigarettes and plenty of matches. One by one the lights flickered and died at the windows, and all became very still.

He smoked and watched the stars, seeing them

393

reduced to insignificance as the brilliant moon rose high in the trees. I hope I'll be able to stay awake, he thought, resting his back against the gnarled bole. He heard a badger yapping across the valley, a high, excited note, repeated many times. Then silence again, apart from the interminable rustling of leaves and stealthy wild things. He was no stranger to night-watches. Many a time when a boy, he had wandered the dark woods, stalking foxes, badgers, those animals who prefer to hunt nocturnally. Not to harm them, but out of interest, curiosity and a desire to understand.

It was getting colder as the night advanced. He pulled his collar up over his ears, his thoughts turned inwards so that he was no longer aware of the night. Time was nothing then. Perhaps he did sleep on his feet. Then something drew him back, soft, like the touch of a hand. Over his shoulder fell a high silver radiance – silver light falling across the wall, pitting it with dark shadows, silver shine on the earth below, patterned with the outline of the tree. The moon was high. He looked at his watch, clear in that unearthly light. Nearly one o'clock.

His attention sharpened, breath fallen to a soft rhythm inaudible even to himself. Footsteps on leaves. Coming closer. Then the sight of a figure, flitting from patches of moonlight, patches of shadow. Nearer it came, and nearer, leaving the trees, gliding up the drive towards the flight of wide stone steps. Giving himself no time to question whether it was something real or supernatural, Shawn leaped out in pursuit, gaining on it, launching himself in a rugby tackle.

It was a female body that lay beneath him on the gravel, a female voice that screamed in fright. In the bright moonlight he was looking down into Gladys Lacey's terrified eyes. 'You!' he grated. 'You're the one writing those foul letters! Get up, woman, and give an account of yourself.'

He hauled Gladys to her feet. She sagged against him,

almost fainting with fear. 'Don't tell anyone, Mr Brennan,' she gasped as his hand clamped around her arm. 'I couldn't bear the talk! Whatever would my mother say if she knew?'

'Give me that!' Shawn tore the envelope from her gloved hand. He could feel her shaking. 'How could you do such a thing, Gladys?'

'It was Elsie's idea!' she protested, but did not try to get away, standing passive, trembling, under his hand. 'She's wanted to get her own back on Lady Camilla for helping Lady Alison steal her husband. She wasn't able to come herself – too upset!'

'Too drunk!' Shawn growled. 'And who put her up to this, eh? Was it Selden Ruthen?'

'I don't know.' She was crying now, on the verge of hysteria.

'You *do* know!' He gave her a hard shake, that bony, trouble-making creature who was probably enjoying having him bully her.

'All right! Don't hurt me! Yes, Lord Ruthen is telling her what to do. He wants to drive Lady Camilla away from the village. And he's right! She's a witch! A wicked, evil foreigner, with her looks and her money! Why should she have everything whilst some of us have nothing? Why should I have to spend my life in that shop, never able to go anywhere or do anything – only chapel on Sundays with my mother watching me all the time! It's not fair!' Gladys's voice was a hoarse whisper, filled with resentment, envy and despair.

She did not attempt to free herself from Shawn's grasp, indeed she was leaning towards him, into him. Heat seemed to be radiating from her lean body. She had lost her hat in the struggle, and her hair had come undone, straggling around her face. Her eyes burned as she stared up at him. Holy Mother of God! she wants me to kiss her! he thought, and if I did she'd cry rape and kick up one hell of a hullabaloo!

395

'Damn it, Gladys, find yourself a man for Christ's sake!' he muttered.

'A man?' she gave a strangled laugh. 'What man would look at me now? I'm getting old. I've missed my chance of marriage. Mother saw to that. She needs someone who'll look after her – nurse her when she's dying. But at least I can help his Lordship. He's so kind, so considerate – treats me like a lady – almost.'

That cunning bugger! Shawn thought grimly. Selden makes damn sure that he has the support of all the frustrated spinsters, widows and unsatisfied wives in the area. He knows that women can be vixens. Influence one, and you'll have the rest eating out of your hand. He was sorry for Gladys, but she taxed even his customary empathy with the female race.

He relaxed his hold, but not entirely, then proceeded to give Gladys the lecture of her life, telling her precisely what he thought of her, of Elsie Turner and Lord Ruthen. By the time he had finished she stood like a dead thing, staring at the ground, thoroughly reduced. After he threatened that if he ever heard the slightest rumour that Camilla was being harassed in any way, he'd broadcast Gladys's deeds to the whole of Wessex, she gave him her solemn promise to desist, but could not resist adding:

'You're so forceful, Mr Brennan. Would you like me to meet you sometimes? I'll tell you what Elsie's plotting. Please, say I can. I could come to your cottage any time. Like Lady Josephine's been doing.'

'Gladys, go away!' he groaned, then marched her to the main gates and watched her as she fled towards the village.

He prowled around the sleeping manor house. Not sure of his motives, he only knew that he must see Camilla, must tell her that the letters would stop henceforth. At last, he saw a narrow chink of light at one of the lower windows. He tapped on the glass. When there was no response, he tapped again, harder.

396

The curtains were drawn back, the casement pushed open. He saw Camilla's face, her eyes, heard the alarm in her voice:

'Who is it? What d'you want?'

In answer, he made a jump for the sill, swung a long leg over it and dropped down into the library. The lamplight was blinding. She stood there in a long white robe, her face strained, guarded. Where once she had been as transparent as a rocky pool, now she was opaque. They've done this to her! He burned with rage, longing to crush her in his arms, to protect and keep her safe always.

'Camilla, it's all right. I'm here now. I'll look after you,' he gasped, words tumbling over one another. 'No one shall hurt you again. The letters will stop. I've caught the culprit. Selden's at the bottom of it, but if he tries anything else, I'll kill him!'

BOOK THREE

The Native

. . . A voice as bad as Conscience, rang interminable changes
On one everlasting Whisper day and night repeated – so:
'Something hidden. Go and find it. Go and look behind the Ranges –
Something lost behind the Ranges. Lost and waiting for you. Go!'

'The Explorer', by Rudyard Kipling.

Yes, weekly from Southampton,
Great steamers, white and gold,
Go rolling down to Rio
(Roll down – roll down to Rio!)
And I'd like to roll to Rio
Some day before I'm old!

'Beginning of the Armadilloes', The Just So Stories, by Rudyard Kipling.

Know'st thou the land where the pale citrons grow,
The golden fruits in darker foliage glow?
Soft blows the wind that breathes from that blue sky!
Still stands the myrtle and the laurel high!
Know'st thou it well, that land, beloved Friend?
Thither with thee, O, thither would I wend!

'Mignon's Song', by Samuel Taylor Coleridge.

1

Camilla was curled up on the window seat in her room, legs tucked under her, reading Alison's letter that had arrived with the morning post. They corresponded regularly now, and she had received long missives expressing sympathy and offers of assistance but, over-all, Alison's own happiness kept bubbling through. Camilla shared that gladness, though it emphasized her own lonely state.

This lastest epistle was an account of her excursions to the art school, of new friendships, of the room that had been turned into a study for Frank.

He's writing so much. You'd never believe how industrious he is. We've bought a typewriter and he's learning to use it. I'll do so too, then I can help him with the final draft of his novel. In the evenings, when we're not entertaining, he reads aloud what he's written during the day. The book's very outspoken. It will shock some people when it's published. And of course it *will* be published. One of our friends is a publisher and he's most enthusiastic.

Oh, Camilla, you've no idea how wonderful it is living in Chelsea. The people we've met! Such a lively bunch! Artistic, merry, a trifle raffish, very amusing. Such freedom of thought and expression! No one gives a fig because Frank and I aren't married. You simply must come and meet them. I insist. No ifs or buts. My nearest neighbour is a most remarkable lady. She must be fifty if she's a day, but still beautiful. She holds incredible parties, and I've become quite friendly with her. Her name's Mrs Lilly Pearl Webster, and she used to be – well, how can I describe it? Shall we say a lady of easy virtue? Her lovers were politicians and wealthy, titled men. I think she still receives one or two. Funny thing is, she told me the other day that she knew your father years ago.

That sentence stood out in letters of fire on the paper. 'She knew your father years ago!' Camilla read it several times. Lilly Pearl! The name rang a bell in her head. She flew to the bedside table and took up the exercise book she had found in the attic. How many hours had she spent since poring over it, and the letters too? Love letters written to Edgar Ruthen by a girl who signed herself Maisie Hughes. It was her signature on the cover of the red book – a round, childlike scrawl. The letters, though full of erasions, ink blots and grammatical errors had, nonetheless, been written with blazing sincerity. Maisie Hughes, whoever she had been, had loved him with a deep and abiding passion.

Camilla thumbed through the book, which had proved to be a rather erratically kept diary, searching for the name. She was certain she had not been mistaken. Yes, there it was – and the year was 1883 –

Tonight, I went out to dinner with Edgar. He had asked me to fix up a friend for his pal, that funny lawyer bloke. I asked Lilly Pearl to come and, as she wasn't doing nothing else, she said yes. He got off with her. Paid well, so she told me later.

Could it be the same person? It seemed very likely. An unusual combination of names, Lilly Pearl, and both Alison and the mysterious Maisie hinted that she was a member of the oldest profession in the world. Camilla had read the diary with a sinking sense of apprehension. The entries were sketchy, covering a year, from the time Maisie met Edgar until they suddenly petered out, but during those months they turned from ecstatic happiness to fear. Camilla had been struck by the similarity of his treatment of this unknown woman to the way he had behaved towards her own mother.

402

I wish Edgar wasn't so grumpy. I know I'm not brainy, but he gets so cross. He hit me the other night, just 'cause he thought I'd said something stupid. Then he made love to me and I thought everything was going to be all right, but he wanted to do it *that* way, and it hurt. I don't like it, never have, and gentlemen used to pay me extra if they wanted it. Don't seem right and natural somehow. He marked me something rotten. My back's all covered in scratches.

This had been written in London, but later he had obviously brought the girl to The Priory.

We got here today, and the servants are a stuffy lot. They haven't got no time for me. The only person I know is his man, Gibbs. He's a sly one, I can tell. Up to all sorts of tricks. The house is dark and gloomy. It scares the blooming life out of me, specially the big bedroom, and that creepy study. Edgar shuts hisself up there and won't let no one in.

Camilla had hardly been able to believe the evidence of her own eyes when, on the night of the discovery in the attic cupboard, she settled down in the library to peruse her find. One passage in particular had riveted her attention.

Edgar keeps on about the book and wants me to let him wear my ring, but I won't do it. My Pa give it me. Didn't see the old bugger very often, but he kept in touch. Told me to hang on to that book and the ring, said it might be worth a fortune one day. Fat chance! Funny ring. Too bulky for me really, but Edgar's always looking at it, and reading that book. Don't know what he sees in it.

403

And now this letter from Alison. It seemed that the pieces of the puzzle were coming together. Is everything that happens to us preordained? Camilla wondered, not for the first time. Alison going to Chelsea, meeting with Lilly Pearl. Could 'that funny lawyer bloke' be Rufus Godwin? If so, why hasn't he mentioned Maisie?

She had had much time for thinking lately, avoiding contact with the outside world, seeing no one, except Shawn. Wandering through the house, she had sensed the presence of all those who had lived out their lives within its walls, as if their emotions had seeped into the brickwork, remaining for ever even though they were long dead. In addition to all Leila had taught her, there was a kind of memory that transcended anything she had learned, something that had been passed down through her genes. In her flowed the restless blood of the Ruthens which had always driven them to take risks. Had she returned there for an appointment with destiny? For days now she had mulled over questions in her mind, questions at once burning and remote. The answers were coming, and she had no choice but to receive them.

She returned to the window embrasure, kneeling there and looking out over her land. It glowed with the colours of autumn, a culmination of the seasons that had gone before. The hills were yellow, the shadows purple, the copper beeches flared to the sky like flames, red and bronze and gold. The grass seemed greener even than in spring. The heather had faded to a pinkish-brown, though a few late clumps flaunted mauve tufts to the low-hanging orb of the sun.

Had Maisie crouched there too, during her stay at The Priory, staring at a landscape that must have been alien to her, city-bred as she was? Camilla suddenly *knew* that she had done so. Lonely, weeping because Edgar Ruthen had hurt her, missing gay companions like Lilly Pearl, but unable to leave him, bound by chains of love,

404

no matter what cruel acts he performed. The final pages of that incomplete journal were sad indeed. Smudges blotted the scribbled words. They had been made by tears.

Why is he so nasty to me? I try to please him, but I can't do nothing right. I know he can't marry me. I've not asked him to. I can't help it if I'm in the family way. I won't go to one of them backstreet hags and have it took away. All I ask is that he'll buy me a little house somewhere. I can bring up the baby. I want it. It's Edgar's. He says he will if I give him the ring, but my Dad left it me. I can't do that –

They were the last words that Maisie had written.

Tragedy oozed from the yellowed paper. Pain and suffering and humiliation. Camilla had read it to Leila who shook her head and said: 'I think it's her *duende* we hear, missy. Oh, men! They've a lot to answer for. What you going to do about it?'

'We can't be sure of this, Leila. There's no proof that she's dead. She may, like Lilly Pearl, be a settled, middle-aged woman – possibly married. Who knows?'

'*I* knows.' Leila refused to be swayed.

Camilla had brooded on the problem, discarding one solution after another. But Alison's letter had made her course clear, and when Shawn called later in the morning she ran down to the Hall to meet him, saying:

'I'm going to London.'

'Can I come with you?' He stood bareheaded before her, his hair glinting like the beeches outside, a look in his eyes that made her ashamed, because she knew she was using this good-natured young man.

She had talked to him for a long time that night in the library, finding herself unable to stop. He had heard it all; Darcy's departure to seek the lost city, the finding of Maisie Hughes's diary, the contents of the love letters

405

and the haunting. It had been as if a dam had suddenly burst. He had proved an excellent listener, believing every utterance. He did not offend her intelligence by saying that she was mistaken or foolish or imaginative. They had gone down to the kitchen where all was quiet, save the steady tick-tock of the wall clock. After making cocoa, they had sat by the range and toasted their toes. She had not thought of him as anything but a sympathetic ear, someone prepared to support her and seriously consider every theory she put forward, no matter how outlandish.

He had called many times since, bringing her news of the village, sounding out the temper of the inhabitants. The scandal had died down somewhat, though Beryl and Wilf were treated with cold civility in the pub and Lacey's store. Selden came and went, spending the majority of his time in town. Elsie Turner had moved into the cottage he had provided, and kept much to herself. Such tranquillity was disconcerting. There was no knowing what Selden was planning to do.

Now it seemed the most natural thing on earth for Shawn to suggest himself as Camilla's travelling companion. She was glad, smiling up at him. 'I want to leave at once.'

'That's all right. Just give me a couple of seconds to pack a bag.'

'But what of your work? Selden employs you. Won't he have something to say about it? Josephine too?' This was the first time she had made any direct reference to his involvement with her cousin.

Shawn met her eyes steadily. 'Selden's in London, and so is Josephine. But even if they weren't, they'd not stop me. I'd tell him what to do with his job.'

'And Josephine?' It was none of her business, but to think of him making love to that promiscuous shrew was distasteful.

There was nothing Shawn wanted more than to look

well in her eyes, but even so, he had determined that there must be absolute honesty between them. Nothing else would suffice. 'I haven't been alone with her since the night I came here.' There was an unusual seriousness on his handsome features, then it was mitigated by a wide grin. 'I've decided to become halibut.'

Camilla's laughter rippled through the hall. She had a wonderfully infectious laugh. 'You? Celibate? I don't believe it! Think of the girls you'll disappoint!'

He struck a pose, hand on his heart. 'It's the truth I'm after telling you. Halibacy is the only way for me, until the colleen who's stolen my heart says "yes".'

'Oh, so there is a colleen, is there? In Ireland, maybe?' Camilla could feel her depression lifting. His was a gay, sky-larking nature and no one could remain miserable for long in his company.

He tapped the side of his nose mysteriously. 'I'm not prepared to divulge her name, even to you. We'll say no more about it. Come, whisk me off to the wicked city in your magic coach, before midnight strikes and it turns into a pumpkin and myself into a frog.'

'You lunatic,' she chuckled. 'Be back here double-quick, and we'll get going. I intend to take the car and we'll drive all the way. Should be there well before the witching-hour.'

He promised and was as good as his word. By the time she had flung a few things into a case, he was back. Leila objected, naturally. 'Why you rushing off like this?' she demanded, planting herself resolutely in Camilla's path.

Knowing there was nothing else for it, Camilla explained about Alison's letter, as she swept jewellery and toilet articles into a reticule and swung her coat over her shoulders. 'I want to meet this Lilly Pearl person. Maybe she'll be able to fill in the gaps about Maisie. Look after things here for me, Leila. I shan't be away long.'

'How you going to manage without a maid?' Leila

accompanied her downstairs, still grumbling but carrying the case.

'I'm on serious business.' Glancing down into the Hall, Camilla could see Shawn's tall form, his Inverness cape making him look larger. 'I shan't have time for gadding, so won't be climbing into evening dresses or suchlike.'

'Where you staying? Mrs Amy's or Lady Alison's?' Leila did not like the idea at all, though she had no objection to Shawn accompanying her mistress. She liked Shawn a lot. He was constantly bringing her small presents; a bar of chocolate, a bottle of rum, a gaudy gewgaw to wear. Yes, she thoroughly approved of him.

'Probably Lady Alison's, though I'll be seeing Amy. I intend calling on Mr Godwin too. Must jog his memory about the gay ladies of the town twenty-odd years ago. There's little doubt that he knew Maisie and Lilly. He was my father's best friend, after all. I'm a bit surprised that he hasn't told me about them.'

'Too ashamed of himself, I guess,' Leila sniffed contemptuously. 'Gay ladies, indeed. Them was whores, and you shouldn't go meddling with such trash.'

'I'm not a child, Leila.' Camilla heaved an exasperated sigh and made a distress signal in Shawn's direction.

He read it correctly, coming forward and whisking a large bunch of flowers from behind his back. 'For you,' he said, bowing low to the Creole. 'Now don't you be after fretting about Missy Camilla. Sure and I'll take good care of her, so I will. Just you put your feet up and enjoy a well-earned rest. We'll be back before you know it.'

They left Leila beaming and waving from the top of the steps. As they got into the car, Camilla turned to him, and her laugh was more light-hearted than he had heard it for ages. 'Shawn Brennan! You'd charm the birds right out of the trees!'

*

Camilla's phone call from Dorchester where she had stopped to have lunch, put Alison in a state of high excitement. She was nervous too. This would be the first time anyone had visited from Abbey Sutton. Oh, she had invited her, to be sure, but now that her arrival was imminent, she was overjoyed but slightly apprehensive.

Even to think of the village made her stomach churn. Though Camilla could hardly be said to be a part of the life Alison had once known, the memories kept flooding in, memories that she had put behind her, so happy with her new existence. As soon as she replaced the black receiver on its gilt stand, she rushed to the door of Frank's study. He did not like to be disturbed, not even by her, but this was important. Throughout the quiet house travelled the sound of her imperative rap.

'Who's there?' His voice was sharp, impatient, enough to quell the courage of an ordinary intruder. Alison smiled, decided that he was a cross old bear and knocked once more.

'It's me.'

'Go away!' shouted the irate author.

'Oh, darling, let me in, please.'

In a fury of impatience he dashed to the door and stood scowling on the threshold. 'Alison, you know very well that I hate to be interrupted. I've only just collected my thoughts after lunch. Weren't you attending a life class this afternoon?'

'I should've been, but Camilla's just phoned. She's arriving for dinner, and staying a day or two. Isn't that marvellous?'

His scowl vanished at the sight of her, and with it the fret of composition. His deep-set eyes glowed, his hands stretched out. In an instant she was within the forbidden room, and he had his arms around her. 'Well, I'd hardly call it that,' he teased, resting his lips against the top of her silky hair. 'Are you sure you really want Abbey

409

Sutton brought into our Eden? You're not to get upset, darling. The doctor said you must rest and keep calm.'

'Pooh! I'm as fit as a flea,' she retorted, looking up at him, delighted at his concern for her. 'Never felt better in my life. It'll be lovely to see Camilla. I won't let her disturb your work, I promise.'

He grinned crookedly, sweeping an arm towards the papers scattered over his desk near the bulky, black Imperial typewriter. 'It's painfully easy for a writer to be disturbed. One seeks an excuse to stop working — anything. Haven't you noticed? I sharpen a needless number of pencils, go out for a packet of cigarettes, play with Effie, have a cup of tea, talk to you. Self-discipline isn't easy. That's why I'm like a rhino with a sore backside if I do get down to it and anyone comes along with a pleasant distraction. I have to battle with my laziness and tell them to go away.'

'I understand,' Alison said, caressing him with her eyes. She did understand. Her own work pattern followed much the same line.

Not that this was her lodestar any more. Her pregnancy was taking over, and she was entering that placid, complacent state where her dreams and thoughts were almost entirely absorbed by the foetus developing within her body. She attended art school because she enjoyed it, but also to prove to herself that it could be done. Her work had benefited and she was becoming a most competent artist. But whereas Frank needed to be successful, both financially and to justify the enormous step he had taken, with Alison it was a less vital issue. Her satisfaction lay with him, her home and the longed-for baby. So a great deal of her time was taken up with managing the servants, planning menus, sewing infant garments and knitting them too. She had ordered a magnificent baby carriage from Carters', and it already stood in the nursery which had been painted white and hung with bright wallpaper on which story-book

410

characters were depicted. A cradle had also been delivered, a lovely thing swinging on a stand and draped in white muslin. Everything was white, thus practical for either boy or girl.

I still can't believe it, Alison would say to herself whenever she entered that light, airy room where her child would spend its early years. I can't believe that I'm really pregnant. Why, only a few months ago I would never have dreamed it possible. And she would stand sideways-on, staring wonderingly into the mirror, pressing her loose gown close to her body, seeing the fruitful swell of her belly. She loved to feel the child kicking within her. Such a strangely exciting experience, that heaving and humping, as if it was determined to make her aware of its presence. It had the habit of starting to wriggle when she lay in bed at night, and these antics amused Frank. He was so thrilled about it that it might have been his first-born, and she his one and only love.

Sometimes, when she stopped to consider, she became afraid of going through childbirth. Many women died during the ordeal. She comforted herself by the remembrance of Josephine's confinements. Even though her sister took shameless advantage of so much fuss and attention, she confessed afterwards that there had been really nothing to it.

'The nearest I can describe it is being frightfully constipated!' Josephine had said, sitting up in bed looking radiant and remarkably healthy, when Alison had tiptoed into the main bedroom of Erwarton Hall to see her and the new arrival. 'Quite honestly, darling, to put it crudely, it's just like having an almighty shit.'

The services of a reputable midwife had already been booked. She would move in when Alison's labour commenced and remain for a full month after, as was customary amongst those who could afford such a luxury. This briskly efficient, no-nonsense nurse visited her every week and put her mind at rest on the details of

411

parturition, telling her something of what to expect. Also, she and Frank had become the patients of a competent doctor who lived in Cheyne Row, not far from Cheyne Walk. But despite these arrangements which were the best that circumstances and money could provide, Alison still felt nervous.

By now she had stopped failing to respond when anyone addressed her as Mrs Turner. For long periods of time she could conveniently forget that she was living a lie. Only one person succeeded in bringing her down to earth with a bump, and that was Effie. Not that she had much to do with the child. A nanny had been engaged as soon as they took over the house, and a wing had been allocated as a nursery area. There was a small kitchen where light meals could be prepared, a bathroom, a sitting-room for Nanny Marks, and a playroom for the child. Nanny had one bedroom, and Effie's own room had been tastefully decorated and filled with toys. Close by was the newly equipped nursery for the expected baby. Nanny would take the infant under her wing when the midwife finally departed.

It was not that Effie was unusually naughty, she behaved no worse and probably far better than most four-year-olds. Nanny Marks was firm and Effie knew exactly where she stood with her. It was only Alison who found her difficult and she half suspected that the fault lay with herself. Effie was her conscience. Every time they were together, she thought of Elsie. Fast on the heels of this memory, came an upsurge of guilt difficult to banish with logic. Whatever the cause, if Effie decided to succumb to a show of temper, it was invariably in Alison's company. She had a strong suspicion that there was more behind it than a natural jealousy of a rival who vied for her father's affections.

In the main the child was formally polite and dutifully obedient. She accepted the presents that Alison showered upon her. She played with them quietly and

412

with apparent appreciation. Everyone praised the pretty, well-mannered little girl. To those who asked, Frank had implied that he was a widower and Effie the child of his first marriage. He had not lied in so many words, but had said enough to make questioners withdraw, out of sympathy. Effie called Alison '*Mamma*', because she had been instructed to do so. She kissed her when necessary, but there was always something withheld. It was as if she was acting a part.

Alison and Nanny Marks had attempted to prepare her for the arrival of the baby, saying that Doctor Gough would soon be bringing her a little brother or sister to play with. Effie made no comment, quietly staring at the perambulator, the crib, the tiny garments. For a reason she could not explain, Alison had wanted her to leave, filled with the illogical desire to lock the door of the baby's room against her.

Camilla and Shawn reached London in the early evening and, after driving past Hyde Park and through Brompton, came to the Embankment and Cheyne Walk. It was an interesting riverside area, filled with houses built in the reign of Queen Anne. There were a few shops, a public house or two and several restaurants. Camilla could well understand how such famous artists as Turner, Whistler and Rossetti would have wanted to live there. The Thames flowed swiftly past, its wide surface dotted with shipping. Tall spars and masts stood out starkly against the evening sky and the spires of London shimmered in the distance.

Alison was at the door of her imposing terraced house as soon as the car stopped. She had obviously been watching for them. In a moment, Camilla and she were hugging each other. 'I'm sorry – so sorry –' Alison kept repeating, and there were tears in her eyes.

Camilla was not quite sure of the origin of this sorrow. Was it shame because she was pregnant and had run away from home, or did it mean sympathy for her over

413

the loss of Darcy? It embarrassed and bewildered her and she found herself patting Alison and murmuring: 'That's all right. Don't cry. Please don't cry –'

Meanwhile Shawn brought in the luggage. Frank advanced to shake his hand and help him. There was a small, blonde, blue-eyed child in a smocked dress and white pinafore peeping through the banister rail and Frank bounded up to fetch her, sweeping her high in his arms, showing her off proudly.

How very domesticated. They're like an old married couple already, thought Camilla, as a pert maid in a neat black dress took her coat and they were ushered into a large drawing-room. The house was charming, with high narrow windows and a wealth of early eighteenth century detail. Alison had not really changed her lifestyle at all. True, she was an unmarried mother living in sin, but money still continued to cushion her. No poky rented villa for her. She had purchased the Cheyne Walk establishment. As Camilla sat down on the settee and removed her hat and gloves, she listened to her friend's excited chatter and shrewdly deduced that the only thorn in her flesh was Elsie Turner's daughter.

Alison did not say as much, indeed the child flitted around the room like an animated doll, but her precocity set Camilla's teeth on edge. She could see that Alison found her equally irritating, though did not dare to reprimand her with Frank present. Soon, however, a large woman in a spotless grey uniform came to announce that it was bedtime. Effie stared at Alison, then at Camilla.

'Off you go with Nanny Marks, poppet,' Alison said, smiling at Frank, at the child. 'It's getting late. I'll be along to kiss you good night very soon.'

'I want to stay up. I want to talk to your friend. I don't want to go to bed,' Effie announced loudly.

'Now, now, Miss Effie –' Nanny Marks began, warningly.

414

Effie stepped back and after carefully looking around to ensure a clear floor space, threw herself backwards in a tantrum. Her dramatic performance would have done credit to Sarah Bernhardt.

'Take her away, Nanny,' ordered Frank and, when still kicking and screaming, Effie was tucked under the big woman's arm and carted off to the nursery, he added, with a half smile: 'Can't think what's got into her. She isn't usually like this, Camilla. Jove! Just listen to her! Don't have any children. That's my advice.'

'You don't seem to have followed it,' she smiled, nodding towards where Alison sat, radiating contentment now that Effie had retired.

She was pleased to see her friend looking so well. Gone was the plain, rather gaunt spinster. Alison had filled out. Her shoulders, displayed by her flowing silk dinner gown, were plump, her breasts ripe, her face rounded and rosy, her hair having that lustre often associated with pregnant women. Love had made her beautiful.

Frank too had changed almost beyond recognition. His hair was long, curling about his ears and over his unstarched collar. A light brown moustache adorned his upper lip, a clipped beard covered his chin. He sported a floppy cravat. His trousers were tight and of a rather loud check, and he wore a burgundy velvet smoking jacket with frogged buttonholes, even when they sat down to dinner. He talked a lot, and was an engaging table-companion. Camilla saw the light in his eyes whenever he looked at Alison and asked her opinion, which was every sentence or so. They did not ask Camilla much about the village. Their conversation dealt mainly with in-consequential things; the latest plays, new books, the exhibition at the Royal Academy of Art, amusing anecdotes concerning their Bohemian friends who, by all accounts, gaily flouted social conventions.

Just before they finally retired, Alison drew Camilla

aside and said: 'I popped in to see Mrs Webster this afternoon. She was most interested to hear that you were expected. She's suggested that you call tomorrow evening, about seven.'

Next morning Camilla went out with Shawn. They left the car behind and travelled by horse-drawn bus. This was an entirely new experience for her, and a splendid view of London was obtained from the top of it. Shawn insisted on paying. In fact, he would not permit her to spend any money that day.

'This is my treat,' he said, as he helped her up the winding stairs of the bus. 'You'll see how the other half live, for a change.'

Next he insisted on taking her on the underground railway, where they flew along, rattling and ringing, far beneath the foundations of London to Liverpool Street and the Bioscope Theatre, which had only been open since May.

'Have you ever seen a moving picture show?' he asked, a hand under her elbow as he guided her through the crowds.

'No,' she replied, walking along at his side while all about them people pushed and jostled as they left the station. 'Do you think I should?'

'Of course. A marvellous invention. Like the camera. I've one of those myself. I'll show you my photos one day. I've even taken some of you without you knowing. But moving pictures are something else. I tell you, live theatre'll be a thing of the past one day. Come on.' And he took her across the road into the lobby where, at the ticket office, he paid fourpence each for two seats.

It was a most entertaining performance, and they derived a great deal of amusement from the reactions of the other members of the audience to the over-dramatic or slapstick comedy films. Shawn poked fun at the pianist who, with the flare of a concert artiste, played music appropriate to the silent action on the large white

416

sheet hanging in front of the stage. Seated close to Shawn in the darkened hall, Camilla could not but be aware of him, his shoulder brushing hers sometimes, his deep-throated chuckle, the way he leaned nearer to whisper yet another outrageous remark. The show concluded with the National Anthem when everyone shuffled and coughed and got stiffly to their feet, facing a coloured portrait of the King which wavered on the sheet.

'Time for a cup of tea, I think,' said Shawn as they stood outside, blinking like owls in the sudden daylight.

Camilla shivered. The air was cold after the stuffy hall. She was aware of a drop in spirits. It should have been Darcy accompanying her around London. This is what they had planned to do after their honeymoon trip. Never, even in her wildest dreams, had she anticipated being there with the Irishman. Most of the time, she managed to steer her thoughts away from what might have been, but she missed Darcy cruelly. There seemed to be a bleeding wound in the region of her heart. It was her test of fire. She had come to England to find herself. Perhaps she was doing just that. The days were not too bad, for she kept herself busy, but at night she lay still and tense until sleep came at last, a restless, fitful sleep torn by anguished thoughts.

Shawn was kind and she was grateful to him, but no one could take Darcy's place. It was as if his darkly handsome shade stalked at her side. Even in the bustling tea-shop to which Shawn took her, she felt isolated and lonely. The chatter of customers, the brisk, black-and-white clad waitressess taking orders at the round tables, the feathered hats, the people coming and going, all seemed like the distant, jerky figures of the bioscope. Unreal, colourless, reduced to monochrome.

Shawn was sensitive to her withdrawal and did not attempt to rouse her from it. He talked unendingly, his soft brogue running on lightly. 'I'll be mother,' he insisted when the silver-plated teapot and hot water jug arrived.

417

He ate his round of toasted buns with relish and swallowed two cups of tea, managing to keep up a conversational flow at the same time, concluding with: 'Poxy small little things these. Give me a good big mug any day. You've not drunk yours. It'll be stone cold.'

Then Camilla came back to the present. The cafe swung into focus, bright, cheery, and Shawn smiling across at her. She was aware that women at other tables were looking at him approvingly and at her with a tinge of envy. It was as if she was seeing him for the first time, suddenly struck by his attractive appearance. He was extremely presentable. At Abbey Sutton he had usually stamped about in worn jodhpurs and muddy boots, a spotted scarf knotted about his tanned throat, his hair wind-blown. Today he was spruce and smartly dressed. He wore a cinnamon suit, a broad white stock and polished brown shoes. His grey Derby hat hung from a branch of the mahogany stand behind them.

'That's better.' His green eyes stared directly into hers, and he was no longer smiling. 'You've returned. Sure and I don't like it when you go wandering off into realms where I can't follow.'

'Sorry, Shawn. I'm not very good company.' She dropped her gaze, fidgeted with the handbag on her lap.

'I'm not expecting you to be. You've a lot on your plate.'

'You don't have to stay, you know.' Her voice was beautiful to his ears, a low contralto with lovely modulations. He listened to its timbre more than to her words. 'Call a cab and I'll visit Amy. I'm not expecting you to act as nursemaid and can find my way there perfectly well. Why don't you go off and enjoy yourself?'

'Good company or not, I'd rather be with you than anyone else,' he responded gently. 'And I'll not have you roaming around London by yourself. We'll go together.'

It was warm in the hansom-cab. It smelled of leather, dust, stale cigar smoke and Camilla's pungent French perfume. A little enclosed world with its bowler-hatted driver seated outside, on his box high above. Such an intimate atmosphere was hard on Shawn's self-control. He had ridden this way before, spinning through the traffic with a girl at his side, and knew that such vehicles were an invitation to sexual adventure. On one occasion he had actually managed to make love between one destination and another, on a similar worn, dusty seat.

He and Camilla sat side by side in silence. He was embarrassed by the evidence of desire that her nearness evoked, whilst she was absorbed in her thoughts. Unable to stop himself, he adventured an arm behind her waist. She was leaning forward and seemed unaware of this advance. He longed to close his arm about her but was afraid to make a move which might startle and disgust her. Her state of mind was too delicately balanced to accept male attention at the moment, yet to control such an urge made Shawn sweat. The cab stopped outside the Marchant house, and he experienced relief mingled with regret.

Amy and John lived in Finsbury Park and their house was more modest than Allison's. It was a four-storeyed, bay-windowed villa, with lace curtains and a small front garden behind iron railings. Inside it was comfortably furnished and redolent of middle-class security. Amy employed a maid, a cook and a nurse for Harriet. She and John were attentive as, seated in the parlour, Camilla told them of the latest developments. John was sceptical of supernatural happenings, but Amy listened gravely, more than convinced that her child's baffling illness had been caused by malicious magic. She had visited a medium recently, a woman who was renowned for her powers, impressing Amy with her communications with those who had 'passed over to the Other Side,' as she had put it. So impressed was she, in fact, that she had joined the Spiritualist Association. John was inclined to scoff at such things, but he was content to go along with it, if it made his wife happy.

'You'll call again?' Amy wanted to know as Camilla prepared to leave.

'I don't know. It depends on what Mrs Webster says.' Camilla picked up her muff and swung her fur tippet around her neck. 'I'll probably get in touch with Rufus Godwin. I'd like to know what he has to say regarding the letters I found. If I decide to go straight back to The Priory, I'll phone and tell you what's happened.'

'Do that, my dear, and take care.' Amy accompanied her across the tiled hall and, as they kissed goodbye, she looked beyond Camilla's shoulder at Shawn, wondering precisely where he fitted into the scheme of things. Lady Josephine's lover? Or was that over? It seemed that Camilla had a penchant for inheriting Josephine's cast-offs.

Dusk was settling over London when Camilla mounted the steps of the house next to Alison's. An elderly maid, opening, said to her: 'Lady Camilla Ruthen? Mrs Webster's expecting you. Please come in.'

Camilla waited in the echoing hall, with its panelled dado and statues in alcoves, cunningly interspersed with potted palms. The place wore an air of wealth and luxury. It was centrally heated, and a telephone stood on a marble-topped side table. If what Alison said about Lilly Pearl was correct, the wages of sin were definitely not death. Rather a pathway to riches, she decided.

Within a few minutes, the maid returned and conducted her into a room on the right of the imposing staircase. A woman rose from a deeply cushioned couch to greet her. She was Junoesque of figure, a red-head with an alabaster skin, though as she came closer, Camilla could see that the hair was dyed and her youthful appearance owed much to skilfully applied cosmetics. She was dressed in a blue taffeta gown whose lace-trimmed bodice had stoles reaching to the hem of her bell-shaped skirt. Her waist was small and confined in a corset so tight that her bosom swelled above it.

420

'Welcome, Lady Camilla,' Lilly Pearl said. Her accent still bore traces of her Scottish origin. 'Alison's told me so much about you.'

She extended her hand. It was large, strong but soft-skinned. Camilla took it in her gloved one, then allowed herself to be led to an upholstered chair near the coal fire in the white marble grate. 'It's kind of you to see me,' she said politely, giving herself time to absorb the atmosphere and observe Lilly Pearl.

'The pleasure is mine. Would you like a drink?'

Camilla nodded, and Lilly Pearl swished around, finding two glasses in a cabinet and filling them from a decanter. Then she seated herself on the couch and arranged her skirts around a pair of small feet encased in high-heeled silk shoes. Camilla found that she had been given whisky. She sipped it slowly, looking around the room. It was of similar proportions to Alison's drawing-room, but whereas she favoured simple decor, plain and beautifully balanced, this was filled with pictures, ornaments and draperies of the style so popular in the century not long passed, when Victoria was on the throne, not her son, Edward VII.

Lilly Pearl was watching her and, guessing that she must make the first move, Camilla said: 'Alison tells me that you knew my father.'

'That's right – knew him well. Once seen, never forgotten. That was the kind of man he was. You resemble him. As alike as two peas in a pod. In fact, it gave me quite a turn when you walked in.' Lilly Pearl leaned forward suddenly, staring intently into Camilla's face. 'Was your mother called Maisie, by any chance?'

This question knocked Camilla off balance. She had not been expecting it. 'No. She was French. Her name was Hélène, but it's Maisie I want to talk to you about – Maisie Hughes. You knew her, didn't you, years ago? She mentions you in a diary I found at The Priory, that's my home in Wessex.'

'You don't need to tell me about The Priory. I never went there but Edgar was always boasting about his manor house.' Lilly Pearl's eyes were alert, even though she had topped up her glass and her breath was tainted with whisky.

'Why did you think I might be Maisie's child?' Camilla held out her cigarette case. Lilly Pearl took one and inserted it into an ivory holder.

'She was very much in love with your father. I've never seen a woman so badly smitten. She went to stay at The Priory, and later wrote and told me that she was pregnant.' The flame of Camilla's lighter shone briefly on Lilly Pearl's face. There was something in her heavily mascaraed eyes that struck her as odd. Was it fear peering from beneath the blue lids? A reluctance to dig back into memory?

Camilla clicked the lighter off and sat back. 'I can see that she loved him by the letters, and the diary. She writes of you, and of a lawyer. I think it may have been Mr Rufus Godwin. Tell me about it, Mrs Webster.'

'Why d'you want to know?' Lilly Pearl shifted a little uneasily. 'Why should you be so interested in your father's past? He was no worse than any other gentleman when he came to town. Rufus Godwin, you say? The name rings a bell. Yes, you're right. Oh, it's years ago, but I remember him too. A nice fellow, and a free-spender. Alison tells me you've inherited The Priory and are having trouble with your cousin, Selden. Can raking over old, dead, long-forgotten things really help you?'

'Mrs Webster, I need to know about Maisie Hughes.' A rose-shaded lamp stood on a low table between her chair and the couch. Within its thrown golden aureole, Lilly Pearl saw Camilla's glittering amber eyes and it was as if she was looking at Edgar Ruthen. The same sense of authority, that air of command emanated from his daughter as it had from him. It was rather frightening.

422

She stood up and went to a desk near by. In a moment she returned, carrying a photograph in a silver frame. 'This is Maisie. It was taken around the time she was having that affair with your father.'

Camilla took it in her hands and stared down. It was an oval print, brownish, faded, a head and shoulders composition. A delicate face, the expression wistful, the head slightly tilted, poised on a slender neck, the hair swept up into a coronet of dark curls, banded by pearls, a curling fringe lying across the broad brow. Pearl studs adorned the small ears, a pearl choker with a cameo encircled the throat. Dark brows, a direct stare from eyes that might well have been blue, a straight nose and cupid's bow mouth, faintly smiling.

'She was beautiful,' Camilla said, speaking low as if she was in church.

'She was indeed.' Lilly Pearl stood at her shoulder, looking at the picture. 'Very popular with the gentlemen. We met shortly after I'd come to London from Edinburgh to seek my fortune, and she had run away from home in Wales. We'd both tried honest work, in the factories, or as skivvies, and came to the conclusion that we'd do better by walking the Burlington Arcade. That's where gentlemen went if they wanted a female companion. It wasn't long before we had enough money to set up a small house of our own. It seemed pointless that half our incomes should be taken by the bawd who rented us a room. We decided to work for ourselves.'

'That's how she met my father?'

'Yes. It was when we went to the Café Royal one night. She was with another man, but Ruthen quickly took her over. Nothing ever stood in the way of what he wanted.'

'And he wanted Maisie Hughes.' Camilla was staring intently at the faded impression in her hands.

'For a while.' Lilly Pearl held out her hands to the fire, her gaze on the greedy flames devouring the lumps of black coal. 'But I think he was growing weary of her when they went down to the country. I warned her. I said: "Don't be so possessive, Maisie. You know he can't ever marry you. He'll wed a lady with pots of money. That's what his type always do. They use girls like us for their pleasure and then take a virgin to wife." She wouldn't listen. "I can't live if he doesn't love me!" she would say and then cry her heart out. Pathetic, it was, and I was sorry for her. It's fatal to fall in love. I've never done it, though I've been married three times. Outlived 'em all.'

'What happened to her when she came back from The Priory?' Camilla asked slowly, her fingers smoothing Maisie's photo as if she could somehow console her.

Lilly Pearl turned sharply, her shadow flung against the panelled wall, darker than the oak, darker than the night closing in outside. 'I don't know. I never saw her again.'

'You mean she didn't return to London?'

'Not that I know of. I heard that Edgar had gone abroad and presumed that she was with him. I hoped that he'd had a change of heart and was prepared to provide a home for her and the baby she was expecting.'

'But was there no one who wanted to find out? A mother? Family?' Camilla laid the silver frame on the table and went towards Lilly Pearl, her long skirt whispering over the deeply piled carpet.

'She had no one, only that drunken old sot of a sailor who called himself her father. He was always off abroad somewhere.' In Lilly's eyes she read questions – questions with dire answers.

Camilla gripped Lilly's hand with a fierce pressure. 'Did you ever see her wearing an unusual ring?'

'She had quite a lot of jewellery. Gifts from gentlemen.' Lilly looked down at the strong fingers digging into hers. 'That was after we started to make money. To begin with we had nothing but the clothes we stood up in.'

424

'Wasn't there one piece? A ring from which she'd never be parted?'

'Yes, there was, come to think of it.' As Camilla's grip relaxed, Lilly withdrew to a safe distance. 'I remember asking her once, when we were desperately hard up, why she didn't take it to the pawnbroker. She got quite funny about it, and said that she'd never sell it. Thought a lot of it, she did. I think it was because her old man gave it to her. She clung to it even more after he was knifed in a pub brawl down Limehouse way.'

'Can you describe it to me?' Camilla took another cigarette from her bag. Her fingers shook as she lit it.

'Oh, dear, it was a long time ago.' Lilly passed a hand across her brow. 'It was a clumsy, heavy thing, much more suitable for a man. A thick gold band, if I remember aright. And a yellow stone, set with a few diamonds.'

'A tiger's-eye?'

'Yes, that's right – that's what she said it was – a tiger's-eye. Sort of semi-precious stone, isn't it? But how did you know?'

2

Dick Gibbs was perhaps the most unsavoury man that Camilla had ever seen, and it had been her misfortune to meet many disreputable individuals in her time. It was not so much his appearance, for he was reasonably clean though shabby, it was more an aura that hung around him, bringing a whiff of dank alleyways and despicable acts. When Rufus accompanied him into the library of The Priory, it was as if the crisp November morning darkened visibly.

He stood, bowler in hand, as Rufus introduced him, a lean, stooped elderly man, with a ragged moustache and thinning hair, a few dun-coloured strands of which had been brushed across his crown in an attempt to conceal its baldness. His movements, his manner, suggested a mangy wharfside rat, and the look in his sunken, crafty eyes filled Camilla with the gravest misgiving.

She had been anticipating his arrival, for Rufus had been as good as his word, declaring that he would lay the fellow by the heels and bring him down to meet her. It was Lilly Pearl who had suggested that Gibbs might be able to throw some light on Maisie's disappearance. He had been Edgar Ruthen's valet at the time of the Maisie affair. Though Lilly had lost contact with him, Rufus's memory had been given a terrific nudge when Camilla bearded him in his chambers and recounted the story, in so far as she had been able to piece it together. He had seen or heard of Gibbs in an occasional, somewhat random fashion down the years. The man had left Edgar's service, refusing to go abroad with him. After that, he had drifted from post to post, at first acting in his capacity of valet, then gradually sliding down the scale.

Rufus had eventually traced him to a lodging-house in Whitechapel, where he kept body and soul together by dubious means, mostly petty crime. Even when Rufus knew him in the early days, he had suspected that he was a thief.

At first, Gibbs had positively refused to return to his old stamping ground, Abbey Sutton. His unhealthy complexion had turned a shade greyer, and there had been a pinched look about his lips. The shifty way in which he avoided Rufus's eyes had made him even more determined. Gibbs was perfectly willing to see Lady Camilla anywhere but at The Priory. Rufus was adamant. If he wanted the sum of money offered for information, then it was essential that they go to Wessex. Lady Camilla had just returned there and he saw no reason why she should be called back to town. Gibbs fidgeted, looked anywhere but at Rufus, sweated profusely, though the mean room was damp and cold, and showed all the classic symptoms of fear and guilt. It wasn't a question of money, he had declared stubbornly. Then Rufus had produced his ace. The threat of exposure. The lawyer had a network of spies in the seamy underworld. Reports had come in that Gibbs ran a flourishing sideline, that of receiving stolen goods. Rufus had written to tell Camilla when to expect them.

'It's years since I set foot here,' Gibbs declared, eyes darting round the big, comfortable library as he edged towards the fire. 'And you're Lord Ruthen's daughter. Well, well, I've often thought about him. The best master I ever had. A fine gentleman, your father, milady. Very fine indeed, never had a better. I was most upset when Mr Godwin told me he'd passed on. The poor master, I always think of him as that, never gave my loyalty to any other. A proper gent, he was. Knew how to treat his servants. Generous to a fault.' He dragged a grubby handkerchief from an inner pocket and blew his nose resoundingly, overcome with emotion.

427

'Stow it, Gibbs!' barked Rufus, thumbs hooked in the watch-chain that spanned his broad stomach. 'That sickly slop may deceive some, but it doesn't cut any ice with me. Devoted manservant my eye! You did damned well out of it. Lived soft and easy, my lad! I can remember all too well! You did his dirty work for him, didn't you? Your perks of the trade were always rather more than a little quiet feathering of your nest.'

'I don't know what you mean.' Gibbs was looking not at him or Camilla, but at the decanter and glasses on the table. 'I was his valet, that's all.'

Rufus heaved an exasperated sigh, his formidable eyebrows almost meeting above his aquiline nose. He straddled the hearth rug, coat-tails flipped back to warm his thighs. His temper had not been improved by having to spend hours on the train with Gibbs, an uninspiring companion. Frankly, he didn't believe a word the fellow uttered, disliking his voice that varied from a nasal Cockney twang to the more refined accent that he had acquired during service. He used this when he re-membered, as now, attempting to impress Camilla.

'Stop beating about the bush, Gibbs.' Rufus hunched his forceful shoulders and turned his head very quickly and decisively, giving the man a keen bright stare. 'We want to know what happened to Maisie Hughes.'

Gibbs swallowed hard, twirling his hat slowly in his hands, staring unhappily at the floor, the ceiling, anywhere but at the lawyer. 'I don't know, sir, and that's God's truth. Lord Ruthen told me he was going abroad and did I want to come. I said no, and he gave me a month's wages in advance. I helped him pack, he dropped me off in London and that was the last I ever saw of him.'

'You're lying.' Rufus jabbed an accusing finger at him.

'No, I'm not! I swear it!' Gibbs eased his collar away from his scrawny throat nervously. 'I don't know nothing.'

428

'Let me talk to him.' Camilla silenced Rufus with a gesture, rising from the wingchair which she had occupied. Her head was high as she spoke, and Gibbs thought, a haughty piece, this, and she's a carbon copy of her father. Too tall for his idea of womanhood, with wide shoulders, strong hands. Wouldn't like to get the wrong side of her, any more than I would've done that bastard, Ruthen.

She was wearing a high-collared blouse with ruched sleeves and a long full skirt of embossed velvet, her small waist girdled by a wide leather belt. Her rich corn-gold hair was swept rather austerely away from a central parting to a large chignon at the back. Gibbs shivered as he met the uncompromising stare of her eyes. They were like Ruthen's too, as distant and reserved and every bit as hard.

'What d'you want of me, your Ladyship?' he spluttered. His tongue crept out from between blackened teeth and licked over his slack lips. He was dying for a drink, but none seemed forthcoming.

'The truth, Mr Gibbs.' Her clear, deep voice rang across the afternoon stillness of the library.

This damned house, he thought, aware of the shadows in the corners, the deepening twilight. I never dreamed I'd have to come back here again. 'I've told you the truth, milady,' he lied. By natural aptitude and inclination, Gibbs was an accomplished liar.

'No you haven't, Mr Gibbs.' Camilla was calm but implacable. For days she had been preparing for this interview, studying Maisie's diary, staring at Maisie's photo that Lilly Pearl had given her, opening her mind to Maisie's influence, almost becoming Maisie.

'You're obsessed with her,' complained both Alison and Amy before she left London.

'Obsession seems to run in the family,' she had replied grimly.

The truth was that although she was anxious to lay the

429

ghost, she welcomed anything that would occupy her and blot out thoughts of Darcy that festered like a sore in her mind. She had not heard a word from him since he went. Every day she had looked for a letter, though not really believing that he would write. Why should he? He must have reached Brazil by now and become a *quaquero*, like many another before him, including her father. It was a contagious, virulent disease and men succumbed to it as if they had been bitten by some invisible bug. So Darcy was now infected by the pathological urge to search for a fabled hoard, following the alluring will-o'-the-wisps supposed to dance by moonlight over Inca gold hidden in the depths of the jungle. Obsession? There was nothing anyone could teach her about obsession.

Gibbs's eyes filmed over with confusion. 'It was years ago, Lady Camilla. Maisie Hughes was only one among many. Oh, yes, he was a lad for the ladies, your father. How can I be expected to remember her especially?'

'Blah, sir! Waffle!' snorted Rufus, losing patience with this slippery customer. It had been embarrassing having to take him into his own first-class compartment on the train. In the normal way the fellow would have gone in another carriage, along with servants and other lesser mortals, but he had not dared let him out of his sight. 'Don't talk such twaddle. Maisie was far more import-ant, and you know it.'

'Maybe I do,' Gibbs conceded, then added as a doubtful afterthought: 'And then again, maybe I don't.'

Camilla stalked to the scarlet worsted cord hanging by the fireplace and pulled it. 'You give me no option but to jog your memory, Mr Gibbs.'

Leila came in almost at once. 'Yes, Missy Camilla?' she asked as she stared across suspiciously at Gibbs.

'Will you tell Mr Brennan to join us upstairs?' Camilla was already moving towards the door. 'Come yourself. I shall need you.'

430

As Gibbs followed her through the Great Hall and up the staircase all manner of remembrances were running through his mind. Camilla's work on The Priory had restored it to how it had been when Edgar Ruthen resided there and to his ex-valet it was terrifyingly familiar. He paused when they reached the Long Gallery. The huge bay windows gave a sweeping view of the garden and a part of the L-shaped building. The setting sun burnished the fluted wands of smoke which wavered above the roof. Beyond was a reddening sky. He could see the pool in the distance. It was like a lacquered mirror, fired and bloody.

Camilla was waiting for him to catch up, tapping her foot impatiently. He scurried in her wake. God, but she *is* like her old man! he thought. What a tyrant he was! But what times we had, to be sure. Ruthen didn't give a damn for anyone, man, god or devil. And when he was away, I lorded it in his place. Had 'em all running around in circles to do my bidding – footmen, grooms, cooks and maidservants. Ah, those maids! A spasm tightened in his loins at the memory of the girls he had seduced. They had been frightened to refuse him, scared of losing their jobs, and the master had just laughed if any dared complain. And money! There had been plenty of that, for Ruthen was rich, unthrifty and negligent. It had been a paradise for an unscrupulous man. But I couldn't stay, Gibbs remembered with a shudder – not after what happened. He'd gone too far, even for me.

When Camilla entered the Master Chamber, Gibbs very nearly turned tail and ran. As if reading his mind, Rufus stood one side of him and Leila the other. He had no option but to enter. The room, though a trifle more feminine since Camilla's occupation of it, was the same. Sombrely furnished, sumptuous and magnificent. Gibbs recognized objects, knew the feel and smell of the place, dreaded venturing further. Just then Shawn came in at the door and cut off all hopes of retreat. One glance at

431

that strong young man told Gibbs that they had called in reinforcements and he didn't stand a dog's chance of getting out of there.

Like watching a scene in a recurring dream, he saw Camilla head for the arched door over which there had once been an arras. 'Come along, Gibbs. Don't hang about, man.' Rufus was prodding him in the small of the back.

'I'd rather not, sir – if you don't mind!'

'I do mind. You'll oblige me by stepping inside, or I'll be forced to visit a certain police inspector who'll be more than interested to hear what I know about your nefarious activities.'

Gibbs's face had turned a ghastly hue. 'Please, Mr Godwin. I'll do anything else, but don't make me go in there.' His voice was hoarse with frenzied entreaty. A cold sweat broke out of all his pores. The hairs at his nape stood up eerily.

'Having a spot of trouble, are you, sir?' Shawn addressed the lawyer, and his grip on Gibbs's arm was vicelike.

The portrait was the first thing Gibbs saw when he was thrust unceremoniously into the secret room. He gasped and his knees buckled. Only Shawn's hand stopped him from falling. Leila positioned herself by the fireplace, arms crossed over her breasts, her great, liquid dark eyes never blinking.

'Take a chair, Gibbs,' advised Rufus, watching him intently.

'Could I have a drink?' Gibbs gasped, collapsing on to one near the table. He kept his shoulder turned to the portrait, staring away into the dimness, willing to look anywhere, but not at *that*.

'Later.' Camilla stood over him like an avenging angel, completely merciless. 'After you've told me what I want to know.'

'I don't know nothing. Please, don't keep on at me,'

432

muttered Gibbs miserably. He cringed in the chair, an old, shrivelled man, terrified out of his wits.

Camilla yielded to no stirrings of compassion, no pity for this whining, treacherous creature. She felt Maisie's presence strongly, could almost see her sad, wistful smile, her imploring eyes, and thought of the years her spirit might have spent, chained to this house, unable to progress, locked in timeless limbo. For by now Camilla feared that she had never left The Priory alive. Until she had visited Pearl, and even for a short while after, she had tried to convince herself that the girl must have gone back to London and given birth to her child. But since her return, she had spent hours sitting there alone, steeping herself in the evil atmosphere of the room. Sometimes, it seemed that corruption had taken possession of her own body, in her hair, on her skin, under her fingernails. Was it Maisie's ghost that walked? If so, then Camilla needed Gibbs's confirmation so that she might free her.

Her eyes met Leila's and the *mambo* came nearer. 'Look at me,' she said to Gibbs. He trembled, shook his head and hid his face in his palms. 'Look at me!' she repeated.

Slowly, every movement one of painful reluctance, Gibbs lowered his hands and stared up into her eyes. The room fell into an agony of waiting, protracted and nerve-wracking. Rufus and Shawn were on the alert, lest Gibbs try to escape. Camilla stood like a statue, feeling the psychic pull in her solar plexus, hearing the throbbing of her heart, of the drums. The noise shook the walls, the roof, the very foundations of the manor. A deep, reverberating sound, the compelling voices of the gods of heaven and earth beating through her vitals. But she knew that she shared this with no one but the *mambo*.

Leila's eyes widened. They filled the space between her and Gibbs. He felt himself falling through them, sucked into them, lost in velvety blackness. He began to talk.

'He was sick of Maisie Hughes. She was getting too clinging. "That damned little slut's up the spout, Gibbs," he told me after we'd come to The Priory. Very angry he was. "She won't get rid of it!" "Send her packing, sir," I advised, but he said he couldn't, not while she had the ring.'

'Tell me about the ring.' Leila's voice was a soft, soothing murmur.

'Ah, that bloody thing.' Gibbs's face twitched and he stirred restlessly. 'Mr Hughes brought it back from South America. He told me about it. Got it from a bloke named Dawkins, who'd been searching for gold there, on the trail of the Lost Mines of Muribeca. Instead, he and the mate who was travelling with him, found something else deep in the jungle – a deserted city. A mass of ruins, so he said to Hughes, like there'd been an earthquake, hundreds of years ago. There were a few buildings left standing, all overgrown with vines and trees, full of snakes and I don't know what. There's got to be treasure here, thinks Dawkins and his pal! So they pushed their way into what looked like a temple.' Gibbs stopped, running a hand over his sweating face, his eyes glazed as he recalled everything that Maisie's rascally father had recounted. It wasn't easy to remember as they'd both been rather drunk at the time. Then he continued:

'It was an amazing place, the walls covered in beaten gold, and at last they came to a shrine glittering with jewels. The native bearers who'd gone with them were scared to death. Warned 'em not to touch the gems or they'd be cursed. But Dawkins wouldn't listen. He and his friend took a ring from a big stone idol what stood on an altar. But they soon started to quarrel over it, and Dawkins drew his revolver and shot the other man dead. After that, the bearers deserted and he had a terrible trek to Bahia by himself. There he gave out that his companion had been slaughtered by savage tribes of Indians. He tried to get men to go back with him, but

434

they didn't take him seriously, thought his sufferings had
turned him loopy.'

'Inca gold. Sacred to the sun-god,' whispered Leila.
'Cursed gold if touched by impure hands. Fatal, bringing madness and death.'

'Maisie's Dad stole it from Dawkins's body after he'd
been stabbed to death one night in a brothel in Rio,'
Gibbs droned on, his eyes wide and vacant. 'He helped
himself to a book too, a sort of log, in which Dawkins had
written down his adventures. He'd even drawn a map in
it, showing how to get to the city.'

'Why didn't Mr Hughes search for the treasure?' Leila
asked silkily.

'He was too frightened. Sailors are a superstitious lot
and he knew enough about old legends not to risk his
neck. He gave it to Maisie, along with the book. He knew
she wasn't likely to go tearing off to Brazil, not the
adventurous kind.'

'He could have sold it.'

'Yes, but he'd only have spent the money on booze,
and wanted to leave something to Maisie. Not a bad old
stick at heart. Fond of her in a funny kind of way, though
he was always borrowing cash and never repaying it. She
didn't really understand the ring's value, but Lord
Ruthen did.'

'He wanted it?'

'He was determined to get it. Oh, why couldn't he
have left the damned thing alone!' Tears formed in
Gibbs's eyes and made furrows down his hollow cheeks.
'Why couldn't he take heed? Her father died a violent
death too.'

'And did *she*?'

Long shudders shook Gibbs's body. He flung himself
from side to side in the chair but, under the spell of
Leila's hypnotic gaze, he could not rise. 'No one who
owns it prospers, and if they go looking for that bloody
city, they're done for. Maisie was clever. She knew that

Ruthen wouldn't send her away as long as she had that ring. When she found out there was to be a child, she became even more convinced that he shouldn't have it. Then, one night – ! Oh, God! I was here, in this room! I helped him!'

'Tell me about it. Don't be afraid.' So sibilant, Leila's voice – the hiss of Damballah, the snake-god.

Sweat and tears mingled on Gibbs's face. Now he was back, re-enacting the past. 'They're quarrelling again. I can hear 'em from where I'm working in the bedroom. Take no notice, Dick, m'lad. Light the candles. Lay out his nightshirt. Why doesn't she stop? She must know by now that tears aren't the way to get around him. I'll be glad when she's gone, moping about the place, wandering through the passages at night, crying. I'm fed up with it. Up the creek, is she? Serve her right. Wouldn't have nothing to do with me when Ruthen was away that time. Got all prim and proper. There's no way he's going to marry her, him being a toff and her a tart. I hope he gives her the boot. She's too damned nosy, haven't had so much freedom since she came. Christ! What's that? He's hitting her. She's screaming like a stuck pig! Better go in.'

Gibbs stopped, gasping for breath. He was hunched in the chair, arms clasped about him. 'Go on,' commanded Leila.

'I push open the door. The screaming has stopped. She's lying on the floor, all twisted. Her face is purple. He's kneeling over her, his hands still tight around her throat. He looks up at me and there's the devil in his eyes. "I've killed her, Gibbs," he says. "Strangled her! You must help me. I've got to get the ring off!" I goes over and looks at her hand. The fingers are swollen. She's been ill, getting fat, sort of bloated. Women do get like that sometimes when they're in brat. Kidney-trouble or somesuch. We both tug at the ring. It won't budge. Then Ruthen cusses like fury, pulls out his knife

436

and, with one blow, severs the hand at the wrist, then chops at the finger. God, he's crazy. There's blood everywhere. The ring's swimming in it, but he doesn't care. He puts it on his little finger, holds it to the light. It gleams like fire. His face is terrible. Smiling. Triumphant. I feel sick, but I'm so frightened of him. He's mad! Mad!'

Gibbs was weeping. His words were jumbled, indistinct amidst the great tearing sobs that seemed to come from his very guts. Leila knelt by him, taking his hands in hers. 'What happened next? You must tell me!'

'We've got to get rid of the body. It's night and all the servants in bed. We wrap her in a blanket and carry her downstairs. I fetch two horses and we tie her across the back of his saddle, then we go up to the moors. It's dark – so dark – I've never been there at night before. He knows it well though, weaving a way through the bog. I can feel it moving, hear it squelching, see that blood-stained bundle. We take her to a marshy pool, and weight the body with stones. She disappears with hardly a ripple, sucked beneath the black water.'

He slumped in the chair, trembling, exhausted, but Leila had not done with him yet. 'And then?' she asked remorselessly.

Gibbs roused, and started to speak again, his voice a faint whisper. ' "Clear away the mess," Ruthen orders. "Then pack. Her things too. I'll write a letter telling the housekeeper that Miss Hughes and I have returned to London." I go to the room to wash the floor. Then I see it – ! The hand! We had forgotten it in our haste. What can I do with it? Where to hide it? The chimney! It's big, wide – I feel around inside. Yes, there's a ledge high up. I thrust the hand on to it.'

Leila rose, her face strained, showing new lines that betrayed her years. Gibbs wept on, and part of that weeping was relief. Debased and amoral character that he was, the awful memory of the crime to which he had

437

been a party had haunted him. Drink and the company of loose women had helped obliterate it, but there were times when, if he was alone and sober, the vision of that small, mutilated hand seemed to point at him accusingly. Useless to shut his eyes. It was still there against the blackness behind his lids – pallid, dripping with blood. Hard on this would come the sight of a shrouded body disappearing beneath the mist-clouded surface of the gurgling water. Gibbs had known that he would see it until the day he died. He had never told anyone, neither priest, confessor nor friend, until now.

Camilla was the first to break the silence, coming back to the present, for she had accompanied Gibbs on his journey, witnessed the scenes he had described as if they had been happening then and there. Dreading to face it, she had somehow known from the start that her father had murdered the wretched Maisie Hughes. In that moment of truth, there was but one thought uppermost in her mind.

'Darcy has the ring. I must warn him.'

'*Murder most foul,*' grunted Rufus, his eyes misted as if he had just awakened from a trance.

'Can I have a drink?' begged Gibbs.

'I think we could all do with a drink,' Rufus nodded.

Shawn glanced anxiously at Camilla. Her face was pale, and there was a tension about her which he did not much like. Even now, in the midst of this crisis, she's concerned about that bloody sod, Devereaux, he thought angrily, then went off to fetch a bottle of brandy and some glasses.

'Well, Gibbs, what a dreadful tale. You're in it up to the neck, you know. You were the accomplice, which makes you just as guilty as Ruthen,' said Rufus sternly, frowning down at the ex-valet as if he had him in the dock at the Old Bailey.

Gibbs came to life, fear peering from his mean eyes, already feeling the hangman's noose about his throat.

'What d'you mean, guilty?' he blustered. 'It was years past. I can't be charged now. Where's your proof?'

Rufus looked towards the massive chimneypiece. 'In there, I should imagine, unless you dreamed up the whole story.'

Shawn returned, placing a tray on the table and pouring out five tots. Gibbs drained his with the avidity of a babe at the breast, holding out the glass for more. 'What next, Camilla?' Shawn turned to her, controlling the longing to pull her in his arms and hold her tightly.

'We must find the hand,' she said calmly. 'And he'll help us, won't you, Mr Gibbs?'

Gibbs was on his feet in an instant, slopping brandy as he did so. 'Me? Oh, no! I'll not touch the horrible thing! It'll be rotted away by now. The rats will have eaten it – the birds! I can't stay here. I've told you what you wanted to know, now I'm off. You've no right to keep me!'

'I've every right.' Rufus put down his glass and nodded to Shawn. 'You concealed a murder – let the killer escape. How much did he pay for your silence, eh?'

'Pay me? Nothing. I got no payment. I did it out of loyalty – to save the family name!' Gibbs was frantic now, running around the room like a rat in a trap. Shawn leaned against the door, arms folded, booted feet crossed at the ankle.

'How much did he pay you?' Rufus was relentless, giving him no quarter.

'All right! A hundred pounds, that's all. A measly hundred quid to keep a secret that would've cost him his life! Now will you let me go?'

'You took blood-money! Not only was that poor girl brutally murdered, but her unborn child too.' Rufus was glaring at him as if he was indeed a particularly repulsive specimen of rodent. 'It's high time you made some recompense.' He marched across the room to where Gibbs was cowering, seized him by the collar and forced him towards the fireplace.

439

Kindling and logs were neatly laid between the andirons though they had not been ignited. The aperture was so large that Shawn had no difficulty in standing within it, his head touching the blackened supports. 'Which side did you put it?' he asked Gibbs who, held firmly by Rufus, was staring upwards, eyes bulging with terror.

'To the right. If you reach up and feel around, you'll come to the ledge.'

A shower of soot fell on Shawn's head and shoulders as he began his search. His fingers encountered rough stone. More soot covered his hand, trickled up his sleeve. He grimaced, but continued to probe. Then he touched something. It felt like a bundle of rags. He drew it out into the fading light of the room. At once, Rufus asked Leila to take a match to the candles. They threw a sickly glow over the dirty package that Shawn placed on the table.

Gibbs was making whimpering noises, but Rufus compelled him to look down as Shawn unwrapped the piece of rotting silk. It stuck in places, had to be tugged. Then, with a suddenness that drew a gasp from the onlookers, a gruesome object fell out. It was a part mummified, part skeletal hand. The flesh had gone, only bits of tendon and ivory bones remained. As the horrified onlookers watched, the middle finger, separated from the rest, rolled across the polished wood.

Leila muttered something in an incomprehensible tongue, her fingers at her talisman. The room was pervaded by a dreadful stillness, yet filled with invisible things. It was Leila who broke the spell. 'It must be taken to the moors and placed in that same pool wherein lies her corpse. Spirits don't rest if a part of their earthly body is missing. But first, I must carry out the proper ritual.'

'I want to go home,' wailed Gibbs. 'Let me go – please!'

440

'Not yet,' Rufus said sternly. 'You must guide us to the spot.'

It was not until the early hours of the next morning that the party set off for the marshy ground. Leila's ceremony had been long and complicated. The Priory had vibrated with the notes of Sam's *assoto*. Because the ritual could only be performed by initiates of Voodoo, Rufus, Shawn and Gibbs had waited downstairs. Camilla had ordered supper to be served for them in the dining-room, but partaken of nothing herself. Fasting was an essential element of solemn magic and, anticipating such an event, she had not eaten for two days. The servants had accepted Sam's drumming as part of their daily lives, hardly noticing it now. Their quarters were some distance from the Master Chamber. They had retired to bed long before the rite commenced.

Shawn had thought it just as well, for Camilla had made a strange request of him. Would he go to the hen house and capture the black cockerel? He had sworn never to question her actions and did as she asked. Going to the rear of the night-filled garden, he had disturbed the sleepy hens and robbed them of their husband, the proud rooster with the ebony feathers and flaming red comb and wattles.

Leila had taken the indignant bird into her arms, crooning to it until it became quiescent, then bearing it away upstairs. There, in the haunted death-room, she had commenced her work, bringing with her the objects essential to her task. She had begged the aid of Baron-Samedi, Guardian of Graves. Sam's drums had assumed a mesmeric beat. The cockerel had played his part, the blood from his severed throat pouring in a scarlet stream into a sacred vessel. Energy had been focused on the remains of Maisie's hand.

The hours ticked by, seeming endless to those who waited in the library. Rufus slept, stocky legs stretched out to the fire, hands clasped about his stomach, a

441

handkerchief covering his face. Gibbs too dozed, head down on his folded arms on the table, but Shawn was wide awake, listening to every sound. The drums beat endlessly. At one point he went to stand by the window, pushing back the drapes. The milky light of the moon flooded in. It seemed pregnant with a stillness that reached up to the stars.

I want to be with her, he thought. Whatever pagan devilry she's about up there, I want to stand at her side, even though I risk damnation. He returned to his chair, lit a cigarette and sat there thinking. How could she take part in it? The cock would be slaughtered, of that he was convinced, and the idea of her performing the unpleasant task was repulsive. He mentally crossed himself, though a very lapsed Catholic. And yet it never occurred to him to condemn her. He respected her beliefs even though they might be poles apart from his own.

Then Shawn became aware of a silence so complete and vast that it was as if the world had died. The drums had stopped. He looked at the grandfather clock on whose painted face was represented the sun and moon and Death with a scythe. It was half past three. He turned his head when Camilla came in. Her green robe was smeared with blood, her expression rapt. She seemed either drugged or entranced. Leila was similarly garbed, Sam too, and the *mambo* carefully carried a strange-looking jar between both her hands.

'It is time,' she said.

The lawyer's lids snapped open and he was instantly alert, but it took both his and Shawn's concerted efforts to rouse Gibbs, even though they punched and shook him. When he did wake, his eyes were bleared and he was totally confused. They got him to his feet and propelled him through the house and out to the stables. There Shawn harnessed the horses.

November on the moors and pitch-dark. A cloud covered the moon like a hand over a mouth and the silence became blackness. The ground was crisp with frost under the horses' hooves. As they penetrated deeper into the bogland a thin mist lay in the air, not shrouding it, but giving a weird luminosity.

'We must leave the beasts here and walk the rest of the way,' said Shawn quietly.

Treacherous ground now. How well Camilla remembered it. It was here that Darcy had rescued her on a day that now seemed an eternity ago. This was where she had first realized that she loved him. The small party inched along, single file, led by Gibbs who moved with the greatest caution, finding a tussocky path amidst the morass on either side. He stopped at that black slimy pool near the monolith where once Camilla had crouched with Jeddah. What had she seen in that hour of fear and awakening love? Had it been Maisie's spectral arm rising from the murky water?

'This is the place.' Leila's voice was confident. 'This is where her bones lie. I'll give the consecrated vessel to the *loa*, so that they may bear it down and reunite her hand with her body.'

Raising it on high, she chanted a liturgy in a language as old as time itself. Sam and Camilla made the responses, facing the pool, arms uplifted. When Leila finally committed the jar to the gurgling black depths, it disappeared from view instantly.

At that moment, a bird called, high up in the darkness. Its cry was echoed by those of others. The night air trembled. A little gust of wind stirred the mists. The dawn was near.

'Josephine! What on earth are you doing here?' Alison stopped dead as she entered the drawing-room at Cheyne Walk.

'I thought I'd surprise you! Darling, how well you're looking – positively blooming!' Josephine rustled over.

443

Alison was enveloped in sables, in exotic perfume, in her sister's arms.

She was astonished, then frightened, suspicious of the warmth in Josephine's smiling eyes. What was she up to? She half expected to see Selden lurking in the background. There was a man standing there, but it was not her brother. Alison had met him several times at Lilly Pearl's informal gatherings. Blake Saunders, the artist. His work was controversial, dynamic and unusual in concept. It had been refused by the Royal Academy. His political views were equally radical. He caused a furore wherever he went. He was of a haggard, tormented type of distinction, contemplating the world with great, ravaged eyes, and his face wore an expression that was half amused, half sardonic.

Alison freed herself from Josephine's enthusiastic embrace. 'You're the last person I expected to see. How did you know I lived here?' Camilla could not have betrayed her, surely? With a sinking heart Alison remembered that Frank was out, lunching with his publisher.

'Merest chance, my dear.' Josephine was in such a good mood that Alison suspected she was either beginning a new love affair or planning to play a cruel trick on someone. She prayed that she was not about to be the unfortunate victim of her sister's malice. In the next moment, she realized that Josephine's motive was the former. She darted back to where Blake stood, smiling up into his face with that expression of simpering admiration which Alison knew all too well. 'Blake's painting my portrait. Selden's had this absurd notion that I simply must be painted and hung amongst the rest of the Ruthens. Silly man!'

'I see,' Alison replied for something to say, whilst her mind was running around in circles. Should she summon the maid and order afternoon tea? Or would they prefer something stronger? Housewifely pride was urging her to show Josephine that she had everything under control. She was glad that the drawing-room looked so elegant.

'So, as Blake is the most sought after artist in Europe now, it was absolutely essential that he was commissioned,' Josephine continued, and Alison felt suddenly drab in comparison. So beautiful, so vibrant was her stunning sister, dressed in the height of fashion, swaddled in furs against the cold of early December, a smart velvet hat perched atop her golden curls, its veil like a black mist rendering her features sultry and alluring.

'Cut the flattery, Josie,' Blake said, his deep voice echoing round the warm room. 'Your brother hasn't seen the portrait yet. He may refuse to pay for it or hang it when he does.'

Josephine giggled and fluttered her lashes. 'It *is* rather shocking, I'll admit.' She swung back to Alison. 'I've had to pose nude, darling, lying on a tumbled bed – rather like Goya's "The Naked Maja".'

'It's nothing like it,' Blake broke in, offended. 'What I paint bears no resemblance to anyone else's work.'

'Oh, you're so touchy!' she pouted, tapping him lightly on the arm. '*Really!* You artists! Don't you find them fascinatingly temperamental, Alison? Blake's an absolute beast if I don't do exactly what he orders. Works me like a galley-slave, my dear! And it's positively freezing in his studio.'

'It was you who told Lady Josephine that I lived in Cheyne Walk?' Alison smiled at him uncertainly.

He was rather an alarming individual and his reputation was fearsome. Frank, who had also met him, had voiced a certain disapproval to Alison. 'The fellow's a charlatan,' he had said as they were undressing for bed after one of Lilly Pearl's soirées where the young artist had burst upon the scene like a whirlwind. 'I don't think he's all that talented. But he has a forceful personality,

445

and sweeps all before him, including the women.' He certainly had the kind of showy looks which would appeal to Josephine.

He turned the full power of his fine dark eyes to her. They contained a kind of slumbrous fire which could mean that he lived constantly on the edge of inspiration or might have been nothing more than a happy accident of genetics. 'I happened to mention that I knew Frank Turner.'

'Of course, I leaped on it straight away,' Josephine butted in, unable to bear him paying attention to anyone else. 'Wasn't it a wonderful coincidence? So here I am, wanting to hear all about you and to be shown around your house.'

'Does Selden know?' Alison needed to sit down. Josephine was an exhausting person at the best of times, and her sudden appearance had been a shock.

Alison sought a chair and sank down into it. She had awakened that morning with a dull ache low in her back. I've been overdoing it, she thought, unusually busy over the past few days. But there's so much to be done this time of the year. Christmas will be upon us soon. There's been shopping to organize, gifts to decide upon, extra food to be ordered, and I've not yet finished preparing the layette for the baby.

'Don't worry, I've not told Selden about your hideout. I don't know where he is at the moment. Gone to ground somewhere.' Josephine's lovely face was exposed in its full glory as she tossed back her veil.

'Will you tell him?' Alison knew that she should be playing the hostess but could not summon the energy to ring for the maid.

'It depends.' Josephine was drawing off her gloves thoughtfully and glancing at Blake the while. She took the cigarette he gave her, leaning closer, her hand steadying him, so that he might light it.

Yes, much depended now on Blake Saunders.

446

Josephine was in love again. Angered by Shawn's brusque dismissal and subsequent devotion to Camilla, she had sulked for weeks. Then she had met Blake and forgotten everything else. He had made love to her after the first sitting in his large, bare north facing studio. Fiery and passionate? Yes. Intensely difficult to manage? Yes and yes again. But then, as she had long ago decided, a man wasn't really worth his salt unless he *was* difficult. The conflict made it so much more exciting.

She did not know where she stood with the moody painter with the burning, fanatical eyes. Sometimes he could not wait to push her down amongst the draperies of the couch, whilst at others, he wanted nothing but to stick his palette on his thumb and daub away like a man demented, as if she was merely an object whose impression must be transferred on to canvas with pressing urgency. He could be jealous and demanding or cold and uninterested. She knew that she was not his only paramour. He took his pleasure whenever he fancied and with whom he fancied. Not only women. She had discovered early on in their relationship that he was bisexual. Sometimes she sighed for Shawn. With all his rather sinister sexual intensity, Blake was not such a considerate lover. Too selfish by far, too concerned with his own image, and his own needs.

Alison was beginning to wish that her uninvited visitors would take their leave. Her back was aching constantly and she could not sit comfortably. The baby had decided to be active and she was embarrassed lest they should notice the thrusting moments that were stirring the loose smock that covered her bulging stomach. Yet, despite herself, she was longing to hear what was happening in the village. She had missed it, and this was odd considering how badly she had wanted to leave. Selden occupied her thoughts more often than she cared to admit. After all, one can't housekeep for a brother for eight years without wondering how he was

447

managing without one. There was no denying that he had been awkward and unkind, Josephine too, but as her pregnancy had advanced so Alison had found herself wishing that she had been closer to her family in every way.

'How is Selden?' she asked, glancing at Josephine who had flung herself on the chaise longue, swinging her legs up and arranging her skirt over them.

'Angry,' she answered lightly, patting the space beside her, an invitation that Blake ignored, remaining in front of the fire with an elbow on the overmantel. 'You see, he's found it impossible to pin the blame on Camilla for her father's death. There's no evidence of foul play. All he achieved was to put the villagers' backs up and send Darcy away.'

'Wasn't that enough? Poor Camilla,' Alison began.

'I think she was well shot of Darcy,' Josephine commented airily. 'He's rushed off to Brazil. Always was a restless being. I doubted that he'd settle down. It sounded too good to be true.'

Not long before, Alison had received an extraordinary letter from Camilla. She had read it with growing amazement shot through with alarm, then shown it to Frank and discussed it with Amy and John. Neither could decide whether the rather garbled account of ghosts and murder were true or if the shock of Darcy's jilting her at the altar had turned Camilla's brain. Whichever it was, Alison had wanted to see her very much, particularly as she had stated that she was making plans to visit Bahia without delay. And now, to top it all, had come the unexpected arrival of Josephine.

Oh, dear, I wish Frank would come in! Alison could feel herself beginning to panic. All along she had feared that life was being over-generous. Everything had gone almost too smoothly; finding the house, engaging staff, making new friends, shocking herself by the ease with which she had manipulated the truth about her relationship with Frank. The threatening letters from Elsie had stopped. She accepted the money sent her regularly, though steadfastly refused to consider divorce. Alison had tentatively begun to believe that her troubles were over, happiness complete now that Frank's book was about to go to press. But, as usual, fate had been holding a trick up its sleeve. Blake Saunders to be exact. A slight acquaintance, someone she had only fleetingly met but he had proved to be the link with Josephine, bringing the unhappy past into the present.

She listened to her sister's prattle, watched the play of light over Blake's lean features, saw their mouths moving but was unable to concentrate on what they were saying. Nothing was of any importance but the increasing discomfort of her body.

At last, unable to endure it further, she struggled to her feet. 'If you'll excuse me. There's a household matter needing attention. Frank should be in at any moment to entertain you, and I shan't be long.'

She could feel Josephine's curious eyes boring into her back, hear her saying: 'My dear, are you all right? You've turned very pale. Shall I come with you?'

'No – no. Stay here. I'll have the maid bring in some tea.'

The door. Freedom. Escape watching eyes. She sought her bedroom. Went into the adjoining bathroom, fearful of the dampness she could feel on her underclothes. What was it the midwife, Sister Glasson, had said? 'Call for me at once if you get pains or a show.' What was a show? Alison had been too embarrassed to ask.

A quick examination of her knickers gave her the answer. A brownish-red stain marked the silk at the crutch. Alison dropped her petticoats into place again and leaned against the bathtub. Nausea swept her. She made for the lavatory and emptied the contents of her stomach into it. Faint, weak, bathed in sweat, she clung to the cold china rim. The eyes of blue ceramic flowers stared back at her from the glaze. It's too early! she panicked. The baby shouldn't be coming till January!

Pain leaped on her then, great iron pincers gripping her stomach, turning it into a rigid ball, forcing a groan from between her lips. Frank, where are you? She hauled herself up. Saw her hands clenched so tightly that the knuckles turned chalky. The pain receded, fanning away into the distance, giving her a breathing space. Thank God, thank God! Now I can think, plan, send for the doctor, the midwife! She moved very carefully. The pain did not return but she was aware of its presence somewhere just beyond reach. It was waiting, like a beast lashing its tail, ready to spring at her again. I wish I knew more about childbirth, she thought miserably. Maybe this isn't it. Perhaps it's a false alarm. She tried to buoy up hope, but race-memory, the deep awareness of woman was telling her that her time had come.

She went back to the bedroom, opened the box which contained the articles Sister Glasson had instructed her to collect for the lying-in, and took out a linen cloth of the kind which she had once used for her monthly periods. At least she could protect her clothing while she decided what to do.

The dull ache in her back increased. Pain began to radiate from it, spreading out across her belly, reaching a crescendo then dying back. So this is what being in labour means, she thought, holding on to the heavy mahogany footboard of the bed. I know it. I've been there before though never in this existence. Perhaps Amy's right and there's truth in the theory of reincarnation. She's been telling me about the group run by her medium friend. They believe we're born again and again, learning life's hard lessons, paying off karmic debts, developing our souls. Frank's interested in the idea. He's convinced that we've known each other before

450

somewhere. It might account for the fact that none of these sensations are new to me.

Then speculation was eclipsed by terror. My baby's on its way too soon! she gasped. I don't want anything to happen to it. Oh, God, I don't want to die! Help me, help me! Please God. I'll be good, I promise, only let everything be all right! In the next instant pain kicked with a force that doubled her up. She forgot everything but its fierce torture.

'Alison! What's happened?' A voice penetrated the fog of agony. 'My God! Are you going to have the baby?'

Leaning over the rail like an old, bent woman, Alison looked up to see Josephine coming in at the door. 'I think so,' she panted. 'But it shouldn't be arriving yet.'

'You were such a long time that I told Blake to stay put and came to look for you.' Josephine put an arm about her, took out her handkerchief and wiped the sweat from her face. Alison was glad that she was there. Josephine was so strong. She would know what to do.

'Is Frank home yet?' she asked weakly. She was feeling better now. The pain had gone away. 'I may be making a fuss about nothing.'

'Nonsense, my dear.' Josephine was busy taking off her hat, laying it on the dressing-table. 'Where is he? I'll send Blake to fetch him. And one of the servants must telephone for the doctor and the midwife. You get undressed and hop into bed. Leave everything to me.'

'But Josephine, you can't stand babies or anything to do with birth,' Alison protested, obeying her, starting to struggle with hooks and buttons.

Josephine was hauling on the bell. 'This is different. You're my sister, aren't you?' She nearly ripped the cord from the wall. 'Damnation! Where's that bloody maid? Swigging your port in the kitchen, I suppose! She'd better get herself up here fast!'

All animosities and misunderstandings had miraculously vanished. They were sisters, no matter how much

451

they had disagreed throughout their lives. When it came down to it, blood was thicker than water.

'Oh, Josephine, thank you.' Tears of gratitude stung Alison's eyes.

'Tosh! Save your strength. God knows, you're going to need it.' Josephine was helping her out of her clothes and into a white lawn nightgown. The maidservant poked her head around the door and was briskly dispatched, round-eyed and gawking, with messages for Dr Gough, Sister Glasson and Frank.

'Get out the baby clothes, they're in that basket over there. And could you ask someone to bring the cradle from the nursery?' Alison settled in bed, felt much better now. Josephine was taking the practical burdens from her. Josephine being so helpful and nice, as only she could be when she set her mind to it. Josephine who, in common with Selden, possessed a charm that made one forgive her faults.

'Don't jump the gun, old thing.' Josephine looked down at her with an amused smile. 'Plenty of time for all that. How often are you getting your pains? Every ten minutes? It'll be a while yet before anything happens.'

What a heaven-sent opportunity, she was thinking as they waited for the doctor. I've a wonderful excuse to delay in London now. What could be more natural than my desire to remain with my sister during and after her accouchement? Douglas was becoming ever more boring, the children increasingly tedious and her life at Abbey Sutton devoid of excitement. She longed to stay in Chelsea, with its parties, its free-living inhabitants, wanted to remain with Blake and friends of the same kidney. Oh, yes, she'd be sweetness itself to Alison if, by so doing, she could achieve this end. Selden could go to the devil. He'd not bully her anyhow, and would be pleased that she had tracked down the love-birds. She was all angelic solicitude when the doctor arrived. He was a mature, experienced man who exuded confidence.

452

Handsome too, grey-haired and distinguished. Better and better, thought Josephine, looking up at him in that rather breathless, big-eyed way to which men from all walks of life invariably responded.

The afternoon drew to a frosty close. A sprinkling of snow covered grimy London and, in the bedroom of Cheyne Walk, Alison laboured to bring her child into the world. So much pain. She had not realized that the human frame could stand such agony and still live. They gave her something to drink, sweetish, strong-smelling. Frank, trying unsuccessfully to hide his concern, said that it was laudanum and that she must take it.

A period of confusion that resembled sleep but wasn't. More pain, never-ending now, washing over her like a stormy ocean, crushing her so that she screamed. Sister Glasson, face intent under her crisp white coif, thrust the end of a towel into her hands. It was fastened to the rail at the foot of the bed. She was telling her to pull on it when she got the next pain.

'Pull, my dear. That's right. Then push – go on, push! Harder! Push right down to the bottom of your spine. Good girl!'

They had sent Frank away. Someone said that he was drinking brandy in the library with Blake. It was Josephine who held her hands and encouraged her as she strained on the towel. Dr Gough was there, bending over her as Sister Glasson supported her legs. Inch by slow inch, her womb gave up the child, thrusting it out, a tiny, pink, squeaking scrap, no bigger than a skinned rabbit, which it rather resembled.

'It's a girl,' Josephine announced.

'Fetch Frank. I want Frank,' Alison mumbled, too weak with relief at the cessation of pain to register any other emotion.

Doctor Gough hadn't finished with her yet. His hands were pressing on her flat stomach. Oh, why couldn't they leave her alone? She was so very tired. More discomfort. The afterbirth slipping out into the kidney-basin, like bloody offal, like something from a butcher's slab. The midwife was sitting by the fire with the child in her hands, holding it out to the flames. Josephine stood by her side, watching that small creature fighting for its life. So premature, so incomplete. No layer of warm fat beneath the wrinkled skin. But she was struggling hard, minuscule toes reaching out towards the life-giving heat of the fire.

'Will she live?' Josephine said softly, adding on a note of wonder: 'Good grief! She's my niece.'

Sister Glasson did not look up, concentrating on the child. 'We'll give her some brandy,' she said, a navy-blue-clad spinster who had delivered a multitude of infants and, maybe because of what she had seen, had never offered up her own body to be sacrificed on the altar of motherhood.

Josephine took up the bottle and poured a few drops on to a spoon. While the nurse held the head, which was no bigger than an orange, Josephine dribbled the brandy into the open mouth. The tiny tongue moved. The brandy went down. The baby gasped and started to cry, feebly at first, then more lustily. Sister Glasson swaddled her in flannel and a thick Shetland shawl. Only that red, cross-looking little face peeped forth, crowned with dark brown fluff.

Frank was on his knees by the bedside, concerned only for Alison. 'My brave, brave girl,' he was saying, his voice choked with emotion.

'Let me take her,' Josephine said, holding out her arms. The midwife gave her the feather-light bundle.

She carried the baby across to the parents, very aware of the drama of the moment and her own role in it. The doctor was smiling at her. Everyone was smiling. Elation filled the room. A child had been born. Death had been defeated and life renewed. It was as if they had been warriors helping Alison to fight a mighty battle. It brought them close. They laughed, made a few jokes, were as relieved as the new mother. For Josephine it had been a shattering experience. She had never watched a baby being born before. She realized even more than at the birth of her own children that there was no place for false modesty, no time for conventions or embarrassment about the functions of the human body. It was a raw, primitive act. No matter where it happened, the very basic, fundamental nature of it made those involved face their inner selves.

Frank looked up and Josephine, cloud-high and excited, suddenly realized why Alison had left everything for love of him. In the village, she had never really noticed the rather nondescript curate, but now he was bearded and long-haired, a writer, a part of the Chelsea existence. For the first time ever, Josephine envied her sister.

'Here's your daughter, Frank,' she said.

Doctor Gough was giving the nurse her instructions. Josephine listened closely too. All through the birth he had carried an air of authority that appealed to her. She always had been partial to members of the medical profession. One could be so open with them and talk of personal matters without a blush. The fact that he had just delivered her sister's baby and that she had been present, threw them into an intimacy and comradeship which thrilled her. He was explaining that the child was premature and would need extra care, but he saw no reason why she should not grow strong and healthy.

'She's too small for her crib yet,' he said, as he washed his capable, well-shaped hands in the bathroom, talking through the open door to Sister Glasson, but eyeing Josephine in the mirror. 'Warmth is essential. Find a shoebox, line it with cottonwool and lay her in it. Keep a good fire going and place the box close to the hearth. Disturb her as little as you can, but put her to the breast. If you find that she hasn't the strength to suckle, then express Mrs Turner's milk and give it to her from a feeding-bottle.'

455

He came out, still drying his hands on a towel, virile and masculine in his waistcoat and shirtsleeves. Josephine watched his hands, fascinated. She had the sudden urge to go to bed with him. He shrugged his shoulders into his coat, closed his medical bag with a snap, picked up his hat, smiled down at Alison and nodded to Josephine. He knows what I'm thinking! The idea dizzied her.

'I don't know how to thank you, doctor.' There were tears in Frank's eyes.

Heavens alive! One would think this had never happened to him before, Josephine observed to herself. What about Elsie and the four other children? Men are quite ridiculous, and yet they dare to call women illogical.

'Tuck her in with her mother for a minute,' Doctor Gough advised, as she strolled with him towards the door. 'It will keep her warm whilst Sister prepares the box. You've done well, Lady Josephine. Have you ever thought of taking up nursing?'

It had never occurred to her, but she did not tell him this, enthusing about it, expressing regret that a woman in her position could never do so. 'I think you're all wonderful,' she breathed. 'Masters of life and death. I do so admire doctors.'

Alison took her child into her arms, exhausted but starry-eyed. Such a tiny little thing, and how adorable. She hugged her to her breast, smiling at Frank, at Josephine, at the doctor, radiant, still drugged, deliriously happy.

'What shall you call her, my love?' Frank whispered, looking at them both with something akin to awe.

'Camilla –' Alison whispered. 'I want to call her Camilla.'

Bloody hell! thought Josephine. That bitch gets in on everything! But she smilingly agreed that it was a lovely name. She kissed her sister on the brow and crept out of the room, wondering if the doctor had gone yet or was he

456

still below? She listened. Heard the front door shut. Decided to return to Blake, knowing his restlessness and suddenly worried in case he had become impatient and left without her. Then she saw a figure on the staircase, a child clad in outdoor garments, a wicker case in one hand, a large china doll in the other.

'Where d'you think you're going at this time of night?' she asked, bending down and meeting the stare of cold blue eyes. Their unblinking scrutiny was disconcerting, as was the pointed, pixie-like, rather vicious face.

'I'm not staying in this house with that baby,' Effie announced, chin up, rigid with indignation.

'You're Frank's daughter.' Josephine felt a sudden warmth towards this rebel, recognizing a kindred spirit.

'He's my Papa, yes.' The child carried herself with an oddly adult dignity. It gave Josephine the uncomfortable feeling that she was far, far older than her years. 'But *she's* not my mother.' Her face twisted into an expression of rage. 'She likes me to call her Mamma, but I won't any more. She bought me this stupid doll, but I hate it. I hate it! I hate her too! And I hate the baby!'

Before Josephine realized what she was doing, she climbed on the lower rung of the banister, raised the expensive, gorgeously attired French doll and threw it over the edge. It fell through the air and smashed on the marble tiles of the hall below, lying there with its head broken. Christ! thought Josephine, they'll have to watch the baby night and day or this little fiend will harm it.

'That was rather a silly thing to do,' she said aloud. 'Now you've ruined something valuable. It's unwise to look a gift horse in the mouth, child. It might have been better to have traded it with a friend for something you wanted.'

'I haven't any friends,' Effie replied, climbing down from her perch.

'Well then, might it not be nice to have a sister?' Even as Josephine spoke, she was remembering what a bore she had found Alison, resenting having her trailing

457

around behind her and Selden. She'd always been the odd one out, and they'd made her suffer for it.

'No. I've three brothers and they're much more fun.' Effie tossed her flaxen ringlets beneath the pork-pie hat.

'But you don't see them now.' Josephine had never had much time for children, but this rebellious mite was different. There was something about her that awoke an immediate response. She's selfish, she thought. Like me.

'I shall. I'm going to the station and I'll get the train home. They can't keep me a prisoner here.' Although she spoke so confidently, Effie's lower lip trembled.

'How old are you?' Josephine took her hand and they began to walk down the staircase together.

'I was five on the eighth of November. I'm Effie, and you're Lady Josephine, aren't you? You wear lovely frocks and you smell nice. I shall wear frocks like that one day.'

'I'm quite sure you will, Effie. You can call me Josie, if you like.'

They stopped in the hall and a startled maidservant paused, saying: 'Miss Effie, you've no business being down here. You should be in bed. Does Nanny know?'

'Nanny's busy with that baby. She doesn't care about me any more. None of them care!' Effie's voice rose shrilly, and she started to cry.

The crafty little devil! They're nothing but crocodile tears, mused Josephine, with a grin. She knows damn well that she won't be allowed out of the house but, by God, she's going to make sure that she gets her fair share of attention and makes their lives as difficult as possible into the bargain. I used to get up to just such capers myself. Come to think of it, I still do!

'It's all right,' she dismissed the maid coolly. 'I'll speak to Nanny about this. Miss Effie is coming into the library to meet a friend of mine. Will you send in a glass of milk for her and sherry for us. Oh, and make sure there's a plate of cakes as well. D'you like cake, Effie? Good. We'll have a midnight feast.'

458

3

'And what will you do when you find him?' asked Shawn, resting his elbows on the ship's rail close to Camilla's, and bending towards her with a keen interrogative glance. He was very conscious of her proximity, the bare shoulder gleaming against its jewelled strap, the hands so near his own.

'Darcy?' Camilla spoke softly, turning dreamy eyes to him, eyes in which he saw reflected the brilliant moon of that magical night where everything was clear and dramatic. 'I don't know, Shawn, and that's the truth. Tomorrow we'll land in South America and, for the life of me I hardly know why I've come.'

She did not speak like a woman in love who was anticipating seeing the object of her desire. Hope soared within Shawn. His heart started beating heavily, the blood pounding at his temples. Control had been so hard during the weeks when they had been preparing for the trip and actually on shipboard. He had cursed himself for a fool for helping this woman to reach her lover. She had not asked him to accompany her, but that she should go away without him had been unthinkable. He wanted to protect her, though Rufus had already offered his services, saying that a lawyer would be invaluable should the authorities cause trouble, and passages had been booked for Leila and Sam. So he had thrown up his job with Selden, not too great a sacrifice as he disliked working for Camilla's enemy and for some time Colonel Pinnegar had been angling to employ him, glad to promise him a post on his return. Selden had taken it remarkably calmly, considering. Merely subjecting Shawn to his withering sarcasm, and hinting that

Camilla would be walking into trouble. All in all, the master of Armitstead House had been keeping a suspiciously low profile, and Shawn had caught the distinct odour of treachery in the wind.

The journey had been uneventful, but Shawn had found it fascinating. He had never been on a large liner before, soaking up impressions like a sponge, his enthusiasm infecting Camilla who had regained some of her old sparkle. They had called in at Lisbon, then Funchal and Tenerife. After that had followed nine empty days, where they seemed to live in a state of suspended animation surrounded by blue skies and blue ocean. Now this was the last night. God only knew what lay ahead of them.

Very aware of this, aware too that once she saw Darcy, Camilla would change, Shawn had seized the opportunity, treasuring each fleeting moment. They had spent a most pleasant evening together. The purser's table was at one end of the dining-room and the captain's at the other and they had sat somewhere between the two, in company with Rufus who was thoroughly enjoying this unexpected vacation and looking forward to the adventures in store. He had let Camilla know that he'd once served with the army in India and was thus no stranger to foreign climes.

'It was some years ago, I'll admit,' he had added gruffly, making light of his age lest she might think him too old for hacking his way through jungle territory. 'But I was good with a rifle. Did my bit for Britain on the Khyber Pass. Wasn't there long, unfortunately. Stopped a bullet and was sent home.'

Shawn, with chameleon-like ease, had adapted himself to life aboard ship, playing deck games, dancing, flirting, doing all the things expected of a handsome, well-heeled young man travelling first-class on a luxury liner. He could just about afford to give that impression. Selden had provided him with a roof and food over the

460

months and he had sunk his savings into the venture, equipping himself and buying his ticket. Camilla had offered to pay, but Shawn would have none of this.

'I'll not be labelled a kept man,' he had replied, with his quirky grin. There were only a few sovereigns left in his bank account but he had shrugged philosphically. Something would turn up. He had the luck of the Irish.

Camilla had attracted a great deal of interest amongst her fellow-passengers throughout the journey, so beautiful, so unconventional in dress and attitude. Men had pursued her, and Shawn had let it be known that he was her escort, warding off the most persistent of her admirers, resisting his hotheaded inclination to punch them on the nose. That night, she had seemed more lovely than ever as they ate the fabulous meal and listened to the ship's orchestra playing the gayest of tunes – French *chansons* and American ragtime dances calculated to charm away shadows from the soul. Later, the tables had been moved back and couples had begun to dance. Hardly had the music struck up when a smart naval officer had bowed before Camilla and led her to the floor. Shawn watched them go through narrowed eyes, seeing how the other women looked her over and gossiped spitefully amongst themselves.

The officer was not a good dancer, pumping Camilla's arm up and down and whirling her around and around. She was hot and flushed when she returned, and Shawn had suggested that they go on deck. It was a balmy night, and they were not alone in seeking its privacy. They passed lovers with clasped hands and gentlemen busy, no doubt, with ambitious schemes, planning business ventures as they paced there, smoking quietly in the darkness and the peace. There was the sound of singing from the saloon, borne faintly on the breeze, with the throbbing of stringed instruments.

The beauty, the life on the sea, stole into Camilla's senses. It was as if the spirit of the mighty ship wove a

461

spell about her. The air was cool and scented with spices and, as she leaned on the rail, watching the white spume race by, she felt the quickening wind lift a strand of her hair and brush it across her cheek. She did not move or speak for a while, lost in reverie. She longed to stay there for ever with Brazil a mirage, always hovering ahead but never reached, yet every revolution of the screws, every beat of her heart was bringing it nearer. She yearned to see Darcy but feared his rejection. Why couldn't life stand still sometimes?

'D'you think Darcy will have gone into the jungle? How d'you propose to find him?' Shawn looked down at her with steady scrutiny, then straightened and drew a cigar from his breast pocket. He needed to occupy his hands, lest they move of their own volition and touch Camilla. The physical craving within him was as fierce as the claws of a wild beast, tearing him, not to be pacified by anything except complete possession of her.

'I'll go directly to Rubera and make enquiries,' she said, as he passed her a cheroot from his flat, silver case. 'Ranger Hogan will know if any stranger has arrived and formed an expedition. He's my manager, and was involved in my father's trips.'

'If he has already gone – ?'

'I'll follow. I know the route.'

'Oh, Camilla, must you do this? Think of the danger. Is it really worth it?' There were large Chinese lanterns lighting the deck, fragile painted paper spheres, and in their orange glow Shawn was regarding her with apparent laziness, though there was a coiled alertness in his indolent stance.

'It will be worth it if I can divert him from his madness. You heard what Gibbs said. He's doomed if he follows that chimera which has lured so many others to their deaths.' There was that stubbornness about her which he knew nothing would sway, but he had been drinking a good deal of wine and, emboldened by it, became equally obstinate.

'You're wasting your time,' he growled, the tip of his cigar glowing against the shadowy rise and fall of the sea.

'I must try.' Her face wore a determined expression, turned up towards his, eyes slanting, red lips slightly parted.

Shawn was bewitched by them, seeing their fullness, their promise. He ached to kiss her. He threw the cigar butt over the side impatiently and clenched his fists. 'Supposing he doesn't listen – doesn't want anything to do with you?'

'I must try,' she repeated and Shawn, unable to stop himself, reached out and gripped her upper arm. The flesh was smooth as gold-brown silk, yet firmly muscled. The touch of it drove him almost insane.

'You'd still have him back, after the way he treated you?' he ground out harshly. 'Where's your pride, Camilla? How could you even contemplate it?'

'I love him.' She said the words like a catechism, almost automatically. 'I'd be prepared to try again with him, if he's willing.'

'Camilla!' he groaned, thinking desperately: Christ, I've gone this far so I might as well continue. He seized her other arm, turned her towards him, forced her close to his chest. 'Be sensible. The man's a cad. You'll never be happy with him.'

Strange emotions were streaking through her, baffling things that defied reason. Of course she still wanted Darcy. She did not give her love easily, and when she did it was for ever. He had hurt her grievously, yet she told herself that it was the curse which had changed him. Break that enchantment and he would be hers again, the old Darcy, the farmer, the countryman, filled with plans for his lands, her lands, their continuing future at The Priory, together. Yet Shawn – ah, Shawn! She had become accustomed to his presence, warm, genial, ever-supportive. He was that rare thing, a handsome man who was also a fine and decent human being. It was he who had stood by her through the trauma of Darcy's desertion and the horror of finding that her father had been a murderer. He too who had helped organize the trip, making sure that everything would run like clockwork during her absence. Beryl and Wilf had been left at the helm.

They had been much thrown together on the ship, and she acknowledged to herself that they had reached a degree of intimacy which she at least had never before experienced. There was not a subject which had engrossed her attention, not a problem that baffled her, not a hope or fear, an ambition or dream, which she had not talked over at length with him. Each fresh discussion left her more conscious of help and sympathy, and of profound admiration for his broad-minded, open-hearted character. He made her laugh, and this too was a blessing. She had become solemn of late, losing her optimism, her faith in life. Shawn was gradually restoring it.

Recently the high point of friendship had been reached when silence could be prolonged without apology, a vibrant silence broken at length by a remark that put into words what they had both been thinking. Camilla had at first been amused and delighted at this similarity of thought. But gradually she had grown afraid. Instinct told her that Shawn was in love with her, and the very last thing she wanted was to hurt him.

'Let me go, Shawn,' she said quietly, though her own heart was beating in rhythm with him. 'I don't want to do anything I'll regret later. I'm flesh and blood too, you know. It's a beautiful, romantic night, and I'm so very fond of you.'

'I'll settle for that, for the time being, acushla,' he whispered. 'Let me show you that Darcy's wrong for you, always has been.'

464

This is madness, she thought, shocked by her bodily response to him. Madness! I can't! I won't! I love Darcy! How cruel it would be to let Shawn make love to me and then, when I meet Darcy, tell him it's over. I'll not be like Josephine, using men for my pleasure. It wouldn't be right or fair.

'Shawn, I've too much affection and respect for you,' she began, gently pushing against his chest. 'You're my friend, my very good friend. Let's leave it at that.'

'Ah, there you are!' cried a voice behind them. Rufus came stumping up the companion-way. 'Care for a last noggin, Shawn, old chap? One for the road, as it were, seeing as how we'll be disembarking in the morning.'

He had taken in the situation at a glance, shrewd enough to guess which way the wind was blowing. Camilla was in his charge too and he considered it unwise for her emotions to be complicated further. Time enough for all that when she's sorted out her feelings for Devereaux. They had enough on their plate without him and Shawn fighting over her like two dogs with a bone. She needed time, space and peace of mind.

Camilla turned, feeling herself blushing like a school-girl caught out. Shawn dropped his hold, grinning at the short, stout lawyer. 'What a capital idea, Mr Godwin. But I'll be after returning Camilla to her stateroom before I drink you under the table, or Leila will be scalping me.'

Camilla was stabbing about in her mind for a suitably witty retort when she was pulled up short, aware that there was someone on the upper deck. A man stood there, shrouded in darkness, staring down at her, his hands resting on the rail. She was startled, though unsure why she should be. There were still several passengers taking a final turn about the decks. She was conscious of two sharp emotions, firstly that shock of surprise, followed closely by control. For some reason which she could not explain, she did not draw her

465

companions' attention to him. In an instant she had recovered, gathering up her skirts in order to negotiate the steps leading below. At the same time, she saw the man change position, passing to the opposite angle of the deck above and never taking his eyes off her as he did so. It was unnerving, and not the first time she had felt that someone on board had her under surveillance. Despite Shawn's jokes and Rufus's stalwart presence, gloom descended upon her, unbidden and totally unexpected.

They reached Bahia at sunset two days later. Leaving the liner at Rio they had taken a steamer, hugging the dark-green coastline where the charging jungle stopped short only at the sea. The little craft seemed lost in the big bay of Todas os Santos. Against a tawny sky the wooded hills stood out fiercely. Frigate birds flew over the darkening sea. Forts, docks and warehouses lined the beaches, whilst higher up lay private residences and administrative buildings. Lights twinkled everywhere in gay disorder as the swift, tropical twilight died, plunging the world into dark blue night. The fussy little steamer, overcrowded, smelly and insanitary, manned by what looked like a crew of buccaneers, edged its way around two or three warships and a mass of small frigates flying all flags, and chugged into the harbour. There now ensued a scene familiar to every traveller, a repetition of that which had taken place in Rio. A number of officials came aboard, swarthy, mustachioed, looking pompous yet villainous at the same time, throwing their weight about as they examined passports. This caused an irritating delay, but at length Camilla stood on her native soil.

There, amidst the bustle of the dockside where they were immediately besieged by porters, all jabbering away in Portuguese, all eager to carry their luggage, it was as if she had never left Bahia. The smell of it, the heat, the spice laden air overlaid by rotting fruit and fish, made her gasp with recognition. Rio had never been her home, she had merely visited it on odd occasions, that city of vivid contrasts where the poor were so deprived and the rich lived in all the opulence of royal princes. Dutifully, she had stayed a day or so, permitting the entranced Shawn and Rufus to explore that gay, sad, carnival-mad capital, where there were always fireworks exploding at night in celebration of the birth of a saint or the death of a patriot, and the slum-dwellers sang and drummed and starved, a conglomeration of cultures.

Now she had come home, and knew that it really was her home – not Wessex, not The Priory, or London or Paris. She hated it and its memories, yet was bound to it. They took one of the many horse-drawn carriages that waited for hire, each in charge of a straw-hatted native driver with an ancient nag between the shafts, and soon left the narrow quayside alleys, coming out into wide plazas surrounded by magnificent homes and richly decorated churches built in the golden age of Bahia when it was one of the busiest ports in the Americas.

'That was years ago now,' Camilla explained to Shawn, who sat on the edge of the seat of the open, canopied vehicle, staring around him with avid interest and curiosity. 'From the sixteenth century to the early nineteeth, sugar from the north-east and the gold and diamonds from the mines in the south all passed through the town. It was the capital of Brazil till 1763 when this was transferred to Rio de Janeiro.'

Even Rufus was impressed, though he had been fully prepared to find Bahia a run-down trading post. Far from it. It was an attractive place, swarming with foreigners of all nationalities, but the majority of the population appeared to be negroid or mulatto, quite distinct in every way from the people he had met briefly in Rio. He made a remark to this effect to Camilla. Her face darkened. She seemed to withdraw into herself

467

suddenly, eyes filled with remembered pain, the origins of which she did not communicate.

'The better-class Bahian families keep themselves aloof. I knew a number of them – once,' was all that she said.

'There are so many churches!' Shawn exclaimed, as they bowled along the well-paved streets. 'Sure now, it's even worse than Ireland! Looks as if the inhabitants do nothing but pray.'

'They are very religious,' she agreed, then added with a tired smile: 'But not all pray to Christian saints. Don't forget the *condomble*, the Voodoo ceremonies.'

'Am I likely to forget?' His green eyes switched to hers and in them she read memories of that terrible night at The Priory. 'I suppose Leila and Sam will be off to one just as soon as they can?'

'No doubt.'

'And you?' There was uneasiness in his voice, and she knew his dislike of the subject. Even though she had done her best to explain Voodoo to him, she had been unable to make him understand why it was a part of the warp and weft of her life.

'I just want to sleep and then leave for Rubera in the morning.'

The memories were more overwhelming than she had anticipated. At every corner, in every tree-shaded plaza, she thought she glimpsed André, a dandy in his white suit, gold blazing on his hands, at his wrists, his black hair crisply curling, his dark eyes seeking hers. André for whom every girl in Bahia had sighed, and yet it was to her that he had given his love for a fleeting moment, a dangerous moment that had brought about his death.

The hotel lay in the old section of the port. It had once been a convent but its former cells has been transformed into comfortable rooms for guests. Camilla had stayed there sometimes with her father, and was recognized and welcomed by the host. In his swarthy, widely smiling

468

face she read no suspicions or condemnation. He treated her as an honoured visitor and her companions too. The best the hotel could offer was placed at their disposal.

Next day Shawn was amazed at the transformation in Camilla when she appeared in the small, inward-facing courtyard for breakfast. She was wearing a man's khaki shirt tucked into fawn riding breeches ending in boots. A leather belt clasped her waist, from which hung the holster of a service revolver. A strange, pungent odour wafted from her as she took her place at the white-painted, wrought-iron table.

'It's to keep the mosquitoes at bay,' she told him, reaching for the bowl of fruit. 'A potion concocted by Leila. It seems to work. You must try some. Mosquitoes are awful pests, and make life out here a misery, particularly for strangers. I've become acclimatized to some extent.'

'I was careful to lower the nets around my bed last night,' he assured her, then grinned: 'You'll have to teach me the laws of the jungle, Camilla. Bedad, but you look the part of the Intrepid Leader of an Expedition this morning, damn me if you don't. Why the pistol? Aren't the natives friendly?' They had fallen into the habit of speaking like the heroes of boys' comic papers when they discussed the excursion into the wilds, covering the danger by jokes.

Her eyes were cool, shadowed by her broad-brimmed canvas hat. Her longer fingers held the coffee cup to her lips and she regarded him over the rim. 'It's not the natives I'm bothered about. I think we're being followed, Shawn. Have been ever since we left The Priory. Get into sensible gear after we've eaten, and arm yourself. You too, Rufus.'

'Anything you say, my dear,' he grunted, missing his morning cup of tea, staring at the coffee with dis-approval. 'You're the boss. What makes you think we're being tailed? And by whom?'

469

It was hard to explain that instinctive feeling that made her skin creep. Only someone who had spent weeks in the thick forests, miles from civilization, would have understood. No doubt he thought she was talking nonsense, for the courtyard was peaceful. The sun poured in a great beam through the open roof, as into the nave of one of the cathedrals close by, from which bells had rung out since dawn. Parakeets flew above the tiles, awakening the echoes with their screeching.

Camilla took a cigarette from her pack, lit it and considered the lawyer through the smoke haze. 'I can't tell you that yet. There were several unscrupulous men who probably knew of the log and the map. Though he was secretive about it, my father may have talked too much when he was in his cups. You don't know this part of the world, but I do. For centuries it's been the happy hunting ground of fortune-hunters, slavers, pirates, escaped convicts and ne'er-do-wells. The prospect of wealth has always drawn them like a magnet. There are gold mines, silver mines, diamond mines, a boom in rubber, besides fantastic tales of cities of gold, thousands of years old, left by civilizations who ruled long before the Incas of Peru. As I've told you, my father made several attempts to reach such a ruin, enlisted the aid of adventurers, both native and European. I'll be better able to assess the situation when we get to Rubera. Meanwhile, I advise you both to keep your eyes peeled.'

She had already hired a car and driver. He was a tall, thin, leathery-looking man who saluted them with a great sweep of his sombrero as they came from the hotel into the heat outside. Camilla took the seat beside him, with the others piled in the back with the luggage, under the tattered canvas awning. They took the road which meandered north along the coast and, at first, their spirits were high, with Shawn wanting her to enlighten him on everything they saw, but as the morning advanced and the sun climbed higher, so a hush fell over the party.

470

The road stretched ahead, a rough, swooping empty road. The dust was inches deep. Sometimes the surface was smooth, sometimes pitted and scarred and tortuous, like the bed of a stream. The driver rested his hands on the wheel, a cigarette drooping from between his lips, controlling his jerky, uncertain machine with commendable skill. Camilla lifted her wrist and consulted her watch. It was almost noon. No wonder it was so hot, the great, liquid bubble of the sun sucking all life from the earth. A wet heat, like a Turkish bath. Vapour hung over the trees and within minutes of putting on fresh clothing, they were again saturated with sweat. Camilla had forgotten the unpleasantness of living permanently in damp garments, and it was a new experience for Shawn and Rufus, who complained about it, chiding her for neglecting to warn them.

'But I did,' she protested. 'Why d'you suppose I took you shopping to the most reputable outfitters in London, who specialize in tropical kit? Aren't you glad I insisted that every single garment be made of cotton? And you'll be thankful for those high-laced boots that you're grumbling about. They'll protect you from snake-bite, and possibly stop jiggers from making homes in your feet.'

'And what are jiggers, *capitão*?' Shawn asked, leaning over the front seat and admiring the set of her shoulders outlined where the sweat had soaked into her shirt, making it cling.

'The real name is *chigoe*, but we call them jiggers. They're nasty little beasts, a sort of flea. The female buries herself under the skin and lays her eggs there. The larvae hatch and burrow in deeper, causing unpleasant sores,' Camilla answered, smiling because of the way he had addressed her. 'Only one of the nuisances that abound here.'

They had lost sight of the sea some time before, and with it any chance of a cooling breeze. The track wound

471

steadily upwards. Presently the forest thinned and Camilla drew in a sharp breath at the sight of the familiar panorama spread out below, where a brief vista of campos undulated and shimmered in the heat haze.

'God, what a place!' breathed Shawn from behind her. 'It's marvellous! Jiggers, snakes and all. What a country!'

'It was much more difficult to travel before the motor car,' she answered, mopping across her wet brow. 'It took ages on horseback, but of course we shan't be able to go much further this way. We'll make for the *estancia*, which lies beyond Rubera and, if we find Darcy's not there, we'll have to journey on foot towards the Sao Francisco River. There are no roads and not enough grazing for horses or mules. Bearers will carry our stores and guns. Once we reach the river, we can travel in canoes. We'll be going into the heart of the *sertao*.'

'The what?'

'The bush, or more accurately translated – the wilderness. I'll really have to settle down and teach you the language, Shawn.'

He sat back, filled with admiration for Camilla's pluck and knowledge but still doubting the wisdom of her mission. He prayed that Devereaux would be at the plantation. Prayed for it yet prayed against it too. She was already almost a stranger, tougher somehow, and harder too. Her eyes were shuttered against him, revealing nothing. She had reverted to the role she had once played with her father, losing any feminine softness, once more independent, shouldering the responsibility of the party. And Devereaux? What would he do when he saw her? What would he say? Would he sweep her into his arms and claim her?

Shawn stared out at the view. He could see for miles across scrub-covered plains to remote blue hills, then the road twisted around another hairpin bend, becoming an

472

aisle barred by the shadows of huge trees. Flocks of green parrots darted overhead and, from one steep wall of forest to another pairs of toucans, beaks making them top-heavy in flight, drifted across the valley. And whichever way he looked, the scene was quickly obliterated by forest, tangled, matted, a solid green wall. There was hardly any traffic, though once they passed a horseman and had the fleeting impression of white teeth grinning in a black face, a sturdy pony with a saddle-cloth of gaily dyed sheepskin. Later, they came upon a cart, high and primitive, travelling with infinite leisure behind two mules.

The road began to descend, and soon they drove down into Rubera. It proved to be no more than a huddle of adobe dwellings. The orchreous coloured walls of the tiny church that dominated the single square, cast back the sun's rays in a savage glare. Its shadow sliced the dust with an uneven scar. Vultures sat on the bell tower like bald-headed, drably clad witches, on the lookout for carrion.

Camilla and Leila climbed from the car, stiff and yawning, longing to stretch their legs, wandering over to the *posada* which was kept by an old, active woman with a hairy upper lip, who greeted them warmly. She bared her blackened teeth and smiled, welcoming them like long-lost children, asking eager questions about England, the geographical location of which was beyond her comprehension. They sat with her on the wooden verandah, drinking tepid red wine, munching bread made of cassava flour and waiting for the men who had gone inside to buy provisions, aided by the driver.

It was afternoon and no one indulged in activity. The place wore a poverty-stricken air. Its weedy alleys were littered with old bottles and rotting bananas. Illness abounded, and the populace spent most of their time drunk on potent *kachasa* spirit. Camilla's arrival caused hardly a ripple of interest, though they knew her.

Women watched them from windows, without any expression on their passive, Indian faces. The glum-looking men glanced across, squatting outside their huts, wearing dirty shirts and hats of woven palm. Dogs sprawled, panting, in the shade. Hens and pigs rooted about amongst the garbage. Small, naked, grubby children with pot bellies sidled up, staring at the newcomers with round black eyes from their solemn, round faces. Camilla fished in her pocket and produced a tin of sweets. They scurried away with this prize, and began to squabble over it like a pack of wolf cubs, shrill voices raised. One of the men looked across to snarl out a reprimand. And everywhere there was heat and sweat, dust, flies and apathy.

'A white man, you say?' The old woman wrinkled her eyes at Camilla. 'Yes, such a one passed through several weeks since.'

'He was alone?' There seemed to be a lump in Camilla's throat. Darcy! So close, ah, dear God! The blood ran hot in her veins, then fear chilled it.

'No, there were others with him. They asked about porters, and offered money, cloth and guns in exchange. Several of our men went with them, and we women mourned for we knew their destination was the Bad Lands. The tribes are savage there. They eat human flesh. We went to church and prayed.' The crone crossed herself and drew her dingy black shawl over her straggly grey hair.

I too must go to church, Camilla thought, resting her hand on Leila's shoulder as she rose. The small stone building was cool, dim and incense-fragrant. Camilla paid for two candles, lit them and carried them to the altar, placing them before the tortured figure of Christ. But it was to the Virgin that she turned – the Holy Mother who would forgive her sin, knowing her pain and heartbreak. The Virgin Mary, or was it Erzulie, the Venus of Dahomey? For long moments she knelt there

474

with bowed head and clasped hands, tears running down her face. Then she went out softly, hit by the heat which had the force of a physical blow, and found her way to a corner of the churchyard. Beneath a thorn bush, a tiny mound marked her baby's grave. André's was not there. His grief-stricken family had taken his body back to Bahia, to be laid to rest in the de Jaham mausoleum, but not far away her father had been interred. She could not bring herself to pray for him.

I should have some flowers with me, she thought, seated on the sparse grass under the tree. Poor baby, was your ghost cold in the stream? Did you cry for your mother? Perhaps the *loa* is merciful to the innocent stillborn ones and bears them in soft feathery arms to heaven. Overcome with sorrow, she stretched out across the grave, laying her face where her child's would be, in that shallow trough beneath the soil.

Leila came for her, a black shape against the dazzling sky, speaking to her gently. 'Come, Missy Camilla. It's time to go. Don't weep. Bless him, the little one. He's lucky. He'll never know the cruelty of the world. You must travel on, completing that task which fate has set you, *Si Dios Quize*. If God wills.'

Rufus and Shawn had not yet reappeared. Camilla entered the shabby, fly-blown room behind the verandah to find them. It was a wine shop and general store rolled into one. The proprietress, one of the old woman's many daughters, was a plump half-caste, brown-eyed and pregnant, seated behind a rough counter breast-feeding her youngest child. Recognizing Camilla, she gave a flashing smile and then shouted over her shoulder to the rear. A large, fat Negro waddled out, wiping his greasy hands on his sacking apron. More greetings, more handshakes. He smiled constantly, even though swamped by his large family of grubby children, his wife, his mother-in-law and several aunts, all of whom clustered around the visitors.

475

Shawn and Rufus sat with the men gathered about a table, peons in soiled white trousers, of mixed Indian, black and European blood, of the sort employed on the Ruthen plantation. Shawn waved and beckoned her over and another man rose from amongst them, a white man whom she immediately recognized as the overseer.

'How you going, Miss Camilla! All right?' he cried, advancing towards her. 'I got your letter, but I wasn't expecting you yet.'

'I managed to book an earlier passage,' she explained as he took her hand in his hard, firm one and shook it vigorously. 'What's been happening here? Did Mr Devereaux arrive?'

Ranger Hogan was an Australian who had wound up in Bahia many years before. He was whipcord lean, his skin darkly tanned, his hair bleached almost white by constant exposure to the sun. Once a whaler, his forearms were heavily tattooed. He had been one of her father's most trusted men, accompanying him on many a hazardous venture, and Camilla had left him to manage the crops, when she left for England.

'Yes, he arrived right enough.' Ranger led her to the table, shoving a couple of peons aside so that she might sit between him and Shawn. Rufus, looking slightly dazed and somewhat confused, was seated on the other side of the knife-dented boards. 'I've been telling Mr Brennan about it.'

'Drop the formality, Ranger,' the Irishman said. 'Call me Shawn.'

'Shawn it is, m'old mate,' Ranger grinned. 'You're dead right. There won't be time for formality where we're heading. Of course I insist on coming with you, and these two beauties here'll come along too.'

He jerked a thumb towards his companions. They were of Latin origin, dressed in patched clothing. One of them, introduced as Renko, was a puny, dirty little man, with heavy, slanting eyes, a long curved dagger and a

476

rakishly tilted slouch hat, whilst the other, José, was squat, bow-legged and grinned a lot, showing long, yellowish teeth. They were strangers to Camilla and she guessed that Ranger had press-ganged them into service during her absence. The overseer was of a different mould, carrying an air of command. His eyes were light blue-grey and his age was difficult to judge. The left side of his intricately seamed and wrinkled face was cleft by a deep scar, maybe a knife slash, which pulled the outer corner of his eye a little crooked, and lifted his lips into a sceptical expression. He was wearing a red plaid shirt, his battered trousers held up by a leather cord, his boots studded with nails, a large-calibre Colt dangling from a belt slung over his shoulders.

'Is Mr Devereaux at the *estancia*?' she asked, as the café owner walked about pouring maté tea from an aluminium kettle into tin mugs. Camilla produced a bottle of rum and the men added generous slurps to their measures.

'No, Miss.' The Australian shook his tousled head and grimaced. 'He's long gone into the forest. Wouldn't listen to reason. Hell bent on seeking his grave, if you ask me. As mad to find that bloody treasure as your father was. I fixed him up with guides and sent him on his way.'

'Has anything been heard of him since?' Camilla was seeing visions, knowing the terrain Darcy would be covering.

A maze of thick jungle, scrub land and impassable mountains; a climate that bred fever and a thousand and one species of hungry insect life; rivers boiling into rapids at one moment, then lying turgid, alive with alligators and carnivorous piranha fish; primitive tribes who lived in the depths of the forests, shy, savage if provoked, nervous of the whites who still took them as slaves if they could.

Ranger shook his head. 'Nothing lately, Miss. We did get a report that he'd reached the São Francisco and hired canoes, but all's been silent since. I gather that you're all set to search for him?'

'I am.' Nothing would have stopped her now.

'Then we'd better stock up and get going.' Ranger uncoiled his long limbs and hauled himself to his feet. 'Time I got back, anyway. I've been hanging around here for a couple of days, making enquiries about your friend, waiting for news of you. Nothing will've been done in the fields. The peons're a lazy bunch of wombats, left to their own devices.'

'How's Marieta?' Camilla asked, as Renko and José, under Ranger's orders, lugged the boxes of stores to the car.

'Fine, just fine. Still laughing and singing. She's a great girl,' he answered with a wide grin. 'We've got six kiddies now, you know. She had another while you were away.' Ranger lived with an Indian woman, a bright little thing, happy as a bird, surrounded by her bevy of coffee-coloured children.

Darkness had already fallen when they came to the wooden fence that surrounded the house. The mosquitoes were out in full force, whining around their heads as they made for the yellow rectangle of light at the open door beyond the verandah. Slapping them away and cursing, Camilla's heart was thudding as she climbed the wooden steps that led to her old home. For one ghastly moment she thought that the figure of a man which suddenly loomed against the light was that of her father. How often had he swayed there, drunk and aggressive, hurling abuse at her? After this vision came another. His dead face contorted with agony and terror.

Just for an instant she thought it must be Darcy, but then a voice coiled out to meet the deep blue darkness. 'Good evening, cousin,' said Selden Ruthen.

Camilla heard Shawn's angry intake of breath just behind her, felt the tension of Ranger and his men at the sight of this intruder, knew that their revolvers were

478

already halfway out of the holsters. The presence of these tough cohorts was comforting and gave her a split second to recover her senses. She was on her own ground now. Selden was the interloper.

'What the hell are you doing here?' she snapped, chin up, eyes flinty. Selden gave a light laugh, standing back from the door so that she might enter. Still that solid wall of armed manflesh at her back, Camilla stalked in like a bandit chief with his henchmen.

'After all my trouble in tracking you down, I expected a warmer welcome,' he remarked, a smile twisting his thin handsome features. 'You've put me to a deal of trouble, my dear.'

'Why did you bother?' Camilla came to rest in front of him, hands on her hips. In the smoky light of the oil lamp hanging from the ceiling she looked almost as untamed as the surroundings outside the house. Selden's blood sang with excitement.

'To look after you and help you in your quest for Devereaux.' His smile became fixed, and his grey eyes flashed to Ranger and his scowling men.

'But I don't understand. How? Why?' Camilla eased further into the room and, taking their cue from her, the men positioned themselves at vantage points, one against the door, the others at the walls, never taking their eyes from Selden.

'My dear girl, did you really think I'd permit you to escape me? I heard that you were going to Brazil. I also heard a rumour of treasure. If there's gold to be had in this god-forgotten country, then I want a slice of the pie.'

'And how did you learn of this?'

'My informant was a man called Gibbs. He came to the village, did he not? Lingered in the Red Lion, ran into my man, Jenkins. The rest was easy. A couple of bottles, and he was telling him his life story.'

That's why Selden's activity had died down, thought Shawn, watching the man as one might watch a

479

dangerous snake. He was too busy preparing to steal a march on us. But he's put himself at a disadvantage. I could kill him out in the forest and no one would be any the wiser. I'd have no compunction about doing it either, any more than I would at squashing an obnoxious bug. Why can't he leave Camilla alone?

'You should've come to The Priory and discussed the matter with me, Selden,' Camilla said, thinking: So I was right. It must have been one of his men who had been ordered to follow me.

She seated herself in one of the basketwork chairs and allowed the atmosphere of the house to penetrate her consciousness. It was in much better shape than when she left it. Ranger had obviously set the peons to work. It had been repaired and decorated. Old Gomez and his wife had taken their duties as caretakers seriously, but some things never changed. Despite the trellis of fine gauze wire placed at the windows, clouds of mosquitoes and furry moths circled around the lamp.

'Would you have let me in? I suspect not.' Selden sank himself into the chair opposite her, and nodded towards Shawn and Rufus. 'I see that you've brought your faithful watchdogs with you.'

She ignored this thrust, calmly taking a cigarette from his case. His lighter flared momentarily. She drew the soothing smoke back into her lungs. 'So you decided to act alone. Coming here without being invited.' She was wondering if Gibbs had also told him about her father and Maisie Hughes.

'I left before you, arriving in Rio a couple of weeks ago. I was fortunate to meet up with a certain Dominican missionary, Friar Johnson. Nice fellow, talked a lot about Harrogate, where he hails from. Seemed delighted to help a fellow Englishman. He works amongst the Indians.' While Selden talked and smoked, seemingly at ease, this was given the lie by a nervous tightening of his jaw. 'Naturally, I'd brought along a few stout chaps of my own, Captain Martingale amongst them.'

'Ah, your tame spy!' put in Shawn, unable to contain himself any longer.

'I prefer to think of him as my agent in foreign parts,' Selden replied coldly, shooting him a look of pure venom. 'To continue: Friar Johnson was kind enough to suggest that we travelled with him. He took us to his mission. We rested for a while, then I received word that you'd landed in Rio. I thought you'd like to see a friendly face on your arrival, so I didn't delay. Saddled up and rode here. Your overseer was away, but the caretaker let me in, made me very welcome when I told him that I was your cousin, and accepted the little handout I gave him with touching gratitude. Money talks, the world over, doesn't it, my dear?'

He was managing to undermine her faith in her servants, hinting that he could buy the whole lot of them, if he desired, and have them eating out of the palm of his hand, stripping away her authority. Just for a moment, this ploy succeeded and she began to wonder if Ranger was implicated and if Selden had bought the silence of the villagers in the *posada*. Then she remembered that no one would have taken any notice of a stranger accompanied by a missionary, probably thinking that he was another priest.

She stood up suddenly, pushing aside the chair. 'I want you to leave, Selden. I'll provide an escort to Bahia. It will be wise to do as I suggest.'

He lounged back, his legs in their beautifully tailored riding breeches stretched out before him. 'I've no intention of doing that. Don't let us argue about it, Camilla. I'm here, and here I'm going to stay. When you leave to find Devereaux, I shall accompany you.'

'If the gentleman's so keen, then I suggest you let him come, Miss.' Ranger was looking at Selden with a peculiar smile on his scarred countenance, and in his

481

eyes she read his thoughts. This soft, indulged English milord should be permitted to taste the secretive fury of the tropical forests. There he would either win his spurs or die.

She nodded her head. 'So be it. We leave at first light, Selden. But there's one thing I must make clear. I lead the expedition. You'll take orders from me and from Ranger. You'll do as we say immediately and without question. If you fall behind, we'll try to help you, but not at the risk of the whole party. D'you understand?'

Shawn, listening to her and watching her face, smiled inwardly. He knew next to nothing about it but could hazard a guess at the rigours of the campaign on which they were about to embark. Selden was a fool, a conceited, vainglorious fool who'd soon find that his cunning, lack of integrity and reliance on wealth would stand for nought when face to face with the wildness of nature that awaited them along the trail.

Later that night Camilla undressed in the room that had been hers for so much of her life. It was beautifully equipped with goods purchased in Bahia by her mother who had used her innate sense of fitness and good taste to enhance her daughter's surroundings. It was the chamber of a well-born Creole lady, the solid mahogany furniture heavily carved and ornate following the style popular in France in the last century during the reign of the Bourgeois King, Louis-Philippe.

Leila was there, unpacking a few items. Camilla sensed that she was not very happy, and this surprised her, for she had imagined she would be overjoyed to be home. Thinking about it, she realized that she had been unusually subdued throughout the voyage. Sam, however, had taken on a new lease of life. They had lost him temporarily in Rubera when he had run off to meet some of his erstwhile companions, impressing them with stories of his exploits in England.

It was like taking a journey back into the past as

482

Camilla sat on the brocaded stool before her dressing-table and Leila began to brush her hair. The continual song of the chicadas, the hum of the mosquitoes flinging themselves against the mesh, the cry of a nocturnal bird, lulled her, banishing temporarily the apprehension occasioned by Selden's appearance in their midst.

'He had to come, Missy Camilla.' Leila picked up on her thoughts. 'Fate willed it. Three men want you, but only one will succeed.'

'Darcy?' The words leaped to Camilla's lips. 'I must find him, Leila. He'll be far ahead by this time, if he's survived.'

'Why don't you take a look in the crystal, missy? It may show you what's become of him.'

'No, I won't do that, any more than I would ever agree to help my father find the ruins by this means, though he asked me, sceptic that he was. You know very well that one shouldn't use it to profit oneself, don't you? I'll leave it here with you.' She glanced away from the mirror, suddenly afraid that it might take the place of the scrying-glass, showing her visions that she was unwilling to see.

Leila did not answer, her eyes veiled. The oil lamp purred and moths committed suicide at its golden bowl. Behind them, the vast high bed waited, shrouded in a pall of netting. 'Tomorrow night you'll not sleep so soft,' she commented after a pause. 'A hammock slung beneath a tree, eh, missy? I'll spend my time performing ceremonies for your safe return. Demons await you in the jungle. Watch out for the dreaded, flesh-eating ghoul who walks with his feet turned backwards. He has slavering jaws and great big teeth. Take no heed of the singing enchantress who appears as a beautiful woman in distress. She's a terrible monster who'll lure you to your death.'

Camilla shivered, the fears of childhood returning. Leila had often recounted tales of these dreadful denizens of the forests. She tried to tell herself that danger was more likely to lie with poisonous insects, or anacondas able to crush bones like match-sticks in their tight, constricting coils. Even more dangerous than all these would be Selden. She was certain that he had come there either to seduce or to murder her. The latter seemed the most likely for, even if Darcy no longer lived, there was no way she would ever marry her cousin. Wed her or get rid of her he must, if he was ever to be sure of possessing The Priory.

I can't really be here! Suddenly the room seemed to be closing in on Camilla. All evening she had held the dread at arm's length, but now everywhere she looked she saw her father. 'I should never have come back!' she cried, impatiently escaping Leila's ministrations and pacing up and down over the teak floor, her white nightgown billowing about her. 'I killed him, Leila! I killed him – here – in this house! I never wanted to see it again!'

Leila straightened her wide shoulders, looked at her for a long moment and then spoke so solemnly that Camilla paused to listen. 'You didn't kill him, missy. I did.'

'You, Leila?' Camilla stood stock-still, her hand at her throat. 'What are you saying? I asked you to perform a death-rite. Didn't you do so?'

Leila's eyes were filled with an immeasurable love as she stared at the girl whom she prized above all else. 'Yes, I did, missy, but on my own account, not yours.'

'What d'you mean? Tell me, Leila. What did you do?'

To her astonishment, the Creole went down on her knees before her, head flung back, the gold hoops of the *mambo* glittering against the purple shadows of her hair. 'Oh, *ma pauvre petite*, my baby! I knew you wanted him dead but I wouldn't endanger your soul in the doing of it. A death-wish can be fatal to the sender if it doesn't reach its target. Like a boomerang, it'll fly straight back.'

Camilla could not bear the sight of that bowed,

kneeling figure. It was not like Leila to be humble. She raised her to her feet, held her in her arms, said: 'So you risked damnation for me. Oh, Leila!'

The *mambo* freed herself, standing with all the quiet, tragic dignity of her race. 'Not for you alone, *ma belle*, for me – and for Samuel. Listen, and try not to be angry. Remember that I was a young woman when Edgar Ruthen married your mother – a woman filled with lust and dreams and longing. Ah, if you could have only seen him then! He was like Mr Darcy – just as handsome, every bit as manly. They're too alike. That's why I tried to stop you.'

Pale beneath her tan, sensing what Leila was about to confess, Camilla took her hands. 'Tell me. I promise not to be angry.'

'I loved your father.' In the dark-skinned face there gleamed a ghost of that long-dead passion. 'Can you imagine my anguish? I was devoted to Missy Hélène. I would've died for her and yet I let her husband, my master, make love to me. That's how low I'd sunk. I done bore him a boy-child.'

'Samuel?' Camilla's lips formed the word almost soundlessly.

'Samuel,' Leila nodded. 'Your Pa, he was furious. He hated the blacks, you see, but couldn't leave their women alone. "Black flesh," he used to say. "Black satin, perfumed as no white woman's ever is – fragrant with spices and oils, steeped in the mystery of Africa."'

'My God! Did my mother know?'

'Ah, no! Never!' Leila cried. 'I couldn't wound her so. It would've killed her. She adored him. I told her that I'd been playing around with several men and didn't know which one to blame.'

'But *he* knew.' Was there no end to his iniquities? Camilla wondered. It will be as well if the strain dies out. I should remain childless. The Ruthen blood is rotten and corrupt.

'Yes, and he hated me for it – hated the child even more. It shamed him to have a nigger son. Shamed him so bad that he tried to kill him. That's how Sam got crippled. Ruthen ran him down when he was riding one day, let his brute of a stallion trample and kick him. I prayed to Mâitresse Erzulie, and she done saved him. It was a miracle and he lived, but it left his body twisted.'

Camilla clapped her hands to her ears, shaking her head from side to side. 'Don't! I can't bear any more! Would that anyone had fathered me save him! You were right to kill him. No one could condemn you for it! How was it that you waited so long?'

Leila passed a hand over her eyes. 'There are some men who command love even though they're evil. I couldn't free myself from his spell, not till he drove my poor mistress to her grave and then turned his wickedness on you. When you lost your baby I swore that I'd be revenged. My love had turned to hate, and that sure is a mighty powerful force, missy. You asked me to kill him by magic. I did just that.'

'How?' Camilla was remembering that night when the drums had beat out of the darkness and she had stood for hours listening, praying to the *loa*.

'I knew there was something that he feared – something he'd done that haunted him. Sometimes, when we'd spent nights together, he'd wake up, sweating, crying out, wringing his hands as if to wash 'em clean of blood. He never told me what it was, but at the height of the death-rite, I called that dreadful thing to him here – out of the past, out of its grave – made him look at it. The strain was too much for his heart.'

'Maisie Hughes!' Camilla gasped.

'I didn't know who it was, but when we reached The Priory, I started in to thinking that it was her *duende* that had reached across the sea to scare her killer so bad that he died.'

'Justice. It was the hand of justice.'

486

'That's right, Missy Camilla. Justice, which we *mambos* and *hungans* are sometimes given the power to use.' Leila looked incredibly tired and yet the fire smouldering in her fixed and steady gaze was like a resin torch. 'The white man, he came to our homeland, wrenched us from it, made us slaves to satisfy his greed. We were tortured and humiliated, but we waited, knowing that he would reap as he had sown. The gods revealed the future to some of us. I've heard the wise men speak of it. I've seen it. Done it. We've used our wisdom to bring about his downfall. We've seduced him with our music, potent magic that he don't understand, only hearing the rhythm, deaf to its deeper meaning. We'll seduce him even more in the years to come – with music that he'll try to copy – with our herbs that he'll crave for, using them for pleasure, not to open his mind to wisdom. Oh, yes, Missy Camilla, through the cunning of the blacks he despises, the white man'll grow weak, sick, helpless, then our people will rise and come into their own.'

187

4

Darcy woke abruptly at the sound of yells. With the web of broken sleep still binding him, he could almost feel curare-tipped arrows tearing into his flesh. He rolled out of his hammock and reached for his gun.

'*Mein Gott!* What was that?' A kerosene lamp flared up, and in its sickly light he saw the scared face of Schultz, the German doctor who had accompanied him into the interior.

Everyone was awake now, including Medina, that sleepy-eyed, rather effeminate young botanist from Chile who, with his specimen jars and butterfly nets, had also attached himself to the expedition. The half dozen natives of mixed blood, engaged as bearers, were chattering and gesticulating. They were so frightened that the whites of their popping eyes showed up clearly in the gloom, while the dogs barked, darted into the bushes, and generally added to the uproar.

'Where's Manoel?' Darcy shot the question at them whilst strapping on his pistol and checking the magazine to make sure it was full. The headman of this gang of amiable, idle and wildly superstitious porters was missing.

Round eyes regarded him. Dark heads shook. No one knew. It was nearly dawn. The weird wailing of a bird shocked through the misty air. The monkeys joined in, heralding the day. The canoes had been drawn up on a sandbank for the night, their occupants camping on the soggy ground. Now there came the sounds of loud splashing, and a bedraggled figure hauled itself out of the water. Darcy was still trying to force his swollen, ulcerated feet into his boots when Manoel appeared.

'I'm sorry, *capitão*,' he moaned, his filthy trousers and shirt clinging to his bony body. 'I slung my hammock in that tree, by mistake, never realizing that it was a Palo Santo. Legions of black ants crawled along the ropes and covered me as I slept. Eating me alive they were!'

His friends began to laugh, tension cracking in the relief of knowing that they were not being attacked by savages. They poked fun at him for preferring instant death by piranhas, instead of providing fodder for vicious fire-ants.

Darcy watched them gloomily as they stirred the smouldering logs and prepared a meagre breakfast of maggoty tapir meat. Groaning and complaining, Schultz and Medina were struggling into their damp clothing and lacing up their boots. The netting was removed from the hammocks and the flies shaken out. The daytime mosquitoes took over from the noctural variety, equally persistent and ravenous. This damned, fever-haunted, plague-shot country! he thought savagely. Would to God that I'd never set foot in it!

But, like a reproof, the firelight shot across the ring which glistened on his finger. He crouched there, staring at it, and knew that whatever happened he would never turn back. The place fascinated him and lured him on. He had gleaned much during his short stay in Bahia, stories that corroborated the evidence of the logbook, and others connected with various parts of South America; the *Cidade Encantada*, or Enchanted City, said to draw one on and on, until it vanished like a mirage; the *Aldeida de Fogo*, the Fire City, so named because it was supposed to be roofed in gold. Darcy was ready to believe almost anything.

Searching for men to go with him, he had strayed into many shady areas of the port where, seated in sleazy wine shops, rubbing elbows with adventurers, gold prospectors, the dregs of many nations, he had become even more convinced that marvellous treasures lay in the depths of those secretive forests. It had not been hard to muster men, though the delays, the inevitable *mananas* of the country, had caused him fearful frustration.

Driven on by his obsession, he had hardly thought of England, though sometimes, when waking in some flea-infested village shack on the way to the river, he had lain for a few moments dreaming of the incredibly secure lanes of Abbey Sutton, its temperate climate, the rolling vistas of green hills dotted with sheep. And Camilla? He had not forgotten her, but could feel little but impatience because she had not sunk her fortune into finding her father's City of Gold. Occasionally, when the going had become particularly bad, when he was tormented by ticks and flies and his feet were rotting within his wet boots, he would wonder if he should give up and return to sheltered Chalk Farm, but something told him that thoughts of this wild place would give him no rest. With all its pests and diseases, its misery and discomfort, it would haunt him, disturbing his peace and calling him back.

He had set out with such high hopes, finding Rubera, arriving at the Estancia Esperança. There Ranger Hogan had accepted that he was Camilla Ruthen's fiancé and, whilst trying to dissuade him, had eventually given him all the help he could. From this tough, travel-scarred veteran, he had learned a great deal. Many an evening was spent over glasses of maize beer as the hours ticked by and, to the never-ending accompaniment of the ubiquitous mosquitoes, Ranger recounted his experiences under the command of Edgar Ruthen.

'And you never found the city?' Darcy would ask again and again.

'Not a glimpse of the bitch, though out there the mind becomes sort of open to any kind of imagining, especially if you adopt the old Indian habit of chewing on a wad of coca leaves and lime,' Hogan would reply, lolling in a cane chair, observing the eager Englishman with a shrewd and cynical eye through the fog of tobacco smoke intended to keep the bugs at bay. 'Christ above! You should hear some of the bloody tales! F'rinstance, there's supposed to be a tribe of white Indians with red hair and blue eyes, big buggers who wear kind of old-fashioned European clothes. And another wild lot, called Moregos – the Bat people, reputed to be barbarous savages, hairy ape-men who live in holes in the ground and only come out at night.'

'D'you believe this?'

With a lift of his sinewy shoulders, Ranger would always reply: 'I believe anything can happen in that goddamn poisonous hell,' then go on to add stories of his own to supplement this. 'I know for a fact that the yarns about the size of anacondas are true. I shot one once that was sixty foot long. And I've seen animals unknown to zoologists. The *milta*, for example, a black cat about as big as a foxhound. The natives swear there're enormous beasts that they've sometimes disturbed in the swamps – sort of primeval monsters who leave huge tracks.'

Hearsay? Superstition? If anything such talk had only served to inspire Darcy more, and once he had entered the enormous expanse of wilderness, he had accepted that it contained a reality in which all things were possible, no matter how far-fetched and extreme. The atmosphere was hostile and threatening, the brooding forest jealously guarding its secrets. He knew now that Camilla had been speaking the truth when she tried to warn him.

After a gruelling trek overland, they had reached the river and bought canoes from the half-starved peons who scraped a living on its banks, mostly runaways escaping from the brutality of the plantations. After this they paddled for days, following its meandering course through the silent curtains of dripping trees and lianas. It was a sluggish river full of death which, with little warning, could be transformed into a series of rushing,

491

perilous rapids when disaster was only averted by the skill of their boatmen. As it was they soon lost one canoe containing valuable stores and medical supplies.

As far as Darcy could ascertain, they were heading in the direction given by the map, which was becoming ever more tattered and dog-eared. He kept it close to him and would not let anyone else take a single glance at it. Food was getting short. Any game seemed to have vanished from the swampy landscape, and they were glad to bag a monkey for the pot. The bearers said that alligator meat was good, but these slumberous beasts who lay loglike on the sandbanks were maddeningly elusive, sliding effortlessly into the water if disturbed, making it hard to shoot them. So far there had been unmistakable signs of forest Indians but they had not sighted any. Manoel and his gang were glad of this, declaring that they were cannibals.

Day had followed day, filled with river and forest, all monotonously alike, apart from a variation of weather. Hot sometimes, with that soggy, humid dampness that penetrated the very marrow and sprouted mould on everything, be it human or otherwise, then enveloped by a low, dripping ceiling of cloud. In such a climate the insect and reptile population proliferated – hungry, omnipresent. The dogs never stopped scratching. Bald patches appeared on their hides. They foraged, acted as guards, warned of the nests of large wasps that inhabited boles of trees and attacked without provocation.

Schultz proved his mettle. It was not his first expedition. He was keen to find a disused diamond mine, reputed to have once been worked by slaves for the conquistadors. He was planning to open up and exploit it. Medina, on the other hand, was what Darcy described as a pain in the arse. He had started out as a neat, enthusiastic young man, very keen on ornithology, but once on the trail, he had lapsed into anxious silence, appalled when he discovered his skin to be invaded by ticks, the bites of which became badly infected. Unfortunately, he seemed to attract these troublesome pests more than any other member of the party.

Fired by reading the books of Alexander von Humbolt, the early nineteenth century naturalist who had spent years in the jungle for the sake of science and lived to the ripe old age of eighty-nine, Medina had almost begged Darcy to take him along. However, his head spinning with dreams in which he discovered some hitherto unknown bird and having really no notion of what lay in store, he had neglected to bring much in the way of a change of clothing. What with his suppurating sores and garments reeking of sweat, fever and fear, he became an object of detestation. Tempers were short in the narrow canoes. Annoying habits became exaggerated. It did not need much to ignite an already explosive situation. Darcy calmed his nerves by following Ranger's advice regarding the coca leaves. It dulled pain and disappointment, mitigated hardship and gave him added stamina.

'We derive medical cocaine from it,' remarked Schultz. 'Don't overdo it, my friend. It'll drive you crazy.'

Long ago they had left behind the scattered homesteads in which a few settlers eked out a wretched existence. Heads were shaken when it became known that they were intending to penetrate even deeper into the forests. The locals said that few ever returned and if they did, they never recovered, driven stark, staring mad. The going became harder, and there were fresh tracks of Indians on the sandbanks. Then one morning, as he stood in the prow of the leading canoe as it rounded a bend, Darcy saw a large encampment.

In an instant there was pandemonium. Women shrieked and snatched up their children, fleeing for the bush. The men pounced on their bows and arrows and made for their canoes, shoving them into the river.

Arrows winged towards Darcy. They struck the canoe in a shower. He picked up his rifle and began firing. Several Indians fell backwards into the water. It immediately began to boil, a shoal of piranhas attracted by the scent of blood, homing in for the kill.

'Oh, God! God! We're going to die!' bleated Medina, crouching at the bottom of the boat.

'Get up, man! Where's your gun?' Darcy aimed a kick at him and fired again into the war-canoes which, undeterred, were advancing steadily towards them.

He caught a glimpse of brown skins dyed in patterns of red and ochre, of glossy coal-black hair cut low, pudding-basin style, over foreheads and the tops of ears, of lips distended by discs and noses through which quills had been thrust. The boat-crew were panicking.

'They're Kalapalos braves!' they babbled. 'We're already dead meat! We'll fill their cooking-pots tonight!'

Darcy issued brisk orders to Manoel and their craft were poled fast on to a sandbar on the opposite bank. He and Schultz leaped out, followed by the gibbering bearers. He ducked down behind the cover of the beached canoes and took aim while arrows smacked into the ground all around him. It was then that the miracle happened. Darcy saw someone coming out of a clearing to his right, a tall, fair, slender figure that walked down to the edge of the bank, facing the Kalapalos and addressing them in a tongue which they obviously understood. The barrage of arrows ceased abruptly. The attitude of the braves changed dramatically. They stared, then answered. They waved their bows in greeting. They threw their arms in the air, grinning with delight.

'Tell your men not to fire, whatever they do,' Camilla ordered Darcy over her shoulder, never taking her eyes from the war-canoes which now skimmed across to run aground.

Almost paralysed with astonishment, Darcy issued

the order, watching as the leader of the warriors leaped ashore and, going straight up to Camilla, touched her lightly on each shoulder. She smiled in return and presented him with her canvas hat. This evidently pleased him greatly. Speaking their language fluently, she gestured towards Darcy's party and presently she beckoned them over.

'*Himmel!* A woman! I can't believe it,' muttered Schultz, his eyes goggling behind his thick-rimmed spectacles, sweating face astounded.

'That is no ordinary woman,' Darcy assured him, suddenly realizing that indeed it was not.

'Allow me to introduce you,' Camilla glanced at him calmly, though in reality she could hardly control the shaking of her limbs. Facing warlike Indians was nothing in comparison to looking into his eyes again after so many months. 'This is Queiroz, the chief of the tribe, a friend of mine.'

Darcy found himself staring down into an intelligent, good-looking face. Queiroz grinned. He brandished his bow which was a full six foot in length. His high-cheekboned countenance was painted in square patterns with berry juice, and he wore a shirt of woven grass with a design worked on it in purple dye. Quills, from which dangled bird-of-paradise feathers, transfixed his ears. Some of his warriors wore long dark robes, whilst others were completely naked. Their muscular skin was smooth as burnished copper and they had little facial or body hair.

There was much laughter and chattering amongst the braves as they all piled back into the canoes. 'Where are your boats?' Darcy asked Camilla.

'A little further downstream. I made better time than you, taking one of the river's tributaries. Don't forget, I know the terrain,' she answered. 'I suggest that you get aboard your own craft. It will be expected that we visit their encampment. They'll be offended if we don't, and

495

the situation is already dodgy as you shot some of their warriors. Make sure your men leave the women alone and keep their opinions of Indians to themselves. These are fine people. They have their own codes, their own rules and morals, far more intelligent than the average white man likes to believe. And they have cause to hate him. He's done his best to enslave them and drive them from their lands. Do as I tell you, and you won't be harmed.'

Their position was indeed delicate. Horrified, she had heard the sound of gunfire as her canoes approached the camp. She guessed that it would be Darcy's group, and doubted that he fully understood the peril in which such action would place them. Hating the indiscriminate use of firearms, she had already had much trouble about this with Selden's men, and bitterly regretted allowing him to bring along Martingale, an insolent negro, called Pedro, and two loud-mouthed, excitable mercenary soldiers. They were always blasting away at anything that moved, wasting precious ammunition and likely to scare off more game than they caught. Worse still, it had alarmed the wary Indians. Ever since they reached the river, she had been aware that braves were in the vicinity, watching these invaders of their privacy, though keeping well hidden.

If Darcy thought himself immune to further surprises, he was mistaken. From out of the bush now emerged someone who he would never have imagined seeing in such a spot and at such a time. 'Selden Ruthen!' he exclaimed on a note of wonder. 'I must be dreaming!'

'No dream, Devereaux, old chap.' Selden still retained a little of his swagger but most of it had vanished under the strain of travelling for weeks in the most difficult conditions, urged on by the indomitable Camilla.

Still in that state of disbelief, Darcy caught sight of Ranger and then Shawn, followed by two ruffians who looked exactly like Mexican bandits. The sensation of dreaming was exaggerated further when Rufus Godwin marched through the trees, suntanned, booted and carrying a Winchester rifle. His grizzled hair hung down beneath a pith-helmet. All the men were bearded, giving them an entirely new aspect. Working with the top half of his mind, Darcy collected his own dazed troops and was soon standing on the far shore. The waiting members of the Kalapalos gathered around, examining their clothing and baggage, curious, lively, seeming to find everything amusing. It appeared they all knew and trusted Camilla. She walked amongst them as if they were her own kin, patting a child here, stroking the cheek of a woman there, pausing to admire a new baby who clung, bare and brown, to the breast of a young mother who was sharing the bounty of her milk with a tiny piglet taking its fill at her other nipple.

Camilla's like a pagan queen! thought Darcy, thunderstruck. She loves these savages! It flows from her in a warm, vibrant tide. By God, I don't think it would take much to make her go native. He had heard it said in Bahia that it was usually the most educated and sensitive amongst the Europeans who decided to throw away the ties of civilization and live amongst the tribes, finding peace and contentment in a simple life spent close to nature. Camilla, standing in the middle of a circle of well-constructed huts of wood and palm, seemed entirely in her element. Not so Selden. Never had a man looked more out of place. The sight of that arrogant aristocrat brought down a peg or two afforded Darcy an ignoble satisfaction.

Serve the crafty devil right! What the hell was he doing in Brazil anyway? And Christ, wasn't the shifty figure beside him that nasty piece of work, Martingale? There was another man with them, black as the ace of spades, followed by two scurvy-looking characters, bristling with weapons and giving the Indians nasty looks. Trust Selden to fall in with cut-throats and employ them as his bodyguards!

Preparations for a feast were put into operation, the women running about filling cooking-pots with chunks of meat and fish, merry, talking ceaselessly, peeping at the strangers shyly with wide glistening eyes. Whilst this was happening, the chief led them to the largest hut of all, used as a general meeting place. Camilla squatted down in the dusky, smelly interior and gave him cigarettes. She indicated that the rest of them should also sit and politely exchange gifts with Queiroz. The hut entrace became blocked by small children and inquisitive adults. Pottery was produced and wickerwork baskets, blowpipes, cudgels and stone hatchets.

'What have you brought that you can give them in exchange?' Camilla asked, seated close to Darcy, now daring to glance at his lean, bearded profile. He looked ill. His skin was of an unhealthy yellowish tinge, scabbed with insect bites. His face was sunken and cadaverous, his body dangerously thin. His companions looked in no better shape. It seemed that she had found him in the nick of time, Indians or no Indians. The relentless jungle was taking its toll.

He opened his pack and spread out the contents. There was not much to give. Although they had left the *estancia* well equipped, it had not been long before the burden of carrying baggage through the bush had made them throw away anything not strictly necessary. What remained had been sacrificied to those river-demons who had made their presence felt by lowering skies and downpours of rain. He gave Queiroz a Swiss army knife which seemed to gratify him enormously, especially when all the hundred and one little gadgets were revealed. He still possessed a folding shaving-mirror and this was presented to one of the chief's wives. Camilla, forewarned, had brought along several yards of red cotton cloth, knowing how much this was prized by the

498

Kalapalos. In return she was given a shell necklace which she promptly hung around her neck.

Schultz was now introduced to her and, digging back into the mists of memory, he unearthed a few fragments of long-forgotten Prussian manners. 'Lady Camilla,' he said, clicking the heels of his nearly disintegrated boots. 'Charmed to meet you, most charmed. I'm a doctor, you know. I understand that the Indians have many cures for ailments which they cull from plants. I'd like to learn about these. Our friend here, is in a bad way, poor fellow.'

She insisted on examining Medina's sores, enlisting Queiroz's aid. While the incredulous doctor looked on, the chief made a curious chirruping. In response, the whitish head of a grub issued from the largest, most painful boil on Medina's back. Queiroz pounced upon it, gave a quick squeeze and ejected it.

'This must be done to every one of them,' Camilla explained solemnly. 'If you kill them under the surface, you get blood poisoning. Tobacco juice sometimes helps.'

'Your party seems in pretty good fettle.' Schultz was still watching with wonder as she proceeded to cleanse the botanist of parasites. 'How have you done it?'

She looked up, brushing aside a lock of hair that had escaped from the thong with which she had bound it. 'I was born here, Doctor. I was reared by a very wise woman, a *mambo* who also knows the secrets of the herbs. I spent many months in the *sertao* with my father. I've lived amongst the Indians. When food gets short, I know which grubs to eat and which to leave alone. They're nourishing and contain fat, but they do have a rather soapy taste. And I use the natural antidotes for sickness.'

The meal was set on the floor and the tribe gathered around. The women carried in calabashes containing liquor made from fermented cassava roots. Camilla warned that this should be treated with respect as it was

199

highly intoxicating, and threw Martingale and Pedro a meaningful look. She trusted Selden's followers about as much as she trusted him. It was a relief to see that the French mercenaries had put away their weapons.

An atmosphere of conviviality prevailed. The Indians seemed to have forgiven them for the deaths of several warriors, and the female dependents of these had stopped wailing. Manoel and the porters gorged themselves, suspecting that his might be their last square meal for some time. Soon José and Renco were dead drunk, snoring on the earth. Ranger, after glancing over at them watchfully for they were his responsibility, sank on his hunkers teaching some of the boys to roll dice, with colourful beads as the stakes of play. The chief relaxed with his guests. He produced a leather pouch and tipped out several lumps of brown substance. After crushing it, he inserted a small, hollow reed into one of his nostrils and sniffed up the powder.

He offered it to Camilla. She smiled and shook her head. 'What is it?' Darcy leaned forward, elbows resting on his knees, taking a pinch when it was his turn to do so.

'They call it *niopa*,' she answered, needing no drugs to add to the strangeness of her sensations.

How odd it was, yet how right it felt, to be sitting in the hut with Darcy, as she had done so many times with her father. A dreamlike state possessed her which arose from the odour, the darkness, the cassava brew as sweet and strong as rum. Darcy met her eyes, and there was confusion in his. He was obviously uneasy and several times she waited with baited breath, sure that he was about to speak to her of personal matters. He *must* do so, mustn't he? They'd been engaged to be married, had made love. They'd not seen each other for months. He couldn't go on treating her like a stranger, could he?

A man started to play a flute, the elders chanted. Dark fingers beat a light tattoo on taut drumskins. Leila would be at home here, she thought, while Darcy lapsed into

500

silence and her spirits took a downward plunge. She'd join in the litanies, debate with the medicine-man, and convince the tribe of her superior powers with a neat sleight of hand or two. The gods of Africa, the gods of South America, how they mingled and merged, sometimes diverging but usually running in parallel lines. Was there any foundation in the theories bandied about by geologists, mystics and men of science that once, aeons ago, the two great continents were linked by a huge landmass that disappeared beneath the Atlantic Ocean during some cosmic upheaval? It seemed an answer. Old wisdoms rising out of mutual dark forests. Those of Voodoo would not seem strange to the Indians.

She had dwelt much on Leila's revelation at the *estancia*. Relief had been uppermost. No longer did she carry that terrible burden of guilt. To discover that Sam was her half-brother had made her feel good. It was merely an extension of the closeness she had always felt towards him. Now examining the situation with hindsight, she saw that it formed a pattern, interwoven and mysterious, but unmistakable. Leila and Maisie Hughes had both been Ruthen's mistresses. If my father hadn't met Maisie, neither Sam nor I would've been born, she thought. He wouldn't have gone to Haiti, or known about the map or the ring.

'Give it back to me,' she said suddenly, turning to Darcy. Covered by the general noise she assumed that their conversation would not be overheard, and hope such a request might galvanize him into talking to her.

Under the influence of the drug, he was slowly but surely moving into the nebulous world of dreams. His eyes switched to her, and they were misted. 'What d'you mean?' he muttered.

'The ring. It's cursed. It came from a people who lived years before the Incas, and centuries before their predecessors, the Toltecs.' In her anxiety she reached out and seized his hand, turning it so that she might look

501

at the tiger's-eye. 'Let me have it and I'll throw it into the river, return it to the spirits from whom it came.'

Speaking quietly and quickly, she told him everything that had happened at The Priory. Darcy was aware of her voice, her presence, the hardness of her fingers. He listened, yet did not attend. In his mind he could see nothing but the pinnacles of that shimmering city. He shook his head, dragged his hand away, covered the ring with the other, jealous of it, possessed by it.

'No,' he snarled. 'It's mine now. Even if, as you say, I'll die of it.'

'Darcy, Darcy, give up and go home,' she pleaded, but even as she said the words she knew it was hopeless. In desperation she cried urgently, 'D'you feel nothing for me any longer?'

His eyes focused for a moment. He saw her in all her natural beauty, a brave woman who had come out to find and try to save him. He had desired her once, had planned to live with her for ever but it was as if all natural passions had become atrophied in him. Oh, there had been one or two mulatto women in Bahia who had satisfied his basic sexual urges, but since reaching the jungle he had forgotten lust, forgotten everything except the tantalizing chimera that danced before him. The news about Ruthen murdering his mistress did not shock or appal him. He accepted it as right and natural that anyone who stood in the way of achieving that mighty goal should be removed.

'You don't love me?' she said sadly. A chill wind cooled the sweat on her back, yet nothing stirred. Darcy did not love her. Her father had not loved her. They loved nothing but their vision.

'You'll help me?' He was eager now, pressing against her, willing to let her believe anything if only she would put her knowledge and resourcefulness at his disposal.

'You don't love me,' she repeated dully.

The seeds clattered in the shaman's rattle. He danced

slowly from one foot to the other, circling the crowd. The drums vibrated. In the rafters above her head tarantulas and snakes rustled.

'Then I'll go alone.' Darcy leaned back on his elbows, dreaming again. She could not reach the regions of time and space in which he now wandered.

Selden edged closer. He had been eavesdropping. 'This is exciting, Camilla. You've filled in the gaps left by old Gibbs. Why don't we go with Devereaux? We can make up a strong team between us. What a find that city would be! We'd be world-renowned and,' he continued as a pious afterthought, 'add greatly to the scanty knowledge about those prehistoric civilizations.'

All she could see in his face was greed. Ah, dear God, the poison had spread to him too! 'I'll think about it,' she replied.

'Do that, my dear girl. I'm game, if everyone else is.' He was so eager that it sickened her. His thin face gleamed with avarice, his thin hands worked together feverishly. 'If we find it and mark out the area, then we can go back to Bahia and organize a proper search. I'll put money into it. Will you?'

It was as if the hut was filled with the whispering voices of the hundred ghosts of once equally ambitious adventurers. Camilla put a hand to her head, dizzy with their incessant pressure. She rose and staggered outside the hut where the deep blue of the night was darkened here and there by the shadow of a clump of trees. The great silence was broken by the distant coughing of a jaguar, night-prowling, searching for prey. The mosquitoes whined steadily and a bullfrog croaked. Darcy was lost to her, and he was going to die. She was now forced to accept it, and acceptance brought a spiritual malady that shrivelled the life within her, like a plant that could no longer draw nourishment from arid soil.

Out of the darkness from the direction of the river came Shawn. He was there, his arms about her, letting

503

her cry against his shoulder. She cried for a long time, silently, shaking. He did not expect her to speak. He already guessed what had happened. One glance at Darcy's ravaged face and fanatical eyes had already told him all he wanted to know. There would be no marriage between him and Camilla, ever. And she was there, held close by *him*. All the tenderness of his nature welled up. He soothed her as if she was his hurt child, he caressed her as if she was his beloved wife. Yet he was afraid lest he frighten her.

'I'll go with him,' she said at last, quiet now. 'I'll take him as far as I can. My father travelled towards the hills.'

'We'll go together.' His lips were against her forehead. 'Send the others back. Medina can't take much more.'

'You go too. Why stay in this hell?'

He gave her waist a squeeze. 'It's hell all right, but a hell one sort of gets to like. You won't get rid of me so easily.'

'Selden wants to come. He overheard me talking with Darcy and now he too has become a treasure-seeker.'

'*Three men want you. Only one will succeed,*' whispered Leila's voice out of the rustling trees.

'Let him. With any luck he'll be after tumbling down a precipice and breaking his neck.' Shawn was smiling, teeth and eyes flashing in the gloom.

He, above all of them, was thriving on the hardships. He had not lost weight, had even put on a pound or two, seeming bigger, more robust than ever, with his unruly chestnut hair curling about his neck and a splendid red-bronze beard. He looked like a rascally soldier of fortune, acted like one too, loud, laughing, getting on well with the native bearers, commanding obedience through his geniality. His freebooting Irish ancestors would have been justly proud of him. A good shot, with cool nerves and an agile mind, he had found his forte, proving to be the ideal comrade to have on hand during any crisis. He was Camilla's mainstay and friend. She knew that she needed him more than she cared to admit but: I'll not fall for him on the rebound, she resolved. I don't need a man. I can stand on my own two feet.

The river was flat and oily. All they could hear was the murmuring of the forest hemming them in. Soon a chill rain began to fall steadily. All around the canoes settled a grey vapour in which confused forms reared up, took shape and then dissolved. They were many days' journey away from the Kalapalos camp. At first several warriors had accompanied them, then seeing that they were intent on entering areas where even they dared not venture, they had saluted solemnly, turned around and gone back.

Following Shawn's suggestion, Camilla had insisted that Medina return to the *estancia*. He was running a high fever and needed the expert nursing of Leila. Rufus had, so far, stood up manfully under the strain but he was old and she feared for him. She did not wish to offend him or indicate in any way that she thought he was not fit enough to continue with her, so she put him in charge of the sick man, and ordered José to guard them with his life on the way back. Queiroz consented to provide guides.

The lawyer and the Australian had struck up a firm friendship, much of it based on their mututal respect for Camilla, and on the morning that the two parties split up, he had made a request. 'Look here, Rufus, m'old mate, will you go and see that woman of mine? That'll leave me free to keep an eye on Miss Camilla. Known her since she was knee-high to a grasshopper. Always was a spunky girl. She's had her troubles, mark you, and old man Ruthen was a right bastard. Seems like she's picked another in Devereaux, if you ask me. Any road, Marieta's used to me going off, and I've told her that I've made provision for her and the kids, if I don't come back, but she may forget or be afraid to go to the bank in Bahia. You'll see to it for me, won't you, sport? Half-breed young 'uns don't stand much chance unless they've got a bit of cash behind 'em.'

Rufus had solemnly given his word that he would personally visit the bank and make quite sure that Marieta received money regularly. Ranger had slapped him on the back and pronounced him to be a stout fellow, then jumped happily into one of Camilla's canoes.

Schultz had wanted to journey further and, as he seemed strong, experienced and well able to fend for himself, she had agreed. She entertained serious doubts as to Selden's ability to keep up, but no amount of persuasion on anyone's part had convinced him that it was unwise to try. Although he and Darcy had never had much time for one another, they had now become almost inseparable. She was astonished, thinking Darcy would have been able to see through Selden's schemes, but he was either too far gone on coca to care or filled with that feeling of more than human supremacy which the drug induced. Whatever the reason, she could not make contact with him.

Shortly after the departure of the braves, the mercenaries vanished overnight, but Camilla heaved a sigh of relief. Short of oarsmen, it became necessary for everyone to take turns with the paddles. The river carved its way through gorges, still, humid places, sometimes very wide and towering, at others narrowing so that creepers met over their heads, shutting them into an insect-filled tunnel, dark and horrible and menacing. At times the stream became so shallow that they had to get out and push, their feet quickly becoming chafed by the soggy leather of their boots. Why are we doing this? Camilla would think, as she slipped on the mud, heaving at the heavy canoes, blistering her hands. But one glance at

506

Darcy's set face would convince her that it was no use suggesting that they admit defeat and retrace their steps.

Sometimes, to ease the monotony, she would think about England, but it was an elusive memory. It seemed as if she had never left Brazil, had dreamed up London and Wessex or read about it in a book, without actually going there. Against the brown water, the green foliage, she tried to picture Alison's face but found it near impossible. She had visited her before she left, bearing gifts for the baby, flattered because they had made the tiny creature her namesake. Outside the cosy nursery snow had been falling fast, filling Cheyne Walk with fairy floss. The Thames had sparkled, concealing its filth beneath this pristine mantle – that waterway of which Britishers were so proud. It was a mere stream compared to *her* river, the mighty Amazon.

'Will you be her godmother?' Alison had asked, a mature woman now who had come into her own, full-bosomed and confident. With that affectionate intimacy of a loving relationship, she had leaned on Frank's shoulder as the three of them peeped into the white muslin-trimmed crib.

'If you'll accept a *mambo* for that role,' Camilla had replied, half jesting, half serious.

When I get back to Bahia, I'll buy my goddaughter a string of Brazilian amethysts, she decided as the canoes slipped soundlessly over the water. Strangely, it never occurred to her that she might not touch civilization again. She did not think about dying, yet death was all around her; a moment's carelessness, a fall resulting in a broken limb, an injury causing blood poisoning, the striking of a bushmaster and she would be no more. Though she had witnessed such accidents many times, it was difficult to realize her own mortality.

They went as far as they could go by river, but soon came to ravines where the rapids were fierce, the force of the current growing stronger every minute. 'We'll have

507

to leave the boats. It's too damned dangerous,' concluded Ranger. 'This is about the spot where your Daddy abandoned them on our last trip.'

As they turned a bend they saw the river hemmed in between two walls of high rock with the forest on either side. The water rushed towards them, boiling and roaring. Ranger barked an order and they quickly turned the canoes into a little creek that offered shelter from the swirling torrent. There they climbed out on to the bank near a spot where there was a slight thinning of the trees. The canoes were concealed in the scrub, then the stores were loaded into packs. Shortage of porters dictated that no one could avoid carrying a substantial bundle on his back.

'We don't need all this stuff!' Darcy spoke for the first time in hours. 'It'll slow us down.'

'Don't be ridiculous,' Camilla answered brusquely. 'Our resources are already perilously low. There's no sign of game, so we must take all we can or starve.'

'Is this the way?' He was already forging ahead, crashing through the bushes, taking no heed of what she had said.

'As far as I know.' Her anger boiled like the rapids as Shawn helped her hoist the heavy rucksack across her shoulders. 'You're the man with the map, after all.'

'But you remember it! You must! How could anyone forget such a place?' he shouted above the scolding of a disturbed family of macaws.

He's quite insane, she thought. It's no good trying to reason with him. Selden was only a few paces behind Darcy, afraid to take his eye off him lest he suddenly stumble across a shining hoard. The delirium raged in him too, so that he attempted tasks he would once have considered far beneath him, if not downright impossible. His friends at the London clubs would never have recognized in this mud-spattered, unshaven tramp, the

508

spruce financier, once absorbed in stocks, shares and property.

'I'm going up there,' Darcy pointed to the distance where the sombre green was broken by masses of white and grey. 'We don't have to follow the river any more. We can get out over the hills.'

'I hope to God we can!' muttered Ranger. 'Ruthen couldn't find a way through. You didn't come with us that time, Miss Camilla, but you must remember it. He went down with Yellow Jack out here, and I had the devil's own work getting him back to the *estancia*. Thought we were goners!'

Remember it? How could she forget, or the reason for her absence? She could tell by the set of Ranger's shoulders that he too was remembering. She'd been seven months pregnant when her father decided to try to find the city once again. How glad she'd been to see him go and how much she'd longed that he would meet with an accident en route. Clever? Oh, yes, he'd been clever. Providing himself with the perfect alibi. André had been done to death ten days after Ruthen's departure. No suspicion fell on him, and though Camilla was certain that it was his bullies who'd killed her lover, the general opinion was that the young Creole had been cudgelled and then robbed.

'We're going to get out! I know it! We're almost there. Can't you feel it in the air? Can't you smell it? Come on!' Darcy's wild shout made her aware of him, another madman following a crazy dream.

It was as well that the party was depleted, for the porters were greedy and those who had remained had made short work of their own rations and attempted to steal more. Ranger set a guard over the stores when nightfall came and they halted. A little cassava flour mixed with a small portion of condensed milk formed their supper. Hammocks were quickly slung and nets adjusted while the half-castes lit a fire. Its smoke drove away the flies that were already hovering overhead.

509

'Are you asleep, Camilla?' whispered Shawn from the shroud of his hammock placed not far from hers. He looked like a giant caterpillar in a cocoon.

'No,' she replied softly. 'I was thinking with my eyes shut.'

'Thinking of what?' He lit a cigarette and passed it under the netting to her.

'Oh, many things. Mostly of the people who inhabited these regions once upon a time.'

'The Incas?'

'Perhaps, if Incas strayed so far from their homeland, Peru. I believe there may have been a race much older than them, ruling a world beyond anything we can begin to imagine. A world capable of building long, straight causeways and massive temples. I think they must've been as skilled as the Romans, maybe even more so.' She was picturing ruins that had been found near Bahia, the proportions of which were staggering, the masonry standing after the ravages of the centuries, still intact, designed by master craftsmen.

'The conquistadors left accounts of their wanderings, didn't they?' Shawn was content, listening to the night sounds and her voice.

'They did, but they were destructive, wanting only to subjugate the land for their king, to make converts for their church. Who knows what harm they did to the surroundings in their endless search for riches?' She looked at him through the gauzy veil. 'The Indians speak of towers with stars to light them that never go out. They're terrified of such places and, according to the Kalapalos hunters there are some in this area. What d'you suppose powers these mysterious lights, Shawn? Could it be that the science of antediluvian days had advanced far beyond that which we've now reached, before it was destroyed by some almighty cataclysm? The fall of a meteorite, perhaps? In every culture

510

there're tales of a flood. Even the Christians believe this. Think of Noah and his Ark.'

Shawn's eyelids grew heavy as she continued to speculate on wonders that stretched the limits of imagination. His dreams were fitful, filled with visions of gold-covered buildings, riches beyond price, a powerful seat of government, elaborate religious ceremonies for the worship of a divine Emperor, Son of the Sun.

The escarpments proved further away than they appeared. For many days the party struggled through spongy forest and over slimy rocks thick with moss. Every step of the way was an undertaking in itself as they moved slowly forward in a perpetual dim green light. The vine-like tangles of undergrowth crept over the ground, smothered the trees and climbed towards the high-flung terraces where the sun blazed. There was not an inch of dry earth anywhere. Through a blanket of straggling leaves and matted grass their feet sank into mud with a sucking sound, and the effort to drag them out again became increasingly arduous.

The forest was claustrophobic, hot, steamy and full of insects that swarmed in clouds, stinging any portion of bare flesh, sometimes even penetrating clothing. To perform simple bodily needs was a trial, even more so for Camilla who, as the only woman amongst a party of men, was forced to seek privacy in the bushes. But, years before, she had devised ways of doing this. First, she made certain that the ground was free of ants and that no snakes lurked in the branches overhead, then she draped mosquito netting over her head and body and lowered her breeches beneath it. This kept the flies away long enough for her to relieve herself.

Her period had come upon her twice since leaving the *estancia*, but she had her own method for dealing with this inconvenience, something she had learned from the Indian women. Though from puberty to middle age they were either pregnant or nursing an infant, should they

511

have a monthly flux they were immediately segregated from the rest of the tribe for as long as it lasted. To contain the flow of blood, they made tampons from specially selected moss. Camilla had found cotton-wool more comfortable and effective, so much so that she habitually used it, scorning either cloths or the so-called sanitary-towels, which were now being widely, though discreetly, advertised in ladies' magazines.

The jungle never changes, she thought, tramping by the hour through the perpetual damp. The long beards of greyish vine hanging from every branch conveyed a weird air of menace, and the gnarled limbs of the massive trees seemed to be waiting to grab those who ventured too close. In some parts a fallen forest giant had crashed to the mud beneath it, and daylight reached down through the space made by its demise. Sometimes the density opened out to flat swampland, broken here and there by little islands, crowned with thickets of bamboo. These were vile places, a haven for snakes seeking refuge from the water.

In this accursed wilderness no animals offered themselves to the gun. Camilla thought it likely that the noise of their approach, as they beat their way through with machetes, accounted for this. The stores were no more, the last handful of oats, the final tin of sardines consumed. The bearers had lost heart. Every morning, Shawn and Ranger had to almost beat them to make them rise from the slime into which they had sunk, exhausted, the previous night. All they wanted to do was stay there and die. The dogs were long gone, sleeping to wake no more. Had there been anything of them but skin and bone Camilla would have ordered them to be cooked, but it was not worth the effort required.

The way became steeper. As far as the eye could see was a wall of massive grey rock lying amidst great avenues of forest converging towards its base. They heard the continuous sound of running water. Camilla's throat was parched and she tingled with heat, leading the frenzied search for the source, tracing it to where it gushed from high up amongst the rocks. Heedless of the others, she dropped to her knees, plunging her hands into the icy water, scooping up the drops in her palms and drinking deeply – holding her head under the torrent, eyes closed in ecstasy – letting it soak into her clothes, trickle into her boots.

Thirst assuaged, she saw that the rest were doing the same. It was the first fresh water they had come upon for some time, forced to drink from stagnant pools whose brackish contents gave them stomach cramps. She met Darcy's eyes across the fine mist flung up by the cascade. A fire smouldered in his fixed gaze.

'This is a good omen,' he gasped, hair black with water, beard glistening with it, eyelashes spiky. 'The gods smile on us. They're about to reveal their wonders.'

Camilla glanced up and around. It was dim in the gully, though the sun still shone high up on the tree-crowned tops of the escarpment. The cliffs were pitted with caves and glacial fissures. On all sides there was a wild confusion of tumbled boulders, mixed with a tangle of vegetation. Great butterflies passed across the open space. Camilla had never seen their like. They were yellowish-grey in colour, and the hind wings had dark brown tails about six inches long with spiral ends. Above the tumult of the waterfall that rushed down the sheer face of a precipice, came the clear warble of a bell-bird. She thought of Medina. He would have been enraptured by both. Had he reached the *estancia*? she wondered, sending a prayer winging to the *loa* for Rufus's protection and safety.

'We'll sleep in there tonight,' Shawn declared, making for the largest cave mouth. 'Imagine it! Firm ground strewn with dried grass! What bliss! I swear I'm getting curvature of the spine through lying in a hammock!'

Ranger's long face became even longer and he

declined, slinging his hammock between two trees. 'You won't catch me kipping in any bloody caves. They'll be full of bats.'

'Bats! Rats! I don't care.' Shawn was already exploring the possibilities.

'What are we going to do?' Camilla asked, walking over to Ranger.

'Don't know, Miss. Never came so far before, not heard of anyone else who did. That crazy idiot may be right after all and we're really on to something.' He lit a cigarette, glancing ruefully down at the meagre contents of the packet. It was his last but one.

'Even if we find the city, we don't stand much chance of living to tell the tale, do we?' Depression swamped her. Although refreshed by the water, she was hungry and weary, her feet hurt and her legs ached. The thirty pound pack she hefted felt as if it weighed a ton. I should have left Darcy to his fate, she concluded. I'm as mad as he is. I've risked the lives of the others for nothing, falling into the trap again, like I used to do with my father.

Selden was sitting with his back against a boulder, staring unseeingly before him. For miles now he had become morose and uncommunicative, and she wondered uneasily what was going on in his head. In some way, she was not quite clear how, the party had divided into three distinct factions: Selden in cahoots with Pedro and Martingale; Darcy and Schultz with Manoel and his lads; herself and Ranger leading Shawn, Renco and the natives. Each clique eyed the others warily, whilst appearing not to do so. Tempers were short-fused. There's nothing like hunger, thirst and exhaustion for stripping away the thin veneer of civilized behaviour, she thought. Couple that with greed and you've got a keg of dynamite.

Shawn tramped out of the bushes, holding something aloft triumphantly. It was a bunch of berries. They were edible but permitted of only one per person. It was better than nothing, then:

'I've found an armadillo's burrow!' shouted Manoel excitedly.

'Good, but be quiet,' grunted Ranger. 'We'll have to dig the little bugger out.'

Using machetes and their bare hands, the porters started enlarging the hole, talking in whispers. At last there came a scuffling in the earth. Manoel thrust in his arm, then rose to his knees, drawing out a black, frantically kicking thing. It was not a glorious hunting foray, but useful all the same. The beast was small, rather like an armour-plated rodent. Manoel, proud of his achievement, skinned then stewed it. The resulting broth, with small lumps of meat floating in it, tasted like chicken. But there was not enough. Camilla knew that they would have to do better than that and soon, if they were to survive.

Evening shadows filled the gorge and the noisy bird life began to still. Darcy was clambering about the rocks, seeking a way up. Even when it became too dark to see, he still refused to rest.

'Can't waste time sleeping,' he mumbled. 'Got to get on!'

A camp had been pitched by a large fissure that penetrated deeply into the rocks. The porters made a great fire of brushwood at the entrance. They huddled there miserably, frightened of ghosts, of demons, of the little vampire bats that hung, motionless, in their hundreds high against the arching cave roof.

'Don't venture in too far, *capitão*,' warned Manoel, as Darcy snatched up a burning brand and darted away into the darkness. 'And don't try to sleep on the ground without your netting. You'll wake soaked in blood – your own blood – veins tapped by those fiendish little night-things.'

'Sleep outside, Shawn, and you too, doctor. It's safer,'

Camilla said, for they were amused by the natives' fears, thinking that they exaggerated. 'I was camping with my father once near caves like these. The area was free from mosquitoes and we left off the netting. I woke in the night and saw a bat whirr down and drop on his hand, waving its wings in time with his breathing, so silent and gentle. The rhythmical movement kept him motionless as it began to lap his blood.'

Manoel shuddered. 'That's right, *senhorita*. The beating of their wings lulls a man, so that he doesn't wake until the vampire's drunk its fill. It happened to me. I couldn't move. I liked the feeling. I wanted to go on sleeping and let it have its way.'

Outside the dancing glow of the firelight the dark forest crouched, filled with the rustlings of hidden, hunting creatures. The humans trapped there crept a little closer to one another, hostility temporarily forgotten. Then Shawn guffawed, his voice awakening mocking echoes.

'Bedad, Camilla! I've read Bram Stoker's book, *Dracula*, but this is ridiculous! Vampire bats indeed! Pull the other leg, it's got bells on it!'

Schultz grinned too, though glancing above him apprehensively. 'I've heard that they attack cattle and horses, but not men.'

'Believe what you like, doctor,' she answered with that forthrightness which he admired so much. 'I've seen what I've seen.'

'All right, I'll take your advice.' Shawn sobered at her earnestness. She was wise, that one, and his laughter had been only bravado, like whistling in the dark.

'You'd not catch the Indians risking it. There's a legend about a creature, half man, half god, who has a dark blue skin. When he sees a woman who he desires, he flies quietly down, made invisible by his waving wings,' Camilla said.

'What a useful adjunct to seduction!' put in Selden

lightly, though he was watching the interplay between her and the Irishman, weighing it up, wondering how he could turn it to his own advantage.

The half-castes were nodding, familiar with the story, and Camilla continued: 'He takes her to a wonderful world of dreams and becomes her lover. When she wakes, she remembers nothing, but nine months later gives birth to a child – a child with dark blue leathery skin.'

'Well, no one's likely to make me pregnant,' said Shawn, breaking the chilly silence that had fallen. 'And if they do, I'll be after selling my story to the papers and coining in a fortune!'

Ranger, Camilla and Shawn had long since adopted a policy of taking it in turns to stay on guard, in full agreement that Selden needed watching. Darcy, for all his insanity, would hardly do anything likely to prevent Camilla from helping him. The danger would not come from him until she had outgrown her usefulness. It was Selden who might cause trouble. There was nothing reassuring in the way Pedro stared longingly at the guns and fingered the blade of his machete.

Martingale offered no real threat. Camilla almost found it in her heart to forgive him for ruining her wedding day. In every way he was temperamentally and physically unfitted for this ordeal. Only Selden's constant bullying had kept him on his feet. He had recently begun to complain of stiffness in his right leg, and there was a swelling in his groin. The fever had grown more and more severe and he was half-delirious. In the night, she would hear him groaning aloud in pain. Camilla knew that if she could only find the right herb she could make a poultice to draw out the infection but, though she had searched, it was in vain. Only poisonous plants flourished in this evil place, things with suckers and barbed leaves, flaunting lurid blossoms that stank, attracting regiments of voracious insects.

517

She took the first watch, wrapped in her poncho, rifle across her knees, seated on a boulder by the cave entrance. Shawn and the doctor were sleeping near the fire, and she could see Ranger's humpy shape as he swung in his hammock. Martingale groaned from his place on the earth. Time slipped away, and she was thinking of The Priory. That midsummer party she had given – it was if it had happened to someone else in another existence. Had she ever really worn a gown designed by Paul Poiret, and delighted in Lalique's jewellery? Had there been a time when she cared if her hair was in order, or it had mattered a jot how she looked?

Her breeches were reduced to rags, shirt too, and her boots had become instruments of torture despite the balm she rubbed into her feet. Every inch of her skin had its own particular itch – she was fly-bitten, tick-infested, in desperate need of a bath. Oh, how wonderful that would be! She closed her eyes, dreamed of hot, scented water, of perfumed soap and Leila standing by with a soft white towel.

'Camilla.' A voice broke into her reflections.

'What d'you want, Selden?' Her fingers closed over the rifle.

He came into the circle of firelight. He was smiling at her, a cunning, ingratiating smile. 'I want to talk to you. Listen, I've a plan. We're in desperate straits, aren't we?'

'Things don't look too good,' she answered cautiously.

'Right. And the more mouths there are to feed the less likely our chances, eh?'

'True.' She leaned across to poke another stick among the embers. Fire brought comfort and she never liked to let it die.

'Well, then – why don't we get rid of Darcy and Schultz? Their porters will run off once they're dead.'

'You're talking of murder.' She played for time, hearing him out.

518

He eased closer and his stench took her by the throat. 'That's right, though I prefer to look on it as mercy killing.'

'Merciful for whom? For you?' Points of light in her eyes, points of flame. They were like a cat's.

Just for an instant a bolt of fear shot through him. This woman was strange, had always been strange, from the very first moment she walked into Armitstead House. He had known instantly that she was like no one he had ever come across. He had wanted her then and he wanted her now. Secrets. He suspected that she held the key to many. Occult powers? A means to power? Why not? He would have liked to have killed her, visualized standing with her dead at his feet, those mesmeric eyes closed – her body still warm, still pliable.

The thought shocked him, pleasured him. Christ! What foul longings from the pit did this damned jungle bring to the surface of the mind? We're all monsters under the skin, he thought. In our subconscious roam vile beasts whom we loathe but who are part of us. I could eat her afterwards. Chop her up and roast those lovely limbs and satisfy another form of hunger. With her blood I would absorb her power, her knowledge.

He's dangerous. Camilla was listening to her senses, and the voice in her head was Leila's. Kill or be killed. No mercy. No hesitation. Raise the gun and shoot him now! Do it!

5

'My turn for sentry duty, I believe.' Shawn tipped his hat back from his eyes and sat up. He had not slept, but had mastered the art of relaxing every muscle, therefore even a short rest refreshed him. This was a weird place and it gave him the creeps. His senses were honed razor-keen, registering any shift in atmosphere or slightest movement. When Selden approached Camilla, warning signals flashed across Shawn's brain although his lids were closed. Now his finger coiled around the trigger of the Winchester pressed close against the length of his thigh.

With the snarl of an animal baulked of its prey, Selden rounded on him. 'Goddamn it, Brennan. I'm talking with Lady Camilla!'

'Don't try pulling rank with me!' the Irishman advised, a taut smile touching his lips. 'Out here the only commander is someone who knows exactly what he's doing. I don't think you qualify, Ruthen.'

'You're wrong! I know precisely what I'm doing.' Selden permitted himself a superior sneer but did not elaborate. Since childhood he had always liked to surround himself with an air of conspiracy which accompanied his most trivial actions. It had paid off, intriguing the gullible, women in particular.

Camilla's heart was beating normally again. The instinct to kill had gone. Tension eased out of her. It was good to know that she was not alone. 'The best thing you can do, Selden, is to get some rest. Tomorrow's bound to be taxing. If we can find a way through or climb the cliffs, there may well be grasslands on the other side. I've a feeling there'll be game about. Let's think no further than filling our bellies.'

As Selden passed her, he leaned down to whisper: 'Don't forget what I've said. I'm serious, Camilla. We should be the ones to discover the treasure. We're both Ruthens. It's our inheritance, our right. We can build an empire together, you and I.'

Camilla had lost the habit of sleeping on the hard ground and it was some time before she dropped off. Her dreams were hag-ridden, filled with voices murmuring words which she could not quite catch, and scenes of blood and destruction. She thought she saw Maisie. The girl's face was tragic, her pale lips carrying some urgent message. But what? I can't hear you, Camilla shouted in her dream. There's too much noise!

It seemed to come from all around. A loud, clear cry, rising to an unearthly shriek. Before that blood-curdling scream died away, it was jointed by a booming chorus. She opened her eyes on faint light. Pushed aside the netting that covered her. The branches close by shook as if struck by a tempest, and that roaring continued. I'm awake! She knew a rush of relief. The leaves parted on a large monkey, with a wide open mouth and inflated throat. It was a family of howlers exercising their vocal cords. They vanished before she had time to grab her gun and shoot one for breakfast.

Damn! she swore, sinking down again, and then became aware of warmth at her back. Shawn lay beside her, fast asleep. She stiffened and made to move away, but his hand came across, resting on her waist. She curled up into a ball within that encircling arm. Dawn was near. The stars went out as she watched them. A pale blue film stretched over the sky, turning pink. Shawn's chest rose and fell with the evenness of his breathing. Camilla stayed still, quietly waiting for the sun to come up over the ridge and dry the dew that lay heavily everywhere. The scene was one of rugged grandeur. Giant trees stretched up towards the escarpment. Vivid orchids swung from the branches sixty feet

521

above the ground. The waking noises of animal life increased. A bevy of parakeets rocketed out of the foliage and fluttered noisily over the clearing.

How beautiful it was! As day had passed day, and they penetrated ever deeper into the *sertao*, so the wounds had healed within Camilla. All thought, all energy had been grimly concentrated on staying alive, vendettas forgotten, hopes and ambitions too, other emotions of little consequence. Terrible, remorseless and magnificent, the jungle had welcomed her back. More jealous than the sea itself, it never let go. Few who had entered there ever left for good. You win. I've come home, she whispered. I accept your awesome domination. I'm less than nothing compared to your age-old majesty. King Forest, your daughter pays homage and loves you.

The sun was already brilliant overhead, drawing a white mist from the trees, but in the ravine the air was still cold. Camilla could hear Martingale's teeth chattering. He was stirring restlessly, feverish, muttering. 'My leg! Oh, Christ, it hurts!'

'Shut up, you damned moaner! You've done nothing but whine ever since we left Rio.' Selden, the sleepless, had his back against a rock and was lighting a cigarette, watching with his snake's eyes.

'You didn't tell me it was going to be like this, your Lordship.' Martingale never once neglected to accord Selden due respect. In plain fact, he was more terrified of displeasing his employer than he was of the jungle. Selden knew too much about him. One word in the wrong places when they got back to civilization and he would find himself clapped in jail.

'I didn't know, you bloody fool!' Selden found him a convenient whipping-boy. He liked to see him cringe. 'Pull yourself together. There's work afoot today. The turning point's been reached.'

The natives had awakened with curses and yawns. They squatted near the embers, warming their hands.

Manoel stood over them, scratching and rubbing his knuckles in his eyes. A billycan reached boiling point and this was poured over a scant supply of guaranam seeds. Pedro, with rolling eyeballs and teeth gleaming in a wolfish grin, pointed with his machete towards Selden, making sure that his master had a share.

'Leave some for the lady,' barked Ranger, who had taken the last watch so that Shawn might rest.

'What about me?' whimpered Martingale, his face grey with pain.

'Give him mine.' Camilla slid away from Shawn, suddenly aware that he was awake, embarrassed that the others might see, though she was partly concealed by a rock. 'I'll have water.'

'Probably better than this muck anyway.' Selden contemptuously tossed the contents of the tin mug on to the ground. 'I'd give a fortune for a cup of Earl Grey right now.'

'Or coffee! Ah, for some good, strong black coffee.' Schultz was kneeling by Martingale. When he opened the man's ragged trousers and removed the dressing, the abscess was revealed. It was as big and hard as a cricket ball, purple, livid, the surrounding skin inflamed and taut. Martingale cried out under the doctor's examination. 'If I only had something to use as a compress,' Schultz sighed in exasperation. 'I'll have to lance, I'm afraid, if it doesn't open soon.'

Camilla had gone over to take a look. 'I could cure it,' she said. 'But I need a herb that, as far as I know, only grows in the Putumayo.'

'He'll have to put up with it.' Selden showed not the slightest compassion. 'Or we'll just leave him here to rot.'

Darcy came out of the cave at that moment. There was such a strange look about him that all fell silent, then the porters drew away and crossed themselves. Camilla heard them muttering about the evil eye. He ignored

523

everyone but her, hurrying across the clearing with outstretched hands. Just for a moment she was transported back to Wessex. He was as he used to be when he called to take her out – his eyes alight and really seeing her, his smile warm. It was as if he was courting her all over again.

'Camilla!' He took her hands in his and lowered his voice. 'I've found a wonder in the caves. Come and see. Just you. No one else. This is for your eyes only.'

Ranger, noticing them turn towards the entrance, exchanged a glance with Shawn and gave a quiet order to break camp. The sun was gaining strength. The mists in the gully became wisps and then dissolved completely.

'What is it, Darcy? What've you found?' Camilla's fingers were linked with his. She followed him along a narrow, shale-strewn track.

She could feel him trembling. His grip was painful. He did not answer, face working, eyes like burning pits in his sockets. A fire smouldered just inside the cave, one he had lit during the night. He released her hand and picked up a flaming branch, holding it aloft.

The cavern opened out into a huge amphitheatre. The flickering light did not penetrate the gloom of its vaulted ceiling. The walls were pitted with galleries running in all directions. Darcy darted into one of these corridors. The silence was complete, apart from the continual drip of water. Then, disturbed by the light, the bats awoke, chittering, scrabbling, retreating further into the darkness. The stench of droppings, heavy with ammonia, took their breath away. Camilla clapped her hand over her nose, hating this oppressive place that filled her with foreboding, but she said nothing. Darcy was obviously in a great state of agitation and excitement. A dangerous, unpredictable frame of mind in which there was no knowing what he might do.

They passed bracken-filled holes in the rocks which

were jaguars' nests, fortunately unoccupied, and advanced more slowly through the dripping darkness. The coarse sandy path began to slope upwards and the roof lowered until they were forced to go on all fours. 'Nearly there,' panted Darcy.

Struggling along behind him, Camilla suddenly found herself emerging into a cavern that resembled a crypt. There was light, though by now Darcy's torch had died. Not much light, just a cone shining straight down from a hole far up above them. She straightened, stood there in amazement. On the face of a natural chimney at the far end, she saw two gigantic red paintings of men, raising their arms in worship of a representation of the sun. The white surface was covered with drawings of animals and human beings and symbols, captured for ever in frozen dance by a primitive artist. Heedless of the sweat drying on her face, Camilla controlled the urge to bend the knee before this masterpiece, executed hundreds, maybe thousands of years before. The red pigment looked as fresh and bright as though applied yesterday. A solemn hush permeated the place – held her in awe. This was sacred ground, where rituals to ensure good hunting were once carried out, where the souls of the dead would have been appeased and the gods propitiated.

'Proof, Camilla!' Darcy's head was thrown back as he looked at the natural canvas with rapturous eyes. 'Proof that the city can't be far away.'

Camilla entertained a doubt which she wasn't about to voice. Yes, the find was wonderful, steeped in religious meaning, but it was too crude to fit into her idea of a far advanced civilization. These drawings had been done by simple people, similar to the Kalapalos Indians, perhaps. Maybe the slaves of those who had once held sway over the entire continent. What she sought was something quite different and, in the next moment, she found it.

Her eyes had become accustomed to the diffused light

525

and Darcy led her to an archway which she had at first taken for a rock formation. As they approached, she saw that it had been man-made, a massive gateway built of blocks placed precisely one on the other. Steps led beyond it – wide, regular steps, rising upwards towards a small patch of blue sky bordered by a tangle of branches.

'Are you all right, Miss Camilla?' Ranger's voice rang along the corridor at their back and bounced off the walls. 'Hang on in there. We're coming.'

'Hurry!' Darcy hissed urgently. 'We've got to get to the city before them.'

He was already taking the steps two at a time, and she ran behind him, gasping with exertion. 'Have you already been through?'

'No, not yet. I wanted us to see it together.' He stopped, turned, and revolver in hand, stared down in the direction where they could hear the others already exclaiming over the wall-paintings.

Knowing that he was in the mood to shoot if anyone tried to follow too closely, she ran ahead. 'Come on, Darcy.'

The opening was blocked by a huge tree, old and gnarled, its roots twisting in the soil like deformed limbs with shadowy crevices between. Something moved within it. Camilla froze. There, crouching like a night-mare, was a tarantula – bloated, ugly body, jointed legs covered in blackish fur. It was big enough to eat a bird or a marmoset. A macabre joke invented by the Almighty Prankster. It crawled a little way, then paused, barring the exit, as if aware of her presence – demon guardian of the secret place. Of all the creatures that haunted the forests, Camilla dreaded spiders most of all. Glancing up into the low branches, she saw a mass of sticky webs. Her nerve cracked. She lost control and started to scream.

A shot silenced her, and Darcy was at her side, the spider a bloody pulp at her feet. She was in his arms, clinging to him. His hands were gentle and firm, running

526

over her back and shoulders. He was murmuring reassurance, his voice warm with remembered tenderness.

'It won't hurt you, Camilla. It's dead. I'll protect you, darling, never fear.'

She kept her eyes closed for a second, dreaming that it was as it had once been. Darcy loving her, wanting her. Then she dared look into his face. His expression was almost normal, but not quite. With a sinking in her stomach she saw that his eyes were unnaturally bright, the pupils dilated. The dream vanished as the rocks reverberated with another shot, and another. Selden was standing below them, rifle raised to aim at Darcy again, thinking that he had been firing in his direction.

Then Darcy was crashing through the undergrowth, past the tree, dragging Camilla with him. They tumbled out on a plateau at the top of the escarpment. On one side the forest had changed into great rolling plains, on the other it lay beneath them, a giant's quilt, broken here and there by a hardwood rearing its head above that emerald canopy. A river sparkled far below, curling its way through the jungle like a brown snake. Two great black ridges formed the horizon to the north, a long, low-lying mountain range. The sight was so awe-inspiring that they stood still, enthralled and speechless.

Close at hand was a great cleft in the rock, a split caused by some primeval volcanic eruption, and on the far side frowned a mighty grey bastion. 'Look!' Darcy shouted, pointing to it. 'The city! Can't you see the towers? It's glittering! There it is at last!'

She stared, and for an instant it seemed like a fantastic, barbaric palace, complete with shining pinnacles. Then she blinked and the mirage vanished. All that remained was worn stone, eroded by time. 'It's a rock, Darcy – only a rock. There's no city. What you see glittering is nothing more than quartz.'

Selden burst out of the entrance. He was shouting and

527

waving to those just behind him. Shawn's head and wide shoulders appeared, then Ranger, mustering the others.

'Get back!' Darcy rounded on them, revolver aimed true.

'Hey, there, cool off, matey!' Ranger strolled towards him, hand at his holster, distrusting the look in Darcy's fever-bright eyes. 'What's all the row about? We need to hunt.'

Darcy fired. The dust at Ranger's feet shot up in a shower. The Australian leaped for the shelter of a boulder. 'Keep away. I mean it.' Darcy's face was grim. 'I'm going to find a way over to the city and I'm taking Camilla with me. Don't attempt to follow us. I'll shoot again if you try, and shoot to kill.'

'Do as he says,' Camilla shouted.

She knew that she was safe just as long as she played the game as Darcy saw it in his distorted imagination. She looked across at Shawn, saw the horror in his face, the fear for her. Selden barked out a clipped order to Pedro. The big Negro moved. With a savage roar he leaped at Darcy. His machete swung up in a dazzling arc of fire. Darcy sprang to one side. The swiping blow missed him by a fraction. Sparks flew as the axe shivered against a rock. Pedro slipped, lost his footing, rolled down a steep slope, crashed against an outcrop. He lay still. Blood was spurting from the back of his head. Schultz scrambled down towards him. Ranger and Shawn came pounding towards Darcy who mounted the rim of the precipice and began running along the narrow edge.

'Don't shoot!' Camilla begged, keeping up with the men.

'No, don't shoot. He has the ring – the map!' exclaimed Selden, and he was in the lead.

Darcy, with a speed and dexterity engendered by madness, was taking the path like a chamois, heedless of the drop that fell sheer for hundreds of feet. The city! He must reach the city! It shone before his bemused eyes, luring and alluring, promising all. It was *his!* He would be its emperor!

He was not aware of heat, of discomfort, and the dizzy heights inspired him. He was as invincible as the condor. He could see one, far up, drifting effortlessly against the wide blue expanse. I'm with you, brother! he shouted in his soul. I too can fly! Shadows of light and dark whirled hypnotically about him, creating in his mind an illusion of devastating clarity. His head began to throb as he almost danced across the perilous inclines, leaping over fissures, jumping gaps that spanned gulleys cutting straight down into the treetops.

Amidst the blood rushing in his ears, the wind, the beating of the condor's wings, he heard singing. A woman's voice, sweet and strange. He saw her just ahead – the most beautiful being ever created. Warmth and music and pleasurable excitement flowed through his veins. She floated just in front of him, smiling, graceful, with delicate features and small hands. Naked, but covered in glittering jewels, her skin was honey-coloured and masses of silky golden hair undulated about her as she moved.

Selden had followed closely behind Darcy. He had forgotten fear, blank to anything but the urgent need to get his hands on the map before it was too late. He saw no city, but thought Darcy had the key to treasure. He must have something to take such risks. A noise ahead now, the thunder of water falling from a great height, rushing down into the canyon. Darcy was there, poised on a crag, and Selden eased his way along the slippery, treacherous path towards him.

'Devereaux!' he shouted through cupped hands. 'Wait for me! I'll help you!'

Darcy could not hear him above the roar of the falls. He was staring across the ravine at something on the other side. Selden edged closer. Spray hit him, icy, forceful. Then Darcy suddenly spun around and his fingers closed on his throat. 'Got you!' he snarled. 'Thought you were being very clever, didn't you, Ruthen? You're out to rob me. I know it! Very well, then – come with me! See her? The Golden Woman? She'll take us over. That is the song she sings – I'll be master there and you'll be my slave.'

Camilla and Shawn reached the spot where the water gushed from the rocks. Looking along it, they saw Selden and Darcy struggling on the brink of the abyss. She lurched forward but Shawn pulled her back. 'Don't, Camilla! There's nothing you can do.'

'Crazy bastards! What the hell do they think they're doing?' shouted Ranger, clambering down behind them.

Darcy felt himself to be invincible. The woman was smiling at him so beautifully. She stood on a misty bridge that spanned the gap, a shining bridge covered in beaten gold. Great statues ornamented its balustrades. All he had to do was step out and place his feet on the wide causeway, then enter his city in triumph. Selden was screaming, unable to prise himself free. Darcy's stranglehold tightened. He jerked Selden's body, twisting it this way and that, dragging him closer to where the crumbling brink joined the beautiful bridge. The woman laughed, a light, musical sound. She came towards him now. Her body floated gently, her hair billowing about her in soft, sensuous motion. Her mouth was wet, open, calling his name. Behind her the city glowed with molten fire. She stopped, then moved back – teasing him. He felt the blood in his veins, in his groin. He stepped towards her into open space, taking Selden with him.

The ardent sun, lying low, breathed crimson flame over the jungle that spread like an undulating carpet below the plateau. Never had Camilla witnessed such a variety of green, shading from sage to emerald, from emerald to

530

peridot, with deep blue shadows between. She rolled over on her stomach on the short, springy turf, chin cupped in her hand, filling her eyes, her senses with the peace and beauty of the tropical twilight, that brief moment when day and night changed places.

In the distance the monkeys greeted the darkness – a vast, eerie moaning sound. Close to Camilla, a flock of olive-brown *amarillos* were retiring to roost, uttering a confused chorus of notes. The long clear cry of a lemon-coloured *ventevea* rang through the foliage, and bats whirled out from crevices in their thousands. The forest was settling down to its nocturnal activities and here, on the escarpment, her companions were gathered around the camp fire some distance away, talking, laughing, replete at last.

As she had suspected, there was no shortage of game. The natives had gone off hunting, returning triumphant after a while, carrying a brace of carcasses. Nothing had ever smelled so good as the antelope haunches roasting over the open fire. They had eaten for hours, slept for hours, waking to eat again, fortifying their starved bodies against the return journey which they must soon take.

I don't want to leave, she thought, watching the black shape of an eagle drift across the bloody sky on motionless wings. This period of my life is mine. I'll share it with no one. I should loathe this place, but it's like paradise.

The shock of Darcy's abrupt disappearance had stunned her. By the time she and Shawn peered over the precipice, both he and Selden had vanished, plunging down into the foaming cataract far below. A unanimous decision had been reached, concluding that it was pointless risking further lives in an attempt to find their bodies. Dry-eyed, deadened to all feeling, she had done what was necessary to ensure the safety of the survivors. Then Ranger had taken over, leaving her recovery to

531

Shawn. With Selden gone and Pedro dead, the remaining natives were meek and obedient and Manoel, though he was a shade too glib and rather cowardly, seemed to have their well-being at heart. It was amazing how spirits rose and good temper revived with the advent of food.

Schultz and Camilla had spent some time examining the bushes that grew in abundance on the gentle slopes. She taught him everything she knew about the plants and their prophylactic properties. It had become imperative that they aid Martingale. Terrified of being abandoned to die alone, he had crawled in the wake of the cave explorers. The effort had caused the abscess to burst with all the violence of an erupting volcano. The crater in his groin was huge, pouring forth a stream of blood and pus.

Even in the midst of her own anguish, Camilla found a measure of satisfaction in discovering the herb she needed growing near the waterfall. She had made a paste from the crushed roots, spread it on leaves over the fire to heat and then applied it to Martingale's wound. This had drawn out more thick yellow fluid, and his fever had begun to abate. Schultz was eager to take a supply back with him, praising her skills, saying that she should become a doctor or there would be a great loss to the medical profession.

It's too late, she mused, dreamily. I've too much to think about, too much to do. I must pick up the pieces and soldier on. The stars began to come out, bright with that radiance only found at such an altitude. The full moon began to rise. The same moon, the same sun that shone over Brazil and The Priory alike. She could hear the gentle trickle of water as a crystal-clear stream emptied itself into the pool behind her. Fresh water had been theirs in abundance. They had been able to wash away the accumulated dirt, scrub their clothes and lay them over bushes to dry. To feel really clean again was

532

an experience in itself. Packs had been opened and precious contents overhauled. Camilla had found that her diary was intact, and had begun to add notes about their adventures. She had tried to write in it every day. Apart from anything else, it had provided a calendar. She liked to know what day of the week it was. Shawn rejoiced that his camera and rolls of film had come through unscathed.

It amused her to think that one day she might read of her adventures to her children and grandchildren, and perhaps show them the snaps he had taken. But the idea was also sobering. Would she ever marry? Would any man penetrate her protective barriers and gain her confidence? It seemed doubtful, and yet –

'There you are, *patrão*,' said Shawn. 'I've been looking for you. Don't stay out here on your own, Camilla. It worries me.'

She smiled up at him in the gloaming. 'You said once that you never worried. Why bother about a tough old campaigner like me? You know I'm perfectly capable of looking after myself. It's lovely here.'

'It is indeed.' He threw himself down on the grass beside her, resting on his elbow, chewing reflectively at a long blade of grass. 'How much longer can we stay?'

'A few days, perhaps, then we must start back before the rains begin again. Can't risk our canoes being washed away or we'll be really scuppered. I saw the smoke of distant fires again today. There are Indians out there, Shawn – probably tribes who've never even heard of a white man.'

A night-jar called wistfully from a bush and the cicadas chirped. There was no hum of rapacious mosquitoes. They had been left behind in the swamps. Brilliant moonlight filled the little glade with a soft radiance. Her face was touched by it, white, gleaming, framed by a cloud of hair. It was fine-drawn, the cheekbones like carved ivory. Though she was filling out

533

again, her body still seemed fragile, but her indomitable spirit lit it from within.

I'm going to lose her soon, he thought. If and when we reach the *estancia*, she'll change again. 'What are your plans, when you get back?' he asked quietly.

Camilla had been brooding about this and her course had become clear. 'I can't leave South America for good,' she replied, sitting up and clasping her arms about her knees. 'I realized this when I reached Rio. The country claimed me again, as it always claims its own. I'm a native, Shawn, just like the Indians.'

His heart sank and he grew very still and watchful. 'But The Priory? Your estates?'

'Rufus will take care of that.' Her voice reached him, with its magical cadences, that odd accent which was a mixture of English, French and Portuguese. 'I shan't give it up entirely. Maybe I'll bequeath it to Alison's daughter. That is if I don't marry and have children myself, and I can't see that happening.'

'You think she'll ever be able to enter Abbey Sutton?' Shawn was remembering the Gladys Laceys of the world.

'In time. People forget, even if they don't forgive. There'll be plenty of money. This always helps. Darcy once said that he'd willed Chalkdown Farm to me. Perhaps I can have a new village hall built or some other amenity.' Though she spoke lightly, she was well aware of the difficulties of her proposition. But she knew that the only way to true happiness and peace of mind would be living at the Estancia Esperança and working amongst the local people.

She had suspected as much in Rio, and the feeling had grown stronger when she woke in the *estancia* on the morning after their arrival. To lie hearing the familiar sounds all around her, the rustling of waking parakeets, the voices of the peons on their way to the fields, had finally convinced her. Oh, she loved The Priory too, had tried hard to adapt to the English climate and way of life, but it was no use. This was her home, no matter how she had striven to deny it. Familiar thornbushes and vegetation and tall trees, the lush, exotic flowers, the plantations of sugar and cocoa, and in the midst of all the large, square house of white stone, built by some earlier colonial, an impressive place with a wide verandah in front supported on wooden pillars. This is where I was born and where my mother died, she had thought. This is where I stood one dawn, convinced that I'd murdered my father.

'What of Alison and Josephine? Will they inherit from Selden?' Shawn's voice broke across her memories. It was a strain even bothering to think about matters so far removed from this enchanted night, but he had to try. His own hopes for the future hung in the balance.

'I've no idea, but I should imagine he's made provision for his beloved Josephine at least. There's no one else to leave his money to, though he was the sort of person who thought himself invincible. But he was beaten by a power far stronger.' Camilla was comforted, yet wary of this agreeable man who crashed into her thoughts, demanding that she take her future firmly in hand and stop daydreaming.

With a humorous slanting of his eyes, he looked at her. 'Don't you want to see England again? Are you all set to venture into the great unknown with another expedition? What *are* you going to do, Camilla?'

She gave a nervous laugh. She had thought herself invulnerable but he had an unsettling effect on her. She might lie to herself, but never to Shawn. 'Of course I want to see England, or at least my dear old manor house, but I'll only visit there. As for exploring – no, I think my father was deluded, but there's much work to be done charting the courses of the Amazon's tributaries, working out proper maps and aiding the Indians.'

'They don't seem to need any aid.' Shawn was

535

remembering the Kalapalos village. 'It seems that they cope with their environment admirably.'

'I'm not talking about the ones who live deep in the forests. It's the half-breeds, the peons who need help. They've been so terribly disturbed by the whites, and forgotten the art of survival. But the filth and disease introduced by foreign invaders can yield to proper care. This is how I'll spend my fortune. I've already discussed it with Schultz and offered to set him up in a proper hospital.'

She spoke so earnestly, her voice running on almost frantically as she avoided the kernel of his question. Camilla the benefactress! he thought cynically. But what of Camilla the woman? It was time this nonsense stopped, but how to reach her? She was throwing up words and ideas as shields. She's been so badly hurt, he thought. I must be careful not to alarm her or she'll be off like a startled deer and I'll never get any sense out of her.

The sky was sequinned with stars and numberless fireflies were flitting about, making a lovely show. One landed near his hand and he took it up. It lay sparkling on his flat palm, though its brilliance was beginning to fade. He felt Camilla stir and heard her say:

'Put the little *linterna* down on the grass, for if you should hurt it, the spirits of the jungle will be angry with you. The Indians believe that the spirits wander at night, and love the fireflies who keep them company.'

'You and your spirits,' he said, and the warmth in his voice made her look at him. 'You believe these tales, don't you? You have a direct and simple faith that's very touching.'

'It's not all that simple.' She shook her head but did not withdraw her gaze. 'Voodoo can be complicated – the beliefs of the Indians too. You'd be amazed at the hierarchy of gods and under-gods who have to be given their just dues. But yes, I've much to thank Leila for. Even here, over the past days, I've sent my thoughts

536

back to her. I've seen her in the still waters of the pool. I know she'll be aware that I'm safe.'

'I envy her. She's closer to you than anyone else.'

Shawn was her comrade. Together they had bled and sweated and cursed and laughed. But she was afraid. Go on talking, she lectured herself. If you talk he won't touch you, won't make you do something you'll later regret. Don't lose your head! And to keep the flow going, she told him Leila's story and the secret of Ruthen's death. He said nothing, letting her talk herself to a standstill. I'll kiss her when she runs out of steam, he thought.

'So now you've heard it all, Shawn,' she concluded. 'You know my past and that I had a child whose father was black.'

'And Leila had a child whose father was white,' he broke in and his calmness steadied her. 'It doesn't seem to make much odds. What's done is done. That's behind you. I haven't exactly been a saint myself. We all make mistakes. Take Josephine for example. I'm not proud of my affair with her. But it's the future that concerns me – our future – and the immediate present, Camilla.' He drew in a deep breath. The words could no longer be unspoken. 'I love you. Give yourself to me.'

'I haven't much left to give,' she whispered and turned her head away. With her eyes tight shut, she felt him move, felt his fingertips on her lids, opening them. His face was serious, carved with shadows.

'It's enough, acushla. Later there'll be more, when this madness is finally done with.'

Camilla could not answer him, and she knew that if she stayed there silently for much longer it would be over. He would go away quietly and never mention it again, but she was too afraid to speak. It was as if she was paralysed. With a stupendous effort, she forced herself to look at him. Miraculously, the chains fell off and she found that it was easy to smile, to press her body to his,

537

her arms holding him close, face hidden in the warmth of his neck.

He was on his knees, raising her to kneel before him, and his hands were in her hair, loosening it. He held the tawny mass of it in his palms, pressed it to his mouth, then began to undress her. He laid his lips against her body, breathed in her perfume. With her face upturned to the moon, Camilla arched her spine and bit her lip to stop crying out with longing. Her fingers stroked his hair, the silky beard. He moved aside and spread his jacket on the ground, and they lay down on it.

His caresses were slow and each one had its own ecstasy. He touched her everywhere but so gently that she could not be sure that he touched her at all. Not the urgency of André or Darcy, but controlled, her pleasure of prime importance, lips and fingers trailing down her spine, over her breasts, her thighs. The tension was mounting in her unbearably. She moaned and shivered, reaching for him, wanting him. He smoothed her hair, withdrew a little, then he was naked too. His skin was smooth as a boy's. He lay on his side as she began to caress him in return. He watched her with a look in his eyes that drew her to him, drew out her soul and united it with his, drew her down as if she was drowning in a bottomless pool of love. In her nostrils was wood-smoke and wildness, Shawn and the night.

'They're here! Frank! They're here!' Alison cried from the top of the stairs where, for the past hour, she had been anxiously watching the length and breadth of Cheyne Walk. 'Oh, quick! Go and let them in!'

She did not wait for him, but ran down to the front door herself, getting there before him, before the parlour maid, before they had even rung the bell. Then she paused, did not recognize her – then knew it was her. Camilla, clad in floating white, bronzed, beautiful, obviously pregnant. And Shawn with a hand tucked under her elbow.

'My God, you've changed!' Alison breathed at him, smiling, in tears. 'That beard!'

'A wild man from the wild woods!' and he was grinning, wearing a lightweight suit, a straw hat cocked rakishly on his curls. The same old Shawn, yet older, tougher, more responsible.

Then they were in the hall – in the drawing-room and Frank was there, clapping Shawn on the shoulder, pouring whisky, wanting to hear about their adventures – all about *them*. Everything. The author in him taking command.

'How's the baby?' Camilla pulled off her hat, shook out her hair. She was more beautiful than ever, and Alison loved her for it.

'She's flourishing, getting a real porker – and so artful. A proper little minx,' Alison said, thinking, I mustn't blab on about her. The proud Mamma. It'll seem small-minded and provincial after what they've lived through.

'I want to see her.' Camilla was halfway to the door. 'Take me to the nursery. I've simply got to learn about babies. As you can see, we're expecting one soon.'

'When?' Alison raced after her up the stairs. 'Slyboots! You kept that a secret. Why didn't you write and tell me?'

'My son will be born at The Priory at Christmas, then we'll take him home to Bahia.' Camilla was already pushing open the nursery door.

'How d'you know it will be a boy?'

'Leila told me.'

Leila had indeed known about it long before Camilla herself suspected that she was pregnant. When the return party staggered into the *estancia*, the *mambo* had taken one look at her and said: 'There's a man-child growing in your belly. He was conceived in a glade near a stream at the top of the mountain. A jaguar fetched his soul from the celestial plains to enter his new body. He'll be like the jaguar – lithe and swift, brave and fierce.'

Leila had already been dispatched to Wessex, determined to act as midwife. She would receive the child into her hands, love and care for him throughout her remaining years, imbue him with her skills and wisdom. As for Sam, he had stayed with Ranger, learning to run the plantation, unaware of his status. Leila had thought it best that he be kept in ignorance of his close connection with the Ruthens. Sam was content. Why fire him with ambitions that could only bring disaster? A little knowledge was sometimes dangerous. Leila had seen the harm it could do to Creole bastards whose fathers had been powerful Europeans.

How small England seemed to Camilla. This had struck her when they docked yesterday at Southampton. London first, friends to visit, and then Abbey Sutton. Rufus, leaving for England earlier, had been looking after the estate for her, whilst Beryl and Wilf were now its caretakers, having a place to live for as long as they wanted. After Camilla had married Shawn, she had realized that she could not shrug off her responsibilities. Before they settled in South America for good, a visit to Ireland was necessary, there to put Four Oaks to rights. Shawn wanted to start a stud-farm.

'Are you happy with him?' Alison asked, sweeping up the small Camilla and staring at her friend over the child's fair, curly head. 'Is he good to you?'

'He's wonderful.' Camilla held out her arms and Alison placed the baby in them. 'Oh, it's not all plain sailing. We fight sometimes, and argue terribly. He doesn't let me have my own way about everything, you know. This idea of raising thoroughbreds for example. He's bullied me into lending him the money. But he's shrewd and knows his horseflesh. Shouldn't be surprised if we end up with a Derby winner or two.'

'But you love him? You don't regret it?'

Camilla's eyes misted and there was the suspicion of a blush on her cheeks. 'I love him madly. He's everything that I want in a man, but I daren't let him get too cocksure. Ah, Alison, I hope that you're half as happy with Frank. Shawn's my comrade, you see. We went through a lot together in the jungle. I saw Darcy die, imagined I was strong, but couldn't have survived that without Shawn.'

She was indeed happier than she had thought possible. She had found a man she could trust, someone who did not criticize or blame, who supported her in every way, yet took her to task when he thought she was being too domineering. His skill as a lover had been a revelation. In his arms she had learned to become a woman, loving, giving, receiving the bounty of his ardour, the warmth of his tenderness, the unselfishness of his desire.

'And now you're going to have a baby. I'm so pleased for you,' said Alison.

Camilla replaced the infant in her crib, where she sat contentedly, playing with a rattle and staring at her mother with wide eyes. She resembled a miniature Frank. As Alison had said, she had never looked back after her premature birth, had grown amazingly and was already trying to haul herself to her feet aided by any handy piece of furniture.

'It means that I'll need to retain The Priory for my son.' Camilla turned to Alison. 'I've asked Rufus to arrange that the deeds of Chalkdown Farm are given to this little lass. Who knows? Maybe one day my children may turn their backs on Brazil in favour of England. You'll let me know if you need money, Alison. Don't hesitate to ask. What's happening with regard to Elsie?'

Alison's face darkened and her fingers played restlessly with the fringe of her shawl. 'She still won't divorce Frank. Money is no problem. His book is doing awfully well and he's working on another. Besides which, I have investments and Selden didn't cut me out of his will. Elsie's drinking a great deal, so I hear, but really quite comfortably off with our support. I can see the situation dragging on for ever. Little Camilla, and any other children Frank and I may have will be illegitimate. That's Elsie's revenge.'

Camilla laid an arm about her shoulders, and expressed her sympathy, though painfully conscious that words were of little consolation. Time alone might bring about a solution. Elsie could not live for ever and alcohol would speed her end. They must play the waiting game and leave it in the hands of destiny. It was a sin to wish for someone's death. How well she knew this, and how sorely she had been punished for it.

'How's Effie behaving?' she asked at last.

'Much better.' Alison brightened. 'She's really quite sweet these days. Spends much time playing with the baby, that's when she isn't occupied with Josephine. They've become the best of friends. Strange, really, for my sister usually has little interest in children. But you haven't told me about your wedding. I want to hear every detail and wished so much that I could have been there.'

Camilla was glad to do so for it had been such a happy occasion. 'Rufus was actually able to give me away this time, and the best man was my overseer, Ranger Hogan. He's a good friend of ours. The service was held at the little church in Rubera, followed by a Voodoo ceremony where the *hungan* and Leila officiated.'

Voices from below interrupted them, a woman's laugh, the deeper tones of the men. When they went down it was to find Josephine in the drawing-room. A new Josephine, trailing black draperies and exotic scarves, her hair glittering with jet and cascading over her shoulders – a Josephine who talked about art as if it was something she alone had just discovered, as she

542

fawned on the saturnine Blake Saunders. She had carefully fostered a new persona, discarding whaleboning and that hourglass shape, even more racy now, posing for other artists, entertaining radicals at her dining-table. It was such a wonderful way of being the centre of attention. They called her Josie. She was dressed in mourning for Selden. Both his sisters were in black, but whereas Alison wore it as a mark of respect, Josephine was well aware of the dramatic effect of sombre hues contrasting with her blonde beauty.

'Darling!' she cried, as Camilla came in. 'My God! Such a heroine! And poor Selden dying out there! When the news came, I couldn't believe it! I still can't believe it! Give me a cigarette someone before I faint!' Her eyes switched to Shawn, ran all over him, took in his lean, rugged appearance and found it stimulating. 'I love the beard, Shawn, makes you look positively piratical!'

'Sorry about your brother,' he said, but only because it was the right thing to say. 'My condolences, Lady Josephine.'

'Poor darling Selden. I miss him,' she sighed, and raised a sable handkerchief to her eyes. Her grief was genuine. With his passing she had lost a twin-soul. There was no one left with whom she could plot, scheme and connive. Only Effie and she was but a novice, though learning fast. 'Are you quite certain he was killed? Is there no hope that he may be alive somewhere?'

'Not a chance, I fear. You read the detailed account I sent to Alison?' One of the first things Camilla had done when they reached the *estancia* was to sit down and write a long letter.

The journey back had been hard, with the additional problem of Martingale, slow to recover from the abscess. Once again they had suffered dreadful privations, but at least they had marked the trail and, with compass bearings, had made a correct map of the route. It had

543

rained almost incessantly, lashing, storm-ridden rains that fell upon them like a pack of snarling wolves. The river had swollen, bursting its banks and, though they found the canoes, these had turned over in the rapids more than once, with nearly fatal results.

It was impossible to convey the thrills, excitements and terrors of their travels to these sheltered people who had not the slightest conception of the hardships involved, but she tried, producing photos taken by Shawn, that dedicated cameraman. He had guarded the equipment diligently. Even when struggling in foaming torrents, half drowned, he would be seen, arms above his head, clutching his pack, holding it high out of the water. How little they could know, Josephine, Alison and the others, how little guess what it had cost in suffering and sweat to preserve this record now being passed so casually from hand to hand, along with drinks and cigarettes.

'My dear! Are these your savages?' Josephine exclaimed, staring down at the prints. They had been taken in the Kalapalos village. There was Queiroz, looking rather apprehensive, spear in hand. 'Is it true that they're cannibals?'

'They're *some* of my savages,' Camilla replied, wanting to snatch them back. There was something unpleasant in the way Josephine was staring at the chief as if he was less than human. 'And yes, they sometimes eat human flesh. It's part of their religion.'

Josephine shuddered. 'How disgusting! I can't think why you want to roam amongst them, darling girl! Really! Can't the missionaries do something about it?'

Camilla's eyes snapped with temper. 'The missionaries have done quite enough damage already, starting with the Jesuits in the fifteen hundreds and carrying on ever since.'

Josephine shot her a glance and decided to ignore this, thumbing through the pictures. 'Oh, look – there's Selden and Darcy!'

544

The photos lay on the blue, heavily fringed chenille tablecloth. Unreal somehow, flat and lifeless. They held nothing of the heat, the noise, the smells of the Indian camp. Shawn had taken them on the journey out, shortly after Camilla had found Darcy's party in conflict with the warriors. The explorers had posed rather self-consciously, but they were all there, wary eyes staring out from under pith-helmets and bush hats, faces gaunt and bearded. They leaned on their rifles, on spears borrowed from the braves, against a backdrop of vegetation and hutments. Mangy dogs, pigs and chickens, naked children, naked women. Camilla fought for words, but there was no way she could explain the innate dignity of the people, their gentleness once their trust had been won, their generosity, their absolute affinity with their surroundings.

'Here's one of a bit of the river and the forest,' Shawn put in, seeing that Alison was about to cry again as she gazed at this last memento of her brother. 'It doesn't matter where – they're all monotonously similar.'

'How wonderfully unspoilt,' Blake remarked, with visions in his dark, glowing eyes. 'What a great pity the photos can't be in colour. Tell me about the colours, Lady Camilla. I'd just adore to go there and paint.' He picked up another. 'And where's this? It looks like a mountain. So gloriously untamed and rugged!'

It was the top of the escarpment, and Camilla did not have the heart to tell them that it was near the precipice where Selden and Darcy had fallen to their deaths. That spot which, after the tragedy, had become like the Garden of Eden before the fall, where she had made love to Shawn and conceived her son. There were other pictures of the ruins they had later discovered here, broken pillars and jumbled stones. No treasure, no gold or gems but satisfying nonetheless, proving that there was a grain of truth in the legends of lost cities. It was worth further investigation. Perhaps they hadn't reached the destination shown on the map? Who could tell what wonders lay hidden further off in the forests or beyond the next range of mountains?

'I wish we could've photographed the wall paintings, but we didn't have the necessary equipment. I did some rough drawings of them, but I'm no artist.' Camilla produced some loose pages that she had torn out of her diary, knowing that she must at least make some record of the marvel of the caves, just in case they never returned. 'When we go back there, we'll make sure we've everything we need to make a detailed study. Your skills would be most helpful, but would you be able to stand the pace?'

'You surely don't intend to dash off into the wilds, do you, Blake?' Josephine butted in anxiously. The way in which she leaned her blonde head against his dark one as they pored over the photos was very noticeable. 'Wouldn't that be pushing the cause of art beyond the limit?'

It was difficult to make Josephine take anything seriously and, as Alison remarked privately to Camilla, she was getting worse. Her emergence into the Chelsea set had done nothing to improve her. Douglas spent most of his time at Erwarton Hall, drinking himself into a stupor, while Josephine amused herself in London with Blake and any other man who took her fancy. Selden had left her Armitstead House, and she had promptly sold it to Reginald Claypole.

'Can you endure him as a neighbour, Camilla?' Josephine asked from behind a screen of cigarette smoke. 'He's a perfectly frightful little man and so common, but he paid over the odds for the place. It's made me financially independent.'

'I don't intend to be there often,' Camilla answered, seated on the couch with Shawn beside her. Though he was smiling at Josephine's antics, his eyes were stern. With his hand linked with hers, Camilla knew she had no cause to feel jealousy. The question simply never arose. No one else could possibly share their intimacy.

'Well, I think you've been most awfully brave,' Josephine went on. 'Don't you, Alison? You're something of celebrities, you know. The papers have got hold of the story and I've masses of friends agog to meet you.'

Meet them they did, and for over a week Camilla and Shawn were rather unwillingly lionized. Even when they sought refuge with the Marchants, it was to find that Amy had arranged for some of her spiritualist friends to call. One of them, a rather stout lady who was a medium, claimed that she had had a strange experience when she looked at Camilla's photograph in the *Sunday Times*. Seated by her in Amy's darkened parlour whilst the others listened in rapt silence, Camilla had wondered just who had been talking to the reporters, for she had been careful not to mention the lost city. How much had the medium learned through perfectly ordinary means? She would have been more impressed had she received a message from Maisie Hughes.

The woman's voice had been dreamy as she spoke of her vision; a vast land mass reaching from the coast of Africa to South America – elaborate temples – religious processions. A powerful hierarchy of kings and priests, masters of the world, who became greedy and cruel, giving themselves over to the black arts. They had been destroyed when a holocaust swept the land. A tidal wave had washed over it and Atlantis had sunk into the sea.

'They simply don't understand, any of 'em,' Shawn said for the hundredth time as he and Camilla rattled along in the dim, musty-smelling cab that was taking them to the railway station. 'Even that old biddy with her "psychic visions". I think she was cashing in on the story, to boost her reputation amongst her followers. There's nothing new about the Atlantean myth, is there?'

Camilla smiled, her face tranquil beneath the brim of

547

her fashionable hat. 'Did you understand before you actually went into the *sertao*?'

'No, I'll have to be admitting that I did not. But those idiots we've been plagued by all week! Damned newshounds, and silly ladies with nothing better to do, wanting you to speak at their wretched guilds or Women's Bright Hours or whatever! What do they know or care?'

She stared out at the colourful view of London sweltering in the August heatwave. The crowds, the traffic, the parks and shops and houses – for days she had felt the strain of it, longing for Wessex. 'Amy and John are the only ones who really understand, and they never want to return to Uruguay. South America either gets under your skin or it doesn't. You love or hate it. It's that sort of place.'

He grinned puckishly. 'I'm glad it doesn't appeal to the likes of Josephine and her boyfriend. Begorrah! I thought for one dreadful moment that Saunders was serious when he said he wanted to come back with us. Put him off straight away. I can tell you. He turned quite pale when I told him about the creatures lurking in the rivers. Didn't like the sound of the stingray at all, nor the electric eel. And had to leave the room, poor little feller, when I mentioned that tiny, thin little fish with the swept back barbs, who has the nasty habit of wriggling into the orifices of the unwary bather, preferably up the penis. I was quite proud of my graphic description of the agonizing operation necessary to remove it.'

'You're wicked, Shawn Brennan.' She turned to smile at him and his arm slid along the back of the leather seat behind her.

'That I am, Mrs Brennan,' he agreed, then dodged under her hat-brim to plant a kiss on her cheek. 'D'you remember how we rode in a cab just like this one when we spent that day in London?'

'I do. I knew you wanted to kiss me then,' she said,

548

relaxing against him as the taxi halted abruptly, the driver honking his horn and exchanging brisk insults with the hackney-carriage barring his way.

'Did you, begob!' He widened his eyes and tightened his hold. 'You didn't let on. Did you want me to?'

'Yes, Shawn, I wanted you to. But I guessed that it wasn't the first time you'd made love to a girl in a cab, and I had no intention of becoming just another notch on your bedpost.'

'So, you kept me dangling all that while – dragging me off to risk my neck in the backwoods? You're a hard woman, Camilla.'

'Are you sorry?' She was serious now, worried lest he regret the adventures they had taken part in or the life on which they were about to embark.

'Not a bit of it.' He too was grave. Unsmiling. Holding her carefully yet firmly. 'I love that damned barbarous, violent, wonderful country as much as you do. There's such a lot I want to see there – so much to learn.'

'Including Portuguese. You're not very good at it, Shawn,' she teased, thinking, how lovely it is to have a companion like him – someone I can laugh with, romp with, make mad, passionate love with.

'Will you stop your nagging, woman, and be after giving me a chance?' he protested loudly, scowling at her with mock severity. 'How's a son of The Emerald Isle supposed to get his tongue around such a fanciful lingo as that, when he can't even speak the King's English correctly?'

Camilla bounced up on the seat, half kneeling across him, seizing his handsome, bearded face between her hands and shaking him. 'You'll learn it, my lad! You'll become good at it, and the Indian dialects too.'

'And why should I be doing that at all, Miss Bossy-boots?' His green eyes stared up into hers with a look that made her tingle.

'Because –' she began, but his hands were performing

magic on her neck – her ears. She sank into his arms. 'Because I love you.'

'That's the best reason of all,' he murmured, contemplatively poking a finger amongst her curls.

'Oh, Shawn, there are a million things I want to show you,' she whispered. 'We've not yet visited Peru and stood on the Roof of the World together.'

'We will, acushla, we will,' he promised, as the cab jerked into motion again and they entered the stately precincts of Paddington station. 'And our boy will come too. Meanwhile, Camilla, my Amazonian Queen, I'm about to make up for lost time and kiss you, here and now.' And he did, very thoroughly.

Epilogue

He was short, slight yet muscular, with frizzy hair, and he wore nothing but a bunch of black feathers attached to his left arm and a narrow strip of liana around his loins. He grunted as he came cautiously out from the sheltering bushes on to the sandbank, a solitary figure amidst the tumbling waters, the high cliffs. His name was Kalo, and he was a member of the Quenoroa tribe. He had seen fourteen summers and was a brave, newly initiated into manhood.

Kalo was proud of himself. He had stood up well under the ordeal, fortified by fermented cassava juice and a trance induced by five days of drumming and chanting. No scream of agony had escaped his lips when the sorcerer had passed the wickerwork square filled with angry fire-ants over the sensitive parts of his body. The two hundred abdomens of the giant black ants had touched his flesh and the stings had penetrated simultaneously, injecting their venom.

I didn't move, he thought and danced a triumphant jig. I didn't scream, though they nipped me with their pincers and stung like bees. There had been a hush as the sorcerer took away the ants, and Kalo had opened his eyes. Then from all parts of the great, crowded, smoky hut, had come a long, shrill cry. It was the tribe's shout of welcome to him, the new man in their midst, another hunter, another warrior.

To prove he could hunt, he was sent alone into the bush. For two days now he had been stalking game and, that morning, his blow-pipe had discharged its poisoned dart into a wild pig. He dragged the kill to the water's edge and gutted it, singing to it, saying that he was sorry and explaining his need. He wanted to take a girl to wife, Muhoham, the chief's youngest daughter.

First he must show the elders that he could provide for her. He was not the only young man who wanted Muhoham, but knew that she liked him best. She was always laughing when he was near, looking at him slyly from the corners of her glistening black eyes, giving a toss of her straight ebony hair. Small, like him, with brown skin and short limbs. She was twelve, but already a woman.

Kalo drank at the river, and bundled up the carcass, slinging it across his shoulders. Squinting upwards, he saw that the sun was high. Vultures floated down and perched on the rocks, bald heads turned, attuned to the scent of bleeding guts. They hopped closer, croaking and quarrelling. Waddled across the pebbled bank, eyeing him. He threw a stone at them, scattering their evil conclave.

Seated by the rushing water, he wondered if the pig would be enough proof of his prowess. There were two other contenders for Muhoham's favours. Slightly older than him, equally courageous. If one of them caught an alligator or a jaguar, this would count for much, giving the hunter the power and cunning of those beasts. A pig was too stupid – good meat, but lacking in bravery.

Kalo robbed a bird's nest, cracked open the eggs and ate them. Still hungry, he turned over a rotting log and scooped up a handful of squirming grubs, stuffing them into his mouth. The dead pig lay there like a reproach. It made him feel gloomy, so he prayed to Sumba the rattlesnake god. His mother had told him that Sumba had appeared in their hut at the moment he was born. It was Kalo's totem. He asked Sumba to give him his heart's desire.

He listened. He looked. There was no sign of the snake. The forest creatures chattered and called, mocking him. Reddish-brown monkeys jeered from the high

552

branches. Kalo rose angrily, shouting at them. Then he saw something glint in the gloom between two rocks on the far bank. It flashed momentarily, disappeared, then flashed again. The eyes of Sumba? Kalo shivered, then gripped his bow firmly.

Laughing defiantly, grunting warnings, he hopped from boulder to boulder fording the river, the carcass across his shoulders. Sure-footed, agile, he ran up to where he had seen the light. The cleft was deeper than had at first appeared. He stood above it, squinting down into the gloom. Something gleamed there, not flashing now. He jumped on to the sandy ground and picked the thing up. It was a human skull. There were other bones – a skeleton. Bits of cloth clung to it. Long bones – thigh bones – the ribs – the hands. The flash again, from something circling one finger where a few scraps of flesh lingered.

Kalo bent, muttering incantations, shivering in the sudden chill of the fissure. The dead man's ghost was about. He could feel it. He gently pulled the ring from the finger. The bones fell apart with a soft rustle. Kalo sniffed it, looked at it, turned it around. It pleased him, shining, golden, with a big yellow stone in the centre, like the sun – no, like the eye of the jaguar. Nothing happened. No angry spirit pounced upon him demanding vengeance. Emboldened, Kalo slipped the ring on his own hand. It felt hot, strange, like the ants' stings. He didn't like the feel of it so dropped it into the pouch hanging at his waist.

He kicked the bones aside, searching. Was there something else he could take to Muhoham as a gift? Something that would make her laugh and glance at him in that way which made the blood rise thick within him. Shreds of cloth. Useless, ripped and rotting. Then his hands closed on a package. It was wrapped in a strange material that had kept its contents dry. He opened it and found something even stranger within. It looked like leaves bound together, and it was covered in strange symbols, like those he had seen in the caves of his ancestors. The sorcerer, who was very old and very wise, had told him that it was the thoughts of men made visible.

Kalo shook his head doubtfully. This would not delight Muhoham. She would rather have a jaguar-tooth necklace, or quills to adorn her ears. But he took his finds back to the sandbank, playing with the ring as he squatted there, musing. It was a pleasing thing. The sorcerer had talked much to him about the white man. An idea began to take shape in Kalo's mind. There came a noise behind him, the warning whirr of a rattler. He turned and looked at the flat, bright-eyed head of Sumba, and knew that the thought had been god-inspired.

Older braves who had ventured to the limit of the jungle which they thought to be the edge of the world, had come back with tales of men with white skins. They said that these strangers hunted with terrible sticks that spat fire and rained death on everything in their path. Strange beings indeed, who lusted after gold and gems. They searched for them in the forests and mountains, bartering knives and cloth in exchange.

'I thank thee, O great and cunning Sumba,' Kalo said politely, and the snake coiled itself round a warm rock and dozed. 'I'll find the white men and trade these useless things for a thunderstick, then I'll kill a jaguar – two – three jaguars, and show Muhoham's father that I'm the mightiest hunter of all. He'll give her to me, and I'll take her into the bush to do to her what the other men do to their women. I'll put a child inside her. A son – another hunter – another warrior!'

Nodding at the snake, satisfied that it blessed his endeavours, Kalo dropped the ring and the log book into his pouch and, hefting the pig, headed downstream to find his canoe and begin his long journey towards the mission. The dense green forest hushed, watching him go, listening and waiting.